THE AETHER UNRAVELS

This book is dedicated to the power of love and spite.

The Aether Unravels

C.G. WYNN

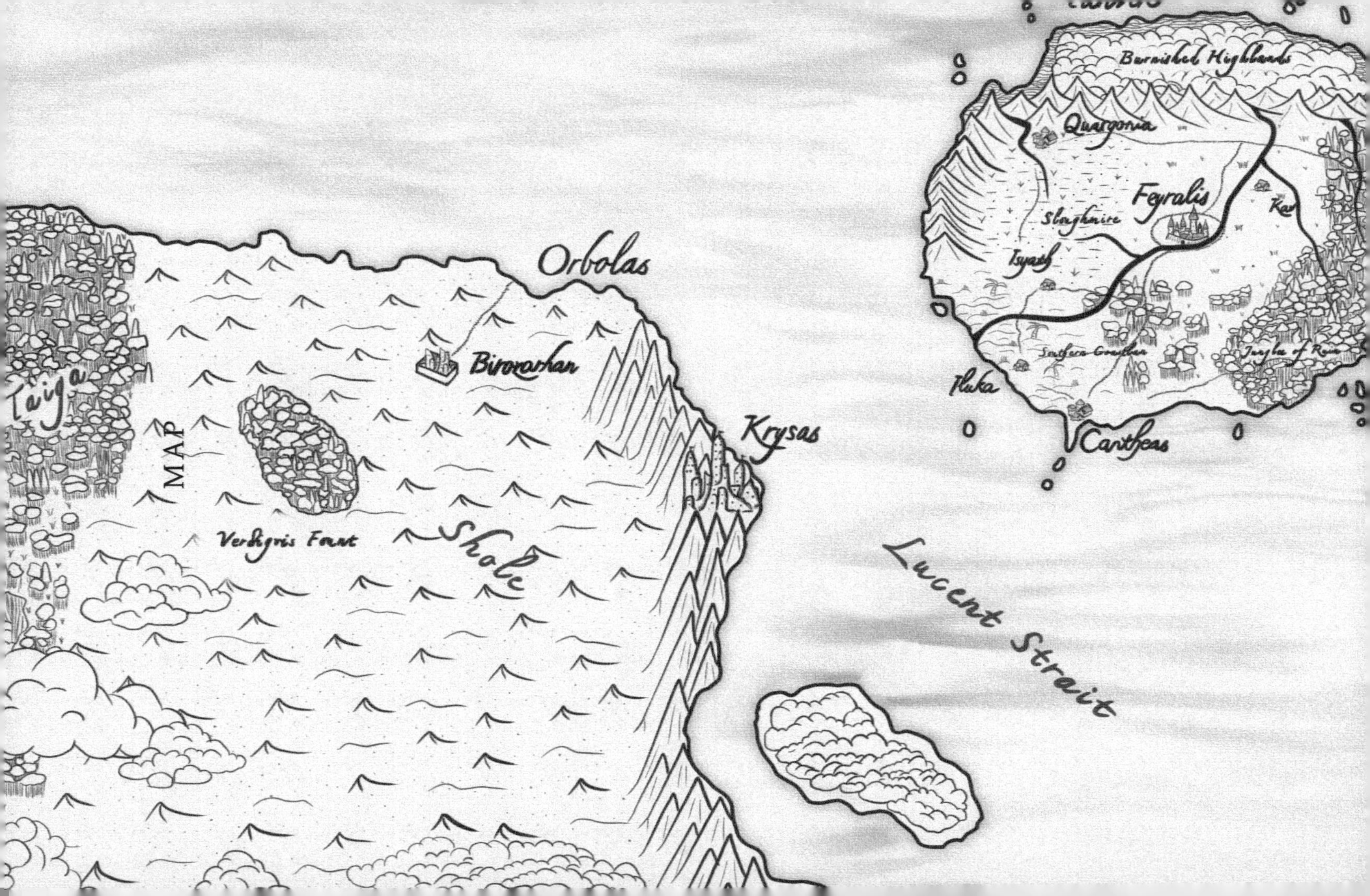

Orbolas
Burnished Highlands
Quargonia
Feyralis
Kar
Slaghrire
Isyads
Birrowlan
Taiga
MAP
Krysas
Verdigris Fault
Shole
Pluka
Southern Gauntlet
Jungle of Rain
Cartheas
Lucent Strait

~ One ~

RELINQUISH

"Lass, yer gonna drink me out of house and home," Lotus said before snatching away the freshly drained stein.

Ophiera looked down at her now empty gauntlet, barely buzzed and mildly annoyed. She didn't think they were nearing that time of the night yet when Lotus would start to get sassy; they were only five pints in...

As she rolled her eyes to the rafters above, she silently prayed he would at least have the decency to give her a refill before starting in on her.

"Tell me what's got on ye nerves this time, lass."

"My hands are empty," she muttered.

For a moment, she feared she had overstepped. But after a frozen minute, Lotus turned around to the keg, and the thick sound of trickling mead echoed through the bar. Her shoulders relaxed a bit before he slammed the worn stein in front of her. When the golden, frothy liquid threatened to spill over the edge, she nearly smiled.

Nearly.

Another splash of the honeyed libation fell across the bar as Ophiera brought the brimming stein to her lips. Briefly, she mourned lost ounce of oaken mead, now seeping into the aged wooden bar top. Another stain to the old collection, absorbed and soon to be forgotten in the grains—which was precisely the same fate she hoped to achieve this night.

"Can't ye at least talk to me *and* drink? That's what me regulars tend to do, ye know."

Avoiding his dark gaze, Ophiera swallowed the entirety of the sweet, malty beverage before taking a breath. Her cold gauntlet grazed against her skin as she wiped the dribble from her chin and slid the empty stein back to the glowering barkeep—silently.

"Can't serve ye if ye can't speak," Lotus said, crossing his thick arms over his bulging belly. "Magistrate law, n'all."

She chewed her lip a moment, absorbing the mention of *law* as if it were a curse. Her claymore shifted heavily against her back, reminding her what she was and why she was here.

"I don't wish to speak," she whispered, not breaking from his gaze, "And you know exactly why."

"Aye, lass, I do," Lotus sighed. "But yer in a strange way tonight...stranger than usual. And since it's me house, and me rules, I ain't giving ye another drop till ya tell me why yer so particularly sour tonight."

For a moment, Ophiera imagined herself stepping behind his bar and filling her own stein with drink. It wasn't as if he could stop her. He was sizable, for certain—a few fingers taller and nearly twice her own width—but so was her blade and her thirst to forget. Overpowering him would be much easier than what he was asking of her now.

"I'm not good at these things, Lotus," she said.

"What things?"

"Talking."

"No, no, yer not, lass," he said with a gentle smile, "but ye get better each time ye try. And thas all I'm askin'."

Ophiera groaned, rolling her eyes again like some petulant child. They were only six drinks in and already he drew the line in the sand for a trade—another one of his interviews for more of his mead.

She hated this nonsense. She wasn't asking for anything but a drink—well, several drinks, but certainly not counsel or advice or conversation. But she'd never met a more stubborn man, and truth be told, he always ended up dragging the words from her despite her kicking and screaming.

"I'm tired," she said flatly.

He uncrossed his arms, gripping the edge of the bar tightly. As he leaned forward, his auburn beard dangled above the bar top.

"Of?"

Ophiera sighed. "Look, I answered your question, so pour me a drink."

"Tired of what, lass?"

"I'm tired of..." she began, staring intently at the thick grains of wood in the bar. Maybe they would provide her with some answer instead of having to consider why she was so tired. The last time she sat at this bar was over a month ago..."Traveling."

Lotus kept his dark eyes on her, eyebrows raised expectantly, as he took the empty stein from the bar.

"That's all?"

She licked her lips to prevent herself from swearing. So damn close to having a drink.

"I'm tired of the weight of my armor."

"And?"

She heard the tap pour forth, gurgling gently into the stein.

"And of the Magistrate's orders."

"And?"

"What else do you want me to say, Lotus?" She growled, breaking with frustration. "I'm tired of being a paladin! I'm tired of being me!"

Lotus set the full mug in front of her as the words she spoke settled in. If anyone heard her speak such heresy, let alone knew she'd thought it, she could be charged with treason. How the hell did Lotus always make her *say* words she shouldn't have even thought? Sliding her gilded fingers around the fresh stein that no longer seemed quite as appetizing, she damned Lotus and his interrogations.

"So, there's the real reason yer tired," Lotus said, watching her slowly drag the mug to her lips. "Now, what do ye want to do about it?"

Ophiera nearly spat her drink but somehow managed to swallow instead. The sweetness of the mead was beginning to churn her empty stomach, unhelped by another pointless question.

"I am what I am. There is nothing that can change that. "

"Doesn't mean ye can't do nothing."

Again, she nearly choked. After all these years of frequenting the Lonely Iris, Lotus knew more about her than anyone else. He knew what she was...he knew what she did...and he knew damn well which lines not to cross. And yet, he chose to ignore them all tonight.

Ophiera lowered her drink without breaking the barkeep's sad stare. She removed the golden gauntlet from her arm, revealing the swirls of blistered scars marring her skin from fingertips to elbow. The subtle pain in Lotus's eyes as they fell upon the marks of her Oath satisfied her annoyance. To the unacquainted, her disfigurement might look like a tragic accident with a hot iron or boiling oil. But those who recognized the runic symbols within the welts knew precisely *why* there was nothing to be done about being a paladin. And Lotus knew better than anyone.

"This mead is all I can do about it," she said, flexing her scarred fingers before wrapping them around the stein. "At least *this* quiets the pain in my heart. At least *this* allows me to sleep, knowing what I must do in the days to come."

She brought the stein to her lips and began to drink, confident that the conversation would end here. There was nothing left to say.

"Do ye really have no choice?" Lotus said, his voice graveled and low.

This time, Ophiera actually choked on her drink, spitting a good amount out onto the bar.

"Lotus, *you* know the consequences of breaking my Oath! The fact that you're even asking—"

"Aye, lass, but I'm not suggestin' ye *break* it—I'm suggestin' ye *avoid* it."

She cocked her head, causing the room to wobble alongside her sanity. Perhaps she was nearing her required quota of mead to sleep peacefully. But Lotus continued to stare at her with expectation, and she knew his words weren't a dream.

"I'm not in the mood for your games."

"Lass, this isn't a riddle," Lotus sighed, pinching the bridge of his nose with thick fingers. "Haven't ye ever heard of a 'loophole'?"

"No," she said flatly.

"What if ye were un-conscripted from the Magistrate?"

"Un-conscripted?"

"Yer Chaplain o' the Cloister served the Magistrate before as a Hand of Retribution, didn't he? He *was* conscripted at one point. Then he went back to the Cloister to do whatever it is he does as Chaplain. Ye think he still answers to the Magistrate's calls for Retribution? Ye think he gets many opportunities to enact his Oath surrounded by priests and clerics, locked away in the Cloister?"

Ophiera straightened her spine, feeling the ache of her eyebrows as she listened. She hadn't ever thought of the Chaplain's Oath before, nor what it meant after his service was complete to the Magistrate. While she and Uzziel were the only two kindled to bear the Oath of Retribution, she was only conscripted to the Magistrate after he'd been made Chaplain of the Cloister. Meaning…were there ways in which someone could be released from duty to Tanvik? And if so, what did it mean for his Oath?

But these were heretical questions. She should have known better than to bother having them.

"I don't understand your point, Lotus."

"Me point is the Aether hasn't claimed him yet, has it? Even though he ain't fulfilling his Oath? So, that must mean his Oath wasn't broken by leaving the Magistrate's conscription. So…what if the Magistrate could release ye too? Like a…I don't know, like a *retirement.*"

A horrible feeling bloomed in her gut. A feeling she hadn't felt in years and, truthfully, never wished to again. Questions and curiosities were one temptation, but the emotion she felt now welling inside her could only come with a promise of punishment, disappointment and pain. She had sworn her own oath to herself to never give in again to the temptation of hope. And yet here Lotus was, dangling it in front of her like a freshly filled stein, knowing what it would do to her to even dream of it.

"You don't know," she growled, standing with such force that her seat crashed to the ground. "You never knew a damned thing if this is what you suggest to me now!"

Ophiera didn't wait to hear any of Lotus's protests before storming off, leaving the stool rocking on the floor. She knew how much he hated it when her temper flew off like this, but tonight, *he'd* been the one who overstepped. Tonight, *she* had every right to be furious. After everything he'd witnessed, after everything she had told him of the Cloister! Of the souls she'd claimed for the

Aether, of her life and her Oath...how dare he even suggest this *retirement* nonsense.

How dare he speak such blasphemy?

How dare he dangle such a lure before her.

How dare he try to make even an ounce of sense...

Didn't he see that even without conscription to the Magistrate, her Oath would still demand Retribution? The only reason the Chaplain hadn't claimed a soul for the Aether since assuming his position was that there were no anathemas in the Cloister. But if he *had* crossed a soul who sinned, someone who'd murdered another, his Oath would demand their own in recompense. The same rule applied to her...Magistrate or not, she was bound to comply with her Oath. If she crossed the path of an anathema...

As Ophiera reached the bottom of the steps, she stopped in her tracks. Is that what Lotus's point had been? If she never encountered another tainted soul...But no matter what, she could never return to the Cloister. Her memories of that place were distorted by pain, little more than brief flashes of a reality she wished never to recall. Where else could she go? There was nowhere she belonged. Not even here, in his vacant inn.

Even her scars agreed, itching with a furious burn. But as she eyed the raised runes against her skin, she realized she had foolishly left her gauntlet behind. The precious armor she couldn't allow to leave her sight, let alone possession, was sitting back on the stained bartop.

Damn him!

Ophiera turned back to the bar, ready to shout one last curse before gathering her armor and ascending the stairs for good this time. But as the room wobbled, churning her gut, both Lotus and the gauntlet were gone.

"Lotus?" She called, taking a clunking step back towards the bar.

He didn't answer.

Their steins remained on the bar top, and her stool still rocked back and forth gently across the floor. But neither barkeep nor gauntlet was in sight.

"Lotus! Give me back my gauntlet!"

Again, her calls were met with silence. He must have gone back into the kitchen, she thought, but even there, he should hear her.

"Don't make me come back into the kitchen!"

The quiet deafened her now.

No clang of armor as she walked.

No knocking as the stool rocked back and forth.

Even her own voice sounded as if she spoke while submerged beneath water.

Perhaps she really had drunk too much.

She reached her scarred hand to pick up the stool when a sudden pain bloomed across her brands. Blinded by the flash of light, she stared in horror as white flames erupted from the bubbled blisters. Without chant, the holy flames poured from her searing skin in an agony she hadn't felt since the day she was kindled. Panic matched pain as the bright fire flowed up her arm beneath her armor.

Desperate, she shook her arm as if to snuff out the flames, but she should have known better. Unlike true fire, the Aether couldn't be snuffed or stopped.

A whimper escaped her trembling lips as the blaze continued to spread, burning beneath her armor as it reached her massive pauldron. In horror, she watched the golden plate warp, distorting and discoloring before melting to slag against her burning skin. The remnants dripped into molten pools on the ground beneath her feet.

"Lass?"

Pain held her voice hostage as the flames spread across her torso, her skin erupting in fire as the armor continued sloughing off. She dropped to her hands and knees, her entire body engulfed in agony. The moment her enflamed hands touched the floor, it burned beneath her until she fell through ash and onto the cool soil of Erum itself.

Power and rage roared through her as the Aether below awakened.

"Lass!" Lotus cried. "Stop!"

Screaming, Ophiera dragged her eyes up, only to see the flames spread across the floor like a spidering river.

She tried to stop them from flowing out to the walls of the tavern.

She tried to stop them from burning the tables and chairs to ash.

She tried to stop them from erupting beneath Lotus's boots.

His dark eyes widened as the flames crawled up his legs, burning his clothes to ash.

Burning his flesh to ash.

With one last tear-stained stare, she watched as Lotus's face disintegrated into a cloud of gray ash.

***

You destroyed it.

Screaming, Ophiera awoke to the dreadful whisper in her ear. She only stopped when a metallic gurgle wetted her tongue, spitting crimson on the dirty floor. At least it wasn't mead, she thought, gasping for breath and resisting the urge to gag.

The taste of blood nauseated her as much as the silhouette of Lotus, crumbling to ash, still lingering in the shadows of the dim room she awoke within. To the soul, the difference between dreams and reality meant little. Despite the lack of ash and flame, she had a difficult time convincing herself she wasn't still at the Lonely Iris.

Destroying the Lonely Iris, rather.

Ignoring the voice in her head, she focused on the crashing waves nearby. The constant rhythm brought her frantic thoughts back down to reality.

She never burned like that in the Lonely Iris. Hell, she wasn't even traveling in the Sloughmire. But most importantly, she had never killed Lotus. Stupid, pointless dreams...At least her mind had the sense to wake before his imagined vesper rose from the ashes of his body. If only it had allowed her the peace to sleep without murdering her oldest friend.

Still caught in the dregs of her nightmare, she focused her thoughts and eyes on her trembling hands. There were no signs of white flames, only golden gauntlets shining in the moonslight. Following the path of the light, she peered through the hole in the damaged roof. Pale, eerie starlight trickled in through a damaged roof, only barely illuminating a place she barely recalled.

The abandoned hut had seemed like a safe place to rest for the evening when she had stumbled upon it earlier. But Ophiera should have known she would never find peace in a place like Neno. Another village, destroyed and forgotten. While the blood may have washed from the sands, the remnants of the once-inhabited abodes stood. By the look of the place, it would be easy to assume a storm took the village by surprise. But to anyone of the Southern Coastlands, it was obvious the village had been taken by quite an *unnatural* disaster.

As the first village to fall to the Gray Marauders, Neno had become the example of what happened to those who resisted Aud. Back then, when Ophiera had stopped the pirates from taking Iluka, she had no idea the actual threat she faced. As she claimed their vespers for the Aether and Iluka, she had no idea the souls she claimed were the predecessors of the Vespula Brotherhood—the followers of Aud.

How had Lotus described them again? More cultists than bandits, they worshipped the supposed god they called Aud by stealing the souls from the Aether and sacrificing them to the Abyss Mother. Ophiera still hadn't entirely wrapped her mind around the threat of Aud, an intangible being she had never faced. But the Brotherhood—those unfortunate souls *were* tangible, and there was one which would burn within her grasp soon enough.

She grimaced at her thoughts, causing blood to dribble from the corner of her mouth. She brought a shaking hand up to wipe the trickle, but the sight of her reflection, distorted by the bloody streak on pale gold, reminded her of a more pressing problem. If her screams had been enough to draw blood, then she may have drawn the Aether as well.

Despite her earlier confidence that she had not burned in her sleep, a sudden doubt drove her to search around the hut. Unlike true fire, the holy flames left no blackened char or dark soot behind as evidence; rather, only the pale ash of whatever or whoever they consumed. Like Lotus...Like Iluka...shaking her head, she focused on the waking moment, finding a sliver of relief in her unburned rucksack beside her. She couldn't find a trace of ash anywhere the moonslight illuminated.

Perhaps the abandoned hut *was* the best choice of shelter, after all.

Like most homes of the Southern Coastlands, the abode Ophiera chose to occupy was built on stilts, standing nearly half her height above the sands. This far off the ground, she had no chance of connecting with the Aether and, thus, no chance of burning down the remnants of Neno. Yet, even from this distance, she could still *sense* the Aether below, like hearing the water beneath a dock in the dark. The whispers of power from below seemed to grow louder the farther she traveled. Ever since leaving Myronor...

Clang.

She clenched a hand over her breastplate as if it would stop the pain from catching her breath now. It felt as if a fishing net had snagged her heart and dragged it through the choppy seas. Every time she thought of *him*, the pain of her soul, connected and yet afar, drove her to misery. The lump forming in her throat was worse than the lingering taste of blood on her tongue. She swallowed hard, settling her sadness beneath the large, rounded scar on her chest—the scar that bound their souls in the first place.

After departing the *Mistral*, she noticed the way her soul dragged, as if she carried an anchor in tow. She knew it must be the ekath, the bond between souls, that drew tighter and tighter as she distanced herself from the soul bound to hers. She couldn't stop her thoughts from lingering on ice-blue eyes and flowing blonde hair, only serving to exacerbate the ache. Every breath stalled in her chest as every fiber of her being drew back to him. And yet, despite the pain, all she had to do was remember the aftermath of Iluka to resist the urge to return to him.

Every step of her departure from the *Mistral* had held doubt of her decision until her eyes fell on the ruins of Iluka. The village she once protected had been swallowed whole by white fires and shaking sands. Whatever had awakened inside her, she couldn't control it, and with it, she had leveled a village...*her* village. When her eyes fell on the crater she once called home, she knew she must leave Myronor's side. She had sworn to protect him, even if it meant from herself.

The Brotherhood is to blame, not you.

Her armor clanged as she started, unsure if the voice was her own cracked sanity or a whispering of the Aether. Ever since the voice of the Aether had bestowed her with the adamantrium armor she wore, she'd yet to *converse* with it again. But that seemingly hadn't stopped the intruding whispers, real or imagined. Regardless, they did have a point. She had only destroyed the body of Iluka with the holy flames; the Brotherhood and Aud had murdered its soul.

The Aether was not the only one that demanded Retribution.

She had vowed to the flames to seek out Marvena, Reverend of Aud, along with every last member of the Brotherhood, and had every intention to fulfill it. Her Oath to Myronor and his late mother would still be fulfilled in due time. But for now, the churning of her gut told her that the path of Retribution was the only one worth following. No matter how much her heart protested what she left behind.

~ Two ~

COURSE

Since closing her eyes only resulted in burning nightmares and flashes of brilliant blue eyes, Ophiera gave up on sleep entirely. In return, she'd made great gains on the Reverend's path along the coast in the last two restless nights. With haste, she trailed Marvena's tainted steps.

As she pursued Marvena's tainted steps, the tether continually dragged on her heart. But with each hour that passed, the tension seemed to ease a bit, replaced by an ever-growing call forward. The Aether compelled her steps rather than weighed upon them, as if the holy flames themselves had set a bounty upon Marvena's soul. She had to keep moving to avoid the burn beneath her feet from overwhelming her, but at least it distracted her from the ache beneath her breastplate.

As Lotus would say, she had traded spoiled mead for rotten vegetables, but at least the Aether was a familiar pain. Hunting anathema had been her existence, after all, and falling back into old habits felt nearly relieving after everything that had happened.

Her body and mind fell in line, focusing on the task at hand and ignoring all other demands, even those for basic necessities. Flashes of blue eyes still lingered in the periphery of her vision, but nothing would interrupt her search for Marvena's sandy footprints.

Who knew how many souls the wretched Reverend had claimed since Ophiera last saw her? As if the destruction of Iluka wasn't enough reason for her scars to burn, she only fueled the fire with memories of Marvena's past crimes. It was Marvena who tortured Myronor in the Brotherhood's encampment—Marvena who shot the arrow through her heart—Marvena who inherited the terrible power of a Reverend, opening the gates for Aud to enter Erum. If Ophiera had considered all the trials and tribulations she had faced since being conscripted again by the Magistrate, Marvena would have been the cause of most of them. And the Aether unquestionably agreed, quickening her steps.

From the moment Ophiera had been kindled, she could always *sense* the Aether. Like a presence waiting just outside a door, the holy flames had been easy to forget about until the need to call upon them arose. But ever since she'd *awakened*, the pressure of the Aether had grown. Now, as she trudged the sanded path toward Marvena, the flames no longer sat quietly behind a door but instead pounded like a fist that rattled the hinges.

She still didn't understand exactly what had happened to her. And yet, there was no one she could turn to for answers anymore. The Cloister was out of the question—not only was she ignorant of its location, like all of Tanvik, but truthfully, she knew they wouldn't help her. When she had been kindled as the Aspect of Retribution, they had no answers or advice, only pain and punishment. The only other person she'd ever trusted was Kaikora, the shaman of Iluka. And though she had revealed much regarding the Cloister and her Oath, more than even Ophiera understood, there was only one answer she needed from Kaikora now.

Ophiera stumbled against a flare of her scars in what she could only interpret as a not-so-gentle reminder of where her priorities lay. Despite her heart's need to find and demand an explanation for Kaikora's abandonment of Iluka, the Reverend was her target now—a target that left a surprisingly obvious trail of broken reeds and overturned stones.

As Ophiera marched on, she noticed that, on occasion, the trail went cold or veered off the main path. But the tracks Marvena left were relatively fresh and quickly regained. Whether an attempt to shake Ophiera off or in search of something unknown, the erratic nature of Marvena's trail did little to slow her. Only when the sand dunes of the coastlands began to mingle with the edge of the escaping jungles did she start to worry about the destination.

If she neared the Jungles of Ruin now, it meant Marvena had traveled southeast...and if she had traveled southeast, there could be only one destination—Cantheas.

The premier city of the Southern Coastlands was the last place she wished to find Marvena. Like Feyralis, Ophiera had avoided the city completely during her retirement. The port had grown significantly since Tanvik began trading with Krysas, and with more people came more anathemas. She wondered if Myronor had already set sail from Cantheas...but with that pointless thought, she refocused on the task at hand.

Marvena's steps seemed to quicken the further she followed them. Between the odd trees that encroached on the sandy path, the gnarled roots began to obscure some of the trail. As Ophiera scanned without blinking, a pearly white flower caught her eye. And for the first time that day, she slowed her steps to a near halt.

Creeping up one of the thicker tree trunks, she gazed upon the familiar dark crawlers overburdened with long, trumpet flowers. They were undeniably beautiful, just as she remembered, and yet, thanks to Lotus, she knew a single pale frond caused devastating effects. Of all the realms of Tanvik, the Jungle of Ruin was the most sparsely inhabited by people while remaining home to countless dangers unseen elsewhere in Erum. Even along the border, the hazardous wilds spilled forth into sandy forests, ever encroaching on the coastlands. Here, quicksand claimed more lives than any beast. And the true peril came from the poisonous plants that flourished outside the dense shade of the jungle proper. Lotus had even gone as far as to transplant some of the species into his own garden at the Lonely Iris. She never thought to ask him why, but then again, she didn't want to know exactly what went into his signature curry, either.

Bending low, Ophiera took the first and only pause in her hunt since leaving Neno to admire the vanusvine flowers. She ran a gold-clad finger along the edge of a trumpet, wishing to feel the delicate warmth of the pale petals as she remembered the song Lotus had taught her.

In the jungle, a vine grows bright.
Flowers herald a dangerous plight,
One petal to forget,
Five for deep regret,
Any more, and the Aether, you'll fight

Her lip trembled as she recalled the deep tenor of his voice singing the song with equal promise and threat. Lotus had been furious when she asked if she could try one little petal and suggested mead instead. Now, nothing stood between her and the pale flowers. A single petal was all it would take to erase everything that had come to pass. A little frond beneath her tongue, and she'd forget the Brotherhood...she'd forget Aud...forget Iluka...forget Myronor.

More intrusive than her darkening thoughts was a vision of Lotus with his black eyes carrying a look of concern he reserved only for her. She could nearly hear him grumbling, *now Lass, is that really what ye want?*

"No," she said aloud, her voice rough.

Her eyes pricked as she pulled away from the devastating flower, straggling tears washing away her delusions. Despite everything that had happened and the lingering woes it left behind, she didn't wish to forget anymore. She might have abandoned Myronor, but she wasn't ready to let him go. How could she, with his soul tied to hers? She'd take the stab of pain to her chest at every thought of him over nothing at all. But she wasn't ready to forget what was owed to Marvena, either.

Again, the Aether burned with a surge of approval as Ophiera continued her march.

For some time, she followed the sporadic trail over intermingled roots and sand, creating a slippery mixture. Eventually, Marvena's trail led through the brush to an open, sanded shore. Framed between two leafless trees, choked out by the salt water, lay the sight of Cantheas. With the entirety of the peninsula city in view, she had to admit it was a prettier sight than Feyralis, at the very least. Cantheas protruded into the sea on a naturally formed pier of stone. Stretching out into the deep waters off the coast, the pier was ideally situated for large ships, negating the need for smaller ferrying vessels. Dozens of wooden piers protruded from the peninsula, striped with the pale salt of high tide and darkened with waves towards the bottom. As always, there were more ships berthed than buildings on the horizon.

From her vantage, it was easy to observe the ships and crews that had docked, at least those facing this side of the coast. Ophiera could even discern which were on their way to departure by the configuration of the sails. To her disappointment and relief, none looked like the *Mistral*. Perhaps this meant that Myronor was already on his way to Krysas.

And with that thought, her stomach sank.

Marvena had stopped here, meaning she surely had some interest in the ships of Cantheas. Departures from Cantheas traveled in all directions, and while most traded with Krysas, many supplied the coastal villages of Tanvik and the surrounding islands. If the wretch planned to stow away aboard a ship or, worse, had a contact at the docks, the trail could be lost for good. At least a trail of footprints, she thought bitterly. No matter where Marvena went, she was likely to leave death in her wake.

Ophiera's scars flashed with white-hot pain, and a wisp of smoke seared her nostrils. The thought of Marvena escaping was about to push her over the edge into flames, but she couldn't lose control here. Not when she could pursue instead. Inspecting the sands again, she followed the trail back into the forest and towards the city. It wasn't too difficult to muster the energy to force her pace, though the exhaustion of days without food or sleep weighed more than the claymore on her back. She was painfully reminded of her days in the Cloister, fasting and training without rest. At least this time, she suffered by choice.

The evening sun dimmed quickly in the thickening woods, obscuring the trail in shadow. But any worry she had of losing the path faded as she recognized the building looming through the trees. The Tattered Sail Inn was the only infrastructure outside the main gates of Cantheas, and to her surprise, it hadn't changed, at least from this view. Even from this distance, she could hear the loud voices and laughter permeating out through the windows. She couldn't see much from behind the inn, but she could hear everything. The sounds of traders' conversations permeated the woods, ricocheting off the stone walls of the city nearby. The last time she had been to Cantheas, the Tattered Sail Inn primarily served the tradespeople traveling to and from Feyralis and other nearby villages who wanted a quieter rest than the inns in the city could offer. Once, and only once, had Ophiera tried to stay the night there, and she had learned her lesson far too quickly. She must assume the public's opinions of paladins had only diminished further since that time, as they had in Feyralis.

While a myth to many, paladins remained a point of contention for others. Before her retirement, she'd always been met with stares and whispers, but that was to be expected. The paladins of the Cloister had fallen to near myth in Tanvik, at least as of late. Many knew of the clerics of the Cloister, given that a Magistrate Justicar had been kindled a Hand of Mercy. But the priests almost never left the Cloister, nearly all kindled as Keepers of their Oaths of Sacrifice. As far as Ophiera knew, she was the last of their order to be bestowed an Oath of Retribution from the pillar of flames and the last to be conscripted by the Magistrate.

Her experience in Feyralis proved just how the perception of the Cloister and their paladins had further soured since her retirement. Stares became glares, whispers became shouts, and the last time she had entered a city, an angry mob nearly attacked her. If it hadn't been for Myronor...

Ophiera shook him violently from her thoughts.

Marvena was the reason she was here, and if she were to catch her before she escaped on a ship, she needed to move with haste. By the look of the tracks beneath her, it seemed Marvena also found going inside the inn out of the question. The hurried footprints turned from the main path, leading behind the establishment towards the stables.

A sudden sense of relief washed over her—a feeling she hadn't felt for days. It was hard to reconcile *why,* as the Aether still burned beneath her feet, but perhaps it was calmer...satisfied? She could only interpret this as a sign she was nearing her quarry—that today, she would find Marvena in Cantheas and finally feel her ashes instead of Iluka's in her hand.

With a firm step, Ophiera set off from the thicket toward the city gates. She kept her head low as she crossed the sandy yard behind the inn, avoiding the crowds, just as the tracks she followed had done. When she reached the stable hand shed, she saw Marvena had paused. Perhaps to scope out the gate, she thought, which she now had in clear sight. Ophiera watched as several self-appointed guards shook down a few new merchants. She heard the outraged cry of "entry fee" before a trickle of awareness crawled down her spine.

She was not the only soul observing nearby.

Crouching low, she inspected Marvena's tracks again and noticed another set of footprints in the sand. Softer and longer strides traveled in the opposite direction of the city, crossing paths with Marvena's as they went. It seemed several people found the path behind the inn preferable to the main road. But as she followed, the newcomer's steps led into the shed while Marvena's continued past it. The weathered wooden door hung slightly ajar, an unforgivable mistake for any stablehand near the jungles. How hadn't she noticed this before?

Listening a moment, she thought she heard a faint scuffle from within, but now that a full-on shouting match had broken out by the gates, she couldn't be sure. But she needed to be sure.

With one hand on the hilt of her sword, she used the other to push open the door slowly. The tiny shed was filled with a few stacks of hay, but otherwise, completely empty. She loosened her grip on her sword, only to realize her error far too late. An unseen force dragged her forcefully into the shed, armor and all, slamming the door behind them.

~ Three ~

CAUGHT

He couldn't believe, even with the strength of his invisibility spell, that the paladin hadn't sensed him before now.

To no surprise, she re-adjusted her grip on her claymore the moment he dragged her into the shed. But he was far too aware of what she could accomplish with the enormous blade, and with a dance of his fingers and a flash of light, he bound her weapon to her back and her hand to the hilt.

She growled against his magic, sending shivers down his spine. Wildly, she fought to pry her arm free from behind her head, her thick braid whipping through the air. Her bloodshot eyes danced around, searching for what bound her to no avail.

He watched amusedly as she thrashed her unbound fist before her, searching for him with violence. That had always been her default, hadn't it? And yet, if she could just stop a moment and focus, she'd have her answer about precisely *who* bound her now.

Dodging another golden fist, he cast again, this time catching her swinging arm around the wrist with his invisible hand. He'd been careful not to touch her this entire time, only using magic to manipulate her. The cold of her golden vambrace provided enough of a barrier that she still didn't connect exactly who he was or why he was doing this. And while he remained slightly impressed that he'd managed to catch her so off guard, any pride he might have felt was overshadowed by her relentless attempts to break free of him.

"Show yourself, coward!" she spat through clenched teeth, "or I will reveal your ashes!"

A burn of rage shook through him, a terrible promise of her threat reverberating through the ekath. But despite her claims, he *knew* her...she wouldn't claim a soul without reason, without *knowing* their guilt. And thus far, he'd done nothing to warrant the Retribution of a paladin.

As if she read his thoughts, he sensed her strength and resolve wane like the dust now settling in the shed. Yet again, she was giving up...

With a sigh and a flash of blue light, he lifted the invisibility spell from himself. As her jewel-like eyes fixated on him, and only him, he watched all the ire drain from them, only to be replaced by a look that was and would forever be his damnation.

"M-Myronor?"

All of his anger burned to ashes the moment she pressed her full lips together to murmur his name. But the rawness of her voice shook him back to frustration.

"I don't want to hear my name on your tongue just yet."

"W-why?" She asked hoarsely.

He sighed, irritated by the roughness of her voice. At least her injuries had healed enough for her to speak, but she still sounded ill. Damaged.

"Because you almost sound as if you missed me."

Though he still bound her in place with magic, her body fell lax in his grip. He didn't think the truth alone could defeat her so thoroughly, and yet he found no sense of victory in this moment.

"I did..." she breathed, swallowing hard, "...miss you."

Of all the responses he had expected, *that* was not one. Why did she have to make everything so difficult? A constant contradiction that he was never prepared to navigate...but he supposed that was part of her charm. Much like her wrists, his anger was becoming harder and harder to hold on to now. Seeing her, touching her, *feeling* her through the ekath again nearly overrode his righteous rage.

Nearly...

"You have an odd way of showing it," he said. "The worst, in fact."

"I—" she began, but stared at the ground in a moment of silence. "Myronor, you don't understand—"

"Exactly!" He growled, failing to keep his voice down. "I don't understand!"

As her eyes welled with tears, her thoughts flooded the ekath. With the tether re-established, her emotions crashed through it like a tidal wave, drowning him in her grief and pain.

The loss of Iluka, the slights of Marvena, and the fear...so much fear of...*for* him. As their pain synced, his grip on her faltered, and by means he still didn't understand, he knew the words repeating in her mind but never spoken aloud.

"What were you protecting me from by leaving me?" He asked.

She closed her eyes as another wave of fear and pain surged through her. Despite the despair of her unspoken thoughts, Myronor found relief in them.

When she'd first left, he feared she only wished to be rid of him. It was too easy to understand why she wouldn't wish to be burdened by him. But when he read her letter, he had held on to a sliver of hope between the lines that her misguided onus was to blame.

Through the ekath, he sensed the truth in her heart. Through her eyes, he saw the suffering endured. And throwing his pain to the wind, he lifted the binds and took her face firmly in his hands.

She didn't fight his lips crashing against hers. The warmth of her mouth, the movement of her jaw, the burn of her soul...he couldn't *feel* enough of her after suffering her absence. And seemingly, she felt the same.

As their mouths melded, so did their thoughts in a cacophony of regrets, worries, and reliefs. She, like him, longed for this moment. She, like him, desperately wished for their reunion. But she, unlike him, still held a thread of wariness, of fear.

He admitted before this moment the bitterness that had overtaken his heart was of a depth he never thought he could be rid of. But how could he feel bitter now, with her so near? When her lips were moving against his with the same need, the same passion? She *had* actually missed him, and that truth healed his heart more than he knew it needed. Ekath or not, *this* was how they were meant to exist—together.

But their moment of relief was suddenly tainted by a flash of fear he couldn't understand. Her passion turned to panic through the ekath as burning fires churned within her soul. It wasn't until he sensed the flames beneath her feet that he understood.

She pushed against him, relatively weakly considering her strength and stature, but with a flash of his mana, he refused to release her. Never again could he let go, even with the threat of the Aether encroaching quickly on them.

With another cast of blue light, Myronor levitated her greaves off the ground, never parting from her lips. Hands glowing, he dropped them from her face to her armored waist, holding her above and against him, away from the ground.

He could sense her immediate relief from the Aether, and to his contentment, she continued to kiss him. But her racing thoughts of flames and Iluka tainted the moment and brought him back to reality.

Beyond his soul's constant cry for her, there were more pressing reasons he needed to find her. Like Feyralis, when they first met, Cantheas was no longer how she remembered.

"Why are you here?" She whispered.

He raised his eyebrows at her, wondering if she purposefully ignored his thoughts through the ekath.

"For you, of course." Despite her own chosen ignorance of their bond, Myronor relied on it. Not only to sense the questions hidden behind her eyes but to answer them as well. "I followed the draw of your soul, and it led me here."

She dropped her gaze, staring at the ground with her brow furrowed. Every angle of her face held a look of defeat as if she had spent the last days battling far more than the tether. And yet, she had no idea the fight she was about to walk into in Cantheas.

"I felt it, too, but I didn't realize...regardless, you shouldn't be here," she said, her voice gaining strength. "You shouldn't have come."

Still casting her above her power source, he took her frustratedly by the chin and dragged her gaze back to his. "You shouldn't have left."

A flare of defiance flickered behind her gaze, relieving as it was terrifying. Rarely was he so bold to challenge her, but that was before their souls were bound. Now, in their connection, he felt all of her emotions flare to life. The guilt of abandonment, the grief for Iluka, the rage for Marvena—all storming beneath her miserable expression. Flashes of white flowers and an abandoned village, of flames and stormy sands filled with debris, leaked through the bond, showing him exactly what she had faced to leave her in this state. But the further back her thoughts traveled, the more desperate her soul felt for reprieve. Like a caldera, she had buried all that had happened to them beneath her hunt for Marvena. But even he could sense the dome cracking.

"Why couldn't you just tell me?" He asked.

"Tell you what?" She asked guiltily.

"Your plans to leave."

She closed her eyes, breaking their gaze. "Because you would have stopped me."

"You're damn right," he hissed, anger suddenly tensing his throat. "And somehow, even knowing that you thought I'd just accept being left behind?" She bit her lip as a bit of color returned to her cheeks, but did not speak a word. It was a clear answer enough for him, and yet he needed her to know just how much she had wounded him. "You called *me* a fool, but abandoning me with the expectation that I would simply *comply* is by far the most foolish choice you've ever made! And that's saying a lot after watching you fight a troynt with your bare hands!"

As her glare turned on him, more of the fire returned to her eyes. Despite being the target of her ire again, he found far too much relief in seeing that look in her eyes again. The burning fire was an improvement from the defeated woman he'd dragged into the shed moments ago. He needed to see the fight in her before he'd let her go.

"I fought off that troynt to save *you!*" She hissed, her voice breaking harshly. "Every decision I've made has been to keep you safe, to keep you from harm!"

"I know," he said, his voice faltering under the weight of her emotion. "But I don't need to be saved from *you*."

Her eyes widened at his words. And just like that, the fight behind them was extinguished. Even with her feet off the ground, she tried to pull away. To flee. To run.

"Why?" He begged.

"Because I can't control the flames!" Ophiera cried, wincing as she pressed a gauntleted hand against her throat. "Every moment, I fight against the call of the Aether! Each day, it grows worse, churning beneath me, threatening to ignite at any moment. Don't you understand? I *destroyed* Iluka because of my lack of control! I destroyed my home—*your* home—all because I cannot quell the power I now wield! I am nothing but destruction, a threat to anyone near me, a threat to you! Imagine what would have happened just now if you hadn't...if...you..."

Myronor watched as the realization struck her, and he couldn't help but smirk. Her greaves clanked gently as he lowered her back to the dirt floor. Through the ekath, he felt her reconnection with Erum as she closed her eyes against the surge. Even he felt the weight of its power, like trying to stand still in a rushing river.

"Kaikora said, 'Your ekath may serve you well if he is willing to help.' And Ophiera, I'm more than willing to help...but you have to let me."

"My failures are not your burdens to bear," she argued.

Myronor placed his hands on her pauldrons, somehow resisting the urge to shake her. Again, he felt her thoughts darken with purpose, and an urge to flee overtook him. Images of cold, dead eyes and yellow robes revealed all he needed to know, and yet, did she not think he felt the same way about Marvena?

"Do I not have a say in what burdens I choose to bear?" She gazed at him confusedly, forcing his frustration into his voice. "You left without asking me what I wanted—you chose for me! And you, of all people, understand the unfairness of someone else deciding your burdens for you without choice."

Both of their eyes fell to the scars, hidden beneath the gleaming gauntlet now. They both knew they were a fate thrust upon her. A decision made for her that she regretted every day.

"I couldn't bear the thought of hurting you," she whispered. "I needed to keep you safe."

"I know," Myronor said. "But no matter the threats we face, Ophiera, even if it is you yourself, *my choice* will always be you. Always."

His voice cracked on his last word, forcing him to bite his lip to keep it from trembling. Again, the ache in his heart proved he wasn't good at fighting. And from the looks of it, all the fight had left her, too. With her head hung low, she looked worse for wear than ever. As if she were wasting away before his very eyes...

He had been so caught up in his reunion with her that he hadn't realized just how poor a state she was in. And in the midst, he'd nearly forgotten the danger they were in. Well, the danger *she* was in.

"Let's continue this discussion inside," he said quietly. "I rented a room at the inn, so you can—"

"There's no time for discussion," she said in a harsh hiss. "I must continue to Cantheas, Marvena—"

"Take advantage of the ekath and rest your voice," he said, not bothering to hide his irritation. She sounded raw and frantic now, the exact opposite of what she needed.

She glared at him, lips pressed together. *I tracked Marvena here—she entered the city within the last hour, and I must find her before she jumps ship!*

"No," he said, still holding her pauldrons. "Ophiera, you can't enter the city."

She looked annoyed by his attempt to hold her in place again. *Why not?*

"Let me explain inside, please. You have no idea what will happen if you show your face out there. Please, trust me."

She eyed him as if she were to argue, but did not speak through lips or ekath. Myronor sighed in relief.

"Alright, first things first, we need to get you out of that armor."

He followed her thoughts as they went in several different directions, the first and foremost relating to his lips pressing against hers moments ago. The vivacity of the images she conjured in her head took him by greater surprise than a navarra.

"It's hard to be angry with you when you think perverted thoughts like that," he said with a shaky smile.

I'm not a pervert!

"Well, you have claimed me one on several occasions, so I'll step outside while you change. I brought some options that should fit—"

But as he reached for the minimized satchel on his belt, she halted his wrist in her grasp.

I'm not taking my armor off until you explain why it's so damn important.

Myronor had hoped she would simply agree, but he should have known better. Still, he hadn't wanted to break the news to her quite yet—not when she already looked so defeated. But he supposed protecting her from the truth of the storm on the horizon would be quite hypocritical of him.

"Ophiera, news of Iluka has reached Cantheas," Myronor said, knowing he couldn't speak the word without despair in his voice.

"Already?" She hissed out loud.

He nodded, pulling a tattered piece of parchment from his robes. "Rumors have already spread far down the coast. It's not safe for you in Cantheas."

"Why?"

Myronor rubbed a hand over his face, debating on whether or not now was the right time to show her. Stuffed in the dingy shed, he supposed this was a better place than in the middle of the busy tavern.

"Because *these* have been hung everywhere in Cantheas."

Ophiera reached for the parchment without question, and he watched as her eyes darted across the notice. He wasn't adequately prepared for the sense of disbelief, rage, and fear that overwhelmed him as she read the words he had already burned to memory.

Wanted!
The Magistrate seeks information on the location of two individuals wanted for questioning in regard to the tragic destruction of Iluka.
Any relevant information will be rewarded.
The shaman, Kaikora Skwol, is described as tall, muscular, with bronze hair, gray eyes, and armed. Last seen in Iluka.
The Warden of Iluka and former paladin of the Cloister, the Aspect of Retribution, is described as tall and of a muscular build with white hair and violet eyes, wearing golden armor. Informally goes by Ophiera. Last seen in Iluka. The Cloister is offering additional rewards for information.

~ Four ~

CONTRITION

Left standing by the tavern stairway, Ophiera waited impatiently for Myronor. He claimed he was requesting food and drink to be delivered to the room, but the line at the bar was outrageously long. Considering the sun hadn't even set yet, it was surprising how many frequented the establishment. But then again, she rarely set foot in places like the Tattered Sail, so perhaps this was normal these days.

While Feyralis was known as the city of beauty and beast, Cantheas held a different dichotomy: a city of friend and foe. As the premier city of the Southern Coastlands and the largest seaport in Tanvik, Cantheas had been politically usurped by Feyralis for use as a trade port—namely, trade with Krysas. When the foreign city-state opened its borders to trade over two decades prior, the trade had catalyzed economic growth and prosperity throughout Tanvik. However, the traditions of the Southern Coastlands could not be shaken by profits and progress.

Cantheas natives, regardless of gains, still clung to conventions of the realm over the years. The old fought against the new, the poor against the rich, and even the sea against the land. And anywhere there was unrest, anathema lurked; murderous souls whom the Aether required returned as recompense. Needless to say, Ophiera had frequented Cantheas often while under Magistrate conscription and avoided it entirely during her retirement.

As Ophiera watched Myronor move up in the queue, she studied the patrons with a weary eye. Though most were merchants, evident in their Feyralis-style flowing garb of endless layers, there was a smattering of local fishers and laborers sitting at the corner tables and bar, dressed in scant, plain leathers. Both parties kept to themselves, segregated in pockets across the tavern, pretending the others did not exist. At least it was easier to hide amongst a crowd of avoidant gazes, but even in the worn set of leathers Myronor had provided, Ophiera felt exposed. She couldn't stop her boot from tapping against the dirt floor and rolled her eyes impatiently, catching a glimpse of a notice board hanging near the door.

Plastered with fragments of parchment, one small area remained open. She guessed it had recently held her own wanted sign before Myronor had removed it. The rapid turn of events had kept her head spinning and her blood boiling. Despite Marvena consuming her thoughts for days, a new worry took hold. Only Ophiera, Myronor, and Berwyn had witnessed the destruction of Iluka. Only they knew it was Marvena and the Brotherhood behind the carnage. So, how in the flames had word reached the Magistrate before they had even arrived in Cantheas? Not even the best courier could have reached Cantheas quickly enough. And why did they want her and Kaikora to question? Nothing made sense, and with that perpetual thought, she dug her nails into her palms, clenching her fists to quell the Aether now threatening to spill forth.

Try to stay calm, Ophiera.

Myronor's thoughts brushed her own, snuffing out her ignition. His alarm mingled with her irritation, both silently agreeing they needed to hurry upstairs. Damned dirt floor, she cursed, trying to reign herself in again. Closing her eyes, she rested the back of her head against the wall. The conversations in the tavern blended together like a roar of flames, indiscernible and yet comforting at the moment. As Myronor said, she just needed to stay calm...to avoid thoughts of...well, everything.

"Right shame about Iluka, eh?"

Ophiera's eyes snapped open, focusing on the bar. The murmur of other voices fell away as she focused on the words she dreaded to hear.

"Aye...the real shame is losing all them pearls."

Trying to keep her stance casual, she leaned forward, eyes falling on two fishers drinking at the end of the bar. They were older, leathery men with several finished pints to each of their names. For a few moments, they drank in silence, sloppily picking a bowl of chipped, roasted ink kelp. She watched them with bated breath, waiting to hear more. An uncomfortable tug in her chest told her Myronor's attention had also turned down toward the end of the bar, listening intently.

"How in the Aether's name ye think an entire village disappeared off the map?" asked the first man with a gravelly voice. "Ain't never heard the likes of it."

"Aye," sighed the other, sounding tired and bored, "hard to say what happened."

I happened, Ophiera thought miserably.

Stop that nonsense.

Myronor's mind recoiled against hers, but she ignored him to focus on the gossipers.

"C'mon, tell me what yer theory is..."

The tired man groaned, drinking deeply before wiping his mouth on his sleeve. "Don't know, and don't care. Got what they deserved, and that's all that matters to me."

I'm almost done at the bar, Ophiera. Just head upstairs now!

Ophiera bit her lip, tasting a faint tang of blood. She needed to listen while keeping the flames and her tongue at bay.

"Hah! Allergic to shellfish or somethin', eh? Weren't they just oyster farmers?"

"Aye...but didn't ye hear about their Warden?"

"Heard they had a fierce one to match the gargantuan shaman they had, too."

"Aye, that's not all. Rumor has it she was a former paladin—abandoned her Oath and never faced judgment for some reason. No one knows why the Magistrate and Cloister allowed it, but now they're paying the price. That village was cursed the moment they let someone like *that* become their Sea Warden."

Ophiera clenched her fists tighter still, her knuckles cracking in the effort to remain composed. Very few knew that she, the Warden of Iluka, was a paladin. The shaman and the villagers had an unspoken rule never to mention it, mainly to avoid unwarranted attention from thieves. But if these two insignificant men knew, how many others did too?

Regardless, her identity didn't change the fact that Iluka *was* her fault, just as the tired man had said. She had failed as Warden—failed to protect them against the Brotherhood and buried her failures in a white, flaming cataclysm.

Stop with that nonsense! Please, Ophiera, go before...before you regret staying.

Ophiera winced against the bite in Myronor's voice in her mind. And while she knew she didn't deserve his forgiveness, *feeling* his own frustration mix with her worry, all while trying to quell the flames and eavesdrop on these men, taxed her control.

She knew any moment now, she would bubble over, and yet, she needed to listen.

"Ya know, I remember hearing about their Warden once—went berserk, but I didn't know she was a paladin. Apparently burned the whole beach against some shipwrecked sailors, claiming they was pirates or some such nonsense. Guess you're right—she probably killed them all, filthy anathema."

The cursed word broke the dam, and white, hot anger rushed through Ophiera. Her scars seared, threatening with the fire filling her insides, a fire she was tempted to release on these horrid men.

They knew *nothing* of what happened. Nothing of her, nothing of the village, nothing of the world, for that matter. While they sat at the bar, drinking their afternoon away in gossip and games, the Brotherhood stole the lives of countless, rending their vespers from the Aether. *They* were the anathemas. And while this darkness had spread across Tanvik, all they could do was gossip. They lived their lives free of duty, allowed to choose, and yet *this* is what they chose: to waste away at a bar while spreading lies and discourse. Ungrateful, entitled, disgusting people.

A flash of pain was her only warning of the ignition. But just as her scars flashed, a cooling sensation of magic replaced the fire within, lifting her from her feet and into Myronor's arms. Dazed by the abrupt disconnect from the Aether, she barely registered how he held her now—his arms under her back and knees, cradled against his chest by the tingling of magic. She looked up at him, lips parted with confusion as he smiled down at her, nearly stopping her heart.

"There you are, my love," Myronor said, his voice steady and jovial. "The honeymoon suite is finally ready."

She nearly choked as all eyes fell upon them. The two old fishers stared at them with furrowed brows before raising their steins, followed by a few other cheers. As her face burned, not with the

Aether for once, the crowd disappeared in a blur of blue as Myronor rushed her upstairs.

He carried her past several rooms as the murmur of the crowded tavern below faded away. Cheek pressed against his chest, Ophiera could hear Myronor's heartbeat match his quickened stride. At the end of the hallway, they stopped under the light of the oil lamps, washing out the pale glow of magic still cast upon her. Only once inside did Myronor set her down to lock the door behind them.

Upstairs, the call of the holy flames was as quiet as the bustle from the tavern. She took a few breaths of silent relief, at least from the Aether.

"Are you well?" Myronor asked.

"No," she said, her words turning into a growl. "They think *I* killed everyone in Iluka!"

Myronor sighed, meeting her gaze with rare worry. "This is why I needed to find you before you marched into Cantheas, unaware. Thanks to the flyers, everyone now knows the Warden of Iluka was a paladin *and* that they are hunting you for questions—it's easy to see how the people interpret that as guilt. "

"This is precisely why we must find Marvena now!" Ophiera snapped, fear overtaking her for a moment. If the Cloister...if they thought she truly abandoned her Oath and claimed the souls of innocents...An icy dread flooded her insides.

What did the Chaplain have to say about these rumors?

Did Aleksander believe them, too?

What punishment would she face?

Isolation?

Extinguishment?

Warmth surrounded her icy hand as Myronor pulled her from her thoughts. The fear subsided as she focused on the sensation of him and him alone.

"I promise we will find Marvena, but—"

"You don't understand! If the Cloister is searching for me...if they think I'm at fault...if they..."

The words clamped down on her chest, squeezing all the breath from her lungs.

She couldn't return to the Cloister.

She couldn't face Uzziel.

She couldn't breathe.

She couldn't stop the room from spinning.

She couldn't...

"Ophiera, please, calm down," Myronor said gently, stroking her knuckles. Again, the sensation of his touch calmed her, even if the ekath was clamped shut to his thoughts. "You're not going back to the Cloister, I promise. But there is a reason I was so desperate to find you, beyond the obvious; I have an idea of what's happening and what we can do to avoid a potential mess. Please, sit down, and I'll explain."

Myronor released her hand and gestured to the small wooden table and chairs beside the door. With her thoughts still lingering on the Cloister, she did as she was told and slunk down into a chair. Her body felt as heavy as her heart, even without her armor.

In the middle of the wooden table lay a tattered journal, which she recognized with a pang. It had felt like ages since she had watched Myronor write in it.

"Luckily for us, I kept exquisite notes throughout our journey," he said, seating himself across from her and flipping open the journal. "First, a curiosity that has stuck out is *both* of the Reverends referring to this Mistress person. At first, I thought it was simply another name for Aud, the entity or god or whatever the Brotherhood serves beyond."

Ophiera frowned as her Oath scars itched again. "I always interpreted the Mistress and Aud as two separate entities. Even Marvena claimed the Mistress sought to capture you alive while Aud desired my death as if they were distinct."

Myronor smiled at her, making her heart skip. "Well, I'm now in agreement with you. I believe that while Aud resides in another plane of existence, I'm quite sure that the Mistress is part of our world, of Erum, and manipulates events unseen. It would explain how quickly information has spread regarding the destruction of Iluka. And it would explain more if the Mistress was, in fact, someone within the Magistrate."

Ophiera stared at him, dumbstruck. "Isn't that a slight stretch?"

"Is it?"

"I mean, I agree the Mistress is resourceful, but fast news doesn't mean the Magistrate has been infiltrated by the Brotherhood. Does it?"

She hated how unsure her question sounded.

"I assume you do not wish to review my journal in the depths I have," Myronor said smugly, "so I simply ask you to check the date on the notices."

If Ophiera hadn't been quite so exhausted, she might have rolled her eyes at his sudden academic tone. But curiosity won over her annoyance, and she unfolded the tattered parchment on the table. She scanned the irritating posting for the mandatory date of notice that all Magistrate writs carried. Her fingers trembled as she ran them along the impossible ink strokes.

"These are dated the same *day* Iluka was attacked..."

"Precisely," Myronor said with a frown. "Meaning—"

"Someone knew Iluka was to be attacked," Ophiera began, trying to quell the fire within from seeping from her scars. "They informed the Magistrate and posted notices before the village was even destroyed."

Myronor nodded. "The Magistrate certainly knew of Iluka's fate before it had actually happened. Worse, they could have been involved in planning it. Hence, my suspicion is that the Mistress may be linked with the Magistrate. There is no other way the

Magistrate, or the Cloister for that matter, could know of Iluka's demise the very day it occurred."

Ophiera blinked, staring at his journal.

The string of lies was becoming too complicated to track. She shook her head, searching for the distant sensation of the Aether. From afar, she felt more compelled to listen to its whispers without fear of losing control. And just as the unspoken fire led her to Cantheas, something in the muffled blaze settled the conflict in her heart.

"I...think you're right."

He looked at her with raised eyebrows. "Convinced that quickly?"

She smiled, half-cocked with exhaustion. "I found it strange that the Brotherhood referred to me as the Aspect of Retribution. Few outside of the Cloister know me by that title...Really, only those within the Magistrate. Uncommon knowledge means an uncommon source. Someone within the Magistrate makes sense."

"I hadn't thought of that," Myronor said, his voice growing in fervor as he flipped a page. "But it all adds up."

Ophiera nodded in agreement.

"How else could the plague in the Sloughmire have gone unnoticed for so long? Lotus claimed Eliana knew of the Brotherhood, and yet you were conscripted to escort me to another country rather than actually uphold your sworn duty of Retribution for the sins they committed?"

She shrugged, wondering why he was continuing his point when she already agreed. But she supposed it didn't hurt to hear him out—she had missed the sound of his voice.

"Tasking me with escorting you made us easy targets—known location, known paths...The only folly I see in this theory *is* us."

"Us?" He asked with a drop in his voice.

"If the Magistrate has been corrupted by the Brotherhood and the Brotherhood wants *you*, why did they not just take you in

Feyralis, at your tower? And why not simply kill me in Iluka during my retirement? Instead, the Magistrate conscripted me with the Cloister's blessing and tasked me to escort you overseas. It doesn't make sense that this Mistress would knowingly allow you to be so well-protected in my custody."

Myronor's mouth twitched. "So, you're admitting that I'm safest with you now?"

Ophiera chewed on her cheek before taking a deep breath. She both hated and admired his ability to skew any conversation in his favor.

"I'm speaking from *their* point of view, not my own. Plus, everything was different at the start of this journey. *Everything.*"

Myronor smirked at her, running his hand through his hair. Something about the motion plucked at her heartstrings. But not enough for her to open the ekath again. It was best they stayed in their own heads for now.

"Much has changed, hasn't it? But even regarding *us*, the narrative still fits from their point of view. We were still easier targets together…They knew to use your Oath against you, to force you to exchange your life for mine. I'm sure it was the only way they could ever hope to kill you." His eyebrows knit together, and though she kept the ekath silent, she could see the discomfort of his thoughts. "I'm sure the Mistress never expected me to fall from the wall of Feyralis…never thought we would be bonded as ekatma. Not even Kaikora foresaw what we are now. "

The doubt in Myronor's voice at the end of his thought made her heart still. He spoke as if he himself did not know the answer to what they were now. When they had first met, he'd been an unwanted charge. But far too quickly, he became far too meaningful to Ophiera. From a kind traveling companion to a soul-bounded savior, to now a…a what? A lover? Were they *lovers*? Despite abandoning him, there was never a doubt in her mind that she loved him. But they hadn't...well, there was the necessary step of making love to become lovers, wasn't there?

A knock on the door caused Ophiera to jump from her chair and reach a hand for her nonexistent claymore.

"It's just the food," Myronor said, rising from his chair.

Ophiera settled back into the wooden seat, though her heart hammered on. Whether it was exhaustion or the discussion, she felt her paranoia peak even with Myronor smirking at her.

A young woman stood outside the room, holding a tray of drinks and a platter of food balanced on her shoulder. The sound of clinking stoneware matched the rhythm of her shaking arms, offset by her high-pitched pants.

"S-sorry for the delay—C-Cyntia is swamped—a-asked me to drop these off for y-you and your b-b-betrothed."

"Ah, splendid!" Myronor said jovially, retrieving the tray of food. "Thank you...?"

Ophiera didn't understand how he could give the young woman such a warm smile when, moments ago, he had looked at her with such...disappointment. The woman flushed under his gaze, returning his expression with a beautiful, coy smile.

"M-my name is Blythe."

"Ah, well, thank you, Blythe," Myronor purred, setting the tray down on the table. From a pouch on his belt, he pulled forth several coins and placed them in her palm, holding her hand in his own for what Ophiera felt was far too long. "Please tell Cyntia that I appreciate her hospitality and the privacy allotted to me and my betrothed in her fine establishment."

As Blythe flushed vividly, Ophiera couldn't help but admire her beauty. Wild, tight curls of red hair radiated in all directions, matching the shade of her cheeks and accentuating the warmth of her dark brown eyes. Eyes that were staring at Myronor in a way Ophiera very much disliked.

"Have a good night," she giggled before Myronor released her slight, delicate hands and closed the door with a sigh.

His face fell as he turned to Ophiera.

"What's wrong?"

She couldn't really describe *what* was wrong, but she was undeniably troubled. Something about the interchange between Myronor and Blythe left her stomach unsettled, even more than the pang of her gut at the sight of the food.

"I'm just hungry," she mumbled.

"When was the last time you ate?" he asked, handing her a stein.

She chewed her lip for a moment. "I'm not sure."

"Ophiera," Myronor said, sitting down again across from her. He sounded quite disappointed saying her name. "When was your last meal?"

She kept both the ekath and her mouth shut. As if his gaze wasn't guilt-ridden enough, she couldn't tell him that the last full meal she'd had was the one he'd conjured for them onboard the *Mistral*. In her hurry to depart, she hadn't packed a morsel of food nor bothered to look for any.

"Never mind," he said quietly, pushing a plate of food before her with trembling hands.

She looked down at the platter of food. Though her insides churned with need, the same coiled sensation that blocked her voice seemed to negate her desire to eat as well. Another old habit from the Cloister—she had learned to cope with long fasts by convincing herself she didn't even desire to eat. Before, food had never been more than a necessity, a weakness to overcome. It wasn't until she met Lotus that a meal meant anything more than sustenance, and even then, it took persuasion.

"Please, Ophiera—eat."

The pain in his voice compelled her to pick up her fork. She wasn't sure why her eating habits caused him such disdain, but she wished Myronor would stop looking at her with quite so much distress behind his eyes. After a few forkfuls of meat she couldn't identify and half a loaf of partially burnt bread, he seemed to relax his glower. But a lump in her throat prevented her from swallowing another bite, and she set her utensil down shortly after.

"That's all you're going to eat?" He asked quietly.

She nodded.

Myronor ran both his hands over his face before sinking his elbows to the table. He pressed his palms against his eyes, obscuring half his face before he spoke.

"Ophiera, I'm not sure I can forgive you."

The words cut deep, dragging across her heart like a serrated edge. She had been waiting for the moment he would admit it, but she still didn't wish to hear it.

"I don't expect you to," she said, refusing to look up from the picked-apart plate before her.

"Do you even know the reason, with the ekath clamped shut as you have it?"

She'd never heard such harshness in his voice before.

"I swore I would never give up on you, and I broke that vow."

He made a chuffing sound, nearly like a laugh but without any humor. "Oh, I forgave you for abandoning me the moment I pulled you into that shed. What I'm having a harder time forgiving is you abandoning yourself."

"What?" She choked out, confused. "I didn't."

"No? What do you call going four days without a meal?"

"I've gone much longer without food or sleep before—"

Myronor stood from the table abruptly, shaking the plates and steins. "You haven't slept either?"

She chewed the inside of her lip, feeling far too defensive when she knew she should feel shame. "It wasn't for lack of effort. But I found staying awake to be far more productive and far less painful."

Myronor pushed his chair back, stepping away from the table. For a moment, Ophiera thought he was about to leave, to abandon her as she had abandoned him. But instead, he rounded the table and knelt before her, taking both of her hands in his own.

"Open the ekath," he said softly.

"W-why?"

"Because I need you to understand, to *feel* what I feel right now, seeing you in this state."

"In what state?"

With a shaking hand, he retrieved a silvered egg spoon from the tray of food and held it to her face. "Look at yourself, Ophiera."

Confused but compliant, she peered into the upside-down reflection. Dark circles drew from the violet of her eyes, leaching over sharp, sallow cheekbones. Stray locks had escaped her braid as if she wore a frayed rope instead, the plait tinted dark with dirt. She looked down at her hand, still clasped in Myronor's, to examine the dirt beneath her nails.

Ophiera placed the spoon on the table. Despite his request, she kept the ekath closed. She didn't need to feel his thoughts to understand why he looked at her with disappointment and pain. If the situation were reversed...well, she had burned down the entire Brotherhood encampment after watching Myronor suffer at the hands of his captors, hadn't she? Yet she had no one else to blame for her current state but herself.

"I was focused on Marvena and all else fell by the wayside," she said in a low whisper. "It's a pathetic excuse, and barely even an explanation. But before you, my Oath was all that mattered—all that I was—and all that I seemingly still am."

Myronor stood, still holding her hand, dragging her up with him. He pulled her against his chest, pressing his lips against the top of her head as she inhaled deeply. The scent of his robes, the warmth of his embrace, everything about him incited her to wrap her arms around him, sating the need of her own heart. They both shook with emotion, neither speaking for quite some time as he held her.

"We both made mistakes," he murmured into her hair. "So let us leave our mistakes behind. Together, we can mourn Iluka. Together, we can find Marvena. And together, we will destroy the Brotherhood."

Ophiera nodded against him, wishing for nothing more than what he spoke. Yet, in the back of her mind, an old worry sprang anew. Though far below their feet now, the Aether called ever louder every day. She nearly burst into flames at the bar below, and while Myronor may have prevented catastrophe, how often would that fall on him if they remained together? It wasn't his fault she couldn't bear the burden of flames, and yet it would fall upon him if they remained together.

"I can sense your doubts, even with the ekath clamped shut," he continued, drawing her tighter against him. "But Ophiera, I need you...I need you to understand—these last few days, I barely know what I've done or who I've become. You and you alone have consumed my every thought, my every action. While you have sought Marvena, all my efforts have been dedicated to finding *you*." With a softness she did not deserve, Myronor placed a knuckle beneath her chin and drew her gaze up to his. The sight of his pale, blue eyes filled with moisture reminded her far too much of the day they met, causing her heart to stammer. "I need you to accept that I would rather burn by your side than stray from it again. So please, I am begging you, don't abandon *us*."

As Ophiera stared unblinking into the eyes that matched his soul, she recognized the pain of abandonment. Regardless of how she'd operated before, the path before her was now shared with another. Despite wishing to break this bond of souls, she couldn't fight its existence. Rather than resist her circumstances, perhaps it was time to embrace them.

Together, she and Myronor had been through much. They'd battled man and beast alike. They had survived the ichor of the swamp and the fires of the cliff cave. For too long, she had viewed him as a burden—something to take care of, to watch out for, to protect. She hadn't realized just how much he had done the same for her.

"So...what's *our* next step?" she asked.

She felt his body relax as a genuine smile crossed his face. He ran his hands along her back and tugged gently on her frayed braid.

"Please don't take this the wrong way...but first things first, you really need a bath."

~ Five ~

FOUND

After days of concentrating on the draw of the ekath, Myronor could finally relax. Perhaps it was naive of him to assume that struggle must always serve a greater purpose, but their recent suffering had truly been for nothing. Had Ophiera simply been honest with him, they could have worked out a plan moving forward together and avoided these last days of turmoil. Because that's what they were—pure, torturous turmoil. But bitterness served no one.

While Myronor would forever remain sympathetic to Ophiera's nature, he still struggled to understand her. It had been her choice to leave him, and yet, she seemingly suffered as much, if not more, than Myronor in their separation. At least he had slept and managed a few meals while chasing the pull of the tether. He still could hardly believe she had reached Cantheas in such a short time. Any normal person would have been bedridden, if not dead, had they traveled as she had without rest or sustenance. His frustration stemmed from her suffering a pointless journey, only for them to be reunited again now—*that* was what he struggled to understand.

But at least now, things were closer to right.

They were together again, and both would reap the benefits of Myronor spending the extra coin for this particular room. Against the wall sat a large, four-poster bed piled high with straw pillows and knitted blankets. He was much looking forward to sprawling out and getting a good night's sleep with Ophiera beside him again. Before they could rest, however, she needed to finish bathing.

The presence of the large copper bathtub in the corner was rare, much like the woman within it. Tempting as he found their situation, he certainly wasn't a pervert and remained seated at the small table near the door, far behind the paper room divider. He could just make out her silhouette cast in the fiery evening light as steamy tendrils rose from the basin.

"Marvena has sailed from Cantheas by now while I sit here stewing like some pampered clam," Ophiera said from behind the divider.

Myronor stopped writing in his journal, smirking to himself. "And what makes you think she sails?"

"I don't think," she said tersely. "I can feel it; the wretch is fleeing, and I might lose her trail overseas..."

Her gut instincts were often correct, Myronor admitted, but the conviction with which she spoke made him wonder if something more drew her toward Marvena.

"If she is sailing anywhere, it is most likely to Krysas," Myronor said, feeling the twinge of doubt reverberating through the dampened connection. "Berwyn and I caught glimpses of sailors wearing yellow bandanas near the docks at night—often boarding ships bound for the mage city."

"If the Brotherhood is already here, then we should sail tonight!" Ophiera hissed with a particularly violent splash.

Myronor sighed. "There are no vessels *officially* departing to Krysas tonight—the ones that are are smugglers, and none would accept us as fare, at least not without selling you out for the reward. The ship Berwyn found us is our best bet for discretion and speed—it leaves tomorrow morning and, according to him, will sail us there in half the time of any other ship in port."

He waited, half expecting an argument, but her silence proved just how much she trusted the old man.

There was no ship or captain within the Southern Coastlands that Berwyn didn't know of or know personally. Even Myronor had been surprised at how quickly his father had used his contacts at the docks to find them a ship to Krysas. Besides the exorbitant fee and the speed of the ship, the only information Berwyn would share was that the captain was a distant relative of the former inn owner of Iluka, Yelena.

Gentle splashes from the tub distracted Myronor from his musings. He tried his best to keep his eyes on his journal, but the silhouette of Ophiera's arched back as she ran her hands through her endless hair made him drop his quill.

"Damnit," he muttered, trying to mop up the smear.

"What's going on?" She barked with a splash.

Only Ophiera could remain tense while submerged in hot water.

"Nothing at all—I just spilled some ink."

Myronor took a calming breath as her shadow settled back into the tub. He understood why she was on the edge, even with the ekath still silenced. The only benefit was that she couldn't judge his inappropriate thoughts. And at least now, the connection no longer ailed him.

When she had left him on the *Mistral*, nothing could have prepared Myronor for the physical pain of the ekath stretched thin with distance. While he had grown used to the tether, he hadn't realized how strenuous her absence would weigh upon it. Neither had Ophiera, it seemed, and now he wondered if the pain of their separation would only further convince her to sever the ekath.

Before Iluka, she had made clear her desire to break the bond, and though the thought hurt him deeply, he would support her decision as long as it was hers and not another misplaced intention to save him.

"Do you think someone may have recognized me downstairs?" Ophiera asked quietly.

"I doubt it," Myronor said, trying to sound as if he didn't share the same worry. "I took the notices down the moment I set foot in the inn. Plus, you didn't speak to anyone, and you weren't wearing your armor."

"But you knew I was a paladin, even without my armor."

Myronor smiled in recollection of her sopping wet form, chanting atop him near the riverbank. It was true; he had known precisely what she was the day she'd revived him. But to his dismay, he had forgotten how she had chanted in that strange language to evoke the holy flames. Since awakening, she commanded the Aether wordlessly at will, or rather, against her will.

"I'm exceptionally well-read and a great deal cleverer than most," Myronor said, keeping his voice light-hearted. "I doubt anyone in Cantheas would have the sense to see your scars for what they are."

Ophiera chuckled throatily before muttering, "The arrogance of mages."

"Can only be matched by the stubbornness of paladins," he retorted.

He heard Ophiera snort from behind the room divider and wished he could see her expression. But he supposed if he *could* see her bathing at that moment, it wouldn't matter much what facial expression she wore. By the flames, he had missed her.

"Where is Berwyn now?" she asked.

"Still on the *Mistral*. He wants to stay docked in Cantheas for now."

Another splash of water caught his ear. "He's not coming with us to Krysas?"

Myronor was pleased to hear her say 'us' again. "He wishes to keep an eye out for any survivors...and for Kaikora."

Ophiera *tsked*. "He will need to get in line for the shaman."

"You've quite the list of people to find—Marvena, Pyra, and Kaikora?"

The silence that followed made him regret his tongue. Why had he thought mentioning Pyra would be a good idea, considering her current mood? His mother was the reason for their entire journey, after all. Ophiera had been re-conscripted because of *his* request for an investigation of Pyra's death. It had crossed his mind on several occasions that everything Ophiera had been through was truthfully his fault. Pyra's death had set a series of events in motion that neither he nor anyone else could have predicted.

"I have a suspicion that where I find Marvena, I will find clues to Pyra's fate as well."

Myronor wished she'd allow the ekath open so he could follow her thoughts better. "What connection do you think Marvena has to Pyra?"

"Marvena and the Brotherhood are searching for you," she began, her voice subdued. "Both you and the Reverends possess magic that connects you to other worlds...a gift of spanning that you and your mother also shared. So, if they're interested in capturing you, isn't it likely for your power? And if that is the case, then why wouldn't they be after her, too? Why wouldn't they have *started* with her?"

Myronor gripped the side of the table, trying to still his hammering heart. She so quickly discerned the connection he still avoided making. After his captivity by the Brotherhood, he had suspected a possible link between the portals the Reverends summoned and the dark realm he traversed when spanning. He and his mother were the only mages he knew of who possessed spanning magic—the ability to travel near-instantaneously between locations on Erum. The only problem was that to use this magic, he needed to traverse into the dark place—a realm he now thought may be inhabited by Aud themself.

"We can only hope to find answers in Krysas," he said, trying to sound composed.

But clearly, he wasn't a very good actor, as he and Ophiera fell into silence. Lost in their thoughts, Myronor resumed working in his journal. Though he genuinely hoped to find answers overseas, he still had much to reevaluate from his writings.

One question that remained unanswered was how many in Tanvik truly *knew* of the Vespula Brotherhood. He and Ophiera could not be the only unfortunate souls to have discovered the new faction of cultists disguised as thieves. According to Marvena, the order itself had existed for centuries under many names. To what end, he didn't know...but he had a feeling of who might.

Lotus, Ophiera's oldest confidant, seemed to have known *exactly* what the Brotherhood was capable of, though he seemingly withheld that knowledge. The innkeeper reminded Myronor much of his former mentor, which wasn't necessarily a good thing. Rheta, the famed mage scholar and alchemician, had also held knowledge close to her chest. He wouldn't have been surprised if she had known some, if not all, the truths about the Vespula Brotherhood before they'd even departed Feyralis. Though he would have greatly appreciated her sharing that information, he expected no less after everything she'd put him through.

Knock. Knock. Knock.

Myronor jutted an ink line across the parchment. He heard Ophiera's startled splashes from the tub but made a "shh" sound under his breath. It was nearly dark outside, and he thought he had been rather explicit with Cyntia about their privacy.

"Who is it?" he asked loudly through the door.

There was a pause before a squeaky voice called back. "C-Cyntia asked me to d-drop off extra drinks, on the house."

Myronor smiled, letting out a sigh of relief. But that relief was not shared by the bathing paladin. Even with her thoughts obscured, he could sense her unease. But good hospitality was rarely nefarious, and he could certainly use a drink.

Through the room divider, he saw Ophiera's silhouette settle back down in the water as if trying to make herself unseen. Given her reaction the last time Blythe delivered, it was probably for the best.

When he unlatched the door, he'd barely cracked it open before a hand shot out from beyond the threshold. He couldn't see who pressed the thick swatch of wool over his nose and mouth, but he knew it wasn't Blythe.

Instinctively, Myronor inhaled to yell to Ophiera, but the dizzying mixture of stringent alcohol and metallic sweetness caught his voice in his throat. His limbs suddenly fell limp, and he collapsed into a strange set of thick arms.

It was terrifying how aware he remained while entirely unable to move. And more terrifying was Ophiera's absence behind the paper divider. Only when her head rose from the water did he realize she had been submerged during the altercation.

The same set of strange arms lowered him helplessly to the ground as a second person rushed into the room. As they shut the door, his head lolled against the wood-planked floor with a thud.

"Myronor?" Ophiera called. "Have you spilled your ink again?"

He fought desperately to scream again, to warn her, but his lips wouldn't move. Nothing would move. No matter how he struggled, his body would not heed him. He could only watch in horror as the second man, burly and broad, moved straight for the paper room divider.

Ophiera!

But with the ekath still silenced, he had no way to warn her.

"Make sure she can't chant!" hissed a voice above him.

"Myr—" cried Ophiera before the burly assailant wrapped both his hands around her neck, pushing her forcefully beneath the water.

He watched in horror as the water sloshed onto the floor and her legs kicked out. With gruff movements, the first assailant began binding Myronor's arms behind his back, forcing him to watch the struggle. Forcing him to watch her legs go limp, draped over the copper edge.

Ophiera?

No.

Ophiera!

Not again.

He couldn't witness her die again!

Like the arrow that pierced her chest, he could do nothing but watch as the life drained out of her. Again, helpless to stop her from slipping away back to the Aether.

Panic overrode reason as he screamed through the ekath, unable to comprehend why the tether remained...calm.

He felt no pull, no thoughts, no feelings at all, yet he sensed a tranquility that began to calm his heart. She...

A flash of blinding white light filled the room.

Tears poured from Myronor's eyes, unable to avoid the flare in his state. He remained dazzled by the light for a moment until his vision finally adjusted to the pile of smoldering ash lying beside the washtub.

From the water, Ophiera stood with sopping white hair flowing over her bare body. Steam rose from her runic arm, the source of her mana, glowing like the fury in her eyes. The droplets of water ran down every groove of her musculature as she leaped out of the basin, dripping from the curves of her shoulders and hips.

She landed with a thick thud, immediately falling into stride as she crossed the room and disappeared out of sight.

Myronor could only hear a few thuds and grunts from behind him. But with his eyes fixated on the pile of ash, he wasn't worried. In fact, he was relieved by the loud *bang* of flesh against wood, and even more so when he felt the ekath open in full.

Are you hurt?

The concern in her thoughts quelled some of the rage coursing through the ekath, but only slightly. Though her fury overwhelmed the tether, he relaxed into the sensation of her mind against his again, burning away all the fear he held moments ago.

Can't move, but otherwise, unharmed.

"What did you do to him?" Ophiera growled out loud, her attention no longer on Myronor.

"P-p-paralysis...p-p-po..." a voice stammered and squealed at the end.

Of course, Myronor thought. At least it made sense now why he vaguely recognized the metallic, sweet taste lingering in the back of his throat. As her apprentice, Myronor was often subjected to testing new formulations and concoctions of Rheta. He remembered clearly the one day she'd had him drink a paralysis poison, claiming it was a lesson in the potencies, but he knew it was a punishment for not returning her books to the proper shelf.

Is there an antidote I can beat out of this bastard?

Myronor heard the man sputter and groan, assuming Ophiera tightened her grip. While he greatly appreciated her enthusiasm, there were far more pressing matters to address than his ability to move.

No, it will wear off. Just press him for as much information as you can while you have him.

"Who the hell are you?" She hissed.

Though Myronor couldn't see the man directly, he *saw* through Ophiera's perspective thanks to the ekath. Flashes of an older, bald man pushed against the door with a scarred hand. Though her runes no longer burned, he felt the smoldering energy just beneath the surface. As Ophiera squeezed tighter around his throat, the man's face turned a splotchy purple.

"Hhhiired," the man gurgled.

He was at the bar earlier! Myronor thought, recognizing his voice and face now. *One of the drunks talking about Iluka...I'm assuming the other is the pile of ash by the washtub.*

"Who hired you?" Ophiera hissed.

The man could only spit incoherent noises.

You might need to loosen your grip a smidge.

He heard the man release a great breath and pant for a moment. "A-a woman...dressed in black..."

Marvena! They both thought bitterly in unison.

"And what were you hired to do?" She asked each word enunciated as if a struggle to say.

"C-capture the mage...k-kill...you."

Myronor felt her fingers squeeze for more as the man clawed desperately at her hands. "Did she say why?"

"No-o...only said...if he couldn't cast...and you c-c-couldn't chant...e-e-easy money."

"Not so easy, I'm afraid," Ophiera whispered.

Myronor felt her mana catch flame before white light filled the room. As her power and rage poured through her scars, a fraction of that energy back-drafted through the ekath to him. Even with her feet far above the ground, Ophiera held a reserve of the Aether, a powerful, vengeful mana that seared painfully against his mind. It was an agony unlike anything he'd ever felt, and while he internally cowered from it, Ophiera let the pain drive her flames.

Through her, Myronor saw another cloud of ash fall to the ground as she shook the grit from her hand. Dazed by the pain so suddenly relieved, he stared through his own eyes now at the vesper of the first man, slowly scattering and dimming. Within the fragments of the returning soul, foreign, dark streaks clung to the hazy yellow light. Myronor was immediately reminded of the leech worms that often parasitized the rubyfin schools offshore of Iluka.

The sound of furniture scraping across the floor broke his stupor. Ophiera dragged the table in front of the door as her frantic thoughts seeped incoherently into the tether. Dropping to her knees behind him, he felt her shaking hands undoing the binds that held him.

Ophiera, I promise I'm fine.

"Nothing about this is fine!" she snapped, rolling him onto his back.

To his surprise, she took his face in her heated, trembling hands as her burning gaze fell over him. Her wide, amethyst eyes lingered on his for a moment before she crashed her lips against his. Through the ekath, he felt her frustration, but through her kiss, he could only feel relief. And while her affection was everything he needed at the moment, he wished he could move a muscle to match it.

"You're quite sure this will wear off?" She breathed, running a scarred thumb over his cheek. "If I couldn't hear your voice in my head, I would be sure you had returned to the Aether."

It was strange to think the hands that held him so tenderly now were covered in the ashes of those she'd returned to the Aether moments before. And yet, he felt no disgust, no fear by this thought—only appreciation that it was her hands on him now and no one else's.

Quite sure. But you could keep kissing me, you know, to see if it helps move things along...

"This isn't the time for your jokes," Ophiera mumbled before standing. "And I'm sorry."

For what?

"For making you watch that."

Watch what? Returning two souls to the Aether after they wished to do the same to us?

Myronor felt her resistance through the ekath, but he was relieved to find a lack of guilt. Good, he thought, careful to keep it to himself.

As Ophiera crossed the room, Myronor was quickly distracted by her...well, her *everything.* She wasn't even attempting to hide her nudity from him now as she flexed her scarred hand, examining the room. If their lives hadn't been in mortal danger moments ago, he would think she was trying to torture him. Ash clung to her full figure, hugging every curve like highlights from a dark paintbrush. He had the insatiable urge to brush the grit from her glorious skin, if only to run his hands over every inch of her. By the flames, it was a blessing he couldn't move right now and embarrass himself. To think she had apologized moments before...

"You're most certainly still the pervert between us," Ophiera said as she reached for a creamy white tunic slung over a chair.

Appreciation isn't the same as perversion.

With a roll of her eyes and seemingly little effort, Ophiera dragged his limp body over her shoulders and carried him to the bed. His legs twitched incessantly as she laid him back on the pillows, a sign that the poison was already waning. His jaw, however, remained slack, and he prayed he wouldn't drool too much before he regained control.

"How the hell did they find us?" she said, staring between the ashen piles by the door and the wash tub.

Myronor followed her gaze to the glowing vesper still hovering near the door, pale green with swirls of black. Myronor knew the blackened corruption proved they had been deserving of Retribution, but it was a shocking sight, nonetheless.

They must have been staking out the bar...just like I was.

"So much for the armor giving me away," Ophiera growled audibly. "And how many more will follow them?"

I doubt anyone else—

"You doubted anyone would recognize us the first time! These fools knew I was a paladin—they even tried to prevent me from chanting."

Myronor smiled to himself. An indignant paladin, indeed, was an enjoyable cliche.

This might actually be a good thing, Ophiera.

"What could possibly be good about two men, hired by the Brotherhood, trying to kill us?"

To be fair, they were only trying to kill you...but details aside, think about it—they assumed you still needed to chant, meaning they don't know you've awakened as an Aspect...

Ophiera stopped her pacing. "But Marvena knows I don't need the chants to burn anymore. She's witnessed my cataclysms twice now."

Maybe it wasn't Marvena who hired them? We assumed a woman in black must have been the Reverend, but that's hardly a unique description.

"Or she knew that no one would follow her command if they knew the truth," Ophiera said. "Kill a paladin capable of leveling a village without speaking a word—not even a dedicated follower would take on that task. Perhaps Marvena sent them, knowing they were throwing their lives away on a slim chance they would reveal us."

Ophiera began pacing the room again, leaving Myronor paralyzed on the bed to watch. Her still-damp hair flowed behind her like a cape of white tendrils. She looked so different in clothes instead of armor and without the long braid...

"Ophiera, you were right," he said out loud with a slight slur in his voice. His tongue moved, but his lips would not obey in full. *I was arrogant and believed no one would recognize you. But maybe it wasn't just the scars they recognized. You are...quite distinct in appearance, Ophiera.*

Her eyes snapped to his, full of doubt. "How so? White hair isn't uncommon in Tanvik, and surely many others share my eyes. I doubt anyone would recognize me based on features alone."

When are you going to accept the fact that you are unique amongst the rest?

Myronor felt her embarrassment seep through the link. She had always been a constant contradiction, but he could never understand how she could be so unaware of herself. He knew from the moment he'd met her that he'd never forget her; he imagined he wasn't the only person to feel that.

"You cast magic down in the bar when you picked me up," Ophiera said with a tone of accusation. "They may have recognized me by my features, but traveling with a mage likely solidified the connection. Neither of us was careful, and we nearly paid the price."

Myronor's eyes fell on the pendant that hung around his neck, the inherited heirloom that named him Ambassador to Krysas. He hadn't ever considered casting a spell to be a threat to their safety. Magic had always been celebrated, not feared, in Tanvik. But he could see her point.

"I won't be so flagrant with my magic, at least until we reach Krysas," Myronor said, hoping to smooth her furrowed brow. "That said, our charter tomorrow is already aware they are transporting an Ambassador to Krysas, which heavily implies a mage."

"We should depart tonight, then, on another ship."

"We've already discussed why we can't," Myronor said, rolling his eyes.

"But—"

Trust me when I say I have thought this through, Ophiera. No ship sails tonight that would be worth the risk. Only bootleggers and pirates, and half of them are probably already in league with the Brotherhood. We would trap ourselves out at sea with the likes of them, alone on a ship and away from the Aether. I know I was wrong about you being recognized, and that is the problem we should be discussing, the leak we should address before jumping ship.

The effort Ophiera put forth to hold her tongue was remarkable and, frankly, proved to him how much she truly cared for him. Her instinct was to argue, but instead, she took a deep breath before mumbling, "So what do you suggest we do?"

Myronor thought to himself for a moment, finally able to properly furrow his brow. He might be able to render her invisible with magic, at least for a time. But even with his staff alleviating some of the cost, he didn't possess enough mana for the task. Plus, captains of the trading vessels didn't tolerate stowaways, no matter how honorable Berwyn might think them. It was clear now that removing her golden armor would no longer be enough to escape Cantheas unrecognized.

"I must remain as I am for us to board that ship," Myronor started, the words falling from his mouth nearly as fast as his idea came to mind. "But we could find some disguise for you before we set sail—a new identity of sorts."

Ophiera whipped her head to him. "An identity that includes my sword, I hope?"

He smiled at her, unsurprised. "Subtlety is more important now. You going unseen is more important than protecting me."

"I don't know," Ophiera continued, along with her pacing. "I'm not sure I can be anything other than what I am."

And that was precisely why he loved her so.

With considerable effort, Myronor sat himself up on the bed. Thankfully, the lush pillows proved quite supportive as he leaned back against the headboard. With the grace of a drunk, he beckoned Ophiera with his hand.

"Come here, please."

"Why?"

By the flames, she was difficult.

"You're making me nervous with all this pacing. Come sit with me."

After a moment's pause, as if by some miracle, she listened. She threw herself down onto the bed with unwarranted force. He took her scarred hand in his own and felt the relief of the ekath fully connected again.

"You're not the only one who can keep us safe, you know," he said. With his free hand, he concentrated his mana on the door. Blue light surrounded the frame, and the sound of squelching wood filled the room. When the light disappeared, the melded door continued to waver as if heat emanated from it. "The seal will last through the night, so let's try to rest a bit before our early morning departure."

"I won't find sleep here, seal or not," she growled, watching the door.

Leaning back against the pile of pillows, he tugged at her hand, hoping to coax her to join him. Though she still scowled at the door, she leaned back against his chest. As if by old habit, he wound his arm over her waist.

This moment was all he had desired lately. Feeling her body relax against him, he knew she, too, felt the relief of their closeness. He pressed his face against her hair, breathing in the damp scent of the ink-kelp soap mingled with traces of ash.

~ Six ~

DEPARTURE

Beside the sea, the early morning mist hung heavily, leaving everything slick and damp. Already, Ophiera's newly acquired clothing had become soggy as she leaned against a stack of cool barrels. Tugging down the hood of her cloak, she shifted her shoulders, hoping to reposition to a dryer spot. Like everything else of late, the effort felt futile.

No amount of disguise could ease Ophiera's paranoia while waiting along the crowded port in Cantheas. After last night, walking into the city proper without her sword was worse than losing a limb. She had managed a compromise with Myronor after much discussion, but the presence of the short blade stowed in her boot gave her more doubt than reassurance. What good was a five-inch blade against the Vespula Brotherhood?

From beneath the cloak, her eyes darted up and down the street that ran alongside the docks, searching for any hint of a goldenrod armband amongst the small morning crowds. Everything in her bones told her Marvena had already fled the city—but that didn't mean other anathemas of the Brotherhood weren't left behind.

Worse, the two who had attacked her and Myronor in the night had worn nothing to affiliate them with the Brotherhood. Had this city just become a nest of murder? Watching the bustle of the docks, she wished to believe not. But ultimately, she could trust nothing now.

Despite the hour, the port grew busy with fishers and shippers, traders and merchants, and all the in-betweens preparing for their long day of work. So far, no one paid her any mind where she stood alone against the barrels—no one but the man tethered to her soul up the peninsula and a few docks over.

All the way to the very end, her charge's blue robes blended into a view of the sea. He spoke animatedly to a man shrouded in dark clothes, but even if she had left the ekath open, she would struggle to read him from this distance.

By the flames, she should have just accompanied him. Since when did she just let Myronor take the lead on anything? But their situation was far more precarious than it ever had been before. She was a fugitive in Cantheas, and the Brotherhood was here. Not to mention, the Aether continued to grow unwieldy, perpetuating a constant itch from beneath her wrapped leather cuffs—an attempt to hide her scars from sight while fitting with her new *disguise*.

When Myronor insisted she wait behind while he negotiated their passage, she didn't understand. But through his thoughts, she had pieced together a complexity of reasoning that led to one conclusion. He was trying to protect her. Whether from being recognized *before* they made a deal or from bursting into flames, she wasn't sure, though the latter was the most pressing threat now.

Ophiera shifted her feet against the stone path, leaning heavily on the barrels. She needed to ensure as little of her touched the ground as possible...The Aether had grown even more challenging to quell after last night. Each minute felt worse than the previous, as if she were on a countdown to another disaster.

Staring at the ground, she tried to center herself against the urge to burn. She had thought unleashing her fury on the two assailants last night would calm the need, but the call of the Aether only grew more enthusiastic. It was as if the Aether needed to claim Marvena more than herself, as if it craved Retribution more than she alone. Was it trying to tell her more anathema were near? Or was all this rage for the Reverend alone?

She shook her head.

When had she begun talking about the Aether as if it were sentient? As if it had thoughts and feelings? The Aether wasn't a person but a collective of souls, the lifestream of Erum. Then again, she *had* heard a voice within the holy flames. The same voice that had threatened to return her to the Aether in the cave. The same voice that answered her call against Marvena.

"We're set," Myronor said, clapping his hands together.

Ophiera twitched, the closest she'd come to a jump. She'd been so deep in thought that she hadn't sensed his return. At least she hadn't caught flame in her surprise, though the effort was enormous.

"When do we depart?" She asked, swallowing her shame.

Myronor leaned in, peering at her face beneath the hood. "Within the hour. Are you alright?"

She nodded weakly. "And what do the accommodations look like?"

"We have a private quarter," Myronor said, looking up and down the port. At least she wasn't the only one uncomfortable out in the open. "Small, but discretion is guaranteed."

Ophiera tried to hide her doubt, but even with the ekath silenced, Myronor seemed to read her clearly.

"There will be no notices in Krysas...no chance the Magistrate or Cloister will find you there."

"And the Brotherhood?" she whispered.

His silence was answer enough.

He may have been confident that they would find refuge from the Magistrate and Cloister in Krysas, but if Marvena traveled to the foreign mage city too, it meant she had allies there. It was hard to imagine how many institutions the Brotherhood had infiltrated, but at this point, Ophiera must assume all. Krysas included.

To be hunted by so many was quite the change...usually, it was she who did the hunting. Her task from the Magistrate, after all, required her to hunt down the fate of Pyra Ebontide, a potential victim of an anathema or willful sacrifice to the Aether. Yet she couldn't forget that the very same Magistrate who demanded her obedience was likely corrupted by those who sought to kill her. The same Magistrate who now held a bounty on her life with blessing from the Cloister.

If the Brotherhood *had* infiltrated the Magistrate, was the Cloister aware as well? After the many lies Kaikora had revealed, it was hard not to view the Cloister's support of the bounty as anything but a threat. Her experiences since awakening had forced her to admit that some greater power influenced her fate. But those same experiences also fueled her uncertainty now. Did her Oath truly mean nothing? Was everything she knew a lie?

"Ophieraaa..." Myronor said in a sing-song voice.

"What?" she said with a bite, looking up at him from under the thick hood.

"Did you fall asleep standing up?"

"Of course not," she hissed. However, she had lost her attention again in a spiral of hidden thoughts. When had she grown so careless?

"You weren't answering me, and you do look rather tired—"

"I was thinking for a moment," she snapped. "Try it sometime."

He stared back at her, momentary feelings of hurt relaxing to exasperation. "Well, I *think* we should board the ship sooner rather than later. It's getting rather crowded around here."

Ophiera pushed herself off the barrels and took a pointed step towards the dock. All she could do was cling to the promise of relief from prying eyes and the Aether that the sailing ship offered. But Myronor caught her by the wrist, turning her to face him. Without her greaves, he was slightly taller than her and looked down at her with a frown.

Perhaps her snappish nature was too much for him at the moment.

But as he ran his fingertips against the welted bruises collaring her neck, she realized why he looked suddenly furious. From where the brute tried to drown her last night, her injury looked three days healed, thanks to the ekath. The bruises were a fair exchange for their lives, as were their souls. Odd, how much it used to bother her to claim anathema...but where Myronor's life was involved, she felt nothing but satisfaction, untainted by regret.

"They deserved to burn and then some," Myronor said in a whisper as he ran a caressing thumb across her collarbone.

Again, though she kept her thoughts to herself, he sensed and shared her sentiments. But unlike the Aether that purred beneath her scars in response, Ophiera recoiled against his words.

"Don't speak like that," she said.

"Why not?"

Ophiera scowled, dragging his hand away from the fading bruises. "We both know violence doesn't suit you."

He said nothing and, after an awkward moment, silently led the way toward the dock. She followed, still uneasy with the callousness of his words. The Myronor she knew had nearly fainted when faced with a troynt. And he had resisted wielding a quarterstaff but for his own detest of violence. While she had always found it difficult to believe he loved her, a being of pure violence, it was more difficult to imagine him wishing for retribution as she knew it.

"There's our ship," Myronor said.

He smiled again as usual as he pointed ahead, unaware of her thoughts.

Ophiera squinted from under her hood, reading the coal-black lettering painted alongside the smallest hull in the dock. The *Berserker* was a strange name for an even stranger ship. Long and narrow, the vessel was clearly older but well-kept. The shapely hull and unique pattern of sails were indicative to Ophiera that the ship was built for speed, not cargo like the trade behemoths beside it. And for neither the first nor last time, she doubted this plan.

"How can we be guaranteed discretion on a ship smaller than the Tattered Sail?" She asked. "Wouldn't we be better off blending in with a crowd on one of the larger ships?"

The briefest wave of irritation rolled through her before Myronor chuckled, holding up the pendant bouncing on his chest. "As an Ambassador, I'm kind of a big deal—*very* influential."

"So, they agreed to a discreet charter simply because you're some sort of Magistrate dignitary?" she asked.

"It certainly helped," he mused with a crooked smile, "but I also paid them quite a hefty sum."

Ophiera rolled her eyes. "If only our pockets were as rich as your wit."

He laughed, though she wasn't trying to be funny.

"Nothing can compare to my wit. Just like nothing can compare to the beauty of my consort."

Ophiera felt the flames surge beneath her at the mention of her new role. The breadth of the disguise was mostly hidden beneath her cloak, begging the question as to why she must wear the ridiculous outfit in the first place. But she supposed it wasn't just today she needed to play the part, but rather the entire journey.

"I will fool no one as a consort, no matter the clothing. I should have worn the leathers, so at least I could be comfortable."

"Comfort is a high demand coming from a fugitive," Myronor said light-heartedly. At her scowl, he sighed. "Come now, no one would expect...well, *you*, to be dressed as you are now. However, we should work on your candor if you wish to be convincing. Feyralis consorts are usually more...*demure*," he paused, trying to hide the chuckle breaking his voice.

"And what does that mean?" She snapped.

He laughed so hard that a tear pooled in the corner of his eye. But she didn't understand what was so damned funny.

"On second thought, it would be best if you didn't speak with anyone at all."

The briefest flicker of flames itched beneath her skin. Luckily, none broke through this time. But between the Aether and Myronor's chuckles, everything seemed to prick at her senses like hot needles.

"And try to smile," Myronor said, winding an arm around her waist and pulling her close to him. Despite the comfort of his touch through the ekath, the sensation of being handled made her feel as if the air was thinning.

"Oh, and maybe don't make eye contact with anyone; you look like you're trying to set me on fire right now."

First, a betrothed, then a consort; she wasn't sure which was more ridiculous. Both identities were ill-fitting for her demeanor and personality. She danced better with a blade than a partner and tended to burst into flames when angered. Hardly the temperament of a hired companion. She was more uncomfortable than she had ever been in her life, which said a lot given the days she spent in confinement in the Cloister. Yet, Myronor only felt amusement from this situation. Here she was, allowing him to dictate her choices, her actions, her everything, and all he could do was smirk.

She couldn't unclench her jaw enough to speak aloud.

It is taking all my self-control to avoid setting you on fire right now! She began with a flood of irritation rattling through the ekath. *You have no idea how horrible this feels—fighting against the Aether—exhaustion—my own mind—with every step! I'm glad you find my lack of charm and grace amusing, but I am walking a fine enough line as it is without you prodding me. So please, stop and let me concentrate on not bursting into flames!*

She breathed heavily through her nostrils as if she had screamed the words aloud. And despite her hopes, it seemed losing her temper only made the flames burn worse beneath her scars.

"I'm sorry," he whispered, dancing his fingers across her back. "I don't wish to make this harder on you, I promise."

His circling hand on her lower spine, this time, did soothe her soul while winding up her heart. It was difficult to believe she ever had the strength to leave him, and even more so, how quickly she allowed him to dictate their path forward. As she fell into old habits, perhaps she fell again into the worst one of all—obedience.

But no, she reminded herself. *This* obedience was different from the Cloister, where her compliance hinged upon fear of consequence. But with Myronor, the only thing she feared was hurting him again. In her heart, she knew his intentions, desires...love. And that was it, wasn't it? Love and trust drove her choices to follow his lead, not fear and pain.

The *Berserker* was beside them now, and the moment Ophiera stepped onto the wooden planks out over the cerulean sea, the pressure of the flames all but disappeared. It reminded her of that dreadful first step onto land after a long voyage at sea. Disorientating and relieving at once, she nearly stumbled with the shift in sensation.

Easy now, I'll keep you steady, Myronor thought to her, holding her tight enough not to sway. The situation caused her face to warm unnecessarily. But at least her flushed cheeks would only serve to enhance her cover.

Near the ramp to the boat, Ophiera only now noticed the man dressed in black. But as he turned to greet them, she didn't understand how she could have missed him before.

"Captain Jasper!" Myronor called with a raised hand.

For a moment, she had a hard time believing her ekath addressed the right person. Shipping captains were usually older and gruffer, with a bit more around the middle than a regular sailor. But the man before them stood nearly as beautiful as Myronor, only a few fingers shorter but quite a bit broader in the shoulders. His dark, loose curls fell beside a clenched, heart-shaped jaw with a shadow of stubble that couldn't hide his youth. As he looked them both over with eyes of liquid copper, his gaze lingered on her for far too long. A sudden heat of recognition washed over her, and she couldn't understand.

"Ambassador and your...consort, was it?" Jasper said. His voice was deep, yet lacked any warmth. If Ophiera had to guess, she'd say he was barely out of his second decade, too young by most standards to be a captain. Yet his inured expression, still fixated on her, was one of a soul who had seen a lifetime and then some.

"We are grateful for your hospitality," Myronor replied, tugging Ophiera closer to him with a tightening hand at her waist. Jasper's gaze shifted from hers to Myronor's, and for an awkward moment, they glared at each other silently. She couldn't understand exactly what was being exchanged between them, but whatever it was, she was beginning to doubt her charge's claim of hospitality.

"And I'm more grateful for your coin," the captain said, patting a worn pocket on his old leather overcoat. His amber gaze returned to hers without a hint of gratitude, but something far more empty. "Collette will show you to your quarters."

Myronor nodded and led her up the ramp without another glance at the captain. As they approached the top, Ophiera left the strange man's antics behind and sighed in relief at the open wooden deck.

A few stacks of cargo were tied down in various holds near the center of the deck, but otherwise, it remained clear. Barrels and crates of odd shapes littered the deck as well, with some tied and covered under canvas. She found it odd that not a single container was branded with any of the common trading companies in Cantheas. While not illegal, it was unusual, and she had a suspicion they were not the only cargo traveling discreetly.

Beside a stack of wooden crates stood a short, curvy woman with cropped, wild hair of deep plum. She held a sweet expression, quite the opposite of the captain's, with wide, dark eyes set in a perfectly round face. Though her smile glimmered in the morning sun, the orders she barked were far from kind.

"You're telling me that barrel won't roll with the first cross wave we hit?" she sighed, dropping her hands to her ample hips. The young ginger deckhand beside her remained silent but slowly gathered up the barrel and skulked away. "Yeah—that's what I thought. Tie it down, Felix—*correctly!*"

Myronor cleared his throat, smiling bemusedly as he garnered her attention. Her dark eyes roved over them in appraisal, her cloying expression never faltering.

"Ah, you must be our fancy fare this voyage, eh?"

"And you must be Collette, the fancy and *fair* first mate," Myronor said with a wink.

Ophiera glared down at the ship deck, focusing on a particularly large knot in the wood to prevent her eyes from rolling. The overtly obvious flirtations would never be charming, at least to her. Especially not when directed at someone else. The fake interactions between people of society often vexed her, but rarely annoyed her this greatly. But she supposed he had been appointed Ambassador for some reason beyond nepotism.

"Aye, that I am," the first mate said with a giggle. "Follow me, and I'll show you and your fairly fair fare to your quarters."

She winked at Ophiera before leading them across the deck. With a gentle grunt, Collette lifted a hatch in the deck and descended first. Myronor wobbled slightly as he descended the crude staircase while Ophiera tried her damnedest to maneuver gracefully in the billows of material hidden beneath her cloak. How anyone functioned in a dress, she would never understand. Luckily, Collette seemed unconcerned by their struggles as she led them along a narrow passageway.

Myronor slowed his steps to observe several glass orbs hanging from the low ceiling. They illuminated the dingy corridor in a blue-green light rather than the familiar orange glow of true flames. Ophiera thought she recognized the teal hue of the infamous sea but didn't see how it was possible to...

"How did you bottle the light of the Lucent Strait?" Myronor asked Collette, reaching up to brush his fingertips across the dusty, glowing glass.

"I fancy myself a bit of an alchemician," Collette said with a crooked smile. "Can't divulge the recipe, but I'd be happy to sell you a few. I call them flameless candles—mighty useful on a ship where true fire can be the death of us."

Myronor laughed, though Ophiera could sense the thread of discomfort shared between them. It was surely a pure coincidence that she'd mentioned true fire as if it were a common term.

"While they are exquisite, I can't foresee a need for them where we're going."

The first mate's girlish giggle echoed as she stopped before a door blended in against the paneled walls. Nearly hidden in the dim light, Ophiera could barely make out the small latch Collette flipped before flinging the door open.

A cloud of dust kicked up into the air, and through the haze, Ophiera couldn't help but grimace. There was room enough for two to stand beside each other next to a narrow, lumpy bed, and that was all. No flameless candles had been spared for these quarters, but a small porthole provided a surprising amount of light, filtering hazily through the dusty air.

"It's lovely, Collette, thank you," Myronor said, taking the first mate's hand and bending at the hip.

Ophiera refused to watch his lips brush against her knuckles; her stomach was sour enough. Why was she so suddenly averse to a customary show of appreciation, a benign act of charm? Yet she held a burning desire to smack his face away from the first mate's hand that could only be sated by closing her eyes.

"Oh, my pleasure," Collette giggled again. Her eyes sharpened as she looked at Ophiera. "It's not every day someone offers such coin for *discreet* transit. That said, there are a few rules to be upheld."

"Naturally," Myronor smirked.

"The captain requests you not wander beyond your quarters and the main deck. The crew knows not to disturb you, but discretion goes both ways, so please leave them be. We should arrive in port in three or four days' time, depending on the winds and storms. The captain or I will let you know when we are close to landing in Krysas, so if you ask either of us how much longer the voyage is at any point, we will be forced to throw you overboard."

Ophiera scowled, not realizing the first mate was joking until she winked.

"Sounds reasonable," Myronor said, returning the wink, "I'll be hard-pressed to leave my quarters, anyway, with my consort here."

Before Ophiera could kick him in the shin, he'd nudged her into the room. After a final goodbye to the first mate, he closed the door, leaving them barely enough room to stand. She felt Myronor press against her back, his lips grazing her ear with the lightest kiss.

"See? We made it aboard with no problems," he whispered. "All will be well now."

Ophiera turned to face him, unconvinced. "Both she and the captain mentioned *such coin*...exactly how much did you pay them?"

Myronor chuckled, though the expression didn't meet his eyes as he ran the back of his knuckles affectionately over her cheek. "My consort shouldn't worry about such trivial things as money."

She smacked his hand away. "Money is the only weapon we have right now since I'm not allowed mine."

He sighed, pressing his lips together with a look of exasperation. Something about the expression stirred something within her, neither good nor bad, just...had he ever looked like that before? Exhaustion and worry mingling as he avoided her eyes?

Suddenly uncomfortable, Ophiera unfastened the neck of her cloak. She agreed to wear her hair down rather than braided, yet the knee-length waves of untamed snowy hair acted like a secondary cloak, trapping all of her warmth. As she threw the garment to the bed, she gathered her swath of hair and pulled it off her neck, savoring the moment of air against her overheated skin.

"And I've told you there is no need to worry," he said, smiling and taking her bare shoulders in his hands. "I carry more than enough coin with us, and Ambassadors receive exceptional compensation for their services. Didn't I mention that?"

"You certainly did not," she said bitterly. "Anything else you care to share before we set sail?"

To her surprise, Myronor's smile faltered a moment. "Why don't you get some rest? You didn't sleep last night, nor have you in too many nights."

Even without the ekath, she could sense his unease toward her question. Rarely had he ever been avoidant, even with the most personal of questions. So what was he avoiding now? Or was exhaustion simply warping her thoughts?

"I don't see how I'm supposed to sleep in this damned dress."

She glanced down at the skirt, slit up to her hips, and nearly touching the floor. Her thick, muscular thighs peaking between the dark purple fabric seemed a dead giveaway that she was no consort, but Myronor seemed to think that detail wouldn't matter. Given the heat of the room, she could have forgiven the skirt, but the black leather bodice held her torso far too tight, making her pine for the bulky weight of armor. The same black leather covered her arms from wrist to elbow in decoratively wrapped straps, obscuring her scarred arm in the name of Feyralis fashion.

"You're free to take it off in the cabin," Myronor said thickly, his smirk returning from previous discomfort.

Swallowing hard, Ophiera fought against her wandering thoughts.

"I admit I need sleep," she said, removing her boots and stuffing them beneath the bed. "But I will only rest if you—"

"I promise to stay awake and stand guard, Ophiera. But please believe me...we're safe here."

She heard the calls up on deck to depart as she slid down onto the mattress, sinking into a surprisingly soft bed. They would be out at sea soon, with only storms to fear. She left room for Myronor to sit if he wished, pressing her back against the cabin wall. Not even the night in the Sloughmire compared to the wariness that dragged at her now. Myronor sank beside her on the edge of the small bed. Despite his words of assurance, she couldn't help but notice the ghost of a frown pulling at his lips as he watched her eyes flutter closed.

~ Seven ~

OBEDIENCE

Drip. Drip. Drip.

Ophiera focused on the familiar sound of melting ice falling on cold stone. She couldn't see or move or feel, but unfortunately, she could still hear. Out of pure boredom, she tried matching her shallow breaths with the quiet rhythm of the dripping. Or perhaps it was desperation.

The air drew thin and damp through her slack mouth. Musty and cold. Her chest ached with each scant breath, and with every weak exhale, she felt more fluid pooling in her lungs. Usually, it was the unkindled that drowned in their sickness. A disease of elevation was easily avoided with the proper breathing exercises. The breathing techniques were one of the first trainings she had received at the Cloister—exercises she now avoided, purposefully and diligently.

Darkly, she wondered if she would be the first kindled to succumb to the death within. By the flames, she hoped so. Some might call it self-pity. But the only pity she felt was for the water trapped in the cell alongside her.

Drip. Drip. Drip.

She assumed the water originated from the snow melt atop the peaks, seeping into the ground over time. It had escaped the frigid mountains only to find this chamber by chance—a sad story—freed from one hellish fate only to be trapped in another.

The sounds were her countdown now, a metronome of her life, slowly melting away as she drew closer to the flames of the Aether. She wondered if the priests knew how close to the Aether she was now. Would they try to heal her? Or would they finally let her meet her end freely? Would the Aether consider a death by neglect murder? The priests had placed her in this cell after all; if she died under their care, was that not an unnatural death? At what point did neglect become murder? Would another paladin seek Retribution for her soul? She despised the thought, even though she bore the scars. In this room, in this state, none of the teachings made sense anymore.

"You're not practicing your breaths," a voice called from the dark.

She couldn't raise her head enough to see the door, but she knew instantly who spoke through the bars on the door. From the tone, she guessed his forehead was creased above two narrow, hazel eyes, and his lips curled in a mirthless smile.

"I never do in here," she wheezed, taking a rattling breath.

How many times now had she been *here*, chained to this floor? Before her kindling, many times, though many of the memories blurred together now. After her kindling, well, she had spent more time in this cell than out. Each time the silent priests had forced her to the ground and wrapped the cold chains around her, Uzziel had visited. And each time, she wished he hadn't.

"What offense did you commit this time?" Uzziel asked.

Ophiera pictured his face, jaw tense with an arrogant expression. The golden armor he so treasured was likely freshly polished, shining even in this faint light. She was glad she couldn't see him.

"Snuck into the Archives," she said in a huff.

"Idiot," he hissed.

She didn't argue.

Idiot was the least offensive insult she'd suffered of late. Granted, the priests couldn't break their silence, but their actions said it all; leaving her to die spelled out something far worse than *idiot*. And the clerics...well, they were always glad to deem someone *unworthy*. She could hear their whispers outside the door, and yet not a single one set foot in this chamber to alleviate her suffering. To think she had been so desperate for the Oath of Mercy, and yet the clerics wasted their gifts here in the Cloister. What was the point of the healing rites if they hid away in the mountains? Was there meaning behind any of it if they allowed their brethren to drown inside themselves?

"Why were you in the Archives again?" Uzziel asked.

In the silence, she thought he had left. Or desperately wished he had.

"You know why," she wheezed.

He scoffed in the dark, and involuntarily, she winced at the sound. She was glad the barred door stood between them. At least he could only verbally torment her now.

"How many times must you be locked in here before you accept your fate?" he groaned.

"Don't—" she began, but a fit of spasmodic coughs overtook her words.

Between the string of hacking breaths, she couldn't draw enough air, and each time she tried, more coughs followed. A viscous fluid bubbled past her lips, coating her tongue in a salty, metallic taste before dribbling over her chin. She slowed down, taking in air deliberately through her nostrils as the instinct to breathe overtook any desire she had to return to the Aether. It was a few moments before the chains finally stopped rattling.

Even as Ophiera's cough settled, the iron shackles dug uncomfortably into the raw scars of her Oath. Nearly a year old, and still, they felt as tender as the day she'd been kindled. Her recovery from the Sacramentum had been long and arduous, flitting between fevered dreams and burning alive. Perhaps her time spent in this cell had prevented the blistered symbols of Retribution from scarring over.

Despite her suffering through the Sacramentum, no one could tell her what the branded writ on her arm meant. No one would even acknowledge the word Aspect. The priest's only concern was her Oath, the one that claimed her for Retribution, and rightfully so. Decades had passed since the last paladin had been kindled from the flames, let alone two within the same cohort. She and Uzziel had been sent to the Sacramentum within days of each other, and yet everything afterward had gone quite differently.

While she suffered for months against the holy flames, Uzziel recovered within days. He began his training first as a new Hand of Retribution, the only echelon allowed to leave the walls of the Cloister. As if he hadn't been arrogant enough before the fires burned their writ into his skin, now, his head was as heavy as his armor. The armor *he* had received, while she still had not.

"If you would accept your Oath, you would be free."

At least he had waited until she was done speaking before starting on her again. Ophiera took a calming breath, testing if she had the capacity for speech.

"Why are you even here, Uzziel?"

His snort echoed against the walls of the dark chamber. "I came to say goodbye."

"Am I that close to death?"

"Don't speak so brazenly," he hissed. It was good to know she could still get under his skin, even chained to the floor. "Ophiera, I leave tomorrow for Feyralis; the Magistrate has conscripted me."

Drip. Drip. Drip.

Ophiera held her breath. Her arm, scarred and shackled to the ground, itched for a moment. She tried to refocus her thoughts on the water droplets, ignoring the burn of disappointment coating her insides. So Uzziel would escape this place while she...

Drip. Drip. Drip.

It wasn't as if she wished to be conscripted, to enter into service to the Magistrate. She never wished to be a Hand; she only dreamt of escape. It was best that Uzziel would be the next paladin of the Magistrate.

"Congratulations," she rasped.

"It *should* have been you," Uzziel said quietly, all the arrogance lost in his voice. "Had you not been so reckless—"

"I'm not reckless," she said, ignoring the protest of her lungs. Pacing her breaths with her words, she pressed on. "Reckless implies...I haven't considered the consequences...when I simply find...the consequences...worth the risk."

She heard him sniff judgmentally in the dark. "So, you'd rather live your days in this cell than out in Tanvik? You'd rather die alone in the dark than accept what the holy flames gifted you?"

Now it was Ophiera's turn to snort, though it came off more like a wheeze. "Retribution is not a gift! After...my searches...in the Archives...I'm beginning to...believe all...Oaths are curses."

From the dark, she sensed Uzziel's frustration by the change in his breath and continued silence. Again, she relished in the small victory of disrupting his surety. He had always been accepting of his fate, even before they were kindled. While she had prayed for an Oath of Mercy, he dreamt of Retribution. At least one of them had received exactly what they wanted.

Today would be her sixth night in this wretched cell without moving, without food, without water. And yet she would still rather be here, allowing the coughs to chip away the remaining fragments of her soul, than seeking Retribution for the Aether. If there really wasn't a way to change one's Oath, why did the priests keep her away from the Archives? Why punish her so thoroughly if there was nothing she could do to change her fate?

"Do you have any idea what I would sacrifice to have been kindled as an Aspect?" Uzziel said in barely a whisper.

"What do you mean?" She barked too forcefully, given the air left to her. Coughs wracked her body again.

"Nevermind," Uzziel said.

"U-z-z-what—" she managed before the spasms smothered her voice and air.

No one had been able to explain to her what it meant to be an Aspect. Yet, seemingly, he knew something. What did he know that she did not? And what in the world could he possibly sacrifice for it? After everything he'd put her through, he owed her at least one answer, even if she could not utter the question again. Her chest ached with the need for air.

"Ophiera, I need you to stay alive."

She could barely understand his words over the sound of her futile gasps. Regardless of what he wished, she knew it was too late. The foaming bubbles no longer trickled but poured from her mouth, preventing any draw of breath. There was no more air in the room, no more in her lungs—nothing but a searing pain blooming from deep within her chest.

Her body began to jerk, fighting against her fate. The sound of greaves clanking on the stone grew distant. He was leaving her to die alone. Good riddance, she thought bitterly.

Foam poured from her mouth and nose as her chest jolted with her last reflexive breaths. The chains dug into her scarred flesh as her body convulsed without control. And despite the pain, she found the fire in her chest relieving. It was the same sear of agony imparted by the flames, and she could only take that as a promise to join the Aether soon.

Any moment, she would be free.

But rather than consume, the burning only spread. She felt the crawl of flames beneath her skin, the controlled burn of a path down her arm. Blinded by the flash beyond her eyelids, she felt the holy flames burst from her scars like steam from a kettle.

She couldn't stop herself from looking through the slits of her eyes down at her ignited arm. Unable to breathe, let alone chant, she didn't understand how the runes of her Oath could have ignited. But the proof lay in the melted chains pooling beneath the shadow of her fiery arm.

The holy flames spread from her scars, crawling over her skin like a breeze across a field of grass. Though she caught the flame with ease, the pain was beyond anything she could withstand.

This must be the extinguishment, she screamed in her mind. The final judgment of the Aether. She expected it would be excruciating, but what she hadn't expected was the hot air that began to fill her lungs. The flames alleviated the weight from her chest while propelling the screams from her lungs past her lips. Echoing throughout the chamber, her agony roared as her body burned, and yet, she felt more alive than she ever had in this cell.

Like the flames, Ophiera rose.

Enflamed in white, she dragged herself to her feet and stumbled towards the door. Through the haze of fire, she saw neither Uzziel nor priests beyond the grated window. She touched her burning hand to the door and watched as her fiery handprint scorched through the wood.

She could escape...But then what?

Burn them.

The voice in her head offered a compelling argument.

The Cloister wanted her to evoke her Oath, did they not? Retribution was her duty, they claimed. The priests and the clerics *were* guilty, perhaps not of murder, but of sins of equal detriment. Neglect and arrogance returned more souls to the Aether than any anathemas. Where was the Retribution for the souls lost to the Sacramentum? Or better yet, for her?

Burn them all.

The holy flames coursing through demanded more than retribution for her suffering. As she stepped forth from the dank cell, the dripping water served as her war drum, setting a slow and steady rhythm.

~ Eight ~

EXPOSED

Ophiera couldn't remember the last time she had awoken to the sway of the ocean. The sound of wood creaking to the rhythm of waves splashing against the hull set a tempo of incredible speed. While the rough rocking of a rapid pace made the green sailors ill, for her, the cadence had only lulled her into a deep and peaceful sleep. She hadn't felt this well-rested in ages.

Myronor lay with his back to her, and by the rhythm of his breaths, she knew he wasn't asleep. The glow of sunset trickled in through the small porthole, illuminating his fair hair like true fire, rather. But the sight triggered flashes of a dream she had successfully forgotten until now.

"Did I really sleep the entire day away?" she asked with a slight rasp.

"Clearly, you need it."

Myronor rolled over to face her, inches away, with a half-hearted smile. He plucked a lock of her loose hair and twirled it between his fingers. Though the gesture wasn't something out of the ordinary, the furrow in his brow and avoidant gaze surely were. Taking a leaf from his book, she searched the ekath for the source of his unease. But to her surprise, she realized it was *he* who blocked her from their tether.

"What's wrong?" She asked.

He shook his head, mind still closed and eyes still distant.

She stilled his hand with her own. While she wouldn't push him too hard, she refused to let go until he answered. It took him longer to comply than she had expected.

"Your dreams..." he started, pressing his lips together before continuing, "Do you ever remember them?"

She eyed the leather binds overlaying her scars, relieved they'd remained intact. No smoke. No burns. But the skin felt overly sensitive beneath the leather straps as if she had truly been bound in chains moments ago.

"Why are you asking about my dreams?"

Myronor interlaced his fingers with hers, the smile falling from his lips. "You know, according to the Phratries, dreams are a requirement for the soul to remain healthy. While the body requires rest for longevity, the soul cannot sleep...thus, it remains active while the body sleeps, evoking what we know as dreams. But few remember them. The Phratries say—"

"Please don't," she whispered. "Why ask about what I dream?"

His expression relaxed, sheepish, yet still pained. "I discovered a new facet to the ekath...it seems that I can see...well, I suppose more like *live* your dreams while you sleep."

"You saw my dreams?" She asked. Myronor nodded with a pained expression. "How much of them?"

"Everything," he breathed, biting his lip. "I saw everything, felt everything." His eyes fell to the twirling lock of hair as he took a deep, shuddering breath. "I felt your despair, your sickness, your flames, your pain."

Ophiera swallowed, trying to remember precisely what she had dreamt. Bits and pieces came back, but nothing with the weight that Myronor described. She didn't know what to say.

"As much as I hate to admit it, I had to block the connection," he confessed. "I...once you started burning, I couldn't withstand the agony. While you slept soundly through it, I nearly collapsed, resorting to biting down on my robes just to stop myself from screaming. I couldn't withstand even a fraction of your pain..."

Ophiera closed her eyes, unwilling to see the tears pooling in his pale blue eyes. She had brought this pain, and so many others, upon him. Even in her sleep, she was capable of nothing but hurting him. Just when she thought she had finally accepted their bond...their connection...their *love*, something as fleeting as a dream made her doubt her decisions.

She shouldn't have ever agreed to travel with him again.

She shouldn't have ever agreed to bring him to Krysas.

Her instincts had been right from the start; she only put him in harm's way, even leagues away from the Aether. Her clouded memories were danger enough.

"Don't," he said, "I'm not telling you this to fault you—I'm telling you this to apologize."

Ophiera opened her eyes and saw Myronor wore quite a different expression than when she had closed them. The pain was gone, replaced by a look she didn't understand.

"Apologize?" She asked confusedly. "For what?"

"For being the fool you've always known me to be, even if I seldom admit it myself. I never understood...and I'm sorry."

"Understand what?" She mumbled.

"Anything. The brutality of the Cloister, the pain of the flames, and just how out of control you felt...feel rather still."

She smiled softly. "I don't expect you to understand something I barely can."

"It doesn't change the fact that I am sorry, Ophiera."

"I don't want pity."

To her surprise, Myronor smiled sadly. They were close enough that she could feel his breath against her cheek as he sighed. His eyes darted over her face as he released her hair and brought his hand to her jaw. The jolt of his emotions, strengthened by the physical connection, only served to confuse her further.

"I'm not offering pity," he whispered, brushing his thumb across her lips. "I'm offering compassion."

"Same difference," she murmured.

To her surprise, he leaned forward and gently pressed his lips against hers. The moment they kissed, she felt the connection established in full, relieving her of guilt and replacing it instead with an emotion she couldn't place.

They are very different, he said, continuing to kiss her. *Compassion requires one to care, and I care more for you than anything else. Before, I wished so desperately to alleviate you of your burdens—to free you of your binds. But I'm beginning to realize that was a rather naive approach...I can't undo what's been done; I can't change the burdens you've been dealt. But maybe I can help you bear them.*

The sensation of his words, combined with the motion of his mouth, overwhelmed her thoughts. If he was trying to make her feel better, it was working. But the moment his tongue slipped past her lips, the briefest flicker of fire burned within her, and she pulled away.

"The only burden I cannot bear is hurting you," she said, trying to hide her frustration. Despite her distance from the Aether, she couldn't fully control her Oath. And yet, some foreign and growing part of her didn't actually wish to control herself. Not with him.

She wanted to taste him again.

She wanted to feel more of him.

And yet, if she let go, the flames within might...

"Ophiera, being without you hurt me more than burning with you," Myronor murmured before lacing his fingers in her hair and pulling her back to him again.

Despite being so close, their noses touched, he didn't kiss her. The tease of his breath mingling with hers without the touch of their lips caused a burn in her belly distinct from that smoldering beneath her scars—warmer, painless, and unhindered. His hungry blue eyes bore into hers as he smirked again.

"I'll happily risk the latter."

This time, his lips found hers with a fervor that tempted her out of sensibility. When his tongue danced with hers again, all doubts and flames were promptly replaced with a more frantic, weightless burden of need.

With his hand still woven into her white hair, Ophiera pushed him onto his back, rolling over the top of him, still kissing him from above. The long slits of her skirt made it far too easy to slide atop and straddle against him.

Myronor danced both his hands in unison down her shoulders and waist, finally settling on her bare thighs. His fingers dug into her exposed flesh, squeezing and pulling her down against him. It was unfair that he could touch her skin, but she couldn't feel him through the deep blue robes.

A sigh escaped his lips as she began undoing the ties of his robes. As the blue fabric peeled open, she ran her hands against his bare chest. He had the lithe musculature of a fisher by birthright, but his hands held the softness of a scholar. Hands that traveled up her legs and settled on her bottom, rocking her back and forth against him.

Whether the ekath or her heart drove her need, she didn't care to know anymore. Whatever reason there might be for how she felt about Myronor, the coil tightening deep within her over-rode all. Every sensation flowed freely between them, and as their breaths grew ragged, she felt his hand wander again. His intentions boomed through their link in imaginings, she urged him to make a reality. She needed him to touch her like she needed air to breathe.

But as Ophiera trembled with excitement, so did the flames within. Threatening to burst forth, she felt a fire inside her ignite that she could no longer control. Panicked, she threw herself from Myronor, landing hard against the wooden floor. The pain quickly dampened the burn, but she stared down at her Oath, wrapped in leather binds. Though she feared the worst, the leather bracer remained intact, with only a whisper of smoke smoldering from beneath. It may not have been the worst-case scenario, but it *was* disappointing.

With heavy breaths, Ophiera silenced their link and tried to compose herself. She had nearly lost control again, though it took her longer to wrangle her heart into calmness than it did her mana. After the smoke settled, she dared a glance up at the pale eyes she knew bore down on her.

Myronor smiled, slightly lopsided with a flush coloring his cheeks. His robes remained undone, and Ophiera found difficulty looking away from the rise and fall of his chest, beading with sweat. He said nothing but continued to study her as if she were a brand new book he'd never read before, and the lewd thoughts she had moments ago returned.

"I need some fresh air," she mumbled, standing and fleeing the room.

Without looking back, she leaned against the door in the hall, straightening out her dress. As she examined herself, she wished she'd thought to take her boots or, at the very least, her cloak. The neckline of the dress revealed far more than she was comfortable with, but at least her scars remained hidden beneath the leather wraps.

Down the hall, away from the deck, she heard the low voices of the crew exchanging words. Likely in the mess if she recalled the layout correctly. Merchant trade ships varied much in design and purpose from the traditional fishing vessels of the Southern Coastlands. Fishers had to actually work while they sailed; meanwhile, traders could sit back more and enjoy the ride. She had half a mind to wander down and see if they had any ale to spare. A drink sounded wonderful at the moment. But with a flash of Lotus's face in her mind and Collette's warning in her ear, she chose the discretion of fresh air instead.

As Ophiera emerged onto the deserted ship deck, she took in a deep, salty breath. The day's warmth clung to the smooth wooden planks beneath her bare toes even as the sun began to sink into the sea. Not a soul was in sight across the deck, meaning their course must be set for quite some time, and she could be guaranteed some much-needed solitude.

She made her way toward the forward bow, enjoying the foreign sensation of the sea breeze dancing through her loose hair. The sway of the ship didn't bother her balance, a surprise given their speed and the length of time that had passed since the last time she sailed. But even barefoot, she'd never forget how to walk with the waves.

As Ophiera crossed the deck, it became even more apparent that the ship had been well cared for over the years. Reaching the prow, the wind rushed at her again, whipping her loose hair and skirts like the sails above. It was a terribly strange sensation, given her usual style of hardened leathers. Still, she admitted it was terribly freeing at the same time.

She leaned over the worn wooden rail and took another deep breath. It was more challenging with the wind blowing against her, but relieving just the same. The sinking sun burned a path of shimmering crimson onto the surface of the water, guiding their sail west. And like many times in Iluka, she found more tranquility in the crashing waves than anywhere else on Erum.

And, just like Iluka, her tranquility disappeared in an instant. There was no returning to the only life she had ever chosen. But with the ekath... even if she hadn't destroyed the village, would the tether have allowed her to return to Iluka? The drag of the tether was nearly intolerable after a few days of trudging along the coast while Myronor sailed to Cantheas. They hadn't been that distant, and yet she had suffered his absence more than she cared to admit.

"Good evening."

Ophiera whipped around, reaching for the hilt of her absent claymore. The disrupting voice belonged to Captain Jasper, watching her with a questioning, molten copper gaze. She didn't understand how exactly he had snuck up on her, but he had. And like a fool, she pretended to adjust her hair, longing for her sword instead.

"I'm surprised to see you out on deck." His eyes fell to her bare feet, hiding his judgment. "Most passengers we ferry become quite seasick from the speed of my ship."

A tingle shot down her spine when his voice dropped to say *my* ship. Possessive and prideful for that moment alone, his tone returned to neutral before he ended the sentence.

She shrugged, not trusting her tongue. Myronor had told her consorts were demure. Didn't that mean quiet?

"Does he not allow you to speak?" he asked with derision.

To say she didn't appreciate his tone was an understatement. She straightened her spine a little, accepting she actually had no idea what demure meant.

"I choose to speak when I deem it necessary."

A flicker of annoyance crossed his face, and she worried she'd overstepped. She thought it was the most honest answer she could provide. But it was clearly not the right one.

"Given your occupation, I thought you could at least entertain me with conversation," he said, gesturing to the deck around them. "Tell me what you think of the *Berserker*."

Ophiera couldn't understand why he would want her opinion of his ship. Is this what Feyralis dignitaries did with their hired consorts? *Conversed?* Why the ridiculous dress, then? She supposed she should have clarified her assumed tasks with Myronor before...

But it was too late now. The captain watched her with a scrutinizing gaze, waiting for an answer.

"It's a beautiful ship, though I find the name to be quite peculiar."

Jasper smirked this time, but unlike Myronor, there was no pleasure behind the expression.

"You must be familiar with the old proverbs, then, if you find it *peculiar*. How does it go again? 'The winds guide those with heavy hearts, but the sea rewards those who sing to her.'"

Ophiera nodded, a small smile escaping her lips. She was surprised that anyone beyond the village fishers knew that particular saying. The Southern Coastlands held many traditions, including conventions for naming ships. Fishing vessels were traditionally named after the sea, like Berwyn's ship, the *Mistral*—an intended tribute to the sea in hopes of bountiful harvests. Meanwhile, trade vessels were more often named after a lover or loved one, a hope that swift sails brought them home safely.

"I don't believe in superstitions," Jasper said, clicking his heel on the deck of the ship. "Lovers are fleeting, and the sea is impassive; neither felt right when it came time to name this particular ship."

Ophiera watched him with narrowed eyes, calculating why he said the things he said. She had spent enough time at the Lonely Iris, watching Lotus interrogate travelers with his own opinions, to suspect what the captain was attempting on her now. The man rarely asked a direct question and more often provided his thoughts, counting on friendly company to ease people's tongues. It had worked on Ophiera in the early days of her conscription, but she knew better now.

"Then *Berserker* refers to nothing of significance, then?" She asked carefully.

Jasper snorted hollowly. "Oh, she's still named after someone significant, just not a lover. The *Berserker* is the nickname I chose for a person who nearly killed me."

Ophiera said nothing, hoping to keep her expression placid. Murder was not often discussed in a normal conversation in Tanvik. To speak of an attempt on his life so nonchalantly would be considered taboo to most. But maybe he knew she was not most.

"I hope this *Berserker* doesn't attempt to take the lives of your passengers, too."

Jasper said nothing for a moment. And again, she worried she'd been too blunt. If it hadn't been abundantly clear that she was no consort before, it certainly was now. She held her tongue as the sun descended halfway behind the waves, unappreciative of his position between her and the hatch below deck.

"I assure you my ship is in prime condition," he finally said, smiling slyly again. "Speaking of, do you know which part of the ship you now stand upon? I'd be happy to educate you."

His patronizing tone was the perfect flint to ignite her temper.

"I don't require any maritime lessons, thank you," she snapped.

"My apologies. I simply couldn't imagine *you* having sailed before."

She quickly decided she didn't much care for this captain, nor for what a consort was supposed to say.

"You must have a fairly weak imagination, then."

"Perhaps," he chuckled coldly without even an attempt to hide his gaze descending lower on her neckline. He took a shadowing step towards her. "Though I daresay it depends on the topic."

Ophiera refused to react to his pathetic attempt to assert dominance. Consort or not, she wasn't a coward. A spark of pride tingled beneath her scars as she decided that the dress itself was not nearly as embarrassing as how easily distracted grown men became by the slightest show of skin.

"Now that you've been entertained, may I finally be left alone?"

The captain looked momentarily taken aback before the blank, indifferent facade washed over him again. He took another step closer to her, but again, Ophiera held her ground.

"If I recall correctly, this is my ship," he said with a flash across his amber eyes, "I go where I please."

Ophiera took a deep breath through her nostrils. "And if I recall correctly, the Ambassador paid you quite well for our discreet transport. So, unless you have something else you need of me, I desire the discretion of solitude."

He cocked his head, eyes dipping again to her neckline. Irritating, young bastard, she thought, but before she could voice her irritation, his haughty expression flitted to a sneer.

"Those bruises," he growled, reaching a gloved hand towards her. "Has the Ambassador harmed you?"

Before his glove could graze her skin, her hand shot out, twisting him away by the wrist. A grunt of pain escaped his pursed lips, and she loosened her grip only slightly.

"Of course not."

"Then who?" He asked, not even trying to pull his hand away from her grip any longer.

She didn't understand why he was so concerned about a wound she barely felt.

"A dead man," she said, throwing the answer at him along with his hand.

"And the scar on your chest?" He asked, rubbing his wrist. "A wound like that should have been fatal."

If only she had thought to cover that one as thoroughly as those on her arms.

"Obviously, it wasn't," she said, trying to sound indifferent.

They stood tensed, silent, and staring as Jasper rubbed his wrist. He didn't act much like a captain, though she didn't act much like a consort.

"Are all consorts in Feyralis as *spirited* as you?"

He may have called her a consort, but the sly smirk playing across his face told her he thought otherwise. But she wasn't the only one between them with something to hide.

"It's an occupational requirement when serving mages," she said, annunciating the last word.

A flash of anger crossed his face, and she nearly smiled. At least she had interpreted something about him correctly. The young captain of the *Berserker* wasn't very fond of mages.

The winds shifted, and for a moment, she caught the scent of sea salt and the aged leather of his overcoat. He stood far too close for comfort, and yet, she found something oddly calming about his scent.

For what felt like hours, they remained silent, matched in height and ire. She wished for nothing more than to return to the cabin below, but his broad stature blocked her path. Maybe he sensed her tension or finally decided to be a decent human, but he relaxed, taking a step out of her space.

"Do you have a name, or should I continue referring to you as his consort?"

With a single breath, she quickly decided on a name. Since Lotus had been on her mind of late, it wasn't hard to think of one she liked.

"Iris."

Again, the captain's demeanor shifted. His amber eyes warmed despite the sun disappearing beneath the waves. It was the first genuine smile she'd seen pass over his lips. She realized at that moment just how young the captain was...and how suffered. As quickly as it appeared, the innocence fell from his face, replaced by the indifferent facade she'd come to expect. His change in mood was jarring, to say the least.

"What a rare flower to be named after," Jasper said, meeting her gaze. "They used to grow in the Southern Coastlands when I was a child. I always found them quite beautiful."

"And poisonous."

His lips quirked with the hint of a smile before he bowed. "Well then, *Iris*, this has been entertaining. I suggest you retire below soon...after dark, these seas are no place for a consort or anyone else, for that matter."

Jasper glared out at the setting sun, a disquiet settling over his features before he turned away. With silent steps, he crossed the deck and disappeared below.

While Ophiera breathed a sigh of relief, she knew if Lotus were here, he'd tell her to steer clear of that man. As much as she desired solitude, she also recognized there was little point in loitering. The calm of the sunset was tainted now by what had just unfolded.

She returned below deck, thankfully avoiding the captain and his first mate as she navigated the narrow hallway. In the small cabin, she found Myronor fast asleep in the narrow bed. Sprawled out as a sea creature washed ashore after a storm, he snored gently on his stomach.

Though his peaceful expression had a soporific effect on her, she resisted the urge to crawl into bed beside him. Hadn't she already slept the entire day away? That, and the captain's last words, still echoed in her mind.

While surely the sea was a dangerous place at night, it was so during the day as well. When she served as Warden of Iluka, she often sailed with deep water vessels, where the night sea was no different from the day. Shifts of fishers worked around the clock to keep the catches coming in and shorten their time out at sea. Never once was she told to stay off deck at night, and never once did she see a sailor look as disquieted as the captain did this evening.

Ophiera peered out the small porthole of the darkening cabin, blinking until the only light from the stars could be seen. Maybe the captain was just trying to keep her off the deck, knowing they would soon be sailing through the Lucent Strait. Many of the ships in Cantheas contended with what they called tourists—people with more money than sense who booked passage on ships only to see the glowing seas. It had been years since she'd witnessed the bright waters during the last Moon Tide that reached the shores of Iluka.

Every decade or so, the currents would shift and bring the glowing waters closer to Tanvik's coast. It was a wonderful celebration to remember as the villagers flocked to the beach, along with the shaman. On the rare nights of the Moon Tide, the shaman was constantly summoned to perform the union rites between young lovers, hoping for the extra blessings promised by the illuminated waters. Yet another tradition of the Southern Coastlands that she never understood and yet longed to know.

The union rite was not as damning as an Oath and yet far more foreign. It was a bond of love, only formed and broken by choices. As Ophiera watched Myronor's lips quirk in his sleep, she imagined the two of them standing hand in hand before the pale, luminescent surf while Kaikora declared their hearts bound in this life and the next.

But Ophiera shook the silly imaginings from her head. She didn't need any more binds, nor did she need the reminder of the shaman. Kaikora had abandoned Iluka to its fate, just as she had abandoned Myronor. She didn't deserve his forgiveness, and Kaikora certainly did not deserve hers.

Myronor stirred again, and Ophiera saw his lips pulling into a contented smile. Rarely did one of them sleep while the other remained awake; perhaps this was why he had never witnessed her dreams before. If her soul was only capable of projecting images of destruction and pain, she wondered what the mage's dreams held instead.

But his eyes fluttered open before she had the chance to see, bright blue even in the dim dusk light.

"Why are you down there?"

"There was nowhere else to go," Ophiera said, her lips twitching at the corners. "You know you sleep like one of those giant hexapus creatures, limbs draped everywhere."

Myronor laughed and extended a hand to her. "Well, you weren't here for me to hold on to."

~ Nine ~

RELIANCE

Awakening beside Ophiera again, even on the cramped bed of a rocking ship, brought Myronor wondrous comfort. As they slept, their souls fed off each other's presence alone, reconstituting and healing his heart in ways he didn't know he needed.

She still slept soundly, even after sleeping the entire previous day and night away. Myronor couldn't help but study her—rarely could he see her face without the furrow between her brow. She no longer bore dark circles beneath her eyes, and the bruises on her neck were nearly healed. The only imperfection in sight was the circular scar between her breasts, rising and falling in a slow, restful rhythm. It was hard to believe she was the same person he saw stumbling from the woods, exhausted and filthy; the same person he'd watched level a village in white flames; the same person who had jumped atop him yesterday and driven his flesh to madness.

And yet, the person who fell asleep in his arms last night was not the same person who awoke midday. When Ophiera finally rose from bed, it was very clearly on the wrong side. Despite her angelic features while asleep, she refused to speak to Myronor with more than grunts and nods for the first hour after waking. With the ekath clamped shut, he couldn't understand in the slightest the reason for her sour mood. Before, he might have left her to stew on her thoughts. But they were in this together now, far beyond the immediate fact that they would be spending three days in a cramped cabin together. And so, he pried and prodded until, eventually, he wore her down.

Without words, she opened the ekath and flooded his mind with the conversation she'd had with the captain. Myronor admitted the questions the captain had asked were suspicious for a man who acted as if he cared for nothing but coin. And from Ophiera's memories, he watched as Jasper's eyes had roved over her with an expression Myronor both recognized and despised. Ophiera *was* stunning, so he couldn't much blame the captain for wandering eyes, but how naive had he been to assume a simple dress would be enough to convince others she was nothing more than a consort? The captain had correctly suspected she was much, much more.

"That is why my mood is foul," Ophiera said. "It's best I stay away from him and the crew until we land in Krysas."

She curled her knees up to her chest as she settled against the wall. When her amethyst gaze fell to the porthole, she closed the ekath again in finality.

As the day progressed, it proved to be as uncomfortable as the morning. For the entirety of the time, Ophiera remained seated, agitated, and restless. She kept the ekath silent, and her brow furrowed, all while continuing to stare out the porthole with barely a blink. No matter how Myronor tried to engage, he was met with a cold shoulder or an unamused snort.

It wasn't easy to witness this cloistered version of her again. No matter what he tried—questions, jokes, or even humming, hoping she would join in, nothing seemed to reach her. She had spent so much time imprisoned, physically, mentally, and spiritually; what could he possibly have to say to offer her comfort? A cage was a cage, no matter the purpose. And he didn't wish ever to be the cruel outsider rattling the bars.

So, in dread of repeating past mistakes, Myronor kept to himself all day. Ophiera brooded, perched on the bed, while he wrote in his journal on the floor. The only change to their routine came when the sun finally set outside the porthole. He noticed her glare shifted away from the sea and lingered on the door instead. She must have heard something long before Collette's high-pitched voice called from outside.

"Weather conditions are just right again, Jasp! I'll need your help harvesting a few more barrels tonight."

"Again?" Jasper asked. "I'm busy."

"Busy doing what? You always say nothing is more important than coin, and last time we ported in Krysas, I sold out in a day!"

Jasper snorted. "You sold more than half your inventory to the Yeoman alone. That was luck, not business, Col."

"Coin is a coin, and I'm only asking you to fetch me two barrels. After everything I've done for you, you can't do this one tiny favor for me?"

The hallway remained silent for a moment. Myronor could imagine the glare Collette directed at Jasper. He was beginning to understand who really captained the *Berserker.*

"Fine," Jasper sighed. "You're the only person I'd ruin my night for, you know that."

"Oh, and what a sacrifice you're making," Collette said in a mocking tone. "You'll have plenty of time to sulk and drown yourself in booze *after* you get me my ingredients."

Their voices died down as they walked away, but Ophiera's eyes remained glued to the door. He wished she would open the ekath, if only so he could know what was going through her head. But he wasn't sure it was time to push his luck yet.

So, the evening hours continued to pass in painful silence.

Myronor kept himself occupied writing in his journal as Ophiera continued her silent brooding. He didn't look up again until the light outside the porthole had disappeared completely, blending the ink invisible against the parchment in darkness.

Myronor tugged on the crystal from beneath his robes, holding it out in his palm. The crystal flickered with aversion.

"Don't worry, Mallow, I won't ask you to come out again."

Though he wished for nothing more than to see his fluffy familiar prancing around the tiny cabin, the poor dear couldn't stomach the sea. Yesterday, when Ophiera had fled for the deck, he coaxed Mallow from her crystal to keep him company. But within minutes, he was cleaning vomit from her cream and blackened-blue pointed fur. No, it was quite clear her four legs were meant for solid land, squishy armchairs, or crystalline worlds only.

"But I could use a bit of light if you don't mind," he said, running his thumb over the crystal.

This time, Mallow's crystal glowed steadily and brightly, filling the room with pale light. Myronor saw Ophiera's foot jiggling back and forth off the edge of the bed in a constant, irritated rhythm. Her eyes look painfully glazed in the light, fixated on some thought far beyond the sea. Though the ekath remained closed, the room felt filled with her ire, and he could bear it no longer.

"Ophiera, are you alright?" He asked.

She nodded without looking at him.

Shut down again; he wasn't sure what to say anymore. But as his eyes fell to his journal, an idea struck him...in this situation, did *he* necessarily need to *say* anything?

"How are you feeling?" He asked.

She raised her eyebrows, still staring at the porthole. "Fine."

"Nothing else?" he pressed.

Her glare softened slightly. "I suppose I'm bored."

"And?"

She sighed. "That's it."

"What do you think about when you're bored?" He asked, hoping to coax more from her.

Ophiera closed her eyes. "I don't know."

"What don't you know then?"

She bit her lip, frustratedly, giving him hope that his tactic was working. With her eyes still closed, she spoke under her breath.

"My thoughts wander constantly, so it is hard to pin down one of them to describe."

"Well then, where do your thoughts wander?"

"To places I wish they wouldn't."

Now, they were getting somewhere. As always, she was never one to volunteer information. Thus, he needed to do what he did best: question her. Relentlessly.

"Are your thoughts on Iluka?"

She froze for a moment. Perhaps he had been too direct. Speaking of Iluka tore at his own heart, and he worried the wound would force her to shut down again. But in her silence, she nodded ever so slightly.

"What are your thoughts about Iluka?"

Ophiera's eyes snapped open, glaring at him as if he had spoken another language. "What do you think?"

It was hard to keep the tremor out of his voice. "I don't know what you're thinking, Ophiera. That's why I'm asking."

Her eyes dropped to her shaking foot as if only realizing now it had moved.

"Why do you wish to know?"

Myronor sighed. Questions with questions, she'd learned a bit too much from him. "So, I can understand."

Her eyes fell to the floor, laden with guilt. "If you must, I will show you through the ekath."

"No," Myronor said, smiling at her as the idea struck him. "I want you to *speak* your thoughts aloud."

"What difference does it make if I speak or show?"

Myronor closed his journal and replaced the cap on his ink bottle. Mallow flickered amusedly, understanding far too well the point he was about to make. "Sometimes, putting your thoughts into something tangible helps process them rather than simply experiencing them. Speaking them or writing them requires intention—that's why I carry my journal everywhere. Writing down my thoughts forces me to reflect rather than feel, to draw conclusions rather than avoid."

She held his gaze for some time before speaking again. "I can't write very well. And I don't know if I can put anything into words properly at the moment."

"Why not?"

With thumb and pointer finger, she pinched her eyes. "I...often find my words go missing when I feel like this."

"Feel like what?"

"Trapped."

Myronor stood, stretching his stiff legs. "What if we go out on deck?"

Her eyes flashed dangerously. "The entire reason I stayed cooped up in here all day was to avoid the captain and crew."

"We will," he said, extending his glowing blue hand to Ophiera. "I'll keep us hidden."

"We're supposed to be acting discreetly...and besides your mana—"

"Is at full capacity with little purpose other than to feed us. So, what could be the harm in using it for this?"

The wrinkle between her brows smoothed over for the first time since she woke, and he pushed his advantage. Without asking, he took her hand and pulled her to a stand beside him. She barely resisted and nearly smiled as he pushed the spell over them both. While her body wavered as if heat rolled off, a glance at their nonexistent shadows cast by the crystal confirmed the invisibility spell had worked.

With an unnecessary "shh," Myronor led her from the room.

On the abandoned deck, the night was only lit by starlight, for now. Both knew their way around a ship and reached the forward bow with little trouble. With a tightening grip, Ophiera held his hand as she leaned over the railing into the wind, her invisible hair dancing across his chest and shoulders.

"It's the Moon Tide," she said with a gentleness he rarely heard in her voice.

Myronor leaned over her shoulder to watch the faint light trail along the ship, brightest where the water met the hull. As the boat disturbed the sea, the light ignited by the churning waters spread in the wake, leaving behind a glowing path cut through the waves. It was a beautiful, miraculous sight, only trumped by the wide-eyed look of wonder gracing Ophiera's gentle expression beside him. To his delight, she leaned back, pressing her bare shoulders against his chest, leaving one hand on the rail while the other remained in his. With a deep inhale, he brushed his nose against her long, loose hair, inhaling her scent along with the sea.

"Can you tell me now what's been on your mind?" He whispered.

It pained him to ask a question that so quickly returned the look of worry to her eyes. But she did not feel nearly as agitated leaning against him as she had in the cabin.

"I'll remind you again," she said quietly, "the knowledge you seek isn't pleasant."

Myronor set his hand atop hers on the railing, bracing her against the shifting wind. As if it were yesterday, he remembered their first night camping alone after departing Feyralis. He had asked her how one became a paladin, and though her warning had been just, given the discomfort her story evoked, he had no regrets.

"I used to find that unpleasant knowledge was often the most important to seek," he replied, adjusting his words from before. "But now, I only seek you and your thoughts."

She took a deep breath against him, taking her time to inhale the cool, salty air.

"I'm starting to believe that I may be an anathema now."

Myronor held his breath a moment. That wasn't what he'd expected her to say in the slightest. Anathemas were those who had committed the ultimate sin against the Aether. Murder. By killing another in cold blood, an anathema robbed the Aether of a soul for reincarnation. Memories of the Brotherhood encampment bubbled into his mind, reliving the day he witnessed the Reverend claim three souls for the Void. Their vespers, free of any trace of corruption, had imploded in on themselves before being claimed by the Reverend.

"I *know* you're not," he said, trying to keep his voice steady.

"How can you know?"

"Because I've seen your vesper with my own eyes, I feel it tied to my own at every moment. Something so pure could never harbor the taint the anathemas carry."

"But it is the intention that matters," she said, a shiver traveling across her shoulders. "Death has been my duty, but regret and my Oath are the only exemptions I can claim. Yet now, I find myself craving Retribution for Iluka. Now, I *want* to kill Marvena, not for the Aether but for myself. The intensity of that desire, devoid of pity or mercy, frightens me. What does that make me if not an anathema?"

The strain in each of her words ached his heart. He draped his arm around her, placing his hand over the scar between her breasts. Beneath his caressing fingers, he could nearly feel her heartbreak.

"Anathemas only seek the pain of others with no purpose or remorse. That's what makes them anathema and what makes you different."

Ophiera felt stiff in his arms, silently watching the glowing waters sliced cleanly by the hull's travel. The light was growing brighter as the ship sailed onward.

"I don't regret killing the Reverend," Ophiera said in a cold voice. "And I won't regret killing Marvena. So now, all I have left is my Oath keeping me from becoming what I hunt...and after everything we've been through, I don't know if that can truly exempt me from my intentions."

Unsure of what to say, Myronor instead studied the waters in thought. The sea now left a trail of pale teal light behind the *Berserker;* only the past remained visible while they sailed onward into the darkness. But at least they were together.

Tonight was one of the very few times Ophiera admitted any doubt surrounding her Oath. While he had always questioned how much power her scars honestly held over her, she rarely expressed her concerns. Whether by the power of the Aether or fear of consequence, he was never sure what exactly bound her to her Oath. And no matter how often he tried to process these thoughts in his journal, he could never reach a conclusion. No book had ever revealed more, and Kaikora had failed to provide insight. Ophiera was his only reliable source of information on the matter, and if she believed her Oath held her to duty, then that was what he must accept.

Accept. His mind reeled again.

"I want Marvena's death as much as you," he said, tightening his grip around her. "If the intention is all it takes, then I'm an anathema as well."

Her hair brushed against him as she shook her head. "But I *have* killed, Myronor. Time and time again, in fact. You have not. You *could* not."

He watched the shifting seas for a moment, mulling over her doubt. It was true he detested violence. The staff was the only weapon he'd agree to wield, and even then, he preferred it more for its magical properties than its violent potential. Yet when he thought of Marvena, his thoughts became confused.

"I could for you."

She turned in his arms suddenly, taking his face in her hand, trembling yet not cold.

"No, you couldn't. And I wouldn't allow it."

"Why?" He asked, slighted by the hypocrisy.

"Because I have already risked the purity of your soul enough by proxy alone."

"I don't care about purity—"

"I do!" She cut in, her voice breaking. "Myronor, I need you...I need your vesper to stay just as it was the day I laid eyes on it beside the riverbank. It's the reason my thoughts have been so tumultuous today...why I worry so much I am an anathema. Not for what it means for me, but what it means for *you*. What happens if your soul is bound to one so tainted?"

"I...don't know," he admitted, not having ever considered the scenario.

"Exactly. So if we don't know, how can we risk it?"

"I don't understand, Ophiera—risk what?"

"Keeping the ekath intact."

His heart sank as she loosened her grip on him.

"I...we don't even know if breaking it is possible," he faltered, trying not to scream his protests.

"But someone in Krysas might. Kaikora said...well, suffice it to say, she hinted there might be people who know how to sever the bond. Myronor, my worst fear is that my soul will destroy yours on the path ahead...if there is a way to prevent that, I must consider it."

All day, she had brooded over the fate of their souls in silence, yet again excluding him from the conversation. Again, she had plowed ahead, making choices *for* him. And while he knew her intentions were from a place of love, a love he felt through the ekath every day despite her denials, he wouldn't let her do this again, not without contention.

"Ophiera," he said, taking her face in his hands. "If breaking the ekath is truly what you want in your heart, then I won't stop you. I'll still love you just the same, ekath or not. But it needs to be for *you*, not for me. My mind won't change; I'll tell you again and again, I would rather burn alongside you than be without you. I need you to start accepting that no matter the consequences, I will always choose you. But you must make the choices that feel right for you, not for anyone else."

Tears wet her cheek, rolling over the backs of his hands. "It's hard for me to accept and make these choices."

"What do you mean?"

"My whole life has been dictated to me by law and flame. You were one of the few choices I've ever made...And a choice I continue to make. I don't want to choose *for* you again, but I struggle to accept that what's best for you is me. If I break the ekath, I go against your wishes...if we remain how we are, I risk damning your soul. Either path is hopeless, and I feel as trapped in my own choices as I did in the cabin below."

Ophiera wrapped her arms around his neck and leaned into him. If Myronor had known that one day she'd seek his arms after speaking her heart to him, he'd have laughed heartily at the joke. But he had finally learned the appropriate time for laughter, and it wasn't now. In truth, he had learned much over their journey, most importantly that despite her constant denial, *he* had loved Ophiera from the moment he'd first laid eyes on her. Only when he held her lifeless body in his arms did he fully acknowledge the depth of that love and just how pointless existence would be without her. The reverie of that painful reckoning brought an idea to his mind.

"Open the ekath," he whispered in her ear.

Without an ounce of protest, he felt her conflicted heart flood the connection.

Ophiera, I want you to imagine there is nothing here on Erum—a blank slate—no Tanvik, no Magistrate, no Oath, no Iluka, no Marvena, no Aether, nothing but an empty void left behind where this world once lay.

A vision of a vast white space flooded her mind, surprising him slightly. When he thought of the void, he imagined darkness.

Imagine, in this emptiness, you could conjure one thing—a person or place—any one aspect of your previous existence to accompany you in the void. What would you choose?

The whirl of her thoughts was near incomprehensible at first, like the spokes on a wheel blurring as it rolled. Slowly, some images began to take form—of waterfalls and dark marshes, but in each of these locations, he saw himself until all that remained was a mirror image of him.

Ophiera pressed her face into the crook of his neck without saying any more. Her streaming tears soaked into his robes, causing his eyes to prick, too. Holding on tightly to her and her thoughts, he savored this moment beneath the night sky as the surrounding waters illuminated in a pale, green light. He felt her gaze shift to the spectacle of the Moon Tide, their breaths in unison as they witnessed the trail of light spread further out to sea.

His memories fell to Iluka. Before Pyra left for Krysas, there was a spectacular Moon Tide. He remembered walking along the lighted surf as Pyra explained the source of the glow. Small creatures, invisible to the naked eye, produced the light so often confused with magic. What had she called them again? Thecaphytes? A term no one but Pyra knew. She had known everything, it seemed to Myronor at the time, and yet so very little beyond her motivations.

Berwyn hand, had claimed another explanation. Together on the beach, Myronor remembered the way his father had so boldly declared Pyra "ruined the mystery with such dry discussions" and proceeded to tell them the myth of the two moons.

In the Southern Coastlands, the legend behind the Moon Tide described the two moons as spiritual entities—two beings forever cursed. In the sky, they hung close but always apart. The smaller moon, which shone the brightest of the two, grew weary of the endless fate and plunged itself into the sea, lighting the waters with its sorrow. But without the smaller moon, the larger could no longer shine and disappeared into the night sky. One could not exist without the other.

That was why, when the Moon Tide occurred along the coast, tradition demanded the villagers flock to the shorelines. Unions occurred to encourage the small moon to return to his lover—to remind them what they left behind.

To this day, Myronor couldn't understand why both myth and reason could not coexist. Weren't the thecaphytes that caused the glow just as magical as the tale to explain it? Wasn't the myth of the Moon Tide a more thought-provoking lesson? Perhaps he was the product of myth and reason himself. Pyra had been absent for most of his life, yet Myronor resembled her in spirit more than he cared to admit. He always wanted to *know*. And while his mother perpetually sated his curiosity, it was Berwyn who taught him to appreciate the mystery.

And now, he was sailing through the glowing waters towards Krysas, dreading what he might find there. Try as he might to pour his worries into his journal rather than the ekath these last days, he couldn't help but stare at the vast, glowing sea and wonder if he should have never accepted the Ambassadorship...never questioned his mother's disappearance.

"I feel your thoughts souring, even if you won't share them," Ophiera breathed against him.

"Nonsense," he said, shaking off his worries in an instant. "Nothing could sour this moment—"

"Did you hear voices?"

The question wasn't Ophiera's, but another voice from across the deck. It took Myronor a moment to recognize Collette's sweet voice carried on the wind.

They can't see us, right? Ophiera asked, her alarm transferring through the tether.

No, but they can certainly hear us...

"It's the wind, Col. Let's get this over with so I can sleep."

Collette made her way on graceful feet toward the starboard bow. She stood three, maybe four, arm's length away from where Myronor held Ophiera tightly against him. He couldn't believe they had arrived without either of their notice.

We should leave, Ophiera said.

Why, when we can watch what they're up to?

I don't like sneaking, and I especially don't like the prospect of getting caught.

Myronor sighed to himself.

Your honor, as always, is admirable. But I'm fairly certain we have a higher chance of getting caught if we try to sneak around them now. It's a narrow ship, and my footsteps are most certainly not as quiet as theirs, even if yours are.

"Grab the barrels, Jasp, and I'll set up the hoist."

Truthfully, Myronor did have enough mana to cast the charm that lightened their feet, muffling any sounds they made while maintaining their invisibility. But why bother when he could simply sit back and watch whatever it was these two were scheming? Coin might be *one* of their only weapons, but so was information, and if the captain suspected something of Ophiera, the best they could do was gain something on him.

You're quite conniving, you know, Ophiera thought with more admiration than disappointment.

Myronor watched in earnest curiosity as the first mate began assembling a complex pulley system that hung near the stern's edge. He had assumed these were used to haul cargo on board, but Collete, it seemed, had other uses for the apparatus.

The sullen captain joined her shortly, carrying two empty barrels thrown over his broad shoulders. Jasper looked damn near graceful as he hoisted the two casks beside Collette. With a grunt, she rolled them into position, clearly struggling against the weight. He felt Ophiera's intrigue through the link but didn't quite understand it.

"Why did you need my help if we were just going to use the hoist?" Jasper asked, sounding sullen.

"Because not everyone can haul a barrel full of seawater on board even with the help of modern technology," Collette said, pointedly running a rope through the assembly. "I need your biceps, captain."

"You need to ask Felix to help you with this nonsense next time," Jasper snorted, sounding bored for such a cutting comment.

"If you hire a deckhand strong enough, then I won't ask you for help ever again."

"I'm not helping you again, regardless," Jasper said. "Between that Ambassador and the *other* cargo, we shouldn't need your side hustles anymore to keep afloat."

Collette laughed. "Oh, Jasp, people like us always need a side hustle. You say not to count on anything but coin. And these flameless candles are a quick, easy payday."

"I will admit they are a bit more profitable than the burn bombs you were selling before. Less of a hazard, for sure."

Myronor listened to the pair bicker while watching Jasper rig the barrels with rope. With little thought or effort, he twisted a complex weave to hold the bucket firm.

"Is your rig ready?" Jasper asked, testing the ropes with a few tugs.

"Aye, captain."

Jasper rolled his eyes before heaving the barrel overboard, the rope whipping behind with a whirl. The slack tightened to a straight line as the cask towed behind the speeding ship, lighting the sea.

After a moment, Collette began winding the handle, and the pulleys moved in a synchronized manner. Again, Myronor was quite impressed. The weight of a seawater-filled barrel was immense on its own, but considering the drag of the ship sailing at full speed, it was a miracle the rope did not break.

As Collette cranked, she pivoted the arm of the hoist, dangling the full barrel above the deck. A few splashes of glimmering water escaped in the process, fading quickly as they hit the deck. Myronor recalled Rheta's complaints about the light of the Lucent Strait being difficult to bottle due to the nature of the thecaphytes. And yet he knew Collette had somehow mastered the task. His curiosity only grew as he watched Jasper help guide the barrel down, lifting it in his broad arms before setting it firmly on the deck.

From her bosom, Collette pulled forth a small glass dropper and added a full decant of mysterious fluid to the barrel. Brighter light exploded from the barrel as the surface bubbled violently. When the waters finally stilled, the luminescence remained much brighter than the sea below. Collette dipped a hand into the barrel, returning with a viscous fluorescent coating over her fingers.

"See?" She exclaimed. "I knew tonight would be a good haul!"

The captain began harnessing a second empty barrel while Collette placed a lid on the first. She hadn't bothered to clean her hand and left a trail of glowing fingerprints behind as she worked. It was an impressive material, Myronor thought to himself, and he wondered if perhaps he should buy a bottle just to send to Rheta as a tease.

As Jasper finished tying the barrel, the first mate glared back in his direction. When he moved to the hull's edge to haul the second barrel overboard, she shadowed him with feathered steps. The moment Jasper tossed the second barrel overboard, Collette raised her sticky, glowing hand, aiming at Jasper's head.

In a blur of movement, Jasper turned, grabbing her by the wrist and eyeing her tainted fingers.

"Don't you dare."

"Dare what?"

"Col—Don't."

"Let go, I need to crank the hoist."

"The second I let go, you're going to smear that glowing crap all over my face."

"You never have fun anymore," Collette simpered before flicking her fingers at him. The sullen captain's face was speckled with glowing water.

"You'll regret that," Jasper growled, releasing her wrist to wipe his face.

Myronor nearly laughed aloud before he remembered they were not meant to be there. But he felt Ophiera relax a bit beside him, watching the interaction between the two. Her thoughts lingered on Pellucid Falls, and he could understand why.

Collette giggled girlishly as she ran around the deck, remaining a few steps out of Jasper's reach. They were both exceptionally quick on their feet and acted more like children playing now—not at all like the captain and first mate of a respectable ship. It was clear he and Ophiera were not the only ones on this ship who weren't quite what they presented.

A loud crack pierced the night, and the two halted their dance. Ophiera tensed against Myronor as he watched the pulley drag across the deck and snap away from the hoist. The large wheel began to bounce violently as it flew towards Collette, led by the rope out to sea. Her dark eyes went wide as she stood unmoving from its path.

With a fluidity like water, Jasper spun in a blur, stretching out a gloved hand as he dipped low to avoid speeding debris. Amidst the chaos, he grasped the rope, dragging the pulley away from Collette. With a grunt, he twirled his arm around the free end, bracing himself against the drag of the barrel on the other end.

It will take him overboard! Ophiera cried through the link. She was already pulling away from him towards the captain, but Myronor dragged her back against him.

Oh, I don't think he's going anywhere.

Not only had the captain held his own against the drag of the barrel, but he had begun pulling it aboard, one arm's length of rope at a time. Collette stared at the broken pulley, her breath slowing as calm returned to her round face.

Jasper hauled the barrel over the railing, spilling much more glowing water than the first but far less than he should have. Myronor couldn't imagine how much that barrel must have weighed, and yet the captain set it upon the deck as gently as an empty cask. The only person he'd never known to possess even near that strength was Ophiera, and he was quite certain even she would struggle against the task.

Covered in fading seawater, Jasper turned to Collette. "*That* earned me a hell of a lot more than *a* drink."

Collette snorted shakily. "Aye, aye. Though I do wish you'd find another way to reward yourself."

She approached the fading barrel, adding her tincture as before and placing the lid atop. Without looking at him, she murmured something that Myronor couldn't hear.

Jasper smirked. "What was that, Col?"

She growled before grabbing Jasper by the ear and dragging him down to her height. "I said thanks for saving my arse!"

Jasper broke free, rubbing his ear. "Well, we really need to sell those candles now if we hope to replace the hoist."

"So my arse is just worth coin now, eh?"

The captain turned to his first mate, the smirk slipping from his face. He placed his gloved hand on her head and ruffled her hair. "Come on, Col, you know I couldn't survive without you."

She pushed his hand away with a scowl, though her eyes were kind. "Right. I'll get Felix to move these below deck; should keep him occupied for several hours, the poor lad."

Collette and Jasper trudged below deck, leaving Ophiera and Myronor undiscovered on the deck. Through the ekath, he knew they were both pondering the strength of the captain. It seemed everyone on this boat had something to hide.

~ Ten ~

BEREFT

A loud knock awoke Myronor, face down and nose crushed against the pages of an open tome. Yet again, his late-night reading with sweet Mallow curled in his lap had resulted in the perfect recipe for sleep. He knew he likely had ink streaked across his face and had seemingly drooled on the parchment, but his familiar's gentle purrs were already lulling him back to the edge of slumber.

Whoever was at the door could wait.

But the knocking persisted, dragging him away from his dreams. He ruffled a few scrolls aside, searching for the small desk clock he so seldom used. When his vision finally focused on the small, silver hands, he could see it was exceptionally late. Or exceptionally early, depending on one's prerogative. Regardless, it was an inappropriate hour for anyone to be calling on him.

The knocking continued, growing to a thunderous volume. Rudely awakened as well, Mallow let out an irritated mewl.

"Care to come along?" Myronor asked, stretching his stiff neck and shoulders.

She closed her eyes, pretending to sleep.

"Please don't make me go alone," he sighed, reaching a finger to scratch her cheek. "What if they're trying to sell me something?"

She mewled another protest but jumped from his lap, shaking out her fur. The look she gave him could only be interpreted as, "Get moving if you're going to make me do this."

As he descended to his living space, he passed an ornate mirror hung on the wall. Sure enough, his most recent notations were stamped across his face. With the sleeve of his blue robes, he wiped the scribbles of lettering from his jaw. He had tied his blonde hair back in a messy bun but didn't bother to fix that; he wished only to look presentable, not decent.

The knocking continued, testing his tolerance as he strolled toward the door. Warm but without flame, the massive hearth still held smoldering coals as he passed. With the wave of his hand, he conjured a few pieces of wood atop. Though winters were mild in Feyralis, he had an aversion to being chilled that only Mallow seemed to understand. Creatures of comfort, as Rheta called them both, evident by the blanket-laden couch beside the hearth. The nest was quite a bit more comfortable than sleeping at his desk, and once this knocking business was sorted out, he'd very much like to curl up here with sweet Mallow and return to sleep. He wasn't sure if he'd ever be able to stomach sleeping in his bedroom again.

After a few more stone steps, Myronor found himself in the entryway to his tower, resisting the urge to return upstairs. He had no obligation to answer the door when someone called this late, and yet his curiosity would always triumph over any other need. Besides, robbers didn't knock.

He stared at the solid oak door, hung inset in the curved stone wall, rattling with each series of knocks. Taking a breath, he unlatched the lock and opened the door to the brisk night. A thin frost clung to the crystal lantern hanging outside, and another chill ran across his skin as he faced a cloaked figure waiting in the shadows. As they stepped into the lantern light, bright, green eyes flashed beneath the hood, and for a moment, he wished it *had* been a robber.

"Eliana...don't you usually require dinner before calling at this hour?"

Without a word or invitation, the newly minted Justicar of Feyralis stepped past him into his home. Myronor's stomach clenched, knowing he could do nothing to stop her. Even before she had become Justicar, he could do nothing to stop her.

Eliana threw back her hood, revealing sleek, black hair that fell in curtains framing her elegant face. No one could deny her beauty, but what lay beneath the surface caused bile to rise in his throat.

"Myronor," she said in a dulcet tone. "It's wonderful to see you."

"You don't have to lie to me anymore," he said, trying to keep his voice from shaking. "Just tell me what you want so I can say no, and we can move on with our night."

Eliana looked momentarily taken aback, nearly as surprised as Myronor himself by the coldness in his voice. It wasn't in his nature to act cruelly, but the bitterness coating his insides now felt powerful and protective, even if it was a slight against his character.

"I apologize for the hour," she said, not sounding sorry at all. "I've just received a notice from the Consortia, and I assumed you'd prefer hearing the news sooner rather than later."

He felt a strange stillness in the air. She didn't move or speak but instead watched him for a reaction. Yet again, he was being baited. And yet again, he couldn't resist the urge.

"Well then, what news?"

She dropped her gaze to the floor, and a façade of grief washed over her expression. "The Ambassador to Krysas, Pyra Ebontide, is dead."

The abruptness of her words felt like a punch to the gut. Eliana was calculating and cruel, traits she proudly put on display. She had lied, she had consumed, she had pulled every string Myronor had revealed to her. But this...this was not another of her manipulations. His mother was truly dead.

A strange numbness settled in his chest, preventing any words from escaping his mouth.

Eliana removed a scroll from her cloak and held it out to him. Myronor snatched it from her, ignoring her indignant expression and managing to keep his hands steady as he unfurled the expensive parchment. Through the standard bureaucratic pleasantries and formalities, he read as fast as he could translate. The entire document was written in Krysan, the language of the Consortia. Much of the message consisted of wasted text concerning self-important governances.

He skimmed ahead, looking for Pyra's name and the answer he sought. He re-read the same line four times over before he could comprehend it.

"Self-destruction?" He breathed.

"It's a literal translation," Eliana answered, misreading the question in his voice.

He knew the meaning of the word. What he could not believe was that any of this was happening now.

"I must make arrangements," Myronor said.

"Is there anything I can do to help?" she asked, her voice sickly sweet again.

"You've done enough," he said.

Eliana slinked towards him on feathered steps. "Myronor, I wish to help you bear this terrible loss in any way I can." She reached for his face, but he jerked away from the coils of her icy hands. Despite his disgust, a part of him sought her embrace. The power she still held over him...

"The best you've done for me was to leave."

But Eliana would not be thwarted. She pressed her hands against his chest, pushing him backward until his spine touched the wall. His heart was running away and breaking at the same time. She could always sense his weakness and pounced upon it.

"I can provide comfort to you in this time of need," she simpered.

Against the wall, he took her hands by the wrists, trying desperately to keep her claws from him.

"I want nothing from you, least of all comfort."

While he held her wrists at bay, Eliana craned her body against his, molding to him like she had so many times before. Myronor shivered, his body reacting against his will as her breath danced across his neck.

"Are you certain?" She whispered. Her body tensed against his before she bit him on the neck and proceeded to kiss the mark. The pain of her touch pulled him from the stupor.

"Get out," he spat, pushing her away. She caught her balance quickly, glaring at him with a haughty grimace. The expression was her true nature revealed, and witnessing it yet again only fueled his resolve. "I appreciate you acting as the late-night messenger, *Justicar*, but as usual, you have overstayed your welcome."

Eliana drew the hood back over her dark hair, framing her furious face.

"Few would dare to treat a Justicar with such blatant disrespect," she hissed.

"Few would tolerate being treated with such cruelty by any person, regardless of title," he replied.

She pursed her lips. "You can't have it both ways forever, Myronor. There will be consequences for your flippant audacity."

"And this is the consequence for yours," he said, opening the door to his home and gesturing for her to leave.

He half expected another round of vitriol before she would take her leave, but with a final parting glare, she slammed the door behind her with violence. Unlike the last time she'd stormed from the tower, the painting of Iluka managed to cling firmly to the wall.

Mallow peeked her head out from behind the large chest, her eyes wider than usual. The sight of his familiar alone melted away the tension Eliana had left behind. He scooped her up before ascending the stairs, and she gave him a reproachful stare.

"Yes, yes, I know...worst mistake of my life," he sighed, watching Mallow's expression. Her ears flattened as her slitted pupils dilated, darkening her pale blue eyes dangerously. "I agree...I should have known she was evil the moment she claimed to dislike familiars."

Myronor walked with Mallow cupped in her arms, past the sofa, where he had intended to rest until they reached the center of the spiraling bookcases of the library. He accepted there would be no sleep for him tonight. After tenderly placing Mallow in her favorite plum-colored armchair, he unfurled the scroll concerning his mother and read it again. And again. And again.

According to the Consortia, multiple eyewitnesses reported Pyra leaping to her death. From the dark cliffs of Krysas, the Ambassador had thrown herself into the sea. No parting words were spoken, no letter was found, and nobody could be recovered.

The Consortia's primary concern had little to do with the circumstances of her death but more with the vacancy in her position. As it stood, there was no Ambassador of Tanvik to Krysas. The bureaucratic formalities Myronor had skipped over before now held his attention as his own name appeared in the script several times over. It seemed that prior to her death, Pyra had nominated Myronor as her successor as Ambassador to Krysas.

As if her death was not shocking enough, the thought of becoming a diplomat, of assuming his mother's stature, left him queasy. He was a scholar by training with little interest in politics. Though he served as a low-level advisor to some arbitrary committees, his primary involvement with the Magistrate was mistakenly falling in love with the Justicar of Feyralis. Or at least he had thought it love.

But fretting over assuming the role of Ambassador was pointless. As it stood, a complication arose in the laws of succession. Along with her body lost at sea, so too was the Ambassador's medallion, the symbol of her status. In Krysas, the former emissaries chose their successors, and the medallions served as a symbol of that succession. Like a crown passed on by kings—except now the crown was lost. Regardless of Pyra's request, there would be no heir to her position without the medallion. The loss of the literal heirloom posed an irrecoverable issue. Historically, the Consortia interpreted the loss of a medallion as a flaw in the Ambassador, often resulting in Krysas cutting ties with the representing country. If such a precious gift were lost or damaged, how could they be entrusted to represent an entire nation? While Myronor understood the logic, he wasn't convinced he could agree with the rigidity.

At least Eliana's involvement in this affair made more sense now. The Justicar of Feyralis was about to lose her nation's relation with Krysas. Without the mage-city's trades, Feyralis would suffer greatly. All the growth and prosperity realized in the last twenty years since Pyra had taken the mantle of Ambassador would come to an abrupt end, much like her life. And yet again, Myronor had to accept that Eliana's actions tonight were never about him.

Another bang on the door echoed through the tower. He wondered how long he could ignore the knocking this time. If it was Eliana again...But the knocks sounded different this time.

He descended the stairs and flung the oak door open to find no one in sight. Gazing into the cold, darkened street, he wondered if someone was playing a prank.

"Myrny! Let me in."

The deep, familiar voice came from a tiny figure, two heads below him in a dark cloak.

"I shouldn't be surprised," he sighed, gesturing Rheta inside.

His former mentor often showed up unannounced, though usually at more reasonable hours. But the news of his mother must have passed through Rheta's ears, and he did not mean the fleshy bits sticking out from beneath her chocolate curls. No, his former mentor had informants everywhere. Nothing occurred in Feyralis without her knowing, and while he typically found this amusing, tonight, it left him bitter.

Rather than returning to his study, Myronor escorted Rheta into the kitchen on the living level of his tower. In an act of muscle memory, he set a kettle on the hearth as Rheta took her usual place at his small kitchen table. Her legs dangled from the chair as she twitched her ankle agitatedly.

"I see the harpy left you in a fine state."

Myronor grunted, not wishing to say any more about Eliana. But under Rheta's unrelenting golden gaze, he continued. "She tested me tonight...and it has been more difficult than I'd care to admit to rid her from my heart."

"You sure it's your heart and not another organ she ensnared?" Rheta asked with a smirk.

Myronor couldn't laugh, as amusing or truthful as it may be. Their *physical* relationship had never been the problem, only everything else. Trying to forget, he busied himself with nothing, staring at the kettle, wishing it to boil. Usually, he enjoyed the drawn-out process of making tea without magic, but tonight, it failed to soothe him.

"I'm sorry, Myrny. I tried to get here sooner. I didn't want you to hear about your mother from her."

"You knew already?"

"Long before Eliana, I daresay," Rheta said. But when Myronor opened his mouth to inquire further, she made a tsk-tsk sound. "Don't ask for my sources. It doesn't matter because dear Pyra is the reason I'm here now." With delicate hands, she pulled a small paper parcel from inside her cloak and placed it on the table. "This arrived in my latest shipment of supplies from Krysas."

"And what do your alchemicians have to do with me or my mother?"

"Just open the damn parcel."

Usually, Myronor appreciated her candor, but not tonight. Still, he knew better than to argue and hesitantly unwrapped the parcel. He didn't much care for what was in the box, even as he gingerly lifted the cover to find a neatly folded note with his name atop in beautiful script. His heart clenched at the sight, stalling him from unfolding it for quite some time.

My dearest son,

I'm afraid time has finally caught up with me. Our shared gift is one of many incomprehensible powers, and it is one you must finally begin to understand. I know I've asked much of you these last twenty years to keep a promise to a mother you barely know. But I swear the sacrifices have been made for a purpose. I have only ever wished to provide you with a future free of darkness. But I foolishly underestimated my time, and now my work is incomplete.

My only child, I have named you my successor in more ways than title. As Ambassador to Krysas, you will inherit everything I have built, everything I am, and everything that must be done. Share this letter with our mutual friend—she will explain everything she knows.

I'm sorry this is the last letter you'll receive from me. Please know I always have and always will love you more than this world itself.

Your mother,
  Pyra

Myronor ran a finger over the inked signature before examining the contents of the parcel. Inside lay the pale medallion, shining with silver and gold, an inlaid crescent moon curving around three stars. He stared at the glimmering trinket as he handed the letter to Rheta. As she read, he silently turned the medallion over and over in his hand, not truly seeing it.

Pyra's letter disturbed him more than her death. His thoughts were struggling to catch up with his emotions, and he needed their *mutual friend* to provide context. At least before his whirling mind imploded in on itself.

A whistling kettle gave him something to do at least, but his hands trembled as he poured them both tea. Why...but no, he wouldn't start questioning yet. Rheta would clarify before long. But her brow remained furrowed over eyes completely focused on the parchment until he placed the cup before her. Only then did she lift her gaze from the letter, only to fall on the cup of tea instead of Myronor himself.

"Well...that is interesting."

"That's all you have to say?"

She pursed her lips but continued staring at the cup, unblinking and unspeaking. Normally, he was rather tolerant of Rheta's enigmatic nature; like himself, she thought about things quite differently than other mages he'd met. She had a seemingly limitless memory, as demonstrated by her success as both an alchemician and a mage. Sometimes, it took her an inordinate amount of time to sift through the density of her thoughts in the library of her mind. But tonight, he could not suffer her idiosyncratic silence.

"Rheta," he snapped, finally drawing her eyes to him. "Either you have an explanation for that letter, or Pyra went mad before her death."

With a deep breath, she began in a pitiful voice, "I know this can't be easy, Myrny."

"I'm not asking for easy! I'm asking for honesty!" He continued, voice rising far above any volume he had ever dared use with his mentor.

"What you have to understand about Pyra's research is—"

"How do *you* know what her research was concerned with?" He said, dropping into the seat opposite her, his legs suddenly numb.

Rheta didn't speak, answering him with her eyes. "There was a reason we couldn't tell you."

"We? You mean Pyra?"

"Yes."

"You were in contact with my mother?"

"Yes," she said with caution. "But again, you must understand the importance of—"

"For how long?" Myronor interrupted. His breath started to come in short, rapid bursts.

"Many years now."

"Years?!" he exclaimed in a rare temper. For the past twenty years, all he had known of his mother was a few letters exchanged per year. And they were nothing terribly personal, or meaningful for that matter. She was always more interested in his achievements, training, and studies, but not in him. And not once did she ask about Rheta.

"It was important—"

"Not important enough to tell me, her own son—your apprentice!"

Pyra knew Rheta was his mentor...*she* had requested the arrangements. And the infamous alchemician mage who swore off taking on multiple apprentices knew he was the son of the Pyra Ebontide when she had accepted him under her tutelage. He assumed it was by her name and name alone that Rheta agreed to take him on; he never guessed they had actually known each other.

"Myronor, you must understand her studies required the utmost secrecy."

"Isn't the point of research to share knowledge?" He spat.

"Not always, not when so much is at stake. The work Pyra started—"

"I'm sure whatever it was, it did not require you, my friend and mentor, to lie to me!"

"Stop acting like a child!" Rheta growled, slamming her fist on the table. He set down his tea in silence, no longer trusting his hands to remain steady. She took a breath. "People *lie*, it's part of life. And I know you haven't always been truthful with me either."

"When have I lied to you?"

"About your gift. Oh yes, Pyra told me all about the spanning magic and the dark place you both traverse. But I also understand *why* you never spoke of it! You knew well before now that the consequences of truth are often greater than those of a lie."

Myronor's gut twisted with the betrayal of it all. Was it not by Pyra's instructions that he had never revealed his true magic to anyone, not even his mentor? Why would his mother require his secrecy yet divulge everything to Rheta without him knowing? He felt like a clueless fly caught in a web of lies.

Draining his teacup, he, in a flash of blue light, refilled it with a more potent drink. The warm, golden liquid he conjured was a poor imitation of ember whiskey, but it did the trick in washing away the tightness in his voice.

"Why then, after refusing to tell me anything, did Pyra tell you *everything*?"

"Because she asked me for help," Rheta said quietly. "You know the currency I work in. We exchanged, mutually, in rare tomes, scarce ingredients, knowledge, and discretion. My interests became more academic than industrious when she began work on that dark realm you visit."

"She was studying our magic?"

"Yes, but more specifically, *where* spanning takes you when you use it. I even found her a name for the place you both traverse; the Enclave clans called it Umbraxus."

Giving a name to the place didn't ease Myronor's anxiety surrounding it. Even if he hadn't promised his mother to never span again, he would have chosen never to return there. The mere thought of the dark, suffocating realm sent a shiver down his back.

"So, what exactly was she researching?" Myronor asked.

Rheta pinched the bridge of her nose, her usual habit when lining up her thoughts.

"She was trying to open a permanent path to Umbraxus."

"Why?" He choked.

"I don't know."

"How?"

"Magic, of course. This spanning business is unheard of here in Tanvik, but when Pyra learned the Consortia had used gateway imbuteria in their cities, she sought knowledge there. In Krysas, some of the city's oldest infrastructure was built around the use of short-distance portals, a defensive strategy adopted during the ancient wars. But the gateways only provided limited movement, a limitation Pyra sought to overcome. She reasoned that by combining her own magic with the gateway imbuteria, she could establish portals between two very distant places."

"That is...impossible..."

"How can you be so certain when you have spanned great distances on Erum? And when your precious Mallow herself hails from an entirely different realm?"

Myronor sniffed, annoyed by how quickly she'd poked holes in his bitter disbelief. "Were you successful then?"

"Yes," Rheta said. "We started by establishing a portal between Feyralis and Krysas."

"You *started* by trying to connect continents?"

"It made the most logical sense."

Nothing made sense anymore. While the implications were not lost on Myronor, he was quickly becoming overwhelmed. Instantaneous travel, instantaneous information...the exchange rate could progress everything, not just magic, at an exponential rate.

"Cities, I understand, but why create a portal to Umbraxus? There is nothing there but darkness."

"Suffice it to say, Pyra had theories, backed by some minimal amount of evidence, that there was more in Umbraxus than met the eye. Or rather, what didn't."

Myronor leaned back in his chair, absorbing the absurdity of it all. While he pretended the dark world didn't exist, his mother had been traipsing around Krysas, trying to discover how to open a permanent doorway. *This* was what she had abandoned him and his father for?

"Did she succeed in opening a portal to Umbraxus?"

"No. After we established the portal from Krysas to Feyralis, our work toward Umbraxus, paradoxically, slowed down. We exchanged goods and information through the portal regularly, but anytime I asked about Umbraxus, she grew agitated. Then, a few weeks ago, she stopped her correspondence with me. Nothing came through the portal, and I could no longer open it from my end. Then, this morning, I received one of my *standard* shipments, you know, through the ports of Cantheas, and found the parcel at the bottom, addressed to you."

Myronor stood abruptly, finding himself in dire need to move. He wasn't sure if the pacing helped or not.

"Rheta, since I've known you, I've considered you more friend than mentor," Myronor began, his voice shaking. "You were more akin to a mother to me than my own. And yet, never once did you mention anything of Pyra or this research! I may have kept quiet about my spanning magic, but you kept me in a darkness far worse than any I encountered in Umbraxus!"

Rheta sighed, shaking her head of dark curls. "Myrny, your mother swore me to secrecy. And once I understood the potential of her work, I knew the danger was just too great."

"Oh, even better. It was all her decision that I remained unaware?"

Rheta said nothing in her defense. He glared at her for as long as he could muster, but bitterness was not in his nature. Still, he refused to speak. Eventually, Rheta broke the silence.

"I'm not here to argue the past but rather ensure the future. It's imperative that we save and continue her research, now more than ever. We must—"

"We?" Myronor chuffed.

"Myrny—"

"Twenty years, Rheta! I barely knew her or remember what she looked like! I would have preferred never to know these secrets. There is no *we*, Rheta. You and Pyra don't get to dump this on my doorstep just because she's dead."

"You're the Ambassador now!" Rheta scolded. "Only you will have access to her library, to her notes, and all her research. You know the succession laws!"

"I will simply deny the Ambassadorship," he said, pushing the parcel with the medallion across the table. "You can have it since you're so involved already. It will be perfect, Rheta, you can move to Krysas and never return, just as she did!"

Myronor turned away from her, watching the hearth fire burn like his throat. If his mother could pretend he didn't exist for twenty years, he could easily pretend tonight had never happened. He could continue with his research on conjura magics. His work was just as important, wasn't it? It was more practical for certain. Finding magical ways to prevent food shortages would do Tanvik a lot more good than forging a path to the dark realm.

Yet, no matter how many times he repeated the words in his head, they failed to convince him. The questions he'd asked himself over the years resurfaced with the hope of answers. Answers to be found in her library, answers beyond her research. In Krysas, the most powerful mage nation on Erum, endless knowledge would be at his fingertips.

Rheta joined him by the hearth, brushing her shoulder against his elbow.

"I know it seems hypocritical...almost cruel, but there is a purpose for everything Pyra has ever done. Her love for you is unmatched."

"Love?" Myronor spat. "That word holds little meaning."

People spent their entire lives searching for love, desperate for a taste. Yet Eliana's love was a guise for control. And Pyra's love bore more anguish than joy. How did love drive her to abandon her family in Iluka? How did love convince her to stay away for twenty years? How did love entitle her to expect so much of her son now? Myronor may not have had the best grasp on love, but he knew it could not be so selfish.

"She's dead now," he said bitterly. "It doesn't matter how she felt."

"Is that so?"

Myronor nearly cricked his neck, turning to face her. "What do you mean?"

"Myrny...I'm not yet convinced Pyra is dead."

~ Eleven ~

EVINCE

Somehow, the tiny cabin felt even more cramped when Ophiera was left alone.

For once, it was Myronor who was too restless to wait patiently. He had left for the deck to inquire about their arrival time nearly half an hour ago and still had not returned. Ophiera reasoned that the likelihood Collette would *actually* throw him overboard was low enough that she could keep the ekath closed. Moreover, she did not wish for Myronor to read too far into her thoughts while she was stuck below deck.

The hypothetical scenario Myronor had asked her to conjure in her mind last night was just that: hypothetical. She was not in a void, and until moments ago, she had not been alone. She was, in fact, on Erum, with multiple tasks pulling her in all directions. That was the reality they faced. And while Myronor would forever be her *choice,* for now, duty clouded her mind.

After arriving in Krysas, their paths would once again become unclear. Myronor was meant to take on the role of Ambassador, and she remained Oath-bound to investigate Pyra's death. Though Myronor had pledged his effort to track down Marvena and the Brotherhood, she wondered how realistic that task might be once they'd landed. She was neither Oath- nor Magistrate-bound to hunt Marvena, and yet, even disconnected from the Aether as they sailed, she felt the draw towards the dark continent, knowing without knowing the wretched soul awaited her there.

The unending circles of thought running through her mind were beginning to exhaust her.

Closing her eyes, she attempted to center herself on the ebb and flow of the ship. Like a cradle for a babe, the *Berserker* rocked her, freeing her of some anxiety. She had always loved sailing, even as Warden. The lengthy stints out at sea on the fishing vessels, protecting the villagers as they ventured into deeper waters, were never long enough for her. And none of those voyages had been on a ship quite so well-built as the *Berserker.*

Perhaps it was Myronor's influence or simply cabin fever, but she began imagining what her retirement might have looked like if she had chosen a life at sea rather than merely near the sea. If she had found a ship like the *Berserker*, with a different captain, of course, or perhaps none at all, she might have had a very different retirement indeed. Away from the Aether, away from people—it sounded ideal until she imagined, instead of being alone, sailing with Myronor instead.

Suddenly, something shifted in the ship's course—the gentle rocking became a shudder as the wood creaked and torqued. Ophiera's eyes snapped open, gazing straight out the porthole. It didn't make sense to change direction now, when they were so close to Krysas, nor to slow their speed, and yet, from both the feel and her view, the *Berserker* had done both.

A shadow passed over the room, quick enough to be confused for a blink, but she had *not* blinked. Perhaps a bird, she thought, but by the looks of the size of the waves, she wasn't sure they were close enough to the shores of Krysas for any seabirds to venture out this far. Staring through the small glass porthole, she waited, unblinking and searching for the shadow's return.

Just as her eyes began to water, the porthole blackened again. Drowning her in sudden darkness, her eyes took a moment to adjust. She thought she imagined shining, obsidian scales pressed against the porthole. But as the dark diamonds undulated across the glass with a squeaking scrape, she suspected this was more of a nightmare than imagination alone.

Opening the ekath, a crashing wave of panic overwhelmed her the moment she connected with Myronor. She couldn't make sense of his thoughts, only the fear that drove his hurried steps away from the deck and down into the hull.

The darkness let up, the scales replaced by a single yellow eye. The twitching gaze hung against the glass like a golden moon on the dark sea, and she quickly realized why the ship had changed course. She held absolutely still under the yellow gaze, hoping that without movement, it would be without sight. When the room grew bright again as the navarra slithered away, she quickly slipped her feet into boots, securing them as swiftly and calmly as she could muster. Myronor's frantic energy was leaking into her hands, shaking as she reached for the knob of the door.

The ship jerked violently to the side as a loud bang deafened her ears. Even braced against the door, the tilting floor forced her footing to fumble. She held on tightly as the ship rocked back to an even keel. The sounds of creaking wood and shouts from above kept her heart racing.

Behind her, the sunlight flashed with another pass of the navarra.

Bang.

The room grew dark again as the ship teetered sickeningly. She fumbled for the doorknob, but the constant sway made escape impossible.

Bang.

These relentless attacks would tip them soon, or worse...

Crack.

The last sound stopped her heart. No matter how well a ship was constructed, a wooden hull could take only so much.

Crack.

She clung to the moment of silence between attacks, but a new sound of trickling water drowned her hopes.

"Ophiera!"

Myronor's voice reflected the terror she felt through the ekath. At that moment, she realized it was not herself who was afraid.

"The door's jammed!" She growled, yanking at the knob again to no avail.

Beneath the small porthole, a steady stream of seawater poured forth a promise of certain doom.

"Hold on!"

In a flash of blue, the doorknob shrank within her hand as the door warped and twisted before her eyes, contracting to the size of a playing card. Myronor stood beyond the threshold, a faint glow of blue illuminating his terrified features. But the joy of seeing him unharmed lasted only a moment.

"Myronor, I need my swor-*dargh—*"

She managed to stutter the words out before another blow sent them toppling into the hallway. The attacks had slowed but not stopped.

"My sword! I'll fend off the beast while you keep the hull sealed."

She felt his questioning protest through the ekath, even as his eyes fell to the leaking porthole. Berwyn raised him to know what even a tiny leak meant for the fate of a ship. But she felt the worry of exposure lingering beneath the fear.

With a resolved nod, Myronor held out a glowing hand toward the porthole. In another flash of blue, the water ceased trickling as the wood began to seal itself. And yet, he had not yet given her the damned sword.

Crack.

Another attack sent them both toppling over in a spray of seawater. As salt and moisture clung in the air, a new, more significant split formed beneath the porthole. Myronor cast again, sealing the breach with a grunt.

"This won't end until the beast is dead," she spat, grabbing his wrist. "Discretion be damned, if this ship sinks, we *all* die!"

By the pain that flashed across his eyes, she knew he understood the depth of her meaning. Though the ekath tethered their souls together, it only worked as long as the other lived. If she and Myronor drowned together, they would both return to the Aether as one.

Silently, Myronor continued channeling his spell while using his free hand to untie the bag from his belt. He expanded the bag, revealing the gleaming hilt poking through the top. With her leather-wrapped hand, she retrieved the gift from the Aether, noticing the golden swirls glimmering even in the dim hall.

Myronor wrapped his hand over hers, joining her grip over the hilt.

"Remember the third eye," he said in a shaking voice. "The gray between the yellow."

She nodded. "I'll make quick work of the beast. Keep us from sinking in the meantime."

As she turned to leave, he jerked her back to him and crushed his lips against hers. Through them, she tasted his encouragement and promise, yet his fear tainted all else.

I promise I will protect you, Myronor.

His grip faltered as he released her, smiling sadly. "That's precisely what I fear."

Without looking back, Ophiera rushed to the deck, her dress flowing irritatingly around her legs. As she emerged onto the bright deck, the sounds of frantic chaos dragged her attention in all directions. The small crew was scattered wildly across the deck, some trying to hold the sails, others chasing after rolling cargo. At the center of it all, the young captain barked orders, his dark, curly hair blowing askew in the wind. All indifference was wiped from his expression, leaving behind only rage. And despite the peril, Ophiera found the sight of him quite...beautiful. But a terrifying screech dragged her eyes from the captain to the starboard bow.

She expected to see the navarra head rise over the edge, the size of a small wagon, baring teeth the length of her forearm. What she had not expected was a second beast to rise alongside it. As far as she knew, these creatures were known to hunt alone and, even then, were encountered only very rarely. Even as Warden, she had never sighted a navarra...but she still knew how to kill it.

"Order everyone below deck!" Ophiera yelled, marching toward the captain with her sword drawn.

"Get more of Col's burn bombs ready!" Jasper commanded one of the crew, blind to her until he turned to face her. "I-Iris?" His eyes fell on her golden sword, lingering there instead over her whipping dress. At least he could prioritize adequately when the time called for it.

"I said order everyone below deck," she repeated, brandishing the blade.

"Y-yes, you most certainly should be below deck," Jasper growled, ignoring her request and turning back to his crew. "Someone find the damn harpoons!"

Ophiera growled. Was it the dress that undermined her demands of Myronor and Jasper? Perhaps her loose hair whipping in every damned direction sent the wrong message as well. With a loud *thunk*, she drove her sword between two boards of the deck, catching the captain's attention and fury.

"What in the bloody—"

"For the last time, order everyone below!" she commanded, allowing her sword to stand on edge while she began tying back her loose white hair. The dress, she couldn't do much about at the moment, but damned if she would let anything else get in her way.

The hair on the back of her neck stood on end, her body sensing the danger before her eyes had time. Jasper was drawing a hissing breath, distracted by her blow to his ship and ego. Focused on her, he hadn't noticed the curved spine of the first navarra unsnap towards them.

With her runed hand, Ophiera pried her sword free of the deck and, with the other, pushed hard against the captain's chest. His eyes widened as she shoved with all her might, clutching his leather overcoat in the process. The man was young but built like stone, and her boots squeaked against the deck in her efforts to ensure neither of them ended up in the jaws of the beast.

As they tumbled, a spray of seawater stung her eyes, thrown from the attacking beast. The smell of leather and smoke consumed her senses as she dragged Jasper against her, rolling them both onto the deck beneath the snap of fangs. She somehow managed to hold onto her claymore in the process, but as she rolled to her feet to attack, the beast had already retreated into the sea.

"By the flames, they're quick," she said, resetting her grip on her golden sword. Though the first beast had recoiled, the second was ready to spring, almost as if they had *planned* the attack. She knew the navarras were known to be intelligent, but a coordinated attack required they possessed far more consciousness than she was comfortable admitting.

With a hiss, the second navarra lunged. Ophiera twisted, surprised by the speed at which it came for her and only her. The sound of tearing fabric preceded the *snap* of its jaw, and as she turned to face it, she saw a piece of her dress dangling from its lips. Ignoring the close call, she raised her sword, commanding every muscle in her body to swing. But her sword hit the deck with a reverberating clang as the beast retreated to the sea long before she could swear.

"Everyone, off the deck!" Jasper yelled from behind her.

Ophiera turned to see his eyes burning with a wisp of fear as he glared at a growing stain splashed upon the deck. Following his gaze, she immediately recognized the dark ichor. The viscous excretion burned and sizzled into the beautiful wood, just as it had burned through her armor and flesh alike before. Like the awakened death in the Sloughmire, like the power summoned by the Reverends, these navarra were tainted by Aud.

"Jasper, hurry!" Collette yelled, ushering the last two crew members below deck.

Ophiera returned her attention to the two sets of yellow eyes gazing hungrily down at her. At least now, she wouldn't have to worry about collateral damage. From behind, she heard the *schwing* of not one but two blades abruptly drawn.

"Go!" she spat at Jasper. "I don't need another distraction."

"My ship, remember?" he laughed, brandishing his two curved knives.

She didn't understand what he thought he could accomplish with two blades, barely the length of his boots, against two monstrous beasts out at sea. And yet the expression he wore was somehow more dangerous.

"You're absurd!"

He looked her up and down, eyes lingering on her torn, flowing skirts before shrugging. "Not any more than yourself."

Before she could draw breath to argue, the leading navarra snapped forward again like an arrow from a bow. As Ophiera twisted left, Jasper stepped right, and both skirted the blackened scales by less than an inch. She growled as the jaws began to retreat while she still readied her claymore. But already, the beast was out of reach.

A blur of metal and leather flashed as the beast screeched deafeningly. While she spun, continuing to build her swing in what felt like slow motion, Jasper moved at the speed of the navarra, driving both his blades into the beast's snout. Its body wriggled against his hold and yet did not retreat—rather, it could not retreat. Jasper groaned as he held his ground, boots squeaking against the deck, fighting the drag of the beast. And winning.

Ophiera didn't waste a second of thought and swung her claymore down with a scream. The grind of metal against bone reverberated through her leather hand wraps but did nothing to slow her cleave. A familiar *thunk* of her blade against the deck assured her this time.

Warm blood poured from the divide, spraying her in sticky crimson. She had only a moment to be grateful it held no trace of the ichor before dodging the long, muscular body as it jerked back into the sea. Held firmly by Jasper's blades, the severed head remained behind, leeching black and red viscosities from its mouth onto the deck.

Panting, Ophiera stared at Jasper in disbelief. With a quiet grunt, he pulled his blades from the head, wiping the blood on his already-tainted overcoat. She couldn't believe the young, apathetic captain held his own against the beast. The strength required to pin the monster was far more than a few barrels laden with seawater. His narrowed eyes remained fixated on the blackened ichor, sizzling as it ate away at the wooden deck.

She didn't understand how the plague of the Sloughmire had made its way to these beasts. As far as she knew, the navarra were dangerous for their bloodlust, not their venom. And this venom was the same that tainted the Sloughmire. The rotting corpse of the giant troynt haunted her thoughts.

"Impressive swing," Jasper said, pointing a knife at her bloodied claymore. His amber eyes bore into hers, almost accusatory.

"Nice pin," Ophiera replied with a curt nod. She wanted to ask how he had acted so quickly or how he had the strength to hold the beast still. But those were curiosities for another time. Now, her mind needed to focus on the remaining navarra.

As if sensing the same change in the air, Jasper turned his attention upwards. Strange, she thought...the beast now kept its distance. The yellow eyes darted across the deck as if searching and, she couldn't believe it, plotting.

"Maybe its friend will make the same twice," Jasper muttered, flourishing his blades.

As if in answer to his query, the navarra recoiled in the air, dancing like a charmed snake about to strike. Ophiera could only hope the beast might be so foolish, but she knew better than to hope.

With a sudden roar, the beast charged, but this time, not with its head and not toward the deck. The navarra screeched as it resumed bashing its tail against the hull, the splintering wood audible from above deck.

Panic took over her heart as she sought the link.

Myronor!

I'm fine—hull is resealed, he replied through the ekath. *But I can't hold much longer.*

Ophiera sensed his dwindling mana, spent on repairing the hull and reinforcing it still. If the beast broke through again...

Time quickly became their newest enemy.

Searching the deck, she looked for anything to grab its attention. But given the coordination of the two navarra and the gleam in its eye as it attacked the hull, it *knew* not to come close to her again.

She needed to kill the beast swiftly. If she timed herself, she could jump off the deck and onto the body of the navarra. But it only came close when it assaulted the hull and would see her long before she could climb to its head. She might be strong, but not strong enough to carve through the thick, coiled body. Within her chest, she felt the Aether roar with need, her mana desperate to end this threat. If the ichor was in the head, then it was the head she must target. Perhaps Myronor could levitate her up to its head, and she could dispatch it with the holy flames. But he needed to focus on the hull. As she studied the navarras head, reeling back from the next attack, her eyes caught sight of the sails.

"How far are we from Krysas?" Ophiera asked Jasper.

"Close enough for the currents to carry us but too far to swim if that's what you're thinking."

"Hold this," she said, thrusting the hilt of the bloodied sword toward the captain. He looked mildly horrified as he took it unquestioningly from her grasp. "And if you can think of a good way to distract it, that would be a great deal of help."

She tore off toward the center of the ship before giving him the chance to question. The singular benefit of the now torn dress was that she moved far more quickly and quietly as she made her way to the center mast.

Using the ropes wrapped tightly around the mast for footing, she began her climb. The wind threatened her pride, blowing the stained and torn fabric in all directions. But nothing was as threatening as the screeching navarra preparing for another tail attack.

At the top of the sails, she wrapped her legs around the wooden mast, freeing her arms to untie the smallest piece of canvas. Luckily for her, Jasper's crew didn't tie knots like Berwyn, and with hands still covered in navarra blood, she undid the ties of the sail with ease.

The captain glared at her from the deck, strapping her sword to his back. She supposed she should have told him what she'd planned. But it was either his sails or their lives.

The navarra's eyes flitted to her like a piece of meat on a skewer, ready for dinner. She was exposed in far too many ways up high on the mast, but the clever beast knew she could do no harm where she hung. Instead, it hissed as it released its coiled tail against the hull again.

Ophiera held on tightly with her legs as the ship tilted with the blow. High on the mast, the exaggerated sway sickened her gut. Despite the nauseous angle, she continued wrapping the last bit of rope around her wrists, securing the sail to her hands.

Hoping for a distraction, she watched below as the captain pulled a small, round bottle from his belt. The flask shape suggested a flameless candle that Collette concocted. But as he flourished the bottle, she saw a dark, viscous fluid slosh beneath a tight seal of wax.

Jasper glanced at her with an unreadable expression before kissing the bottle and hurling it at the creature. In a blur, Ophiera could barely follow, the bottle landed directly between the beast's eyes. The navarra roared as the dark liquid splashed across its yellow eyes, recoiling from the ship as smoke began to rise. Trickles of blood ran down its snout, pouring from its blinking eyes. But as the smoke cleared, the bomb, it seemed, had little effect on the gray third eye.

She knew it couldn't be that easy, but damn if she didn't wish it had been. With a resolving breath, she threw the loosened sail into the wind and released her legs from the mast. She dropped sickeningly through the salty air before catching the wind to begin gliding towards the blinded navarra.

You know I can see exactly what you're doing, right?

The rippling thought nearly caused her hand to slip from the canvas. She wondered if it would be crueler to block Myronor from the ekath or allow him to watch.

Cruel is acting so recklessly again, regardless of whether I can see or not!

Ophiera took a deep breath, ignoring his upset and concentrating on her landing zone. The nape of the neck was far more reasonable to reach now that Jasper had blinded it.

None of this is reasonable!

The roar of the navarra in her ear matched Myronor's voice in her head. But it was too late now to turn back.

No, it's not! Turn back!

Her eyes watered as the wind stung her unblinking glare. She needed to wait until the absolute last moment to release the sail.

Don't you dare...

Just a little further...just a little...

Ophiera!

She dropped.

Only a moment passed before she collided with the writhing creature and began sliding down its glossy scales. Desperately, she grasped for anything to keep her from falling into the sea. Thick, thorny protrusions served her purpose, but even the leather wraps failed to protect her hands against the sharp spines. Pain permeated her slippery grip as she began scaling the back of the navarra, unable to differentiate blood or sweat.

Only when she neared the top of its head did the navarra begin thrashing violently. She held tight as wet warmth pooled beneath her leather wraps, threatening her grip. Every ounce of strength was spent on remaining atop the navarra. And through the ekath, she felt Myronor's fear pulsating as he watched.

Like a signal from a war drum, his terror ignited Ophiera's scars in a blaze of white. The creature's spine disintegrated in her Oath hand, along with the leather of her arm, all burning to ash in the wind. With only one hand still gripping the navarra, she was left with little choice. Drawing her scarred hand high, she allowed the pain to propel her white-hot fist down. As she plunged into the center, gray eye, she found herself elbow-deep in a warm, viscous fluid. The creature screeched as its innards boiled and burned around her fiery arm, whistling steam and acrid smoke. In one final thrash, the beast flung her from itself before clouding into a pillar of ash. As she fell, she watched the dark remains rain into the ocean, churning in the wake left behind by the *Berserker*.

Not her best plan, she thought to herself, plummeting towards the water. She hadn't thought of her return to the ship or how to avoid drowning in the sea. The impact alone from this height was guaranteed to be painful and maybe even mangle her. Would Jasper turn the sails around to fetch her?

She really should have thought this through a bit more before jumping.

You said it, not me!

With her nose only inches from the surface of the sea, her body suddenly jerked upwards, back into the air. It felt as if a rope had been tied around her waist, yanking her painfully back along the path she had fallen. Only when the deck was in sight did she notice the blue light surrounding her.

Casting with an ill-fit grimace, Myronor stood waiting for her with outstretched arms. The moment her toes touched the wooden deck, both he and his spell collapsed. Despite being covered in grime and grit, she caught him in her arms, supporting more of his weight than she feared was needed. His breath felt erratic against her ear as his entire body trembled against hers.

"Is the hull sealed?" She asked.

"Yes," he breathed. He took her face in his hands, assessing her with worried eyes. "I don't need to ask if the navarras are dead. Are you injured?"

"More filthy than anything," she said, looking down at her blood-covered dress. "How is your mana?"

"Drained, but not nearly as much as my heart," he said, holding her hand against him again. "You have a bad habit of jumping to near-certain death! And my heart cannot take it again."

"My success rate is higher than yours," she teased, trying to avoid facing the pain behind his words.

To her relief, Myronor chuckled, though his voice rasped with exhaustion. He ran his thumb across her lips affectionately, leaning in close. She closed her eyes, ready to feel the relief of his kiss, when an enraged growl cut through the air.

"You!"

Both she and Myronor turned to see the captain holding her sword beside the still-twitching head. Despite the anger in his voice, his eyes looked desperate as they bore into hers.

There was something painfully familiar about the way he stared at her now. The look in his eyes, the trembling of his hands, pointing at her with blood and seawater.

"Who the hell are *you*?!"

~ Twelve ~

GNAW

The captain's eyes seemed to hold nearly every emotion at once as he glared at Ophiera. Copper swirled with tears and anger—the sight alone was jarring enough without him covered in blood and holding her sword at his back.

Myronor's arms tensed around her. "Did you hit your head or something, captain? She's my cons—"

"I wasn't speaking to *you*!" Jasper hissed, his eyes never leaving Ophiera's. "Who are you?"

She couldn't find the words to respond. The entire point of the consort's guise was to hide who she was. A paladin of the Cloister, the Warden of Iluka, a fugitive of the Magistrate. But lying felt equally pointless after what she had just done.

Jasper stepped forward, ignoring her silence. "I knew from the moment you set foot upon my ship you were no consort."

I told you, Ophiera communicated to Myronor in private.

He ran his hand down her back, smiling through his exhaustion. *To be fair, slaying two navarras is far beyond a Feyralis consort's skill set.*

Jasper closed the space between them, now close enough that Ophiera caught a waft of leather, sea salt, and blood. She couldn't understand why he looked as if he'd seen a ghost. It was reasonable to ask *who* was on his ship, but the way his coppery eyes shimmered caused her heart to falter.

"What else could she possibly be?" Myronor asked, rolling his eyes. He was trying to avoid the truth as desperately as Ophiera, but neither had much to stand on.

"I've seen those flames before," Jasper whispered with a tremble. His eyes dipped to her hand, scars raw and exposed after burning with the holy flames.

And with that, Ophiera knew she had nothing left to stand on. Miraculous as it may be, if Jasper had recognized the holy flames, it was a short sail to link her to the wanted posters in Cantheas. And while she trusted Berwyn's judgment of a discrete ship, coin ruled the seas as much as the storms. Unlabeled cargo and mysterious skills, there was no guarantee that the Brotherhood did not have influence over Jasper or his crew.

"It's you, isn't it?" Jasper said, his voice growing in strength. "The berserker Warden of Iluka!"

Myronor twisted his shoulders, placing himself between her and the captain. While she appreciated the gesture, there was no point denying her identity any longer. She squeezed Myronor's shoulder with her now-exposed scarred arm. His eyes fell on her, worry and exhaustion tainting the brilliant shade of blue.

Let me handle this...

He nodded solemnly and released her.

"I *was* the Warden of Iluka," she said. Scars and all, she faced the captain, prepared to demonstrate exactly who she was if the conversation turned sour.

"I knew it," Jasper croaked before dropping to his knees. She couldn't tell if his strength had failed him or if...was he groveling? Nothing he did made sense, not even the desperation in his eyes. His...eyes...

"I knew your eyes—" he started as if reading her thoughts. "That shade of violet stood out even in the darkness. I've never forgotten, never."

"I'm sorry, but I don't know *you*," she said, the words feeling wrong even as they fell from her lips.

Jasper's eyes widened painfully as if she had slapped him across the face. He licked his lips and narrowed his gaze before lifting himself from the ground. As he rose, his demeanor changed, his eyes narrowing and his scowl returning. By the time he stood, matching her in height, only a burning rage was left behind his stare.

"I am both captain of this ship and the only survivor of the culling of the Gray Marauders—the only soul you left unclaimed from the white fires on the stormy beach of Iluka."

Ophiera felt Myronor's shock before her own through the ekath. And a flood of memories hit her like a cross wave. A young man alone in a boat...Sopping, dark hair and amber eyes full of regret...drifting amongst a sea of vespers.

She studied the captain who now stood before her and saw the reflection of the boy adrift. Tormented and afraid, only this time, stained with blood instead of rain.

Something within her stirred, tangling into a mess she could not undo.

She was the source of his terror and tears alike, both then and now.

She couldn't imagine anyone but an anathema causing such an expression.

Even the sight of the navarra had not had this effect on Jasper, and yet she...she was a monster, wasn't she?

Her worst thoughts bubbled forth, despite Myronor's muffled protests through the ekath behind her.

But her silent implosion was interrupted by a terrible, gurgling squelch.

The bodiless jaw of the navarra twitched before it first snapped, the head bounding forward with a jerk. Her mind was pulled in too many directions to react to the unfathomable action of the dead beast. Black ichor dripped from its teeth as it opened its bloodied, dark mouth; she wondered if its bite would hurt as badly as the troynt.

A sudden blow to her back sent her tumbling forward, away from the jaws and towards the captain's open arms. Jasper caught her and rolled with her onto the deck. Dazed by the jostle, her back scraped to a stop on the wooden deck with the captain pressed hard atop her. Overwhelmed by the scent of leather and blood, she didn't understand...What was he protecting her from? And what was that horrible squelching sound?

Excruciating pain erupted from her leg, though she had fallen nowhere near the snapping jaws. In concert, she heard Myronor's anguished cry.

Over Jasper's shoulder, she confirmed her worst fears. The severed navarra head was clamped down upon Myronor's leg, where he stood heavily on the other. Black ichor oozed from its mouth as his hands glowed blue, laboring to prevent it from closing further while prying himself free. His mana flashed blue as he freed himself, stumbling backward and crashing against the deck.

Ophiera shoved the captain away from her and scrambled to her feet. Her flames within had all but dwindled against the second navarra. But seeing Myronor was enough to summon forth the dregs of her mana to burn the twitching head to ash. She dropped to Myronor's side, avoiding the splashes of black ichor while hastily examining him. To her relief, his eyes were still open, but he stared back at her with a set jaw and pallid complexion.

"No, no, no," she mumbled, watching the viscous poison bubble and smoke through the blue cloth of his robes. She resisted the urge to burn the foul taint away. Even if she had the mana left, Myronor would not survive the flames as she could.

Myronor groaned through his clenched teeth, the agony transferring through the ekath and acting as a focus for her thoughts. She began tearing the pieces of the ichor-stained robe from his body.

"Hardly seems the time to undress me," Myronor said, trying to smile but only managing a grimace.

Beneath the scraps and smears of blood, she clearly made out the small row of three punctures, momentarily thankful the bite had not managed to close upon his flesh. But the mixture of ichor oozing from the most central wound was cause for concern.

"I need my armor," she hissed to him.

Myronor bit down on his lip to manage the pain while a trembling hand threw the gem fruit-sized bag to the deck. She knew she had asked too much given his state, but there was little other choice. With a flicker of azure light, the bag maximized to full size beside her. Frantic, Ophiera dragged her cloak from the pack, finding it wrapped around the pieces of gleaming gold paladin armor.

With her dress in a deplorable state, she instead used the cloak to wipe away the blood near the bite, taking care to avoid touching the ichor to her skin. Bile rose in her throat as she saw the dark tendrils spread beneath his flesh.

"Jasper!" Ophiera growled, snapping the captain out of his stupor. He'd done nothing but stare at the black ichor eating away at the deck since she'd escaped his grasp. But now, a void of hopelessness lingered behind his gaze as he stared at her. "Find him something to bite down on, and then hold him down!"

"Are my jokes really that ba-bad?" Myronor said, his voice fading to a groan of pain.

Jasper neither acknowledged nor ignored her as he approached, placing his leather knife sheath between Myronor's teeth. His eyes darkened as they fell on the wound, his lips tightening as if holding back a curse. It was clearly no one's first time encountering the ichor; a sentiment echoed in the ekath as Myronor's tension rose. Jasper placed two firm hands on his shoulders, and both men stared at Ophiera, expectant.

I'm sorry.

She pressed the adamantrium plate against the wound but couldn't hear the hissing and boiling of the ichor over Myronor's screams. Beneath Jasper's grip, he writhed and jerked, his pain tearing through the ekath like a broken blade. The black smoke rising strengthened her resolve to keep pushing, to keep causing him agony. His survival depended on it, no matter the pain.

Jasper restrained him as best he could, but even the captain's strength faltered against Myronor's agony. His amber eyes looked dead as he winced against the screams as if he felt the same pain as Myronor. She couldn't understand...*she* was the one who had to feel every facet of his agony through the ekath. And though it broke her heart in ways she knew not possible, the alternative was a far worse fate.

When the smoke stopped, and only crimson blood poured forth, she withdrew the vambrace. Myronor's screams quieted to whimpered breaths as she examined his leg. For a moment, she felt relief, only for it to be slashed by a sliver of darkness still writhing within the deepest puncture. A tendril of black squirmed beneath the skin, retreating deeper within the wound.

She couldn't reach the taint with the obtusely flat, golden plate. And yet, if she didn't stop it...A vision of clouded blue eyes and a seeping smile of black ichor flooded her vision.

From the pile of armor, she pulled forth a golden greave and strapped it against Myronor's calf. As she suspected, the tendrils shifted beneath his skin, traveling *away* from the adamantrium.

She next fastened her heavy belt tightly across his upper thigh, cutting off its path while slowing the bleeding. The darkness festered in the wound but did not travel further. For good measure, she laid her golden cuisse atop the wound, praying she had done enough to contain it for the moment.

Sweat ran from Myronor's pale brow as he breathed raggedly through the gag. She was impressed he'd remained conscious throughout the ordeal. With shaking hands, she removed the saliva-soaked sheath from his mouth and handed it back to Jasper.

"How do you feel?" She asked.

"Been better," Myronor replied with a weak smirk. "I don't suppose I'm wearing your armor for a good reason, eh?"

Ophiera closed her eyes. "Some of the ichor remains in the wound—it's contained for now, but I cannot say for how long."

"Could be worse, I suppose."

"Could be better," she snapped. "What the hell were you thinking, pushing me away like that?"

Myronor winced as he chuckled, gripping her hand. "You'll be unsurprised to learn that I hadn't really thought at all."

At her glare, he slipped into the ekath.

I couldn't bear the thought of you getting hurt, Ophiera.

Better me than you!

That's a matter of opinion.

Not opinion, fact! It is a fact that I could have cleansed the ichor from myself!

Maybe.

Not maybe. I've done it before!

Let's call it even for foolish decisions today and leave it at that.

Jasper stood abruptly, interrupting their silent argument. With a swift step, he stood before her as if yet again shielding her from something. As she looked up at him, all traces of fear and hopelessness were washed from his face, replaced by a stony, neutral expression.

Only then did Ophiera notice the crew reappearing from below deck. They stared at the scene with equal terror and curiosity. She dragged the remnants of Myronor's blue robes over the armor, hiding any trace of gold and wound.

Your scars, Ophiera.

With a pang of annoyance, she tucked her Oath arm behind her. While she doubted the crew had witnessed her fight against the navarras, she couldn't risk any hint that she was a paladin. But Jasper still held her bloodied blade on his back, dangling before her eyes.

She felt exposed in more than one way as Jasper turned an eye on her, glaring as if debating himself. With a sigh, he turned back to his crew.

"I've slain the beasts!" he shouted, his voice commanding and confident. He was suddenly a vastly different man from the weeping, lost boy only moments ago. Though the crew cheered at his words, with a gently raised hand, Jasper silenced the lot. "But there is nothing to celebrate! We must reach Krysas with haste or face more navarra! I need two of you to carry our injured diplomat to my cabin while the rest of you prepare to sail. Now!"

With not so much as a raised eyebrow, the crew called out in unison, "Aye aye," and set to work.

"Col!" Jasper shouted amidst the flurry. "I need you!"

The first mate approached, slightly disheveled but otherwise composed. Her dark eyes scanned Myronor, and her gaze flicked to Jasper in silent question.

"His wound needs tending, but..." he said, setting a gentle hand upon the woman's shoulder, "he is tainted."

Ophiera couldn't believe the tenderness of his voice as he addressed his first mate. Nor could she believe how violently Collette began to tremble.

"But that means..." she choked before getting a hold of herself. "My apologies...I never imagined the navarra would carry the ichor."

Jasper nodded. "Are you able to handle it?"

"Aye-well, I'll do my best," she murmured. But despite her agreement, Ophiera clearly saw the hollow fear in her gaze.

"Keep his leg hidden until you're below deck. And don't speak of the armor or the ichor to any of the crew. Tell them it is a flesh wound, and that is all. They don't need to know what dangers we really face now."

Jasper patted the diminished Collette on the shoulder, the touch seeming to perk her up slightly.

Two crew members approached as Jasper gestured them towards Myronor. They lifted Myronor from the deck, and she felt the pain of his wounds as they shifted him with rough hands. Ophiera stood on shaky legs, ensuring her Oath scars remained hidden behind her. Collette eyed her bloodied dress before turning her attention to the crew.

"Get him to the cabin."

As Ophiera moved to follow the procession, a blood-encrusted blade blocked her path. *Her* blood-encrusted blade.

"Let Col take care of him," Jasper said in a dead voice. He dropped the blade and held the hilt out to her. "We have matters to discuss."

"What exactly is there to discuss?" she hissed, snatching her sword. She wasn't sure what hurt her pride more, the fact that he'd wielded her beloved blade with such grace or the grimy state she had left it in.

"Don't play coy, *Iris*," he growled. The amber eyes that bore into her now no longer belonged to the boy in the boat but instead to a cold and indifferent beast. "We need to discuss the Vespula Brotherhood...and why they want you dead."

~ Thirteen ~

CONFLUX

The hull groaned as the *Berserker* sailed at full speed once again—a sound that always brought Jasper a great deal of comfort. But after the attack, it brought him far more than comfort alone. Each of the navarra's attacks against the hull had felt like a personal slight against him. An attempt on his life and that of his crew was a threat he could not easily overcome. And though he celebrated their survival, now, a bitter part of him wished the two guests on his ship had remained just that.

Jasper had suspected the blonde bastard was a mage, but at least he'd had the common decency to keep his magic to himself thus far. As captain of a private vessel, Jasper often refused transport to innaturals, preferring to keep his sailing company free of magic. But now his ship had been tainted by the worst kind of mana on Erum, and it had saved their skins to boot. He hated feeling indebted, though admittedly, the mage wasn't the only cause of the bitter bile bubbling in his gut.

The so-called consort now sat at his cartography table, caked in dried blood and the remaining scraps of a dress. She scowled down at the ancient leather map in front of her, at once both beautiful and terrifying.

Why did fate torment him so?

The moment Jasper had first laid eyes upon her, cloaked and clinging to that mage on the Cantheas docks, the hair on his neck had stood on end. But like a comfortable idiot, he had brushed off his instinct as a misplaced reaction. It had been a long time since he'd encountered anyone quite so alluring, and yet, he should have known a pretty face could not intimidate him so easily. Usually, he didn't dismiss his gut instinct quite so readily.

After their first conversation, he had known she was far more than a consort. Yet even as he watched the fateful swing of her massive sword, he still believed her to be a sort of bodyguard hidden in a skirt. Only after those pale flames shone brighter than the sun in the midday sky had he known it was *her*. The Warden of Iluka. The berserker who haunted his dreams.

Though her snowy hair fell in a loose foxtail over a dirty, scant dress, her eyes remained the same. Jasper watched her stillness as he mulled over his options, mesmerized by the manner in which she glared at the map. Her gaze held that same terrible purpose, smoldering beneath her violet eyes. It was no wonder the Vespula Brotherhood found her a threat enough to eliminate.

"So, Iluka truly is gone..." Jasper said, breaking the awkward silence.

The paladin nodded, refusing to tear her eyes away from the map.

She had only just finished confessing her story to him. He had heard the rumors of Iluka's ill fate long before she'd explained the unfortunate series of events that had led her and the mage to his ship. It was hard to believe the Brotherhood was capable of the level of destruction she described. And now, he found himself suppressing a grief he had no right to feel.

"I assume Iluka is the reason the Cloister seeks your bounty?" he asked.

Ophiera's brow pinched together at the mention.

"Your guess is as good as mine," she growled.

"Is it now?"

"I don't *know* anything more than what I've told you," she said, turning furiously on him. "Maybe the Brotherhood seeks to frame me for Iluka. Perhaps the Cloister considers my failure to protect Iluka a violation of my Oath. Or, as you suggest, perhaps they blame me entirely. I truly don't know why the Cloister searches for me, but I know that whatever the reason, it cannot be pleasant."

She was quick to anger, but Jasper actually found it amusing. Now that she no longer had to act the floozy consort, her proper temperament shone through. He decided it suited her far better.

"And the shaman? You know nothing of her whereabouts?" Jasper asked, studying her eyes carefully for the signs of deception. If they could locate the shaman, he mused, at least his crew could claim one of the bounties.

"Trust me, if I had a clue as to where she was, we would be sailing in her direction, not towards Krysas," she said with a glare.

"You're not exactly in a position to decide where we sail."

The way she bit her lip told him she was holding back more than just her tongue. It was good to know how easily he could get under her skin.

"And what position am I in, exactly?" She asked. "You asked me to tell you everything, and I have. I believe it's your turn to explain yourself."

With an irritated smile, Jasper leaned forward. He found her claim to be quite bold; she'd barely told him anything. From the way she hesitated to the words she chose, it was apparent she kept many secrets hidden behind her avoidant eyes.

But it no longer mattered. Her body language betrayed her thoughts clearly: the way her eyebrows twitched, the direction her eyes darted, and the way she fidgeted with her fingers. Every single tell revealed *everything* to someone like him.

"I should begin with the night we met," Jasper said, taking a slow drink. "After you killed the Gray Marauders, I stumbled down to Cantheas and worked my way up through the docks until I could afford my own ship—this ship."

In acknowledgment, Jasper sloshed a bit of ale on the floor, watching it absorb into the scarred wood of his pride and joy. He had never expected his ship's namesake to set foot on her deck, let alone be the reason she almost sank *and* still sailed. Fate indeed tormented him.

"What does any of this have to do with the Brotherhood?"

Impatience seeped from her pores, but he supposed he couldn't blame her. He had at least removed his soiled overcoat, leaving him in the comfort of his untarnished undershirt and somewhat clean pants. Meanwhile, she remained caked in the visceral remains of the navarra, her dirty flesh revealed in places he was certain she never intended. Uncomfortable as she was, he also decided the mixture of darkened blood and ash smeared across her cheeks suited her as much as her ire.

"Everything," he said quietly. "I learned an important lesson that night: in order to stay alive, it is best to be inconspicuous. I purchased the smallest and fastest cargo vessel I could find in Cantheas, recognizing the *Berserker*'s potential while most others scoffed," Jasper continued. "The ship has served me well, carrying me and my crew across these waters more times than any other vessel. Yet, we draw little to no attention. We're not affiliated with any of the trade companies, nor are we openly freelance. It's amazing what you can learn about the world when you build a business on *discretion*."

She snorted but kept her thoughts unspoken, though certainly not to herself. He wondered if she was aware of how obvious her expressions could be read.

"A year or so ago, ships began disappearing in the Lucent Strait," Jasper continued, ready to satisfy her impatience with his point. "More than what storms accounted for, but still few enough to easily ignore. Well, for *others* to ignore. It didn't take much for Col and me to discover the Brotherhood's involvement...and to find our fortune within it."

Her eyes widened without subtlety. She was so reckless with her emotions; he could hardly understand how she'd survived this long. Then again, in her existence, it didn't much matter how she felt or what she thought. That was the way of the Cloister, was it not? That was the way of life.

"Are you—"

"No," he replied, cutting her off. "Despite my former affiliations, I hold no allegiance to the Vespula Brotherhood." Admittedly, the look of shock spread across her face pleased him. "I simply know their business and mind my own. I know they're responsible for the missing vessels. I know they bend the navarra to their will and taint them with a dark ichor that consumes everything it touches. I know they transport large quantities of goods to and from the mage city-state of Krysas. And I know the lofty price they pay upon delivery."

"If you knew the Brotherhood was at fault for so much, why do nothing to stop them?"

"It is not my business to stop them."

"And that justifies turning a blind eye to the atrocities they commit?"

He could feel her anger bubbling, resonating with something hidden deep within himself. A bitter demon he had suppressed for years had shivered free, filling him with a mirrored discourse he no longer controlled.

"You say atrocities as if some are *better* than others," Jasper snarled. "Yet I am forced to watch two dozen people burn alive on the shores of Iluka in my dreams. The screams, the ash, and the glow of their vespers against wet sand—it's as if I'm there again. You may have had justice on your side, but what I witnessed that night was still an atrocity. How can I possibly judge which acts of violence are right or wrong, which sins are necessary or cruel, when they leave the same marks on those who bear witness?"

Avoidant eyes, slumped shoulders, tensed jaw—Jasper saw that his words had indeed struck a nerve. The bitter demon purred, enjoying the pain he'd caused her with words alone. Her eyes suddenly hardened as they met his.

"Then what is your judgment for me, now that you know who I am? I assume you plan to turn me over to the Brotherhood? Or perhaps to the Cloister? Which benefits your pocket more?"

Jasper found it both intriguing and frustrating—she wouldn't refute his words.

"Don't misread me," he replied shortly, rolling his eyes. "Factions come and go with the tide; power changes hands like the weather, and the difference between right and wrong shifts with each storm. But the sea remains indifferent, and I admire—no, *require* the consonance it offers. I let the currents take me where they lead."

"I care about your intentions, not your life philosophy," she growled. "So tell me, what fate befalls us in Krysas? Which is the path of least resistance?"

Jasper sighed, pressing his lips together. He hated decisions like this. In these moments, he often left his choices up to a simple question: what threatened his immediate survival most?

Between the Brotherhood and the berserker, he wasn't certain who posed the greater threat. He now sat in a room with an irritable paladin who had trounced two of the Brotherhood's navarras.

Granted, he might have helped a bit, but he had a sneaking suspicion she could have bested the beasts solo.

She *had* saved his life and the lives of his first mate and crew. And while he certainly did not consider himself moral, he did hold *some* honor. Though he tried to search for any other way out of this scenario, the truth was that the choice had been made the moment her sword came down on the navarra.

"I will deliver you and that innatural to Krysas with discretion, as agreed."

Her lilac eyes widened, and he realized she honestly had expected him to hand them to the Brotherhood. To his surprise, the thought stung him.

"That's all I care to know," Ophiera said as she stood suddenly. "I'll take my leave then."

She towered over him in the chair, intimidating and yet familiar. Jasper was forcibly reminded of the boy on the boat again, shaking in fear as the berserker approached. He had been so confident she was about to kill him that night. Sometimes, he wished she had. Memories from the beach flashed through his mind again, but this time, he wouldn't let her walk away.

As Ophiera stepped to leave, he reached for her, taking her by the wrist. A desperate need broke through his indifference—a need for her to...The glare she turned on him was reminiscent of a cat whose tail had just been yanked. Yet she neither bit him nor ran away.

"Stay a moment," he said, barely recognizing his voice. It was almost as if every word he uttered held a question hidden within.

"I must see to Myronor," she whispered icily.

He tightened his grip involuntarily at the mention of the mage. "Col is likely still working up her concoctions—it would be best not to interrupt them."

She continued to glare down at him. "Is that why you stopped me?"

"Not exactly."

"Then what else could you possibly need of me?"

It was a valid question. A part of him knew this would likely be the last chance he had to ask her. And yet, he wasn't convinced he wanted the answer.

For years, he'd honed his dissonance into the perfect mask. And the protection of his apathy was only broken by bouts of fear and anger. 'Fire cannot burn those who feel no pain,' as the proverb went. He had worked so very hard to master himself, to *cope* with the dark hand fate had dealt him. Yet by her presence alone, Ophiera had dredged up the worst parts of himself. Memories bubbled to the surface of his mind—memories he couldn't ignore as the demons of his heart awakened. Memories he thought long buried.

"Why did you spare me?" he whispered.

Her arm slackened in his grip. With full lips parted, she let out a breath as if in disbelief. And for the first time since entering his cabin, he could no longer read the intention behind her gaze. He couldn't read her at all.

"I spared you," she breathed, "because you hesitated."

Jasper sensed something break deep inside him. "I don't understand."

Ophiera took another deep breath. "Whether from fear of death or love for your home, I saw regret in your eyes. Every time I...I searched for that look, only to be disappointed. You were the first and only soul to meet my sword with contrition."

Jasper felt his throat tighten.

When he'd fled the beach of Iluka that night, he had assumed he'd been too pathetic to finish off. Later, he wondered if she simply spared him to serve as a warning to others. On his worst nights, he even feared she would return to finish the job. But the truth she shared now...the answer provided was not at all what he'd expected.

She had *seen* something within him worth sparing.

Again, the sense of something gone awry within him hit with full force. Like a raw nerve, he felt suddenly exposed in heart and soul. The memories flashed so violently in his mind that they clouded the vision of the cabin. As his heart thundered in his ears, he wondered if he would be able to separate the past from reality this time.

His hand slipped from her wrist down into her lax hand. To his surprise and need, she wrapped her fingers around his own, holding him afloat amidst the waves of reveries.

"My dreams always start with the dock," he murmured before taking a gasping breath. "It hadn't changed since I'd been overseas...ten years away and...I didn't know...the Marauders at the time...I didn't know...I thought they wanted the pearls...I didn't...I was trapped...long before the flames...loathing everything I did and didn't do...And after...after I witnessed their deaths in white fire and steam...I bobbed in that sea of ash, wondering if my vesper would match theirs when you came to claim it. I hated myself that night...and for so many more after..."

To his surprise, Ophiera placed a hand against his cheek. His face was wet with tears, and her skin rough from battle, but it brought him inexplicable comfort.

"You weren't the only one who hated yourself on that beach," she said.

Her confession calmed the storm in his heart. Not even Col understood the pain of despising one's own existence. But he could see in the depths of her eyes that Ophiera knew that feeling all too well.

Outside himself, Jasper pulled the berserker closer to him. And unbelievably, she obliged. The metallic scent of blood filled his nostrils as she stepped before him. He remained seated at his cartography table, looking up over the torn dress through wet, dark lashes.

"I apologize for my words earlier," he said. "Your actions that night were not an atrocity."

She laughed bitterly. "No, what you've said is correct."

"I don't—"

"I accept that my very existence is an atrocity," Ophiera hissed. "There is no point in hiding from it any longer."

"Hiding?"

Her eyes darkened as she stood before him. "I tried to avoid my Oath by retiring somewhere like Iluka. I chose to hide from my duties instead of accepting myself." Her hands clenched within his. "But no longer; no Oath compels me to take my Retribution against the Brotherhood now. I choose to claim their souls in recompense for *their* atrocities."

Her words sent shivers down his spine. He couldn't remember the last time he'd felt fear, but in her presence, it came to him with ease. Years of apathy were unraveling now in Ophiera's hands, burning away as if never existing. The effect she held over him was undeniable, despite his wishes to deny everything.

"You speak of choice as if everyone has the power to do so," he said, more defensively than intended. "Those choices become burdens to those without the strength to carry them."

Ophiera looked at him with a sad smile. "Conviction is a power we all carry. For as long as I've been alive, I've been convinced I did not have choices. But I *chose* to hide in Iluka; I chose to spare your soul...I chose to protect Myronor...and now I choose to destroy the Brotherhood, regardless of the burden of atrocity."

Jasper considered her words for a moment. Experience had taught him what power really was, and it had never been conviction. Power was destroying a navarra in a blaze of pale flame. Power was Collette's talent to remedy nearly any ailment. But conviction? Conviction was a scam—Cloister rhetoric fed to the masses to ensure righteous behavior. Conviction was simply a tool to manipulate people into choices that ended their lives prematurely.

The only conviction *he* required was to survive, and even then, it sometimes waned. Some nights, when sandstorms and cold winds crept into his sleep to torment him through the morning, he wondered why he still bothered with the business of survival.

Still hand in hand, they sat together in silence as he stormed within. Still so close. Still so warm and firm against his grip. Despite years of mastering himself, his emotions, his *fear*, his hands shook within hers. How could he have survived this long only to have his suffering incarnate before him now, holding his hands? Her gaze still brought a shiver to his spine, but there was something more dangerous than fear causing his heart to stutter.

Jasper didn't think as he dragged her hands onto his shoulders. He held them down against his linen shirt, watching as her eyes widened, yet she didn't recoil. Instead, she dug her fingers into the thin fabric, gripping the muscle above his collarbone tightly.

As if pulling the cat's tail had not been enough, Jasper *dared* place his hands on her waist. Beneath the grimy bodice, her body felt firm and sculpted, far different from any consort he'd ever touched. Following the glorious curve of muscle, Jasper slid his hands lower to her hips, admiring the power of her build beneath the thin, filthy material.

She tensed against his touch but remained within his grasp. Even with his gifts of strength and stealth, he knew she could overpower him in an instant if she wished. And yet she remained wary but curious.

When Jasper had imagined the berserker, it hadn't been like this, and yet he wanted nothing *but* this now. The demons within him roared with need, wishing to tear the dress from her and expose the god-like woman he could feel beneath. To conquer her would be to conquer fear, would it not?

"I am *not* the path of least resistance," Ophiera suddenly said, pushing him back into the chair with force, wooden legs scraping loudly against the rough floor. She turned on her heel and stormed from the room without a backward glance, heading down the stairs to his quarters. And for a moment, Jasper considered pursuing her before he came to his senses.

What in the blazes had come over him?

The demons Jasper kept buried crawled forth again, destroying his delusions and reminding him of himself. Why did he desire *her*? He shouldn't be pining after her—he should *hate* her.

Steps echoed from below. Despite coming to his senses, Jasper wished to see white hair and a bloody dress rise from below for a moment. But he was equally disappointed and relieved as Col rose into the room from his quarters.

She wore her black leather apron, stained and burned over the years with her alchemicians. Though she didn't speak a word, Jasper could read in her raised eyebrows and pursed lips that she was about to ask him what he had done to aggravate the consort so dearly.

"How is our diplomat fairing?" Jasper asked, hoping to deter her.

"He'll make it to Krysas," she said, wiping her hands out of habit. "Though I can't say how long after landfall. I've never seen anyone or anything survive that ichor..."

Her voice trailed off to a place Jasper had never been but knew well by the hollowness in her eyes. He rose, heading towards his private reserve stowed near the wall. Filling two steins with ale, he assumed Col's needs matched his own. She took a seat at the cartography table, replacing Ophiera's vacancy. The thought of the berserker made him drop the overfilled drink a little too forcefully.

"His survival won't be our problem once we land," he said, raising his cup in a bitter toast.

"No? I'm quite certain it will be one of many," she replied, taking a drink from the stein before continuing. "We lost eight barrels in the attack…both the Yeoman *and* our other clients will want an explanation. We're looking at garnished wages *and* an injured diplomat…no Jasp, our problems are just beginning."

Jasper sighed. "We'll tell the Yeoman of rough seas or blame Felix as usual," he said, waving his hand dismissively. "We can throw in some of your flameless candles or something to sate the deficit."

"And why are we throwing Felix under the ship again?" Col hissed. She had become rather protective of the kid, even if she used him as a scapegoat the most.

"The Yeoman can't know about the navarra."

"Why?"

"Because I rather enjoy getting paid!" Jasper snapped, his frustration instantly boiling over. He usually refrained from yelling at his first mate unless he was drunk. And unfortunately, he was far too sober for the moment.

Col's shock faded to worry before she spoke again.

"Jasp, you know where those barrels come from—"

"I know nothing other than what is on the manifest, particularly the details referencing price per parcel."

Col slammed her hand on the table, spilling ale in the violence. Without flinching, Jasper dropped his gaze to their merging puddles of drink spilled in anger.

"Wake up, Jasp! Navarras have never bothered us before! We've been delivering our *excess* to the Yeoman for months. The gig is up! Maybe the Brotherhood isn't too happy about your scheming—maybe they've finally come to see *us* as a problem."

Jasper gazed at the map, tracing the familiar course to port with his eyes. He silently considered how much truth might lie in Collette's conclusions, especially after he had so willingly and conveniently blamed Ophiera for their current woes.

He hadn't become wealthy by keeping secrets or picking sides. Neutrality was something to capitalize on, and his latest scheme had done just that, or so he'd thought. The *Berserker* had been hired through third parties and with a careful lack of documentation to transport goods. He wasn't supposed to know who they were for, but he did know, nonetheless. He made it his business to know. And while he discreetly transported their cargo as requested, he also skimmed from that cargo, selling the excess to the Yeoman in Krysas, at double the price. Neither party could report him to any authority without exposing themselves, and until now, the waves he made had been small enough to be ignored. But perhaps no longer.

"What would you suggest we do?" he asked Collette.

She sighed, staring back at Jasper with the warm pity she only held when she knew she was right.

"I know your biases, but if the mage survives, he holds a powerful position with powerful connections, and we could ask—"

"Absolutely not," Jasper spat. "I will not be indebted to some filthy innatural who stumbled upon my ship, dragging havoc along with him." Col winced at his tasteless use of the derogatory term, but Jasper didn't think twice about her reaction; mages *were* innatural.

"We're already indebted to him. For helping to save the ship," Col said quietly.

Jasper ran a hand over his face, trying to compose himself. "And you've paid him in full by tending his wounds. Besides, the navarra might have targeted him for all we know."

While he had promised to keep the truth of Ophiera's tale secret, Col had seemingly drawn her conclusions on suspicion alone. But despite his baiting, the first mate laughed back at him in a girlish mockery he so despised.

"Why would the Vespulas want him? An Ambassador is too high profile and too risky for their operations. Open your eyes,

Jasp—we've been had! That mage and his feisty consort are our only friends in Krysas now, regardless of your prejudice."

He scowled at her. "And regardless of my prejudice, he'll likely not survive the night, anyway!"

"He may well survive!" Col hissed, hushing her voice with a glance at the stairs. "I simply said I don't know. And those burn bombs I made you are unnatural, same as all the other concoctions I've whipped up over the years. Even your abilities are..." She trailed off, knowing damn well how close she'd just approached an unspeakable subject. "Look, you always say, 'who are we to judge,' so stop being a hypocrite."

Jasper closed his eyes, weighing the options.

In their line of work, they seldom had friends. On the wrong side of the Vespula Brotherhood, they would have even fewer. Perhaps his first mate had a point. The *Berserker* could extend its stay in Krysas and lay low for a time. The crew would probably appreciate a bit of shore leave, especially after the navarra attack. And it might give him a chance to find out who had put a target on his ship. *Someone* was expecting the ship to be sunk and not float into port.

"Fine. We dock in Krysas until things settle down," he said gruffly. "We'll see what the Yeoman has to say before we ask the innat—the *mage,* for anything."

"Aye, aye," Col replied with apparent relief. She drained her ale before pushing her chair back to leave. "I'll make sure he's extra comfortable until then."

Jasper waved her to stay seated. "You might as well relax; wouldn't want to interrupt him and his consort." The bitterness of his words surprised him more than Collette.

She grinned like a demon. "Oh, captain..."

"Stop, Col."

"Never did I think I'd see the day you fancied anything other than drink."

"I don't *fancy* anything," Jasper replied acidly, crossing his arms. He knew from experience that Col would not let up until he gave her *something* to think on. "I just...I've met-er-Iris before."

The flowery name sounded pathetic on his tongue, but he swore to uphold her disguise.

"By the sea, what fate is this! Was she a consort then?"

"No," Jasper said. He was uncomfortable with this conversation. He hated lying to his first mate and usually refused to do so. Withholding wasn't a lie, though, was it? "She was quite different then, as was I."

"Sounds like she was your first," Col chortled between girlish giggles.

"Get your head out of the latrine. It was nothing like that." However, her words sparked his imagination from only moments earlier. He wished it *had* been something like that. "Frankly, she nearly killed me."

"Funny how many people have tried to kill you, Jasp."

"Hilarious."

"Aye, but I understand now why you've been behaving so strangely," Col said softly, no longer mocking. Her dark eyes stared past his own, the only person who ever truly saw him. "She's reminded you of a time you weren't so numb, hasn't she? And now, you're starting to feel *something* after you've gone so long feeling nothing. Her presence alone has yanked you from the depths, but now that you've surfaced, you can't remember how to breathe the air."

Jasper stared blankly at his first mate. "I can't say I appreciate your insight at the moment."

"Aye, you'll never appreciate me," she said, smiling, and stood from the table. "I'd still prefer you to *speak* your thoughts rather than force me to read them from your pretty face."

Jasper once again felt the foreign constriction around his heart.

"You're the finest first mate on these waters, Col."

"That I am, captain, which earns me a solid rest before we arrive in Krysas." She stood, stretching for dramatic effect. "You'll let me know if Myronor or his consort need anything, aye?"

"Aye."

With a mocking bow that almost caused her excessive bosom to tumble free, she left his cabin.

Alone with his thoughts, Jasper began to brood almost immediately. He found his mood strange, and in the turmoil, he had forgotten the most basic rule of subterfuge and secrecy—never act without reliable information. He wasn't sure who was to blame for the navarra attack on his ship, but for now, he would gather information. In fact, he could start right now within the confines of his cabin.

~ Fourteen ~

PERCEPTION

Ophiera dropped the filthy rag into the filthy bucket of filthy water. It was amazing how much blood and ash remained caked on her skin, even after removing the dress. Pulling an unsullied shirt over her head, she turned her attention back to Myronor with a pit in her stomach.

"So the captain believes the Brotherhood manipulates the navarra," he said, the words falling from his lips lazily. Whatever potion Collette had given him had alleviated any discomfort, it seemed, and then some.

"And so do I."

Her eyes fell to Myronor's wound, a burden of irrefutable proof. Now surrounded by her golden plate, Collette had cleaned and bound his wounds without questioning how the armor repelled the ichor. Nor did she question why a consort and diplomat carried with them a complete set of golden plate mail. Given her wit, this lack of questioning from Collette was more worrisome than relieving. Still, whatever Collette suspected or did not suspect, she had left Myronor in far better condition than when Ophiera had seen him last. Eyes glazed, Myronor now lay in the captain's lavish four-posted bed in a pair of underclothes she did not recognize.

"If only he had provided some theories on how they managed to contain the ichor in their bite without rotting the whole, like that troynt," Myronor said. "It's curious, isn't it?"

"It doesn't matter how they had the ichor," Ophiera sighed, taking a seat beside him on the bed. "What matters is it's still festering in your wound."

Even obscured by her plate mail, the presence of the corruption seemed to linger on the periphery of her senses, like faint smoke long after a fire. Though contained for the moment, it was impossible to guess whether the taint would resolve on its own. Perhaps the ichor acted as an infection and could be fought off with the right potions and salves. Or perhaps, like an infection, it would only spread.

"Those navarras were working in unison," he mulled, twirling a lock of her damp, freshly washed hair between his fingers. "I didn't imagine that, right?"

"No, you did not. And yet, even decapitated, they could still bite!" Unable to contain her ire with the last word, she winced as the words grated against her throat. The shouts on deck and the following conversations had left her voice hoarse and strained. Regardless of ekath or rest, it seemed that the wound from Iluka might never fully heal.

"Take advantage of our tether," Myronor said gently. "I'm sure chatting up the captain overexerted your voice as much as fighting the navarra."

Her spine stiffened at the hint of accusation beneath his gentle words.

What do you mean by 'chatting up'?

Myronor sighed with a lopsided smirk. "I merely meant you did a phenomenal job softening him up in his map room. You're quite the flirt, my consort."

She slapped his twirling fingers away from her hair. *Flirt? I was trying to find out if the selfish bastard planned to hand us over to the Brotherhood!*

"I understand that," Myronor said, gazing at her curiously. "And by allowing him to take your hands so sweetly and pour out his pent-up pities of the past, you've ensured he won't turn us over to Magistrate or Brotherhood alike. In fact, we may even have allies now in the docks of Krysas..."

I...but that was not my intention.

The mage's jovial expression faltered slightly. "Then why allow him to put his hands on you? Why continue that *intimate* conversation if not for our advantage?"

Ophiera was searching for the answer herself.

Truthfully, her first instinct had been to throttle Jasper for daring to lay hands on her yet again. But this time, she had found herself startled by the desperation in his grasp. She could not help but compare it to Myronor's touch.

Jasper's grip was rough and calloused, unlike Myronor's soft, gentle hands that had just stopped playing with her hair. The most stark difference, though, was the sensation of being touched without a tether attached. When Jasper grasped her, it was a silent connection that neither caused her heart to race nor the flames to surge. Though she could not deny it had caused something to stir within her.

"Ah...well, I think I understand now," Myronor said, unable to hide the disappointment in his thoughts.

Ophiera's jaw nearly dropped.

She didn't care that Myronor had followed her thoughts, but she did care that the fool had reached such an erroneous conclusion. Even with access to her very soul, Myronor failed to understand her. When Jasper ran his hands over her, it hadn't even crossed her mind that *others* might view her actions as anything beyond pure curiosity. Before recently, she had barely known what it felt like to be touched without harm or animosity. No one shook hands with a paladin, let alone held them tightly through the night. Yet the way Jasper had grasped her hands, without a tether to transfer *more* than pure touch, well...it was something she hadn't experienced much either.

Again, she sensed Myronor following her thoughts with a wisp of disappointment. But this time, her patience for his foolishness was as non-existent as her mana.

Don't you dare draw another misguided conclusion from my thoughts! Ever since we left Feyralis, I've faced challenges to my body, soul, and heart. Everything is new, and it is these new things I'm beginning to fear. On this ship, the Aether may be silent due to distance and drain, but the moment we land in Krysas, I have to contend with my inability to control the surges. Touch, rage, fear, the ekath—all of these potential triggers for the Aether—all of which I struggle against! Of course, I must consider how Jasper's touch felt and how his actions affected my own because, at that moment, I didn't feel the threat of the flames. And...that has given me a sliver of hope that I may one day be able to control this cataclysm that I've become. I understand why you cannot comprehend my burdens, but I cannot understand how you can misread my intentions so severely.

A prickling sensation behind her eyes threatened to break through with her anger. She looked away from Myronor, unable to stomach the look of shock across his sallow features. He was injured and ill, so why was she lashing out at him now? While her frustration was well placed, expressing it felt more challenging than slaying the navarra.

With a gentle tug on the sleeve of her shirt, she heard Myronor say, "Come lie by me."

Lying beside you would be ill-advised with your wound, she said before she could stop herself. Though the ekath thrummed with approval of his suggestion, her heart and mind were pulling her thoughts in all directions.

Myronor sighed. "What if you lie on top?"

Despite her frustration, her lips quirked at the way he maneuvered every conversation in his favor. Before she could argue, Myronor had taken her by the waist, guiding her atop him. And while her eyes focused on his wounded leg, she found his touch difficult to resist. As she carefully straddled him, she felt momentarily self-conscious about just how exposed she was in the linen shirt alone. To avoid his gaze, she laid her head on his chest. Just because the ekath desired his touch did not mean she was ready to face him quite yet.

"Ophiera, I'm sorry," he began, his warm breath dancing against the top of her head. "I...it's not an excuse, but I let my past experiences cloud my judgment, and for that, I truly apologize. It's been easy for me to acclimate to many of the changes we've experienced since we met. But you're right; I don't have the burden of Oath or Aether, and those factors influence much of how you think. While I admire how differently you view the world, I'm ashamed to admit it has taken me an absurd amount of time to realize just how askew my priorities are from yours."

What do you mean by priorities?

He sighed, pressing his lips against the top of her head before speaking. "Ophiera, you were my first and only thought when the navarras attacked."

As you were mine. How is that askew?

"I may have been your first thought, but not your *only*."

I don't understand.

"The first thing you asked for was your sword," he said with a chuckle.

But we had no choice except to fight. If the beasts had capsized the ship, we would have all perished.

Myronor sighed, more exasperated than disappointed. "*You had no choice, Ophiera. When I say you were my only thought, I mean it. I ran from the deck straight to you without concern for whomever I left behind. And when I opened the door to the cabin, I intended to span us away. To abandon the crew to the navarras.*"

Ophiera felt his chest tremble beneath her as if he had relived the fear of that moment by simply speaking it. She hadn't realized what he'd planned to do, nor had she even considered the option of escape. If she had known, though, would she have agreed with it then?

"*It was quite cowardly, I admit,*" Myronor continued. "*My point is that I acknowledge now that there is much you consider beyond me. Which is why I'm sorry for my comments.*"

Apology accepted, Ophiera replied, relaxing against him. But there was an itch in the back of her mind regarding his earlier words. *I admit that I am curious about what you mean when you say past experiences.*

She felt his thoughts cloud and was unable to make out a coherent or clear vision before he took a deep breath.

"I was *involved* with another person some time ago. And well, she treated me quite differently than you do," he said with a faltering voice. His heart began to beat irregularly beneath her ear with the strain of his words. "I was not really a lover, not even a pet to her—just something to be used when she was bored. I came to the conclusion that I simply wasn't enough for her, and let the mistreatment continue for far too long. Sometimes, when my mind isn't in its right place, I worry I'm not enough for you either. But between your Oath and the tether...I never want you to feel *obligated* to me. You should be free to make the choices you wish, with whomever you wish."

Ophiera sighed against him, understanding with painful clarity the feeling he described. She had felt like a tool her entire life, and regardless of the purpose, being used had a way of damaging the soul. And yet, despite the damage and the obligations, he still wanted her love to be her choice. With Jasper, she had claimed conviction was a power held by all, and yet, of late, she lacked much herself. Was her obligation to her Oath truly conviction, even if it represented something she'd never wanted? In the same way, could she truly be *obligated* to Myronor if she desired him above all else?

I may have held another hand in curiosity, but it's your arms I seek now. And while my soul demands our closeness, it is my heart that feels the joy in it, overriding any whisper of obligation.

Myronor's entire body relaxed beneath hers. "I suppose if you *did* feel obligated to me, you wouldn't have left me before."

While Ophiera knew his sentiment came from a place of comfort, she couldn't help but feel ashamed. Her love for Myronor might outweigh any sense of obligation, but her doubts that he was better for it trumped all. Not only had she treated him poorly, but every horrible experience he'd faced was due to her failings.

She felt his hand slip beneath her chin, leading her to face him. The pain in his eyes stopped her breath. From her jaw, his hand slipped over her collarbone, down to the faint scar between her breasts. Through the ekath, she felt a painful swell of memories.

"I know what it meant to live in this world without you," he said quietly. "Just as I cannot comprehend the pain of your Oath, I'm not sure you can comprehend how much it broke me. As I said, my choice will always be you."

Ophiera didn't process her thoughts as her lips found his. To feel despair from a memory of the loss of a soul was something she understood. It was undeniable that Myronor loved her, regardless of whether she could understand exactly why. And after the day they'd both had, she was tired of fighting.

His fingers curled through her hair, and she sighed at the sensation. Though potions and exhaustion still clouded his thoughts, Ophiera caught flashes of imaginings, not memories, racing through the ekath. Images of her without a shred of clothing atop him, of his hands traveling to places they hadn't before, of their bodies melding together in ways she *used* to think were forbidden. But what was once taboo now became her only desire.

The faintest of shuffling sounds distracted her from his lips. She froze to listen while he began a trail of kisses from her chin to her neck. The floorboards creaked ever so slightly, distinct from the ship's groaning hull tossed against the waves.

Myronor, do you hear that?

His breath danced across her collarbone as he continued down.

I can only hear your hurried heart and the creaking of the ship.

While he might have mistaken the sound of sneaking steps for the usual groans of sailing, Ophiera knew better.

Someone is lurking at the bottom of the steps.

Myronor paused his lips for a moment, tugging her shirt collar aside and exposing her shoulder. Before resuming his path of kisses, he smiled up at her. *I see only shadows, Ophiera.*

From her periphery, she eyed the dark corner near the stairs, searching the darkness desperately. There was little doubt in her mind that it was Jasper. Whether he was spying for the thrill alone or in search of something more, she didn't appreciate his subterfuge. But she had caught a faint whiff of leather and whiskey that hadn't been quite so potent in the room before.

I see, Myronor said, following her thoughts. *Well, I am an injured Ambassador alone with my beautiful consort—we should keep up the act for our spy, wouldn't you say?*

With a gentle tug, he pulled her lips back to his and began kissing her with a ferocity she'd never felt from him before. As if his imaginings were about to be realized, she trembled with anticipation as his hands moved to her bare thighs, caressing and squeezing as he held her down against him.

The ruse is pointless. Jasper knows I'm no consort.

Myronor chuckled aloud. *Do you find this pointless?* Her argument fell to the wayside as his tongue slipped past her lips. *He may know you are the Warden of Iluka, but let him learn who you really are to me.*

The possessive tone in his voice was unlike him, yet intriguing. Warmth spread from her chest outward, tingling down to her extremities while pooling at her center.

And what am I to you?

You're my partner, he began, kissing her more fiercely still. *You're my love—my fire—my motivation—my soul—my world. You're my everything, Ophiera.*

If she posed any threat to burst into flames, it was surely after hearing the intensity of those thoughts. And yet, with her mana drained, her need for his touch was the only burn she felt. As Myronor slipped his hands beneath her shirt, his hands danced across her skin as if stoking her flames. She wondered if the way her skin caught ablaze was some spell, but as his hands traveled to her chest, she didn't actually care any longer. Even the threat of a voyeur couldn't stop her from wanting more.

Her breath stopped as he caressed her breast, cupping and squeezing her sensitive spots in a pleasurable kind of pain. A moan escaped her, and she hardly recognized the sound. But she couldn't stop her verbal release of the sensations, especially as he began kissing down the path laid by his lips before. This time, as he dragged his lips down her neck, he licked and sucked, forcing more incoherent sounds to escape her. Her breaths were more erratic now than when she'd fought the navarra, but she held her breath completely when his mouth finally reached her chest. Gently, he kissed the raised scar at the center of her chest.

She bucked hard against the sensation of his lips against her skin. Nothing was in her control anymore, not her body or voice or thoughts. But her taste of an unbound moment was cut short by the shot of pain through the ekath.

Myronor's wound throbbed against her poorly placed foot, and the sensation of the darkness lingering within immediately snuffed out her desire. What was she thinking? Her charge was injured; they were on a ship fleeing after navarra had nearly killed them, and the captain was likely lurking in the corner. This was quite possibly the worst time for them to do what they were about to do.

Maybe now isn't the time for this, she thought disappointed, sliding off Myronor. She was about to stand, but Myronor dragged her back to his side, this time opposite the wound. Careful to lay her head on his heaving chest and away from his searching gaze, she fought against the smoldering burn of his skin against hers. But guilt quickly replaced any lingering lust.

Ophiera, there is nothing to feel guilty about. But you're right; a little bit of patience never hurts, especially if we have an audience.

~ Fifteen ~

RECITATION

"Good news," Rheta drawled, tossing a roll of parchment on the table. "The Magistrate has accepted your request."

Her words barely registered as Myronor unfurled the notice. Since learning of his mother's...

"I didn't think Eliana would actually agree to a formal investigation," he mumbled, reading through the legal jargon.

"The Magistrate is more than just the Justice of Feyralis, Myrny. The Justicar of the Sloughmire was particularly keen on contesting the Consortia's claims surrounding Pyra's death."

"Why?" He asked, relishing the rare flicker of curiosity he felt these days.

"It doesn't matter," Rheta replied with a snort. "Suffice it to say, you're *officially* the new Ambassador to Krysas, and your words hold sway with the Magistrate."

Now, it was Myronor's turn to snort. His word shouldn't hold any sway over anyone, especially any word regarding his mother. They had only ever shared blood and magic. But that, apparently, had been adequate to inherit her problems in full. He drummed his fingers across the worn table, re-reading the same sentence over and over again.

"It says an investigator has already been appointed, but doesn't bother to name them?"

"Who conducts the investigation is the least of your concerns at the moment," Rheta said, looking away from him. "Come, I need to show you something in the library."

Just like in the days of his apprenticeship, Rheta's tone alone was enough for Myronor to obey without question. He slid the notice into his pocket and silently followed her. As much as he hated to admit it, at the moment, it felt good to be led.

Lately, all he could do was what he was told or nothing at all. Distracted, indecisive, hesitant...one might assume he suffered grief. And perhaps it was, but not for Pyra. He hadn't known his mother well enough to mourn. Twenty years of semi-annual correspondence were hardly sufficient to build any sort of relationship. Yet, it was enough for her to deem him a worthy successor as Ambassador.

Politics had never been his interest or forte. He chose to become a scholar so that his only responsibility in life could be knowledge. Mallow had come along and inserted herself into his life, thankfully, with little say on his part; Eliana was much the same, yet to far more detriment. But he was responsible for neither, just as he wished. He had never wanted a say over anyone or anything, but now, as Ambassador, he would have a say over an entire nation.

The medallion bouncing off his chest as he followed Rheta felt more and more like a yoke than an honor.

"By the flames, Myrny, I taught you to put the books *away* when you're done!" Rheta's dark curls bobbed agitatedly as she maneuvered around the many piles of tomes. With a flit of her hand and a pale yellow glow, she levitated the books from their piles.

"I *was* reading those," he murmured as the tomes flew in every direction, each returned to their preordained locations.

"Trust me, you'll be occupied with others now."

Early on in his apprenticeship, he had learned that when Rheta was cryptic, there was no sense trying to press her for clarity. Like a fish on a line, he had to simply wait until she decided to reel him in.

The center study remained just as he had left it: a wreck. More stacks of books and piles of parchment covered his desk and floor. Mallow peeked her head up from the plum armchair, her orb-like eyes following his mentor with curiosity. Rheta began summoning tomes, surrounded by the buttery light as they levitated through the air. With widening eyes, Mallow's pupils expanded, and Myronor recognized the gaze of a hunter. He thought he was about to be entertained, but with a few blinks, the fickle creature ultimately settled on laziness and sank back into the chair. Oh, how he wished he could do the same.

"I knew you wouldn't dare rearrange *my* library, Myrny," Rheta commented as books continued flying and piling onto the desk. He couldn't help but roll his eyes.

When Rheta bestowed the tower on him, she did so with one condition: the library was to remain untouched and accessible to her at all times. As her self-proclaimed favorite apprentice, he had gladly upheld his word, though he regretted it now.

"These are materials I believe you will find integral to understanding Pyra's research," Rheta said. "And one...well, one of these tomes is the reason I'm convinced Pyra is still alive."

With a sigh, Myronor indulged her.

"And how does a book provide any proof of that?"

Rheta reached for a black-bound book, hovering inches away from her nose. When she turned her golden gaze on him, he felt a trickle of anxiety.

"I believe Pyra used *this* to fake her own death."

With a crash, Myronor tripped over the nearest pile of books, catching himself clumsily on the edge of the desk. He wasn't sure if laughing, crying, or screaming was more appropriate at the moment, so he let out a yelp that sounded like all three.

"I thought you were delusional before when you declared she wasn't dead," he said, searching for any indication she was joking. "But Rheta, faking her death? That's ridiculous."

"Is it?" She continued, rolling her eyes. "We agree that self-destruction doesn't fit Pyra's nature. Her letter was oddly cryptic, especially for Pyra. I believe either the Consortia is lying about her cause of death, or she faked it and is still alive."

"And why in the world would Pyra fake her death?"

"There is only one reason Pyra did anything, and that was to protect her research."

"Well, we can agree on that," Myronor added bitterly. "So, how do you speculate she used *that* book to *fake* her death?"

Rheta's thick brow twitched, an early warning sign that her patience waned. "She borrowed this tome from me ages ago and returned it right before we lost contact."

"That's rich—you sent my mother books from *my* library through your little portal?"

"And why wouldn't I?" Rheta said, ignoring his ire as she turned the book in her hands. She frowned as she ran a thumb down the compressed pages. "Upon return, I noticed she had notched a page. And she *knows* far too well how much I hate when a book is defiled like that."

Myronor found himself laughing. It was his only salvation from the encroaching insanity. "Great to know there are books in my library that have spent more time with my mother than I have."

"Here," she said, ignoring his quip and handing him the open book. He had a strong inclination to knock the book from her hands. But curiosity demanded that he take the tome.

The title was the first of many oddities surrounding the book. *The Mana Mole: Useful Spells for Snooping* appeared more like a satirical novel than a how-to guide for anything. And as he skimmed the pages, Myronor found it more difficult to understand why his mother or Rheta would read anything of that nature. The page Rheta had set for him was mostly filled with musings of an old mage who fancied himself a master of spy craft. But Myronor's judgment of the manuscript shifted as he read, resisting his curiosity to continue beyond the marked page.

There must be a reason Rheta—no, Pyra—had selected this particular page. However, the two most interesting sentences he came across only discussed flotation imbuteria in Krysas without any details. The page ended with an interesting rant on human applications, but otherwise, he found the reveal to be entirely fruitless.

"So this mage developed a charm to cause someone to float? Or, in his example, slow his fall when jumping from a chair?" Rheta nodded. "Well, while I find it mildly fascinating, it seems far beneath the level of magic you and Pyra were toying with."

Rheta stared back at him, wearing a familiar expression that told him he had missed the point. He used to appreciate her methods of forcing him to find answers for himself, but now he wished she would simply speak her mind. Unable to resist the years of conditioning, he sighed and began the process of thinking aloud.

"According to the death notice, eyewitnesses reported Pyra leaping from a cliffside terrace in Krysas. But no vesper was seen, and the body never recovered. So, am I to assume you believe she used this spell to fake her death?"

Rheta's dark curls bounced as she nodded. "Precisely. Her letter was written too carefully, revealing nothing in writing other than some suspicion. It was as if she *wanted* foul play to be assumed."

"*You're* assuming so much of what my mother wanted," Myronor said, crossing his arms. "To me, that letter seemed more like a desperate attempt to ensure that someone continued her research at any cost."

"Not just anyone...she clearly wanted *you* to continue that research," Rheta said with a sad smile.

Closing his eyes, Myronor massaged the bridge of his nose, a headache blooming beneath. He hated feeling so bitter and so lost, especially in his own study, beside his own mentor.

"And what if I don't want to?"

"Why wouldn't you?" Rheta said, nearly laughing. It irritated him far more than it should have.

"Because I was happy with the research I was conducting here. It's important, too, and far more practical. Why should her problems become mine just because she died? Or, according to you, faked dying?"

"Regardless of whether Pyra is alive or dead, I'm finding it difficult to believe *my* apprentice would pass up the opportunity to learn so much about his own powers, of his own mother."

"You assume too much of me as well!" Myronor screamed, unable to contain the frustration any longer. Danger flashed across Rheta's eyes before she fell into a more pitiful expression. He'd never yelled at his mentor before, never lashed out...sometimes he forgot Rheta didn't understand people the way most did. Her objective nature left her disconnected at times, as if devoid of emotion. But he knew her better. *He* knew better.

"Rheta, please—this is all too much. I need more information—more time to process everything you're throwing at me. You're supposed to be my mentor and my friend, and now, I feel as if I'm nothing more than a puppet in your and Pyra's schemes. I've grown extremely wary of being left in the dark and used in the process, especially by those closest to me."

Rheta chewed her lip, watching him with observant eyes. "Myrny, first let me just say that self-pity doesn't suit you. And you know better than to compare me to Eliana. I don't know everything that transpired between you two, but I promise you're better off without that power-hungry hag."

The callousness of her voice stung. She really was never good at comforting anyone.

"I'm not disagreeing that I'm better off without her," Myronor began, his voice raw with emotion. "But some wounds take time to heal—time I've barely been allowed before *this* fiasco was thrown into my lap. You expect me to go along with everything because you say so, because *you* apparently know what I want more than I do in this scenario. But even if that were true, how am I to trust you after all of this?"

Rheta's hardened eyes melted into soft pools of gold. "I'm sorry, Myrny. I really am. I know...I know I'm asking a lot of you so suddenly. I thought we had more time, and clearly, so did Pyra. But I promise that what I'm asking of you isn't manipulation; it's desperation, as you said."

She began pacing, tugging at her hands as she continued to speak. "Something or someone threatened Pyra and her research—*our* research. And the wrongful death investigation will flush out those responsible. If Pyra faked her death, it was because someone or something was after her. Word will spread of Tanvik conducting its investigation, perhaps to those who still seek her out. They will come looking for her, too."

He still couldn't believe Rheta thought this more likely. "And what if she is dead?"

Rheta sighed. "Then the Consortia will have to answer for any discrepancies after a second investigation. Either way, *you* gain access to Pyra's library and her research by succeeding her as Ambassador."

"I've already said I don't know if I want—"

"Fine then," Rheta said, stamping her foot in frustration. "Don't continue the research. You can decide once you get there; you can help me re-establish the portal between Krysas and Feyralis. If you still decide you want no part in this, you can make me Ambassador instead. I'll take over her role and research without ever bothering you again. But *you* are the only person that I can trust to reestablish the portal."

The fact that Rheta now offered him a choice in the matter reestablished some of his faith in her. If all that was asked of him were to re-establish this portal, then maybe...maybe it would be worth the hassle.

"Alright," he said quietly. "Maybe some time away would do me good, anyway."

He felt her small hand squeeze his shoulder. "Nothing helps clear the mind like a change of routine. I hope you know I wouldn't push so hard if it weren't necessary."

Her footsteps barely made a sound as she left his study. The front door of the tower closed with a thud, and he realized he hadn't fully expected her to really leave. He hadn't expected to be so alone.

Mallow rubbed against his calf as he slouched in the chair. She left behind a few strands of cream-colored fur against his blue robes as she mewled sweetly. The chair creaked as he reached a hand down to scratch her chin. Her purrs reverberated through him, negating some of the pain of the last few days.

Rheta was right; self-pity didn't suit him. And he was never really alone with his perfect little familiar around.

Just as he was about to scoop her up, the cat slinked from reach with calculated accuracy. He was more curious than hurt by her denial as she instead trotted to his desk. Perched on her hind legs, she gave a curious sniff at the stack of books Rheta provided. Turning, she glared back at Myronor expectantly.

"I haven't even decided if any of this is worth the trouble," he said, waving a dismissive hand.

Mallow mewled and pawed gently at a single tome near the top of an adjacent stack. Her chosen publication was bound in prehistoric pale leather and seemingly lacked any identifying text on the spine. While he'd never seen this particular book before, that wasn't necessarily a surprise. It would take several lifetimes to read every piece of literature Rheta had acquired. But Mallow's demand for *that* particular book piqued his curiosity.

"Alright, alright..." he sighed, pulling himself from the chair. "Any reason for this one?"

Mallow ignored him, returning to her armchair as he slid the tome from the stack. Though she curled herself back into a ball, her orb-like eyes remained fixated on the frail book. The dry, ivory leather was covered in a layer of dust, but at least the front seemed to be tilted. Embossed in flaked, gold lettering, he read the name of the novel several times over before wondering if Rheta had pulled this tome by mistake. He turned to his familiar, now eyeing him suspiciously from her perch.

"Mallow, why in the world do you want me to read about *The Paladins of the Cloister?*"

~ Sixteen ~

INGRESS

A massive wall of city, etched in seemingly endless black stone, shadowed the entire port. Myronor had mentioned that Krysas had been carved directly into the sea-facing cliffside, but Ophiera hadn't expected the view of the monstrous metropolis to be quite so literal. Where Feyralis sprawled horizontally across a verdant landscape in bright steeples and foreign stone, Krysas, it seemed, had implemented a purely *vertical* infrastructure.

Gaze pitched upwards, Ophiera's gut quivered slightly as she took in the chiseled city from the deck of the *Berserker*. They had reached Krysas without further incident, though she hesitated to call it "safe and sound." The sun had already set behind the cliffs, the peaks now obscured in bright pink clouds, creating the illusion of an endlessly reaching cityscape. And somehow, they had to reach the upper levels sooner rather than later. Between Myronor's injured leg and her impending reunion with the Aether, she was beginning to second-guess her enthusiasm to depart the *Berserker*.

But the captain's feathered steps approaching from behind reminded her why they needed to leave as soon as possible. She didn't much appreciate the hovering or the stalking, but simply pretending he wasn't there only forced him to speak.

"Is this your first time to Krysas?" He asked.

"Yes," she said without facing him.

"I assume you'll find a healer first?"

"Ask Myronor," she bit back.

"Ah, so, you're back pretending to be his whore again?"

Ophiera closed her eyes against the hint of venom beneath his apathetic tone. The man tried her patience in a way she seldom contended against—far worse even than Myronor.

"I suppose that depends on the reputation of paladins in this city," she said through gritted teeth. "You might provide insight instead of insult on the matter."

Though she kept her back to him, she nearly heard his spine stiffen.

"The upper Consortia officials may know of Tanvik's Cloister and their disciples. But most will likely see the golden armor as nothing more than a unique, magical artifact."

"Well then, at least I can be a whore in armor."

She found the silence of his discomfort oddly satisfying.

"It was a poor choice of words."

"Poor choices are your bane," she snapped. "Make a good decision now and leave me be."

Ophiera resumed observing the bustling dock, pretending to be interested in the loading and unloading of crates and barrels. The port of Krysas was exponentially busier than Cantheas, assaulting and overwhelming her senses. Smells, sounds, and sights all blended into a flurry of discomforting triggers, amplifying her nerves. She needed to calm herself before setting foot on dry land again, and the captain breathing down her neck, lurking behind her, wasn't helping.

"Why are you still here?" She finally asked.

He sighed. "I need to know your plans in Krysas."

She turned around to face him. "We only have needs of sleep and sustenance, both of which can be overcome with the right training."

"Fine, I would very much *like* to know—"

"Didn't you learn enough to your *liking* while sneaking on us below hours ago? Whatever you overheard from the shadows of your cabin shall be all you get from me."

Jasper watched her, hardly apologetic. "How could you possibly know I was there?"

"I have ears!" she snapped. "And a nose. Whatever magic kept you hidden—"

"Don't you dare confuse my skills for *magic*," he growled, stepping towards her. "I'm not an innatural."

Ophiera bit her bottom lip, struggling to refrain from swinging her fist. "Well, whatever you may be, it disgusts me just the same."

"I'm not the one pretending to be someone I'm not."

"Then perhaps you should try!"

His glower transformed into a sheepish smile, half amused but wholly genuine. The sudden switch shocked her, and for a moment, she was speechless, only left to wonder why, when she fought him, he became more himself. His smile smoothed his harsh features and lit up his eyes like the sun setting on the sea. She might be pretending to be someone else, but she didn't understand why he hid this part of himself from sight.

"It seems I owe you yet another apology," he said, running a hand through dark curls.

"It doesn't matter," she muttered as she heard movement from below deck. Her fists unclenched as she realized Myronor was finally ready to depart, and not a moment too soon. Without another word, she moved to step past Jasper, but as she neared, he gripped her by the shoulders.

"Please, tell me where you're going—how I can find you," he hissed rapidly. "I could help. I know of several healers in Krysas—and I know things that might aid you against the Brotherhood. I just need to speak to some contacts in Krysas before—"

"Before what?" She asked. "Making another *difficult* choice?"

His eyes fell from hers as if she had slapped him in the face.

Again, his true self was shown the moment she challenged him; this time, though, the part of his personality she had a hand in creating. Lost and tormented, she couldn't look at him without feeling sympathy. But the path ahead would be filled with enough problematic choices, and he lacked the conviction to make even the easy ones.

She pulled away from the captain's grip, ignoring his lingering reach as she looked towards Myronor, now rising from the rickety stairs below deck. He looked more himself than he had only a few hours earlier when she'd left him with Collette. Though he leaned heavily against his staff of driftwood and pearl, worrying her a bit. His blue robes hung loosely over his injured leg, hiding her bound armor pieces from sight. He smirked at her, easing some of the tension trapped in her shoulders.

"Ah, Collette's dress is quite lovely on you," he said, eyeing the dark green fabric of her new attire.

"I'm just relieved it covers more than the one *you* conjured before."

She tried to smile while examining the long, tight sleeves looped around her thumbs and covering her scars. The material was adorned in foreign designs of coppery threads, a strange style that Collette assured them was all the rage in Krysas. While Ophiera was thankful for her hospitality, she couldn't help but think there was an awfully high likelihood the dress would end up in ashes.

Myronor cupped her jaw, smiling lopsidedly down at her. "What did the captain say to put you in such a mood?"

"Nothing of consequence," she replied, fixing her expression again. "Is your wound troublesome to walk on?"

"Not really. Collette engineered a clever little splint." He lifted his robes to reveal the makeshift support of wood and twine interlaced with golden armor.

"Don't forget these now!" Collette yelled from below deck. A clinking noise rattled as she hurried up the stairs, thrusting a burlap bag into Myronor's hands. "Remember, the red ones will help with the pain, and the purple ones will help you sleep."

Myronor kissed her knuckles while accepting the sack. "Collette, you have been a true savior. How can I repay you for your expertise?"

"Oh, no payment needed," she said sweetly, though her smile didn't meet her eyes. "Just glad you're feeling better, though you really must find a healer for a second opinion."

"I trust your opinion wholly," Myronor said with a smirk. "I must give my regards to your captain before we depart."

With a slight limp, he strode the few steps towards Jasper with a thudding pace offset between staff and splint. Ophiera hung back, unsure if she wished to engage the captain again. But a strong hand slipped under her elbow, ushering her towards Myronor and Jasper.

"It was a pleasure meeting you, Iris," Collette said softly.

"You as well. I'm grateful for all his improvements after your care."

"Oh, easing that wound seems a minor feat compared to what you've done for our captain."

Ophiera stopped in her tracks. "I've done nothing."

"Common words of a guilty conscience," Collette giggled. "All he'd tell me is that you nearly killed him long ago. Don't worry, I can't blame you; I often get the urge to garrote the sullen bastard myself." Ophiera choked a laugh, hoping to hide her relief. "But the captain has acted more alive since your arrival on this ship than I've seen him in years. So thank you."

Collette's voice trailed off at Jasper's glower. He seemed outright disgusted to touch Myronor as they shook hands, but when his eyes fell on Ophiera, she saw the lingering torment she'd put there years ago. She wasn't sure she trusted Collette's perception of *alive* in regard to the captain.

"We appreciate your swiftness and continued discretion surrounding our travels," Myronor said in a haughty tone.

"And you have my thanks for helping save my ship," Jasper said, but his eyes lingered on Ophiera.

"Anything to keep my consort safe," Myronor replied, drawing the captain's attention back to him. "You can find *us* at the Embassy, if you should ever require my assistance again."

The bite in Myronor's voice was foreign—an intentional prod at the captain. But Jasper's expression remained unreadable. Before anything else foolish could be done or said, Ophiera dragged Myronor away toward the port city.

He hobbled down the ship's ramp, holding her shoulder for balance. She wondered if the wound remained painful or if he was simply clumsy with the heft of brace and armor. It worried her how little she felt from him through the link. Then again, maybe it was her nerves overwhelming both of their thoughts.

While she'd always felt out of place in Tanvik, she had, nonetheless, learned to navigate various cities and cultures alike. But here in Krysas, she was a complete foreigner with little knowledge of local ways. Even the docks felt strange, with many ships berthed hull to hull and of odd makes and designs. She'd thought Cantheas was the busiest port she'd ever seen, but Krysas brought a new definition to the word. The crews shouted and laughed, worked and drank, all in a frenzy to beat the setting sun. She felt almost as if she were back in the crowds of Feyralis again. But there was nowhere to hide on the exposed wooden pier. Each bark, cry, and shout twisted like a knife in her ears.

Myronor took her hand, pulling her closer beside him. "Don't worry. We won't get separated in the masses this time."

She appreciated the sentiment, but it was no longer a mob of civilians she feared. If Marvena had fled to Krysas, she likely had support waiting. Who knew how many amongst the dock workers were in the Brotherhood's pocket? It was growing more apparent that the Brotherhood had infiltrated the Magistrate in Tanvik. What if the Consortia suffered a similar coup?

She pulled the hood of her cloak further up to obscure her face as they walked along the wooden pier. Ahead, the dock connected to a dark stone path that ran parallel to the base of the cliff. It had been worn smooth over millennia with a tideline that ended dangerously near the path's edge. A single bad storm would submerge the entire cliffside road. She supposed Krysas must not endure storms like the Southern Coastlands.

Are you ready? Myronor asked through the link, referring to the dark stone path. She knew he referred to the Aether, which would soon come flooding back when she reconnected with Erum.

I don't have much of a choice, ready or not.

The moment her foot touched the solid rock, Ophiera knew something was terribly wrong. A surge of burning power caused her to stumble, and though Myronor held her steady, she felt his panic racing alongside her own. This wasn't a simple surge of power but a scream. Like a caged animal, the holy flames raged within her, filling her beyond capacity in a desperate attempt to escape, to be free, to consume. She couldn't stop the fire from spreading throughout her. Her scars, hidden from sight beneath the green sleeves, smoldered in threat.

Relief came as her boots were suddenly lifted away from the dark stone. Disconnected from her source of power, she saw Myronor's faintly glowing hand still squeezing her own as she hovered inches above the ground. Her heart pounded against her chest as people continued to flow around them. No one had noticed her fit; no one had realized the imminent threat to their lives.

That was odd, Myronor thought through the link.

The Aether feels...very different here.

Through the ekath, she felt Myronor's whirling thoughts as he led her around the crowd, but she couldn't make out anything coherent. They stopped against the cliff wall near the edge of a stone archway she hadn't noticed before. It looked to be a tunnel of sorts, one of several similar passages lined along the cliff base. The stone was so dark she hadn't noticed them from the ship, hidden within the wall like an optical illusion.

Myronor brushed back the hood of her cloak, examining her face. "Maybe it isn't so different," he said gently. "Maybe you're adjusting from being on the ship for so long? Like when sailors go through withdrawal from land or drink?"

Ophiera considered this possibility but couldn't quite agree. There was something distinctly different in the manner in which the Aether had burned through her just now. It felt tortured and furious. But beads of sweat were falling from Myronor's brow, and she knew it was not the time to worry about the holy flames. They needed to reach the Embassy.

"I'm more concerned about your mana." She looked up at the cliff face, dizzy from the close angle. "The climb to the Embassy appears long and arduous, and you're already strained."

"Ah, about that...we'll get to the top through here," he said, pointing towards the archway. Through the massive tunnel funneled throngs of people walking to and fro between the docks and the archways.

"Are there stairs in there?"

Myronor turned away to stare back at the dock. "I didn't want to say too much within earshot of the captain. He seems like a man who might take advantage of your...naivety."

She scoffed but quickly realized the uncomfortable truth of his words. As she stared back at the docks, it became glaringly apparent that the people here dressed quite distinctly. Most individuals wore a face covering of some kind, a veil for just their nose and mouth. Many were plain, some were decorative, and others remained slack around the neck instead. Rather than the flowing garb of Feyralis, the people of Krysas wore form-fitted attire adorned with twisted metals and polished stones. Their fashion was nearly sculptural, and Myronor's blue robes looked drab in comparison.

"Krysas is the oldest city in Erum," Myronor began, speaking in a low, quickened voice. "And the mages of Krysas hold a mastery over magic that is distinct from that of Tanvik."

"And what does this have to do with climbing up the cliff?" she asked impatiently.

Myronor smiled. "In Feyralis, most mages practice metamagi, which is magic that changes or alters matter, transmuting and conjuring. But here, the mages of Krysas are masters of imbuteria, infusing matter with their mana and endowing magical properties to inanimate objects. The city could not physically exist without the imbuements in the very rock. And these archways," he said, gesturing to the tunnels around them, "lead to a system of imbued lifts that can reach every level of the city above. So...we won't have to climb."

While she rejoiced in the ease of their trip to the top, her temperament was ill-suited for this feeling of ignorance. In Tanvik, she had been the knowledgeable one, leading the city-dwelling mage along familiar roads and known landscapes. But here in this foreign metropolis, his well-read nature put him at an advantage, and it stung her pride more than she cared to admit.

"Come, we can catch a lift to the Embassy," he said, excitement etched across his face.

"Are you sure we shouldn't find a healer first?" Ophiera asked, trying her luck again.

Myronor wouldn't take his eyes off the tunnel. "I feel much better after Collette's potions and a solid few hours of sleep by your side. Besides, I don't know if any healer in this city would know what to do against the ichor. There is no Cloister presence, and if we're worried the Brotherhood is here, drawing attention might not work in our favor. But I have a good feeling that my mother's library in the Embassy could hold some answers…"

He trailed off, eyes glazed for a moment, and his thoughts went somewhere Ophiera couldn't follow. While he eavesdropped on her thoughts with apparent ease, she struggled to find his more and more, as if reaching for a cloud, unable to grasp anything solid. She allowed him a moment to gather his thoughts, but the moment became an uncomfortable amount of time as he remained transfixed on something she couldn't grasp.

Myronor?

"Sorry," he said, snapping his attention back to her. He rubbed his temple before smiling. "I'm sure the Embassy can help us find a healer if needed, so let's get moving."

While Ophiera agreed, his odd behavior concerned her. He'd said his wound wasn't bothering him, but through the connection, she felt something lurking behind his smile. His mood was oscillating nearly as quickly as the captain's, but then again, so had her own. They'd only just dealt with an arduous journey by sea, only to face more hurdles now upon arrival. She should be more understanding of the circumstances, shouldn't she?

"Lead the way," she said reluctantly.

As they rejoined the crowd, Ophiera's nerves grew again despite remaining disconnected from the Aether. She observed smatterings of bronzed hair and swirled designs emblazoned upon the local clothing in the crowd. And not for the first time, she wished she knew what had befallen Kaikora. The enigmatic shaman would likely know how to remove the corruption. She knew everything, after all, except for how to save Iluka.

On that bitter thought, Ophiera followed Myronor through the archway. She'd expected it to be dark, but a dim light illuminated the narrowing passage. Her head spun as she gazed upwards, dizzied by the endless crystals embedded into the high ceiling. They pulsated in a rainbow of ethereal light against the dark stone, resembling gigantic stars in the stone night.

The Consortia mages embed the imbued crystals into the stone to re-inforce the structure, Myronor said through the link.

The small crystal shard dangling on Myronor's chest resonated with the light above. Poor Mallow had been confined to her crystal for so long now. Ophiera missed having the little familiar ride atop her pauldrons as she had along the roads in Tanvik. Back then, she'd been utterly convinced that escorting a flippant mage to Krysas would be her most difficult undertaking since her retirement. She supposed she'd been naive back then, too.

The crystal flashed again, almost frantic. "You'll get to explore soon," he crooned quietly to the crystal. "Just stay put now."

Myronor placed the crystal back beneath his robes, but the crystal continued to flash. Ophiera worried something ailed Mallow, but Myronor placed his hand over the crystal, stroking it soothingly. The affection seemed to calm the familiar but did little to ease Ophiera's growing concern.

When Myronor suddenly halted their progress, she struggled to slow on floating feet. She hadn't realized the queue of people ahead. Chatting merrily in the crowded lines, the people spoke in words she couldn't understand.

Do you speak the language? She asked.

Of course, he smiled. *Most mages trained in Feyralis are fluent. Nearly half the tomes in my library are written in Krysan.*

Another unknown.

How was she meant to investigate Pyra's death when she knew nothing of this place? She hadn't even considered the language, let alone the cultural differences that might hinder her investigation. Had the Magistrate known the difficulty she would face when they'd conscripted her again? Was the Cloister aware they had Oath-bound her to a nearly impossible task?

In the small distance between her boots and the ground, she could feel the Aether stir. Like the warmth of a campfire on a cold night, the Aether tempted her to draw closer with a promise of painful relief. But she couldn't allow herself to be tested this moment, just as she couldn't keep blaming the Cloister for the entirety of her problems.

The priests may have sheltered her in many ways, but Ophiera had voluntarily done the same to herself. She'd been happy to live out her life without consideration of anything beyond Iluka, happy to shelter her head in the sand dunes.

She really was naive.

Watch, here it comes, Myronor said excitedly.

He nodded towards the chamber ahead, where an enormous crystalline disk descended from the ceiling. Defying nature itself in size and weightlessness, the stone sank smoothly from the dark ceiling toward a rounded receptacle carved into the floor itself—the circular crystal nestled within, leveling nearly seamlessly with the platform.

In unison, the crowd moved forward, squeezing as many individuals as possible onto the platform. To Ophiera, it seemed dangerously crowded, but no one appeared discomforted by the density of people shuffling along. Nearly every person wore a cowl over their mouths, matching in style and color to their tight-fitting and heavily decorated attire as if their clothing was designed for closeness.

She stepped onto the platform with the others in the crowd, but the moment her foot hovered above the crystal, she felt herself suddenly drop to the ground. A fresh surge of furious power erupted through her from Erum. She tried to stumble back, but Myronor squeezed her hand, holding her in place as the crowd filled in around her.

Hold on, Myronor said, as if she wasn't employing everything in her power to quell the Aether already. The raging call beneath her feet urged her to spill forth and burn, to purge this anger along with everything else around her. Suddenly, the lift jolted as it began its ascent, and Ophiera let out her held breath.

I'm sorry, I didn't think the lift's magic would negate my spell, Myronor said apologetically. *Are you alright?*

She nodded, teetering a bit with the speed of the lift. Myronor wound an arm around her waist, keeping them both stable alongside his staff. A few people eyed the driftwood and pearl staff with curious expressions. In a city of mages, he was the single individual on the platform carrying a weapon, though she hoped the crowd saw it more as the walking stick it now served as.

After a few moments, the platform slowed to a stop, flooding the packed space with the sounds of a bustling bazaar. As Myronor craned his neck to see, she could feel his thoughts churning faster than a storm. His excitement and her anxiety were matched in energy yet pulled in opposite directions. At least she was glad his leg didn't hurt him too badly.

The lift moved again, and the force of the pull left a queasy feeling in her stomach. She felt a pressure in her ears and instinctively stretched her jaw to pop them. A trick she'd learned while at the Cloister.

Will the air thin at the top? She asked, recalling how the initiates of the Cloister often drowned to death from the inside out. And how she'd almost succumbed herself.

Myronor squeezed her as he followed her thoughts. *There is little risk of elevation sickness, even at the highest level of Krysas. But even from your memories, I cannot imagine where in Tanvik the Cloister must be located, that the air could be so thin.*

She shrugged. *No one is meant to know where it is, but I can certainly attest to the cold, thin air ever present in that place.*

None of the kindled knew where the Cloister was located, mostly because they didn't ever leave. And the manner by which Ophiera had been removed from the grounds at the start of her conscription ensured she also would never know. The only person who *had* traveled between was Aleksander, the Hand of Mercy. As he represented both Tanvik and the Cloister as one of the Justicars of the Magistrate, surely he must return or, at the very least, communicate with the Chaplain.

Before you were conscripted, the Cloister's location was a growing point of contention in Feyralis, Myronor added. *Some thought it ridiculous that they represented the Burnished Highlands with a full seat on the Magistrate when neither they nor anyone else could possibly live there.*

Surprisingly, Ophiera was well aware of this discontent. Since the Cloister represented the Burnished Highlands on the Magistrate, many assumed the order must be located in the nearby region. But the Burnished Highlands were a wasteland, unmapped and untraveled. There were no cities, no roads, nothing but a wall of mountains blocking the caustic, restless land beyond.

Have you ever been to Burnished Highlands? Myronor asked.

Rather than answer him directly, Ophiera simply recalled her memories and let Myronor live them alongside. It was comforting in a strange way. While her travels during her conscription had never brought her to the Burnished Highlands, she'd heard endless stories. Lotus had spun many tales of the place, which she often regarded as half rumor and half imagination. None of what he described matched her memories of the Cloister, except the mountains, of course.

Lotus spoke of a land marred by boiling lakes and poisonous geysers. The air itself was lethal if unprepared, and even then, there was nothing of use to survive on. No plants, no animals, no life, only endless plains of steaming calderas and clouds of death nestled between towering mountains.

Sounds like a lovely place.

It sounds like a myth.

Had I not seen the Cloister through your memories, I would have believed it a myth as well, Myronor said with a smirk.

Ophiera grimaced. *I wish it were.*

Again, Myronor squeezed his arm around her a little tighter but said no more on the matter.

The lift stopped and started several times as they ascended to the very top. Each time the crowds exchanged, Ophiera felt a moment of relief in their departure, only to be agitated again as a new group filled in around her. The only solace she found in this endeavor was continually gaining distance from the Aether.

And yet, even with the disconnect and distance, she felt it whisper to her. Like a breath on her neck, almost as if it were trying to warn her.

Something was very wrong here. Or perhaps something was very wrong with her.

"Next stop is ours," Myronor whispered in her ear as the lift slowed again.

As the stone walls dropped like a curtain, a city shrouded in mist surrounded them. Pale lavender light trapped within the clouds cast a smoky light over the darkened stone. Few citizens meandered about at the dusky hour, leaving the entire cityscape distantly obscured by clouds and clouds alone. It was quite beautiful, yet ominous.

The platform bounced to a halt, and people began disembarking in all directions. Myronor led her from the lift onto another smoothly worn path. Without the float charm in place, Ophiera felt the pulse of the reconnection beneath her boot. The Aether traveled through the stone even to this height. But the edge had been smoothed, or rather, the scream softened. It wasn't comfortable, but it wasn't disastrous either.

~ Seventeen ~

RAMIFICATION

The moment Myronor felt the Aether surge, he quickly pulled Ophiera close, meaning to recast the hover charm immediately. But Ophiera snatched her hand away from his, disrupting the spell.

"No," she said, taking a step away from him. "I...I'll be fine."

Her brow cinched as she took yet another step forward as if testing the stability of the ground. And in a rare moment of doubt, Myronor questioned her decision.

He understood her need to control the Aether, but if she couldn't manage to do so just now, it put them both at terrible risk. It put *everything* at risk. A strong urge to cast the charm, regardless of her choice, overcame him. But he snuffed it out when she turned to him with a weak smile.

Is your wound bothering you? She asked as he joined her. At least, she thought that was the reason he hesitated, as the truth might hurt her too much.

"It's fine," he replied with a thump of his staff, passing her and continuing onwards toward the Embassy.

She followed as they walked the streets of what was referred to as the Exo district. Through the ekath, Myronor felt Ophiera's distraction with quelling the Aether and found he was quite thankful for it. She paid him little thought as she focused entirely on the flames, and for the moment, he took relief in her preoccupation.

He hesitated to admit to himself just how desperate he was to reach the Embassy. Between the discomfort of walking with ill-placed armor and the need to reach his mother's library, it felt as if his entire being depended on crossing the Embassy threshold. The growing need in his chest was as steadfast as the pain in his leg. And yet, neither burden caught Ophiera's attention, preoccupied as she was in her own struggle.

The misty city only added to his fettered state. Power emanated from the very stone, reverberating with his mana like a familiar song. Bright crystals adorned every structure they passed, embedded directly into the dark stone. And though the crystals glimmered through the darkness, the light reflected from the metallic accents hammered into the building facades was somehow more beautiful.

Rheta was the only mage he knew to dabble in the arts of imbuteria. But thanks to his mother's work in Krysas, the practice had gained a small but ever-growing interest in Feyralis. He should have known the two had colluded together by that fact alone; how else could Rheta have learned the arts? There were many questions he'd failed to ask his previous mentor.

"Myronor—what is *that*?"

Startled by her voice, he followed Ophiera's gaze to a structure in the distance. It appeared repellent of the dusky clouds, the only building clear of mist. Strange as it seemed, it all made sense when he recognized the unique structure from a simple line drawing in a book read long ago.

"That's the Aerodock."

Ophiera stopped in the middle of the road, eyes wide in disbelief. "The what?"

Smiling bemusedly, Myronor understood her disbelief—the tall pillar of stone held platforms protruding along the outside, almost like a spiraling staircase. At the end of each of these protrusions hung a ship, like those docked at sea, only now hovering in the air, utterly unsupported by solid land far below.

"It serves as a sort of port for the aerships."

"Air...ships?"

"Yes," Myronor chuckled, enjoying the curious expression lighting her face. It felt like ages had passed since he'd seen that..."They are quite rare to see flying these days in Krysas, especially now that trade routes with the Shole are disrupted."

"Did these...do we have ships like this in Tanvik?"

"Unfortunately, no. Despite Pyra's efforts to popularize them in Tanvik, the Consortia guarded their imbuteria closely, and the Magistrate couldn't justify the cost of construction."

"So imbuement is responsible?"

Myronor nodded but left his explanation there; he did not wish to bore her with details when she was already quite preoccupied. As she watched one of the smaller ships depart from the Aerodock, he found his wound began to ache in earnest again. Sensing the disturbance through the ekath, she turned to him with a scrutinizing glare.

"Which building is the Embassy?"

"I'm not sure," he said, trying to smile but unable to hide the wince. "It's within the Consortia, which is similar to Tanvik's Magistrate...so, I guess it'll be the most extravagant building."

"Let's move then."

Ophiera turned away from the Aerodock and continued along the misty path ahead. Following with a thump of his staff, Myronor felt momentarily guilty that his wound caused her such distress. But again, the feeling of desperation crawled up his spine, and he desired nothing more than to reach the Embassy as soon as possible. Luckily, they didn't have to go far.

With the Aerodock only a few moments of travel behind them, a formidable castle of dark stone loomed through the veil of mist. Myronor knew without a doubt this was the Consortia, and not only from the sketches plastered over every stage of his education in Feyralis. The castle-like structure, carved from the same dark stone as the city itself, exuded power in its structure alone. Resembling a beehive of rock, the building was a series of countless archways carved symmetrically into the circumventing walls. Every surface of the structure was seemingly adorned with metals and crystals; it was almost too ornate, too decorative, too lavish. Hewn from the highest peak of the cliff wall itself, the Consortia towered above all of Krysas.

"It looks like a fortress of sorts," Ophiera said.

Myronor cocked his head, remembering his history. "It was. Krysas has endured more times of war than any nation of Erum, and that is reflected in the architecture."

"War?" Ophiera growled. "Do they not regard murder as a sin against the Aether here?"

Myronor halted before the stone steps, allowing his leg another chance to throb. "The interpretations of the Aether and vespers, and well, the universe itself, are quite different through time and place."

"How so?"

He was about to say, "Because of the Cloister," but only a groan of pain escaped his lips. His knee buckled, forcing him to cling to his staff for balance. As Ophiera caught his elbow with her scarred hand, his wound screamed in agony, far worse than before, throbbing beneath the heavy, hot plates of metal.

"We need to find a healer," she barked.

"No," he replied, forcing weight onto his leg. Her hand slipped from her arm, and the pain dissipated. "I promise I'll be fine. It's more the weight of the armor than anything. Let's find the Embassy within so we may rest."

Her hesitant gaze followed him as he ascended the carved stone steps, but she did not take another step. Somewhere, in the back of his mind, he shared her concern. But they were so near the Embassy now, it would be foolish to turn back.

"Ophiera," he began, trying to hide the exasperation in his voice as he held out his hand. "If anyone knows anything about the ichor, it's Pyra. Our best bet is to reach the Embassy and search her library for a solution. I promise I have a plan, but you must trust me."

Her eyes fell to his hand, lips pursed in unreadable thoughts. For a moment, he thought perhaps she wouldn't join him. But with her cloak flowing behind her, she came to his side without taking his hand.

Accepting this small win, Myronor led the way through the largest archway. He correctly assumed the archway adorned with copper-silver symbols and cobalt blue crystals to be the main entrance. Ophiera hovered behind him as they entered a vast, circular entrance hall. The power thrumming through the building nearly distorted his vision, warping the archways encircling the room like the spokes of a wheel.

With a shake of his head, he cleared his vision on the shimmering, polished floors. Like the Magistrate, the dark stone had metal inlays; however, unlike the Magistrate, the floors here were embedded with large gems and various tiles of stone in a chaotic pattern. He needed a moment to recognize the chaos as a map.

The known world of Erum was depicted in stone across the entirety of the room. At the center, Krysas was represented by a massive dark diamond, glittering beside a pale sea of lapis lazuli-colored stone. To the West, on the same continent of Orbolas, a square white opal sat amidst a gray, marble desert, and he was surprised to see the Consortia hadn't removed Sionnach from the map.

"I've never seen gems this large in my life," Ophiera said, observing a perfectly round garnet centered on an island of agate. She toed the dark crimson gem of Feyralis with a scowl on her face. "Seems a waste to put them in the floor."

Myronor chuckled. "Krysas is quite different, both in culture and resources. I'm sure they'd value the fresh water and the weather we have in Tanvik nearly the same."

She cocked her head to the side, studying the map. "I hadn't really considered...but it doesn't matter. Which one of these doors leads us to the Embassy?"

Though Myronor was content to study the map for hours, he agreed they needed to focus. Above the arches surrounding the room, the names of the Consortia offices had been carved into the dark stone. In Krysan, they listed trade regulations, alchemician societies, arcane resource management, imbuteria laws, and more. And yet, not another living soul was to be seen. Despite the crowds in the lift and on every other level of Krysas, the Consortia was barer than the Exo level of the city below. And yet, there were endless overseeing bodies listed here that collectively governed the city-state of Krysas. In Tanvik, the Magistrate and their five Justicars dictated all laws and decisions for the people, and yet, somehow, a more consolidated rule felt less oppressive than the complicated Consortia.

"This way," he said, taking a heavy step toward the Embassy.

The collection of potions Collette had gifted him bouncing on his belt provided some comfort. He had to endure only a little longer before he could begin his search.

"Search?" Ophiera asked. "For what?"

Myronor swallowed a moment, feeling caught; he hadn't noticed she'd been observing his thoughts. But now that he considered it...he found himself confused as well. What exactly was he searching for?

"For information about the ichor," he said noncommittally

Her doubt matched his own, but he pushed it from his mind. As always, he had never spoken anything untrue to Ophiera, but he also hadn't told her nearly everything.

"Myronor, are you sure you're feeling alright? Your thoughts feel...odd."

"I'm excited to finally be here," he said in a flat tone. "It's been quite a journey, hasn't it?"

His answer must have sufficed because she did not say anything further as they continued along their path. As they walked through another short corridor, Myronor realized their direction didn't quite make sense. Given the shape of the building from the outside, their path within was impossible, especially considering its proximity to the cliffside. But each stone they passed held the evidence of imbuteria, reverberating throughout the building. And with excitement bubbling in his gut, he realized *this* must be the gateway magic Rheta had become obsessed with.

At the end of the hallway, they now walked along, and a single wooden door stood closed. In a city of dark stone and carved arches, the warmth of the pale grain appeared misplaced. A golden plaque above indicated the Embassy, written in several languages, only two of which Myronor could comprehend.

As he pushed open the door, they entered a decagonal room lined with even more archways, here covered in decorative tapestries. A bald man in robes of a deep, luscious pink sat in the center of the room at a desk of glass. His flamboyant garb resembled no fashion Myronor had seen in Tanvik or Krysas. The sleeveless attire was low cut to his navel, revealing his chest and arms in a form fit on his slender frame. Bright bangles of gold, copper, and silver adorned his arms from wrist to elbow and tinkled slightly as he turned the pages of a hefty tome.

A medallion, much like Myronor's, rested on the man's smooth chest. The silver crescent moon with three golden stars overlaid upon a perfect circle was indeed the Consortia's signet. Meaning this man must be the Steward.

Bright emeralds met Myronor's inquisitive stare as he slammed the book shut.

"Ah, finally!" The man said in Krysan, his voice deep but enthusiastic. "Welcome to the Consortia Embassy, Master Ebontide."

Myronor cocked his head, unable to hide his surprise. "I...thank you. But how do you—"

"'Tis my job to know, as the Embassy Steward. But you may call me Glamwell. Now, may I inquire as to the identity of your companion?"

"This is Iris, my Magistrate-mandated consort," Myronor replied in shaky Krysan. Speaking and reading a language were two different feats, the former of which needed much practice.

"Of course, of course!" Glamwell said, rising from his chair to meet them. "Adjusting to life in a foreign country is always easier with someone friendly and familiar." He turned to Ophiera and bowed deeply before speaking in perfect Tanvish. "Welcome to Krysas, my lady Iris."

Ophiera attempted a bow but remained stiff in her delivery. Myronor found it amusing how gracefully she swung a sword, yet struggled with such a simple maneuver in a dress. Still, it must have been convincing enough as Glamwell returned his attention to Myronor.

"Now, sir, I must examine the medallion for proof of claim. I expect you have it with you?"

Myronor reached beneath his robes, separating Mallow's crystal from the chain of the medallion. She had been surprisingly silent since the lift, but he could question her behavior later. While he had planned to remove the pendant from his body, the Steward had no such patience. Grasping the chain around his neck,

Glamwell inspected the medallion closely, the crown of his head nearly touching Myronor's face. Perhaps personal space was a cultural concept unique to Tanvik.

After a moment of study, Glamwell produced a monocle from his pocket that sparkled prismatically. After another few awkward moments of scrutiny, the Steward smiled. "Fantastic!"

The Steward released the medallion and stepped towards one of the archways encircling the room. Only now did Myronor recognize it as the sigil of Tanvik—flames of white and gold embroidered across crimson silk. Though Myronor knew this flag well, it was the first time the heraldry reminded him of Ophiera, enflamed and enraged. His stomach clenched for a moment.

Glamwell cleared his throat.

"This gateway will transport you directly to the Tanvik Embassy as long as you wear that medallion. My lady Iris, you will simply need to hold on to him as you cross." Glamwell nodded enthusiastically between the two, continuing to speak in Tanvik.

"I was told to expect transference of my mother's personal effects; I take it these are within the Embassy?" Again, Myronor despised his act of self-importance, but he needed to know. The location of his mother's research was the entire reason they were here, after all.

"Ah, my apologies. I should have explained more clearly. Usually, the previous Ambassador informs...well, it doesn't matter. The Consortia provide the Embassy dwellings to all of our Ambassadors with equal focus on comfort and sovereignty while they serve this critical diplomatic role. The medallion you wear is key to this, quite literally, in fact. These tokens serve as an imbued gatekey, allowing the wearer and those physically connected to the wearer to pass through the archway. Thus, no one can enter the Tanvik Embassy without that specific medallion, not even I. Because of this, no one has entered since Pyra's passing." The Steward's face fell suddenly grim as tears began to run down his cheeks. "My apologies...the Embassy will be just as she left it..." he sniffed, "...belongings and all."

Glamwell finished and began sobbing in earnest. Flummoxed by the man's grief, Myronor stood frozen, unsure how to proceed. But he saw Ophiera shift beside him, and in her unscarred hand, she held a small handkerchief out to Glamwell. He took her entire hand in his with a shake of appreciation before grasping the cloth and cleaning himself.

"My lady, you are too kind. I apologize for my outburst; it just...seems like yesterday that your mother...well, Master Ebontide walked through that gateway. For twenty years, I looked forward to starting my day with her wit. She would say the most amusing things to me! Like 'wake up' or 'do your job' or 'stop smiling like a fool.' I miss her terribly, as I'm sure you do."

Myronor stifled a laugh, unsure how seriously to take Glamwell. But whether a foolish act or genuine grief, the behavior was wearing down his patience.

"Thank you, Glamwell, for your—uh—condolences. But we are exhausted from travel and would like to take our leave. "

"Yes, of course, sir! I'll be in touch after you've rested some. We might start with a tour of the city, then the Consortia, and we can orientate you to your duties here in Krysas. But alas, rest for now."

The word "duty" always caused Myronor to cringe, but he nodded despite himself. As he stepped forward, the tapestry before the archway parted of its own accord, revealing a darkened hollow. He could see nothing beyond, but they had little choice other than to proceed forward.

As he pulled Ophiera alongside him under the stone arch, it felt as if he walked through cobwebs. An itching, tingly feeling covered his skin until suddenly, he smelled the ocean and heard distant waves. Nausea gripped his gut as pain shot through his leg. But he couldn't let the wound distract him now.

Myronor had finally reached his mother's home.

~ Eighteen ~

SCAITH

A dark shiver passed through the ekath as Ophiera emerged from the archway. Similar in feeling, Myronor shook off her hand as he limped into the room, silencing their tether as he left her behind. She did her best to ignore the pit of hurt forming in her gut, suppressing it by trying to be more understanding in a situation she could not comprehend. Perhaps this was his version of grief. Maybe this cold, distant version of Myronor was how he coped with entering his deceased mother's home.

Thus, she swallowed her pride and gave him space, which wasn't difficult in the vast entry room Ophiera found herself in. The walls were the same dark stone as all of Krysas, with slices of dim light cutting through here and there. Thin windows circumscribed the oblong space, inset into the outer walls from floor to ceiling, reminiscent of claw marks slashed into cloth. Outside, dusk had fallen to an indigo night sky, with an inky ocean churning below. The entire abode felt somewhat like a cage suspended high over the sea.

On the far side of the room sat a cold hearth, cylindrical and metal with a coppery flue to match. Exotic rugs covered the stone floor in haphazard layers, designating a sitting area in the hall. Small cushions, a few large armchairs, and one luxurious fainting couch sat poised around the odd hearth, perfect for conversation.

Myronor ran his hand delicately along the backs of the chairs, studying them intently by sight and touch. The scene was frozen in time: an open book, a crumpled piece of parchment, and a dried-up ink bottle set askew on a low chair. Despite the silence of the ekath, she felt the tension of this moment, of Pyra's last moment.

She wasn't sure what to do or say. Without the ekath, she couldn't begin to imagine the thoughts running through his head. But she understood his need for silence. Pyra had been absent for most of his life, but instead, she had been *here*. What did it feel like walking into the home she had chosen over Iluka? A life she had chosen over Myronor?

Myronor unfurled the piece of crumpled parchment, cocking his head as he examined it.

"What does it say?" She asked, trying to decipher the handwriting from afar.

But Myronor ignored her, running his fingertips over the scrawls of ink. She again managed to suppress the flare of anger that accompanied being ignored. Through the stone floor, the Aether burned beneath her in solidarity, and she felt her arm tingle with repressed flames.

"Argh," Myronor grunted as he sank to one knee. Despite the silence of the ekath, she felt the phantom discomfort in her leg.

"What's wrong?" She asked, rushing forward.

"Nothing," he said in a dark tone. Using his staff, he dragged himself back to a stand, pocketing the crumpled parchment. "I...I need to find the library...quickly."

His eyes looked drawn and distant as he gazed toward the stone staircase opposite the clawed windows. The zigzagged steps led to an upper level, while two archways flanked the broad base. If his mother's library could indeed rid the ichor from his wound, Ophiera wished to find it quickly, too. But as Myronor silently hobbled forward, a burning in the back of her throat sounded alarm yet again. She was forced to remind herself that she trusted him, even if he wasn't acting his usual self.

It was unclear if Myronor knew the layout of the home or simply guessed where the library might be located. But through the left archway, they entered a library that put any and all others to shame. On the far side, the dark stone walls were carved with the same slitted windows as the living space, yet here they reached four stories in height. Beyond the windows, a balcony extended in either direction out of sight, illuminated in the purple light of dusk. She imagined that in the daylight, the atrium would illuminate the multiple levels of books opposite.

Myronor breathed heavily, craning his head at the endless shelves. Ophiera, too, was forced to admire the thousands of books that lined each dimly lit level of Pyra's library. Each floor was interspersed with more shelves and more tomes, and though she couldn't tell how far back the shelves reached in the dim light, if she had to guess, they were *quite* deep. A few small tables and comfortable-looking chairs had been placed near the edges of each landing, laden with scrolls and instruments, bits, and baubles. Thin, spiral stairs connected the levels, matching the ornate metal railing that lined each floor.

"We have to start searching," Myronor said. "It has to be here somewhere..."

She didn't like the urgency in his voice. "Maybe you should take a rest first. If you tell me where to begin, I—"

"No," he said, approaching the closest bookcase. "*I* have to find it."

Haphazardly, he leaned his staff against the laden shelf, where it immediately slipped, falling away from him. Ophiera caught it deftly, though Myronor seemed to pay little mind to what was going on around him.

"Must find it..." he muttered to himself.

At his last words, the Aether screamed beneath her. The sensation disoriented Ophiera, forcing her to lean upon the staff as she gathered herself.

"Something is wrong, Myronor," she said through gritted teeth.

"If you can't control the flames, you shouldn't be in a library full of books," he remarked without turning to her. "Go collect yourself. Leave me be."

The cruelty of his words stung her more than the arrow that had pierced her heart. He had never spoken to her like this before. Never ignored, never neglected. And in that moment, she doubted everything he'd ever told her. Every kindness, every affection, every proclamation of love, and more. She should have known it was all a lie, all a rouse...

But a trickle of instinct forced her to search the ekath. And in it, she found nothing.

No thoughts, no feelings, no Myronor...

"I'm not leaving until you show me your wound," she said quietly, glaring at the back of his head.

Slowly, he turned to face her, and at that moment, she barely recognized the man before her. His eyes were the same shade of brilliant blue as his vesper, but now drawn and empty. Like the nullity through the ekath, his eyes reflected the void within.

Ophiera rushed to him. His eyes widened with panic as she grasped him by the robes and began dragging him from the library.

"Stop!" He cried, fighting her fiercely. "I must find it!"

She ignored his protests, feeling his strength falter beneath her grasp. Though his hands flickered blue for a moment, no spell was cast.

"Release me!" he screamed. "I must find...I must find..."

Ophiera's eyes began to prick as she hauled him to the fainting couch in the living area. His eyes rolled as he struggled to lift himself from the chair, crying out incoherently as if in a fit. Her heart was breaking with each of his screams.

On her knees, her hands shook as she lifted the robes from his leg. Removing the splint with ease, she revealed the blood-soaked bandages as a waft of rot met her nostrils. She hissed in disgust as she unwrapped the soiled linens.

"Don't touch me!" he screamed, kicking his leg away. His voice only vaguely resembled his own, filled now with disgust and hatred.

She ignored him, continuing to undress the wound. Every time her scarred hand touched his skin, he convulsed and screamed.

"Stop, stop, it burns!"

Despite his claim of pain, Ophiera felt nothing through the ekath. Whatever force had taken him had blocked the tether as well. Or maybe...maybe he was lost to her for good...She recalled the day on the riverbank and how she'd nearly walked away when she believed him lost. The thought of abandoning him now caused her even more grief, and she continued undressing the wound.

Bile rose in her throat as she inspected the exposed wound. Black tendrils of corruption vined beneath his skin, reaching up his thigh in a clear path toward his chest. As she feared, the armor had slowed its progress, but could do nothing to stop the vile taint from spreading.

With new desperation, she forced open the ekath in full, searching the nothingness for the tether she knew connected their souls. But what she found was something else...something terribly wrong. A whispering, grating tongue spoke over My-ronor's frantic thoughts.

She will burn you.

Stop!

Not even Iluka was spared her wrath.

Iluka wasn't her fault!

She's only caused you pain.

Let me go!

Never again.

"Myronor!" She cried aloud, shaking him by the shoulders.

His eyes rolled, and the voice continued.

Kill her. Kill her and open the portal.

I...never.

Claim her soul and be free of her binds!

On his belt, Ophiera recognized Collette's collection of potions. With trembling hands, she pulled the satchel away from him and searched for something, anything, that could help alleviate his suffering. She tried to remember what Collette had said about the colors...

Myronor screamed through a clenched jaw, pressing his palms against his temples. The blackened vines writhed beneath his skin, crawling ever upwards.

She was short on time and options.

Ophiera popped the cork on a purple bottle and brought the potion to her lips. The draught was completely tasteless yet left a numbing sensation on her palate as she held it in her mouth. Pre-pared for resistance, she took his face firmly in her hands.

As expected, Myronor recoiled against her touch, though his strength had dwindled significantly. She watched his chest heav-ing and eyes jittering before pressing her lips against his. At her touch, she felt the whispers of reluctance and relief through the ekath. She parted his lips with her tongue and flooded his mouth with the potion. Despite his arms pushing her away, his reflexes betrayed him, and he swallowed everything she had decanted, including one single memory.

With perfect detail, she recalled the pale blue orb hovering above his chest on the side of the river. She'd never told him, never shown him, exactly what had happened the day they met. How she felt the moment she'd laid eyes on his brilliant vesper. How she'd refused to let him leave this world without even knowing his name. She wished she had known then what the feeling was that bloomed in her heart. Now, she felt the same grief clawing in her chest, the desperate plea to the Aether or anyone or anything that would hear her call to save his soul.

When Ophiera pulled away, her face was soaked with tears. But she nearly smiled when she recognized the blue eyes that found her own.

"O-Ophiera, " Myronor groaned.

"I'm here," she said, her voice cracking.

"Forgive me."

"There is nothing to forgive," she said, wiping her eyes.

"My...fault...all my fault."

"You'll be asleep soon," she murmured. "And while you're out, I will rid you of this burden."

He searched her face, terror marring his waxy features. "What if...I don't wake...as myself..."

"I'll be here to remind you," she replied, her voice cracking.

"Don't deserve..." he slurred as his eyes fluttered. But suddenly, they snapped open as he reached for her hands. "Ophiera, it *knows*...it knows everything!"

And as if an overpowering force wrested his consciousness away, his eyes rolled back, and his body fell limp.

~ Nineteen ~

INCHOATION

Today, everything would change. Or at least, that was the plan if the purported investigator ever arrived. For days, Myronor had paced the library, impatiently awaiting the arrival of this mysterious individual the Magistrate had summoned to not only find the cause of his mother's death but escort him to Krysas. The notice of summons had been sent weeks ago via courier, and yet there had been no sign of their arrival thus far. Tomorrow marked the deadline set by the Justicar of Feyralis, and he considered what type of person would risk arriving on the last possible day. Or were they simply never going to come?

When Myronor had been informed of the lengthy deadline, Rheta assured him all would be worth the wait. In Tanvik, it was quite rare indeed to travel with a personal escort. Most dignitaries simply signed on with one of the many trading companies, their comfort and safety directly proportional to the amount of gold coughed up for transport. But as for the investigation...well, the people of Tanvik rarely spoke of death, let alone investigated it.

Most were too frightened to toe the line of taboo. So that left Myronor to wonder…how could anyone possibly develop the skills to *investigate* a death when the mere whisper of a vesper or, worse, an anathema, sent most denizens of Feyralis into a frenzy? But as always, Rheta had refused to share any additional information, instead demanding his ever-waning trust yet again.

Through the windows circumscribing the library, the pink light of an early spring evening shone ominously against the worn shelves. Another day had been wasted then, pacing about, hoping to both solve and quell his wonderings about this supposed escort. He considered what exactly qualified this individual to determine the fate of his mother. Were they a mage? Surely not if they did not reside in Feyralis already, though he did know of a few mages scattered throughout the Sloughmire. Perhaps a hunter from the Jungle of Ruins? That could explain why they were taking their dear time arriving…Or maybe a retired sailor from the Southern Coastlands? Though as quickly as he'd thought it, he refuted himself. He'd never seen a sailor of the South off a boat or out of a tavern.

With thumb and pointer finger, Myronor pinched the narrow bridge of his nose. The endless questions racking against his skull were beginning to give him a headache. Again.

He looked at Mallow, who still feigned sleep on the plum armchair. As her tail twitched, betraying her closed eyes, it wasn't hard for him to guess what annoyed her. His constant pacing and inability to sit, eat, drink, or sleep were disrupting her routine as well—as her routine consisted of *only* those things. Both of their lives were about to be upended, but at least she retained the solace of her crystal world, Nijeka, as a retreat when necessary. Myronor, however, had become a prisoner to this plan—to wait.

An inexplicable paralysis of logic and reason that he now suffered had never struck him so deftly before. Indecision froze him as the arrival of the escort overshadowed all of his choices, seemingly even those as simple as what to eat. His mood demanded something hearty and heavy, comfort food in its finest form. But if his escort arrived and they were to begin traveling soon, he didn't want a belly full of greasy food. Something lighter, then, but nothing seemed appealing to his taste buds, and round and round he went until he had gone the entire day without eating, only *thinking* about eating and souring his mood even further. His thoughts had run in circles like this these past few days, never settling fully on either side of anything.

He truly disliked *waiting*.

But as he watched Mallow stretch and roll to her opposite side, he realized he *wasn't* a prisoner. Rheta had instructed him to stay put so that he may receive the notice of his escort's arrival as soon as possible. But hadn't they made him wait for days on end now? They could certainly wait for a few hours, couldn't they? Especially if it meant he could regain a small sliver of sanity.

"Fancy a walk, Mallow?"

Again, the tail twitched, but her eyes remained closed in a clear dismissal. He wished his familiar could be a bit more understanding, although it wasn't as if he particularly enjoyed his own company at the moment either. Then again, she wouldn't be *Mallow* if she acted any differently—she only rarely ventured out into Feyralis proper, after all.

"Fine," he said, straightening his robes. "Alone, as usual."

Without a clear idea of where he was headed, Myronor let his feet carry him from the tower and onto the cobbled streets of Feyralis. The tall steeples lining the street did little to help him feel any less confined. Colloquially known as the Spire District, mages typically tended to live in this part of the city. Slowly over time, the old sod homes had been replaced by enormous stone towers, an architectural feature that had garnered popularity alongside magic itself.

Despite desiring to leave his tower, Myronor couldn't help but glance back at it from the street. Rheta had built the tower with her mana, and while she had indeed gifted it to him permanently, he would soon offer it back. Though he had every intention of returning to Feyralis once this rumored portal was reestablished to Krysas, he wasn't certain how long it might take. It might be a very long time before he returned home.

But a more urgent destination remained undecided...where the hell to go *next*.

Myronor knew he didn't wish to wander anywhere within the Spire District. Too many people would seek to engage with him, congratulate him emptily on his new position, or provide him with their shallow condolences of Pyra. Though duty-bound to simply reply "thank you" and move on, he knew he wouldn't be able to keep his thoughts to himself. If anyone dared ask him, he would almost gladly disclose that he'd hardly known his mother these past twenty years and that her death brought forth information he wished he'd never known. No one would understand that he was mourning the loss of his comfortable existence rather than the death of his mother.

Perhaps a strong drink would help slow his mind. He supposed he could head over to see Ubel at his sparsely populated tavern down near the markets. The bartender was always ready with a story, meaning Myronor wouldn't have to speak at all...and he could imbibe perhaps the finest cyser in all of Feyralis. But as Myronor imagined himself strolling through the doors of the dusty pub, he realized he wasn't in the mood to listen...or drink...or even say goodbye.

A solitary trip to the evening market could ease his nerves. A new quill or fresh journal had helped him overcome many agitations before. But again, spending coin on frivolous trinkets didn't feel like the best way to occupy his, seemingly, final night in the city he had called home for the last twenty years. But despite that, he couldn't think of a single place in Feyralis that he wished to be in right now.

Myronor took a deep breath, pondering the surprisingly heavy air given the clear spring evening. He found himself as indecisive out here in the middle of the street as he'd been inside the tower. A shadow fell over the cobblestone as the sun disappeared in full behind the wall. The impenetrable stone barrier loomed over the city's residents, providing most with comfort and security. But for him, the wall only filled him with ire. Tanvik was a peaceful land; there was nothing to keep *out*, and instead, the wall only served to keep everyone in.

Since first setting foot in Feyralis many years ago, Myronor had viewed the city wall as a challenge to overcome. Few knew the catacombs that lay within, the multitude of hidden passageways and secretive stairs winding to the very top. He'd spent far too long distracted by his magical studies to focus on the architecture or history of that damned stone wall. And with his eyes fixated on a familiar spot along the edge, Myronor took off at a decisive pace.

He hadn't visited an old haunt like the wall in ages. Avoiding the evening bustle, he trotted down the backstreets, blue robes rustling in his wake. Throughout his apprenticeship, he'd thoroughly explored the wall, documenting the hidden places, the areas of collapse, and those he favored. One particular passage he was fond of lay hidden within a less populated area of the city, in which vagrants counted as the only residents. Hopefully, the stairway remained in usable shape—he hadn't visited this place since he and Eliana...

Stopping the thought short, he came to a sudden halt before the wall; he refused to allow *her* to ruin any more of the time remaining. Running his hands along the stone wall, he searched for the darkened, loosened rock hidden within this section of the wall. He smiled, despite himself, as he found the small boulder, the size of a loaf of bread, and gently slid it from between the other stones. In the dank, dark crevasse, his fingers fumbled for the cold metal switch, rough with oxidation. A snort of relief escaped his nostrils as he heard the distant grind of stone against stone.

Following along in near muscle memory, Myronor arrived at the newly revealed slot along the dark wall, leading to a rugged stone staircase beyond. The past few years of study had dampened his stamina, it seemed, as he didn't remember becoming quite so winded after only a single flight. But pacing his steps and his breathing, he continued to drag his boots upwards. By the time he reached the top, he found himself gasping for breath, robes sticking uncomfortably between his shoulders. He'd never been so relieved to feel the gusting wind as he emerged onto a narrow path near the top of the wall.

Inset within the wall like a shallow canal, the path circumvented the entire city, minus a few sections that had crumbled with age. Centuries ago, watches had patrolled these walls, but in his lifetime, at least, he'd never encountered another soul. Apart from Eliana...but again, he cut the thought short, not wishing to spoil the view.

This section of the wall faced southwest, allowing him a glimpse of the Slumbrous River far below and the beautiful sunset falling over the distant Sloughmire, now covered in a low mist. The snowy peaks of the mountains to the north could easily be mistaken for clouds, but given the rush of the river below, he knew they would soon disappear. Unfortunately, Myronor couldn't make out the mountains from within the confines of the city—the barrier of cliff rock that separated the farmlands of Feyralis from the destitute Burnished Highlands.

Finally, Myronor found the single place in Feyralis that he wished to be. Perhaps it was telling that he felt the most peace he had known in days, looking out over the countryside...and not to the spired city lurking at his back. As intriguing as the city view was from his vantage atop the sprawling capital, little could do justice to the vast, beautiful landscape beyond the wall.

Myronor began his walk along the wall, staying as near as possible to the outer edge to avoid any wandering eyes from the city below. Strictly speaking, people were not allowed in the ruins of the old walls, let alone atop them. Something about historical preservation and the risk of bodily harm. But he'd never been caught before, and this evening would be no different.

The last time Myronor had ventured beyond these city walls was the day he'd arrived nearly twenty years ago. It was...foolish, wasn't it? He had entered his third decade and yet had barely traveled beyond the city. Before, he'd have welcomed any excuse to visit Krysas, to see the greatest mage metropolis in all of Erum and learn from their endless repositories of knowledge. But like many of his aspirations, Pyra had tainted his future with her own.

Staring over the wall, Myronor followed the road along the river, tracing it with his eyes back toward Iluka. The Southern Coastlands were too far from here to see, but he knew where they lay. Only a week's travel by foot from his father, and yet he had never returned home. When he'd first arrived in Feyralis, he had naive dreams of returning for holidays or simply for a visit. But Berwyn had burst that bubble, providing him with a letter from his mother in which he was asked never to use his gift again. Not that he necessarily wished to span...the ominous presence within the dark place was more than enough to keep him away. But now that he'd learned of Pyra's research surrounding their strange magic, Myronor was beginning to rethink his promise.

"Ouch!" Myronor exclaimed, unable to help himself as his toe impacted a fallen stone. Thoughts of Pyra already soured his mood as he examined the cragged stone, which was nearly the size of a chest. He was overcome with the sudden urge to toss it over the wall. Given his struggle to merely reach the top of the wall, he knew he didn't have the athleticism to haul it over. But he did have the mana.

Channeling the spell most recently taught to him by dear Pyra's book, Myronor attempted to levitate the stone. Struggling against the heft of granite, he eventually balanced the correct output of mana needed to lift the boulder from the ground, carefully considering the effects of the blustering wind.

Myronor guided the rock over the wall's edge and released the spell. He waited...listening intently for the splash of water. When he heard nothing, he leaned over the wall's edge, hoping to determine what had happened. But given the depth and height of the barrier, he could see very little. Gathering his robes above his knees, Myronor hoisted himself up onto the stone baluster of the wall and very carefully peered over.

There, floating like a feather in the wind, hung the rock, drifting slowly to the ground as if lowered gently on invisible chains. If his mother *had* faked her death, then he supposed this spell would have done the trick. As he sat pondering this latest development, a strong gust of wind caught his robes, threatening his precarious balance. But it also carried with it something more than panic.

The whispers of a sad song from far below caught Myronor's breath in his throat.

Someone was singing in the distance, carried up the wall by the fierce breeze. He listened intently, trying to decipher the gibberish words that were far beyond comprehension. The despair in the voice...*her voice*...but who...and where...and what?

Like a moth to a flame, he followed the sound, desperate to find the source. He squinted his eyes against the setting sun, searching again. The sound seemed to originate from near the wall itself, too close, perhaps, for him to see. And as he peered further over the edge, hoping to catch a glimpse of the bearer of the haunting voice, a sudden gust of wind knocked his curiosity from him and his body from the wall.

~ Twenty ~

UPHEAVAL

"She's late," Jasper said, tapping his foot against the stone alleyway. The sun had set some time ago, leaving him and Col alone in the dark streets of Krysas.

"Technically, *we're* late," Col said, pulling a pocket watch from her bosom. "By several hours, in fact."

"Yes, but we're always late."

"I'm sure she'll forgive us. After we've explained about the navarras, of course."

"We're not telling her shite," Jasper growled under his breath. "My point is the Yeoman is never late..."

Col sighed, flashing the whites of her eyes as they rolled. "Hold on to your sails. We've been waiting here less time than you spend in the loo."

Jasper grunted as he peered around the alley. No one had yet come from the main street or the back end of the alley. They hadn't met in this specific location before, but that in itself wasn't unusual. The Yeoman typically changed their meeting location each time they rendezvoused.

As Jasper adjusted his sleeves, he slipped a hand beneath his overcoat, unbelting his knives. "This doesn't feel right, Col."

"Maybe you're just jumpy," Col replied while reaching a hand within her cloak and adjusting her means of defense. "Not every day you slay sea monsters."

Whenever Col's words failed to match her actions, it signaled to him that danger was afoot. Jasper chuffed, playing along with her ruse as his hands rested directly over the handle of each knife. It wasn't often that he blatantly lied to Col, but for her, he must. After speaking to the Yeoman, he'd sworn to himself that he'd tell her the truth of Ophiera and the navarra. But until he had a better handle on the situation, of the Brotherhood's reasons for attacking his ship, and of what the Yeoman knew of the new Ambassador, he was not making rash decisions.

"Funny," croaked a voice from the darkness, "the *Berserker* is the fastest ship on the sea, yet has never once delivered on time."

Jasper was shocked to find the elderly woman had slunk into the alleyway without his notice. Strange...she'd never arrived by way of the main streets before.

"Yeoman, nice of you to finally show up," Jasper called out. His voice came across calmer than his senses, and Col subtly shifted her position, sensing danger as well.

As always, the Yeoman carried a small lantern dangling from a knobby stick, illuminating the slightest area before her. Yet even that seemed pointless against the leather blindfold bound across her eyes. The straps of leather had been tied in place for so long that they seemed to resemble her skin, minus the slight variation in tonality. Her gray hair sat in a bun atop her head, loose wisps falling across her sun-scorched face. A thin-lipped smirk stretched her cragged mouth.

"The *Berserker* crew has always been a favorite contract, you know?" The Yeoman said. "Dependable. Loyal. *Private.* That's why I truly regret how this discussion between friends may end."

Jasper sensed movement in the alley long before the Yeoman had finished her abstruse message.

Three sets of near-silent steps approached in the darkness. Whoever they were, their abilities to meld into the shadows were far too like his own.

Nearly invisible, in fact...Which could only mean...

Memories feathered on the edge of his vision, threatening to drag him back into another living dream—a living nightmare—hauntings from a past he drank to forget. His hands shook, paralyzed in fear and unable to reach toward his weapons. The invisible steps were nearing now, and he could do nothing to stop them—he had *never* been able to stop them.

Col flung her cloak open wide. With arms whirling in deadly precision, streaks of silver escaped her hands. One, two, three—sickening thuds echoed against the alley walls, snapping Jasper from his momentary stupor.

Three bodies materialized from the shadows, crumpling forward to their knees.

Dressed in obscuring black cloth, matte and tight against their bodies, each sneak was decorated with a shining hilt, courtesy of Col's throwing knives. She'd perfectly targeted two enemies in the leg and one in the arm...in preparation for her signature interrogation strategy.

"Most haven't heard of drosera toxin," she said sweetly. From deep within her bosom, she pulled a small yellow vial. "Lucky for *one* of you, I have an antidote. The first to speak wins a chance to survive."

Col shook the potion bottle between her fingers, inspecting her nails in a feign of impatience. Jasper watched as the first fallen sneak managed to remove her knife from his arm. Clumsily, he chucked it back towards Col, but Jasper swung his blade upwards more quickly, easily deflecting the weakly thrown blade. The motion had served to spread the poison faster, and the first of the three fell to the ground motionless.

Only then did Jasper see the goldenrod cloth tied tightly about their ankle.

"They won't talk; they're Brotherhood," he growled, hoping to hide the fear that had crept into his voice.

If members of the Brotherhood had acquired the ability to cloak, to move near invisible in the darkness, they likely held markings similar to his own carved into their flesh. He was tempted to see for himself, to peel back their dark coverings...if they bore the marks of...of *him.*

"What a waste of my talents," Col said, shaking her head and placing the antidote between her breasts once again.

The remaining assailants collapsed to the ground, twitching horribly. But even as they lie unmoving, no vespers emerged from their bodies.

The Yeoman sighed as she scuffled beside Col. "How long until they wake?"

"An hour, tops. It's not my most potent batch, still working out the right carrier."

The Yeoman patted Col on the forearm. "That's plenty, dear. You've always outdone yourself with your talents, and this is no exception."

Ignoring the odd placation from the Yeoman, Jasper returned his knives, staring down at the three unconscious Vespulas.

"What do you want done with them?"

"Leave them," the Yeoman replied, nudging the nearest assailant in the ribs. "I'll ensure my people find them long before they wake." She took a step towards the far end of the alley. "Let's get to our business, then."

Jasper and Col exchanged a glance before following the old woman. Moving helped loosen the tension between his shoulders, but he felt Col's eyes on him. Eventually, she would grill him about what had just happened, the threat of his flashbacks, and the Brotherhood's new skillset. And eventually, he'd be forced to explain—but not sober.

He should have brought his flask.

At this hour, the main streets of Krysas lay nearly deserted, apart from a few late-night food stands a level above in the Strato district. Here in the Tropo district, however, few ventured out past dark.

As the population of Krysas grew, the single option had been to build upwards and inwards, delving further up and into the cliffside. Each district level was wrought with its own quirks, but the dark and stuffy inner streets were home to those the Consortia wished to hide. The Tropo district held the worst reputation—precisely where Jasper did most of his dealings in Krysas. As did the Yeoman.

Rumor had it she was a former trainee of the Phratries, but Jasper didn't put much faith in rumor. She was far too straightforward—not a trait typically associated with the shamans. And that was precisely why he maintained such an equitable business relationship with the Yeoman.

The three of them stopped before a narrow archway belonging to one of the many abodes lining the back street. Illuminated by her minute lantern, Jasper was taken aback by the wooden door framed within the arch, a rare luxury in a city of stone, especially in the depths of the Tropo district. Other than the odd door, however, the hovel appeared no different from the surrounding stone slums.

The Yeoman knocked, starting with three taps, a pause, then two more, followed by another pause, then...

Jasper lost interest in counting long before the latches came undone.

The door swung slowly inwards, and they followed the Yeoman down a series of stone steps. Like most of the inner-city homes in Krysas, the room they entered resembled a cave—solid dark stone walls and stale air. Only the wealthy and those on the Exo level could afford the imbuteria required for the structural weakness imparted by windows. But Jasper didn't care—he generally preferred the warm light of oil lanterns and candles over the natural glare of daylight.

This safe house was laid out more like a cheap tavern than a home. An amalgam of furniture had been arranged around the room: tables, chairs, and even a counter bar. However, no bartender or patrons were present. They were utterly alone, or so the Yeoman wanted him to think.

"Sit," said the Yeoman as she gestured to a table in the corner. "I need a drink, and so do you."

Jasper watched her shuffle to the kegs stacked neatly behind the bar, wishing more pubs were like this—self-service, with empty tables. Yawning, he relaxed into his seat, only to feel Col's worried eyes following him.

"Surely you're not upset over the wasted paralysis poison?" He asked. "I'll buy you whatever ingredients you need once we're paid."

She pursed her lips with a look of pity. "Jasp...we can't just ignore what happened."

"Watch me," he replied, putting his boots up.

"You couldn't out there—I saw your eyes, you nearly—"

"But I didn't. So drop it, Col."

"Fine. But we need to address three Brotherhood assassins brandishing cloaking abilities nearly as potent as your own. I nearly missed them!"

Jasper scoffed. "But you didn't, and that's all that matters."

"So, it doesn't matter that the Vespulas have intercepted us twice today?" Col hissed. "It doesn't matter that *he* might be involved?"

A shiver of fear trickled down Jasper's spine. He didn't like that Col had reached the same conclusion he had.

"Concerned about the Brotherhood, are we?" the old woman asked, depositing three overflowing steins on the uneven tabletop.

"Not at all," Jasper muttered, carefully dragging a frothing stein to himself.

"Well, you will be," the Yeoman said, drinking deeply. Jasper followed suit, savoring the familiar flavors of a foreign lager. After a few smacks of her lips, the Yeoman continued. "I don't have to tell you that the Brotherhood has finally caught on to your little scheme. They know my organization has been purchasing the skimmed shipments, too."

"Called it," Col shouted, slamming her fist on the table and glaring at Jasper.

As usual, his first mate had been right. This meant the attack on his ship hadn't been caused by Ophiera, after all. Which meant, perhaps, he could find her again, and...But no. One step at a time, he reminded himself. First, they needed to be paid. He observed the Yeoman, silently calculating which direction this conversation might lead. But without a view of her eyes, he felt nearly as blind.

"What does that mean for our contract?" Jasper finally asked.

The Yeoman shifted, producing a grubby leather pouch from beneath the table. She tossed it beside his drink without speaking a word. With a gloved hand, Jasper dragged the pouch before him and loosened the tie gruffly.

Blush-colored pearls spilled forth, rolling across the dark wooden table in a gleaming frenzy.

"Iluka pearls?" he breathed. It had been years since he'd seen the ocean's most precious and beautiful bounty.

"Aye," the Yeoman nodded. "Should be enough to buy out your contract."

"So *that's* how you do your business," he returned, as critically as possible.

"The Vespula Brotherhood is targeting the *Berserker* now, and unfortunately, you're an easy target. For the sake of my organization's survival, we're going to put our professional relationship aside. Surely you understand."

"*You* contributed to this target on our backs," Jasper spat. "And our reward for risking our necks is to give us the boot? Fend for ourselves?"

He knew he'd likely have done much the same in the Yeoman's shoes, but it didn't stop the bitter demon in his gut from churning. Without the Yeoman's business, they'd be back to hauling timber and stone across the sea for little to no profit. And if the Vespula Brotherhood *had* marked him now, the *Berserker* couldn't sail the Lucent Strait safely again, anyway. He and his crew could be stranded in Krysas until things calmed down. And given that he just delivered the Brotherhood's flaming white nightmare to the shores of Orbolas, he had a hunch nothing would ever be calm again.

"That's the cost of business." The Yeoman drank again, slowly. "But there is one alternative my organization could offer."

Jasper clenched his jaw, unwilling to be baited.

"And what option is that?" Col said softly.

"Join us."

Jasper nearly spat his ale across the table.

The Yeoman smiled. "We offer protection in exchange for *loyalty*. Work exclusively for us, join our cause, and obey our rules, and we will protect the *Berserker* and her crew from the storms rolling in."

Col cut in with a low tone. "Does your organization still intend to destroy the Brotherhood?"

Jasper froze mid-drink. While he had his suspicions and his clues, he'd always pretended not to know the Yeoman's business. In fact, both he and the Yeoman preferred it that way. But Col...why had Col acted so familiar with the Yeoman just now? What did she know?

"Of course," the Yeoman replied without a shred of doubt in her voice. "And we are nearly there. We've increased our coffers and recruits significantly, thanks to some refugees from a village in Tanvik. They want retribution, as does their shaman."

Jasper's heart jumped, but he didn't speak. The way Ophiera had described the attack on Iluka...he'd assumed no one had survived.

"When was the last time you visited home, Jasper?" the Yeoman asked.

It took every ounce of his self-control not to flip the table in anger. She was goading him, and very nearly successfully. He didn't care how she'd learned he was from Iluka, and he didn't care to provide her with an answer. But his silence alone wasn't enough to thwart the Yeoman.

"I hear the new Ambassador and his poorly disguised concubine also hail from your hometown. So, tell me, what was your impression of them?"

Jasper bit his tongue so hard he tasted blood. Either her network of spies was far more skilled than he had imagined or...

"I'll give you my impression," Col said, refusing to look at him. "The captain has been attempting to keep the identity of the woman a secret, even from me. I'm still not completely sure *who* she is, but she's certainly no consort. She took down two navarras in a silk dress but gave this idiot and the Ambassador credit in order to remain hidden."

Anger boiled beneath Jasper's forced calm. He should have known Col was too damned smart to be fooled by his lies, but he never imagined she'd betray him like this.

"How long have you been selling our secrets to the Yeoman?" He growled, breaking the façade.

Col smiled soothingly. "Come now, Jasp, I haven't *sold* her anything; I voluntarily share information that benefits their cause."

If Col intended these words to make him feel better, she was sorely mistaken. Not only had she sold him out, but she had done so without profit. "We agreed to remain neutral, Col! To stay the hell out of this Brotherhood business!"

"*You* decided to remain neutral, Jasp. But I won't sit around as Erum dies!" He watched as the familiar, vacant horror overtook her dark eyes. "You weren't there in the Sloughmire—the night the bog came alive with death. The night I had to..." Col took a deep, stuttering breath. "The Yeoman and her people are taking this *plague* seriously! A blight we know has been caused by the Vespula Brotherhood!"

Jasper chewed his lip, fighting to withstand the waves of fear pouring from Col. He had heard her story only once, and it had been one too many times. She'd survived the Sloughmire, in the same fashion he'd survived his youth, by remaining uninvolved with the fate of others. And yet, between the Yeoman, Ophiera, and Col, there seemed to be no path free of entanglement.

If, indeed, all paths led to war with the Brotherhood, well, he would travel better as a profiteer.

"Pay me," he said to the Yeoman. "I want protection *and* payment in exchange for my loyalty and services."

Unable to stomach Col's disappointed stare, Jasper drained his lager. The Yeoman remained silent, too. For a moment, he wondered if he'd assumed too much, but he didn't regret taking the chance.

"Deal," the Yeoman said. She placed her empty stein on the tabletop and smacked her lips one final time. "Rates stay the same, though."

Jasper nodded, but before he could even be pleased with himself, the Yeoman whistled so loudly that his ears rang. Behind the bar, the stone wall slid with a grind, revealing a crack just wide enough for people to pass. Summoned by the Yeoman, the small throng waved to the Yeoman before filling in the tables of the tavern, glancing between Jasper and Col. Col waved to many with a smile, which they returned in kind.

The demons Ophiera had awakened within him roared to life once again. They screamed of Col's betrayal, of her blame for his current predicament. Perhaps the Brotherhood targeting the *Berserker* was due to her dealings instead, drawing their attention by associating beyond business with the Yeoman. Because of her, his life would yet again belong to someone else. A familiar hatred coursed through him, hatred for everyone and everything.

"We're welcoming a new member to the Ashen Order today," the Yeoman shouted, breaking his intrusive thoughts.

The room raised their hands in a cheer that Jasper interpreted more as a jeer. The Yeoman always referred to her business as "the organization," yet Jasper couldn't help but interpret the name 'Ashen Order' as anything more than a cult. He felt equally trapped and welcomed and wondered if there would be any type of initiation ceremony.

"Now, there is someone you both must meet," the Yeoman said, smiling at Col and Jasper. "She has some urgent questions regarding your fare from Cantheas."

The Yeoman whistled again.

Despite his mood, Jasper couldn't help but stare unabashedly at the scantily clad giant stalking toward him. Her bronze hair fell in dreaded locks down her tattooed, fully exposed, brawny torso. She wore nothing beyond a yoke of sea glass and twine, which left little to the imagination, draped across her ample bosom. The slink of pearlescent scales, rattling like shells caught in the surf, caught his attention as he examined her lengthy loincloth.

"I can tell you've seen the Warden recently," she said in a deep, sultry voice that shivered through him. "Though she clearly left her mark on you long ago."

"You must be Kaikora," Jasper replied, keeping his voice cool. He remembered the shaman from Ophiera's confession—the one who had abandoned Iluka in its time of need.

"Did Ophiera and Myronor inform you of their plans?"

Jasper raised an eyebrow at her. "Aren't you supposed to be some sort of seer?"

A sharp pain across his shin told him Col didn't appreciate his attitude. But he blamed his mood on her. Partially, anyway. And he didn't need a half-naked behemoth interrogating him, either.

Kaikora's gray eyes pierced him like a stone dagger. "I cannot see her fate anymore, nor his. But I need you to tell me where she is."

He laughed mirthlessly. "I am not sure she wishes to be found."

"You don't faze me as a man who much cares what others want."

Col snorted into her cup.

"Then why should I care what you ask me now?"

The shaman smiled as she bent low, meeting him eye to eye.

"I lost sight of them both when you were attacked by navarra. Which means one of them has suffered the black bite."

Jasper felt Col's anxiety clear as day, and his own hands began to tremble in reflection. He couldn't keep her emotions from his head in his current state and felt his ire fold under the weight.

"The mage," Col said in a shaky voice. "The ichor still lingered in his wound when they left us. And they seemed quite uninterested in seeking a healer."

Kaikora's face may have remained stoic, but the fear radiating from her crashed against Jasper. In a single day, years of training had been undone, and now he felt everything as his own. He needed a drink. He needed to feel something other than the desperation permeating every inch of the room.

"If the ichor claims Myronor, it will consume Ophiera as well. If either of you has any care in the world for the fate of her soul, you must help me find them. Now."

~ Twenty One ~

CREDENCE

Pacing in the dark was the only option left for Ophiera.

She had tried frantically to singe away as much of the contaminating ichor from the wound as possible. But as before, it had receded too deeply for the armor's repellent qualities to reach, festering and spreading as the roots of a tree. The Aether beneath her called for the ichor's eradication nearly as desperately as she did herself. Even as she paced, the scars on her arm itched, almost begging her to *burn* him. But she couldn't risk Myronor's soul with any rite, let alone the full force of the unbridled holy flames. Their souls may be tethered, but would their bond suffice to protect him from the Aether? Perhaps releasing Myronor's soul to the Aether would be more merciful than allowing him to become like the troynt in the dead marsh.

The thought alone froze the breath in her chest. If she believed his death a better fate than succumbing to the ichor, what more could she do? If he had told her sooner...but 'what ifs' couldn't help at this point. She now found herself in a foreign land with no knowledge of language or culture; in a city of mages in which she possessed only a rudimentary understanding of magic, at best.

Ophiera studied Myronor's shallow, labored breaths, the only sign he still lived. While his behavior still stabbed at her heart, she knew his actions were not his own. And yet she was terrified to find out *who* they belonged to instead. As his chest rose and fell, a glint caught her eye—the medallion shone gently in the moonslight, the crescent moon, and three barely discernible stars.

Their only escape route from this place was via that medallion, and she had thoughtlessly left it in the possession of the possessed. Carefully, she lifted the pendant over Myronor's sweating brow, moving slowly so as not to disturb him. But as she gazed upon his sallow, sweating face, she couldn't help but graze her knuckles against his cheek.

Overwhelming despair flooded through the ekath. A vision of Myronor alone in the darkness invaded her thoughts, but something obscured her reach toward him. He drifted in nowhere, carried further away from her with each passing moment, unable to sense her soul.

Gong.

Ophiera jumped at the reverberating clang of the bell, searching the room for the source of the sound.

Gong.

Her ears dragged her eyes to the gateway, the entrance to the Embassy home. She approached, clutching the pendant as a voice grew louder and more distinct. Standing before the door, she now recognized Glamwell's voice, though in a language she couldn't understand. His distress, however, required no translation.

She thought best how to answer his call. She *wanted* to relay that Myronor had fallen ill and chastised herself again for not requesting Glamwell to contact a healer immediately upon their arrival. But her instinct had warned her that the Steward would be of no help against the ichor.

"The Ambassador has requested not to be disturbed," she blurted out, hoping her voice traveled through the archway of its own accord.

"I apologize, Lady Iris," Glamwell replied in her own tongue. "But there are some-uh-*acquaintances* of the Ambassador that wish to call upon him."

Ophiera's stomach dropped. They knew no one in Krysas, and no one knew them. This was likely a ploy masterminded by the Brotherhood, but she needed to be certain.

"Who are they?" she asked.

"Well, there's an incredibly tall, partially clothed woman who refuses to provide her name, demanding to see Myronor and the Warden. But when I tried explaining to her that I'm a Steward, not a warden, she grew irate and—"

"I'll retrieve them," Ophiera replied shortly, managing to keep her voice steady.

She could hardly believe the shaman had found her way to Krysas. Ophiera thought the shaman was either very stupid or very lucky to seek her out at this particular moment. Either way, Ophiera needed to know for herself.

Still clothed in the tight green gown Collette had lent her, Ophiera rushed through the archway. With a veiled sensation of delicate silk webs tugged across her body, she entered the Embassy office to find Glamwell at his warped glass desk, contemplating a closed book. Before him stood a devastatingly beautiful woman bearing a massive trident and a glorious grin.

Ophiera nearly burst into flames at the sight of those gray eyes as her stomach burned with resentment and relief. But the sight of Jasper, leaning casually against the doorway a step behind the shaman, snuffed out her flames in cold surprise. Earlier today, these two individuals would have been the last people on Erum she wished to meet, but now, she needed them desperately.

"Thank you, Glamwell," Ophiera said shakily. "I'll escort them from here."

Glamwell nodded before relaxing back into his chair, glowering slightly as he opened his book. By the wrists, she dragged Kaikora and Jasper through the tapestried archway into the residence. As they entered the sitting room, Ophiera released Jasper and turned immediately to Kaikora.

"I can't decide if I should thank the flames you're here or call upon them to strike you down!"

"I wouldn't fault you for either choice," Kaikora replied calmly. "However, I would advise we deal with the more pressing matter of the moment before you decide."

Ophiera's eyes fell to Myronor, splayed on the fainting couch, unconscious and sallow.

"Can you help him?" She asked.

Kaikora didn't answer as she crossed the room. With a grind of metal and stone, she released her trident roughly on the floor beside Myronor, kneeling low over him. She placed a massive, tattooed hand on his leg and lifted the robes.

Bile rose in Ophiera's throat. The darkened tendrils had continued to spread, and the flesh around the wound had begun to fester. She had the sudden urge to sever the afflicted limb from his body, a worthy sacrifice if it meant saving his soul. But if Kaikora could provide a better solution...

"Give me a moment, Warden," the shaman said softly.

Ophiera stepped towards the narrow window, breathing in the deep salty night. In the dark silence, she watched the sea, praying for something, anything to help. The Aether called to her, Myronor suffered beside her, Kaikora reappeared before her, and Jasper lurked behind her. The weight of their combined actions held her pinned, immobilized before the window. She felt on the verge of collapse.

"What happened after you left?" Jasper whispered in her ear.

His voice sent shivers down her neck, compelling her to speak.

"The wound," she began, unsure what drove her words. "I didn't realize it had progressed so far until it was too late."

"Did he hurt you?"

The growl beneath his whisper sent shivers of danger across her skin. While Myronor hadn't physically harmed her, his dark, tainted thoughts had carved deeper wounds in her heart. The way he had screamed when she'd touched him, recoiled, and begged her to stop. It was her worst fear realized: to be hated by *him*.

If she lost Myronor to this darkness...

Jasper's gloved hand fell on her shoulder. She hadn't realized just how much she shook until he held her still. Maybe this tactic worked to quell Collette, but Ophiera felt even more conflicted by his touch. Like Myronor, the captain had also hurt her with words alone before, and yet now he worried for her well-being. Her heart stammered on the edge of control, moisture building in her eyes as she desperately held her composure.

Why was she breaking under the weight of his hand?

Jasper tugged her around to face him, and she lacked the strength to resist. Every ounce of her being was spent on suppressing the Aether and her tears, neither of which were welcome nor helpful. Two thick, leather-cloaked arms pulled her into his chest, squeezing her tightly against him.

"Breathe, Ophiera," he whispered against her ear. "Slow, deep breaths. Feel mine and match them."

She didn't understand what was happening. Wasn't she breathing? Rapidly, perhaps. Erratically, perhaps. The room was spinning, and yet Jasper brought a rhythm back to her ragged breaths. His embrace, the strength of his hold, and the scent of leather and salt—combined, it somehow pulled her back from the edge.

How did he know, she wondered, and why did he bother? The captain had expressed such disdain for her on board the ship, a feeling she believed mutual. And yet, the way he held her now, as if sheltering her from a storm at sea, calmed her heart.

"Warden," Kaikora's voice boomed, causing her to jump from Jasper's grasp. Any peace she'd found was destroyed by the doubt reflected in the shaman's eyes. "Your flames are his only hope now."

"Then he is doomed," Ophiera breathed, dread rushing over her.

"We are all doomed if *you* do not act," Kaikora interjected, her voice harsh. "The affliction threatens his very soul, and if it consumes him, you will be destroyed as well through the ekath."

"So my choice is to let us die in darkness or fire?" Ophiera shouted, stepping towards the shaman.

"You must call upon the Aether—"

"I *must*?!" Ophiera growled. "You've no idea what I'm capable of when the Aether slips from my control. If I ignite again, if I lose control, this entire city will be destroyed!"

Jasper sighed from the far corner of the room. "I don't really understand what's going on here, but I watched you reduce a navarra to ash with that fire. So what precisely is different now?"

"Because now I'm connected to the...Jasper, that's it! If we could get Myronor back to the *Berserker*."

"Why would you need to bring him to my ship?" He stared at her, suddenly cold.

Kaikora's brow furrowed. "Ophiera, I know you fear the flames, but I doubt we can escape the attention of the pink man with Myronor in his current state."

Ophiera thought for a moment. "Jasper, can you extend your cloaking skills to someone you carried?"

Jasper stared at her still, his gaze becoming more icy. "Not only are you asking to use my ship, but now you wish me to carry this half-dead innatural on my back? I didn't sign up for this."

His cruelty shocked her. Only moments before, he had comforted her, calmed her, and embraced her. Yet now, it was as if he meant to wound her purposefully.

"Ophiera, he is nearly lost," Kaikora said gravely. "We must act now. If you fear your connection to the Aether, then I will help you."

The manner in which Kaikora annunciated *fear* triggered a burn of rebellion in Ophiera's gut. *Fear* was something she so seldom possessed, and yet, there was no denying she had lived her life afraid. Afraid of her Oath, afraid of her fate, afraid of everything she could not hope to understand. It was the same fear she saw behind Jasper's eyes as she'd approached him, bearing sword and flame on the beach of Iluka. The same fear she saw in Myronor's eyes as he pushed her from the navarra's bite.

Fear drove so many of her choices, and yet each only led her to failure.

Was she truly going to allow the threat of Myronor's death to prevent her from trying to save him? In the end, his soul was lost if she did nothing...Her scars burned as she considered eradicating the blight, reminding her again that the Aether had not chosen wrong before.

"Help me save him, Kaikora," Ophiera said to the shaman.

With a silent nod, Kaikora placed her thick arms behind Myronor's knees and back, lifting him as if he weighed nothing. She strode to the balcony, and Ophiera followed through a narrow window, ignoring the scoffs emanating from Jasper behind her.

Only pale moonslight illuminated the darkened balcony, carved from the same dark stone of the cliffside. The platform stretched out over the ocean and across the length of the home. As an extension of the natural cliffside itself, Ophiera felt the Aether pulse with each of her steps, drawn ever closer to the surface.

Kaikora came to a stop at the widest point of the curved balcony, at the center of which bubbled a small fountain. Surrounded by large clay planters brimming with exotic flowers and fruits, the vast space seemed surprisingly secluded. It was surely a wonderfully beautiful place had the moment not been so dire.

As Kaikora laid Myronor on the stone ground, his breathing hitched, and a few whimpers escaped his closed mouth. Ophiera sensed a shift in the ichor as if it were imitating the navarra itself, reeling to poise for an attack. Time was slipping away.

"Cleanse him," Kaikora said, gesturing to the font of water. "I will encase you in water, separated from the Aether. However, it is not without risk to your souls. You must be swift."

Ophiera understood the shaman's warning all too well. If she and Myronor drowned simultaneously, neither could serve as an anchor for the other's life. Either she saved him now, or they perished together.

As Ophiera bent low beside Myronor, Jasper's calloused hand tugged her away by the wrist. "There has to be another way to help him that doesn't involve risking your life or mine! This is reckless—idiotic!"

"Idiocy is continuing to touch me without my permission!" Ophiera growled, shoving him roughly from her.

Ignoring the captain, she again knelt alongside Myronor, brushing his long, golden hair from his face. Myronor's pale hair shone as it flowed over Kaikora's arm, but Ophiera was focused on the waxy texture of his skin. She didn't need Kaikora's words to sense he was nearly gone. He had told her once that he would rather burn beside her than be without her, and now, she must hold him to his words.

"Center yourself," Kaikora said. "Remember who you are."

Ophiera nodded, again ignoring Jasper's grunt of frustration. His presence served as a reminder of her own words: conviction was power. As she stared down at the face of her ekath, she knew this choice was hers to make. She had always chosen to protect him, to rescue him, to abandon and return to him. Her soul may have been bound to his without choice, but she had freely given her heart to him. Myronor had always been *her* choice.

The Aether surged beneath her, and in the searing power, she found clarity. She could, no, *would* sacrifice everyone in Krysas if it meant saving Myronor's life. There was nothing she wouldn't do to ensure his freedom from darkness. She was only disappointed that it had taken her this long to solidify her resolve.

With the guidance of the holy flames, Ophiera placed her runed hand over the darkened wound. The vile energy recoiled beneath as if sensing her unshackled intentions. Over his heart, she rested her unscarred hand, and with closed eyes, she searched for their tether. Like a frayed rope beneath the surf, she sensed the thread that bound her to him and followed it into the dark depths.

The ichor obscured everything, darkening the path to Myronor. Like a map, she followed the fault lines of dissemination, all reaching toward his soul. Every tendril was an offense, a revolting contrast to the pure soul they wrapped in darkness. The sensation caused her mouth to water and her blood to boil. And as the flames roared to life beneath her, matching her hatred, she embraced the flow of fire.

The moment the roar of the Aether finally burned through her, Ophiera perceived cool water suddenly enveloping her body. She clung to Myronor against the surf, holding her breath as they were both submerged in Kaikora's sphere of water. Without the pressure of the Aether's rage, the webs of corruption were brought into focus, and she gave herself over entirely to instinct.

Acting without thought, Ophiera clung to the ekath, holding the thread of his soul close to her own as she poured forth the flames she carried within. She guided her mana along the lines of corruption, pushing forth white fire wherever black tainted blue.

The ichor burned.

And as it did, she felt a presence within their bond—a contamination of pain and rage screaming against the purifying fire.

Ophiera.

The sound of Myronor's feeble voice against her mind nearly broke her concentration. But she sensed the parting darkness swarming again, clouding Myronor's essence and silencing his calls to her. The thought of his soul bound and suffocating only served to enrage her further. Fear had no place in her heart any longer as she blazed through the darkness, incinerating every shred of corruption. She burned until nothing remained but an echoing scream of agony, diminishing to silence within the tether.

The next sensation Ophiera became aware of was momentum—she was falling. She felt the jolt in her stomach before the crash against the rough stone. Water flooded the ground as she coughed and sputtered, and she felt her lungs heavy with stinging fluid. Just as it had in the Cloister, it felt as if she might never draw breath again. But as she pondered this, a hard blow was delivered across her back, and with only a single strike, the water poured from her lungs onto the stone below.

She gasped for air as a pair of calloused hands grasped her shoulders and held her upright.

"Breathe through your nose," Jasper said in a shaky voice.

Despite her earlier aggravation with him, she leaned against him for support as she took several real breaths through her nostrils. Beneath her, the Aether was now reduced to a babbling brook in place of the raging sea from only moments before. And beside her, Myronor stirred.

Freeing herself from Jasper, she tore at the wet robes covering Myronor's wound. Even in the pale light of the moons, she could see that none of the black corruption remained. The only concern now was the punctures themselves, trickling red into the pooling water around them. But truthfully, the remaining wounds were superficial in comparison to the risk posed by the ichor.

Ophiera's eyes never left Myronor as she watched him stir. Somewhere behind her, she heard Kaikora shuffle Jasper away. Alone, she waited for Myronor's eyes to flutter open.

Nearly luminescent against the night, his brilliant blue eyes focused on her, wide-eyed and curious. He looked up at her as if...

Suddenly, his hands weaved into her sopping hair and dragged her down against him. His cool, trembling lips crushed against hers, and at that moment, she knew they were his and his alone. With an unacknowledged need, she gripped the robes at his chest, savoring the sensation of him reconnected in full to her very soul. Through the ekath, everything was exchanged and relived from the last few hours. But she broke away, having witnessed enough of his suffering without reliving it again.

Ophiera ran her scarred hands along his jaw, examining his features. His skin no longer held the waxy texture, and though his eyes were darkened by exhaustion, they held evidence of the smile now playing across his lips. He reached a trembling hand to her wrist and wrapped his cold fingers around her hand.

"How are you feeling?" she asked, at a loss for words.

"Better when your lips were on mine," Myronor replied, reaching up to hold her face in his shaking palm.

"I meant your wound. I should have healed it while..." Her voice faded as her eyes fell to the steady trickle of blood escaping the punctures.

"You've done more than enough," he said huskily. "How many times have you saved my life?"

"I don't know," Ophiera laughed, wiping the tears from her eyes. "I've lost count."

"I owe you my next breath. And so much more."

"My Oath—"

He grabbed her hand and pressed her palm against his sopping chest. She knew what he asked her to feel—it wasn't the vesper beneath.

"Even in my darkest hour, you were my only light. Don't tell me it was only because of your Oath."

"O-of course not."

"Then why? Why did you save me again?"

She felt the heat rise in her cheeks as the intensity of his stare grew.

"You know why," she whispered.

"Tell me," he smiled sadly.

"D-don't actions speak louder than words?"

"After spending so long in that darkness, I only wish to hear your voice."

The pain in his voice overrode any embarrassment she may have felt. She took his face in her hands while staring past his calm, blue gaze.

"Because I love you, Myronor."

He craned his neck to kiss her once again. *You have no idea the healing power of those words.*

Together, they remained embraced under the light of the moons until she sensed his fading constitution.

"We have guests waiting inside."

"Guests?"

"Kaikora is here."

"Kaikora?" He asked, raising an eyebrow. "Alive? I mean, you didn't...or did you?"

"She's alive but unforgiven. After this, I at least owe her a chance to explain."

"That's quite...diplomatic of you, love," he said with a smile.

"It's where my diplomacy ends. For some reason, she brought Jasper along."

"Sullen bastard of the sea, Jasper? How the hell—" he paused, closing his eyes against the stab of pain breaking through the ekath.

"You need to rest," Ophiera said, preparing to lift him from the ground. "Then, together, we can press them both for answers."

She lifted him from the ground, throwing his arm over her shoulder and supporting much of his weight. But when she tried to move forward, Myronor didn't budge. His face looked strained, as if he might collapse under the weight of something. But she sensed little pain.

"What's wrong?"

Myronor pressed his lips against her forehead. He was shaking so violently in her arms she nearly thought he was sobbing. But he only whispered through the ekath *I'm so very sorry.*

For what?

For everything.

~ Twenty Two ~

ABEYANCE

Myronor wasn't thrilled to be lying on the purple fainting couch again. This time, at least, he felt wholly himself, though the reminders of the struggle remained. Pieces of Ophiera's bloodied armor lay strewn about the floor, along with broken bits of the splint Collette had fashioned. The living space felt as chaotic as his heart at the moment.

"Stay off the leg for at least a day," Kaikora said, wrapping the wound in salve and bandages. "You need sleep more than anything, but the salve and ekath should take care of the rest."

He nodded, still not convinced he was awake. How could Kaikora be here, in Krysas? And in one piece, for that matter, while occupying the same room as Ophiera? The shaman had always been reticent and cryptic, and despite knowing her for decades, Myronor knew very little about her personally. If she had been so willing to help them now, could she have really abandoned Iluka? It seemed the same question was lingering in his ekath's mind.

Ophiera stepped beside the shaman the moment she'd tucked in the last piece of loose linen.

"Now that the wound is settled, *we* need to settle some matters."

Kaikora wiped the perspiration from her brow. "Tomorrow."

"Now," Ophiera spat.

"Patience has never been your strong suit, but I implore you to give it a chance; tomorrow is a better time for this discussion."

"I don't want *better*—I want the truth!" Ophiera growled, the runes on her arms flashing with ignition. She had burned away the sleeve of the green dress, revealing her raw scars. "I've not thrown you from the cliffside because you aided us tonight. But you abandoned Iluka to a doom worse than death, and as their Warden, I demand an explanation!"

Through the ekath, Myronor felt no threat of the Aether overwhelming her; he could feel only rage. His heart sank as he realized he, too, would be on the receiving end of her wrath soon enough.

"Fine," Kaikora sighed, sinking into one of the rounded poufs nearby. If tensions hadn't been so high, the sight might have been comical. Her gray eyes bore into Ophiera, and for the first time since he'd known her, Myronor saw wariness drawn across the shaman's face.

"To be clear, I never abandoned *you*."

"Oh?" Ophiera seethed. "You sent us to an empty cave, only to watch Iluka burn from a distance! How else would you define abandonment?!"

Myronor felt her memories of that day whirl through the ekath. It seemed like ages ago that Kaikora had sent them to the rainbow cliffs in search of armor for Ophiera. But in that cave, they found no tomb as promised, no armor, no weapon, and to boot, the Aether had tried to claim Ophiera's soul.

"I sent Berwyn to retrieve you, did I not?"

Ophiera scoffed. "Exactly! You *knew* everything and sent us away *knowing* Iluka would be attacked! How can you be gifted with sight and do nothing to intervene!"

"*You* view the sight as a gift," Kaikora said, rubbing the back of her neck. "But like your own gifts, the weight is...burdensome."

"What do you know of burdens?"

"I bear the burden of *choice*, Ophiera!" Kaikora snapped, her resolve breaking. "I had to make a choice, and I followed the path that would save Erum!"

Ophiera sneered as she paced, the hem of her dress dancing with agitation. The exhausted side of Myronor wished she had left this discussion until morning, and yet, curiosity about Kaikora's choices kept him awake and alert.

"How could allowing the Brotherhood to destroy Iluka possibly save Erum?" Ophiera hissed, glaring at the shaman. "There had to be a way to save them both!"

"There wasn't," Kaikora shot back, her shoulders slumped despite the power of her voice. "I chose the path to salvation—the path that would put a stop to Aud."

On her last word, Kaikora's eyes fell to Myronor's wound. The name evoked more fear in him since receiving the black bite, a dreadful reminder of what the ichor heralded.

"All the more reason you shouldn't have sent me away! You should have let me stop the Brotherhood at Iluka!" Ophiera snapped. "If I had stayed—"

"You'd have destroyed the village *and* every soul in it!"

Myronor felt the blow to his heart as if it were directed against him. He chanced a glance at Ophiera, his heart breaking at the sight of her expression.

"You don't know—"

"But I do!" Kaikora shouted, her voice breaking. "As you say, I *knew!* I knew exactly what would have happened if you'd stayed in Iluka! I saw how you would have lost yourself to the Aether again, how you would have destroyed some of the Brotherhood and all of us along with them! I saw the ashes of Iluka *your* hands if you had stayed! So, I sent you away...not on a lie, but on a hope that you would find a means of control within that ancient font before it was too late. And from what I can tell, I made the right choice!"

The silence that followed tore at Myronor's heart. Still as stone, Ophiera stopped pacing, her eyes fixated on something beyond the window. He could feel the tempest of emotions seeping through the tether like ice melting.

Alone on the *Mistral* with Berwyn, Myronor had made his peace with the destruction of Iluka. Perhaps it was the distance from Ophiera or the desperate need to find her, but he knew then that there was only one person deserving of blame.

The discomfort of his bandaged wounds was a pale reminder of Aud's threats. A battle for his soul had taken place within him, all because of that vile ichor that the Brotherhood now manipulated. If Kaikora had abandoned Iluka to prevent Erum from suffering Aud's fate, he trusted it was the right choice.

"For what it's worth, Kaikora," Myronor began quietly, "I think...I think you did your best. And I appreciate you saving us."

Kaikora's gray eyes found his, a hint of surprise breaking past the dry grief. But otherwise, the shaman remained stoic and silent, as did Ophiera. It was a painful silence.

"Any other grievances to air out, or can we retire for the night?" Jasper said from the shadows.

Myronor had forgotten that the captain now lurked around the sitting room as well. He honestly thought he'd seen the last of the sullen sailor when they'd departed his ship earlier that morning. And yet, here Jasper was, in his new residence with dark curls cascading over a bemused expression.

"Why is he still here?" Ophiera hissed.

"You know, I ask myself that every day," Jasper said sullenly. "Why am I here? What is the point? When will this life end? What—"

"Answer me, or I will answer when it ends," Ophiera interrupted angrily.

"Oh, I'd love to see you try *again*. Though I'm certain anything violent you attempt in that dress will pose quite a challenge."

"No more a challenge than two navarra," she growled as Myronor felt her mind focus on her claymore leaning against the wall.

When Myronor had expanded their belongings earlier, it was with the intention to find the salve, not to provide her with a weapon. He couldn't decide if he regretted his choice to lean the weapon against the wall or if his desire to watch Ophiera beat the captain into place outweighed his guilt.

"That is enough," Kaikora growled, thrusting her trident between them. "We are all testy with exhaustion. As I've said, we should retire for the evening and have a proper discussion tomorrow."

Myronor breathed a sigh of relief, hoping to avoid the continuation of this conversation. Despite Ophiera's confusion as to how Kaikora and Jasper were connected, Myronor had a sneaking suspicion he knew why. If the Order were involved, he would have to fess up to Ophiera. He would have to explain *why* he'd accepted the Ambassadorship to Krysas...why he desired nothing more than to search his mother's library.

"I'm no longer waiting for answers," Ophiera spat, dashing his hopes in an instant. "I want to know how you two know each other and why the scoundrel is here!"

Kaikora gave Myronor a sideways glance. It wasn't a question but a warning. Uncomfortable truths were soon to be revealed.

"Jasper has been assigned to aid me."

The captain threw himself down into a nearby armchair and began twirling a curved blade between his gloved hands.

"Assigned? By whom?"

"The Ashen Order, of course—" Jasper replied, his voice dripping in sarcasm. "Didn't your boyfriend tell you all about them?"

Ophiera's eyes fell on Myronor, who couldn't speak under her gaze. The look of a painful question etched across her beautiful face was the precise reason he'd failed to tell her the truth so many times before.

"Again, this discussion would be best left for the morning," Kaikora said. Her gray gaze lingered on Ophiera for some time before conceding with a pinched brow. "But seeing as you will not be swayed, I must at least ask that you sit down and cease this infernal pacing."

After a momentary stare-down with the shaman, Ophiera took a seat, stiffly, in a distant chair. With one last mournful glance at Myronor, she forced the ekath shut. The cold silence felt exceptionally lonely after what they had just endured.

"You know the stories of the ancient wars, yes?" Kaikora asked Ophiera.

Ophiera nodded, but Jasper chuffed. "What do those ridiculous legends have to do with the Order other than being as old as the Yeoman?"

Kaikora pinched the bridge of her nose. "Those legends are our history, despite the great lengths much of the world goes through to forget. The Ashen Order was established in response to the ancient wars...after the first Aspect was forged from the Aether."

Ophiera's head cocked to one side and, even silenced, Myronor could feel her frustration with the shaman. She purposefully averted her eyes from his, wounding him deeper than the navarra bite. There was no scenario in which he could avoid the truth any longer.

When Rheta had explained the purpose of the Order to him, she had given him a more vague and *current* perspective. But Kaikora's explanation began at the dawn of time, revealing a connection he had no knowledge of before. He wondered if Ophiera would accept his ignorance on the matter.

Kaikora gestured with her trident to the pile of golden plate armor near the hearth. "The first Aspect known by the Phratries was born at a time when Erum faced oblivion. Their appearance turned our annihilation into our salvation, but the peace our world has known since is but a lull in a war that continues to be fought to this day."

"We're at war right now?" Jasper asked. "Wish someone had told me."

Another wave of anger shook the ekath, but this time, Myronor was relieved it wasn't directed at him. He, too, wished the idiot would leave.

"Before their death, the first Aspect tasked the mother clans with protecting Erum's hard-earned peace. However, there were...disagreements as to how to best prevent future catastrophes. The Phratries believed maintaining knowledge of our world served peace best...but the Cloister believed maintaining the purity of the Aether was the only answer. For some time, the two factions co-existed, yet drifted further apart as the years went on. The Ashen Order was established decades later to fill in the gaps. As a collective, they saw a flaw in the Phratries and Cloister's philosophies. I will spare you the details, but the Order has one goal and one goal only: to prevent the ancient wars from repeating themselves, this time by stopping the Brotherhood."

So what Rheta had told Myronor *was* true. Much that he had read now fell into place. He knew his mother had been working with the Ashen Order, but when Rheta had explained *why*, he'd thought her insane. Now, Kaikora had confirmed everything and then some.

"The Cloister never spoke of this order," Ophiera said, shaking her head in disbelief.

Kaikora smiled sadly. "The Cloister never spoke of the Brotherhood either, yet you know them to be real."

"All of this makes it sound like I just joined some sort of religion," Jasper mused in a derisive tone. "That wasn't well advertised by the Yeoman now, was it?"

"Isn't your allegiance to the Phratries?" Ophiera asked Kaikora tersely, ignoring the rogue's rudeness. "Why do you serve this Order, too?"

Kaikora's expression became stony. "This is not the Cloister, Ophiera; we do not *serve*. The Phratries and the Order have been allied since the beginning. We recognize that there may be multiple solutions to the problem that deserve their chance to succeed or fail. It is only the Cloister that isolates itself in absolution."

"I don't know, this feels a hell of a lot like servitude to me," Jasper muttered.

The shaman threw him a deadly glare. "You're being compensated, aren't you?"

"Clearly not enough."

Ophiera turned her gaze to Myronor. He could see the pained question in her eyes, a precursor to the betrayal he knew to come. Even with the ekath shut, he knew what she was about to ask of him.

"Who else is a part of this Order?"

With a deep breath, Myronor spoke to the dark, cold floor.

"Rheta was a part of the Order for many years. And upon my mother's death, I learned she was also *involved*."

"So, you knew of the Ashen Order this entire time?" Ophiera asked, her voice shaking.

"By name, but I did not know all of this. The way Rheta explained it, I only understood that they cared about Pyra's research and our spanning magic. I didn't know anything of wars or Aud or the Brotherhood before we met, Ophiera, I swear."

The full force of Ophiera's pain thundered through her eyes. He didn't need the ekath to feel her trust disintegrating in flames before him. If only he hadn't been such a coward and had shared the truth from the start...but even now, the truth felt weak.

Her life had been thrown into disarray because of his hellbent curiosity. If he had simply denied the Ambassadorship as planned, none of this would have happened. He could have continued living his life without interest in what his mother had researched, and Ophiera would be relaxing on the dock outside her cottage, watching the pearl farmers harvest beneath the moonslight. They wouldn't be together here in Krysas, suffering these grim injuries of body, soul, and heart.

"So," Ophiera began in a shaking voice. "I was the only one...unaware."

At Kaikora's nod, the paladin stood abruptly. She removed the medallion from her neck, which Myronor had not noticed was missing until now. She dropped it into his lap and stepped away.

"Ophiera," he begged, reaching for her hand. She recoiled, not meeting his eyes as she marched from him. Before she disappeared through the slitted windows onto the dark balcony, she snatched her golden claymore from the wall.

Myronor recalled how she had dismembered a stone statue in a fit of rage at the Magistrate and feared for the planters out on the balcony. He rose from his seat to follow her outside, but Kaikora pressed the butt of her trident against his shoulder, halting him in place.

"Let her go. You need rest."

Jasper suddenly rose from his sprawl. "I'll ensure she doesn't set the place on fire."

"She wants to be alone," Myronor snapped.

With a haughty grin, Jasper turned to him, walking backward out the window. "I'm quite certain she only wants to be away from *you*."

Again, Myronor started to follow. And again, Kaikora poked him still with the butt of her trident.

"Rest, remember? And besides, it's his funeral. She's warned him already..."

"Warned him?"

Kaikora rolled her eyes. "By the sea, she can clearly handle one handsy pirate."

"Handsy? What the hell happened?"

"It's not important," Kaikora said with a wave of her hand. "What is important is this supposed portal to Feyralis. That is the task the Order has set upon me, to find and reconnect your mother's creation."

Myronor relaxed slightly in the silence from the balcony and refocused on Kaikora's abrupt admission. While he hadn't a clue she'd known of the Order prior to this evening, he would wager a guess that Kaikora knew a great deal more than he did of their intentions.

"What did the Order tell you of Pyra and her research?"

"Only what I need to know to help you. From my understanding, Rheta was a key source of information for the Order, information that only passed through Pyra's portals. While she never *shared* her invention with the Order, she served as the liaison between Rheta's reports in Feyralis and the Yeoman in Krysas. Without the portal, the Order is nearly blind to events in Feyralis."

Myronor chuffed humorlessly. "So they have to rely on the old methods of messages by couriers? Hardly seems worth the effort."

"They are concerned with more than just the portal to Feyralis," Kaikora said darkly. "There is the matter of her work to find Umbraxus as well."

Ice trickled down his spine as his thoughts went to the library. His thoughts lingered in that room on memories of a desperate need. Before the dark voice wrested away his mind, it had...influenced him to seek the library. And the instant he had stepped into the room, it claimed him as if waiting for that precise moment.

Myronor tried to recall the whisperings of the voice, the demands, the fears. But hazy with exhaustion, his mind struggled to piece together the fear burning in his chest with the anger reverberating through the ekath.

"Once you're rested, we must resume the search," Kaikora said in response to his wordless struggle. "Since you and Ophiera left Feyralis, the Brotherhood has grown bold. They openly attack those connected with the Order, systematically cutting off communications and supplies completely within the last few weeks. Without Pyra's portal to Rheta, the Order is blind to the Brotherhood's actions."

Portal.

Blind.

Brotherhood.

The words triggered something in his mind, forcing his next question out before he had time to consider it.

"What is the relation between the ichor and Umbraxus?"

Kaikora stared at him. "Why do you ask?"

Why did he ask? Why didn't she answer? *That* was a more relevant question, he thought. The shaman's knowledge always came at a cost, and this time, he hoped she'd accept his plea.

"When the darkness invaded my mind, I felt a connection. Almost like the ekath, but different. With Ophiera, I'm compatible...But with the ichor, everything in my being rejected the darkness. In this connection, I heard and felt *thoughts*, thoughts that contrasted with my own on every front. The conflict in ethos within my very soul tore me apart...But there was one thought we shared...one tangible *need* I felt in my own heart. We both sought the portal."

Kaikora remained silent for an uncomfortable amount of time. She wouldn't look at him and instead stared out the slitted windows to the darkened, quiet sea.

"The relation between the Aether and Erum is the same as the Void and Umbraxus," Kaikora said solemnly. "In that vein, the ichor is akin to the holy flames—a power originating from the world itself, requiring someone or something to wield it. Through Ophiera, the Aether becomes much more—the holy flames are a power that can give or take life, depending on *her*. The Phratries believe that is what the ichor is: the Void itself wielded by Aud and the Reverends of the Brotherhood."

It was as if Kaikora had dropped a weight on his chest. Myronor's mind raced to comprehend just how close he had been to succumbing to Aud. He wondered...when he had spanned in the past, had the presence lurking in the darkness been Aud this entire time?

"So...Aud seeks the portal to invade Erum?"

"It appears so," she said sadly. "The portals the Reverends produce are but glimpses—momentary breeches between our worlds, and at such terrible cost to the wielders. But with Pyra's portal, Aud could flow into this world and drown us in her darkness."

"Rheta is part of the order, yet not once did she mention Aud or the Brotherhood," Myronor said, rubbing his temples with his hands.

"It's likely she didn't know...or perhaps didn't care. She's always been one to focus more on the process than the results. She'd have helped Pyra with her research no matter the reason. So many of us in the Order are oblivious to others' involvement, motivations, or tasks."

"Except when it comes to Ophiera," Myronor said, recalling the tome, *The Paladins of the Cloister*, that Rheta had forced him to read. "Everyone seems to agree she's important."

Kaikora smiled sadly at him, clasping her thick hands together. "Ironically enough, yes; while Ophiera knew not of the Ashen Order, nearly every member of it knows of her. The Yeoman believes she is the key to destroying the ichor and thus the Brotherhood...even whilst she has been wholly unaware of herself."

"That seems rather unfair—"

"It is," Kaikora interrupted bitterly. "But it is also necessary. We all think the truth is the ultimate answer. But no one recognizes that the truth requires proper timing—proper context. Like a cub weaned from its mother, people must be weaned from the lies before they can digest the truth. It is exhausting, aggravating, and painful at times, but it must be done. Even if it means withholding knowledge from those I care about."

Again, an uncomfortable silence fell between them. He realized he was acting rather hypocritical, having withheld information from Ophiera himself. If he had told her about his mother's research from the start, would they be where they were now?

"I don't think Ophiera will forgive me," Myronor admitted sadly.

Kaikora chuckled softly, which, for her, sounded nearly like a growl. "We're lucky the Aether does not see lying as a sin, else we would all be anathemas, Ophiera included. But I believe one can lie to protect, to shield, to endure, for another. One can lie to someone yet still love them greatly."

Myronor felt a lump form in his throat and looked out to the balcony. Ophiera was out of sight and out of reach through the ekath. Silenced still, he didn't know if she was being harassed or comforted by that abysmal excuse of a captain.

"Why *is* Jasper here?" he asked Kaikora.

"I told you, he was assigned to me."

"But why did he agree?"

"The same reason we are all here," Kaikora smirked. "Her."

A cry of rage tore both their gazes to the balcony. Kaikora stood, trident raised and at the ready. On the terrace, Myronor watched as Jasper's body sailed through the air across the balcony, landing hard against the stone. As the rogue righted himself, Myronor watched him withdraw two curved daggers and brace himself, crossing them over his chest. A blur of white hair and green cloth charged into view, and Ophiera's cry rang louder than the clash of her claymore against crossed blades.

~ Twenty Three ~

DEMARCATION

Steadied by the weight of her blade in hand, Ophiera took in a shaky breath of the dark sea breeze. Though she was as far from the flickering light of the living space window as the wrapping balcony allowed, it wasn't nearly far enough.

Longingly, she gazed out to sea, searching for any semblance of calm in the lonely moonlit waters. As she leaned over the stone banister between two over-fruited white yuzu trees, she breathed in the salty air and the familiar citrus scent. Everything around her was a recipe for calm, and she very much needed it to quell the disquiet of her heart. Still, nothing calmed her like the swing of her sword.

With a firm grip on her claymore, Ophiera scanned the dark, empty terrace, searching for anything that could withstand a blow. But out on the balcony, she only found moonlit planters with overgrown yuzu trees spilling forth. Such beautiful plants did not deserve her ire, though *someone* certainly did.

The shaman may have had *reasons* for her choices, but justification did not equate to forgiveness. And while Ophiera may have demanded her questions be answered, now she was left reeling in the details she'd yet to comprehend. Would she have really destroyed Iluka? But the single person she'd thought she could turn to for clarity had been just as deceitful as everyone else.

How many other secrets had Myronor kept from her? He was her charge and ekath, yet even with their souls connected, she had missed the truth.

Why was she always the last to know?

Because ye never ask, lass.

Even in her subconscious. Lotus's voice spoke the truth she didn't wish to hear.

Obtusely following orders her entire life had blinded Ophiera to most everything outside the tunnel of their will. She had allowed the Cloister and the Magistrate to beat away her curiosity and replace it with compliance. And yet, even in her retirement, in her moment of rebellion, she hadn't bothered to learn or change. Perhaps she preferred not to know. Maybe she preferred not to choose.

Just when she had finally chosen the path of retirement, the Magistrate had forced her back into conscription. After choosing to save Myronor's life, she'd still ended up Oath-bound to escort and protect him. She'd chosen to take the long road to Iluka, ending only with the Brotherhood abducting Myronor from under her nose. She'd chosen to leave Myronor in Berwyn's hands, only to end up in Krysas with him now. And just hours ago, she'd embraced her power as an Aspect, only to discover that, in reality, she hadn't had a choice in anything.

Against the sounds of distant waves, her ear caught a near-silent scuffle on the stone ground. Out of her periphery, she saw a distortion of air in the monochrome moonslight. And just when she was ready to shake off her paranoia, a familiar scent of leather wafted along the sea breeze.

"Leave me alone," she growled into the night.

And for a moment, the night held still. But as Jasper materialized beside her, she knew there would be no peace found tonight. He watched her with an amused expression, his amber eyes surprisingly vibrant in the dark.

"I find it quite remarkable how easily you detect me," he muttered.

"Is that intended to be a compliment?" she bit back.

"Do you wish it to be?" He asked, sidling next to her.

"As I said, I wish to be alone."

"Which is confusing, considering how upset you are after being excluded."

Ophiera glared at Jasper, annoyed by the way he crossed his arms and stared out at the ocean. The moonlight silvered his dark curls, and the sea breeze carried the scent of his leather overcoat.

"I'm upset for being deceived."

He laughed wryly. "Again, confusing, given the company you keep. What else is to be expected from an innatural?"

"Don't call him that!" She spat. While she truthfully didn't grasp the full meaning of the word, the venom with which Jasper spoke made it clear it was offensive.

"Are you still going to defend him after everything he's done?"

"You have no place to judge me or him after what *you've* done."

Silence fell between them as they both glared at the sea, avoiding each other's gaze.

Ophiera had hoped to find calm in the quiet, but a draw was never very satisfactory. Her life had been a never-ending conflict, and Jasper somehow knew precisely how to stoke the fires. She wanted nothing more than to escape into solitude, to be alone with her thoughts and emotions until she could sort them out. But the young rogue remained, silently brooding beside her.

For a moment, she closed her eyes and pretended she was alone. It wasn't hard, given the stillness in which Jasper stood. In her mind, she saw herself alone, sitting upon her dock outside Iluka. Each night she spent on land, she held vigil looking out on that moonlit sea. Yet again, her attempt for peace, even imagined, only ended in discourse.

Her cottage no longer existed. She had destroyed her home and any chance of returning to that dock.

"For such a stoic woman, you truly wear every emotion on your face," Jasper whispered against her ear.

"Is that another poor attempt at a compliment?"

He chuckled in her ear, his shoulder brushing against hers. "I'm not sure it's a compliment...to be as readable as a scroll."

Ophiera held her breath a moment, deciding if it was worth taking the bait. And while she had been searching for peace, she realized now where she found relief.

"Literacy and comprehension are two distinct skills," she bit back. "Just because you can read me doesn't mean you know me."

"Oh, I think I know you quite well, *Warden*," he said in a deep voice, dripping in sarcasm.

"You know nothing!" Ophiera growled, hoping to contain the sear of shame that tore at her chest upon hearing that title.

"I know you were exceptionally irritated with me a moment ago before calming a bit and then becoming distracted by some thought or memory behind closed eyes. Whatever it was, your posture changed quite dramatically. So what are you feeling so guilty about?"

She bit her lips, trying to hide her annoyance with how close he fell to the truth.

"If you know me so damn well, why don't you tell me?"

Jasper chuckled, the sound reverberating far too close to her ear.

"My guess is some self-righteous nonsense of the kind only paladins could torture themselves with. Perhaps you're feeling guilty for failing to save Iluka?"

"Close, but not quite right."

"Tell me where I'm wrong, then," he purred.

But where *she* was wrong was more relevant.

On the *Berserker*, Ophiera never told Jasper that *she* was the one who had leveled Iluka. At the time, she withheld information to keep her and Myronor safe and blamed the entirety of Iluka's destruction on the Brotherhood. Yet she stood on this balcony, furious with Kaikora and Myronor for withholding secrets when she had done much the same. And not only from Jasper.

"I destroyed Iluka," she confessed. "The Brotherhood may have claimed their souls, but I wiped the village off the map. I lost control of the Aether, and if it hadn't been for Myronor...well, I don't know if I could have been stopped. And yet, even after all of that, I don't feel guilty for failing to save Iluka—I feel guilty for destroying *my* home."

Jasper stood silently for some time, allowing time for the self-loathing to sink in. She mourned the loss of her home, yet had taken more from everyone else. Jasper, Myronor, Kaikora...they'd called Iluka home, too.

"I suppose you're not as self-righteous as I thought."

"I'm purely selfish."

"That's not a bad thing—selfishness is key to survival," he said with a dark chuckle. "Though I admit, this does explain a lot."

"What do you mean?"

"I now know why you have such an unhealthy fixation with controlling the holy flames."

If her jaw hadn't been clenched quite so tightly, it might have dropped to the floor. "Didn't you hear me? I reduced Iluka to a *crater...by accident!*"

"Precisely. And you let the fear of that mistake nearly prevent you from saving the one you claim to love. That seems like a control problem if I've ever seen one."

"And what the hell do you know of control?" she hissed.

"I know when to cut my losses," he said, plucking a white yuzu fruit from the overladen tree. "And when to let the currents take me."

She watched as he rolled the palm-sized fruit back and forth in his hand, balancing it on the tips of his fingers all the way back to his wrist. The motion was as rhythmic and consistent as the ocean. And nearly as calming.

"'Only the lost drift with the waves,'" Ophiera whispered.

Jasper smiled. "Ah, you can't use a proverb against me without finishing it."

She didn't speak, silently admitting she had forgotten the remainder. The captain smiled dangerously. "The full saying goes, 'only the lost drift with the waves, but battling the winds ends in torn sails.'"

Ophiera chewed her cheek, annoyed at Jasper and herself. Avoiding his gaze, she fixated on the rolling fruit in Jasper's hand that suddenly stilled as he wrapped his gloved hand over the pale rind.

"See, the harder you try to control something, the harder you tend to grasp it. And the harder you grasp something..."

He tossed the fruit at her, and instinctively, her hand shot out to catch it. As her scarred fingers closed around the cool, waxy skin, the citrus ruptured in her grasp. She hadn't noticed how over-ripened the fruits were until the pale, shimmering juice ran between her knuckles and down her wrist.

"The less you hold," Jasper murmured, taking her wrist in his hand. She let him pull her cold, sticky fist between them, his breath warm against her soaked knuckles. "Keep squeezing, and you'll be left with nothing. Nothing but the knowledge that you, and only you, caused the mess now slipping through your fingers."

With a precise squeeze, his middle finger dug between two tendons in her wrist. The pressure point forced her hand to go limp, releasing the remnants of the mangled fruit. It hit the ground with a sickening thud. His words were gentle, unlike his grip, and though he made his point as clear as the moonlight, she hated him for all of it.

"Don't pretend to understand who I am or what I've done," she hissed.

"I don't need to pretend," he said, drawing even closer. His warm breath and bright eyes mesmerized her as the scent of leather and sea salt filled her lungs. "Few understand the self-hatred that comes with destroying what you tried to protect."

"And you do?"

"Yes," he whispered before grazing his lips against her cold, sticky fingers. "Can't you sense how we *feel* the same?"

The sensation of his warm tongue over her fingertips felt like nothing she'd ever felt before. She didn't understand *why* the way he sucked the juices from her hand felt so alluring and alarming at once. His eyes never left hers as he ran his tongue down her palm, pressing her hand against his soft lips.

"I feel the pain of your soul, Ophiera. And I know the mage will never understand the depth of that pain...or what it takes to control it."

At the mention of Myronor, a fire roared to life within her. With a shiver, she twisted her wrist away, glaring at amber eyes crinkled in a smirk.

"You preach of control," she hissed, "yet you dare overstep again?"

"Is it an overstep when you could have stopped me at any moment?"

"Don't answer me with a question!"

"I thought it might help relieve some tension," he chuckled. "But I can see I've only caused more."

"I told you not to touch me!"

"You told me it was *foolish* to touch you," he said unflinchingly. "And I never claimed to be smart."

With a roar of the Aether beneath her, Ophiera gripped the collar of Jasper's leather overcoat. His eyes widened, and she found his shock far more satisfying than his touch. The only thought burning through her mind was that she wished for him to be as far away from her as possible. And the next thing she knew, she found herself heaving him away with a strength that surprised Ophiera most.

As Jasper rolled across the balcony, she felt a moment of guilt for responding so violently. Only a moment, though. The rogue gracefully recovered into a crouching position as he pulled two curved blades from beneath his coat. Brandishing the blades, she might have resisted his challenge had he not worn a smug grin beneath his burning eyes. Whatever regret she may have witnessed behind those eyes on the night she'd spared his life was gone now.

Without a second thought, she reached for her claymore and dashed across the balcony, the green dress flowing behind her as fury propelled her forward. A battle cry was the singular warning to him before she swung the golden blade down hard.

The clang of metal cut through the night air. Though Jasper blocked the attack with crossed knives, the force of her swing dropped him to a knee. His grin remained frustratingly intact.

"I didn't realize my tongue was so sinful it required retribution," he taunted before twisting free of their deadlock.

Growling while regaining her footing, Ophiera moved for another swing, but like the navarra, he was far out of reach of her counter. Rising to a stand, he flourished his blades again, beckoningly.

The man seemingly wished for death.

Silently, Ophiera adjusted her grip on the claymore, studying his posture and resisting the urge to charge again. He had already proven himself a skilled fighter with questionable morals. Nothing he had done thus far was truly a sin, at least in the eyes of the Aether, so despite her instincts, she couldn't strike him down. And yet, she felt more slighted by his transgressions than most anathema she'd crossed paths with before.

"Or perhaps you're just angry about how much you enjoyed the feel of my mouth on your skin."

The way his lips quirked up at the sides served only to infuriate her more. With sword raised high, she charged again. A deafening ring echoed from the stone cliff as he parried her away to his side. The strength of his defense threw off her footing, catching herself in the tangle of skirts.

He laughed, relaxing his stance as if declaring the end of the bout. But Ophiera wasn't about to let a slip of her balance end this exchange. Using the momentum of her fall and the weight of her sword, she counterbalanced to a twirl. Swinging her sword horizontally, this time straight towards his chest.

She smiled as his eyes widened in shock. The cur had no time to pull his blades to block, but instead, bent backward from the hips. She felt the slightest vibration through her blade as it passed just over his chest and head, slicing through the air.

Jasper exhaled as he straightened his spine, glaring at her darkly. With a twirl of his blade, he tucked it up against his wrist as he inspected the collar of his leather overcoat. Now she saw what her blade had touched; he stuck two fingers through the gash, a scowl replacing the foolish grin.

"And here I thought you cared for nothing," Ophiera taunted.

He readjusted his knife to face her, rolling his shoulders as he assumed a new stance. "Perhaps you should take your own advice and not pretend to know who I am or what I care for."

In a blur of black, he lunged for her quicker than before. Had he been holding back his speed? But as she braced herself for his attack, his body melded into the night. Blood rushed in her ears, muffling the sounds of his movements. Her eyes darted, searching for any sign of distortion or displacement, but she appeared alone on the balcony.

"Only a coward hides!" She hissed, spinning on her heel.

"Another trait we have in common," his voice whispered beside her.

She swung her body and blade, only to face the empty balcony yet again. In the light cast by the hearth inside, she watched the slitted shadows, hoping to catch his movements.

"You and I are nothing alike!" She growled into the empty night. "I may let fear cloud my judgments, but I have the spine to follow through with my choices! You couldn't even see this fight to the end."

A sudden blow to her chest sent her tumbling backward towards the dark stone ground. The scent of sea salt and leather lingered in her nostrils before she slammed hard onto the ground, knocking the air from her lungs. Blood coated her mouth as she tried to draw breath, a bitten tongue the least of her worries.

Still seemingly alone, Ophiera leveraged the last of her strength in another blind swing. An invisible force abruptly halted her arm, the feel of leather gloves wrapping around both her wrists. With a sudden pinch, her sword clanged to the ground as both of Ophiera's hands fell limp.

Though her breath returned, a heavy weight pressed down on her, forcing her to hiss. She wasn't surprised as Jasper uncloaked himself, his dark curls brushing her forehead as he loomed over her. She struggled to free herself, but he only pressed his hips harder against her own, pinning her to the ground. "Do you know whose fault it is that I care for nothing?" Jasper asked, his breath hot against her face.

The pain in his voice fed the guilt in her heart, and for a moment, she heeded her struggle. His eyes fell again to the same expression of a boy in a boat, floating in a sea of horror and regret. The hands holding her down against the stone trembled now, and she wondered if that, too, was her fault.

"I was more than content to live without ever *feeling* like this again," he said, his hair dancing in the breeze against her cheek. "But then I witnessed a consort go berserk to destroy a navarra with her bare, flaming fist. You had that same look in your eyes, a deadly fire that rivaled that which I witnessed on the beach of Iluka years ago."

Suddenly, Jasper's weight atop her filled her with something more than fury. She didn't wish to hear any more of her shame. With all the strength she could muster, she bucked her hips. But he pressed down in response even harder, his lips nearly touching her own as he laughed.

"It's the same look you had moments ago, charging toward me with a golden blade. That look...it's like nothing I've witnessed, Ophiera. And now, all I *feel* is a craving to see that fire again and again."

His lips brushed against hers, revealing his intentions. She didn't understand how the battle had become a confession. A confession that made her feel dirty and used.

Jasper didn't *care* for her; he only sought to use her. Just like the Magistrate...and the Cloister. And the Brotherhood...and the Order...*Everyone* sought to use her. Where was her say in any of the matters at hand?

With a quick jerk of her neck, Ophiera crashed her forehead violently into the captain's encroaching nose. Blood spurted from his nostrils as he reeled backward, cupping his face. One bloody hand that freed her own scarred one.

In a flash of white, she allowed the scars to ignite, heeding the Aether's fury. Jasper's eyes became molten copper in the light, terrified as he watched the flames travel up her shoulder. She bucked him from her before allowing the flames to overtake her in full, disintegrating the green dress to ash.

As the Aether seared around her, she dragged herself upright. She took a fiery step forward toward the young captain, now on his knees. Illuminated in white, flickering light, she saw his knives had fallen beside him. And in Jasper's wide eyes, she saw her reflection: an enflamed white terror dancing against tearful amber irises. For the first time since awakening, she *saw* herself. And for the first time in her life, she owned herself. She was an Aspect—the Aether itself embodied.

"Isn't this precisely what you *craved*?" She hissed, her voice warped by the fires surrounding her.

Unblinking, Jasper shook his head from side to side, tears streaking his blood-drained cheeks. A small part of her heart cooled to his plight, smoldering from fury to pity.

"*This* is who I am," she growled over the roar of the flames. "Not a consort, not a paladin, not a scroll for you to read, nor someone for you to toy with! I *am* the fire you see behind my eyes! To crave me is to crave death! So, embrace the survivor you claim to be, and yield."

Jasper nodded, closing his eyes and collapsing to the ground. Accepting his surrender, Ophiera extinguished. Relieved of pain and fire, she took a slow, steadying breath. The cool sea breeze soothed her bare skin, and she realized with a jolt that the dress Collette had lent her lay in ashes about her feet. She stood bare above the trembling rogue, still collapsed on the ground below.

The ekath tugged her attention away from Jasper. Slowly, she turned and met the intensity of Myronor's stare. Though he leaned heavily on his staff, bearing torn robes and a gaunt face, there was something powerful behind his eyes as he watched her. She couldn't understand the emotion reverberating through the ekath. But with a quirk of his lips and a stare that burned through her very soul, she found her answer.

~ Twenty Four ~

REFERENDUM

Hours passed slowly as Ophiera watched the gentle snores escape Myronor's parted lips. Every rise and fall of his bare chest sapped away some of her tension, though not enough to allow her to join him in rest.

Following her outburst on the balcony, Kaikora volunteered to tend to Jasper while she and Myronor tended to themselves. Ophiera, in need of clothing, and Myronor, in need of rest, managed to find the master bedroom of the abode. Pyra's former bedroom.

Dressed now in a worn pair of trousers and the cream linen shirt borrowed from her sleeping charge, she kept silent vigil over his exhausted body and soul. It was easy enough to blame the ekath for drawing her to him at this moment, but in truth, *her* soul needed this closeness more than his.

Absentmindedly, she circled her fingers over the raised scar between her breasts. While the ekath was invisible, the marks left by the Brotherhood were not. In the breaking dawn light, Myronor's scars appeared evident to her, shining slightly against his otherwise unblemished skin. Different scars from different Reverends, she had memorized each and every one of them as she swore retribution for their placement.

The fact that Marvena still drew breath irritated her far more than Jasper's foolishness. While she wished she'd never let him get under her skin, she supposed it was for the best in the end. There was no longer any question whether she could control the Aether's fury now. Which meant nothing would hold her back from seeking out Marvena and freeing the wretched soul from the ashes of her corpse.

The ichor was the trail left to follow, the proof of Aud's encroachment on Erum. And while Ophiera had focused so much of her attention on Marvena, the ichor would continue to grow with or without the latest Reverend. The plague of the Brotherhood needed to be exterminated.

Opening and closing her fist, Ophiera felt her Oath arm itch. For the first time since receiving them, she saw her scars without disdain. Her entire existence had been spent fighting for and against the Aether. A constant conflict, inside and out. But no longer.

Myronor lay before her, alive and well, because she now chose to accept what fate had bestowed upon her. She now chose to fight *with* the Aether rather than against it. Like denying the bond of her soul and the love in her heart, fighting the fires of her scars had proven futile.

Jasper's taunts lingered in her mind. She'd wasted so much time fearing what she might destroy when, indeed, destruction was her only path to salvation. Before, she'd thought the only way to save a soul was to heal the body that harbored it. And while the rites of Mercy had been exceptionally useful in her life, she hadn't understood how Retribution could be equal in its potential for deliverance.

When she'd felt the first Reverend's skin blister and char beneath her flaming hand, she had saved the souls of many future victims, had she not? How many more would she save by destroying the Marvena? Or by ending the Brotherhood? Or better yet, by destroying Aud? There was no need for Retribution if Erum's souls were otherwise protected.

Footsteps sounded in the hallway, and Ophiera recognized the shaman's heavy gait. With a sigh, she leaned back in the chair and closed her eyes. Perhaps if the shaman thought she was asleep, she'd leave her to rest, keeping whatever storm she carried at bay.

"Come to the library," Kaikora whispered from the doorway. Ophiera remained silent, pointlessly hopeful. The shaman waited almost a shameful amount of time before speaking again.

"It's clear you are not asleep."

With hopes dashed, Ophiera opened her eyes, gazing back at Myronor. She was almost certain she saw his lips quirk in the corners.

"I'd rather not leave his side," she whispered back to Kaikora.

"He cannot help you make your decision."

Ophiera's eyes snapped to the shaman. The sight of her still drew rage from Ophiera despite the explanations provided.

"And what decision do you believe I'm making?"

The shaman's tired eyes fell to her scarred arm, and a gentle smile stretched across her full lips. "Whom deserves your Retribution next, of course."

Without waiting for a response, Kaikora turned and left, her heavy steps falling quiet as she descended downstairs. For a few moments, Ophiera sat in the bedroom chair, watching Myronor stir restlessly. Perhaps her agitation now contaminated his peaceful slumber, and with a reluctant sigh, she decided to take her frustrations with her to the library.

The tether tugged gently as she descended the stairs, leaving behind her an invisible trailing thread back to her ekath. As she passed the clawed windows in the living space, Ophiera found Jasper lingering outside on the balcony. Leaning against the stone banister, the rising sun silhouetting his stance, Jasper sat slumped and defeated.

As she watched him, it appeared as if he shrank in on himself. Only when his shoulders began to tremble did she realize her presence caused this response. Guilt seared her throat as she turned her back on the rogue and continued toward the library.

While she didn't regret setting boundaries, she did wonder if perhaps there may have been a more civilized approach other than threatening him with white flames. Though given his persistence, it was unlikely he'd have heeded anything else. If he refused to look at her now, he certainly wouldn't touch her again. Why, then, did she feel so horrible?

Ophiera entered the library just as the sun broke the horizon. Warm light spilled into the atrium from the multi-story windows facing out to sea. Illuminated before a window, Kaikora stood cross-armed, staring up at the endless shelves of tomes and tables. Though Ophiera crossed the room loudly to stand beside her, the shaman paid her little mind. Waiting for her to speak, the shaman instead stared off in silence; it was as if Ophiera wasn't there at all.

"What is the point of asking me here if you're going to ignore me?" Ophiera mused.

The shaman sighed. "When one is burdened with the sight, it's easy to forget about one's voice."

"Imagine having neither."

Kaikora winced against the bite of Ophiera's words but recovered quickly with a smirk. "I believe all of Krysas heard your voice, loud and clear on the balcony.

"Assuming you *recall* how to listen, I suggest heeding my words then, too."

The shaman remained silent for a moment, studying the exceptional view offered by the library.

"Warden, I know—"

"Don't," Ophiera interrupted with a growl. "The title feels more like a curse coming from your lips."

Kaikora took a deep breath. "I know you are frustrated with me."

"*Frustrated* is an inadequate description of how I feel."

"I am sorry."

"That, too, is inadequate," Ophiera hissed.

"I know—"

"Don't you always!"

Kaikora rolled her lips, the calm façade finally breaking. And in that, Ophiera found...comfort.

"As you say, I always know. But I want—no, I *need* you to know...I'm sorry."

A trickle of ice ran down Ophiera's throat, settling in the darkest pit of her stomach.

"I warned the village of the attack the day before the Brotherhood arrived. Many listened and fled, but you know the coastlander's ways," Kaikora continued as her voice deepened with a shiver. "Those who remained behind knew what fate they faced. And they faced it with honor. But honor means little to the dead. Not a night has passed that I do not hear their screams across the dunes. I can still feel the air as their souls were ripped from Erum."

Warm tears trickled down Ophiera's cheeks before she even knew she wept. It had been too easy for her to hate Kaikora in her absence when she didn't know when she needed someone to blame. But now, all she could feel was sorrow.

"Ophiera, I want to respect their choices...But I know in the end, the choice was mine. *I* chose their fates. And now I live with the burden of their lost souls."

Hearing Kaikora's confession sapped away much of the anger she had used to bury the despair. No amount of apologies or explanations could bring Iluka back.

For so long now, Ophiera had pined after the freedom of choice. Yet until this moment, she hadn't truly appreciated the burden of Kaikora's decisions. Trained by the Phratries, Kaikora had lived with the burden of choice not only for her fate but for each soul she encountered in the Southern Coastlands.

For Iluka, the village shaman and Sea Warden were two sides of the same oar. It was the way of the Southern Coastlands and would remain so, even if they no longer had a village to protect. To blame Kaikora and Kaikora alone for Iluka would be to shift the blame from herself. And as Jasper had said, true cowards only hide from the truth. *She* was the Warden. And she had failed.

They had both failed.

"The burdens of Iluka were always shared between us," Ophiera said, wiping her face dry again. "So shall be its demise."

Kaikora sniffed, her gray eyes fixated on the ground. And Ophiera wasn't sure which was more disturbing, the tears that wetted the stone below the shaman's formidable shadow or the lack of words she had in response. For some time, they lingered in the charged silence.

"Thank you," Kaikora whispered.

"I've done nothing worth praise."

"It is appreciation for providing me with that which I cannot provide myself." Ophiera blinked, trying to recall what she had provided the shaman in this conversation beyond ire and sorrow. A massive, cool hand squeezed her shoulder. "Forgiveness, Ophiera."

Ophiera smiled sadly, her mind flashing to the notices in Cantheas. "Can it truly be forgiveness when we are both guilty of so much? Even the Magistrate finds us in equal contempt."

"Your judgment means more to me than that of the Magistrate," Kaikora said, lifting her hand from Ophiera's shoulder. "Besides, I'm quite convinced Tanvik's leadership truly lacks vision."

"In regard to the Brotherhood?" Ophiera asked.

Kaikora laughed deeply. "In regard to everything. Did you see how they described us in the postings? Yes, we are both tall and muscular, yet I'm a good head taller than you and in far better shape. They didn't even mention my tattoos."

Ophiera snorted, the closest she could manage to a laugh. She wasn't certain how the bitterness she had held towards Kaikora could dissipate from her heart so quickly. Was that all forgiveness meant?

"Perhaps their inaccuracies will only make it harder to find us," Ophiera said. "And perhaps, if I can take Marvena alive, we can prove our innocence."

"You know it won't be that simple."

"I can hope," Ophiera breathed.

"Not anymore," Kaikora said solemnly.

The shaman turned and stepped away without a word. At first, Ophiera only followed her with her eyes, watching as she stepped out through the center, slitted window to the balcony beyond. Kaikora welcomed the sunlight with open arms, her dark tattoos glistening in the burning light. There, she lingered, waiting for Ophiera to make her choice.

Myronor's side was the only place she wished to be right now, yet her scars tingled as she watched the shaman give praise to the sea. As Kaikora said, decisions must be made, and she was done running from fate.

Ophiera joined the shaman on the balcony, relieved Jasper no longer occupied the far end. Leaning over the stone banister, she contemplated the view in the light before speaking.

"I wish to find Marvena," Ophiera said.

"And do you know where she is?" Kaikora asked.

"I don't...but I feel something; a draw, a purpose, a delusion, I don't know...something more than my Oath, or ekath drew me to Krysas, and now it draws me elsewhere."

"There are many powers at play here," Kaikora sighed. "You may hunt Marvena, but remember, it has always been the Brotherhood that has hunted you. They desire your soul, remember?"

Ophiera sniffed, straightening her spine. She hadn't considered the pursuit of the Brotherhood beyond protecting her charge. But in reality, they had continually made attempts on her life since her conscription. Had she been blindly following the bait into a trap?

"All I desire is to feel the grit of their ash between my fingertips. So, their *wants* are of no consequence to me."

"And what of the Cloister's wants, or task rather?" Kaikora asked. "You escorted the Ambassador, yes, but are you not Oathbound to uncover Pyra's fate? How will they view you running amok, chasing after Aud's followers when your Oath to the Magistrate remains unfulfilled?"

Chewing her lip, Ophiera glared at the minute shadows cast by her raised, blistered scars. Kaikora spoke the words she herself faltered on every time she thought of her future. Nostalgia seeped into her heart, recalling similar conversations that had taken place back in Iluka. Always wise, always knowledgeable, the shaman had never provided her clear direction, only questioned and prodded until she'd chosen on her own.

Many powers at play, indeed, she thought to herself. If the Magistrate sought her for Iluka's demise, how would they respond if she ignored her duty further? And the Cloister...she dared not think of the punishments awaiting her for abandonment.

Yet another factor weighed in her mind now, quelling the fear brought on by thoughts of the Cloister. No longer could Ophiera deny the draw of the Aether. Like the ekath pulling her heart back to Myronor, she felt a burning thread leading her toward retribution. Whether that draw was simply her Oath or something far more meaningful, Ophiera accepted that she may never know. But when it came to Pyra and the Brotherhood, the burning wrath beneath her scars was finally settling on a choice.

"I believe where I find the Brotherhood, I will find answers regarding Pyra. Her involvement with the Order and Aud's desire to obtain her research have only confirmed every instinct I've felt regarding the late Ambassador. To search for one is as good as searching for the other."

"So you will pursue Pyra?"

"I will fulfill my Oath while satiating my need for retribution," she replied. "For now, the paths are shared."

The shaman placed a hand on her shoulder and squeezed gently. "And what of paths unshared by your Oath or the Aether?"

"What do you mean?"

"My path is clear as well, Ophiera. The Order needs to access the portal before Aud. Without the holy flames at our fingertips, it is the only way *we* can combat the Brotherhood."

"Then you and I will go our separate ways again," Ophiera shrugged. "You're only tolerable in small doses, anyway."

The shaman laughed throatily. "I'm glad to see his sense of humor has rubbed off on you. However, Myronor must also be considered in these choices. What do you think his choice will be? To follow you toward Pyra or to seek the portals he so desperately clings to?"

"What does the sight show you?" Ophiera asked, unwilling to consider the meaning beneath Kaikora's questions.

"Nothing," she said with a warble in her voice. "It increasingly fails me as Aud's presence grows in Erum. The ichor acts like spilled ink across pages of a book. Whole chapters are illegible, and even when I manage to find a clean page, the ink creeps in yet again. I can only glimpse pieces of a story I no longer understand."

The shaman had never held a more hopeless expression in her gray gaze. Yet somehow, knowing the sight held little sway over their decisions felt relieving in a curious way. What lay ahead was truly of their own making, which meant the options were limitless.

"Whatever paths we take, they will lead to Aud's end."

"And what if those paths separate?" Kaikora asked quietly.

"You once told me the mother clans used the ekatma to ally clans across great distances, didn't you?" Ophiera asked, despite how her heart ached at the thought.

"Yes," Kaikora said. "But those were bonds built over decades; I cannot know how yours might respond."

But Ophiera did know.

When she'd abandoned Myronor onboard the *Mistrel*, it wasn't only grief that had prevented her from eating and sleeping. Looking back, she recognized the heavy drag the ekath placed on her soul—a constant aching yearning for him and him alone.

I felt the same. And it dreads me to think of going through that again.

Ophiera started against his voice, brushing through her mind. How long had he been awake, listening to her thoughts and conversation? Despite being on opposite ends of the cliffside, she followed his whirling mind in perfect clarity...images of Berwyn's trembling hands as he handed over a written note, blurred now to an empty rowboat cast upon a sandy shore.

It won't happen again, she thought gently. *This time, we decide our paths together.*

~ Twenty Five ~

DIVERGENCE

For the past hour, Ophiera had fought a losing battle. Against the warmth of the hearth and the droning of conversation, she could not win against her drooping eyelids.

Tonight was the third and final evening she, Jasper, Kaikora, and Myronor convened around the small table in the living space of the Embassy to discuss their next steps. Naturally, much of what was discussed revolved around the ever-mysterious actions of the late Pyra Ebontide.

Kaikora and Myronor exchanged most of the secrets and knowledge while Ophiera and Jasper listened. She wasn't sure why the shaman demanded *all* of their presence, but at least Ophiera didn't have to participate. The constant verbal circles between the mage and shaman exhausted her. At first, she'd tried to keep track of the details surrounding Rheta's precise role in Pyra's research, the more excellent intentions of the Order, and the flurry of events leading up to her conscription. But she was quickly lost within the network of secrets and details. Her mind only had so much room left in it, and at the moment, it was filled with only one trepidatious purpose.

We can take more time to decide, Ophiera. We don't have to do this tonight.

Ophiera pinched herself to keep her eyes open. Though Myronor was gesturing toward a hand-drawn map and answering Kaikora's endless questions, his heart was always with hers. He was now quite adept at multitasking with the ekath open, but it still cost some of his concentration. She could see his brow furrowed uncharacteristically as he argued with Kaikora, tripping over a few of his words while waiting for her reply.

Time is precisely why there is little other choice, my charge. Unless you've discovered a better solution since last night, this is our only path.

She knew he only delayed in hopes of finding another solution, despite his heart knowing it did not exist. But what they decided today needed to be a mutual decision, not just her own. She needed him to be sure.

As Kaikora growled something about sands and wielders of something, Myronor's resolve shook through the ekath. Their paths were decided then.

Now, they simply needed to convince the other two.

While Myronor continued arguing with Kaikora about some nuance of imbuteria magic, Ophiera turned her attention to Jasper. Seated opposite her at the table, Jasper twirled his knife in gloved hands, eyes fixated on the hearth across the room. This had been his vigil every night they gathered for these lengthy discussions. Though he had yet to look Ophiera in the face or speak to her since their *disagreement*, he at least no longer cowered in her presence.

The steady and delicate movements of his blade in hand were quite mesmerizing. He wasn't even paying attention, and yet he moved his fingers with a speed she'd struggle to match on a good day. No wonder he had been able to find her pressure points so quickly and precisely.

She shifted in her chair, uncomfortably reminded of how his body had felt pressed against hers out on the balcony. At least she was confident that whatever misguided infatuation he held before had burned up along with the borrowed dress. Whatever his feelings were now, hatred or disgust, they would undoubtedly make the discussion tonight even more awkward.

"Well, we've talked in circles enough," Myronor finally said, ending the argument between himself and Kaikora. "It's time to decide our next move."

All attention fell on Myronor now as his eyes bore into hers. The emotions reverberating through the ekath were more than enough to keep Ophiera awake now. Together, they had come to this decision, and together, they would make their case.

"After everything we've learned of Aud, the Brotherhood, the Order, and Pyra, there are two paths left before us," Myronor said, casually flipping the pages of his journal. "The first is to search for Pyra, whether alive or dead, and uncover her fate. This may lead us to understanding her research and locating the portals with any luck. The second path is to instead stay put and attempt to decipher her research in the library whilst searching for the portal."

Kaikora leaned forward. "I agree; those are the only paths left to us. And if we are to choose one, then it must be to remain and search for the portals. The Order *needs* information and aid from Feyralis. Without Rheta, we have been woefully in the dark against the Brotherhood these last few months. It is far more pressing and feasible to search her library for the portal to Feyralis."

Jasper stilled his knife. "Of course, I will do what I am paid to do, but it seems a bit foolish to wander in the dark. Wouldn't it be best to simply find Pyra herself?"

"Unless she truly is dead," Kaikora countered, "in which case we would waste precious time."

Ophiera sighed, her eyes still connected to Myronor's faltering gaze. "There is the issue of my Oath. I am still bound by Cloister and Magistrate to investigate Pyra's death. I do not know what ramifications, by-laws or flames, will befall me if I abandon my task."

"You're still hung up on that Oath business?" Jasper asked, sitting up. "That must be some conditioning the Cloister put you through."

It didn't surprise Ophiera entirely that the first words from Jasper's mouth were rude and callous. What did surprise her, however, was her inability to speak against it.

Her hands went suddenly numb at the thought of the Cloister. Memories of a dark cell and hot chains flickered through her mind. But those punishments, however harsh, were nothing compared to what would happen if the Chaplain were to find her...

A tug through the tether pulled her from dark memories back to a sky-blue gaze. Though Myronor frowned, having felt her emotions as she was lost in reverie, she knew it wasn't *at* her but rather *for* her. He understood why she must obey her Oath even if...even if she didn't fully understand her own compulsion.

"Don't speak on things you know nothing about," Kaikora growled to Jasper. "This is a choice Ophiera must make."

"Doesn't sound like she has a choice, or did I misinterpret the meaning of an oath?" Jasper added, rolling his eyes.

"None of us truly has any freedom in this matter," Myronor said in a voice laced with frustration. "The bottom line is, Erum is in peril. We know Aud encroaches ever steadfastly, threatening our world with darkness. And with knowledge comes responsibility. There is no longer time to dally. Which is why..." he swallowed, pausing a moment. "Our only option is to divide and conquer."

While the necessity and truth of their future hurt to hear, Ophiera felt some relief at the finality. The path ahead was clearly laid; now, it was up to Kaikora and Jasper how they wanted to proceed.

"You're suggesting splitting up?" Jasper chuffed, rocking back in his chair. "I thought you two couldn't leave each other's sight because of the spirit rope business?"

"*Ekath*," Kaikora cut in. "And they can separate—we just don't know how far or how the bond will respond. Though I must admit, time is an enemy matched by Aud, and so, I support this notion of divide and conquer. Am I assuming, Ophiera, this means you will pursue Pyra?"

"Yes," Ophiera said calmly. "And if I encounter Marvena in the process, I will be sure to send her ashes to Aud."

Myronor smirked at her words, though despair clung to his eyes.

"And what the hell are we going to do?" Jasper asked.

Though the rogue clearly addressed Kaikora, the shaman gazed at Ophiera in thought. Jasper's eyes darted between them, trying to read the silent exchange. As Kaikora's lips quirked into the slightest of smiles, Ophiera's mouth crumpled into a scowl.

"My task is the portal," Kaikora said to Jasper. "So I will help Myronor in his search. You, however, have likely not set foot in a library in your life, have you?"

"Not to read, that's for certain," Jasper murmured.

"Then I will task you to aid Ophiera in her search for Pyra."

Myronor's protests through the ekath were far louder than Jasper's scoff. But no one disliked the idea of Jasper joining her in the search for Pyra more than Ophiera. Days ago, she had threatened to set him ablaze. They would destroy each other long before encountering Pyra.

"I will do as I'm contracted," Jasper replied, his voice unreadable.

"Then the plan is clear," Kaikora said with a smirk. "Myronor and I will stay behind while Ophiera and Jasper investigate Pyra."

Are you all right with this? Myronor asked through the ekath.

Ophiera chewed her lip, staring at the table with a clenched fist. *Practically, I must admit his skills could be useful in pursuing Pyra. Personally, I would rather suffer a navarra bite than travel anywhere with him.*

Myronor snorted, catching the questioning stares of the other two. With an agreeing nod, he saved himself an explanation.

"But are we to travel around Krysas shouting Pyra's name with the Brotherhood sniffing at our heels?" Jasper asked dryly, staring at the ceiling.

Ophiera raised her eyebrows, ignoring his contempt for the keenness of his words. The sharpness of his mind matched his tongue, she thought with a shiver and shook away the memory of it between her fingers.

"Glamwell provided a lead to her whereabouts," Myronor said, glaring at the map on the table. "Were you not listening to what Kaikora and I were just discussing?"

Both Ophiera and Jasper shook their heads.

"Shortly before Pyra disappeared, she had returned from a trip to the Shole."

"Why in the blazes would she travel there?" Jasper snapped.

Ophiera had only heard of the place in passing thoughts from Myronor, but the fear that shook Jasper's voice piqued her curiosity. Through the ekath, she sensed a great deal of hesitancy from Myronor as he glared at Jasper.

"She traveled to Birozahran and met with Zadok no Enukaja, the Autarch of the Odestal."

Jasper stood so abruptly that his palm slammed to the table before his chair crashed against the stone. Pinned beneath his trembling hand, the knife he had been twirling moments ago remained still.

"No."

"No?" Kaikora asked bemusedly.

But Ophiera found nothing about Jasper's reaction amusing. Could the shaman not see the storm building behind his darkening eyes?

"I refuse to have anything to do with the Enclave," he said, voice steady.

"The Enclave?" Ophiera asked, trying to understand yet another new term.

Myronor pinched his brow. "Like we were just discussing, they are the mage clans—"

"*Savage* mage clans," Jasper hissed with such disdain that he spat upon the table. His copper gaze fell to Ophiera for the first time in days, yet held nothing but emptiness. "If Pyra was meeting with the Odestal clan, it's more likely *they* killed her than the Brotherhood."

"The Enclave is all that is left of the mother clans after the Purge," Kaikora interjected to Ophiera as if she were meant to know what that was as well. "*Savage* best describes the Consortia's genocide and the disgusting excuse of a peace treaty resulting from it."

Silence hung uncomfortably between them as Jasper remained standing, tensed as if poised to run or charge. And though he did his best to hide it with his blank glare, Ophiera could see the furious terror behind his empty mask.

"The search for Pyra must start in Birozahran," Myronor said solemnly. "If that is problematic, perhaps Kaikora should accompany Ophiera."

"No," Kaikora said curtly. "Jasper knows the Shole and the city well. He can guide Ophiera—"

"Absolutely not," Jasper growled, pushing off the table briskly. He kept his fingers tightly wrapped around his dagger.

Kaikora glared at him, a storm building dangerously behind her eyes. "You will do as the Order commands, captain."

"Not in matters of the Shole," he said coldly.

Neither Kaikora nor Myronor seemed disturbed enough by his behavior. They both watched him with irritation, not the caution required around a wild beast backed into a corner. Ophiera was far too familiar with the fear that was overtaking the captain's demeanor and his reasoning.

"I know little of the mother clans other than what you've mentioned regarding the birzhan," Ophiera said, hoping to steer the conversation away from Jasper, at least.

"The Enclave is not what it once was," Kaikora replied. "There are only a few clans left, and after decades of oppression by the Consortia, their people, culture, and magic have been...warped."

"Derivation magics go far beyond *warped*," Jasper cut in. "The Odestal are nothing more than a band of filthy warlocks—"

"Enough of your bigotry," Kaikora hissed. "Whatever they have become, it's not our place to pass judgment."

The shaman rarely lost her composure, yet twice now, her temper had swelled over Jasper like a stormy wave. Still, it was nothing in comparison to the terror building behind Jasper's gaze. Like the word anathema, it seems warlock had some other meaning Ophiera didn't know.

"Judgment?" Jasper laughed, hysterical and mirthless. He spun the blade in his hand, adjusting his grip. "Is that not what the Cloister has commanded of Ophiera's entire existence? Send her to Birozahran, and she will be forced to reduce that city to a crater as well, just to sate her Oath!"

The room fell silent, eyes falling on Ophiera. Despite her sympathy for Jasper's state, she found it difficult to excuse his insensitivity. But it was Myronor's rage that forced her words.

"Who put this fear in you?" She asked Jasper coldly. By the shock in his eyes, she knew she'd verbally struck too hard. But if she hadn't, Myronor would have, and with Jasper's blade at the ready, she didn't trust how that would end.

"None of your bloody business," he finally spat, glaring at her with contempt.

Whatever he was about to do, she needed him to focus on *her*. The captain despised mages, but his contempt for the Enclave was beyond a *feeling*. It controlled his every action.

What are you doing, Ophiera?

From experience, she knew there was no stopping him from spiraling now. The only thing she could do was rip the bandage off.

"Was it a *warlock*?" She asked.

"Shut up!" Jasper screamed.

With a flash of metal, his blade was at her throat. She held still as the cold steel bit into her skin, and a warm trickle of blood coursed down her collarbone. Despite Kaikora's growl and Myronor's hands glowing blue, the captain continued to bear down on her, hot breath inches from her face.

Don't intervene, she commanded Myronor.

Though the blood had now reached her shirt, she felt only pity for the wild creature before her. With her own scarred hand, she wrapped her fingers around his wrist, feeling the heat of his skin against hers. His pulse was erratic and forceful, much like him. But she knew it came from the heart of a lost boy, not an anathema.

Jasper blinked rapidly against her touch, his strength faltering. And gently, she pushed the blade away from her throat. His eyes darted until they fell to the wound on her neck, superficial but bleeding, nonetheless.

"Berserker..." he muttered, dropping his blade to the table with a clang. Before Myronor or Kaikora could address the situation, Jasper fled the room on fast, feathered steps.

~ Twenty Six ~

SYNCHRONICITY

Alone on the balcony, Ophiera picked mindlessly at the dried blood covering her shirt collar. Since their meeting had abruptly adjourned, she had watched the restless ocean churning beneath the clear night sky. The sea below mirrored her mood perfectly.

After Jasper's meltdown, Kaikora chased after him while Ophiera sequestered herself away outside. It was best for her to stay away from the rogue while he was in this state. Or perhaps, no matter his state.

Through the ekath, she saw Myronor leading Kaikora and Jasper out of the Embassy. It seemed that, regardless of Jasper's earlier objections, they were still moving ahead with the plan. Kaikora only needed the Yeoman's blessing before preparing the *Berserker* to set sail for the Shole.

Regardless of the Yeoman's involvement, Ophiera knew *her* path. The scars on her arm prickled against the breeze as the Aether's call to the Shole became clearer by the minute. Whether by Oath or flames, in search of Pyra or Marvena, she was confident the western desert held answers she would not find in Krysas.

Though she had always known the day would come, little could soften the blow of the encroaching departure from her ekath. After everything she and Myronor had been through, simply going their separate ways now seemed...pointless. And yet, the point of their decision was everything. In order to prevent Aud from claiming Erum, they needed to do what they each did best: this time, separately rather than together.

The two moons hung heavy, reflecting the turbid sea like platters of molten silver. Against the chilled breeze, she listened to the waves crash rhythmically, predictably, and endlessly against the cliffs. A fruitless assault of water against rock, with neither winner nor loser. The evening reminded her far too much of the Moon Tide myth.

She understood the nature of people...to create stories where they wished for explanations. But what was the moral of the two moons? To be contented in their separation, suffering an eternal fate, so others did not? It seemed a poor choice, and yet it was a choice she and her ekath were making, too.

Before Ophiera heard his gentle steps, she *felt* Myronor's approach from behind. With their guests now departed, they were alone for the first time since arriving in Krysas. He lingered in the window while she leaned over the banister toward the sea. And what permeated through their bond now was an emotion that had run high throughout the night, one she hated feeling from him.

"Do you fear me now, too?" She asked quietly, refusing to turn from the sea.

He didn't answer.

But after a moment, she heard his hurried steps and relaxed as his arms wound around her waist. Warmth pressed against her back, and yet, his breath trembled against her ear.

"I've told you, I can never fear *you*. But I must admit, I've never felt so terrified in all my life as I do right now."

His words felt as desperate as his clinging hands. A blur of thoughts confused her through their tether, and again, she was reminded of the night of the Moon Tide—of their night when the sea had glowed brightly.

"Tell me," she offered, leaning back into his embrace. "Tell me what terrifies you so."

He plucked at the dried blood on her shirt before grazing his fingertips across the cut. It was nearly healed, much faster than any wound had healed before. And yet she could feel his sorrow as he examined the remnants.

"I'm terrified to lose you, Ophiera."

Her heart faltered under the pain in his voice. She swallowed, relieving the lump in her throat.

"We knew our paths would become complicated once in Krysas," she said. "But this time, we decided together. Your place may be here and mine elsewhere, but our souls remain together. I cannot be lost as long as my heart remains with yours."

His golden locks fell over her shoulder as he pressed his lips against the wound on her neck. She shivered, but not with the night's chill. Within the ekath, she could no longer feel the silly, carefree man she knew. Fear and anger had tainted his heart just as the ichor had tainted his soul.

"I know," he said with a sigh. "I know this is the best choice. But I fear...I fear so much else along our paths," he said, his lips and breath dancing across her skin.

"Such as?"

"Everything and nothing simultaneously," he said blankly. "I fear the power of Aud...I fear the influence of the Brotherhood. I fear what will happen if they find us...I fear what the Cloister will do if they find you."

At the mention of the Cloister, Ophiera shared a shiver of his fear. But between the burn of the Aether beneath her and his arms still wrapped around her, she resisted allowing that fear to control her.

"The Cloister has never traveled beyond Tanvik, and I doubt they would follow after me. I may be wanted, but the Chaplain made it quite clear my existence was inconsequential. And as for Aud and the Brotherhood, well...it is they who should fear me."

Through the ekath, she felt some of his anxieties ease at her words. But not all. His arms tightened around her as he whispered even more quietly than before.

"Despite all that, I still fear more. Such as what Jasper will do while traveling with you...and if the Enclave will know how to break the ekath...and what your choice will be if given the chance."

Ophiera focused on the reflection of the moons again, churning throughout his confessions. The erratic nature of the captain was a concern, but nothing she couldn't handle. But in all their discussions, she hadn't considered that the Enclave may possess the knowledge to break their bond.

"Truthfully, I wouldn't blame you for wishing to rid yourself of the connection," Myronor continued. "A part of me even wishes it for you. I swore to free you from obligation, and yet, I cannot bear the thought of being without you."

Slowly, Ophiera turned in his arms, facing him against the night. She ran her hands up his blue robes, bringing her scarred hand to his face. He leaned into her rough palm, closing his eyes.

"Would breaking the ekath change your love for me?" She asked quietly.

"Of course not."

"Then what does it matter?"

Myronor pressed his lips against her palm with a hint of a smile. "What if, without a connection to my soul, you decide I really am the fool you thought I was?"

"Then I will be in love with a fool."

Eyes open, Myronor's gaze bore into hers, alight and yet questioning. Though she felt her face warm with the intensity, her gut churned with guilt. The doubt behind his eyes...she had put it there.

"Myronor, it is not my Oath or the ekath that binds me to you. Or rather, I no longer rely on them as an excuse...or...I'm not good at explaining this," she said, closing her eyes in frustration. Perhaps this was why he found it so hard to believe she loved him when she could not articulate her feelings. With a deep breath, she kept her eyes shut to focus on her heart and words. "It's like...a home. I used to think that home was a location, a place in the world I lacked until I found one in Iluka. And I thought that feeling of home couldn't exist anymore now that Iluka is gone. Yet when I'm with you, I feel far more content than I ever did in my cottage. You're the only place I belong, Myronor—the only reason I have to return, no matter what."

She dared open her eyes, wondering what expression could match the surge of emotion through the ekath. The way Myronor studied her with lips parted and eyes wide as the moons caused her heart to stutter. Yet she wished he'd say something in return.

His silence was relieved when his lips met hers. The relief of his response quickly grew to something far less familiar. Even as her tongue danced with his own, she felt a burning *need* to be nearer.

Ophiera gave in to instinct and ran her hands beneath his robes, feeling his warm, bare chest against her scarred hand. She suddenly despised those blue robes.

Curiosity unchained, she kept her lips on his as her hands traveled downwards beneath his robes. As her fingertips grazed over each muscle of his abdomen, she felt his breath hitch and his heart race. Through his pulse, she felt the same need for closeness.

Each touch felt like another cord wove into their tether, another anchor point pulling them closer. As she reached his waist with her exploring hands, she smiled, finally discovering exactly what he wore beneath his robes.

But Myronor broke away, and she feared she had misread his desire. Her instincts were proven incorrect, though, as his hands slipped beneath her linen tunic. His soft hands caressed the bare skin of her lower back before slowly lifting it overhead.

She despised her instinct to cover herself, resisting the response with his appreciative gaze. Topless against the sea breeze, she found the chill touch of air against the sensitive parts of her skin tantalizing, and yet, she wanted *him* more. To think, she had been revolted by the idea of him touching her when they first met, only to crave it now so desperately.

Following her desires, his nimble fingers began undoing the ties to her pants. Once loosened, he ran his thumbs along her waist, peeling the trousers away from her heated skin until they crumpled to the ground.

Stepping back, his eyes never left hers as he undid the fastenings to his robes and let them fall away to his feet. And in the light of the moons, Ophiera's breath caught in her throat.

She felt paralyzed in appreciation of the man before her. Blessed with the lineage of a fisher, she couldn't help but notice how the journey had toughened him. His lithe muscles were more defined, casting alluring shadows in the moonslight like the exaggerated lines of a sketch; his shoulders sat a bit broader, and the veins on his arms thickened with his pulse. Even the presence of the glistening scars in the moonlight couldn't diminish her desire to touch him.

Ophiera reached a trembling hand to his chest, relieved by the connection and yet exhilarated by the sensation building between them. He pressed a hand over hers while dragging his thumb across her jawline.

Every touch of their skin sent a shockwave of heat through the ekath. All worries disintegrated as they embraced, bare to the world. Both of their breaths drew ragged as they ran their hands over each other, simply relishing in their exploration of flesh. She let out a sigh as Myronor cupped her breast, leaning his face down into the crook of her neck. He ran his nose from her ear to her shoulder, leaving a trail of gentle kisses as he traveled.

Her legs began to shake, the building tension too much to bear. Leaning back, she used the stone banister to hold herself upright as Myronor's hand continued to worship her, his thumb circling over her sensitive peak. When his gentle kisses reached the fresh cut on her neck, she felt a surge of anger through the ekath, but it did not linger. Further down her arm, he went until his mouth reached her Oath. And though she appreciated the feel of his reverent kisses against her scars, she still wanted more.

With the power of sea and stone at her back, she ran her fingers through his golden locks and dragged him fully against her. She wasn't sure which was harder, the stone against her back or him against her front, but the feeling of them both brought her lips to his in a voracious call for more.

Ophiera...are you sure you wish to share yet another connection with me?

His thoughts were crystal clear through the ekath, and yet hers were a chaotic blaze. She shivered against him as her mouth moved frantically with his, trying to control the desperate fire smoldering inside her. She focused on her words, though it was a struggle.

Myronor, my soul is bound to you, and my heart has chosen you, but now my very flesh needs you. I have never been more sure of anything in my life, and I beg you, please, do not make me wait any longer.

Myronor's response thundered through their link, more instinct than words. With a glow of blue light, her feet left the ground as he settled her bottom on the stone banister. She knew the ocean churned far, far below, and yet all it did was excite her more. With her hands in his hair again, she clung to him, knowing he would never let her fall. She wrapped her legs around his waist and drew him to her, feeling his need press deep against her center.

Ophiera cried out into the night the moment their bodies melded. The ecstatic mixture of pleasure and pain only found escape through her lips, lips that Myronor quieted with his own. Gently, he held his hips in place, allowing her to collect herself while he kissed her softly. She hadn't expected the pain, but the fullness was foreign and fantastic. Through the tether, their bodies and souls found balance in each other, allowing the discomfort of flesh to be wholly muffled by the pleasure shared through the ekath.

In a rhythm much like the sea at her back, Myronor moved against her. Each time he distanced, she felt a moment of disappointment, only to be filled with a wave of ecstasy. Stoking her flames at a steady pace, the blaze of his thrusts filled her with a fire like the Aether itself. And for once, she feared not losing control of herself. In fact, she wished for nothing more.

Again, answering her call, Myronor wrapped his hand around her braid, pulling her head back to face the sky. His tongue traveled down her neck as his rhythm quickened, pounding her against the stone while her legs clung around him.

The stars swirled as her eyes rolled, a blissful madness building and building within her. Every thrust threatened to burst her from the seams. Every kiss threatened to break her heart. She couldn't stop the heat from spilling over, yet she needed something, anything, to relieve the pressure building within.

Myronor's hand slipped from her breast, caressing down her abdomen until he reached her center. There, his soft, coaxing fingers swirled just above where they melded, sending shockwaves of sensation radiating through her. With every circle he made, more pressure built, coaxing her closer to eruption.

Burn for me, Ophiera.

The world disappeared as she cried into the night. His voice against her mind was the ignition to the cataclysmic eruption quaking through her body and soul. Not in pale flames but in pure, wondrous ecstasy that ignited every nerve in her body.

She held onto him as overwhelming pleasure blazed through every fiber of her being. His embrace was the only force keeping her existence whole, the only dam preventing the Aether from spilling forth along with every other part of her.

Just when she thought she had reached the pinnacle of rapture, Myronor groaned, and another explosion rocked through her. His arms tightened around her as his body quaked with his detonation.

Together, they burned, fusing more than their souls and bodies in the heat.

Myronor crumpled against Ophiera's heaving chest, listening to her heart pound nearly as hard as his. Though her legs trembled, she kept them wrapped around him tightly, holding him against her as if unable to let go. He pressed one last kiss against the round scar between her breasts before raising his eyes to look at her.

Every muscle in her body tensed and shone with perspiration. In the moonlight, he found scars he never knew existed rippling across her thick muscles. As his gaze traveled upwards, his heart fluttered again at the sight of her parted, puffy lips, drawing ragged breaths. But the moment he caught her eyes in his, all air vacated his lungs.

The moons reflected in her jewel-like irises, gazing at him and only him. Bright amethyst above flushed, freckled cheeks, he couldn't help but run his knuckles across her skin, soaking in all of her. She was the most beautiful sight he'd ever laid eyes on. And though he stood by his word that he never wished for her to feel obligated to him, a part of him relished in the fact that the fire behind her eyes was for him and him alone.

I've only ever burned like this for you.

Her words caressed his mind, settling in his heart as she combed her fingers through his hair. Though she kissed him again, Myronor lowered her from the banister edge in a haze of blue light. Touching her felt like breathing, as if he would surely perish if he relinquished for only a moment. But he felt her soreness through the link and the chill against her skin despite her mouth continuing to consume his own.

Myronor began to laugh beneath her kiss.

"What's so funny?" She asked aloud, pulling away to glare at him.

"Nothing," he said, smiling as he ran his thumb over her bottom lip. "I just can't decide if I'm dreaming or not."

To his detriment, Ophiera took his thumb into her mouth and bit down. It was just hard enough to make him flinch.

"You're not asleep if you can feel pain," she said with a smile before running her tongue over the sore spot.

"If my dreams of you had been this perfect, I would have never woken."

Though her cheeks flushed at his words, they quickly paled as she looked away from him. She glared at the spot on the balcony where she had burned away the ichor from his wound. Visions of his unconscious body replaced the passion behind her eyes with despair. And his voice soon echoed in her thoughts, growling hurtful, terrible words that were not of his own heart. So quickly had her fire diminished to dark, cold ash.

Myronor cupped her face in both his hands, drawing her gaze back to his. To his harm, he saw moisture welling in the corners of her despondent eyes. She smiled sadly, blinking away the tears that now fell.

"I suppose the thought of you not waking was too close to my heart."

"Ophiera, my everything," he said in a shaking voice. "I swear, neither distance nor Aether nor Aud will ever come between us again."

She nodded against his hands, and though she smiled up at him, he sensed her doubt; not a doubt in him, but in the unknown of their future. At this moment, he wanted nothing more than to stop time, to pretend the woes of the world had nothing to do with them. And while he had never heard of time magic in all his studies, he did know of one way to forget everything.

With her scarred hand in his, Myronor began to lead her back inside.

"Where are we going?" She asked.

"To the bedroom."

"Wh-why?"

He turned back to her, taking her mouth with his and kissing her as if it were the first and last time. Against his chest, her heart thundered with his, beating away some of the doubt that still lingered.

"So, I may continue to convince you that no power in this world surpasses my love for you."

~ Twenty Seven ~

ELEGIAC

"You packed a hammock, right?" Myronor asked as he conjured a fully laden breakfast tray.

"Yes," Ophiera moaned, still sprawled in bed, a pillow across her face." You know I've spent most of my life traveling. I know what to pack."

He placed the tray on a nearby table before slipping back into the enormous bed beside her. The lavish upper bedroom of the estate mirrored the Embassy residence with dark stone walls and luxurious furniture. Bright sunlight fell through the slitted windows, which was the reason Ophiera hid beneath a pillow just now.

"I'm simply ensuring your comfort *and* autonomy while you're away," Myronor said as the smirk fell from his face.

Her soon-to-be traveling companion had an unappreciated yet understandable infatuation. Each time Jasper had been mentioned these past few days of planning, Myronor felt his blood turn to ice. Not with jealousy or possessiveness, no. Jealousy implied the desire for something another possessed, but Myronor had everything he desired. No, the chill he had felt was good old-fashioned dislike. He'd yet to find a redeeming quality in the young captain, and now the love of his life was to rely on him as a guide through the Shole.

"Jasper won't be a problem," Ophiera said, her face now buried in the pillow.

She'd followed his thoughts more closely since their night on the terrace, and truthfully, Myronor found he loved it. Seamless communication of thought without direct conversation was a more intimate experience in many ways. But Myronor refused to be distracted; Ophiera needed to remember just how dangerous Jasper had become at the mere mention of the Enclave. He felt rather strongly that a dangerous and unstable man who put a knife to her throat was guaranteed to be a problem.

"I didn't say he wasn't troubled...I'm simply saying I know how to deal with him," Ophiera said. "I was fully prepared to make the trek alone anyhow. If he gets out of hand, my flames will always bring him to his knees."

Myronor chuckled darkly. "I'm fairly certain your flames only serve to entice him further."

"Who in their right mind is enticed by someone who catches fire?"

"I was. Still am, apparently."

His mind wandered to the memory of her ablaze, the rogue lying crumpled at her feet. While Jasper had cowered, Myronor had instead admired, burning each licking flame of her curves into his mind. The image of Ophiera, hair blasted from its braid in white fire, commanding the respect she deserved, had made him fall even further in love with her, if possible.

"Stop," she said quietly, still hidden beneath the pillow. Humble as ever, he could only imagine the shade her cheeks had turned. Quickly, he pulled the pillow from her face, and the view did not disappoint.

Her eyes narrowed sleepily over her freckled cheeks, white hair loose and tangled over the bed sheet. He found it more enticing knowing that if she so desired, she could set the bed ablaze and send every person in Krysas to the Aether. But instead, she bit her lip and looked back at him as if he were the only soul in the world.

For the past few nights, she had looked at him like that as they awaited the *Berserker* to prepare for her journey. Messages from Kaikora arrived every so often, but otherwise, they remained locked away in the dark stone mansion, unabatedly exploring their newfound *physical* connection. How many times had he declared her his everything, only to now send her on her way?

"We've made the right choice," Ophiera whispered, following his thoughts again. She took his hand and pressed it over her chest, the circular scar thick beneath his palm. "The portals are both our greatest weapon and our greatest weakness against Aud. And fugitive or not, I'm still the Aspect of Retribution. Oath or not, we need to find out what happened to Pyra."

Myronor took her hand in his, running his fingers across her other scars. He always found the symbols blistered into her skin simultaneously beautiful and sad. The power the Cloister held over her had nearly prevented them from becoming what they were now.

"What if the Cloister comes for you?" He asked quietly.

"They won't."

"But if—"

"Then all the more reason to travel to the Shole," she said sternly.

Through the ekath, he felt her withdraw into herself again. The pain he felt every time she thought of the Cloister broke his heart. And even though he felt it too, he knew he'd never understand. All he could do was ensure they couldn't hurt her again.

"I have a surprise for you," he said, leaning back toward the bedside table. He'd planned to wait until they were aboard the ship, but he needed a distraction now. She watched him curiously as he dangled two tethered crystals before her.

"What happened?" she asked. "Is Mallow alright?"

"Yes, yes," he chuckled. "I fractured the crystal so we may each keep half. Then, when it suits her, she can travel between us."

"And she agreed to this?" Ophiera asked, grasping the crystal and turning it over in her hands.

"Of course."

The shard flickered in response, illuminating Ophiera's corresponding smile. Mallow appeared, unable to resist an opportunity to be the center of attention. As Ophiera ran her hands through the fluffy fur, Myronor felt a moment of relief. As usual, his familiar lightened everyone's mood.

After breakfast, Myronor left Ophiera to dress while he minimized the bags of armor and traveling supplies near the hearth. They agreed it was unwise to don her golden plate until she landed in the Shole. He couldn't risk her being found in Krysas by the Brotherhood or the Cloister alike.

When Ophiera finally strode down the spiral staircase from the upper bedroom, Myronor felt a twinge of regret for suggesting a consort as a disguise. His mother's old wardrobe remained full and untouched, giving the paladin her pick. The new dress covered far more skin than a normal consort's gown, yet somehow rendered her body far more alluring. The matte black material clung to her arms from shoulder to thumb, and an inky leather bodice accentuated her waist and bosom. As she descended the stairs, the dress flowed over her statuesque physique, the material moving like the sea.

"We can't forget to maximize those on the ship," she said with a frown, eyeing the minimized bags held before him.

He laughed. "I wouldn't dare leave my delicate consort stranded without her belongings."

She rolled her lilac eyes before attacking her still-loose hair. As usual, she weaved a complicated plait with little effort. Once the long tendril was woven, she began wrapping it into a bun. With her hands distracted, Myronor looped his fingers into her bodice and pulled her against him.

"I know you prefer the armor, but I *very* much like this dress."

She smiled, tucking away her hair. "I find that surprising."

"How so?"

With a peck on the cheek, she whispered against his ear, "I rather thought you preferred when I wore nothing at all."

Leaving him stunned in silence, she continued adjusting the gown's sleeves and cowl. He could see now why she'd selected this particular dress. In a classic style of Krysan garb, it bore a dark cowl that she now pulled low over her nose and mouth. The traditional style was born from practicality and, in more modern times, served as a fashion statement. The long sleeves looped over her middle fingers, covering her Oath without the need for wraps or gloves.

Together, they left through Glamwell's office. The Steward sat at his desk, reading from yet another tome in his fluorescent pink garb. He kept his eyes glued to the pages as he smiled.

"Ambassador Myronor and Lady Iris! Out to explore the city? I have a wonderful recommendation for some traditional Civ cuisine if you're feeling peckish."

"We're headed to the port, actually," Myronor said solemnly. "My consort must return to Feyralis for a short time and attend to some personal matters for me."

Glamwell closed his book, his face crumpling as he stood. "Oh dear, how unfortunate. I can't imagine how difficult this must be for you both. As always, please let me know if there is anything I can do to assist you while she's away. I mean, I'm not volunteering *those* services. Though my cousin informs me I would make for a popular consort in Feyralis."

"Thank you, Glamwell, but we must make haste to the ship," Myronor said, straining to keep his face straight as he dragged Ophiera from the room.

Once outside, she burst into a fit of giggles that only stopped when they reached the crystal lifts. And while Myronor loved the sound of her laugh nearly as much as her singing voice, the encroaching departure prevented him from enjoying it in full.

He barely registered the descent, caught up in his own thoughts. It wasn't easy to reconcile how he felt at the moment. While he knew in his mind their plan was the best course of action, he found the sense of dread in his heart winning over. To knowingly put themselves through the discomfort and pain of the ekath distanced, to purposefully separate when every fiber of their existence told them to be near...Was this how Pyra felt when making the choice to come to Krysas?

Ophiera took his hand in hers and squeezed without a word. While she must have followed his thoughts down the lift, she did not speak of them. But her touch alone was enough to pull him from despair and strengthen his step off the platform.

Even amongst the crowds of the docks, Kaikora was hard to miss, standing two heads higher than Collette alongside her. They both seemed to be engaged in animated conversation alongside the *Berserker,* and for a moment, Myronor worried they were arguing. But as he approached, he realized they were both laughing.

"Collette, lovely to meet again," Myronor said, greeting the first mate. He took her hand and kissed it, paying close attention as Kaikora's eyes bore into him. He felt, rather than saw, Ophiera roll her eyes behind him.

"Glad to see you're walking on two legs again," she simpered, turning her gaze to Ophiera. "And my oh my, this black dress suits you far better than that grubby green frock I lent you."

Ophiera bowed her head as she tugged down her cowl. "I apologize; I had an accident and ruined your dress, but there is a replacement in my belongings."

Waving her hand dismissively, Collette giggled. "Oh my, you worry far too much over a piece of cloth! The first rule of the sea is never to lend out something you'll miss."

Kaikora set a rough hand on Ophiera's shoulder, shaking her slightly. "I'm glad to see you haven't lost your flair for the dramatic, my friend. Once you stow your belongings, meet me on deck; we must discuss the next steps before you depart."

The word *depart* stung Myronor's heart, even as he followed Collette onto the *Berserker*. The evidence of the ichor's burn still marred the oily deck, another scar left behind by the Brotherhood. Though the plan was for the *Berserker* to sail the shoreline of Orbolas until they reached the Shole, he wondered how close any navarras might swim for a chance to kill Ophiera. Why hadn't he considered this danger before when they were hatching their plans?

Don't think about that, Ophiera's voice said calmly. *Even if the navarras are so bold, I am more so; they won't stand a chance.*

Myronor smiled to himself as they descended into the ship. If only she could understand that her words brought him more worry, not reassurance. Did she expect him to simply forget about her last fight against the navarras? She'd been so bold, in fact, that she'd have been left stranded at sea had he not been there to retrieve her.

Don't think about that either, she added sheepishly.

Unaware of their internal conversation, the first mate swung the rickety door to the cabin wide. Water-stained floors and a small, pristine porthole were the only objects of interest left in the room. Somehow, the lack of any furniture made the quarters feel even smaller.

"The navarra attack destroyed the bed, and the captain...well, he's been troubled with other tasks..." Collette trailed off, rolling her eyes towards the door.

"Good thing you remembered to pack the hammock," Myronor goaded, placing the minimized packs in a corner. With a flash of blue, he maximized Ophiera's packs. Most prominent among them was her old rucksack, worn and packed to the brim with supplies. He'd tried to conjure as many of her favorite pastries to pack along, hoping she'd actually eat this time. Water was another concern in the desert, and much of her pack was consumed by waterskins. Another bag held her armor pieces and claymore, bulky in the drawstring canvas. The sight of it all pained him. If he traveled with her, she wouldn't need to worry about any of this.

"Col!" A loud clang came from down the corridor, along with the gravelly voice. "Col! Where...can't find..." another crash echoed.

The first mate pinched the bridge of her nose as Jasper continued to wail. "By the sea, will you excuse me?"

The woodsy burn of ember whiskey clung to the air as the door shut behind her. Even through the thick wood, Jasper's voice carried through with a slur. "Col, where-*hiccup*-poshun..."

Ophiera glared at the floor with a pained expression, listening to the first mate attempt to calm the captain.

"A drunken rogue should be easier to subdue, at least," Myronor said aloud, trying to break the scowl from her lips.

"And will be useless for the task ahead," she said through gritted teeth. "I don't know why Collette could not simply sail us there without him."

"Isn't he meant to guide you through the Shole?" he asked.

"I don't see how he could in *that* state," she said, rolling her eyes toward the door. "Even so, he clearly never wished to."

A possessive part of him purred at the idea of her traveling without the cur of a captain. He'd proven to be more of a threat than an aid to her already, and he expected that would only grow worse in the desert. But after hearing the stories of the Enclave and the violence of the Shole...Myronor sided with Kaikora—Ophiera shouldn't go alone.

Haven't I proven I can take care of myself?

"Yes," he said, taking her scarred hand in his. "But we don't know what will happen to the ekath this time, with this distance. Last time we were separated, you...you..."

Myronor trailed off, unable to complete the sentence. The images of her worn and weak, sneaking behind the Tattered Sail Inn after days of neglect, caused the air to freeze in his lungs. He'd forgotten, or repressed, just how painful that brief separation had been. And now, they would be much further away, for potentially longer.

She tightened her rough grip. *Last time, my heart was breaking for you and for Iluka. This time, I only contend with the ekath, which feels stronger than ever. I promise, this time, it will be different. This time, I'll return healthy and whole.*

He smiled, feeling the comfort of her words. "I can conjure you a bed, at least...that way you could get some sleep.

She shook her head with a forlorn smile. *The hammock will suffice. A bed would only remind me of your absence.*

Three loud thumps shook the dust from the boards above, and Myronor recognized a signal from the beckoning shaman. With a peck on the cheek, Ophiera led the way from the small cabin to the deck.

Above, the towering shaman played lazily with a small globe of water betwixt her thick fingers. The water-bending abilities of the shamans were no secret, but rarely had Myronor seen her display her power quite so openly. The droplet fell as her gray eyes honed in on Ophiera.

"Dealing with the Enclave will require a delicate hand."

Ophiera nodded. "I assumed as much."

"And yet I've never known you for your diplomacy."

Myronor stifled a snort at Kaikora's jab.

"And I've never known you to be straightforward," Ophiera countered.

Kaikora smiled. "The Enclave does not trust outsiders, and few could blame them after the Purge. They respond quite *violently* to interlopers of the Shole, but luckily for us, they consider many of Tanvik their lost children. With that, they should provide you with hospitality."

"Should?" Ophiera asked. "That doesn't sound very reassuring."

"You know better than to expect assurance from me."

"Then give me perspective. I watched Jasper react like a wild animal at the mere mention of the Enclave, and he is of Tanvik—wouldn't he be a wayward child, as you say?"

Myronor and Kaikora both frowned, though he suspected for different reasons. Usually, the overtly curious Myronor couldn't have cared less why Jasper had behaved like a madman, and he wished Ophiera felt similarly.

"I am not familiar with Jasper's specific experience with the Enclave," Kaikora said, "but you must understand, until very recently, the people of the Enclave were under the Consortia's occupation, and their rule was brutal. The only perspective I can provide is that oppression forces people to do things outside their nature. So, try not to judge them for what the Consortia forced them to become, but rather for what they are trying to do now, free of the yoke. And I would approach Jasper similarly."

Ophiera nodded, brow knitted tightly. Dipping into the ekath, Myronor felt the thoughts racing through her head. Rightfully so, she worried about Jasper's instability when faced with a tormentor. But to his annoyance, he realized she viewed herself as such.

"How, then, is she to earn the Enclave's favor?" Myronor asked, hoping to deter Ophiera's darkening thoughts.

"As their lost children, Tanvik shares language with the Enclave. But their vernacular is quite distinct. For instance, when you arrive, they will ask you *who* you are. But they are not asking for a name or title; what they mean is, what magic do you possess?"

"I possess no magic," Ophiera said quickly, eyes wide with annoyance.

"But you do wield mana. You must tell them you are a Wielder of Erum's Flame."

"Erum's Flame?" Myronor asked.

"The Aether," Ophiera breathed.

Kaikora nodded.

Never had Myronor considered Ophiera's dominion over the Aether a form of magic, at least none that the Enclave might recognize. Krysas and Tanvik had strict definitions of magic: conjura, transmutation, imbuteria, and a smattering of less popular arts. Now he understood it was only those who drew from the Void that were considered mages, but that didn't necessarily mean other forms of magic couldn't exist.

Though the Magistrate did not consider the Phratries' powers over water magic either, Myronor had known better. Raised in Iluka, he witnessed firsthand the power of the mana Kaikora and her order wielded. But the power of the Cloister and their paladins was less known, more myth than magic or mana. Servants to the Cloister, slaves to the holy flames, their power was scarce and under the absolute control of the Magistrate.

"Last call for crew and cargo!" Collette yelled across the deck.

"Ophiera," Kaikora said, grasping her by the shoulder. "The sight may fail me more and more, but you never have. Trust what your soul tells you—I certainly do."

Ophiera smiled before throwing her arms around the massive woman. He'd never seen Kaikora so shocked as she returned the embrace. But he found himself suddenly unable to witness their goodbye. Avoidant, he turned his attention to the busy dock to observe the flurry of mundane and menial activity. Throngs of people who bore no awareness of the threats to their existence. He hadn't until recently. And yet, through them, Aud pressed down on all their future. The thought sobered him up to the choices ahead.

From his periphery, Myronor saw Kaikora depart with one last smile. Alone with Ophiera, Myronor no longer knew how to speak. It took all the strength he could muster to turn and face her. Even then, he could only stare at her, memorizing every feature of her face as she smiled up at him.

"You might find a few days apart to be welcome," she began softly. "You'll be able to read in peace without me distracting you."

"I suppose," he said, his sadness somehow dissipating with her words. "And you'll be able to slay whatever beast crosses your path without worrying about me."

She leaned forward and kissed him, short and sweet, for the last time. Their proper goodbyes happened in the privacy of the ekath as they walked to the ship's ramp.

The door to the captain's quarters swung open, wood bashing wood in a thunderous clap. Leaning against the doorframe, Jasper's greasy curls fell over unfocused, bloodshot eyes. Myronor swore he could smell whiskey and sweat contaminating the sea breeze, even from this distance.

"Weigh anchor!" he yelled to everyone and no one. "If you're not coming with us to hell, this is your last chance to save yourself!"

He disappeared again below deck as Collette emerged, frowning and flustered. But when her dark eyes met Myronor's, she smiled in reassurance, as if a drunken captain was little to no problem. She placed a hand on Ophiera's elbow, promising to care for her. Myronor wasn't sure how he'd assumed so much from Collette's subtle movements, but he knew as he took the hardest step in his life that Ophiera was in good hands.

Down the ramp, Myronor stood by Kaikora, struggling to remain composed. The sparse crew hurriedly finished their preparations for departure, a flurry of activity around his stoic ekath. Her eyes met his in one final promise that she would return, that all would be well, and that she loved him. But as she turned away with Collette, disappearing below deck, the ekath tightened around his heart.

The ship drifted away from the docks, and all his effort was spent resisting the urge to span aboard and travel with her. Every moment of watching the *Berserker* sail away drew from his strength and resolve. It wasn't only the tautness of the ekath that began to ail him, but the emptiness of his heart.

How could he have believed the portal to Feyralis more important than journeying with her?

A twinge of discomfort in his leg quickly reminded him why they chose this path. Aud.

He'd experienced firsthand the deity's darkness slithering into his soul, whispering her cruel intentions that he still didn't fully understand. Ophiera had rid him of that darkness, yes, but the stain it left behind would forever taint his view of their future. No matter what, preventing Aud from usurping Erum was the most crucial task ahead. Regaining control of Pyra's portals, a tool so powerful both the Order and Brotherhood sought, was precisely why he stayed behind now as Ophiera sailed into the horizon. But just because he stood by his decision didn't mean he was fully prepared for the consequences.

As the sails blended with the pale horizon, the pain became unbearable. Every heartstring connecting him to her stretched taut across the sea. The sudden agony of the ekath stopped his breath and caused his limbs to shake as if he were physically resisting the drag of the ship as it pulled away. He couldn't understand why this departure was so much more terrible than the last...

When she had left him in Iluka before, he felt the discomfort and irritation, but not this *burn.*

"Has it begun?" Kaikora asked him gently.

"Seems so," he said, rubbing his throbbing chest. "Though it's a tad more intense than I had expected."

"It will likely get worse."

"Bedside manner...isn't your strength..." he gasped, failing to withstand the growing drag.

The sharp agony in his chest radiated out to his limbs now. He resisted, but it was like trying to fight a harpoon to the chest, chain attached to the ship now sailing out of sight. He fell to his knees, grasping his staff for support. Kaikora's words echoed, muffled in his ear, as he gasped, searching for air that was no longer there.

~ Twenty Eight ~

CINCH

With arms wrapped tightly around herself, Ophiera rocked for hours with the waves. In the corner of the darkening cabin, she took deep, steadying breaths, clinging to herself as the ache in her chest tried to claw its way back to Myronor.

Solitude, for once, felt intrusive and unbearable. The void left behind of his mind against hers left only silent pain in her heart. Though the physical discomfort grew worse as they sailed, Ophiera reminded herself it was still more tolerable than their separation had been before. Luckily for her, or perhaps unluckily, her entire existence had been filled with pain, and at least *this* pain held the promise of purpose.

When the drag of the ekath began, she had been trying to hang her hammock, which now lay crumpled beside her. Collapsing in the corner, she lay cradled on the floor, paralyzed by the tugging of a thousand hooks. She passed the time studying the complex weave of the rubyfin net sprawled over water-stained wood.

A gentle knock on the door surprised her, though she found she couldn't bring herself to respond.

"Ophiera? It's Collette."

She mouthed the words "Come in," but no sound came forth; simply breathing took the majority of her effort.

Regardless, the first mate entered with a tired smile, carrying a small plate of food illuminated by one flameless candle. The crusty bread and dried meat seemed dismal compared to the meals Myronor could conjure, and the reminder squeezed her chest terribly.

Collette plopped herself on the floor beside Ophiera, sitting cross-legged beneath her skirts. With her dark eyes, she assessed Ophiera up and down.

"Not feeling the best, are we?"

Ophiera wondered if the simple nod would convey that she felt stretched across the sea, but it was all she could muster.

"Aye, though moving your head is a good sign. Kai said you'd be mighty uncomfortable, possibly incapacitated by the ekath business."

"K-Kai?" Ophiera asked in a breathy voice.

"Ah, good, you can speak too," Collette smirked. "Managing the deck is easier with short names. Anyway, she instructed me to make you eat and talk, even if you didn't want to, so here I am."

"I didn't realize you two were acquaintances," Ophiera said quietly.

Speaking was undoubtedly an effort, but it did seem to loosen the knot in her chest slightly.

"We've only met recently, through the Order...connected over apothecary topics, mostly. Though I must say, if I had met a woman like that before I joined the *Berserker*, I might have run off to the Phratries instead," she trailed off, fanning herself with her hand.

Ophiera tried to laugh but only managed to sniff through her nose. "Kaikora is great to connect with, regardless of time or topic," she said before her smile fell to a grimace and then to a groan.

It felt as if a troynt had sat on her chest.

"Come now," Collette said, holding out her hand, "let's get you sat up at least, and then we can try a little remedy of mine."

It shouldn't have been so difficult to lift her own scarred hand to take Collette's, but she managed. She tried to ignore the first mate's scrutinizing eyes, fixated as they were on the symbols peaking beneath her sleeve.

Dragging herself up, Ophiera fought against the sway of the boat. The room spun sickeningly, and all her strength was concentrated on not vomiting in Collette's lap.

From her belt, the first mate pulled forth a curious clay jug with a dark cork stopper.

"A potion?" Ophiera asked, taking a deep breath through her nose.

"Of sorts...'tis the captain's favorite elixir for certain."

Collette retrieved two small crystalline cups from between her breasts. Impressed, Ophiera didn't understand how she could fit anything within her ample bosom, but she had an uncanny talent for doing so. It wasn't hard to understand why Kaikora hadn't resisted *connecting* with her.

With her teeth, Collette deftly extracted the cork, and a waft of the jug's contents reached Ophiera's nose. The acrid and malted aroma coated the back of her throat, instantly transporting her to the Lonely Iris. She vividly remembered how Lotus had introduced to her a quicker way to nullity than his honey ale provided.

"Is that ember whiskey?"

"Aye! You really are a sailor, aren't you?" Collette giggled, pouring the dark amber liquid into the small cups and nearly spilling the contents as she clumsily passed it to Ophiera.

"Now, the first drink is *always* to the sea," she said, raising her glass. "May she grant us safe passage through her waters."

Collette clinked their cups together and gulped down the contents in a single gulp. Fighting back nausea, Ophiera followed, holding the liquid in her mouth for a moment to allow the burn to radiate into her nostrils. As she swallowed, the warmth pooled in her chest, easing the tautness of the tether.

Motioning for her cup, Collette poured another round and promptly handed it back. "Second drink is to the ship—may she carry us swiftly across the sea."

Together, they drank the second toast in perfect synchrony. Ophiera tasted more of the libation this time. The smoky sweetness layered on the soothing warmth coated her tongue, smothering away the last remnants of nausea. Again, her chest loosened another notch.

"And the last," Collette said, her voice dropping slightly, "is to those we left behind. May they remain anchored safely until our return."

This last dose of warmth lingered in Ophiera's throat for a moment, stalled by a sudden swell of emotion. Her eyes pricked, but the moisture never broke.

"Well, that should set you right," Collette said, gesturing to the tray. "Make sure you—"

Suddenly, the door was flung open, and a young, red-headed man scurried into the room.

"Felix!" Collette hissed. "I told you to—"

But she cut herself off as the young man put a finger over his lips. He closed the door softly behind him, leaning his back against it. Beneath the door, Ophiera heard the scuffle of dragging boots as a shadow of unstable steps passed by.

"Where the hell is the whiskey?!" Jasper cried, his raspy voice barely recognizable.

All eyes fell to the clay jug on the floor, but the first mate only winked at Ophiera. Keeping quiet, they listened to the muffled clatter of objects being tossed and displaced. Felix alone twitched against the sounds of heavy wood scraping against the floor. A glass fell, shattering into tinkling pieces. Beneath Felix's ginger curls, his eyes stared widely up at the ceiling as if in silent prayer. She noticed now how his hand gripped the door handle, white-knuckled and entirely still. It was difficult to know how to feel about the rampage occurring outside the room; while the deck-hand appeared fearful, Collette only looked...disappointed.

"Col!?" Jasper yelled, his voice faltering along with his steps. A few more crashes shook the door in its frame, but the first mate only rolled her eyes.

"Felix!?"

The young man flinched again at his name.

"Someone better find me a damned drink, or I swear to the sea I will run this ship aground!"

Ophiera's eyes darted to Collette, eyebrows raised in question. But the first mate smiled sadly, as if that alone could reassure Ophiera that the drunken captain wouldn't follow through with his threats.

As his steps faded away, stumbling up the wooden staircase, Felix's slight shoulders relaxed. His wide eyes fell on Collette, whose darkened eyes were fixated elsewhere.

"Sorry, I didn't know what else to do but hide," Felix whispered. "Last time he left his cabin in that state, he threatened to throw me overboard."

Collette sighed. "It's alright, Fel...though it's not me you've intruded on."

The boy's eyes widened as he looked at Ophiera. His cheeks suddenly flushed before he dropped to his hands and knees before her.

"I'm sorry, Miss Berserker, ma'am-er-Lady Paladin?" He took a deep breath and muttered to himself for a moment. "Oh, no, the captain is going to kill me...he said if I bothered her, I'd be burned alive...Um, Great Aspect, please accept my apologies. I didn't mean to disrupt...to intrude...please, please, forgive me, please!"

While Collette cackled, Ophiera recoiled slightly, mouth agape with bewilderment. The sight of him begging like this enraged her.

"Sit up," Ophiera said, and the boy whipped his spine straight so quickly she saw his eyes falter with the dizziness. "The only person on this ship that ought to be begging for my forgiveness is the captain himself."

"I—wait...so, you won't set me on fire?"

Collette cackled, bemused again.

"I will not. As long as you call me Ophiera and never utter the words Lady Paladin again."

His eyes widened as his cheeks flushed, and Ophiera was painfully reminded of an expression Myronor often made when she said something to his liking. The tether tensed, and she immediately placed a hand over her chest, inhaling a deep breath.

"Fel," Collette said quickly, "go to my quarters. Under my bed, there is a loose floorboard, and you'll find several more of these." She paused, gesturing to the clay jug. "Bring the captain *one*, ya hear? *One.* Say something nice to him, either about the ship or his hair, hand over the whiskey, and get out."

"Aye, aye," he said, his gaze lingering on Ophiera for a moment. His mouth hung open as if wishing to say something, but with Collette's purposeful cough, he snuck from the room.

Alone again, the silence hung heavy, like a storm offshore. While Ophiera had been holed away, battling the drag of the ekath, it seemed the captain was having a battle of his own. The last time she had spoken with him was the night he'd put a knife to her throat. And yet, somehow, hearing him shuffle around in that state, seeing the look of fear on Felix's young face and Collette's worry, she could feel only pity for the man.

"Why is he like this?" Ophiera asked, breaking the quiet.

Collette blinked as if waking up before smiling gently. "The captain? Aye, a scholar could dedicate their entire life to that question and still not find the answer. But I take it you mean, why is he acting like a different person all of a sudden?"

Ophiera nodded. "I don't understand what has changed."

Twiddling her thumbs, Collette glanced at the floor, listening to the footsteps of someone she could only assume was Felix fetching the whiskey.

"I reckon you understand...perhaps you just don't want to think about it right now."

"What do you mean?"

Collette chewed her lip for a moment. "Imagine if you had to return to the Cloister. How might you react?"

A different discomfort settled in the pit of Ophiera's stomach now. The thought of the place alone did indeed cause her distress.

"So the Shole is to blame for all of this?"

"Not all of it," Collette replied, twiddling her thumbs again. She hesitated a moment, looking slightly ashamed. With another deep breath, she closed her eyes. "Don't get me wrong, the Shole is certainly not a good place for him, but your presence...well...it doesn't help."

Though the tautness of the tether had loosened with the whiskey, a tightness resurged in her chest.

"So, this is my fault?" She breathed, trying to shake the image of a burning beach littered with glowing vespers.

"Partially, but don't take that as *blame*." Her dark eyes fell to the bottle of whiskey with a pained expression. "The captain...well, are you familiar with the tidal pools that form around Cantheas?"

Ophiera nodded, remembering the stench of rotting sea life trapped in the shallow, mucky curves carved in the rocks.

"Well, until recently, the captain's life has been nothing but a tidal pool—a never-ending influx of bad experiences left to fester in the heat of the sun. But ya know, sometimes, those pools settle out when left undisturbed long enough...the rot sinks, and the stench disappears. All that's left is still, apathetic water floating above the hidden muck. Never truly gone but never acknowledged either. Then you came along, like the storm that you are, and stirred up the rotten sediment. Now, he's trying to ride out the storm, hoping it will settle back, just as it has before...But I'm afraid it can't in your presence."

Ophiera chewed her lip, processing the metaphor Collette had so beautifully painted. It resonated with her in a way that, as Collette said, she wasn't ready to think about at the moment.

"I didn't intend to cause him so much pain."

"People usually don't, but Jasp is particularly attuned to pain," Collette said gently. "That said, there are worse things—like rotting comfortably from the inside out. Like barely surviving instead of living. But maybe now that everything is churned up, the storm can clear him out—cast the muck out to sea and start fresh with clear water."

Confused, Ophiera followed this metaphor with less success. If she were the storm...

"How?"

Collette's dark eyes softened. "All these years, I've helped Jasper survive himself, but after seeing how he looks at you, I truly believe you'll be the one to help him thrive."

Ophiera shook her head, smiling sadly. "You're giving me far too much credit. From what I've seen, *I've* only brought out the worst in him. I'm fairly certain he hates me."

"Aye, he might...but hatred is the most significant thing he's felt in years. You've already given him a reason beyond surviving to act, a sense of purpose he never had."

To Ophiera, the word *purpose* triggered thoughts that were quite unwelcome. Her life had been filled with nothing *but* purpose; as an Aspect, as a paladin of the Cloister, as the Warden of Iluka, so many titles with much purpose. Yet had she ever truly fulfilled any of them? Had any of them fulfilled her? Seek Pyra, destroy the Brotherhood, and kill Aud; those were her purposes now…and all would end in violence. But wasn't violence itself her very purpose? And was it not that violence that forced Jasper to drink to forget?

"Aye, dear, don't think too hard on it," Collette said softly. "Just know that I'm delighted you're here with us, doing what you're doing, and I know the captain is too. Even if he doesn't show it in any sane or comprehensible way."

Instinctively, Ophiera reached a hand to her throat, feeling the slight bump where his knife had nicked. Scarred over now, she was sure it would fade to nothing in time. But the horror behind his gaze, could that ever fade?

"Try to rest, even if it takes drinking more of this," Collette said, pushing the clay jug beside Ophiera as she stretched to a stand. "If ya need more, find me or Felix. And if you need a better place to sleep, I can ask the captain—"

"I've slept on harder floors," Ophiera interrupted with a hollow smile, "but thank you. For everything."

"Aye, aye," Collette said, her mouth twisting into a smirk that didn't quite meet her eyes. The first mate closed the door behind her, leaving Ophiera alone with only whiskey.

~ Twenty Nine ~

MEMORIA

"Are you feeling any better?" Kaikora boomed.

Myronor winced. He wasn't sure why she had to shout everything, especially in a library.

"Same as before."

Her gray eyes lingered on him, unreadable as usual. "You don't look well."

Myronor sighed, closing the book in his hand and allowing his frustration and pain to take over his mouth.

"And how could I be well? I continually find it more difficult to move, think, or sleep as the ekath destroys me from the inside out. As much as I appreciate your offer of wine to soothe the burden, I find my thoughts darken beyond the discomfort with libations. All I can do is lie here and read."

The shaman cocked her head to the side, examining the book now resting on his chest. "Find anything of interest in your mother's journals yet?"

"Concerning the portals? Not yet," Myronor said, raising the journal again in his shaky hands. "But that doesn't mean it isn't interesting..."

* * *

Only months into my new position as Ambassador, and I'm nearing my wits' end with the Consortia. When I accepted this position, I admit it was with motivations beyond diplomacy, yet I still expected the most powerful sovereignty in Erum to be slightly less paranoid. Knowledge is the ultimate power, currency, and liberator, yet the Consortia hoard their knowledge like their wealth and slaves alike. In all my years, I can't remember feeling more lost in a place than here, and given my ability to span, that is saying something.

My first task as Ambassador has been to trade knowledge for knowledge—conjura for imbuteria—and yet I'm beginning to think I've been duped in some way during the exchange. Every bit of information I have been able to share with the Magistrate on the practices of imbuteria has been well-documented and well-received. Yet, despite numerous attempts by the Magistrate's mages, my efforts have been insufficient. Any imbuements cast have been near failures, only weak imitations of the expected products, though the incantations remain without fault. The reports I've received indicate they've been unable to produce anything close to the lowest quality imbued items sold at the poorest of markets in Krysas. Even Rheta's prized apprentice cannot produce more than a glowing dagger. Though truthfully, that may have more to do with her temperament than anything else. I can only hope that Eliana completes her apprenticeship with Rheta before my son's magic is realized, for his sake as much as mine. That woman has more ambition.

Regardless, the Justicars hold me accountable for these failures, claiming I have provided poor instructions. They have now requested that I return to Feyralis and demonstrate the practices in person. And while I understand their logic, as direct observation of magical practices is far better than reading instructions, I cannot return to Tanvik. For those who are dedicated to the pursuit of knowledge, asylum and esteem are often required equally.

Thus, I must find a solution to this problem. While I am not one to skirt responsibility or fault, I do suspect I am not the only hindrance in this scenario. My guess is that the Consortia has been sharing only a portion of their knowledge, providing an incomplete recipe to those who are not wiser. It is an unfortunate matter that I doubt will be solved by diplomacy alone. Any leverage of conjura practices I may have held is gone, having foolishly assumed our exchange was equal. Already, several of the Consortia mages have become adept at conjuring a few basic foods, and some, like Glamwell, have already begun adapting the practices to their own preferences and cuisines. The only solace I can take from this scenario is that there is clearly no deficit in my ability to teach.

But teaching is not doing. Therefore, tonight, I will attempt the imbuements I've passed on to Feyralis. I will gather the necessary materials, prepare the incantations, and focus all my energy on the task at hand. And if I, Pyra Ebontide, cannot achieve the expected results, then I will have confirmed the problem is something other than myself.

* * *

Consortia politics are not the only confusion I suffer here. Of late, primarily when my mind is at rest, I find myself craving the sandy dunes and cerulean waters of Iluka. While the city of Krysas is an undeniable marvel of imbuteria and history, the dark stone and cramped streets remind me too much of my earliest memories. Too much of what I willfully left behind. And while this confirms some of my suspicions regarding the founding of the city, it brings me no comfort. Not as Iluka did.

Strange how little value I first saw in the village, beyond the pearls, that is. And yet, I have left everything I hold dear behind there now. Berwyn writes weekly, updating me on our son and the goings-on in the village. It is distracting, to say the least, but a welcome distraction at times. He begs me to write in return, even if only for our son, and yet each time I bring my quill to parchment, the words disappear like smoke in the wind. In my journals and in my research, the words flow from me faster than I can write. And yet, I struggle to understand why I fail to connect with my kin in the manner they wish for.

Then again, I view this existence through a far different lens.

I can only do my best, and the best for Myronor is the work I'm conducting now here in Krysas. Letters won't secure a future for him. My emotions won't change his fate. I do wonder what is worse: to be forgotten or to be resented by my own flesh and blood. Only time will tell, but in these moments of weakness, I must remember the reason I am here, the duty I must uphold.

I will have to accept that the waves are quite different here, crashing against stone in place of sand.

~ Thirty ~

TEMPERANCE

*G*asp.

A frigid slap of cold caught Jasper's breath in his throat. Violently awakened, he shuddered against the drenched floor. Head throbbing, his eyes remained closed as he prayed to slip back into oblivion.

Another splash, another gasp, forcing his eyes open. Blinking away the bright light, a bleary nail stuck awkwardly from the floorboard, wavering in and out of focus.

"Get up," said Col, her anger stabbing his ears.

He turned his face downwards, hoping to drown himself in the shallow puddle. Just as darkness came to claim him again, he felt the hardened sole of a boot lightly step on his outstretched hand.

"Get up now, or I'll start crushing."

Jasper rolled onto his back, taking a few moments to recognize the underside of his cartography table. Insides churning, he knew of only one solution and reached a hand up in the air.

"Be a doll and hand me my flask."

Instead of his precious relief, she slapped his hand aside. In one graceful motion, she seized him by the shirt and hauled him into a chair. Again, his insides writhed threateningly as the world spun around him. Or maybe *he* spun through the world. Either way, it wasn't good.

"No more flask," Col said as she slid a bucket between his legs.

As always, her timing was impeccable. Suddenly, his body wracked as a vile liquid purged from his gut, searing his nostrils as he spewed into the bucket. Cool, soft hands pulled his hair back, holding him steady as his expulsion continued. And continued. As his body revolted against him, he wondered just how much he'd put away last night and how much he now wasted into the bucket.

"You're disgusting," Col said quietly, wiping her hands clean with a rag before tossing it to him.

He wiped his mouth shakily, not daring to speak. Col removed the vile bucket with an expression that worried him she'd next dump it over his head. But thankfully, his first mate tossed the pail and all out to sea through the open porthole.

As his head lolled to the side, he glimpsed his panacea on the table. She must have found his flask on the floor and set it on the table, just barely out of reach.

Col growled, slapping his wandering hand away from his salvation.

Now that his gut had been purged, he found it filled with self-loathing instead. He was tired of being told what to do...he bore the title of captain, after all. Rising to a shaky stand, he towered over Col with a pointed finger.

"Listen here, this is my ship, and if I want a drink, I—"

A sharp blow to his chest stopped his breath, and he landed hard back into the chair. As he gasped for air, Col bent over him, dark eyes smoldering.

"*Your ship?*" She hissed. "We've been sailing for nearly two days under my command while you've been drowning yourself in whiskey. By the laws of the sea, *I* am captain of this vessel now. And you know damn well who the crew will choose to follow if I call for a mutiny."

He swallowed the foulness on his tongue. "Don't be stupid, Col. There's barely a crew to mutiny."

"I'm not the foolish one! While you've been blacked out like an idiot, Fel and I have been tending to you and Ophiera, all while sailing us to the Shole in near record time! So, how about you shut your mouth and do what you're told, *Captain?*" She kicked another bucket between his legs, this one brimming with soapy water. "Wash up and prepare for landfall."

The bubbles swayed lazily on the water's surface, splashing gently onto the floor. It wasn't hard for his loathsome mood to turn inward now.

"Col, look, I'm s-"

"You're always sorry!" she snapped, stomping towards the door. "And yet, we always end up right back here."

He ran a filthy hand over his face, feeling every bit of her ire burning through him. Ever since they'd set sail from Cantheas, he'd struggled to keep others' emotions out of his own, and Col was no different. In fact, he felt her emotions more intensely than anyone, given the closeness of their friendship. Though perhaps friendship wasn't quite the right label for their relationship. Friendship indicated a give-and-take, but in truth, Jasper only took. He was a parasite, especially during episodes such as this; if not for Col, he would have long ago lost the ship or his life.

"Just clean up," Col said, her voice softening with an effort. "We'll worry about the rest later."

She wiggled her fingers at him before leaving the room, slamming the door behind her. And like a trail of smoke left in her wake, he was overcome by her disappointment left behind.

By the sea, he was worthless.

The first episode he'd suffered with Col would have forced any other person to abandon ship. But she had stuck by him despite the feelings of disgust, terror, and pity that seeped from her after seeing him in such a state. Right now, her low opinion of him caused him more pain than any of the buried reasons he drank.

And for years, that had been his primary motivation to fight off these episodes. It didn't always work, but he had been much improved. Col had helped him develop a routine and a plan of action, and she never failed to see him through to the end. Usually, it only took a single night of inebriated chaos for him to reach the bottom of the abyss and begin his climb back out. But since the night he'd pulled his knife on Ophiera, he had spent every conscious moment drinking himself to the brink, and yet his demons continued to hold him in the dark depths. Seemingly, nothing could offer him a moment of peace, not even enough ember whiskey to drown a navarra. He didn't understand what had changed; what had broken?

Slowly, Jasper undressed. Though reluctant to bathe himself, he recognized the need, and it was the least he could do for Col. As he pulled his grubby shirt overhead, the light reflector above his cartography table caught his eye. Mirrored in the wide, concave disk, he saw the piteous man reflected.

His sickly complexion caused the scars decorating his torso to seem more repugnant than usual. Like a record of his existence, each symbol and slash that decorated his body held intention and consequence. Though he rarely suffered night terrors of their acquisition any longer, he didn't need dreams to relive the pain of each.

Jasper kept his eyes on the floor as he finished undressing. Bare in his cartography room, he reached into the bucket, grasping the cloth submerged near the bottom. The warm water felt uncomfortable against his chilled, clammy hands, and his discomfort continued as he dragged the rough cloth across the raised disfig-urements. Overly sensitive, as usual.

Once his body had been cleansed, he swirled his inky locks in the grayish water several times before wringing them out. He let the air dry his skin, not wishing to aggravate the overly sensitive carvings with another rough towel. Pacing around the room sped up the process and staved off the remaining nausea.

Col had placed a change of clothes in a neat pile on the cartography table beside the forgotten flask. He was surprised she had left it so carelessly, but she had fled rather quickly. Temptation hit him like a tidal wave, and yet, he forced his shaking hand over the dark linen pants and ruddy shirt instead. He knew he was undeserving of Col's care, but his demons reminded him that another undeserving soul was present on his ship.

No wonder he couldn't find any peace while the white-flamed nightmare sailed with him. Ophiera was the reason he was now forced to return to the Shole, dragged along in her search for Pyra. The entire situation only reinforced his surety that all innaturals, even those he had never met, were meant to ruin his life. And while he usually reserved that insult for mages, he now concluded that the paladins and shamans of Tanvik were just as disgusting.

They'd all made his life a living hell.

In the past, when his episodes had been especially terrible, he sometimes wished Ophiera had killed him on the beach along with the others. Back and forth, his ego went, trying to decide why she'd spared him. And though he had his answer now, did it really change anything? Now, it only felt as if she'd returned to finish the job.

Without her interference, he wouldn't need to rely on the Ashen Order to protect the *Berserker* and his shored crew members. Without her presence on his ship, he could block the sensations of others more easily. Without her duty, he wouldn't be sailing to the last place on Erum he wished to venture to. It seemed every one of his problems sparked from Ophiera.

Heavy footsteps echoed outside the door. Usually, Col was a bit more light-footed than that. Suddenly, the door to his cartography room flew open without a knock or sound. And while he expected Col to barge in, berating him for taking so long to dress, he realized far too quickly that fate had indeed cursed him.

Ophiera's dark dress shifted with the shadows beyond the threshold, stark against her crown of white hair. Her violet eyes fixed on him, like death, come to claim him at last, and yet the sight of her incited something far greater than fear. But as her gaze dropped to his bare, mutilated body, rage overtook him.

"Knocking is polite," he growled, pulling on the pair of dark pants held in his hand.

She said nothing, eyes still fixated on the scars burdening his bare chest. He threw the stone red shirt over his head.

With a heavy step, she came inside, closing the door behind her. When she faced him again, though, her expression was purposefully bland.

"I would like to discuss our plan before landing."

"*Our* plan?" he asked, roughly settling himself into a seat at his cartography table. "If I had a say in any of this, I would plan to turn around."

To his surprise, she crossed the room and took the opposite seat at the table. He noticed her gait was off, as if she hadn't quite acquired her sealegs yet. Or maybe it was just the awkwardness of walking in the form-fitted dress. He wished she'd worn her armor instead—it seemed less intimidating than the Krysan-style gown clinging to her muscles now.

"Fine, then, can you at least provide me with advice?" She asked.

"My advice? We should have never set sail."

He noticed her eyebrow twitch violently at his words, bringing a sliver of amusement to his sour mood. She really wasn't good at this...

"I know little to nothing of where we are traveling, but my understanding is the city isn't near the coast, correct?" She asked stiffly.

He nodded, surprised she kept pressing.

"So the plan is to travel on foot from the port, yes?"

He nodded again.

"How many nights then will it take to reach Birozahran?"

"Depends on how fast you walk."

She took another deep breath before gesturing to the map sprawled on the table. "Can you at least show me where we will land and where we must go?"

"Here," he said, pointing a shaking finger. He noticed the flask still teetering at the edge of the cartography table and was tempted to alleviate the weight of this conversation. Licking his lips, he barely heard Ophiera's following query.

"And *what* is there?"

"Sionnach's abandoned port," he said quietly. She cocked her head curiously, and the expression softened the burn in his gut. He guessed her next question and decided it would be easier to answer preemptively. "Sionnach was the name of Birozahran while under Consortia occupation."

She nodded, feigning an understanding he knew she couldn't have. As he watched the wheels turn behind her darkening eyes, he hoped she wouldn't ask the next logical question.

"Why does the city have two different names?"

Jasper bit his lip, knowing he shouldn't answer. Talk of the city and its history could never end well. But she always seemed to compel him to act against his better judgment. She was worse, in many ways, than the flagon of whiskey resting on the edge of the table.

"During the Purge, the Consortia claimed the city, renaming it Sionnach, holding some meaning in Krysan I care not to go into. But when the Enclave overthrew the Consortia occupation, they began calling the city by its ancestral name of Birozahran."

She studied him with rapt attention, and he found the rhythm of his heart changed. It was ridiculous how he could despise and desire so equally.

"Is that a good idea?" Ophiera asked.

Confused, he followed her gaze towards his hand, outstretched towards his flagon. He hadn't noticed his reach, but rather than continue to ponder what lay beneath her black dress, he listened to his instincts.

The first drink always hit the best—a promising burn that soothed his throat while filling his belly with a drop of apathy. And that was precisely what he needed right now. Desperate to fill himself with nothingness, he drank like a man in a desert.

He'd nearly drained half the contents when it was snatched away from his lips. Ophiera glared at him as she put the flagon to her lips, tilting her head back. Dumbfounded, he could only watch as she emptied the contents into herself before tossing the empty flask on the table.

"And why the hell would you do that?" he asked angrily.

"I, too, needed something to temper this discussion," she said, meeting his glare.

He smirked, glaring down at the drop of ember whiskey seeping into the wooden table. What had been left in that flask was enough to put Col under the table.

"You're going to be flat on your arse within the hour."

"Then we best map out a travel route quickly," she said sternly, leaning over the map. "Are we following a road, or will we be traveling cross-country?"

He couldn't believe her nerve.

Then again, maybe he could. Hadn't he watched her jump from his ship onto a navarra, only to kill it with her bare hands? Hadn't he watched her catch fire in white flames and threaten to kill him? Now that he thought of it, if there was one thing she had in troves, it was nerve. Perhaps it was in his best interest to comply with her demands, especially if she were soon to be exceptionally inebriated.

From a nearby stack, Jasper reached for a thin piece of tracing paper and a willow charcoal. He laid the thin sheet over the map and began to trace out a route. "There is a stone road that runs from the port to Sionnach, but like the port, it's been abandoned for years. Given its construction, I believe it should still be intact enough for us to walk to the city, and in that case, we will only have to sleep one night in the Shole."

The corners of her lips twitched upwards, breaking her stoic expression. He tried to ignore it while continuing to trace the map.

"What about water?" she asked. "Kaikora mentioned hidden sources in the desert."

Jasper indicated one of the cairn stones he had previously traced. "There are several aqueduct caves beneath the sand, remnants of the former Enclave civilization. But trust me when I say water is the least of our concerns."

"What else is there?" She asked, leaning forward to study the map.

The way the dress hugged her shoulders reminded him of how easily she maneuvered the giant blade normally strapped on her back. When the ember whiskey hit her, would she be a belligerent or benevolent drunk? His best hope was that she simply passed out, leaving him in the peace of solitude again. And yet, he could barely stop his mind from imagining what she must look like asleep.

"Sandstorms," he grunted with a shake of his head. "Luckily, they shouldn't be too bad this time of year. But once the sun sets, we'll use the aqueducts as shelter, or else the night will be our death."

"Because of the cold?"

He shrugged. "The temperature doesn't help, but I refer more to the creatures. You have no idea the abominations that prowl the sands at night."

She snorted, surprising him momentarily. He'd thought what he described sounded rather horrific, and yet she appeared amused.

"That funny?"

"No, no," she said, stifling a smile. He could hardly believe she was smiling. "You seem to have quite a plan for someone only providing advice."

"You'd prefer I not think about our survival?" he snapped.

She laughed, beautiful and aggravating all at once. It lightened the weight on his heart nearly as much as the ember whiskey. And yet he didn't want this feeling; he wanted nothing.

"I'm just not used to..." She cleared her throat, pressing her hand hard against her chest. "Well, perhaps the whiskey has hit me in a strange way."

He glared at her.

The whiskey may have loosened her tongue, but it wasn't to blame for her faltering smile or hollowing eyes. At that moment, he wished he *couldn't* read her expression so easily. He sensed the pain that drew upon her features and recalled Kaikora's warnings of the spirit rope. Half his heart wished to comfort her while the other half celebrated her suffering.

Giving in to his darker urge, he watched in silence as she struggled against herself. He watched every shift of her expression until she wore the benign mask yet again. It was quite a lesson in picking oneself up by one's bootstraps, and he wondered why he could not achieve the same.

"How do you know so much about the Shole?" She asked, not meeting his eyes.

The demons inside begged him not to answer.

This wasn't something to discuss, not here, not now, not ever.

But after watching her struggle against herself, he felt compelled to answer. Perhaps the ember whiskey was affecting him, too.

"I was born in Iluka, but I lived in Sionnach most of my childhood."

"Before the Enclave reclaimed it?"

He nodded. "I relocated to Krysas after the revolution."

"Is that why you despise the Enclave so much?" she asked.

But no amount of ember whiskey could prevent the demons from roaring at her presumption.

"By that logic, I would despise you just the same for destroying Iluka."

He watched with a pang of satisfaction as the devastation hung on her face. But as he watched her eyes moisten, staring unblinkingly at the map, he felt only guilt.

"You should," she murmured. "I apologize for prying."

She pushed her chair back from the table, resisting eye contact. But before she had the chance to stand and leave, Jasper had reached for her hand. The warmth of her fingers beneath his trembling palm silenced the demons for the moment.

"I shouldn't have said that," he offered quietly.

"Why not? It is the truth," she breathed. "I can't blame you for despising me as much as the Shole."

"I don't—you don't understand," he began, his voice shaking. "The Shole took everything from me and does so for anyone who sets an unwelcome foot within its sands. If Pyra sought the Enclave, then she didn't wish to be found."

"We don't know what Pyra wished for," Ophiera replied angrily, sliding her hand out from under his. With one last glare, she stood from the table, and he noticed again the sway in her stance. As she stepped away from him, the sound of tearing cloth rang throughout the cabin, and she disappeared beneath the table with a loud thud.

"Ophiera?" He asked, leaning over to see her face down on the floor, the edge of her dress caught and torn on the loosened nail jutting beneath the table.

She wasn't moving.

Panicked, Jasper fell to his knees and rolled her over by the shoulders. To his surprise, she wore an embarrassed smile across her lips. And then, the unthinkable happened. The woman who had nearly killed him twice, the berserker, the Warden of Iluka, the Aspect of Retribution, *giggled*.

"I told you that was too much whiskey," he growled, releasing her shoulders and sitting back on his knees.

"You don't even know the half of it," she laughed, covering her face with her hand. "I had already finished mine just before I came here."

Her smile fell into a trembling frown, her mood shifting faster than the winds in a storm. Whether it was the tether or simply the feelings loosened by whiskey that overtook her, Jasper was certain they were difficult to bear. Beneath her hand, he saw tears trickle down her reddening cheeks. He could only sit patiently beside her and let whatever this was work itself out. That was precisely what Col would do for him, though Col didn't have to suffer the sensation of another's emotions rattling their very own. Whatever ailed Ophiera now was a heavy weight indeed.

"You know," she began hoarsely, wiping the moisture from her glistening eyes, "the whiskey helps null the pain of the ekath, but it makes other things much worse."

"Like what?" He asked, resting his elbow on his knee.

"Balance, to start," she said, sitting up slowly. The hem of her dress was still caught on the nail, though she no longer seemed to notice. "And guilt...it's harder to hide from the guilt after drinking so much of that vile liquid."

"First off, it's not vile, just an acquired taste," he said with a slight smile. "Second, you shouldn't take what I say seriously, let alone allow it to guilt you. I know little about anything beyond the sea, and even Col would question that much."

She smiled sadly, staring at her hand. "Yet all I've known is my Oath, and I've never given it a second thought until recently. And no matter if I'm held to duty or not, I'm doomed by the scars it has left behind."

Slowly, she rolled up her sleeve, revealing the blistered scars. He had never realized the symbols burned into her skin resembled his own so closely. Gently, he took her by the wrist, dragging her arm close to him.

"Does it hurt?" he asked, running his thumb gently over the raised mutilations.

"Not exactly," she said with the scent of whiskey on her breath. "I *feel* them all the time, and they only pain me when I burn."

A vision of her surrounded by flame caused him to release her hand. "I'm sorry," he murmured; she had made her stance clear, and yet he still crossed the line of flames again and again.

"I'm sorry, too," she said, her voice slurred ever so slightly. "I shouldn't have questioned you on the Shole. And I shouldn't have threatened to set you on fire before..."

He chuffed. "Col says an apology doesn't count if you're drunk."

"I *am* drunk, aren't I?" she said, surprised. "Damn it all...I'll die trying to get back in that hammock."

"Hammock?" He asked.

"No bed," she mumbled, trying to come to a stand. "I should lie down."

"Wait—"

Fffrrrip!

Before he could warn her of her dress still caught on the nail, she'd toppled again to the sound of tearing fabric. This time, he caught her, falling backward together against the damp floor. She lay between his legs, pressed uncomfortably against his intimate parts. The smell of something herbaceous filled his nostrils as her soft hair brushed against his face. With hands on his chest, she lifted her head, eyes glazed in surprise as she gazed at him. He saw the faintest mark on her neck from where his dagger had drawn blood days ago. In that moment, she could have—no, *should* have killed him. In his moment of fear, he had marred even more of her beautiful, smooth skin, just like the Cloister had done.

"I'm sorry," Jasper said, running a finger against her faded cut. "Often the scars we can't see are the ones that we feel the most."

"You don't have to apologize," she said with a sad smile. "I don't blame you for despising me."

"I don't only despise you," he stumbled, unable to say what he truly meant while meeting those violet eyes. "I mean to say, I despise many things in this world, least of all you. We are just...very different."

Ophiera chuffed, setting her head down on his chest. The weight of her against his markings was oddly soothing, yet her sigh of comfort alarmed him. For someone who had come after him with a sword for touching her, she was surely getting comfortable atop him now.

"We are not so different," she whispered, running her fingers over his shirt, across the scars beneath. "I couldn't...go back...either."

As her breaths grew ragged, slowing in rhythm, he felt her body relax against his own. Warm and heavy, he found himself pinned to the ground by a drunken, slumbering paladin. The scent of her hair and the weight of her body began to affect him as well. He ran a hand along her arm, feeling every curve of hard muscle and every raised symbol. Perhaps she was right—they weren't so different. But given his current state, the moment of peace was quickly turning to temptation.

"Col!" he called quietly, trying to direct his voice under the door.

Ophiera stirred in his arms, murmuring, "Don't...shout...at...her."

His first mate appeared at the door a moment later. She gazed upon Ophiera's limp body, crushing him to the ground, her eyes narrowing furiously. "You scoundrel—"

"She's drunk!" he whispered. "Can you maybe help me instead of judging!?"

"Oh, the poor dear," Col said with a tsk. "Felix already gave her half a flagon today; how much did you give her?!"

"How is this my fault?"

"Because it's always your fault!"

"Shut up...please..." Ophiera murmured, nuzzling her face against his ruddy shirt.

Jasper very much needed to be free of her now.

Col helped to maneuver Ophiera from him, but he knew his first mate didn't have the strength to carry such a woman. Once free, he took Ophiera into his arms, cradling her muscular body against his chest. His heartbeat was far from steady. Her breath may have smelled like whiskey, but it only tempted him to taste the smoky libation from her lips.

"Where are you going?" Col hissed, following Jasper at his heels.

"She can have my bed," he said quietly, descending the stairs to his quarters. "I deserve one more night on the floor, sober this time."

After setting the agitated paladin in his untouched bed, Jasper returned to his cartography room. Col, as was her nature, stayed behind to fuss over Ophiera. As she did with him, he was certain she made sure a bucket was nearby and placed pillows to brace her back, ensuring she didn't roll over and drown in her vomit. Regardless of what he imagined Col was doing below, he wasn't sure he could stomach any of it at the moment.

Instead, Jasper occupied his hands by completing the traced paper copy of the Shole. A mindless, tactile task kept his mind from going deeper into darkness. Thankfully, the tremors in his hands had dissipated by the time Col had rejoined him in the cartography room. She hovered above him for a moment, silent and studying the map he traced.

"You're going into the desert with her, right?"

He inhaled a deep, sour breath. "Seems I have little choice if I want to keep my ship and my crew alive and well."

There was a brief pause; the only sounds were the scraping of charcoal and the crash of the sea.

"How are you feeling otherwise?" Col asked.

"Sober."

She sighed. "You know what I me—"

"How do you think, Col?" He growled, snapping the piece of charcoal on the map. Everything inside him seemed to spill over like the sea, unstoppable and detrimental. "My mood has gone through more heaves and pitches than the damned ship! I thought I had been freed of that forsaken place, and now I'm being forced to return, escorting *her* of all people! I want nothing more than to be blacked out on the floor, and yet I hate myself for needing the whiskey! I cannot win, I cannot *be,* and that is how I feel, along with everything else everyone else *feels* when they are near me!"

He reached for another piece of charcoal and continued copying the map. The shake in his hands had returned, and he hated the wave of guilt that hit him as Col crossed her arms around his shoulders, pressing her bosom against his neck.

"I'm sorry, Jasp," she whispered. "This is all my fault—I went behind your back and got you roped into the Ashen Order. I never wished for you to return to the Shole, and if there had been any other option, you know I'd have chosen it."

Under the weight of her embrace, his anger faded. He placed a steady hand on hers and patted gently. "You have nothing to be sorry for, Col. My misery is my own doing, and I deserve the suffering I've sown."

"Don't you dare blame yourself for what they did to you!"

"I'm not," he said, keeping the visions of *them* at bay. "But just now, Ophiera...she said we weren't that different, and it is true in some ways. She has suffered similar circumstances, and yet, where we differ is in our responses to them. Tonight, she drank from that flask for a very different reason...Doesn't this prove the fault lies within me?"

It was the first time Jasper had admitted such a thing. He'd spent so long blaming the Shole for breaking him, but what if he'd been broken from the start? What if, no matter what he had suffered, he would always be insufferable?

"Just because her suffering weighs on her differently doesn't mean you are faulted by how you carry it. The burdens of the past are sometimes easiest fought, sometimes easiest shared...and sometimes easiest forgotten. She might have drunk that ember whiskey tonight for a different reason, but she has drunk it before for the same. Perhaps she simply learned earlier that it doesn't help in the way you wish it would."

"Col, nothing has ever been how I wished it to be."

She ran an affectionate hand through his clean hair. The feel of her fingertips grazing against his scalp seemed to calm his heart nearly as much as her warmth against his back. "All I can say is you don't have to be like her. But I do think you need to follow her."

"Why?"

"Because since the moment she set foot on this ship, the tides have shifted in her direction. Maybe they always have...like the old proverb says, 'stagnant waters may ease your sail, but never rely on them to live.' When in doubt, follow the current, remember? I believe there is a purpose to our suffering, and I think that purpose lies with her."

~ Thirty One ~

ESTRANGED

The world turned gray.

Dreary clouds hung high in the sky with an empty threat of rain. Dark waters churned against the *Berserker* without a hint of blue. Gargantuan dunes of rolling gray sands loomed on the horizon, blending with the dismal sky and sea.

The only disparity in the monotone view was a massive harbor of marred white stone and rotting wood. Birozahran's seaport stood similar in size to that in Krysas, yet was now utterly devoid of ships. All berths were open, and some of the wooden docks remained intact, but most were to be found in various stages of decay. Any vessel sailing within sight would undoubtedly know this place was abandoned. And any sailor with half a mind would surely have kept their distance.

"Take her in slow around the debris, captain!" Collette yelled.

"I see the rubble just fine," Jasper called back dryly from the wheel.

"That's interesting...since ya seem to be steering the boat right at it."

Ophiera rubbed her temples, closing her eyes tightly in frustration. She had already tolerated their bickering all morning since awakening in Jasper's cabin. While she appreciated the gesture, she wished Jasper had simply carried her back to the cramped cabin—at least there, she couldn't hear the arguing. And yet, they continued to jab at her throbbing head relentlessly. She had overindulged much on this journey in hopes of calming the ekath, but last night...last night she'd acted a fool.

All morning, she struggled to forget the feel of his steady breaths beneath her as she'd fallen asleep. Whatever had been said in the captain's cartography room must remain there; she needed that behind her as she looked toward the journey ahead.

"He's sober enough to steer the ship," Collette muttered under her breath as they stood together near the starboard edge.

"But how does he not suffer any after-effects?" she grumbled, still rubbing her temple.

Collette gasped so loudly that Ophiera nearly reached for her claymore.

"Sorry, I forgot..." The first mate pulled a small vial of emerald green liquid from between her bosoms. "Jasp keeps a permanent stock of these in his quarters. Guaranteed to set you right!"

Desperate, Ophiera drank without question. The sweet and salty concoction tasted oddly herbaceous, but that was nothing compared to its egregious texture. Thick, slimy liquid slid down her throat, nearly a paste, and she struggled to swallow. But almost immediately, she felt a relief of pressure behind her eyes, and the gray light of the Shole didn't seem to shine quite so brightly. With the throbbing reduced to a faint buzz, she refocused her attention on the port again.

"Why was this place abandoned?"

Collette shrugged. "Port fell into disuse as aerships became the preference. Why bother walking through the Shole when you could glide over it in a fraction of the time? Then, after the rebellions, rumor is the Enclave destroyed it out of spite."

With Jasper distracted near the wheel, Ophiera leaned down to Collette's ear.

"Is the Enclave truly so evil?"

The first mate shrugged again. "I can't say for certain, as I've never been to the Shole. However, I've met my fair share of Enclave people in Krysas. All I can say is I mostly felt pity for them. They've been through hell, and it hasn't gotten much easier. But I also know Jasper suffered a great deal in this place, and for that, I will find it forever tainted."

"Prepare to dock!" Jasper called.

The young deckhand Felix began gathering ropes, preparing for the tricky task of docking in a decrepit port. Though he smiled at Ophiera in greeting, his eyes fixated on her armor with a hint of trepidation.

The moment Collette had called, 'Land ho!' Ophiera had donned her golden plate armor. Snug against her musculature, the plate mail fit her body as if it had been forged upon her, which was closer to truth than not. Even in the gray light, the adamantrium metal, born from the Aether itself, shimmered and swirled. The ekath might still discomfort her greatly, but she'd already felt her mood improve from wearing the armor again.

With a graceful lope, Jasper descended from the ship's wheel, stalking past Felix with a glare.

"What are you looking at?" he hissed.

"N-nothing, captain," Felix replied, turning pink again and refocusing on tying off the ship.

Ophiera rolled her eyes, her gaze landing on the torn leather overcoat Jasper now wore. While it looked particularly worn in the gray light, she felt a pang of guilt for the slash she had put in the collar, still agape and unmended.

"Welcome to the Shole," Jasper said, moving to stand before her.

"At least the weather is nice," Ophiera said dryly.

Collette snorted, but Jasper glared back at her, distant and emotionless. His amber eyes were empty again—like the night he'd put his knife to her throat. The man who had drunkenly compared their scars was no longer aboard.

"Abandon this plan," he said darkly. "Please."

At least he'd tried to be polite, she thought with a sigh. But there was no convincing her otherwise. Like her hunt for Marvena along the Southern Coastlands, she felt in her soul that the answers she sought lay ahead. The only obstacle in her path was the pain of the ekath pulling her back to Myronor. But that was far too much to explain to Jasper and Collette.

"I must find Pyra," she said quietly.

"Why?"

"My Oath demands—"

"The Oath that you fear means nothing?"

So, she wasn't the only one who remembered their drunken conversation.

"The Order needs to learn what has become of Pyra, too," she said calmly, "and Myronor deserves to know the fate of his mother."

"You owe the Order *nothing*," Jasper spat, "And you owe Myronor even less."

"Are you naturally hypocritical or do you have to try?" Ophiera growled. Any sympathy she'd felt for the rogue had been sapped away the moment he'd mentioned her charge's name with such disdain. "Haven't you sailed to this wretched place for the Order? I doubt Kaikora holds *that* much sway over you. So why, then, did you come here, Jasper, if you are so utterly convinced it's a mis-take?"

He refused to meet her gaze, staring instead at the decayed port. "Why I'm here doesn't change the fact that the Shole is a death trap."

Stuck between anger and pity, Ophiera took a deep, steadying breath. She didn't need this, and neither did he. His mood was too unstable, just like his creed. And her purpose, like his pain, was far too great in this place.

"Luckily, I'm rather resistant to death," she said through gritted teeth. "Remain onboard the ship—I will continue alone."

"You can't cross the Shole without a guide," he said, his brow twitching with irritation.

"I've lived my life thus far without one; I'll take my chances." She hoisted the large rucksack, heavy with water, onto her back before turning to a mortified Collette. "I appreciate everything you've done for us, Collette, and everything you will continue to deal with in my absence. Please, give me seven nights. If I do not return by then, return to Krysas without me and inform Kaikora and Myronor."

"I can t-take you," Felix offered. "I've been to Birozahran once b-before..."

His words faltered as all eyes fell on him. The slight, wide-eyed lad looked like a lamb surrounded by lions, confused and out of place. Jasper's lip sneered while Collette's eyes widened, but Ophiera knew it fell to her to dissuade him.

"Absolutely not," she said harshly. Stepping forward, her armor clanked loudly against the deck. "Your captain was already a liabil-ity to my task, so what can you offer me in his stead?"

Felix's eyes fell, and the flash of pain behind them was hard to witness. The lad had been nothing but kind to her since they'd set sail, but she needed him to remain on the ship, no matter how cruelly she must convince him. She supposed she understood now why Jasper was so harsh on him.

With one last nod to Collette and a glare at Jasper, she took her first heavy step down the ship's ramp. Her armor pressed uncomfortably against her shoulders as she descended, with the weight of the bag settling in. Ladened with the heft of water and food, the pack carried with it the reminder of Myronor's absence. She'd been spoiled traveling with him before and wished that it was he, not Jasper or Felix, alongside her now. But she could not spare any mind for regret, not when the ekath transformed her longing into discomfort, pinching painfully beneath her breastplate.

At the base of the ramp, the swollen wood of the dock appeared slippery with swirls of sea moss scattered betwixt chunks of rubble. Carefully crossing the wobbling wood, Ophiera gazed down in horror at the countless ships silently hidden beneath the calm gray waters. Thick beds of colorful oysters clung to the surfaces facing the waves, reminding her painfully of Iluka.

When her boots finally stepped off the punky wooden dock onto the stone road, she felt the Aether surge beneath her. The same agonized energy she'd felt in Krysas now pulsated through her again, but this time, it was more relieving than anything. As if reunited with an old friend, the rage quelled the pain of the ekath, all while drawing her onward to the desert.

Ophiera followed the path as it led up the steep dune into the desert above. When Jasper had called it a stone road, he truly meant *a* stone. Instead of cobblestone or gravel, massive slabs of solid white rock lay nestled in the sand. Some pieces were longer than the *Berserker* itself, and if the gray sand had not blown into and filled the grooves between the segments, the path would have appeared as a single solid stone.

Only when she reached the top of the road did she dare a glance back at the *Berserker*. There was no sign of anyone following her, and while she felt relief in Felix's absence, she couldn't help but feel a pang of disappointment with Jasper. The deck lay empty, and she could only guess that the captain was inside his cabin and halfway to oblivion by now. And perhaps that was the best place for him.

The vast desert before her reminded her of the sea, with a horizon of ashen dunes rippling like waves, broken by clusters of coal-colored rocks resembling ships. As she trekked forward, she noticed that despite the stone's dark coloration, there appeared to be a strange sheen upon them, like the spectrum of light produced by oil floating atop the water. It was a place unlike any she had seen before, and in that, she found a sliver of joy.

Against the chilled wind, she found herself hurrying her speed, yet the drag of the ekath prevented her from ever reaching full stride. Without the relief of ember whiskey, there was little to distract her from the constant discomfort. And yet, despite searching the tether for Myronor's voice at every chance, she still felt nothing but the desperate pull.

The stark coloration of the landscape resembled that of a dead fire at the break of dawn. But a ways ahead on the road, she noticed the sands began to change. Something in the geography of the dunes, something more purposeful than the random ebb and flow of the desert thus far. As she approached these more patterned sands, she edged the road, not daring to step from it, following Jasper's warnings. The nearer the road brought her to the sandy mounds, however, the happier she was to remain upon it.

Breaking through the flows of sand, she found odd protrusions similarly gray but distinct in shape. With a squint of her eyes, she eventually recognized what pierced the dunes. Skeletal remains of countless bodies littered the ground, remnants of a great battle or perhaps a ruthless slaughter. Regardless, many souls had been sent to the Aether in this place.

Bleached skulls with sand-filled eyes stared blankly at her as she walked past. She didn't know *how* she knew their souls had been lost to the Aether in sin; she simply did. She'd thought the Brotherhood was merciless, but whatever had occurred here had been an equal, if not worse, atrocity. Unable to stomach the sight, she kept her eyes on the road until the bleak, gray middens were far behind her.

She relished in the solitude throughout the day, only consulting the traced map when she needed something more interesting to peruse than the sand itself. Jasper had clearly marked the road and what she assumed were a few of the aqueducts, but otherwise, it was a fairly sparse map. In bold letters near a drawn stone pillar, he'd written 'camp,' which she assumed was where they were meant to sleep. Well, where *she* would be sleeping now.

As the sky transitioned from gray to lavender, the stone landmark suddenly appeared on the horizon. The dark pillar loomed impossibly tall, hovering over the horizon as if floating. She knew the distortions of the cold desert could present a mirage, but it did not diminish the intimidating imagery.

Night poised itself as she arrived at the jagged cairn. Like the holy flames erupting from the very ground, the blackened glass stone had been thrust through the road, reaching upward towards the austere sky. Cracks throughout the slab provided evidence of the force behind its emergence, now filled with sand and dull spiderwebs.

Only when she stopped walking did she feel the fatigue hit her from an entire day of traveling on foot. She needed a rest, especially now as the breeze continued to blow colder and colder. Though labeled clearly, the map proved useless in her search for the aqueducts—no cave entrance or other shelter was visible from the road, only the stone cairn itself dominating the road.

She searched the sands, wondering if perhaps the entrance was hidden behind an illusion created by the cold, but she found nothing. Damning Jasper with a few choice curses, she eventually surrendered her search for the caves. She had spent many nights sleeping under the stars in Tanvik; what was one night in the Shole?

Bad idea, lass.

Ignoring the inner voice of Lotus, Ophiera threw her bag to the ground before collapsing against the stone pillar. After an entire day's trek, she wished for nothing more than rest. Yet the tight fit of adamantrium armor made it nearly impossible to relax. She loosened the fittings between the plates, hoping to provide her legs a bit more comfort. Yet the chill of the desert air seeped through the now-exposed gaps, trading one discomfort for another.

Begrudgingly, she retrieved her bed rolls from the pack and bundled herself against the dropping temperature. As the light disappeared, so did the clouds, revealing a dark purple sky beneath which Ophiera began to shiver. Reflected in the sparkling sand, the sky exploded in celestial fireworks. More stars than she knew existed emerged from the dark, impossibly bright against the vast, purple sky. The starlight illuminated the landscape more vibrantly than the gray-clouded sun of the day.

Jasper had called the Shole hell, but the beauty of the shimmering dunes bewitched her. For hours, she watched the lights of the night sky dance across the desert, trying to stay warm in thought. Her eyes slipped shut several times, but the shivers wracking her body prevented any proper sleep. This cycle of uncomfortable rest and cold continued until all she could hope for was morning.

* * *

Mewl.

The sound was foreign enough against the wind to force Ophiera's eyes open. She wiped the frost from her eyelashes, only to face the vast, dark, glittering sands. For a moment, she had forgotten where she was, or even who she was, apart from cold.

A flash of light drew her gaze downward. After a few more blinks of her tired eyes, she realized for the first time since departing Krysas that the delicate crystal dangling from her wrist glowed.

"M-Mallow?" she whispered hoarsely.

With another flash of light, the familiar burst into existence. On the stone road, she shook out her luxurious cream-colored coat. Ophiera reached for the cat, her stiff, gauntleted hands trembling in the cold. Warm fur brushed her open palm as she dragged Mallow against her breastplate. Two eyes of pale blue, nearly silver in the night, stared up at her in a worried expression.

"Is M-Myronor well?" Ophiera murmured, her teeth chattering.

The cat lifted her chin, exposing a small roll of parchment tied around her neck with a ribbon of blue fabric. Though her gauntlets rattled, she managed to untie the knot and unfurled the small piece of parchment.

Ophiera, I would have written sooner if not for being at the whim of a familiar. Words cannot possibly convey the yearning I feel in my soul without you. I thought that was all it was when my body fell cold, and I began to shiver, but now I worry that something has gone horribly wrong. Please send Mallow back with some indication that you are well. I've never felt this cold in my life...I need to know you're safe.

A flicker of warmth pierced the cold in her chest at the familiar script. But the sharp ache from the ekath reminded her that she was the cause of his pain. How ridiculous that she could not speak with him in her heart, yet he could feel her suffering from this distance.

There was little she could do about the cold, but at least she could provide him with a response. Without a quill or charcoal, she pulled the knife from beneath her greaves. Mallow's curious eyes followed the blade to her braid as she looped a tendril of pale hair loose from the plat and cut it clean with the knife. The long white strands illuminated eerily in the darkness as she knotted the lock of hair around Mallow's neck.

"T-tell him I'm s-sorry," she said, scratching under the familiar's chin. It would have been more reassuring if her hands had stopped shaking.

Unsure of what to do with the blue ribbon from the scroll, Ophiera reached to tie it to the end of her claymore. But her shaking grip faltered, and the claymore fell to the stone with a clang. In the silent desert, the sound rang out across the dunes, distorting as it went.

And in return, a blood-curdling screech pierced the night.

Ophiera and Mallow scanned the horizon, neither breathing nor moving. She had never heard such a sound in her life, a sound that gripped her spine while chilling her heart. All day, she traveled without seeing another living creature, but Jasper had warned her of the desert at night.

"Go!" Ophiera hissed at Mallow, thrusting the crystal before her. The familiar hesitated, eyes darting as if looking for some way to help. But as the second deathly screech pierced the night, Mallow disappeared in a flash of light.

She quickly tied the ribbon and the crystal to the hilt for safekeeping as she listened to the desert. Like drifting reeds, soft shuffling sounds seemed to emerge from nowhere and everywhere at once. On the horizon, nothing moved except the twinkling of stars.

Rising to her feet, Ophiera grasped her claymore tightly. Another screech pierced the night, louder and higher-pitched than before. Out of her periphery, she glimpsed a trail of glittering dust rising from the dunes like a smoky fault line. Whatever traveled beneath the sand, it was not alone. She counted a dozen trails, all converging on her now.

With her scars tingling, she called upon the Aether to draw a protective circle of runes. Although she felt the holy flames flow beneath her readily, none now heeded her call. She didn't understand. Something prevented her command, her reach, despite feeling the Aether's screams below her. She glared at the white stone road in disbelief.

The first of the dust trails exploded. Small and sharp, a spiny monstrosity burst forward, wailing through the air like a rubyfin breaching the water's surface. The cry turned into a chorus of exploding sand and deathly screeches as the others followed suit. There were many...and yet, *none* were alive.

Atop the sand, their movements disturbed Ophiera; humanoid skulls hung low, devoid of eyes and jaws. The spinal column remained intact, curved backward and upwards with nefarious purpose. Only when she saw their rib cages spread wide and skitter about like legs did she realize the skeletons of the middens had come to life.

Soulless mutilations, just like the victims of the ichor, and yet they showed no sign of the black poison. The only indication of some power beyond death was a singular, glowing bead lodged deep within the eye socket of each creature. As they lined up around her, their lower spines began to curl, pointing toward her with needle-like crystals of dark crimson.

Without the holy flames, Ophiera held little chance of victory. As she shifted her stance upon the slab of stone, she planned to retreat toward the sands. A shrill cry was the only warning as the first creature lunged at her. Its red stinger poised, Ophiera swung her claymore, cutting the beast in half. The remaining creatures were on her before she had followed through with the first swing.

The clash of bone against metal rang loudly through the night air as the beasts attempted to penetrate her armor. They wrapped their ribbed legs around her limbs, intent on overwhelming their prey. Her armor, however, served its purpose, protecting her from the worst of their attacks. Shielding her face with her arms, she dragged her legs in step toward the sand.

A sharp, searing pain shot through her leg. Somehow, one of the crystal needles had found its way between her loosened armor, penetrating the soft flesh behind her knee. She felt the jagged needle rip away from her flesh as a venomous cold spread from the wound.

Another stab between the junctions of her armor brought her steps to a halt. Like ice in her veins, whatever venom or magic the creature possessed spread to her limbs. Another stab. And another. Relentlessly, they concentrated their attacks on her weak spots. The screech of their stone stings between her metal plate deafened the rush of blood in her ears.

Desperately, she tried to call upon the flames within, but the spreading numbness smothered all fire from her as if she were being drained of everything, blood and mana alike. With a sickening crunch of bone against stone, she fell to the ground.

The sandy desert was only an arm's length away. Though her arms were weakening as the venom spread, she continued to drag herself to the edge of the platformed road. No longer covering her head, one creature wrapped its bony spine around her throat, attempting to drag her up and away from the path's edge. She groped desperately at the stone, throwing her whole body forward against the rough collar of sandy bone.

The moment her open palm touched cold, silken sand, she called the Aether forth. To her relief, the white flames engulfed her without hesitation, replacing her body's numbness with a terrible burn. Salvation seared through her, disintegrating the bony grips and relieving her of their weight.

Only after the ashes had settled did she dare extinguish. Frigid once again, Ophiera rolled onto her back, gazing up at the beautiful, glistening sky. For a moment, she felt safe in the silence of ash and sand. But the time between her inhalation and exhalation shortened with each breath. And soon, she realized she couldn't feel anything at all. Though the flames had cleansed the creatures themselves, whatever this poison was could not be burned away so easily. Every staggering beat of her heart brought darkness from the periphery of her vision closer. And in darkness, she groped for the only sensation left to her: the drag of the tether.

* * *

You managed, what, three days without grievous injury?

The sound of his voice ignited her very soul. Suddenly, Ophiera was aware of the cold again, and yet it was kept at bay by his warmth. It was strange to *hear* him without really hearing...to feel him without really feeling. Yet she wanted nothing more than to see him.

I'm here, love. Concentrate.

In the darkness, an image of stark blue eyes and a sad smirk formed like a cloud in the sky. Real, yet untouchable.

You really are reckless when I'm not there to stop you.

They jumped on me this time, she said, trying not to sound as weak as she felt.

So I saw...

How could you see?

It's hard to explain. I was in the library trying to warm by a lamp when I felt a stab of agony behind my knee. I grew cold, colder than I already was, and fell to my knees. In the darkness, I felt the tether pull until I looked down and saw golden armor covered in those vile things.

I'm sorry.

There is no need. I've missed you terribly.

And I you, but...I never wished to cause you suffering.

As I've said, I'd rather suffer with you than without you. It's Jasper who should be sorry. Where the hell was he as you battled those creatures?

I...it's not his fault. I left him behind.

Why?

Pain suddenly replaced the numbness, breaking through the darkness.

Ophiera?

She couldn't think as the tether drew so taut it came close to snapping. Crushed and torn, dragged and drawn, her very soul was being ripped from her.

Ophiera, you need to wake up!

Darkness pressed in as Myronor's voice roared in her mind. The vision of him flickered to nothing as emptiness surrounded her.

Wake up!

~ Thirty Two ~

COMPLICIT

"**W**ake up, damn it!"

Something squeezed Ophiera's jaw, prying open her frozen lips. Despite hearing the words, she could see nothing but skeletal horrors behind her closed eyes. No matter how her heart and mind screamed to fight, she couldn't move a muscle.

Warm liquid gushed into her mouth, dribbling down her chin. She tried to spit out the bitter liquid, but she couldn't prevent it from trickling into her throat. Myronor had told her she needed to wake, but at the moment, she wished for quite the opposite. At least in the numbing darkness, she might find him again.

As the liquid settled in her gut, she felt the hold on her jaw was warm and solid, not cold and hard. With some feeling returning, she felt the sting of pain as something slapped her cheeks. Whatever tormented her now wasn't one of those monstrosities. And the voice she'd heard...hadn't it been in her head?

She found enough strength to open her eyes, though it took some time. The desert sky blurred behind the shadow of a man with two amber eyes, reflecting brightly like the harvest moons. As he came into focus, she wanted to smile, but only the corners of her mouth twitched.

"More will come," Jasper hissed.

"Can't...move," she managed to breathe out. The effort was astounding, and her eyes rolled again.

"No, no, no, stay awake," he said, slapping her cheeks again. With a thumb, he lifted an eyelid and studied her with a furrowed, beaded brow. "How many stings did you suffer?"

She paused, trying to recall in the fog of venom still coursing through her.

"Several."

He swore colorfully, no longer attempting to remain quiet. "Don't set me on fire—I'm going to pick you up."

Armor and all, he hoisted her over his shoulder. She closed her eyes against the jarring movement of his quickened gait. Despite being unable to control her body, the movement caused her stomach to churn. And as if sensing her disquiet, Jasper slowed his pace. Her awareness faded in and out as they walked, and it wasn't until he set her down against a cold, stone ground that she found her voice again.

"Where...?"

"The caves *you* should have found," he said with a grunt.

She became suddenly aware of the sound of trickling water nearby. Everything was coming to her so slowly that she wondered if one of the beasts had pierced her skull. Blinking slowly, she searched the darkness for the aqueducts, more out of curiosity than thirst.

Pale light filled her vision, illuminating a heavily breathing Jasper brandishing a glowing glass flask. The flameless candle reflected against the smooth, obsidian walls of the cave-like blue fire on a blackened mirror. Nearby lay her rucksack and claymore, alongside a pack of his own through which he now rummaged. She couldn't believe he'd carried all that gear along with her fully armored body.

"Open your mouth again," Jasper said, kneeling beside her.

Without question, but with great effort, she parted her lips. He uncorked the bottle with his teeth and brought the flask to her lips. Most of the bitter contents made it into her mouth, though she felt a dribble from the corner of her lips. He lifted her chin, tilting her head back to swallow as he wiped away the excess with a calloused thumb.

Her body twitched against the warmth of his touch.

"That's all the antidote a person can usually tolerate without throwing it back up," he said quietly. "But the stings will need to be cleaned, or else they fester. I don't understand how they even managed to sting you through this armor."

"I loosened some of the plates to rest," she said quietly.

"By the sea," he growled, accessing her armor in confirmation. "Where?"

She paused, assessing the source of her discomfort. All she recalled was the feel of the probing bones covering her from head to foot. With a shiver, she uttered, "Everywhere."

He hissed into the dark, rubbing a frustrated hand over his face. She might have found it amusing had the antidote worked more slowly, but as it stood, she was becoming quite discomforted by the pain and spasms.

"You understand I'll need to remove your armor to treat them, right?"

Ophiera understood the hesitancy in his voice, mirroring the feeling herself. Did she trust Jasper enough to handle her bare body without her control? As it stood, she couldn't fight or move yet, but wave after wave of pain coursed through her muscles. And she was reminded that Myronor likely suffered now as well.

"Go ahead."

Jasper's rough hands began removing her armor, not cruelly, but clumsily with speed. The cold air dragged across her bare skin, and she wished she hadn't regained any feeling. Even after spending years in the peaks of the Cloister, she'd never felt this cold. To her relief, he tucked a leather blanket beneath her bare body, protecting her from the frigid stone, at least.

Every one of her muscles rippled with spasms now. They weren't as painful as the flames, but they certainly brought her more than enough discomfort. She couldn't control the shivers from cold or venom.

"Those are good signs," Jasper said, reaching for his pack. "Even better if they hurt."

"Great," she muttered through gritted teeth.

Like with the troynt in the dead marsh, she was more surprised that she had suffered a wound than actually suffering the agony from it. So rarely had she been injured in her travels, and even less so, an injury so grave she could not heal or treat herself. Unlike the ichor, whatever poison those creatures possessed was potent enough to resist her flames and stop her mana...strong enough to bring her to the brink of death.

"What were those things?" she asked with a clenched jaw.

"Girtas."

"Excuse you?"

"They are called girtas," Jasper sighed. "Abominations created by the Enclave's necromancers to protect the desert from intruders."

She swallowed the bile rising in her throat. The Cloister had taught of the practice of necromancy before, mainly as a guaranteed indication of anathema rather than anything else. The ability to manipulate the vespers and vessels after death was more taboo than death itself. But as with so many of the Cloister's teachings, she now considered how skewed their opinions might be. There was no denying the girtas had meant to kill her, though.

Jasper set a small clay jar on the stone beside her. When he removed the wax top, the cave was filled with an herbaceous aroma that triggered her memory.

"Kaikora?"

"Part of her and Collette's *exchange*. I'm going to start cleaning and dressing the stings, but if it is too much, tell me to stop."

She nodded, and slowly, he began the tedious task. He started by wiping away the caked-on blood, gentle but irritating, nonetheless. The unction itself stung when he applied it to the first wound, though not nearly as painfully as the original stabs. As he moved down her body, from sting to sting, she couldn't help but draw a shaky breath each time his fingers grazed a sore spot. He tore small scraps of linen and laid them over each wound, allowing the salve to hold the cloth against her.

For as gruff and angry as Jasper had been since finding her, his touch was warm and gentle. The pain of the wounds might draw her breath, but the tenderness of his touch was forcing her heart to stammer in ways she knew it shouldn't. Myronor's face still lingered behind her eyes, bringing both longing and guilt to the forefront of her heart. The draw of the ekath had somehow eased since awakening, perhaps too exhausted to drag anymore. But her heart ached with the echo of his voice against the warmth of Jasper's hands on her bare skin.

Instead, she tried to focus on the pain. That was what she deserved, at least. While she'd beat herself up for loosening her plates so carelessly for the rest of her life, she was at least thankful for the armor itself. If she had been wearing anything else, like that silly dress, the girtas would have likely tenderized her alive. She was quite certain the ekath could never stop her from returning to the Aether in that situation.

"Are there more on your backside?" Jasper asked quietly.

She nodded, knowing she had just as many, if not more, wounds there. With a sigh, he began turning her over, only to stop and hiss under his breath.

"Several my arse..."

The pain in his voice did not match the warmth of his hands, burning against her icy skin. He was careful not to place her completely facedown, propping her on her side as he tended to each of the wounds. Though her limbs still refused to move, her heart raced on ahead with each of his caresses, overriding any thoughts of the pain.

"You should be dead, you know," he growled.

She sighed. "It certainly feels that way."

"Most succumb to one sting, and I've counted more than a dozen thus far."

"Funny, I thought there would have been more."

"There is nothing funny about this," he snapped, laying her back on the bedroll gingerly. With a scowl, he covered her with furs and leathers, tucking them tightly around her. "It was pure idiocy to leave the *Berserker* alone."

While she appreciated his touch, his words turned her blood as icy as the venom.

"My Oath—"

"Is one of idiocy!"

Anger returned some of the warmth to her cheeks. She wished to remind him that she wasn't meant to travel the Shole alone to start. That *he* was meant to guide her. But she held her tongue, taking deep, calming breaths.

"My paths were limited," she said quietly. "I either forced you to accompany me or went ahead by myself, and I refused to further your suffering by dragging you to the place you despise so much. So yes, I made a choice to travel the Shole alone, but even lying here, half-dead and at your mercy, I don't consider that choice idiotic if it meant saving you the suffering of what's ahead."

His eyes widened, and she expected an argument. But instead, he stood up and walked away from where she lay. On the far side of the cave, he remained silent, busying himself without so much as a grunt. It was hard to tell if she had offended him further or if he simply had nothing else to say.

But she quickly grew too cold to care.

Despite the layers of furs overtop her, there was no warmth to trap beneath them. Her muscles continued to twitch and jerk as the antidote worked its way through her body. But more feeling and movement only brought with it greater discomfort, especially when her teeth began to chatter. If Myronor had shared the chill of the desert with her before, she wondered how he must be suffering now. No matter how much she shook, warmth eluded her.

It felt like hours had passed before she regained enough control to roll on her side. Beneath the furs, she curled in on herself, trying to condense any heat she might capture in her endless shivers. But her jaw and back only ached worse with the cold tremors wracking her body.

"Are you not warming?" Jasper asked quietly from the dark.

"I-I'll s-survive," she said, attempting to calm her chattering jaw.

A waft of sea salt and leather preceded another layer of warmth on top of the furs. She looked and recognized his leather overcoat.

"T-t-thanks…B-b-ut won't-t you f-freeze?"

"Oh, I'm not staying out here," he said throatily.

"W-w-wait," she protested as he lifted the layers from behind and slid in beside her.

"For what?" He growled, his breath hot against the back of her neck. "For your lips to turn a deeper blue? For your fingers to blacken and fall off? Your spirit rope nonsense might prevent your death, but that doesn't mean you cannot suffer or become disfigured."

She didn't want to concede his point, but the warmth of him at her backside brought such relief to her desperate chill that she couldn't protest. Against the far wall leaned her claymore, blue ribbon and crystal dangling from the hilt. If Myronor had suffered this frigidness with her, would he have suffered more knowing Jasper had alleviated it?

"Just d-don't cross m-me."

"Wouldn't dream of it," he murmured, sliding one arm beneath her head and the other over her waist.

She had never realized how thick his arms were until he dragged her against him. The dressed wounds of her back pressed against his chest, and though it *should* have hurt, the sensation of warmth was too comforting to deny.

"Give me your hands."

With effort, she unfurled her clenched fists and allowed him to wrap them in his calloused grip. He ran his thumbs up and down, creating more warmth in the friction.

"And put your feet on mine."

He hissed a breath as she slid her numb toes against the tops of his feet, but otherwise, neither spoke another word.

Time passed slowly with Jasper cradled around her, but eventually, her teeth finally stopped chattering. Once she was warm, she knew she should have asked him to leave her alone. She should have demanded he unwrap himself from her and allow her to rest. But now that she was embraced so wholly in his arms, she didn't wish to move.

Until very recently, she hadn't understood what it meant to find comfort in touch. While Myronor was the first person she'd met who willingly cuddled a paladin, she also assumed he'd be the last. But it was impossible not to compare the way Myronor held her to how Jasper clung to her now. Her charge's touch was gentle, filled with adoration, and lacked any trace of apprehension. But

Jasper held her with a tension that hadn't left him since he'd lain down beside her.

Without access to his thoughts, her curiosity ran away from her. Perhaps he was revolted by her presence? Perhaps he could barely stand this moment of closeness with someone he despised so much. Or was it simply fear of this place that caused his body to coil around her so tightly? She remembered the look in his eyes as he'd held the knife to her throat and felt a pang of guilt. Whatever the reason for his tension at this moment, it was likely her fault.

"Thank you," she said.

"Don't thank me for warmth," he hissed against her ear.

"Not just for this, but also for finding me."

"Don't thank me for that either."

She couldn't help but shiver against the coldness of his voice. And yet, he continued to caress her hands so gently, pressing even harder against her back.

"Why not?"

His breath froze behind her as she felt his entire body tense. And when he finally breathed again, it was only to whisper, "Because I didn't do it for you."

The bitterness in his voice caused the ekath to twist in her chest. He really hadn't voluntarily come to her aid, just as she'd suspected. And there was only one person she knew of who could make Jasper do what he resisted...

"Then Collette—"

"Not for her either," he said, suddenly squeezing around her. She felt his breath at the nape of her neck before his lips pressed against her cool skin. Heat shivered down her spine as he murmured, "I only came for *me*."

Though his words were quiet, they echoed against the cave walls, matching the rhythm of her stammering heart. Only Myronor had ever made her body react like this, and yet the tether neither drew nor relaxed.

"I don't understand," she lied, allowing guilt to drive her denial.

"Don't you?" He asked with a hint of bitterness. She couldn't see his face behind her, and for that, she was thankful. But as his breath danced against her neck, she couldn't stop her back from arching even harder against him. "When I watched you disappear behind the dunes, I knew that was the last time I would ever see you alive. I returned to my cabin and drank enough ember whiskey to kill an ippomare, hoping to forget *everything*, including you. But I couldn't...you were the only thought on my mind, the only need left unmet, and before I realized what I was doing, I had set off after you. Not *for* you, but purely because of my own selfish need of you."

His words again echoed in the cave as his lips grazed the skin on her neck. But despite how her flesh responded, her heart forced her to shake her head in protest.

"The only needs we suffer are sleep and sustenance," she said shakily. "Whatever compelled you to follow me, I promise you, it is not what you think it is."

He snorted against her ear, more growl than laughter, sending hot shivers down her spine.

"I chased after you into this forsaken place, knowing only suffering lies ahead for us both. What else drives a person to that but desire?"

"Revenge," Ophiera replied, hoping to replace the heat in her gut with everything and anything else. "You've said it yourself...I've caused you nothing but suffering. You're confusing despise for desi—"

"I'm *not* confused," he hissed. "You've haunted both my waking dreams and darkest nightmares since I first laid eyes on you. Like the South Star at sea, you have been a constant presence in my mind, and yet, I've always sailed in the opposite direction. But no longer. You said everyone holds the power of conviction, and I've decided you are the only person on Erum worthy of mine."

"C-conviction?" she stammered. "What does that mean exactly in regard to another person?"

"It means a masochistic disregard for any suffering I will face while standing by your side," Jasper said, a whisper of pain in his voice. "It means I swear to follow you to the ends of Erum, to aid you in any task, to dedicate myself to you and your bidding in whole. I know my heart and soul are too damaged, too tainted to be of any value, and while my flesh may be mutilated, it is all I have left to offer. In battle, in travel, in bed, in everything...I'm yours, Ophiera."

The weight of his words made it impossible to breathe, to speak, to think for a moment. This was no proclamation of love or desire but a promise of dedication. And while he knew her heart and soul were bound to another, Jasper still promised too much. She understood the agony of blind conviction all too well and dreaded becoming his burden, too.

"I don't want your dedication," she said sternly.

"It's too late."

"How so?"

"Because I'm here, aren't I?"

"Yesterday, you wanted nothing to do with me and my problems," Ophiera said, anger lacing her words. "You've been cruel and callous, violent even at times. How is it possible I've gone from the bane of your existence to someone worthy of your life?"

"Because you *died*," he said, his voice dropping to a rasp. His arms tightened around her, uncomfortably and yet desirably so, squeezing her argument from her in a hissing breath. "Ophiera, regardless of the ekath, of the Aether, of all the powers in Erum, I *read* death in every feature of your face when I found you in the desert. I *felt* your absence from Erum and found an emptiness I've never known! At that moment, I found myself lost again, like the boy in that boat, with no option left but to give up and drown in the storm. Yet when you began to breathe again, when I saw the pulse return to your veins, it felt as if the clouds had parted and a lodestar appeared. You, Ophiera, have been my lodestar since we met, and I've simply grown tired of fighting the currents."

~ Thirty Three ~

MEMORIA

Despite many difficulties navigating the Consortia's clandestine policies with imbuteria magic, there is some hope on the horizon. Bloody, violent hope.

The Consortia can no longer hide the stories of Sionnach's rebellions nor the increase in refugees flowing into Krysas. While the Enclave people may be second-class citizens, they are quite distinct citizens. Their pointed ears and marks of the Registry have stirred up quite a commotion amongst the Krysan citizens. The people here are comfortable with the sparse servant bearing the token stamped into their ear, but now, they arrive in droves on aerships, boats, and caravans alike. Something terrible is beginning in the Western desert, and I'm quite certain I can use it to my advantage.

Few know, or rather acknowledge, that the practice of imbuteria originated with the Enclave. Eons ago, the ancient clans of Erum's firsts experimented with every sort of mana and application of magic. And though the Enclave are a shell of their former civilization, within the three clans remaining in the desert, I guarantee the practices of imbuteria are still alive.

Like every other ruling body across time and history, the Consortia has buried the past beneath their power, continuing the cycle of oppression by claiming what they've stolen as their own. But forgetting is not the way of the Enclave, nor is forgiveness.

So, I have begun my search for those born of the Enclave who might be convinced or coerced into sharing their practices with me. The Aether only knows I pressed the Phratries long enough when I was still in Tanvik, to no avail. But now I have both law and conflict on my side. Glamwell confirmed that as an Ambassador, I maintain certain civic rights in Krysas, including the right to indentured servants. And only those born of Enclave, bearing the token of the Registry, are indentured. The simplest of plans would be to take on a few servants and press them for knowledge. But when I shared this idea with Rheta, she kindly reminded me that most servants in Krysas have come from generations raised in Krysas—meaning they are either too cunning to reveal their secrets or they have been beaten from them by the Consortia, more likely the latter.

Of course, acquiring a few of the new refugees as servants is an option. However, it must be handled carefully. The people of Sionnach, whether Enclave or Consortia born, were raised in that lawless city under far different social and power dynamics. Their adjustment to life and expectations in Krysas must be considered, especially when trying to pry something from them as I am. A sound approach and strategy will be key. As much as I hate to admit it, I will be relying heavily on Glamwell to navigate this new pursuit. He may very well come to hate me by the end of all this. Most who work with me do— a small price to pay for progress.

✳ ✳ ✳

After many hurdles and continued resistance on all fronts, I've found the perfect servant.

The Enclave refugees were not suitable for my plan, an oversight on my part. I had no idea conditions in the Shole had become quite so dire, but nearly every refugee I spoke to preferred to be in the camps than indentured to a Consortia dignitary. Their traditions of fair exchange were something I'd hoped to take advantage of, but when a person has nothing to lose, there is little to bargain with. It was actually Glamwell who had the brilliant idea to search the prisons. And there I found my little fox.

She resisted negotiations at first, claiming a preference for death over slavery. But I left my offer behind the ketrite bars with her and patiently waited for her to see reason. The stubborn little thing didn't accept my offer until the morning of her execution. I know I've certainly upset some of the higher-ups in the Consortia with my choices. Many wanted to see her dead, it seems—all the better.

However, since arriving at the Embassy home, she has attempted to escape four times. The ketrite token prevents the worst of her magic, but the little fox has found ways to override that. While my academic interests are simply a flutter, Glamwell has undoubtedly been on his last nerves. He may act the idiot, but I've found myself quite impressed with his capabilities in handling our new house guest. Like a stray, I'm hoping to break her of her feral tendencies soon so we may get to work on what's really important.

* * *

Nothing has gone to plan.

The little fox continually challenges everything, especially me. It seems she honestly preferred death to servitude, and I'm nearly ready to gift it to her.

It turned out she had been hiding a familiar this entire time. Here, I thought the fox emblem engraved on her token was simply a signet of her clan, but it never symbolized something quite so literal. Where she had been hiding the crystal to allow the beast to hide, I do not know. All I do know is I now have two unruly house guests to contend with, two to convince to aid me, and two to fight to contain.

I'm not certain of what the little fox has said to Glamwell, but whatever she has hissed at him has undoubtedly burrowed deep under his skin. He is agitated and avoidant, leaving more of the legwork to me than I had envisioned. Glamwell believes the only path forward is to toss them both into the sea and wipe my hands of the entire endeavor. And I can't deny the idea is tempting. I'm on a running clock now, and if she doesn't bend soon—if I cannot master imbuteria and complete my research, the sea beneath the cliffs may very well be all of our fates.

More than just my career or interests weigh in on these next choices. And the only person who ever understood the weight of these choices I must make, I've left abandoned in Iluka. At times like these, I wish Berwyn were here for no reason other than to have another soul nearby that resonated with my own. But with such care comes weakness.

Perhaps...yes, that's it, isn't it? I should focus on the little fox's familiar—her weakness. Through him, I may convince her we're better off working together.

Or perhaps this has been a waste of precious time.

~ Thirty Four ~

TOWED

Bitter cold wracked Myronor's entire being as he emerged from the nightmare in the desert. The tether was still drawn taut; he hadn't even the strength to open his eyes. All he could do was feel the cold stone beneath him and the lingering horror of what he had just witnessed.

The moment the first sting had pierced Ophiera's skin, Myronor had fallen into her soul, dragged by the ekath across the continent. Like now, unable to do anything but *feel,* he'd watched Ophiera struggle against the skeletal horrors. And only when her life had slipped away was he able to fully connect with her again.

The touch of her heart within his was guiltily relieving in the circumstances. Even now, though he still felt the lingering effects of her suffering, he savored the sensation of *her.*

Finding the strength to open his eyes, he stared sideways over the third-story balcony of the library. On the cold stone in the dim light, he lay numb and shivering beside a small, leather-bound tome. That's right...he had been reading before Ophiera dragged him into darkness.

It was all he could bring himself to do in her absence: read. Obsession shrouded the ache, allowing him to drown himself in research instead of pain. His mother's journals had seemed the best place to start, but thus far, he had been wholly disappointed in their content.

Pyra's library had an entire section dedicated to her journals, and she had been impeccably diligent in logging her thoughts and activities. He had begun reading the account of her life, beginning with the very first day she'd set foot through the gateway as new Ambassador. But the first dozen journals he'd read thus far only highlighted her struggles with the Consortia. And, to his disillusionment, he and Berwyn were mentioned less and less as time progressed.

Slowly, the feeling was returning to his limbs, bringing with it a muted pain. When he was finally able to drag himself off the floor, the room spun in a dangerous way. Aches twitched through his muscles while worry stalled his breath. He knew in his very soul that Ophiera was still alive, but by the fact that he still sat defeated on the floor, unable to stand, she must have suffered greatly. At least when on the brink of death, he had seen her, spoken to her, felt her...Now, he only felt helpless in the unknown of her condition.

After a few moments of concentrating on his limbs, Myronor realized more of his strength had returned. And if *he* was improving, it must mean Ophiera was as well. On shaking legs, he took the chance to stand. But he could only make it to the nearby armchair before collapsing again. With his boot, he dragged the fallen lantern closer, hoping the antracinders would at least provide some warmth. It was a miracle he hadn't broken anything in the fall, bodily or otherwise.

He was beginning to seriously doubt this choice in divergent paths. While Ophiera faced death in the desert, he was simply catching up on family history. Though he browsed the journals with the intention of finding information on the portals, his mother's writings had a more profound effect on his emotional state than expected. Some of her thoughts so mirrored his own, and yet others only proved he had truly never known her. On every page, he found himself unconsciously searching for his name, or at the very least Berwyn's, only to be disappointed.

When he remembered Pyra, he had always envisioned her as she was in Iluka. She had held his hand while walking down the beach, explaining the cause of the Moon Tide. He'd never describe her as warm, but she wasn't cruel either. Yet sometimes, the person who wrote these entries felt…soulless.

He shouldn't have been surprised, he thought bitterly. If Pyra had abandoned her family for duty alone, perhaps she'd never had a heart to begin with. In her final letter, she had proclaimed love drove her choices, and yet it was she, now, who drew away his ekath into the desert. And for the first time in a very long time, he truly felt regret for accepting this ridiculous title and task.

A bright flash of light shocked him from his darkening thoughts. For a moment, he feared the antracinder lamp had caught flame, but as Mallow materialized before him, he only felt relief. But something was very wrong.

Mallow paced furiously across the library floor, not acknowledging him or anything else as she shook her fur out. With tail twitching, her agitation was palpable.

"Mallow?" He asked, sticking out his hand in offering.

She stopped to sniff his hand and relaxed her fur a bit. But when she looked up at him, her eyes were wide and dark.

"You're safe now," Myronor said softly. "Tell me what happened."

The familiar resumed her pacing, her ears twitching now. At first, he thought she was purely terrified, but as he watched his little familiar, he realized she was less fearful and more trying to warm herself. Neither was a particularly good sign, considering where she had just been.

"I saw those horrific creatures, too," he said quietly. "I'm glad you escaped, but did you happen to see...is Ophiera...is she...?"

The words caught in his throat. But Mallow nodded, and through the bond that no scholar seemed able to explain, he recounted the experience with her.

It seemed as though Mallow had escaped into her crystal; she remained there, watching Ophiera closely. In fact, that was where his familiar had been since departing Krysas. So *that* was why the little fluff hadn't visited him until he was shivering here in the library. While she refrained from telling him the full details of the journey to the Shole, she did explain, in her way, what had happened after Ophiera burned the creatures.

"So, Jasper followed her after all? Thank the flames," Myronor breathed, closing his eyes. "I suppose he isn't as much of a scoundrel as I thought."

The news of Ophiera's safety forced the last bit of chill from his limbs. As much as he distrusted the captain, at least he had the integrity to follow after her. But when he opened his eyes, Mallow was looking at him with a very odd expression.

"Mallow? What's wrong?"

Her eyes shied away from his, a guilty twist in her whiskers.

"Aren't they safe now?"

She nodded, but still rather stiffly.

"So then, what is the problem?"

Blinking, she looked up at the high ceiling, avoidant. His familiar might be trying to hide it from him, but the scenario was simple enough to work out. It was no coincidence that he only began to warm *after* his familiar arrived. He should have known the good news alone couldn't have fully alleviated the shivers.

"Jasper is keeping Ophiera warm, I suppose?"

Mallow nodded sheepishly.

A brief flare of envy burned in his throat, but he forced it away just as quickly. Ophiera had been frozen, stabbed, and poisoned—all while he sat in the comfort of the library; this wasn't the time to feel self-pity or jealousy. In truth, beneath the pain of the ekath and the longing it carried with it, he was appreciative that Jasper was there to help. Even if she couldn't return to the Aether, who knew how long she would have lain incapacitated, or worse, if more of those creatures had returned. It shouldn't make him jealous that there was someone else willing to risk their life for her. And even if he didn't enjoy imagining *how* the captain was keeping her warm, he smiled to himself, knowing that Ophiera would never allow anything untoward again. At least, nothing she didn't wish to happen.

"As long as she's safe, that's all that matters," he said to Mallow.

Again, he stretched his fingers out to her, finding relief in the tickle of her whiskers against his fingertips. She purred as she lifted her head for chin scratches, revealing a tendril of pure white hair tied about her neck. With one tug, the lock came loose, still carrying a chill against his palm. He held Ophiera's message between his fingers, no longer feeling an ounce of annoyance at the idea of Jasper keeping her warm.

Mallow mewled expectantly, sitting quite stiffly beside the antracinder lantern. Now that she had warmed, it seemed her appetite had returned. But Myronor's first attempt to conjure a meal ended with only a flicker of smoke. His concentration, not his mana, was to blame, proven by the second attempt in which he managed to provide a small platter of miniature sausages in a pool of steaming cream.

While Mallow ate enthusiastically, he sat back in the chair, relaxing his muscles and glaring at the fallen journal on the floor again. Another fruitless volume, like all the rest. Following his instinct, he flicked a finger with a spark of blue light and sent the journal soaring over the edge of the atrium. The satisfying 'thump' as it hit the other unworthy tomes he'd tossed below allowed him to relax all the way into the chair.

Perhaps throwing the journals three stories over the balcony to the floor below was childish, but it was the most straightforward system he'd worked out for keeping track of those he'd read. Plus, it felt good to hear the *thump,* an auditory indication he was actually progressing on something. Exhausted and still slightly chilled, he was forced to wonder yet again if any of this was worthwhile.

Although he understood the power of instantaneous travel and the unprecedented consequences portal magic could have across all of Erum, he still felt hesitant to believe Kaikora and the Order could seek something so desperately. But Rheta had exhibited the same desperation, even without ever mentioning the Brotherhood. For a moment, he imagined a world in which everyone was honest and upfront about their intentions.

And with his mind on unknown intentions, he watched Mallow lick her plate clean. Familiars were rare in Tanvik, but not unknown. Every apprentice learned of them, even if an entity of Nijeka didn't choose them. Depending on the mage, a spectrum of opinions existed towards familiars. Some thought them mere companions, others viewed them as tools to be used, while many felt their presence in Erum was meddlesome, even nefarious. The only mage he knew with a familiar was the Justicar of Quargonia—an enormous toad she was rumored to ride atop through the swamps.

"Mallow, do many of your kind visit this continent?"

She closed her eyes and began cleaning her paws with her rough, pink tongue.

Ignored, yet again.

"Can you at least tell me if any of your brethren have visited Krysas before? I mean, there are plenty of mages and crystals around here."

Again, she refused to even twitch an ear at him. He'd yet to meet anyone better at writing him off, though Ophiera was now a close second. Absentmindedly, Myronor rubbed a hand over his chest, trying to knead away the discomfort. With one last forlorn look at her cleaned plate, Mallow trotted away towards the stairs. He almost asked her to stay, but she likely needed some time alone after what she'd witnessed in the desert. And maybe he did, too.

Myronor twirled the lock of hair between his fingers. Like a worry stone, the motion brought clarity to his thoughts. She was halfway across the continent, and yet through Nijeka, Mallow was able to carry items from one side to the other. Granted, it was on her terms—the little beast had been absent since Ophiera's departure, unresponsive to his calls or queries. On the other hand, his mother *could* span and had used that gift to create these so-called portals. But hadn't he nearly created a portal himself by using Mallow to transport messages and small objects to Ophiera?

"Myronor!" Kaikora's voice boomed from below.

"Yes?"

"Good. You're awake."

"If I hadn't been, I certainly would be now," he called back.

Below on the ground level, Kaikora toed the pile of books. "You've been busy."

"And horribly unproductive," he said, coming to a shaky stand.

He wondered how much Kaikora knew of Pyra's doings here in Krysas. Or rather, how much the Order knew. Distrust wasn't a feeling he was accustomed to, but perhaps Ophiera had left behind more of herself with him than he'd realized. He felt suddenly cautious, eyeing the half-naked shaman below.

"Your aura is weak," Kaikora said, crossing her thick arms across her chest. "Has something happened in the desert?"

"My what?" He chuffed, hoping to avoid the topic.

"Your soul is shaken, which can only mean Ophiera was in danger."

With fast steps, Kaikora joined him on the third story of the library. He'd never seen so much worry in her eyes as he had of late, and yet now, it was all directed at him.

"Sit," she commanded, pointing a thick finger to the armchair he had just risen from.

With a sigh, he sat back down. "Ophiera is recovering, and so am I."

"Conjure a bit of water, will you?"

He didn't ask why as he held his hand out, conjuring a small glass of crystal-clear water. As he moved to hand her the glass, she merely glared back into it as her eyes became a reflective pond. In his hand, the glass grew warm, bubbling slightly as her eyes returned to gray.

"Drink," she said. "And tell me what happened."

Myronor wasn't about to argue with the seven-foot-tall wall of bare muscle looming over him. He took a sip of the tepid, metallic-tasting water and began describing the events of his collapse. As he drank, the knot in his chest loosened a bit, though the chill of the desert still hadn't entirely left his body. Kaikora frowned the entire time as if he were offending her in some way with the details, and it wasn't until he'd finished that he understood her disquiet.

"I couldn't *see* any of this happening," she grumbled. "Years I've spent watching her fate, only to be blinded at this most critical moment. I'm not one to succumb to frustration, but I must admit I am...perturbed."

"If it makes you feel better, I'd much rather have *not* seen any of it," he said, recalling the spiny beasts overtaking her. "Sometimes it feels as if all I do is feel her suffer."

"That fear talking, not you," she said knowingly. "It's your nature to know rather than not. Just as it was Pyra's."

Myronor stared down at the pile of journals, knowing there was truth to Kaikora's words. He'd traveled here, after all, because he needed to *know*. And yet, what he found most value in thus far was nowhere near this library. She was out in the desert, facing dangers unknown, so that perhaps they had a chance of saving what they truly cared for in this world.

"After reading her journals, Kaikora...I never wish to be like Pyra."

~ Thirty Five ~

ACQUIESCENCE

Dim morning sunlight trickled in through sparse cracks, illuminating the cave of black glass stone. In delirium and darkness, Ophiera hadn't noticed the perfectly cylindrical tunnels shooting from the central chamber where she lay. Nor had she fully appreciated just how smooth the dark mirrored surfaces of the walls, black and curved, reflected the light. Everywhere she turned, she faced distorted images of Jasper curled possessively around her beneath the pile of furs and leathers.

The sound of trickling water echoed through the cave, forcing her to choose between thirst and warmth. Against the frigid air of the cave, she slipped from Jasper's arms, taking with her the warmth of his leather overcoat. With jaw clenched tight, his full lips quirked involuntarily, a shadow of a wince crossed an otherwise peaceful expression. She was impressed he'd remained asleep, even with his heavy curls flowing over his dark furrowed brow.

He looked quite beautiful. But a cloud of guilt shadowed her admiration for him, and she turned to search for the aqueduct. She missed Myronor in ways beyond the tearing at her soul and the drag of the ekath, the least of her pains. His carelessness and humor had been annoyances at first, yet now she wished for the lightness of his presence. While she found comfort in Jasper's arms, it was Myronor's she longed for...and so much more. His lips, his hands, his...

Ophiera shivered with more than a chill. When had she become so perverted? Thoughts of Jasper's lips, hands, and tongue tempted her curiosity too much. Last night, the lingering sensation of Myronor in her soul with the warmth of Jasper's flesh against her own had done something strange to her heart—something she didn't wish to understand.

Following the sound of water, Ophiera eventually came upon a fount down one of many tunneled offshoots. Protruding from the ground, water bubbled from a glassy stone stalagmite, pouring into a carved basin. Behind the wall of the cave had been engraved with ornate pictographs, glyphs, and drawings. Despite her thirst, she studied the wall for a moment, searching for a purpose beyond decoration. Something about the symbols and the layout of the objects held a logic that surpassed language, and she saw a carved city, perfectly square, with deep swirls flowing in all directions from the center. At first, she thought they were meant to depict roads, but she soon remembered that only a *single* road existed.

The sound of the bubbling water quickly won her curiosity, and she decided to save her questions about the wall for Jasper when he awoke. For now, she was more interested in wetting her tongue. In the pool beneath the gurgling stalagmite, she dipped her fingers, expecting frigid water. Cupping her hand, she brought the balmy spring water to her mouth, thawing her chilled lips as she drank. The water tasted ever so slightly mineralized, increasing her thirst while simultaneously satisfying it. She managed to gulp down six palmfuls before another sound echoed through the cave.

"Ophiera?!" Jasper growled. His voice boomed throughout the cave, traveling down each of the tunneled passages in a surreal echo of terror. She couldn't see him from where she was drinking.

"Over here," she said softly.

"Where the hell—" he began, fury burning in every word. But as he glared around the cave, his amber eyes found hers, devoid of warmth, staring at her as if she were a ghost. He ran a shaking hand over his face, swearing under his breath.

With Jasper's shirt unbuttoned, she couldn't help but glare at the symbols marring his muscular torso. Cuts scarred quite distinctly from burns; where her blistered scars were raised, his were deep, and while hers appeared darker than her complexion, his shone a shade lighter. They'd have looked beautiful if she'd been ignorant of the suffering carried with them.

"Why are you wearing my coat?" He asked, the anger returning to his voice.

With a clenched fist, she held her tongue. Though her instinct was to match his anger with her own, she knew this place warped his mood. Despite wearing nothing beneath, she began unfastening the leather overcoat. She felt the cool air against her bandages before Jasper protested.

"Stop! I didn't mean—just leave it on," he barked, yet again covering his face with his hands. He took a deep breath as Ophiera shrugged the coat back over her shoulders.

"How are your wounds?" He asked.

"Nearly healed."

"Already?"

"Between you and the ekath, I feel quite refreshed this morning." His lip twitched beneath his hand, and she realized how strange her wording had been. "I'll be ready to continue to Birozahran soon."

At the mention of the city, Jasper's hands began to tremble in full. By the Aether, she wasn't good at this…how could she communicate that she needed to press on while remaining sensitive to his situation? Without causing him more harm?

"Jasper, I will not hold you to anything you said last night," she said carefully. "If you need to return to the *Berserker*, I understand."

He dropped his hands into his lap, revealing a solemn expression. "You really wish to continue after what you endured last night?"

"Wish? I barely know the meaning," she said with a sad smile. "But I must continue. You, however, can choose for yourself. I promise I won't think ill of you for it."

His amber eyes hardened, but the indifferent facade remained. "Unfortunately for you, I meant what I said last night. I'm following the lodestar—where you go, I follow."

Warmth flushed her cheeks, and she dropped her gaze, unable to continue to meet the intensity of his own. Beneath his loosened shirt collar, she saw a few shining scars peeking through again. Each one was a unique reason for him to hate this place.

"Did you receive those scars in Sionnach?" She asked.

He nodded.

"Who put them there?"

"It's irrelevant."

"Not to me."

"The intention behind them was never my death," he said as horror passed over his eyes. "So it *should* be irrelevant to you."

"My Oath is not the reason I ask."

It was harder to accept the truth than to speak it, but somehow she managed the latter. Regardless of her duty to Retribution, she desired revenge for Jasper. Beneath the glossy stone, she felt the Aether stir in agreement that whoever had carved his body like this deserved death.

"A mage," Jasper began with his eyes closed.

"For what purpose, if not death?" She asked, unable to hide the disgust in her voice.

"Imbuteria."

"What?"

Jasper took a breath, his eyes still closed. "You know the practice?"

"Yes," she said, recalling Myronor's musing. "To impart objects with mana—with magic."

"Right. Well, I was the object in this case."

Beneath her feet, the Aether stirred, matching her fury. She might not know much about magic and the ways of mages, but she was quite certain imbuing a person, particularly against their will, was wrong.

"And no one thought to stop this person?" She asked.

"Sionnach was a lawless place. The Consortia and Magistrate might have declared it illegal to transmutate or imbue anything with a vesper, but you know better than anyone how little *legality* means to the victims. The laws against murder have never slowed your Retribution, have they?"

The truth of his words stung more than the bitterness behind them. Laws hadn't stopped the Vespula Brotherhood from spreading the ichor in the Sloughmire. And neither had her Oath. What good was Retribution applied only to death and not suffering? The more she learned of the world, the more she doubted her place in it.

"Tell me who—"

"I can't talk about *this* anymore," Jasper said sharply and shakily. "I'm sorry, I usually need a lot more ember whiskey to even think about it, let alone speak the words."

She wasn't sure what drove her to stand beside him and place a hand on his shoulder. "I understand, Jasper, I really do. I'm sorry for pressing you."

The tremors seemed to slow with her touch and more so when he placed his hand over hers. She couldn't help but examine the ornate burns peaking through his fingers. If she stood within the Sacramentum again, could she discuss the ritual that had kindled her there? Absolutely not. But someone had once asked her how she became a paladin. And while she had found it difficult to revisit and share with Myronor, it was as if her words alone carried away part of the burden. If she could do for Jasper what Myronor had done for her...

"You should know, before we enter the city, the Enclave have cultural practices of fair exchange," Jasper said quietly, running a thumb across one of the symbols of her hand. "Question for question, answer for answer, pain for pain. So, it's only fair that I ask you...who gave you your scars?"

"It's irrelevant," she said quietly.

"Not to me."

"I gave them to myself," she said, taking her hand from his. The possession in his voice made her uncomfortable, and yet, a small, dark part of her soul enjoyed hearing the vengeful inflection he carried for her.

"Then how do they bind you to anything but your own will?" He asked.

Ophiera stood abruptly. "Now *I* can't talk about this anymore."

In a pile nearby sat her armor, covered in sand and blood that needed to be cleaned before they departed. With her back to Jasper, she set to work.

After each piece had been thoroughly inspected, she began the tedious act of armoring herself. Whether or not she doubted the Cloister, she no longer doubted the Aether. And in her gut, she felt the burning draw of Birozahran. Regardless of Oath, regardless of Pyra, something inexplicable drew her deeper into the desert, calling to her from deep within Erum.

She listened to Jasper pack his belongings behind her while she dressed, unwilling or unable to look. Though she knew it was best for him to return to the *Berserker*, the thought of continuing on alone felt disappointing. As she tightened the plates for the perfect fit, she eyed her claymore still leaning in the corner. To her surprise, Jasper grasped it by the hilt and gave it a swing before stalking toward her with it.

"The balance of this blade is impeccable," he said, handing it to her. "Though, I think the little ribbon might throw it off a bit, don't you?"

She retrieved her sword from him, distrustful of his haughty smile. There was no more tension in his gaze, no more sadness. She sniffed the air, wondering if he had snuck a flask somewhere in their gear. But he smiled as he put his dark overcoat back on, hiding any remnants of his markings.

"If we leave soon, we can reach Birozahran well before dusk."

"Are you sure you're ready?" She asked, gifting him one last chance to leave.

"Are you?" He asked, smiling as he tossed her a full waterskin. "Col says I set a cruel pace, even on land."

* * *

"There's another," Jasper said, pointing to a cairn stone in the distance. "Generally, they mark an aqueduct cavern nearby."

Ophiera squinted at the cragged, glassy rock protruding from the sand.

"They're nearly impossible to distinguish from the other desert stones," she argued.

"Aye, but the entrances aren't. I still can't believe you ignored my warnings and tried to sleep on the road."

"I searched for the cave entrance for a solid hour and found nothing!"

"So what you're telling me is you can't tell a hole from the ground?" He snorted. "I suppose you couldn't be blessed with exceptional hearing *and* vision."

While he had taken the time to point out the various locations of shelter along the route, they always came at a price. She'd spent the morning defending her actions, and yet she knew he would only continue jabbing at her pride.

"The only reason I don't smack that smug look from your face is because you helped me last night," she said, trying to keep her voice even.

Even though the second gray day of travel passed smoothly, Ophiera still looked over her pauldrons at every shift in the wind. The girtas had certainly struck a nerve, inciting a level of paranoia she hadn't experienced since the dead marshes. Jasper claimed such creatures only emerged at night, but the dusky, gray sky tricked her eyes into questioning how far sunset was above the horizon. She had the feeling she would dream about the sounds of the screaming sands for years to come.

"Helped? My dear, on the sea, we call that saving your arse."

"Then, thank the flames, we are in the desert!"

"You mean the desert that tried to kill you? How many stings did they land again?"

She tripped over her boots. Though he chuckled throatily, he matched her silence and said no more.

For a moment, she was relieved that the white stone road blocked her access to the Aether. Otherwise, it would have been too tempting to catch blaze and end Jasper's taunts. Glaring at her greaves, she wondered why the Aether had churned beneath her feet, yet wouldn't heed her call. She had already asked Jasper, early on in the journey, about the origin of the road, but he hadn't a clue. According to him, not even the Consortia knew of its origin. Ophiera wanted to know how rock itself could be powerful enough to blunt the Aether.

"The cairns are intended to blend in with the landscape, as are the cave entrances," Jasper said, stretching his arms. "Not even the Consortia could find them, which is precisely why they lost the city. The aqueducts were the main advantage the Enclave held during the rebellions."

If she hadn't known better, she might think he felt remorse from poking fun at her earlier. She looked out to the cairn stone, her eyes scanning the horizon towards the small, square city in the distance.

"Aren't these caves too far out in the desert to have been of use when taking the city?"

Jasper shook his head. "All the caves connect in one way or another, including those beneath the city. Either the Consortia never knew the cave systems existed, or they didn't care...All their magic, yet the Enclave took them so quickly by surprise. Just another testament to the arrogance of innaturals. "

The disgust in his voice stung her unnecessarily. She didn't quite understand the depth of meaning behind the word, but she felt the hatred in his voice—a hatred for something that she found quite remarkable.

Magic was creation to her, as Myronor had demonstrated again and again. His particular affluence held the power to *add* to this world rather than take from it. Throughout their journey, he had provided her with so much using nothing more than his two hands. Food, water, safety...

Just as the Aether could both claim or heal a soul, it seemed magic held a darker side as well. Jasper's scars remained hidden beneath his leather overcoat, but the idea that a *person* could be imbued drew her ire and curiosity. At least his odd skillset could finally be explained. His strength and stealth were unnatural, and his ability to meld into shadows rivaled Myronor's invisibility charm.

A pang in her chest reminded her that she couldn't linger on thoughts of Myronor right now. Though she had recovered significantly from the girtas attack, something within the link felt frayed with exhaustion.

"How long until we reach Birozahran?" she asked, hoping to distract herself.

"Can't you see it in the distance?"

Ophiera rolled her eyes. His snark was a fine distraction, indeed. "I see it, but I've never dealt with these cold mirages before...things appear larger, oddly floating, making it impossible to tell. I assumed my guide could, but if I'm mistaken..."

"Soon," Jasper said. "But still enough time to turn around."

"I can make it on my own from here if that's what you wish."

"Can't blame me for trying."

"Tell me who I can blame, then," she said with a sudden surge of anger.

His pace slowed a fraction before he mumbled, "We already discussed it—doesn't matter."

"It does to me."

Only their sandy steps and the shifting winds were to be heard. He walked a bit more stiffly but still refused to look at her.

"Blame the Enclave," he finally relented. "While a mage carved the runes, it was the savages that developed the practice alongside their derivations."

"Derivations?"

"Their warped form of magic. Just as you draw your mana from the Aether and Kaikora from the sea, the Enclave experimented beyond all mana with life and soul. I told you the girtas are *their* creations—disgusting necromancy only skims the surface of their twisted practices. To think, there was once more than three bloody clans of innaturals out here..."

As his muttering continued, Ophiera again found herself recoiling against the disdain in his voice. She had performed rites that drew from both life and soul. Reviving Myronor, becoming ekatma...the Aether itself, after all, was the flow of Erum's souls. Did he then view her with similar disgust? The idea bothered her more than she cared to admit.

She was quickly learning there were two sides to every tale, however. While the girtas were horrifying, she found herself repeating what Jasper had once said. Who was she to decide what was or was not an abomination? Kaikora indicated the Enclave suffered greatly under Consortia rule, and Jasper said the creatures were created to protect their people. Hadn't she burned people alive in the name of justice and protection? As Warden, *she* was the protector of Iluka, and yet her actions had affected Jasper more than the girtas last night.

"If you were from Iluka, how did you come to live in Sionnach?" She asked, hoping to change the subject.

"My parents drowned in the oyster beds—storms, you know. My father's next of kin lived in Sionnach, so I was shipped off."

"I see..." Ophiera said, holding her next question. A part of her was beginning to wonder if she genuinely had taken on some of Myronor's personality when their souls joined. It was true she'd always had a flare of curiosity, but usually, she had far more self-restraint in prying into people's business.

Jasper sighed. "I can tell you want to ask, so I'll just say it. My aunt wasn't responsible for what happened to me. Well, not directly, anyway. She barely had enough to keep herself fed, let alone a little brat such as myself. After about a year, she sold me off."

"Sold?" she asked in disbelief. "There was slavery in Sionnach?"

"The Consortia prefer the term indentured servitude, but yes. Took some time for *that* law to go into place and even longer for it to fall out of practice."

"Jasper, I—"

"Don't," he snapped. "It was the luck of the draw, and I was exceptionally unlucky. But when I remember how many didn't escape..." After a moment's pause, his posture shifted yet again, more upright, more confident. "I guess their *gifts* to me were just another luck of the draw."

Suddenly, Jasper disappeared against the gray sands, melding in with wavering air. Ophiera heard the whisper of his shuffling steps and saw a waver of a shadow, but had she not known what to look for, he would have been lost to the desert. It was hard to find a silver lining to suffering, but he had managed, even out here in the sands.

"I find the ability to disappear more desirable than bursting into flame. Would be far more useful, that's for certain."

"Perhaps," he chuffed, curling around her. "But I can't think of anything quite as desirable as your figure engulfed in white fire."

"Don't be crass," she said, stepping away from his presence.

Though his words caused heat to rise up her neck, they also caused her chest to wrench in pain. She had grown familiar with the ache of the ekath dragging at her every step, but each time her thoughts lingered too long on Myronor, the discomfort surged. And he had been on her mind a great deal today.

Last night, as she lay with Jasper, the tether felt the most relaxed since she'd left Krysas. But she was sure that had little to do with Jasper and everything to do with nearing death. In the darkness, they found each other, and some illogical, twisted part of her wished for it to happen again, if only to find relief.

"Is the spirit rope causing you trouble?"

"Yes," she said into the air; he'd yet to reveal himself, and at the moment, she preferred it. She hated how easily he guessed her thoughts without knowing them.

"You've been thinking about *him* a lot."

She nodded.

"So be honest—do you *actually* miss him?"

"Of course I do," she hissed.

"How do you know it's not all this spirit rope thing?"

"Because I know how I feel."

She didn't owe him an explanation for what had taken her so long to realize. The ekath may have changed the pace of their relationship, but from the moment she saw Myronor's vesper, she knew she loved him. With or without the ekath, her heart would hurt in his absence.

"Kaikora said the Enclave might know how to break the ekath," Jasper said, still disembodied against the desert. "Do you plan to inquire about it while we're here?"

"Let's enter the city first, then worry about other curiosities," she said harshly.

"Your freedom is a curiosity?"

She bit her lip in frustration. "Pyra is our purpose here, first and foremost."

"Ah, so you evade like a rogue, too."

"Speaking of *evading*," she said pointedly, ready to turn the conversation. "Why don't you remain cloaked from here on out?"

"Am I that hard on the eyes?" he quipped.

She took an annoyed breath before continuing. "It is a tactical advantage as we near the city. Wouldn't it make more sense for me to arrive at the gates on my own as a Wielder of whatever I must say? You can remain hidden, scout ahead, watch my back..."

Jasper barked a laugh. "My oh my. I didn't think paladins were capable of strategy. But truthfully, that was my intention all along."

"Of course it was," she replied dryly.

And that was something quite different from Myronor. Jasper knew how to survive, how to fight, and how to navigate this place. Though truthfully, while she thought it would be a tactical advantage, she also worried about Jasper's heart. The mere mention of the city had turned him into a flailing beast, and though she didn't fear his knife at her throat again, she dreaded what her response might do to him in this place.

"We should designate some sort of sign in case one of us is in trouble."

"Why bother?" he said, amused. "I can read you easily enough; I'll intervene when necessary."

"But what if *you're* in trouble? I can't read your mind or see you, for that matter. How will I know if you need help?"

"I won't," he said calmly.

"Jasper—"

Invisible, he took her hand, his leather glove cool against the palm of her gauntleted hand.

"As long as you need me, Ophiera, I need nothing more."

"I didn't say—"

"Now listen, the guards can likely see you approaching, even from this distance. I suggest silence from here on out."

And for once, Ophiera couldn't agree with him more.

~ Thirty Six ~

MEMORIA

Progress has been made. Slowly but surely.

Against Glamwell's wishes, I let the little fox off her leash today. Unbeknownst to her, of course. She thought she was so very clever escaping from her cell, only to steal my medallion and flee into the city. Oh, the look on Glamwell's face when I told him I planned to use the embassy pendant as bait was quite priceless. I'm fairly certain he popped at least four blood vessels in his eyes as he reminded me that if I lost the medallion, I would forfeit Tanvik's sovereignty within the Embassy. But at this point, Tanvik's relationship with Krysas is already on the brink. All is on the brink.

We followed the little fox and her familiar to the Strato-District, where several Enclave refugee camps now reside within the Depths, behind the main streets. To be honest, I hadn't visited the camps since I acquired the little fox, but the Consortia truly has outdone themselves in cruelty. Overcrowded, underfed, and kept in the dark, the people of the Enclave suffer more in the name of safety in Krysas than they did in the Shole. Imagine the havoc the Enclave could enact if they didn't have those ketrite tokens punched in their ears. Imagine what they could accomplish. The Consortia are right to fear the Enclave's potential, but they took the route of suppression rather than alliance. The Enclave clans had so much to offer the world, and yet the Consortia treated them like cattle, castrated and herded. Imagine what could be accomplished if mages combined their magical knowledge instead of divide!

The little fox snuck through the alley behind the anvil shop all the way to one of the unmarked hovels. Unseen, I followed her inside while Glamwell kept watch. It was clearly a black market imbuteria shop—stones and sands, maps and incantations. When the shop owner came to greet the little fox, I was quite taken aback by their appearance—two different colored eyes and two gaping holes where their ears should have been—a freed Enclave. My little fox hasn't been brave enough to disfigure herself to remove the token. It's not a simple task, given the imbuteria of the ketrite coins. But given this escape attempt, it's only a matter of time before she chews off a limb to rid herself of chains. I knew I had chosen her well.

Unfortunately, the shopkeep sensed my presence before the little fox could convey why she was there. While the shopkeep fled, Glamwell and I recaptured her and her familiar, but in the struggle, the other refugees took notice. I was left with little choice other than to prove to her why it was best she worked with me instead of against me.

* * *

I'm not meant to nurture.

I've known this my whole life.

The love I had for Berwyn and his for me clouded my judgment into believing I could be a mother. But my choices with the little fox have taught *me one important lesson. The best thing I have ever done for Myronor was to leave him.*

How can my greatest failure also be my greatest achievement?

* * *

Now that the little fox is cooperating, we've been able to reach some agreements, or rather, exchanges. Again, Glamwell is quite unhappy with all aspects of these exchanges, but all is a worthy sacrifice for what I'm seeking to accomplish.

Interestingly enough, the cooperation of my house guest coincides with an odd request from the Consortia. Unfortunately, they have seemingly found my thesis from years ago on the wane of sight across the Phratries of the Southern Coastlands. Apparently, the shamans were unknown to the Consortia before, and now, their curiosity about the illusive order has piqued. As the resident expert, I'm now knee-deep in writing an official report on the Phratries of the Southern Coastlands and their dying traditions. In exchange, the Consortia is offering more knowledge of imbuteria magic, and yet the trust I have for their honesty is gone. Still, the little fox had some fascinating insight to offer...

While the Consortia did not know of the shamans, the remnants of the Enclave have longed to reclaim them as their own. And with this knowledge, an idea has struck me.

In Tanvik, only the Phratries practice an art close to imbuteria; they enhance their attunement to mana through uniquely crafted totems. Usually weapons, but clothing, and even their own person could be manipulated in a fashion to channel their powers. Channel is the key—unlike the imbuteria arts of Krysas, whereby an object possesses magic, the Phratries' practices served more as a conduit to their mana of sea and water. Their teachings also describe the many other manas of Erum—for instance, life, fire, stone, or Aether. They believed all of Erum—the rock, plants, animals, water, and people possessed various combinations of all. To my understanding, this was the key to their practices...finding a balance of mana and material when constructing their totems.

A seemingly endless yet finite list of possibilities that again remain lost to those outside the Phratries. Still, recanting their dithers again for the Consortia report and the little fox has made me wonder...what if the material receiving the imbuement is more critical than the power of the mage? What if it is actually the combination of mana and material that determines the power of imbuement? What if, like in cooking, the wrong ingredient can destroy the dish...unless you change the recipe to compensate. A great chef can do wonders with subpar materials if they have the experience, but it requires adjustment from the original intentions...A balance must be struck.

I think I will return to the black market shop in the Depths and demand fair exchange with the earless shopkeep. The question is, do I trust the little fox enough to accompany me, or do I leave her out of this side quest until she's proven herself trustworthy? Either way, I refuse to leave the Depths empty-handed.

~ Thirty Seven ~

SUBSTRATE

The sun hung high as Myronor and Kaikora made their way through the crowded marketplace. While the tether no longer sapped his energy as it had last night, it ached uncomfortably as he walked through the throngs.

He didn't bother to ask Kaikora how she knew the streets of Krysas so well. Quick as she stepped, it was pleasant walking in her wake. Amongst the Krysan people, her stature was unmatched, and the wide path she carved through the dense crowds eased his nerves. The streets were packed thrice as densely as Feyralis, and he doubted Ophiera could have tolerated it well had she been here.

A bolt of pain shot through his chest, forcing him to lean a little heavier on his staff.

"How is the ekath feeling?" Kaikora asked him from over her shoulder.

"Fine," he said, voice muffled slightly by the cowl he wore.

Glamwell had insisted he wear the customary attire before leaving the Embassy—a tube of decorative fabric hung around his neck, pulled up over his mouth and nose. Fashionable now, the origin of the cowls nearly every citizen of Krysas wore was one of survival, not vanity.

As Kaikora continued parting the densifying crowds of the market, he appreciated the nose and mouth coverings even more. During his apprenticeship, history was a major portion of his studies, and much focused on Krysas. He recalled reading about the history of the city of mages and the limitations of their imbuteria. The Consortia could only tunnel so far into the rock face before it would fall into the sea, and thus, physical space was forever limited. Needless to say, their entire culture evolved around accommodating their ever-increasing population in a city with nowhere else to grow.

Ages ago, when a plague devastated the population of Krysas, the cowls became institutional. Magical interventions had little effect on a disease spread through the air in a city with little room to breathe, and yet, a simple cloth over the mouth and nose mitigated the spread. Since then, face coverings have become part of Krysan culture, serving both to prevent catastrophe again and allowing for individual expression.

The plain, white, silken cloth covering Myronor's mouth and nose filtered out the smog and smells that clung heavily in the Strato District. Kaikora had made a good point this morning that, here in Krysas, he would be far more obvious to identify by the Brotherhood. Covering his face was the final step in a disguise he feared would become his new norm as Ambassador.

"Your new attire looks quite natural on you," Kaikora said with a wry smirk.

With a snort, Myronor couldn't help but look down at the traditional Krysan clothes Glamwell had acquired for him. While he refused to give up his favorite color of blue, he had traded his light, flowing robes for darker, more form-fitted attire. The sapphire material felt almost like leather, tight against his skin, only more breathable. Covered in tarnished silver adornments, the excess of metal reminded him far too much of armor. And the cape...who wore capes anymore? But as they wandered the market, he realized how well he did blend in with the styles of the foreign city.

"If only I could get away wearing what you are not, Kaikora," Myronor replied, smiling haughtily beneath his pale cowl.

"No one has complained so far," Kaikora said, holding her thick arms out in appraisal of herself. The shaman wore what she always wore—barely anything.

Though it was clear she stood out from the crowds, the people truthfully paid her little mind other than vacating her path. Perhaps living in such a crowded, busy place desensitized them to views of anything *other.*

"There's the anvil shop," Kaikora said, slowing her pace as they approached.

Peering around her shoulder, Myronor saw smoke flowing onto the main drag through a shop window. Carved into the rock, the wide-open abode displayed a variety of stone and metal anvils, from red sandstone to copper-laced granite to solid iron, pock-marked and oxidized. A heavy-set woman covered head to toe in black chainmail wrappings worked a forge with green flames. Every so often, a spark jumped from the forge, searing the dark stone floor and illuminating the other anvils in the shop.

Myronor stopped in his tracks as the smithy pulled a small, pale anvil from the fires. She continued shaping the blunted horn with a granite hammer, grunting as she swung. Another woman, wearing attire similar to his own, watched the anvil smith work. With her cowl down around her neck, the smile playing across her lips was one Myronor knew all too well—adoration, not for the craft, but for the crafter.

"Nyr, my gem, can we not break our fast *now?*" Asked the observant woman in Krysan.

The anvil smith shook her head, the chain mail covering her body, the rattling audible outside the shop. "A little longer, Kula. I need to finish this before the customer returns, and if I stop now, I will have to start all over again. You don't want me home late again, do you?"

The observant one, Kula, laughed. "Of course not, but if you don't eat something, gem, there will be nothing left of you to make it home."

Myronor felt the tug of the ekath as he watched the exchange between the two. Would Jasper know Ophiera's tendencies to avoid food and sleep when her mind was set on a task? Would he even care? Myronor had been so relieved to feel her heart strengthening through the night that he didn't bother to think what today would look like for *her*. She probably wouldn't rest more than a single night...she probably was on her way to Birozahran right now, pushing herself when she should be recovering.

The anvilsmith stepped away from the forge and pulled down her cowl. Where her eyes were exposed, soot from the forge had swiped a dark band across her face, leaving her mouth and nose clean. An untarnished smile spread across her lips as she stepped toward her lover and kissed her.

Though Myronor felt sheepish watching this exchange, he couldn't look away. The one named Kula uncrossed her arms, pressing her hands against the chainmail coverings. Nyr kissed her deeply, with a passion that would have been judged harshly in a city like Feyralis, but here in Krysas, only Myronor stared with his lips parted.

"Kula, you are all the sustenance I need," Nyr said, clearly enjoying the way her lover's eyes widened. "But I can hear your stomach growling. Go to that stall you enjoy so much, and bring us back something delicious. I promise I will be done by the time you return, and we can eat together over on the terrace."

Kaikora's sigh interrupted the moment, but only for Myronor. Her gray eyes looked pitiful as she stared at him, irritating him more than they should.

"Shall we find what we came for?"

"Lead the way," he hissed, hoping the two in the shop had not heard her.

Kaikora turned away, taking heavy steps toward the narrow alleyway alongside the shop. They had come to the market with one purpose this morning, and it was not to creep on the romantic antics of the anvil shop owner. Rheta had described Myronor once as 'lovesick' at a time when he was young and not truly in love. But his softness for the affections shared between people hadn't changed with time and, in fact, only grew stronger with the love now tugging at his own heart, stretched across the continent.

The alley proved so narrow that Kaikora was forced to shuffle sideways after her shoulders scraped the stone for the third time. Though illuminated by the crystals above, a sense of claustrophobia was beginning to convince Myronor that the width of the alley was a purposeful deterrent. Even Glamwell himself had warned him to stay away from the Depths, but after reading his mother's latest journal entry, there was no possible way they could avoid it.

At the end of the narrow alley, a crossroad opened, half the width of the main drag but carved high with stone-faced buildings. The backstreet was dimmer than the alley, or rather, the light was simply more diffuse. The ceiling was too high to see, and the only light provided was from the crystals embedded into the walls of the buildings.

On one side of the road were the backsides of market buildings, evident from the smoke of the anvil shop seeping back. The ceilings were high but not tall enough to keep the air from growing stagnant as smoke and everything else clung in the air. Again, Myronor was thankful he wore a face covering. On the other side of the alley stood a mixture of small abodes and what he assumed to be a few stores. There were no windows to browse and no signs of business, but he could see movement within the few doorframes left uncovered.

"Perhaps Krysas should be called the cave city rather than the cliff city," Myronor said, observing the countless, narrow alleyways leading deeper into the stone, away from the sea.

"All cities have facades," the shaman said, steering towards the right, passing the backside of the anvil shop.

Pockets of people loitered about on the backstreet, all wearing cowls and ignoring those who passed. When he had learned of Krysas as an apprentice, he knew the leveled districts of the city had quite distinct class associations. Only the rich and powerful on the Exo level, where the Consortia and aerodocks were located, all the way down to the Tropo level, where the less fortunate worked to move their way up from the sea docks. Now, having left the main streets of the Strato district, traveling deeper into rather than down the cliffside, he wondered what class of citizen lived back here.

"Here," Kaikora said, stopping before a small, tattered banner stretched over a rounded doorway. "I believe this is the shop from Pyra's journal."

"How can you tell?" Myronor asked, searching for some sign or indication that this wasn't just someone's home.

"You'll find out inside; I will wait here."

"What—why?"

The shaman laughed, nodding her head towards his chest. "You know what you're looking for here—I do not. And unlike you, I can be quite a threatening presence to the unacquainted."

Under any other circumstances, he would tout the fact that Kaikora had admitted he *knew* something she did not. But truthfully, nerves twisted his gut at the prospect of stepping foot into an unknown. Working through the journals and retracing his mother's footsteps was the closest he'd been to her in years. There was so much about her he didn't understand and, truthfully, hoped never fully to grasp. If he understood her too well, it would mean he was more like her than he cared to admit.

"Promise you'll come running if I scream," Myronor said with a smile he knew mirrored Berwyn's.

He pushed aside the curtain and stepped through the carved archway. Inside, the only aspect of the cramped room that deemed the place a shop was the counter. There, a set of brass scales and a tattered reckoner offset what otherwise seemed a disused storage room. Stacked crates lined the walls, some covered in burlap, others spilling over with books or lustrous ores Myronor didn't recognize.

Maps centered on the Orbolas continent were plastered over what bits of the wall he could see behind the many stacks. He took a step inside, examining a portion of a particularly colorful map peeking between crates. Overlaid across the terrains were erratic patterns, unlabelled with name or town or road. If he had to guess, he supposed they denoted veins of geological resources, though no map key confirmed or denied his theory.

Still, the place seemed to match his mother's description.

A shuffle caught his attention as a figure appeared from a door behind the counter. They wore an old leather eye patch over one eye, confounding one key identifier...his mother said the shopkeep had two different colored eyes. Pinched between their brow and cheek, the other eye peered through a double-lensed monocle, magnifying a dark blue iris. Braided tendrils of bright silver hair hung loose over their shoulders, hiding their ears entirely from view.

"You lost?" they grunted.

"Perpetually," Myronor said with his broadest smile. "But it seems I may have found the right place at last. I'm looking for imbuteria materials."

"I don't know you," the shopkeep said, watching him through the lens.

The statement caught Myronor off guard, both in the language and content. While Myronor had been careful to begin this conversation in Krysan, the shopkeep replied in his native language of Tanvik. Was his accent truly so atrocious?

"Well, that shouldn't stop us from doing business, should it?" Myronor replied, matching the dialect set by the shopkeeper.

"I don't do business with unknowns," they said before turning away.

"Wait!" Myronor cried, trying not to sound as desperate as he knew he must. They stopped in the doorway but didn't turn back to face him. "I'm the newly appointed Ambassador to Tanvik. My former sent me here...to acquire materials for her research. Pyra Ebontide."

The shopkeep turned back and smiled, revealing teeth coated in metals. Like a cat bearing its fangs, Myronor wasn't reassured by the smile one bit.

"How interesting...Are you a necromancer, child?"

"What?" Myronor choked out. "Of course not."

"That's a shame," they laughed. "But then you should enlighten me—how could a dead Ambassador send you anywhere?"

Myronor clenched his staff, hoping to collect himself. This was going quite poorly, wasn't it?

The shopkeep laughed again.

"Listen, child," they growled. "Based on that medallion bouncing proudly off your chest, I don't think you fully grasp *where* you are right now. So do yourself a favor and head back to the main drag. Go on now."

Without blinking, the shopkeep removed the lens from their eye, brushing a strand of hair back over their shoulder. As they did, Myronor caught sight of an earless hole. One blue eye and one missing ear were enough to convince him this was indeed the shopkeep from his mother's journals.

"What materials did you supply my mother for her research?" Myronor demanded.

While he hadn't found *direct* evidence she'd received materials from this shop, it was clear that her writing took a turn after visiting the place a second time. Her criticisms of the Consortia grew sparse, and the randomness of topics grew abundant.

The shopkeep shifted low over the counter, hunching over without breaking eye contact. Myronor's hair stood on end, and he was vaguely reminded of Mallow hunting swardhops in the grass, though his current predicament was far less adorable. Myronor kept his eyes locked on the single blue iris, refusing to reveal the tremble in his hand.

"Stones."

"What?"

"I gave her stones."

"What kind of stones?"

"The rare kind."

"What were they used for?"

"Haven't a clue."

Myronor breathed. "Well, may I purchase some of whatever she bought?"

"Why?"

"For my own discreet business," Myronor said, throwing a purse of pearls that Kaikora had supplied earlier on the counter. He only hoped it was a currency the shopkeep would accept.

The shopkeep continued to glare at him without even a glance at the payment. Every tactic of negotiation Myronor had learned had been attempted within a five-minute conversation, and still, he was getting nowhere with the Enclave. He thanked the flames he wasn't an Ambassador to them...

"Just like Pyra, I'm a Wielder of Riftwalking," Myronor said, again repeating the words Kaikora had told him to speak if prompted.

A sly smile broke across the face of the shopkeep, and Myronor nearly kicked himself for not making the connection sooner.

"Now that we know who you are," the shopkeep said, taking the bag of gems in their gnarled hands, "We may consider your business. Call us Alzerbez, Wielder of Coalescence."

Myronor didn't understand the sudden switch from singular to plural, nor did he know what a wielder of coalescence meant. But he didn't much care at this point. The pull of the ekath was not the only desperation he felt anymore.

"I wish to continue Pyra's work," Myronor said, licking his lips, "But that has proven difficult without her. The only lead I've found is this shop, but I know not what I'm looking for other than materials she must have been testing for her research."

He realized he rambled more than explained, and worried he had been too frank with the shopkeep. To his relief, they still smiled again as they reached below the counter and dragged forth a battered wooden box. Inside, an assortment of stones rattled about, some dark, some light, some smooth, some jagged. Nearly ten varieties of quarry lay together, all near the size of his palm.

"At home, we believe in fair exchange. Consider these our payment for your pearls—a sampling of every ore we've ever sold to a Wielder of Riftwalking."

Myronor reached a hand to take the box, but Alzerbez pulled it away. "We are, however, willing to make an additional trade. If you tell us which of these stones calls to your soul, we will tell you which called to Pyra's, as well."

Myronor mulled over the question, a distinct feeling that what was being asked of him was not so simple as to which stone he *preferred* the most. Staring at the assortment of stones, he, of course, had opinions; he tended to like lighter colors and smoother surfaces, but that was not his soul speaking, was it? For a moment, he focused on his soul, feeling the tether that shared Ophiera's so far from him now. His soul called for her, not stones, and yet, as his eyes grazed over the box, one that caused his chest to ache. A dark, glossy stone, so smooth his face reflected back at him, even in the dim light of the shop.

"Your answer is the same as ours—a fair exchange indeed," Alzerbez said, sliding the box of stones towards him. "Go. And do not ever set foot in this shop again—at least not without the little fox."

"Wait, what do you know about the 'little fox'?" Myronor asked, but the shopkeep had already disappeared behind the counter.

For a moment, Myronor considered following them, but something in his gut told him Alzerbez was far beyond his reach already. Alone in the dusty place with his parcel and confusion, Myronor took what he could get and left.

In a daze, he held the box of stones out like a platter to Kaikora.

"I see you found *something*," she said curiously.

"Or nothing," Myronor said.

To free his other hand, he minimized his staff, placing the wand-like version of his weapon on his belt. Carefully, he picked up the black stone to inspect. If he had understood Alzerbez's cryptic words correctly, then this was the ore Pyra favored. And in that case, it was most likely the material she used to create the portals. Rheta had indicated she struggled with the formula and that there was much trial and error between materials. And as he held the stone firmly in his palm, he felt an inexplicable draw to the subtle vibrations within the ore. The reverberation he felt through his hand was not one of simple favor—it was one of magic.

"Let's get somewhere with better light," Myronor said, taking long strides back to the alleyway.

Though she huffed a moment, the shaman followed close behind him without a word of protest.

Excitement built in his gut as Myronor rushed through the Strato-District market, darting between bodies towards the bright ocean cliffside. A small terrace hung away from the city, a small platform over the sea with the sole purpose of respite. Small gatherings of shoppers sat together on stone benches, admiring the exotic plants and conversing while taking a break from their spending. Any other time, he would have loved to sit and relax in a spot so beautiful, with a view so splendorous. But right now, it was the only area nearby that was free of shadows.

Anxious to know if his instincts were correct, he held the glossy stone up to the sun in one hand. And for the first time in days, he truly smiled.

"Do you see them?" he asked Kaikora, now leaning over his shoulder to examine alongside him.

Within the dark glass, he recognized the symbolic signature of imbuteria. The strange markings, each distinct, were vaguely familiar. Knowing only little of the art, he couldn't fathom a guess what they might mean but could clearly recognize their presence. Undoubtedly, the ore was not mined from the ground with such markings inscribed within it, which meant a mage had imbued it. And no matter the intention, he was certain *somewhere* in his mother's library, he could find something to decipher the mystery behind it.

"Kaikora, we should head back to—"

Suddenly, the stone slipped from his fingers. Not downwards as if fallen from his grasp, but away. Away from him and into the crowd. The only clue he had to Pyra's research slipped through his fingers. He started forward, panic twisting his stomach, only to be jolted back by a massive, tattooed arm.

"Wait a moment—" she hissed, gray eyes fixated on the crowd. "They've shadowed us since we left the Embassy," she breathed.

"Would've been nice to know sooner," he muttered through gritted teeth. "But we can't just let that stone go!"

Frantic, he scanned the crowd, searching for some sign of magic. Whoever had cast the summoning charm must be near...

"We won't lose it, Myronor."

A loud crack reverberated through the crowd as Kaikora slammed her trident heavily on the stone tiles. The sound alone stunned the crowd, and while the majority froze to ogle the giant woman with wide eyes, a single person began to move. Covered from head to toe in black, form-fitting clothing, their cowl remained pulled up to cover their mouth and head like a hooded mask. Fist clenched tight, they fled into the market, disappearing into the crowd.

"Follow closely and do as I command," Kaikora said before launching into a sprint.

~ Thirty Eight ~

CONVOCATION

Two guards stood at the end of the white road. Before the gate to Birozahran, they had watched Ophiera's approach nearly as closely as she had watched them. The guards were clad in identical attire: flowing robes of deep purple embroidered with swirls shaded like the sands. Both grasped thick, metal staves yet wore no armor of any kind. Only when she stopped mere feet before them did she notice their ears, elongated and pointed, each with an empty hole the size of a coin punched through the cartilage. She tried not to stare as the taller of the two stepped forward.

"*Anathemas* are not welcome here."

Hearing that word stuck her tongue to the roof of her mouth. But the annunciation was different enough to make her wonder if their definitions were the same. Despite how he rolled his r's and the melodic inflection of the vowels, that one cursed word caused her stomach to churn just as it had in Feyralis.

"I seek counsel with the Odestal Autarch, Zadock no Enukaja," she said, repeating the words as Kaikora had instructed.

The guards exchanged glances.

"And *who* are you to make such a request?"

"I uh—" she began, hesitating at the ridiculousness of the question. But an invisible brush against her open palm encouraged her to proceed. "I am Ophiera, a Wielder of Erum's Flame."

The taller guard looked back at his comrade, exchanging an inscrutable expression. As he turned back to her, he glared harshly at her armor and sword.

"Come," he grunted before turning to the gate.

For a moment, she wasn't certain if she should follow. But another breeze across her skin from an invisible Jasper forced her greaves forward. As she trailed behind the silent guard, they passed beneath Birozahran's gate. The pale stone walls mirrored the color and texture of the desert sand as if risen from it. From what Jasper had described, she had imagined only the worst lay within. But as they turned a corner and emerged into a city square, Ophiera skidded to a sudden halt in the sand.

Contrary to the gray desert circumjacent, Ophiera instead found herself immersed in greenery. Thick vines over stone, ferns the size of people, and countless evergreen trees were a surprisingly welcome sight. Despite the density of vegetation, a mixture of buildings stood out within the square. From dark hoodoos of natural stone to smooth, square abodes built of hardened sand and wood, the infrastructure was nearly as foreign as Krysas. However, like Krysas, the hoodoos had been carved into dwellings, untainted by the crystals or metals of imbuteria.

"Keep pace," the guard said, beginning to walk again. "You may ogle at our glorious city after you've gone through the sponsorship."

"Sponsorship?" Ophiera asked, following after him but continuing to stare.

"The Autarchs will decide if you are who you say you are. And whether you are welcome among us."

She instinctively took the statement as a threat, but the guard's candor was more one of simple fact. She held her tongue and judgment, for now, while observing the city square.

Water flowed in proportion with the plant life from fountains of stone, much like the one she'd seen back in the cave. There seemed to be a source of water outside nearly every structure, bubbling away. Near the middle of the square sat the largest fount, centered in a shallow basin of steaming water against the cold desert air. Given the darkness of the stone beneath, it was hard to tell how deep the water dropped until a group of small children ran across it, splashing along with their feet.

How hadn't she noticed the people bustling about before? It was almost as if they'd suddenly appeared from nowhere. Or perhaps because there were no crowds, only scattered pockets of people, it did not strike her nerves the same way.

A small group of young people passed her, staring at her armor with wide eyes and whispers. She chewed her lip, waiting for the jeers and calls she'd come to expect. But none came—not from that group, nor the next, or any passerby thereafter. Soon, Ophiera was no longer avoiding them; instead, she met their gazes, and some even smiled at her.

Their clothing varied as much as their physical appearances; a little bit of everything from brightly flowing robes to dark leather armor, though the trends of Krysas seemed purposefully avoided here. For example, not a single person wore a cowl over their face. And regardless of style, nearly everyone carried a weapon: a knife at the belt, a sword on their back, or a quarterstaff in hand. Even the children bore arms, though they were carved of wood, and they swung them at one another fiercely in mock combat.

The eyes she met were the most varied and vibrant shades she'd ever seen—dark reds, rich violets, deep blues so dark they were nearly black. Paired with their oddly shaped ears, she realized just how different the Enclave was from the Consortia—or

Tanvik, for that matter. And while some ears were pointed, many others were clipped and scarred. The majority of adults bore a large, gaping hole through the cartilage, though most of the children splashing in the fount bore no such mark.

Over her pauldron, she looked for any sign the invisible rogue still followed. She supposed that it was a good thing she detected no trace of him, but an unease crept over her as she followed the guard deeper into the city. Jasper could slip away at any moment and flee back to the ship. Not that she could blame him, but it was hard to accept that she couldn't fully trust him either. For all his talk of the lodestar, she wasn't confident he had the conviction he so declared.

Suddenly, Ophiera felt an invisible nudge, veering her slightly to the left. Her shoulders relaxed a bit at his touch, but she didn't understand why Jasper pushed her to the guard's other side. At least, not until they passed an unmarked hole in the ground. With her eyes wandering endlessly, she'd have tripped down into a cave entrance so similar to those out in the desert.

Below, Ophiera caught a glimpse of cylindrical tunnels brimming with activity. People sat on thick, woven blankets covered in trinkets and wares while others browsed and bartered. A makeshift market in the cave systems explained the sparse population above, at least in part.

The guard paused before an unmarked and otherwise indistinct obsidian pillar. He gave her no instruction before ducking through the large carved archway, and with a deep breath, Ophiera followed. Guards circled the room they'd entered, wearing tabards of varied, beautiful designs. She hadn't time to admire them before noticing the three individuals in the center of the room. In the sand, they sat on woven blankets around a pit of antracinder stones glowing like embers. She nearly ran into the back of the guard as he came to a stop, fixated on the three people, unlike any others, conversing quietly.

"Autarchs," the guard called. "A wayward child has found their way home through the Shole."

The guard bowed towards the man seated farthest right. As Ophiera met his eyes, the hair on her neck rose in protest. She had never seen eyes like his, the deepest crimson swirling like blood in the water. Through curtains of straight, black hair, he glared at her much like the navarra had through the porthole. Every bone in her body tensed, but she stared back, unblinking.

"And *who* is she?" asked the woman seated beside him, refusing to turn her gaze on Ophiera.

The guard licked his lips nervously. "She claims to be a Wielder of Erum's Flame."

"Impossible," the middle Autarch growled, deep and guttural.

Ophiera turned her gaze on the doubtful woman, only to find her stare nearly as disconcerting as the first. Her left eye almost glowed a shade of pale green-gray, and the right, the darkest shade of brown. Half her tawny hair had been shaved and replaced by metallic tattoos across her scalp and neck. And what hair was left hung in braids like leather tassels, dangling above her shoulders. Like Kaikora, her arms were wrapped tightly with sinewy muscle, but unlike Kaikora, this woman's stature was slight, even whilst seated.

"Welcome, wayward child," the third and last Autarch said.

Despite his welcoming words, Ophiera found this man the most threatening of all. Hairless and unassuming, she couldn't understand how he could see with eyes of endless white. And yet, despite the apprehension she felt meeting his empty stare, his broad smile held as much warmth as the cinders before him.

"I am Autarch Thryne Delphius and Wielder of Hollow Vessels. Please forgive my comrades for not introducing themselves. We do not host guests often, or willingly, for that matter. But the Enclave has not encountered Erum's Flame in millennia, and I must say, my curiosity has gotten the better of me."

His tone was kind and gentle, yet Ophiera felt the subtle threat laced between each word. It made sense now why the guard had led her here with no questions or demands for proof of identity. If she were not who she'd declared, there was little chance she'd leave this room alive.

"Child, are you willing to prove to us who you are?"

Ophiera took a breath, letting her pride roll off her shoulders. Though Kaikora had warned her of a possible test, she couldn't help but feel like a pet being asked to perform a trick. In the name of diplomacy, she held her tongue and nodded her compliance.

"Splendid," Thryne said with a smile. "Vaelin, please fetch the two *anathemas* from the hold."

The guard beside her bowed and left the room. Again, the word thrown so casually about churned her stomach. Her disgust must have shown as Thryne laughed gently.

"I apologize, dear child; I should have explained," he said, coming to a stand. "The first law of Birozahran is that only Enclave are permitted entry. However, in an effort to reunite our displaced ancestors and orphans of the Purge, the three remaining clans have agreed to sponsor the wayward children in our city. One of us must agree to take on the responsibility."

"And if none do?" She asked, unable to help herself.

Thryne smiled. "We will come to that when we come to it...but first, we require proof of *who* you are."

As he said this, the two remaining Autarchs rose to a stand. The wild-looking woman wore an outfit of patchwork leather, all varied shades and textures from head to toe. She stretched as the other brushed the sand from his thin, black robes.

Every instinct told her he was the Odestal leader, and she wondered where Jasper was hiding now. Did he know this man, or just of his clan? And why did he fear the warlocks, as he called them, more than the others? There were so many questions she should have put to Jasper before coming to this place.

"Those who were born to wield Erum's Flame have a unique ability to detect *sin*, as your people call it," Thryne said, gesturing to the door.

Vaelin, the guard, entered the room again, this time with two prisoners in tow. Ophiera would have known they were prisoners even without the iron shackles strapped across their throats. Malnourished and beaten, the guard drew the two to their knees before her. They were blindfolded.

Her scars burned beneath her golden gauntlet. Flashes of dark rooms and dripping water threatened her control, but she kept quiet until Thryne spoke again.

"These two *anathemas* infiltrated our city," he said, and this time, all the kindness had left his voice.

"I lived here my whole life!" Screamed one of the chained, only to be silenced by Vaelin's fist against their jaw.

Ophiera hid her disgust as Thryne continued.

"As you can see, they both claim innocence, but we have no way of being certain. However, you may be able to show us which, if any, are truly *untainted*. Cleanse any *anathema* before you and prove to us who you truly are."

Beneath Ophiera's gauntlet, her hand began to tremble. *This* was their test? To cleanse a soul in front of them? To *kill*? She knew nothing of the prisoners' crimes, nothing of this place, and their laws. But that was the test, wasn't it? The Aether knew, even if she did not.

She may have spent nights tormenting herself over her Oath, fretting over the judgments yet to be made, but in all the years spent in the Magistrate's service, she'd not made a mistake. In Iluka, she'd spared Jasper because of a *feeling* and cleansed countless others on the same. Though she never wished to admit it, she had always known when someone was guilty of sin. Doubt had dictated so much of her life—not only in herself but in everything around her. But now, there was no more room for doubt.

Glaring at the Autarchs, Ophiera tossed her bag and sword to the side. The prisoners trembled with each *clunk* of her armor as she approached. Through the sanded ground, she let the Aether course freely through her veins. Without catching flame, she listened to its furious whispers as she circled the two captive souls. Her gauntleted fingers brushed against the first's bare shoulder, and she *felt* so much more than cold, clammy skin.

Fury burned through her, barely contained as she sensed the darkness within. She glared at the Autarchs as she dug her fingertips into the prisoner's shoulders. And the Aether roared through her, nearly pleased at the yelp of pain from the soul beneath her. The flare of white flames reflected brightly in all of their eyes.

When Ophiera released her breath, she felt only ash in her hand. Though the burn lingered painfully within her scars, she felt no guilt in the vesper hovering above the sand. Dark purple and swirling with tendrils of corruption, the orb hung as proof of her justice. She didn't look to the Autarchs as she moved to the next prisoner, shaking the burn from her fingertips.

Again, she felt something more than cold, trembling skin beneath her palm. But as she released the second prisoner's shoulder and stepped away, the Aether quieted. There was nothing to cleanse from the soul of this prisoner. But their chains still rattled as they collapsed to the ground in sobs.

"Cleanse this filth," growled the wild-looking Autarch.

"They are innocent," Ophiera said.

"Lies!" she growled, tossing two pieces of dirty yellow cloth before her feet. "I've yet to meet an innocent who bore these, so finish the task!"

Ophiera managed to control her rage at the proof that the Brotherhood's presence was strewn in the sand. But the second prisoner continued to sob on the ground, dirty and frail, reminding her of a sobbing boy, soaked and alone in a boat.

"Poor judgment is not a sin," Ophiera said quietly. "Have we not all, at some point or another, misjudged who we keep company with?"

Out of the corner of her eye, she saw Zadok's lips quirk. But the wild Autarch stepped towards her in threat, forcing her to reignite her arm in bright, burning flames. The woman growled, dual-colored eyes fixated upon the white fire.

"You asked me to prove who I am," Ophiera declared, keeping her tone respectful but stern. "I have answered by claiming the anathema and sparing the innocent."

Baring her teeth, the Autarch let out another growl that echoed through the ceiling-less room. Ophiera flexed her hand, continuing to burn along with her glare. She knew her actions weren't the most diplomatic, but if they were truly testing *who* she was, they would know one way or another.

With a soft chuckle, Thryne stepped between them. His silvery robes glimmered with the flames, as did his pale, colorless eyes. And to her relief, the crazed woman shrank before him.

"Now, now, Syrina, the child proved herself, did she not? When was the last time any of us laid eyes on the splendor of Erum's Flame?"

The Aether, holy flames, Erum's Flame, Ophiera didn't care what they called it; all that mattered was the pain building beneath her armor. She refused to extinguish until Syrina, as he called her, conceded. But the white flames, while searing, did not pain her as intensely as the ekath.

"*Tch*," Syrina spat, turning back to the strange stone fire. "Proof or not, as the Ailuro Autarch and Wielder of Coalescence, I will not sponsor a child so weak-willed."

"She's burned this long, and you question her will?" Zadok asked, stepping forward. His voice again sounded soft and melodic, as if he sang rather than spoke. "You may extinguish yourself, child."

With a shake of her arm, Ophiera did so, feeling the relief of the Aether now beneath her feet rather than coursing through her flesh. Despite the softness of his voice, his gaze remained unnerving and unwavering. He circled her, dark robes swishing in the sand, assessing her as someone shopping in a marketplace. If he hadn't just defended her, she might have been offended. Zadok turned away, returning to his seat beside Syrina. She glared at the stone embers, refusing to acknowledge his presence.

"As the Odestal Autarch and Wielder of Marrowsong, I offer my sponsorship to a child so rare."

Ophiera let out a breath. While she was relieved to be sponsored at all, she was equally glad it was the Odestal. Her curiosity took hold for a moment, wondering what exactly their titles meant: coalescence, hollow vessels, marrowsong...Like Erum's Flame, the titles must reflect the magic they possess, and yet she wasn't certain which words corresponded to a given mana. Jasper had suggested the Enclave dabbled in derivation magics, and yet the three before her, while intimidating, seemed reasonable in comparison to his description.

"Very well," Thryne said, raising his arms wide. "Wielder of Erum's Flame, you are a welcome guest of the Odestal and, thus, the Enclave. Come, join us by the hearth, and share your purpose for being here."

Thryne returned to his place around the fire, his white eyes hovering expectantly on her. Stepping carefully over the pile of ash in the sand, she sat opposite the three near the hearth. She heard the second prisoner sob quietly as the guard dragged her away. Her fate was out of her hands now, but the guilt of it sat ill with her.

"Do you prefer we call you as they do in Tanvik?" Thryne asked, offering her an ornate vessel.

"I prefer Ophiera," she replied, taking the cup but not drinking.

"That namesake is as ancient as the mana you wield," Thryne said, smiling. "Now, Ophiera, before we begin, I must first ask—is the attire you wear adamantrium?"

She paused, considering how much information to share. In the Cloister, they had her believe her armor was true adamantrium when in reality, it was but a diluted alloy. Still, was there any harm in confirming what they already guessed or knew?

"As far as I know, yes."

"Splendid," Thryne said. "I wondered how it resisted the white flames...but alas, I distracted myself. I should explain our customs, as they are of fair exchange. You provide proof of your claim; thus, we provide sponsorship. You provided an answer to my question; thus, now it is my turn to provide. So, what is it you ask of us?"

The question was so frank that it would have been offensive in Tanvik. But again, she sensed no malice—only curiosity.

"I'm searching for someone—Ambassador Pyra Ebontide. Do you know of her?"

Zadok's crimson eyes widened ever so slightly, but he didn't speak. So much for fair exchange, she thought to herself.

"Why would you look for an *anathema* here?" she spat. "You're lucky we allowed you before us."

"What does that word mean to the Enclave?" Ophiera asked. The three Autarchs looked at her as if she had caught flame again. Fair exchange..."In Tanvik, we use that word to describe those who have committed murder and stolen a soul from the Aether. Does it mean the same to the Enclave?"

Thryne leaned forward, intertwining his fingers. "It means something similar...But now, we consider all outsiders of the Enclave *anathema*."

"Why?" Ophiera asked.

While Syrina growled again, Thryne hushed her with a wave of his hand. "We understand your ignorance of our past, but it is still a delicate subject. I cannot summarize decades of violence and oppression; therefore, I cannot answer this question fairly. What I will say is that we, as Enclave, have rarely met another soul who wished us well. All we have known are those who would do us harm."

Ophiera stared at the stone embers as understanding slowly sank in. It would be akin to calling all navarra monsters; the only navarra she'd met had been violent. So, to the Enclave, all outsiders were dangerous.

"I regret my ignorance," Ophiera said quietly.

Thryne smiled at her again. "Why do you seek this Pyra? Here, of all places?"

She bit her tongue and glanced at Zadok. If she were to say that Pyra was last seen speaking with the Odestal Autarch, it would draw attention to Zadok's earlier hesitation. His terrifying eyes softened as if he understood her dilemma.

"If I may interject, I taste exhaustion from our guest," Zadok said, gesturing to a guard stationed along the walls. "She should rest first and discuss later."

"If this involves the Consortia, Zadok, all of us have the right to know why she's here!" Syrina spat against his ear.

"Come now, Syrina," Thryne interjected. "No clan hates the Consortia more than the Odestal. We must trust each other, remember?"

With a snort, Syrina sat back. "Then I *trust* the Odestal will keep our wayward child safe and out of trouble whilst she is here in our city."

Ophiera fought to keep her expression placid, though each time they called her a child, she wanted nothing more than to catch flame. She wasn't sure exactly what situation she had fallen into, but it was clear Syrina had a bone to pick with *everyone*, not only her.

A new guard approached, clad in different attire from those at the gates, deep black cloth with embroidered droplets splattered unevenly across the outline of an eye with a slitted pupil.

"Iren will escort you to the Odestal Tabernacle," Zadock said, gesturing Ophiera toward the newcomer. "Please, take rest with my people, and I will provide my counsel once you have recovered your strength."

A last glance at the pile of ash blending in with the sands was the only hesitation she allowed herself before following the stiff guard out into Birozahran.

~ Thirty Nine ~

PURSUANCE

The stranger in black tore off far too quickly for Myronor to keep up pace. Luckily, Kaikora's long strides offset her bulk, and she made quick gains on the figure dashing through the crowd. With the throngs of the market parting for the shaman, Myronor was able to keep up the chase, mostly.

Panting as he ran, he cursed himself for allowing his only lead to slip so easily through his fingers. What in the Aether had he been thinking, letting his guard down in a city he knew to be infested by the Brotherhood? If Ophiera were here, she would have some choice words...

As the thief and Kaikora continued further into the marketplace, cries of outrage pierced the bustle. They still ran a good twenty paces ahead of him, leaving Myronor only to witness the aftermath left in their wake. His boot slid against the stone, smashing pastries and nearly toppling him as the baker's cart beside him just had. Grasping the wand on his belt, he cast to lighten his feet, avoiding more mess strewn across the road while speeding his pursuit.

He focused on Kaikora's bouncing dreadlocks, a bronze beacon cutting above the colorful crowds. Gaining on them, he could hear people shouting obscenities and commands to stop. But there was no turning back until he had the stone back in hand.

By the smoke rising in the air, he realized they neared the anvil shop. A familiar face stepped from the crowd, dressed in a garb similar to his, and he recognized the observant lover of the anvil smith. She held a large parcel close to her chest, eyes widening as the thief and Kaikora barreled toward her.

"Out of the way!" Myronor shouted in Krysan, hoping to, at the very least, spare her lunch.

But the woman instead dropped her parcel, the contents spilling onto the street long after her hands glowed pale yellow. The crowd parted around her as she cast, glaring at the thief cloaked in black.

"Stop, by order of the Consortia!" She shouted.

Myronor watched hopefully as the thief slowed, but Kaikora did not. For an instant, he thought the chase over, until a sickening thud echoed through the gasping crowd.

His stomach dropped far past his floating feet as the thief darted into the alleyway. As Kaikora followed, she revealed the sight of Kula on the ground. Gasping air, she clutched the hilt of a knife protruding from the center of her chest. The smell of blood mixed with the smoke from the anvil shop turned Myronor's stomach; everything else froze around him.

The ekath twisted in his chest as visions of an arrow instead of a knife overtook his reality. He could do nothing as the blood spilled from Ophiera's trembling lips...her chest rattling, gurgling against the blood...He could do nothing to stop the life draining from her features...

"No!"

Someone shoved him from behind, knocking him down onto the street. The sound of chain mail rattling focused his attention on the anvil smith, who now dropped to her knees before her dying lover. With soot-covered hands, Nyr held Kula's expressionless face. The crowd gathered, murmuring and shouting as blood pooled over the dark stone street.

An uncontrollable need to run forced Myronor's feet to move. He did not slow as the alleyway narrowed, scraping his shoulders against the stone. The pain helped focus his frantic thoughts. No longer did he pursue a thief, but an anathema now. And though there was nothing he could do to heal or save the woman, who had simply tried to do what was right, he could still *do* right by her.

Ophiera's soul burned within his own, whispering demands for Retribution. And with that fire in his heart, he left the bloodshed behind and followed the dark path ahead.

In the dim light of the backstreet, Myronor searched for Kaikora. His eyes were still adjusting to the dark, and he saw the reflection of the metal adornments that decorated the shaman's hair, which was whipping down a path to the left. With quickened, floating feet, he gave chase.

Deeper and deeper into the Depths, she ran, zigzagging between dim alleyways and narrow paths. Luckily, few people resided this far back into the cliffside, and soon, the only sounds he could hear were their echoing breaths and heavy footsteps. He had to trust that Kaikora still followed the anathema, but he could not see anything ahead of the shaman.

"Myronor, hurry!" Kaikora shouted behind her shoulder. "I need your aid!"

With a glow of blue, he pushed himself to run faster.

As Myronor rounded a turn, he found Kaikora slowing her stride to contend with a dead end. The tall, rocky wall at the end of their path stood four stories tall, illuminated by phosphorus crystals pegged throughout.

Defeat settled in his chest as he searched frantically for any movement. His mind was no longer focused on finding the stolen stone but on finding the culprit who'd stolen the soul back on the street.

"There!" Kaikora growled, pointing her trident up the wall.

A shadow crossed over the crystals, moving upwards. As his eyes followed the intended path of the anathema, he saw another crossroad at the top. If they escaped into another level of back streets, they would surely be lost for good.

"Conjure water at the base of the cliff!" Kaikora demanded.

Without question, Myronor cast the spell, grasping the minimized staff from his belt to soften the blow against his draining mana. A pool of clear water bubbled into existence, reflecting the crystalline light from the wall.

"Jump!" Kaikora commanded as she did so herself.

At her heels, Myronor sprang forward. Without his doing, the pool suddenly frothed as a geyser pushed against his feet. His knees buckled as the pressure propelled him upwards, the flash of the crystals passing by dizzying him. Before he could regain his balance, they'd reached the edge of the next street level. The thief stumbled to a stand, having just cleared the edge as Kaikora leaped forward. And in stride, Myronor followed.

Again, on a narrow back street, they ran. Like the path below, the road here was narrow, and there were no people in sight. He wondered, for the briefest of moments, if these deep places were abandoned after the Enclave camps were dismantled. But his curiosity had no place amongst the fury building in his chest. The anathema slowed, and Myronor wondered if they had finally grown tired of running, for he indeed did. While his mana might compensate for his lack of physical stamina, both were dwindling quickly.

But then he felt the world tear asunder.

In the darkness, a flash of energy cut a rift through the air. The guttural chants coming from a voice in the dark, high pitched and out of breath, waned. Horror gripped his spine, fumbling his feet and forcing him to his knees. The darkness creeping into his mind whispered no conceivable words, yet caused every fiber of his being to recoil. Aud's presence, seeping through the tear between worlds, was poison enough to claim his soul.

"Myronor, cast again!" Kaikora shouted beside him, "Beneath their feet!"

He tried to search beyond the rift for the caster and do as Kaikora demanded. But the vacuous sensation overtaking the alley drew upon his most terrible memories. Innocent screams and disintegrating vespers stole every bit of sight and strength from him. Alone in the dark, awaiting an end he knew was to come.

The rift coiled and churned as tendrils reached beyond the tattered edges. It wasn't magic nor might that crushed him so thoroughly, but fear, and fear alone.

But then, a light ignited in his very soul.

Visions of white flames and violet eyes cleared his mind. Holding on to the image of Ophiera like a talisman, he recovered the strength to cast. Water flooded beneath the darkened portal as he summoned enough to fill the streets.

Kaikora's power radiated in all directions, and under her influence, the water no longer flowed but rose as if blown by the wind. Thick ribbons of waves began to spin, building on themselves as the water funneled upwards and widened. Suddenly, the rift blinked out of existence, and the suffocating darkness disappeared. Near where it had opened, an orb of crystal-clear water spun around a blackened figure.

"C-can they escape?" he sputtered, out of breath and voice.

"As long as my mana holds, nothing can penetrate the surface from within," Kaikora said with a grunt. "But they are fighting quite fiercely. I suggest retrieving the stone sooner rather than later."

Myronor took a few deep breaths, regaining his composure. Again, he'd nearly forgotten why they'd chased down the thief. Heeding Kaikora's words, he broke through the water orb with little resistance, and inside, he cast a summon. As the anathema fought his spell, bubbles broke the surface, though they themselves could not. With a painful smack against his palm, he retrieved the stone, removing himself from the orb to pocket it.

"We should bring them to the Yeoman," Kaikora said with a strained voice. "But I fear I cannot hold them much longer—at least not like this."

Myronor circled the orb, still trembling from the chase. The anathema thrashed within; bubbles reached the top but remained trapped beneath the surface.

"Perhaps we should let them drown," he said in a hollow voice.

Their guilt was clear. Not only had this anathema taken a life, but they had summoned the Void itself. As far as he knew, only the Reverends of the Brotherhood were *gifted* such power. And he only knew of one Reverend at the moment.

"We are not tasked with Retribution," Kaikora said with a gentle strain, still maintaining the orb.

Coming to his senses, Myronor grasped the wand from his belt. As terrible as his thoughts had become, he knew that Ophiera would never forgive him if he did what he desired most at this moment.

"I take it you're good for a secret, Kaikora?" Myronor asked quietly, expanding his quarterstaff back to full size. It was a rhetorical question, of course—he knew she'd never speak a word of what he was about to do.

Closing his eyes, he channeled the dregs of his mana on the wretched life before him. The water frothed and diminished as the figure within folded inward on themselves. He swore he could hear screams trapped within every bubble caught beneath the surface. And when the bubbles finally stopped, only a bright, rubyfin fish remained, swimming in frantic circles around the water orb.

"Brilliant," Kaikora said, her eyes reflective as she shrank the orb down to size. "You might not be fast, but you are clever."

"Tha-argh!"

He hadn't even a moment to relish in the shaman's compliment before his arm seared with pain. Collapsing to the ground, he cradled his arm that held neither injury nor fire, and yet the agony stole the words from his lips.

"Myronor, what's wrong?!"

"O-O-phie-ra..."

Somewhere, she burned—somewhere, a soul was returned to the Aether. And despite his previous wishes for Retribution, he found he could not bear the weight of it now.

* * *

"We're here," the shaman said softly.

Myronor rolled his eyes, blinking to stay alert. From Kaikora's back, he'd barely paid attention as they'd walked. He'd barely been able to stay awake. Since Ophiera burned, he found himself in a haze. The shaman now carried him on his back, along with balancing the transfigured anathema in her hand.

Whether from manasickness or the intensity with which Ophiera burned, Myronor wasn't sure why the power of the Aether drew on the tether so potently. But it had. And now he leaned against Kaikora's broad shoulders, unable to move and barely able to think as she pushed open a painted door.

Beyond the threshold, there was nothing but a wall of stone, or at least it appeared to be, until he looked down. Kaikora ducked them both as she descended the dirty stone steps into the darkness.

The path downwards felt endless, but eventually, they reached a landing outside a large, empty room. Well, not exactly empty, Myronor realized as his eyes focused on the dim light. Three shadows were cast around a large lantern of antracinders. And while he'd never met the Yeoman before, he easily guessed which of the three was her. The leather blindfold seemed to meld with her skin as she turned towards him and Kaikora.

"For a moment, I thought you carried Pyra on your back. But we will get to formal introductions later. For now, Kaikora, my child, show us your catch today."

He found it strange that anyone would refer to the towering shaman as a child. Yet Kaikora dragged the water orb before the Yeoman obediently. The rubyfin danced in circles as the Yeoman craned her neck, inspecting the orb.

"Who are they?"

Kaikora remained suspiciously quiet, lowering Myronor into a chair beside the lantern. Sitting up on his own felt nearly as tiring as chasing down the wretch. But he grew impatient with the shaman's lack of response.

"We don't know, but they are likely a Reverend," he said in a steady voice.

The Yeoman smiled sadly at Kaikora. "Ah, always my most cautious child. Throw them in the cell to the left. The ketrite bars will prevent them from using any mana, no matter from Aud or Erum."

Ketrite...Myronor knew that word somewhere, but in the haze of his exhaustion, nothing came to mind. And truthfully, it didn't matter. Not as Kaikora crossed the room and tossed the watery orb past the odd metal bars lining a cell.

The water splashed to the floor, and the rubyfin fish flopped frantically against the stone. Splashes turned to sputters as the door slammed shut, and like a dark flower blooming violently, a woman in drenched black unfolded into existence. With a gloved hand, she tore the wet cowl from her face as her gasps for air slowly turned to cackles.

"Marvena," Myronor growled. Acid filled his throat as his very soul cried out to strike her down and take revenge for Iluka—for Ophiera.

But Kaikora placed a firm hand on his shoulder, steadying him. "Not yet," she murmured.

"Not yet?!" cried Marvena, still laughing at the ceiling. "Oh, I'd love to see him *try* to kill me...I certainly deserve to die after what I've done."

"Remain silent," Kaikora whispered, even quieter than before. Myronor used all his strength to hold back his tongue, while the Yeoman and others said nothing. He couldn't understand why they'd brought the wretch back here only to ignore her. But it seemed Marvena did not handle the silence well either.

"And here I thought your girlfriend would find me first," she said, sprawling out on her back in the cell. "Where is she, by the way? She was so desperate to claim my soul before, but I suppose you have more reason than she to wish me dead."

His vision tunneled as the memories of Marvena's torment joined the storm. The sacrifices, the beatings, the arrow...he closed his eyes, trying to shake away the sensation crushing around his chest. Kaikora's hand squeezed his shoulder, reminding him he wasn't alone.

"You look as distraught now as the day the white witch bled out in your arms! It was a perfect shot if I do say so myself." She let out another fit of disgusting laughter. Though Kaikora's hand stayed on his shoulder, it could not stop Myronor's blood from thundering. "I've always wanted to ask how you brought her back from the dead. Necromancy? Blood magic? None are very becoming of an Ambassador, you know. Capital offense, in fact—as is transmutating a person."

"You're not a person," Myronor spat, unable to control himself. "You're a monster."

Cackling again, Marvena sat up from the floor. She crawled towards the edge of the metal cage, pressing her face between two pale bars. "And what does that make her, then? Hundreds of souls have gone up in flames by her command. Sounds a lot like something a monster would do..."

As his hands flickered in blue light, Kaikora gripped his shoulder tightly. The pain of her touch brought him back to his senses for a moment. Even if he had enough mana to cast, his magic would be useless beyond those bars.

"Ah, I know why you look so upset now...she left you, didn't she? It must be a hard life, never a priority, and pushed aside for more important matters."

Myronor swallowed his anger and his pride. He wasn't sure if she truly knew the depth to which her taunts struck him or if she simply made assumptions. But after Pyra, Rheta, Eliana, and now, Ophiera...her comments were as well aimed as the arrow she'd shot.

"But you know who does miss you? My Mistress. You've always been her priority, and she would do *anything* to get you back."

"We've heard enough," the Yeoman said. "Let us depart."

"That's it?" Marvena pouted through the bars. "You're not going to torture me for information or, better yet, kill me?"

"Not I," the Yeoman said coldly.

One of the Yeoman's companions carried a bucket of water and placed it near the bars. They tossed a ladle to Marvena before returning to the Yeoman's side. Together, all three moved towards the stairs.

"We're just going to leave her?" Myronor asked Kaikora as she put his arm around her shoulder and hoisted him up.

"I will explain outside," she whispered.

"You already made the mistake of letting me live twice!" Marvena shouted. "Don't learn well for a scholar, do you?"

Myronor couldn't agree more.

Resisting the urge to seize Kaikora's trident and run it through the wretch, he let the shaman lead him back up the dark stairs. He didn't understand...after all that, they were to leave the Reverend of the Brotherhood locked in a cell, unguarded and uninhibited by anything more than metal bars?

Lost in thought, he allowed Kaikora to lead him blindly through Krysas. She supported most of his weight, still, though at least he could walk now rather than be carried. The lingering burn of Ophiera still haunted his soul, and he wondered if he should tell her they'd captured Marvena. Given her hunt for the woman, he assumed she would need to know. But would that knowledge do her any good, halfway across the continent? Would it help her search for Pyra? Perhaps once he knew the Yeoman's plans, he'd send Mallow along with another message. That was if Mallow was being cooperative, and since last night, she had yet to make an appearance.

"You should walk on your own from here," Kaikora said, breaking his thoughts.

His legs still felt shaky, but at the very least, he could stand on his own. Truthfully, he'd been so deep in thought he hadn't paid attention to where they were. He vaguely recalled a lift and now recognized the fortress before them.

"Why are we back at the Consortia?"

"I will explain inside," Kaikora hissed. "It is not safe to speak."

Trusting her, he tried to straighten his collar and cape before entering the Embassy. Inside, Glamwell sat as usual at his crystalline desk, engrossed in yet another book. His nose was nearly pressed against the paper as he looked up to greet them.

"Good evening, sir! How was your shopping...oh dear sir, are you well?"

"I'm fine."

"You look dreadful...Wait! Were you mugged?!"

"No, Glamwell, I—"

"Attacked?"

"No, I—"

"I heard reports of a ruckus in the markets! Did this shaman not defend you? Tell me, and I will file a report immediately—"

"Glamwell!" Myronor shouted, and the man in pink froze. "I'm fine, Kaikora is fine, everything is *fine* other than I'm exhausted, and I pine for my consort. That is all that truly ails me."

"Oh..." Glamwell said, flushing slightly as he brought his book back to his nose. "Well, I suggest a good rest, sir."

"And that's precisely where I'm headed."

Once through the gateway door, Myronor threw himself on the same fainting couch on which the dark ichor had overtaken him. He felt nearly as alone and confused as he had then. Except this time, Ophiera wasn't here to save him.

From his pocket, he extracted the tablet-shaped stone and spun it in his palm. The claw-like windows only provided the dying light of dusk, and so, he turned to the antracinders in the hearth for light. But even they were not bright enough to penetrate the dark, glassy stone and reveal the etchings he knew hid within.

His thoughts lingered on the scene of the market. Would the anvil smith ever recover from the horror of a loved one's death? He knew the answer all too well. And though Marvena had wielded the blade, the guilt of a soul lost because of this stone...So much sacrifice, and for what?

Kaikora joined him in the living space, taking a seat on the floor, cross-legged. In her hands, she held a large stoneware basin filled with water.

"What's that?" He asked.

"A bowl of water," she said matter-of-factly.

"What's it for?"

"You'll see," she replied with a smirk.

He rolled his eyes, both relieved and annoyed by her candor. At least it was familiar in the midst of the day's chaos. She plunged her hands into the basin with a gentle splash and closed her eyes. He watched, waiting for her to volunteer some information, some clue as to what she was doing. But as was her standard, she sat in silence.

"Shouldn't we discuss Marvena?" He asked.

Kaikora sighed. "What is there to discuss?"

He scoffed. "We've captured one of the most dangerous members of the Brotherhood and have left her alone in a cell! And we're doing what, having ourselves a spa day?"

"You give this Reverend too much credit," Kaikora said. "As did Ophiera."

"Too much?" Myronor stood, resisting the urge to kick over the bowl of water. "That woman destroyed Iluka, tortured me, and killed Ophiera! I'm sure the accolades go on!"

"Ophiera's not dead," Kaikora said calmly. "Thanks to you."

"That doesn't take away the pain it caused! The suffering we both have endured since! Marvena deserves every bit of Retribution promised to her."

"And how are you so certain that Marvena doesn't feel the same?" Kaikora said quietly. "Ophiera destroyed her family, her home...Can you fault her for seeking retribution against your ekath?"

Slowly, Myronor returned to his seat, the weight of Kaikora's words dragging him down. Again, the cloud of thoughts buzzed in his mind, and attempting to think was like listening to a bird song in a rainstorm. Shame kept him silent, but thoughts of Ophiera kept him sane.

In his moments of doubt, he always remembered the day she caught flame in the encampment—the moment the world turned white with the holy flames, and she became the Aether itself. *His* suffering had broken her, and thus broke that power free. While she had feared for so long losing control of the Aether, she had never lost her control with him. Her Oath may be one of Retribution, but her nature was protective. She had always sacrificed to ensure he did not suffer...by the river, from the troynt, from the Brotherhood, and even from Aud herself...

"Ophiera and Marvena are not the same," Myronor said to Kaikora. "Ophiera may kill, but it has and always will be to *prevent* greater suffering. Marvena only desires to cause pain, while Ophiera bears it so others don't have to."

Kaikora chuckled deeply, hands in the bowl. "I shouldn't expect any less of a thorough comparison from a scholar such as yourself. But my point is not that Marvena and Ophiera are similar; rather, I think that understanding our opposition's motives may help you predict their next move. Marvena knows what motivates you and Ophiera and targets them at every turn, drawing your weaknesses out into the open. But we know little of what motivates her and her Mistress. It is worth considering all possibilities."

Shame burned in his gut. It was true; Marvena knew precisely where to stick the knife and twist, and he nearly bled for her had it not been for Kaikora. He thought back to her heckling, re-examining the conversation, looking for purpose rather than justice...

Marvena had focused heavily on Ophiera, though she could have easily thrown Iluka in his face to achieve the same reaction. She had harped on Ophiera's location...and yet she seemingly wished to die? That didn't seem right...why, then, had she stolen the stone? She hadn't mentioned the stone a single time...the stone he didn't yet understand ...but maybe...

"What are you even doing?" He asked Kaikora, distracted by her hands still soaking in the bowl.

"Channeling," she said.

"And what does that mean?"

Kaikora sighed. "Water holds all knowledge: the past, present, and future. It is the basis of the Phratries practices."

He closed his eyes, steeling himself into patience. "And what does it have to do with Marvena?"

"All water is connected," she murmured. "Like a sailing ship, water is responsible for carrying it on its journey, but a captain must still steer the boat. I simply serve as the guide."

In an instant, her eyes glazed over, mirrored. Her breathing changed, pointed and heavy as if she chanted or sang without the use of her voice. He watched as the surface of the bowl rippled, pulsating to the rhythm of her breaths, though no one touched it. The water continued to churn as images reflected in the ripples. Like Kaikora's eyes, the surface of the water transformed into a mirror that did not reflect but rather *showed* something.

Distorted like dreams, the images flashing across the surface were incoherent at first. As Kaikora's brow furrowed, Myronor recognized a dark stone ceiling and dark metal bars bubbling to the surface.

"She's here..." said Marvena in a frantic voice. "I know she's here...will come...soon...I know it...mercy...or death? Mercy or death? I failed...oh how I failed..."

Myronor didn't realize he'd crossed the room until he found himself kneeling before Kaikora, staring into the basin in awe. He couldn't believe what he was seeing.

"Can she see us?" He asked stupidly.

"No," Kaikora said. The water in the bowl splashed before returning to perfect clarity. "And I cannot show you for long; it takes much to demonstrate in this way. But I will keep watch over her. It is impossible to interrogate someone without knowing the questions to ask. We will see why she and her Mistress seek Ophiera. And what they know of that stone in your pocket."

~ Forty ~

REPOSE

Iren led Ophiera through a sea of yurts, far past the hoodoos and sanded buildings. The Tabernacle, as Zadok called it, was covered in emblems of the blood-splattered eye, with no paths or order to the placement of anything in sight.

Ophiera wasn't certain why the Odestal chose to segregate themselves from the rest of the city like this, but perhaps the Civ and Ailuro clans had similar territories of their own. It was almost as if she'd entered another city within Birozahran, yet still surrounded by tall gray walls of sandstone.

The guard was young and quiet, efficiently leading Ophiera through the winding tents with few words. She tried to resist the urge to look over her pauldron in search of Jasper, knowing she would find no sign. The sunlight waned below the city walls, but no torches had been lit to provide light—he was quite adept indeed at moving unseen. She hated to admit just how much she hoped he still followed.

Distracted in thought, her armor clanged as she crashed into the back of her escort. Iren turned to glare at her as she rolled her shoulders back to a stiffened posture.

"These are the accommodations, child," she said, gesturing to the yurt beside her. Ophiera chewed her cheek, realizing she would never get used to that term. Iren luckily seemed not to notice. "I will be stationed outside if you should require anything. Otherwise, I will collect you when the Autarch is ready to see you."

She took up position outside the flap of the yurt, digging her staff into the sand.

Ophiera understood the simple yet hidden request—don't leave the yurt. Gazing around, she realized even if she'd wanted to leave, she certainly couldn't find her way anywhere. There were no paths, no signs, and seemingly no reason to the layout of the place...and perhaps that was the point.

"Thank you," she said to Iren before pushing aside the canvas flap. The guard looked confused as she stepped inside.

Again, Ophiera found herself impressed with the so-called savage mage clans of the desert. The abode was far better furnished than her room at the Lonely Iris Inn.

In the center, a shallow fire pit had been dug deep into the sand until it reached the stone, much like the sitting area of the Autarchs. The basin sat filled with the same stone embers that radiated heat and yellow light. Yet despite their warmth, her breath still fogged in the air as the night fell.

She shivered with thoughts of the Shole at night, thankful to be here rather than out there.

Stepping across the sanded ground, she inspected a small stone font bubbling away with fresh water steaming in the cold. A few silvery pots sat against the curved edge of the tent beside a sizable mattress stacked high with furs. All in all, the place felt surprisingly cozy, given the intensity of their emblem.

From the corner of her eye, Ophiera glimpsed the canvas flutter, and a frigid breeze flowed briefly through the yurt. She breathed a sigh of relief as the scent of leather and sea salt wafted before her.

"Do you see now why I despise this place?" Jasper growled into her ear, careful to keep his voice low.

He sounded irritated but not as distressed as she'd feared. Her shoulders relaxed a bit beneath her pauldrons.

"Birozahran isn't what I was expecting, but I'm grateful to be here in one piece," she admitted, throwing her heavy bag on the sandy floor.

"We should have fled the moment they brought in those prisoners," he hissed, still invisible in the yurt.

"Truthfully, I feared you already had."

"Why?"

"I...well," she stumbled, searching for the right words. She had killed in front of him, just as she had on the beach of Iluka.

From the shadows, Jasper revealed himself only inches from her. His amber eyes were the only feature visible beneath his dark hood and the blackened cowl covering his mouth and nose. Even without sight of his face, the pain in his gaze was enough to make her chest ache stronger than the drag of the ekath.

"Every muscle in my body screams to flee this place," he whispered, pulling the cowl to reveal his lips. "My skin crawls against the air, my nostrils burn against the stench, and every ounce of suffering soaked into these sands assaults my every step. But I swore to follow you, and so, here I am."

She swallowed hard, suddenly aware of the heat on his breath. "I never asked—"

"And you will never have to," he said, dropping his voice to a gentle purr. "Now, what is the plan?"

A yell from outside the tent stiffened both their spines. Silent and still, they breathed each other's air while listening for threats. Another scream, and she realized with relief it was laughter.

There were children...

The last time she'd visited Feyralis, the only young she'd seen were the urchins lurking between the buildings, waiting for the vendors to turn a blind eye to their sneaky hands. But here, they roamed free to play in the font or chase each other through the winding tents. She didn't understand why this notion settled her heart.

"We should rest," she said quietly.

"You think we can *rest* in a place like this?"

"We can do nothing else at the moment. And truthfully, this has been a warmer welcome than any city in Tanvik has ever provided me."

Jasper scoffed before quieting again. His eyes narrowed toward the yurt wall, listening as another jabbering group of young voices sounded outside the tent.

"Did you hear?" squealed a small voice. "A child has returned!"

"A child? And *who* are they?"

"No idea, Iren won't tell me."

"Ah, your sister is always stiff on duty..."

"She *is* part of the Autarch's personal guard, ya know. I wouldn't want to upset Zadock either."

"We should find Iku! He always knows what's going on."

"Yeah! Let's go ask him!"

As the voice trailed off, Ophiera and Jasper waited a moment to be sure of silence. She hadn't appreciated how close he stood to her. The collar of his leather overcoat brushed against her pauldron, where he hovered, listening intently. Avoiding the intensity of his eyes, she was distracted instead by a shining object in his earlobe. She'd never noticed before the earring he wore—a raw, jagged gemstone of pale purple and green. The gold metal inset accented the shade of stone, just like the irises that grew in Iluka.

"Take your rest then," Jasper grumbled in the quiet.

With hunched shoulders, he vacated her space and began inspecting the tent's perimeter. She sighed, mostly relieved of the pressure of his presence.

Throwing her braid behind her back, she began the tedious process of loosening the plates of gold. Before, the routine of removing her armor had brought her a great sense of relaxation. She remembered how often she'd caught Myronor's eyes on her, somehow fooling herself into finding his gaze irritating at the time. Now, she only wished to have his eyes on her as she removed each golden piece. He would probably say something like—

"What are you doing?!" Jasper hissed, suddenly at her side again.

She looked down at her bare arms and legs, poised to remove her last armor piece. Setting her breastplate down with the rest, she sighed.

"Have you ever slept in plate mail?"

"You plan on sleeping?" he asked, averting his eyes from her nudity.

"What do you think *rest* means?"

"Not putting yourself at a disadvantage in enemy territory!"

"My armor is far from my only advantage," she grumbled, proud of herself for not mentioning her flames directly. The subject might be too close to the source of his suffering at the moment.

Though she supposed it would be best for everyone if she covered herself. Despite her recent comfort with nudity, she wondered if perhaps it sent the wrong message, undressing with Jasper so near.

In her overpacked rucksack, she rummaged for the single piece of clothing she had packed. Instinctively, she brought the cream-colored tunic to her nose and inhaled deeply. It still held My-ronor's scent, even after all this time, like citrus mixed with parchment and something sugary sweet. Her eyes pricked as she staved off the worst of the pain blooming in her chest. The damned ekath would never stop dragging her heart across the frigid desert, and at the moment, it pulled harder than ever.

But something was different in the sensation. Something was happening to Myronor...not pain or death as she dragged him through, but a sense of disquiet that shook the tether all the way back to her. The tug of war in her soul brought uncontrolled tears to her eyes.

"Are you well?" Jasper whispered, hovering behind her.

His voice was as soft as his fingertips grazing the scar between her shoulder blades. Both somehow relieved a bit of the pain clamping down on her. Shakily, she threw the tunic over her head and wiped her eyes as discreetly as she could.

"I'm exhausted," she murmured, stepping towards the bed.

"Were you—"

"Let us sleep."

"*Us?*"

Her breath hung in the air as she stared at the fur-layered bed. She wasn't sure why she'd said us, but...Would it be so wrong for them to share a bed again? To keep each other warm in a place where they both suffered? For some reason, the thought of sleeping alone plucked painfully at the tether.

"I will admit, your presence brings me a comfort I cannot ex-plain," she whispered, not daring to look at him. "But more so, I wish for *you* to be as comfortable as possible in this place you de-spise. If that is keeping watch all night, so be it; if that is prowling through the city to revisit old places, I will accept; even if it is your wish to head back on the ship, I will understand. Whatever causes you the least amount of suffering, Jasper, that is all I want."

She didn't wait for his response before lifting the layers of furs and crawling into the low bed. Despite being so close to the ground, the stuffed mattress was surprisingly warm. But a genuine rush of heat came to her when Jasper crawled into the bed beside her. And though she did not shiver as she had last night, he still slipped an arm beneath her neck and another over her waist before dragging her against him.

"I admit I slept deeper last night than I have in years," he said against her neck. "But I'm not sure even you can bring me enough peace to close my eyes in this place."

She felt a pang of guilt at the venom beneath his whisper. But curiosity and a need to distract away from his hold of her won.

"Is the city the same as you remember?"

He took a breath. "Much has changed, and yet my gut responds the same. Like nostalgia, without any of the joy, just the bitter reminders of what I worked so hard to forget."

"Sounds like we both could use ember whiskey tonight," she said, massaging the palm of her hand against her sternum. The ache of the ekath had subsided a bit with Jasper's presence, but something burned deep within the tether. A pain she neither caused nor could help. She worried deeply about what was possibly happening to Myronor now.

Jasper ran his fingers across the etched blisters of her arm, following the path of scars to her fingers. Intertwining his own with hers, he pressed her palm against her heart and his lips against her neck.

"Why is your heart racing like this?"

"It may race, but it breaks just the same," she whispered shakily.

"Because of me or the ekath?"

"Both."

She hated herself for the disconnect between the longing of her heart and the yearning of her flesh.

His hand moved from her hand over her scar to graze her breast with his thumb, and she inhaled sharply. Despite her back arching and her skin heating, she hissed, "Don't."

"Are you sure?" He purred. "The way your hips mov—"

"You agreed to respect the boundaries of my heart."

"But what about the boundaries of your flesh?"

"They are one and the same."

"They don't have to be."

"But they are. So heed my wishes or leave."

For the moment, Jasper didn't push her any further, but did not leave the bed either. He remained curled around her, just as he had last night, holding her with a tension that made her regret giving in to this temptation. She just needed her heart to slow, and there she could find rest. With his silence, she found her concentration and focused on the warmth of his embrace rather than the heat of his words. Comfort overcame lust, and in the lull of her heart, she began her search for sleep.

Jasper sighed, relaxing against her as well. "I find it hard to understand how you find *comfort* with me and yet swear yourself to him."

"Finding comfort with someone and sharing your heart with them are two different things. Besides, how can you swear yourself to me while remaining dedicated to Collette?"

"I'm not dedicated to her."

"Lies. I may not be as good at reading people as you, but I see how close you two are."

"Yes, but it's not like this with her."

"Then what is it like?" She asked, more curious than anything. "I don't understand how you can hold her in such esteem and yet still take advantage of her at every opportunity."

He held her quietly as she felt him chew his lip; at least he was thinking about his words first. Perhaps she should have done the same.

"I am and always will be indebted to Col," Jasper murmured against her neck. "She deserves the world, and instead has been given me. For years, she has saved me from myself, and for that, I owe her everything."

"She doesn't seem to be the type to hold you to that debt," Ophiera said.

"No, she wouldn't...which is precisely why I owe it to her."

Ophiera smiled to herself. Perhaps the rogue wasn't such a bad soul after all. If a person like Collette could care so deeply for him, there must be redeeming qualities beyond the feel of him cradled around her now. He might be selfish and apathetic, crude and cruel, but when she remembered the way he so fiercely fought the navarras with her—how he protected his crew, how he comforted Collette, she began to understand how deeply his care matched his suffering.

"Kaikora seemed to have noticed Collette's charm, too," Ophiera said, trying to distract away from her own thoughts.

"Aye," Jasper chuckled throatily, relaxing slightly. "Though I don't think Kaikora fully understands what she's gotten herself into."

"What do you mean?"

"To call Col insatiable is an understatement. I doubt even the shaman has the stamina to match her libido."

Ophiera covered her mouth, trying to muffle her laugh. Though the guard outside had yet to make a noise, she knew how easily sound traveled through the canvas. It was hard to justify laughing alone or laughing at all, for that matter, considering their situation.

Arms tightening around her, she shivered against Jasper's heated breath. The wash of guilt was becoming less and less potent the more she lay with him. And yet, the pang in her chest reminded her of who she truly wished were here as well.

"Col is like family," he whispered. "She and I have never lain together like this; I've never craved her closeness like I do yours."

She swallowed hard. When he spoke, his voice had a gravel that sent a tickling sensation down her spine. And the words he said had a strange effect on her heart and the ekath. She wasn't sure how to put a stop to it or if, in truth, she really wanted to.

"None of what you described sounds like a good thing," she said quietly.

"Neither is ember whiskey, but who says something must be good to be desired?"

She ignored the sultry hiss of his last word and the heat it sent across her skin. "It sounds as if I'm bad for you."

"You are," he breathed against her neck. "And yet you're the only thing keeping me from breaking in this wretched place."

Despite the comfort and heat of his presence, his suffered voice brought with it a rage that superseded all other feelings. Every bane Jasper suffered had begun in this very city; the parts of him that drew her ire were put there by someone else.

In the same way that she wished for Marvena's ashes in her hands, she wondered whose ashes would sate Jasper's suffering. Slowly, Ophiera turned around in his arms. His amber eyes looked terrified for a moment before she took his face in her hands.

"I can't protect you from yourself or from what happened here. But I can seek retribution for your pain. Tell me who, and I will scatter their ashes across this desert without blinking an eye."

To her surprise, he smiled. "That's the kindest offer anyone has made me."

"It's not an offer; it's an oath."

"Doesn't your Oath require a soul to be taken from the Aether? Mine remains, even if the quality is debatable."

She looked at the scars on her hand, now cupping his hardened jaw. It was true her Oath only applied to the souls of the sinful, to those who had committed murder. But then why did her gut churn with the same need to avenge Jasper as she felt for Iluka? Why did her scars tingle with approval at the thought of setting ablaze any who harmed him?

"'There are so many other ways to destroy a soul,'" she breathed, watching the confusion cross Jasper's gaze.

She couldn't explain to him that those had been the words of the Reverend...before he'd beaten Myronor to the brink of death...before she had awakened to the power of the Aether.

What was the point of controlling the flames if she could not prevent suffering with them? The Cloister taught Retribution was reserved for the sinful, but wasn't preventing murder preferable to avenging it? Weren't the scars left behind proof of a sin equal to death? When she thought about Jasper's story compared to what the clerics had put her through, she felt the surge of rage from the Aether itself. The Cloister had claimed her life in childhood and carved her body to do their bidding—in flames rather than magic—leaving her and Jasper marked by the same suffering scars.

"For once, I'm struggling to read your expression," he said, running his hands down the small of her back. "Tell me your thoughts."

Ophiera met his gaze, recognizing the exhaustion and worry behind them. They should rest, and yet, she knew speaking the words aloud would be better for him than sleep. Better for her, too.

"I'm finding the world to be more gray than I ever realized," she whispered. "I've lived with the knowledge that murder is the ultimate sin, and yet for those who bear the scars of a suffered life, perhaps death is more a blessing than a curse. Perhaps...our scars are the marks of death imposed upon us that we simply did not accept."

Jasper pressed his forehead against hers, startling her. For a moment, he simply shared touch and air with her as if drawing some calm from the closeness alone.

"What does that mean for us left scarred, then?" He murmured sleepily.

Ophiera took a breath, considering not what she knew but what she felt. And despite the distance to the sand, she felt the Aether burn in confirmation through her veins.

"It means we deserve retribution, too."

~ Forty One ~

CONSTERNATION

On the dim balcony, Myronor's gaze fell over the dark sea, barely reflecting the pale sky before daybreak. Twirling the smooth stone between his fingers, he'd hoped to find some calm in the fresh air of sunrise. But, as with most of his assumptions of late, he found himself sadly mistaken.

All night, he had fretted. Somehow, he now suffered strange after-effects of Ophiera's brief burn from the day before. The ignition lasted only a few moments—a few unexpected and excruciating minutes. But unlike the night with the girtas, this time he'd remained conscious through the connection, aware of every blister he felt beneath his skin as he writhed on the darkened backstreet in the Depths.

Though perhaps the tether wasn't the only blame for his sleepless night. Visions of the marketplace fiasco from the day before shook his constitution, his nerves now too raw to relax. Mallow hadn't appeared all night, likely avoiding his mood within her crystal. He understood, though he wished she would visit, even if only to tell him how Ophiera fared amongst the Enclave.

"I see you are equally restless," Kaikora called from behind him.

She held the scrying bowl in her hands, though her eyes were their normal stormy gray. While he couldn't be certain, he guessed she hadn't set the bowl down a single time throughout the night.

"I have a good excuse," he said, rubbing his chest while leaning heavily against the stone banister. "What's yours?"

Just then, the sun broke over the sea, igniting the water's surface in a burning orange of dancing water. Instead of the peace he had hoped for, the view reminded him of the flames that still crawled beneath his skin. If the memory alone lingered so potently, he wondered how Ophiera lived with that pain each time she burned.

Absentmindedly, he rubbed the ache in his chest again. Why had he ever thought 'divide and conquer' was the best option?

"Even with the sight, I sometimes forget to look ahead," Kaikora said, shaking her head. "I should have warned you about the Enclave's tests."

"Who could have guessed I would feel her power across the continent?"

"Regardless of how unlikely, it was always a possibility—one I should have seen and voiced. If she had arrived in Birozahran a moment sooner, our chase would have been interrupted. We would still be looking for Marvena, and you would not have that stone in your possession."

Myronor smiled for the first time all night. "Come now, Kaikora, it was no one's fault, only bad luck. Or good luck? Either way, as much as I would love to blame you for all my woes, I can't for this one."

"All your woes?" She chuffed. "You refer to Jasper?"

"That particular bane is most definitely your fault. I wish *you* had traveled with her into the desert instead, though I daresay Jasper would have been far less useful here."

He tried to imagine Jasper chasing Marvena down through the streets of Krysas. The bastard would have likely never left the Embassy, to begin with, let alone run through the Depths of the Strato-District. As much as he hated to admit it, the rogue was better suited to Ophiera's task than any other. Even if that task was keeping her alive...and warm.

"Are you going to tell Ophiera about Marvena?" Kaikora asked, nodding to the crystal around his neck.

Myronor sighed. "Even if Mallow were here to send a message, I can't quite imagine what good it would do. Even if she did decide to return immediately and claim Marvena as she'd hoped, it would take her five days to arrive. And it seems you and the Order have other plans for Marvena. So...perhaps it's best to acquire the information the Order seeks first and leave Ophiera to the task she set out upon."

With a nod, Kaikora stretched, revealing the dark, inked tattoos across the length of her arms and shoulders. As a boy, he'd thought she had painted them on herself when she first joined the village as the shaman. But before he left for his apprenticeship, he learned how the extracts of ink-kelp had been embedded in her skin at the Phratries through needles of bone. He doubted the process was quite as painful as the brands Ophiera incurred, but he'd never asked.

Gong.

Both Myronor and Kaikora turned back towards the home. The sound was pleasant enough but jarring.

"Glamwell has never summoned this early," Kaikora said.

Taking one last blinding glance at the sun, Myronor shrugged. "Well, I am the Ambassador, after all. Surely, I must have tasks or duties to uphold, in addition to chasing Brotherhood members all over the city."

"Do you need me to accompany you?"

"No, no, you keep watch over the bowl," he said, dismissing the idea with a wave of his hand. "I'll be back shortly."

Pocketing the glossy black stone in his awkward attire, Myronor traveled through the gateway to the Embassy.

"Oh, thank goodness!" Glamwell cried, rushing to Myronor's side. "They gave me no time to debrief you, and I wasn't sure—well, just look at the hour! You should be sleeping, especially after your day yesterday!" He started fussing with Myronor's attire, straightening the adornments that decorated his shoulders and providing the medallion a quick polish. "Have you broken your fast yet? Or do you prefer a brisk morning jog like dear Pyra? But no, that doesn't matter—what matters is the complete lack of consideration the Cloister has for—"

"Cloister?" Myronor interjected, stomach clenched.

"I only received word moments ago," Glamwell said, taking a deep breath. "Representatives arrived in Krysas nearly an hour ago—unannounced, unscheduled, and frankly, unprecedented! Their order has never visited Krysas in recorded history, so why, in the name of Nijeka, would they show up midweek at the crack of dawn?"

Myronor couldn't speak as his tongue numbed and his palms clammed up.

Glamwell patted Myronor on the arm and smiled. "Sir, as it stands, they are technically from Tanvik, and therefore, you, as the Ambassador, must receive all emissaries. Though I wouldn't blame you if you simply turned them away or requested they return at a more civilized hour."

He wanted to ask how Glamwell suggested he best force them to leave. But a painfully familiar *clank* of armor echoed from the corridor beyond. With one last apologetic stare, the Steward turned his attention to the two men entering the room.

Aleksander, Justicar of the Cloister, was easy to recognize despite his obscured face. In the traditional garb of the clerics, his white robes covered him from head to toe, veiling his face behind a thin cloth. But he still walked like a snake in the grass. While the Justicar served both Magistrate and Cloister, many viewed his dual appointment with distrust—Myronor included. But Aleksander's close association with Eliana swayed Myronor's opinion of him even more.

Beside him, the source of the clanging armor, was clearly no Justicar, and yet, Myronor *knew* him. His golden armor wasn't true adamantrium but the gaudy, adulterated version peddled by the Cloister to their paladins. Tall, broad, and regal, his severe expression edged him away from handsome and into arrogance. Like Ophiera, he wore his hair in a long plait on his back, but unlike hers, his was a streak of black and white. And in place of a claymore, he carried a worn hammer with a long handle that looked impossible to wield.

"Welcome!" Glamwell proclaimed with open arms.

The two men glared at his bright pink attire unabashedly, and Myronor felt his nerves twitch. While Myronor had remained suspicious of Glamwell, especially given his mentions in Pyra's writings, he felt defensive toward him just the same. He didn't wish Aleksander and Uzziel to treat him untowardly—but more so, he needed to protect Ophiera's identity and location.

And with thoughts on her, a vision of Uzziel informing him of his conscription to the Magistrate bubbled forth in his memory. Shivering in a set of armor too big to protect him against anything but the cold, he remembered being dragged away from the Cloister by two of the priests. But no—that wasn't right—Ophiera was conscripted, not himself. *He* had never met Uzziel—likely, few had given the reclusiveness of the Cloister. But when had he begun re-calling her memories as if they were his own?

Glamwell cleared his throat, his eyes widening alarmingly. My-ronor supposed he was expected to speak. The weight of the medallion against his chest and memories of Ophiera's suffering at the hands of these two gave him strength.

"Aleksander," Myronor said with a curt nod, "I was truly hoping never to see you again. And may I ask who is the wind chime you've brought along?"

Glamwell winced as if Myronor's words had smacked him across the face. At least one of the men here could read a room. Aleksander's veil hid any reaction, and the storm churned beneath the armored man's eyes.

"Ambassador Ebontide," Aleksander said with a sneer, "it is my honor to introduce you to the Chaplain Uzziel, Hand of Retribu-tion."

Myronor nodded to the Chaplain, biting his tongue against an-other choice retort. How poetic it was that Aleksander now served as an escort after damning Ophiera to the task himself. But he needed to keep the conversation away from her and away from the Chaplain, no matter how strongly he wished to prod the cleric.

"Well then, I have a feeling you're not here to sightsee or va-cation, so what brings you to Krysas?" Myronor asked, trying to sound nonchalant. "Or did you lose your way trying to sail up Eliana's—"

Uzziel's growl muffled Glamwell's fit of coughs, both pointedly silencing Myronor. Aleksander was the only individual to remain unperturbed.

"The Cloister is here to request aid from the Consortia," Alek-sander said.

"Aid?" Myronor laughed. "If you are in search of new recruits, I'm afraid Krysas is a city of *mages*—not good starting mater-ial—hardly flammable, you see."

"We are searching for the Aspect of Retribution," spat Uzziel.

Myronor felt another blow to his composure at the Chaplain's words. All his wit, all his sass, was snuffed out in an instant. All he could do was stare blankly at the Chaplain, trying to find the best way to say "go burn" in the most diplomatic way possible.

"Perhaps we should move this discussion somewhere more comfortable?" Glamwell said kindly with a sideways glance at Myronor. "You've traveled a long way from Tanvik, and Krysas is known for our hospitality. We have several—"

"Unnecessary," Uzziel replied. "We are here for her and her alone. Once we have the Aspect in our possession, we will be on our way."

The manner in which the Chaplain hissed *possession* caused Myronor to grind his teeth. Again, he glared back in silence, not fully trusting himself to speak.

Why had he thought they would be safe across the sea? It was true that the Cloister rarely left its hold, only sending a few select liaisons to Feyralis for conscription, and even that was a rare event these days. But Ophiera was special, and clearly not just to him. She was important enough for the Justicar of the Cloister and their Chaplain to sail across the sea and demand from him the one thing he could never give up. He really was the fool she'd always claimed him to be.

"Sirs," Glamwell began again. "You are the first disciples of the Cloister to set foot in Krysas. This is a historic day that should be celebrated, not rushed or—"

"Fulfilling our duty quickly will be celebration enough," hissed the Chaplain. "We received word the paladin with white hair and violet eyes arrived alongside the Ambassador some time ago. She is a fugitive of the Cloister that must be reclaimed. Now, tell us what you know of her whereabouts."

Reclaim, Myronor repeated to himself, the chosen terminology churning his blood again. Anger finally propelled his voice.

"I don't have a clue," Myronor said with a callous smile.

Uzziel clenched his jaw, but this time, Aleksander stepped forward, placing a hand on the Chaplain's chest.

"Did the paladin fail to escort you to Krysas, Ambassador Ebontide?"

The venom in his voice made the intentions of the question clear. If Myronor said yes, then they would assume Ophiera broke her Oath; if he said no, it admitted she had been here, in Krysas. While Myronor chewed over several inappropriate responses, Glamwell stepped in.

"I believe Ambassador Ebontide's presence here is proof he was escorted safely to Krysas. I don't imagine him traveling across the sea on his own accord if you take my meaning." He winked garishly with little response from Uzziel or Aleksander. "Though I must assure you, I'm quite certain no paladin has entered the city of Krysas. Word of someone wearing golden armor such as yours would have made quite the turn on the gossip wheel. Trust me, I follow the gossip in this city *very* closely. You would be amazed at what you can learn beyond the relationship drama between Consortia high houses—"

"You are a nuisance," said the Chaplain, glaring at Glamwell. His attention snapped back to Myronor. "Where is Ophiera?"

"No idea," Myronor said with a shrug.

"Denying information to the Cloister is a punishable offense by the Magistrate, Ambassador or not." The Chaplain took one heavy step forward, imposing over Myronor in ostentatious gold. "Tell us where she is, or face treason."

"I believe the Ambassador has *no* information," Glamwell interjected, all the politeness absent from his voice. "Therefore, he could not truly deny you anything. And even if he did break the laws of your Magistrate, you may not enact charges or punishment here."

Aleksander cocked his head slightly to the side, his swaying veil the only indication of his confusion. Meanwhile, the Chaplain scoffed as if in disbelief at Glamwell's claims. While it was true that Magistrate law required citizens to comply with the Cloister, as far as Myronor knew, it was only in regard to anathema. And if he remembered Consortia laws correctly...well, the humorless chuckle from Glamwell indicated he'd know soon enough.

"The language does usually give it away," Glamwell began, a smug expression somehow enhancing his already handsome features, "but I see I must remind you that you are no longer in Tanvik. You stand here in the grand city of Krysas as a guest of the Consortia, and while we welcome all emissaries from our foreign allies, we have little tolerance for threats or violence by or against them. At least in places of business and most certainly against our dignitaries."

The Chaplain removed himself from Myronor's personal space, but not without a reproachful glare.

"We meant no offense," Aleksander offered, sounding bored as usual. "Perhaps then, we may seek permission for the Cloister to search the city ourselves."

Suddenly, Myronor understood the predicament before him. He knew how the Magistrate operated, the loopholes within loopholes, and vague decrees left open for interpretation. And he understood the nature of the Cloister, thanks to Ophiera and her buried memories. Perhaps it was time to start asking questions rather than evade them.

"Why has the Aspect of Retribution been deemed a fugitive?" Myronor asked.

Behind his clerical robes, Aleksander held too much tension in his shoulders. "She is suspected of breaking her Oath."

"How?"

"She destroyed a village in the Southern Coastlands."

Myronor looked down at the ground, trying to play the part of someone mourning the loss of their home. It wasn't a challenging role to portray.

"You don't look too surprised," he spat.

"And why should I be?" Myronor asked.

"Did you help her destroy Iluka, or are you simply covering for her now?"

"But of course, he already knows this news," Glamwell sighed with no air of silliness. "He is an Ambassador, after all, and the report he received from the Magistrate stated a natural disaster destroyed Iluka. There was no mention of a paladin or Aspect of Retribution or anything related to the Cloister."

Glamwell spoke with significance, hinting at truths and untruths. And though Myronor had read no such report, the inflections in the Steward's voice led him to believe the Magistrate briefing was real. So if the Magistrate had not accused Ophiera, then only the Cloister laid claim to her. But he needed to be certain.

"I fail to see how the paladin is connected to the tragedy of Iluka," Myronor said, feigning ignorance. "What evidence does the Magistrate have against her?"

"It matters not," Uzziel said sternly.

"Oh? Tell me, then, is that how you enact your Retribution, too? Without evidence?"

"Enough," Aleksander interjected before Uzziel could take a swing at Myronor. "Regardless of the evidence, the Cloister is here to reclaim her."

"To be clear, it is the Cloister, not the Magistrate, that holds Ophiera suspect?" Myronor asked.

The silence in the room was answer enough, but Aleksander was a true diplomat after all and cleared his throat defeatedly. "This is a matter of the Cloister and the Cloister alone. My presence here is only to ensure the Magistrate's laws are upheld as I escort the Chaplain."

"I see," Myronor said with a smile. "Well, I wish you had informed us of that fine detail from the beginning. As Ambassador of Tanvik and with my Steward as my witness, I hereby deny your request to enter the city of Krysas.

"On what grounds?" the Chaplain demanded.

"On the grounds that this is not a matter of law or policy between the nations I represent," Myronor began, failing to keep his voice at a diplomatic volume, "I refuse to condone a poorly disguised property dispute from an outdated religion that has no business here. Now, I suggest leaving before Tanvik's reputation is further tarnished by the Cloister's aggressive and misguided actions."

"How dare you?" spat the Chaplain, taking another step forward. With violence in his stride, Myronor prepared to summon any magic he could muster to thwart him. But Uzziel stopped in his tracks as Glamwell stepped between them.

"Sirs, the Ambassador has decided," he began calmly. "And the Consortia will enforce his decision. Now, you are welcome to stay at the aerodock, confined to your ship, of course, until you are ready to depart. As a gesture of good faith, the Consortia will gladly provide supplies for your return journey to Tanvik. But otherwise, I must implore you both to leave the Embassy in peace."

A gentle hand from Aleksander quieted Uzziel's rattling armor. "The decision is regrettable, but we will comply. Good day to you both."

Only when he could no longer hear the clanging armor down the corridor did Myronor let out a sigh of relief. He could hardly believe the Cloister had truly been here. If Ophiera knew how closely they followed...

But it didn't matter.

They would be on their way back to Tanvik soon.

But...if they'd come this far to find her, would they really let him stand in their way?

No...they had to abide by Magistrate law, and for better or worse, he had upheld that law here in Krysas. Legally, they needed to leave the city.

A firm hand on his shoulder jolted him from his spiral. Glamwell stared at him, concern written across his eyes.

"Sir, you look exhausted. I suggest you retire to your dwellings. I will task a few guards to follow them and ensure all protocols are enforced for their departure from the city and afterward—"

"Why did you protect her?" Myronor asked, interrupting the ramble.

"I don't know what you mean, sir," he said innocently.

Myronor opened his mouth to question again, but Glamwell's gaze shifted toward the door. Though the sounds of clanking armor and slinking robes had long disappeared, he got the point.

"I need to know the moment they leave," Myronor said to Glamwell before returning to the Embassy home.

Kaikora awaited his return near the hearth, twirling her fingers in the scrying bowl lazily. She looked exhausted but also curious when she saw his expression.

After explaining all that transpired, he found a new clarity within the chaos of the situation. If Ophiera knew the Cloister had left Tanvik to find her...what would she do?

On the one hand, she had begun to loosen the laces surrounding the Cloister that had subjugated and controlled her for nearly all her life. But on the other, she brazenly went against their laws by finding loopholes in their doctrine, and by loving him. Each time he delved into her memories, whether through ekath or dreams or those vague recollections he now harbored, a fear so intense rippled through his body he could barely hold himself together. It reminded him of the fear he had of Aud—of the darkness of Umbraxus—of losing Ophiera.

Fear had a way of making people do things uncharacteristic of their nature while simultaneously forcing the person to function on instinct. How would Ophiera respond, knowing the Cloister now sought her? What would her Oath demand of her, if anything at all?

Still, he struggled to comprehend how much sway her Oath truly had over her. As the Aspect of Retribution, she was the Aether itself—and yet the scarred symbols covering her arm were an undeniable mark of the Cloister's subjugation. Who controlled whom in this scenario? What did any of it even mean?

Myronor started, brushing past Kaikora as Uzziel's armored stamps echoed in his mind.

"Where are you going?" Kaikora asked.

"The library."

As his rapid steps carried him to his only salvation from the questions barraging through his skull, he found his hands shaking uncontrollably as he pulled book after book from shelves he'd rarely frequented.

"What are you looking for?" Kaikora said, concern lacing her voice.

"Anything on the Cloister, their rites, their Oaths..."

"Aren't you supposed to be looking for a way to understand that stone you retrieved? The portals? What good can come of—"

"Because if Ophiera finds out they are searching for her this desperately, she will...she will..." He took a deep, shaking breath, trying to quell the panic gripping his chest. "Look, I swore to her I would find a way to free her of her obligations. And that is a far better use of my time than sifting through the mess Pyra left behind."

"Myronor, our priority must be finding the portal—"

"Why?" He spat, turning on her with a clenched jaw. "You said it yourself; none of this means anything without her! If those scars truly do dictate her fate, then this stone, this portal, this *distance* means nothing! All of this means nothing!"

Kaikora dropped her gaze to the scrying bowl, and he realized shame was the only thing keeping her from outright disagreeing with him at this moment. She truly believed the portals were the priority, and yet it was his shoulders that the burdens of Pyra fell upon.

"This library has proven useless thus far in understanding that stone or Pyra's research," he continued, tearing tomes from the shelves and tossing any that didn't suit his needs. "Almost as if she never wanted me to know! But Rheta...*thump*...Rheta gave me the book before...*thump*...*The Paladins of the Cloister*...*thump*...and Pyra...*thump*....the paladins are wayward children, are they not? ...*thump*...And Pyra interacted with the Enclave extensively...*thump*...perhaps she has something on how to break a paladin's Oath."

In a heavy silence, Kaikora watched him destroy the library in a desperate fit for answers. Only when the shelf was empty, and he moved to the next, did she leave him to continue his mad search for a way—any way—to break Ophiera of her bonds.

~ Forty Two ~

PACT

Jasper lay awake, listening to Ophiera's steady breaths.

She'd rested soundly with her fingers entwined in his dark curls, holding him against her chest. His cheek rested on her collarbone, rising and falling with the wave of her exposed bosom, the tunic slipping low as she slept.

Although her gesture of lying together had awarded him enough peace for a brief rest, he now lay awake, restless, and yet somehow still relaxed. In the shadows of the yurt, unwanted memories lingered, threatening to overtake his vision each time he closed his eyes. So, instead, he focused on Ophiera as if she were a ward to this place.

For the tenth time, he counted the stitches along the neckline of her tunic. And for the tenth time, his eyes grazed over the shining scar between her breasts. Courtesy of Kaikora, he had heard the story of how she'd acquired the distinct scar. At the time, he refused to believe anyone was immune to death. But after what he'd witnessed in the desert, he finally accepted that Ophiera was the exception to all his assumptions.

The moment Jasper had found Ophiera's cold, limp body covered in ash and sand, he *knew* she was dead. Her heart had stalled, her breath had stilled, and for what felt like an eternity, he studied the blank death mask frozen across her features. It was a look he'd seen far too often in his youth and one he had never mistaken. But by some miracle, he'd watched her warm breath suddenly mist the cold desert air.

Jasper blinked, returning his mind to the yurt momentarily. He refocused his gaze on the stitches of the tunic again, trying to forget her face devoid of countenance. The guilt of abandoning her still stung in his throat. Resisting the truth of Ophiera had only caused him pain, while accepting her as his lodestar had resulted in two nights of indescribable contentment by her side. If only she weren't bound to that helpless innatural...

Something rustled the tent, dragging Jasper back to reality. Instinctively, he cloaked, remaining invisibly pressed against Ophiera. He hoped it would look as if she slept only with a bundle of covers. Blood rushing, he listened, invisible and still, sliding his hand to the knife stowed beneath the pillow. Despite Ophiera's naive optimism about the Enclave, he would never be caught without a weapon in this forsaken place.

The tent flap parted ever so slightly, closing again in a whisper. Someone or something had passed into the yurt, hidden in the shadows, steps muffled by the sand. The antracinders no longer provided light or warmth, but the glyphs carved into Jasper's chest ensured he *should* see almost anything in the dark capable of being seen. But for all he could see now, they were alone.

A chill crept down his spine, recalling the Brotherhood assassin's ability to meld into the dark. The same skill...the same place...but it couldn't be him...

"I do not know the laws of Birozahran," Ophiera called into the night, her sudden voice startling him, "but in Tanvik, you would be trespassing on my privacy."

Jasper remained still as stone, as did the intruder for a moment.

"Impressive," said an invisible voice. Beside the cold antracinders, a figure phased into existence. But what appeared in the tent was no person. Instead, a four-legged red fox twitched its bushy tail. "How did you know I was here?"

Neither feminine nor masculine, the voice of the fox sounded nearly childlike, amused more than anything. But the manner in which their green eyes glowed in the darkness was indicative of a predator—just like everything else in this city.

"I have ears," Ophiera said, stifling a yawn. She sounded neither threatened nor alarmed despite the strange creature sneaking into the yurt. Jasper didn't understand how her heartbeat remained so steady, but her hand caressed his beneath the covers, reassuring him to follow her lead. "If you weren't a familiar, I'd be more upset by the intrusion."

"Ah, you know our kind! That is reassuring." The fox yipped in laughter. "Well, dear child, I'm here on behalf of my ekath, who wishes to meet with you."

Ophiera warned Jasper through a pinch that she was about to sit up. He moved seamlessly with her as she threw the furs beside her, covering him. So far, it appeared the fox remained unaware of his presence, though it was impossible to tell.

"I didn't know your kind could learn to speak," she said, unable to hide her curiosity. "Is that due to being ekatma?"

Another amused yip escaped the fox. "Follow me, and my ekath will explain everything."

Jasper thought he had witnessed all the abominations of magic the Enclave had to offer. But never before had he witnessed a talking familiar, nor had he heard of ekatma before Kaikora had explained it to him recently. All he could see was yet another reason to despise the innaturals.

"I will meet with your ekath, but I require a moment of privacy to dress," Ophiera said.

"Of course, of course," the fox nodded. "I'll wait outside."

Jasper remained cloaked and silent in the bed as the fox slipped from the tent and Ophiera from the bed. She didn't speak, which was for the best, but glanced over her shoulder in his direction before tugging off her sleeping shirt and stuffing it into her pack. Like the night she'd burst into holy flames, she bared herself before him without hesitation or shame. Not that there was anything that deserved shame, but did she even understand what she did to him, exposing herself in such a way?

His demons stirred with temptation, urging him to claim every curve of her. It disgusted him how quickly his mind went from fear to arousal, and yet the way her thighs flexed as she bent low to acquire her armor caused his heart to race.

The beasts within him calmed a bit as she began donning the golden plate. Watching her armor herself was like observing a sultry waltz, the tease of her flesh disappearing behind each golden plate in a predictable and mesmerizing fashion. He couldn't decide which was more alluring, the graceful precision with which she applied her armor or the formidable physique he knew lay hidden beneath it. With her pauldrons in place, she shouldered the gigantic claymore, sliding it along her back in place, and stood before the tent flap.

Her eyes darted back once again to the bed, this time with a look of expectation, before she left.

Jasper gave her and the fox a moment's start before dressing and silently trailing behind. Iren, the guard, was nowhere in sight outside the tent. So much for Enclave hospitality, he thought bitterly.

The fox, however, led Ophiera quickly away, mutely padding against the cold sand. In the Tabernacle, the tents were placed without order, and navigating between them was maze-like. As his breath quickened to keep pace, Jasper saw the cold air reveal his warm exhale. Distracted by Ophiera, he'd forgotten to drag up his hood and cowl. She really wasn't good for him.

Covered in cloth and darkness, Jasper followed the pair into the center of the maze, where the fox came to a halt before one of the larger tents. They entered without a word, leaving Ophiera standing outside alone, perplexed, for a moment. She looked back along the path before entering the yurt, her expression clear as the night sky—she was looking for him. Her trust in him to have her back was like armor itself, protecting him from the haunt of this city.

With the slice of light drifting between the flaps of the yurt, he could observe two figures standing before Ophiera. Both wore draped, flowing robes of the same sheer, black textile, with ornate metalworks intricately woven throughout. Jasper recognized the warlock Zadok from earlier, but the woman at his right was unknown. She'd styled her bluish-black hair relatively short for the Enclave, chin-length in the front and even shorter at the back. The severity of the angle matched the harshness of her gaze, an identical shade to Zadok's blood-red irises and voracious glare. Her darkly painted lips twitched ever so slightly.

"So this is the child who wields Erum's Flame," she simpered in a high voice. The hair on Jasper's neck raised at the raw edge hidden beneath the dulcet tone of her words. Now that she faced the antracinders, her dark opaque robes revealed *everything* beneath that was not obscured by the minuscule metallic breastplate and heavy belt. Her thin arms were wrapped in a weave of metallic wire that continued up her shoulders and around her neck as if a golden vine threatened to strangle her. It was an odd mixture of Krysan and Odestal aesthetics.

"The child has expressed a preference to be called Ophiera," Zadok said quietly, smiling slightly.

"Ophierrra," the red-eyed woman repeated, rolling her tongue with a purr. "I am called Kiela no Enukaja, Wielder of Marrowsong and ascending Overlord of the Odestal. You've already met my father, Zadock, and my ekath, Iku."

The burgundy fox appeared to smile as Kiela ran her long, slender fingers over his black-tipped ears. Jasper's stomach clenched, nauseated by the thought of such a perverse display.

"I admit, I did not realize familiars and mages could be bonded as ekatma," Ophiera said.

He might have thought the same thing but damned if she didn't *speak* it. She shouldn't have revealed her ignorance quite so willingly, he thought, but he could do nothing to stop her here, outside the tent.

"You may know the words of their bond, but there are countless facts of this world the wayward children of Tanvik do not know," Zadock said, stepping forward. As he did so, he revealed a second fox laid behind his black, flowing robes. Like the other, this fox's fur shone burgundy, highlighted with spots of brilliant silver. Its bright yellow eyes followed Zadock as he stood before Ophiera. "Though Pyra, Wielder of Riftwalking, knew even less when she first arrived in our city."

Ophiera stiffened, shock written across her face in bold, beautiful writing. Biting his lip beneath his cowl, Jasper regretted taunting her over her readability, instead wishing he had taught her to mask her thoughts properly. These vultures would take anything she revealed and use it to their advantage. And now they knew just how desperately she sought Pyra.

"I care not of what Pyra knew or did not know—I must simply find her."

Kiela smiled, her dark, full lips hiding her teeth. "You are one of the Cloister's enchained, are you not? Is seeking Pyra some Oath-bound nonsense?"

Even Jasper found himself surprised that the Enclave knew of the Cloister and their paladins. This time, though, he was relieved that Ophiera kept a more reasonable expression.

"If Pyra's death was indeed one of sin, then yes, my Oath demands Retribution."

Zadok's lip twitched. "Except the Consortia has determined her death as one of self-destruction. Your Retribution would be misplaced, though, not undesired."

Ophiera's brow furrowed in the same way Jasper's had regarding Zadok's last words. While the Enclave certainly had a vernacular all their own, this was not one of those phrases he'd learned in his time here. And more confusingly, how did Kiela and her father know of the Cloister? Those in Tanvik barely knew anymore, and yet, all these many years, Jasper had viewed the Enclave as isolated savages.

"I suspect the Consortia may have lied about her fate," Ophiera said sternly, "I only wish to seek the truth."

"The truth? The truth is the Consortia *always* lies," Zadok said quietly, meeting his daughter's eyes. Even Jasper could not read the intent of their exchange without words. And while neither spoke, he could sense Ophiera's growing impatience with the lull in conversation—an impatience the Odestal princess picked up on, too.

"The truth is, Pyra is now gone from this world."

Again, Jasper saw frustration fall over Ophiera's features. But much to his pride, she recovered quickly.

"Has her vesper returned to the Aether?"

Kiela smiled, this time flashing her teeth in a genuine show of contentment. "No. Her soul still resides within the vessel, for now."

Jasper let out a breath into the cold night. So, the idiot mage's mother had somehow faked her death. The fool and the shaman had stayed behind, convinced their answers lay within Krysas. And yet, Ophiera had been right to come to Birozahran after all. At least he knew the lodestar he followed had good instincts.

"If she is alive, then I must find her. Please, tell me where she is," Ophiera demanded.

"Why?" Zadok asked, his thin brows gently raised. "If you no longer seek Retribution for her soul, what other purpose could you have to find her?"

Ophiera remained silent, chewing her lip in frustration. Jasper watched as her mind churned, deciding what to reveal and what to keep hidden. Their questions were a carefully crafted dance of fair exchange, and he wasn't convinced she truly understood. Though her intentions were undoubtedly noble, the two predators before her would read any lies as treachery.

"Her son—" Ophiera paused as if the thought caused her great pain. "He is my ekath."

Zadok and Kiela exchanged looks of mild incredulity, barely perceptible in their scarlet glares. And yet extremely blatant for the Odestal. It was rare to catch their kind off guard, especially the Autarch.

"I thought I sensed the pain of a bond stretched thin, but I refused to believe a child..." Kiela paused her gentle musing, nearly at a loss for words. "How did you accomplish such a rite?"

"By accident," Ophiera said with a sad smile that quickly turned to stone. "But it is undeniable."

The pain of the tether struck her features again as her words fell to silence. As much as it pained him to see her ache, Jasper breathed out a silent sigh of relief. Nothing she had said was a lie, and yet the key details behind her search for Pyra remained buried. Not once did she mention the Order or portals, not even

Myronor's name. She was quite a bit cleverer than he'd credited her.

"Truth is nearly as rare as the white flames you wield, and I greatly appreciate both," Zadock said, clasping his hands before him. "But I am afraid I cannot help you find Pyra. My debts to her were paid long ago, and now, my obligations are to my clan and the Enclave. The Odestal will continue to welcome you as a wayward child—not only do you wield mana, but you bear the burden of soul bond as well. You may remain with us however long you need, take whatever hospitality you require, and if you need support with what ails you, we offer ourselves in full. I, however, cannot help you with your search for Pyra."

Without another word, Zadok strode from the tent, his familiar following close behind.

Jasper barely had time to avoid his path. At first, he feared he'd failed to evade them when the fox familiar sniffed the chilly night air in suspicion. Luckily, he had moved downwind and held still as stone. The fox shook their head and followed the trail of long black robes in the sand, soon joined by an escort of several guards hidden amongst the yurt. Swallowing his pride for not realizing how many guards had hidden nearby, he turned back to spy through the tent flap.

Ophiera stood stoic, a building rage behind violet eyes. To his surprise, Kiela studied her with amusement. Neither woman moved until the warlock crossed her ornately banded arms.

"I'm certain that wasn't what you wished to hear," Kiela said sympathetically.

"No, it was not," Ophiera replied, holding back a growl. "But at least I know my travel here is not in vain."

"Your arrival, while a surprise, is quite the blessing, in fact."

To his detriment, Ophiera quirked her head to the side, just as confused as he was by Kiela's shift in demeanor. He didn't trust the dulcet words dripping from the warlock's painted lips. Why was she acting kind to Ophiera when no such instinct existed behind her predatory gaze?

"While my father may be unwilling to aid you, perhaps I have something to offer."

"*You* would help me find Pyra?" Ophiera asked.

Jasper could hear the desperation in her words and bit his lip to keep from growling. When they returned to the yurt, he was going to show her, whether she liked it or not, how to keep her intentions closer to the chest.

And just as he feared, Kiela's darkly painted lips spread into a dangerous smile. "In fair exchange, of course."

Outside the tent, Jasper felt the air suddenly warm, no longer holding a frigid bite. Sweat beaded beneath his cowl, and he found himself painfully comfortable. But as the sensation reached a fevered peak, the air dipped in temperature again, returning to normal. He shook off the experience and the exhaustion he left behind to focus on Ophiera's growing tension.

"Before I agree to anything, I'd like to know what it is you ask in exchange," Ophiera said.

Kiela uncrossed her arms, reaching toward the tent entrance. Unfurling her fingers, palm up, in indication, she said, "The first exchange is fairly simple—I won't kill that *delicious* man hiding outside the tent if you tell me *who* he is."

With frozen breath, Jasper's eyes locked on Ophiera, who glared at the warlock with only a hint of surprise. He didn't understand how the damned woman had detected him, but there was no chance in hell Ophiera could feign ignorance now. And she knew it, too.

"Jasper," Ophiera said quietly. "Join us, if you will."

He entered the tent but remained cloaked as he gathered himself. Though he had few *recent* interactions with the Odestal clan, their reputation continued to reach as far as Cantheas. The warlocks had led the rebellions, resulting in the borderline derogatory term aimed at their particular specialty of derivation magic. And while Jasper hated all magic, the Wielders of Marrowsong went far beyond the unnatural into pure abhorrence.

Only when he stood beside Ophiera did he feel comfortable uncloaking. He left his hood and cowl up, and like her, he tried to maintain his composure under the crimson gaze.

"There he is," Kiela simpered, "ah, but I can't see his face."

A slender, pale hand reached forward towards his cowl, and his hand twitched over his blade. But with a clunk of armor, Ophiera stepped before him, blocking the woman's reach with her forearm.

"Don't touch him," she growled.

Kiela giggled. "Ah, so, you've claimed him?"

"He is my guide and companion," Ophiera said with a bite. It was not a subtle threat, but he enjoyed it, nonetheless. Jasper wanted nothing more than to belong to her.

"A friend of yours is a friend of mine, as they say. Such interesting talents...so tell us, *who* are you exactly?" Kiela asked, her crimson eyes pinning him in place.

"No one," he replied, knowing the true meaning of her question. "I wield only scars and whiskey."

"Ah, one of the Forged," Kiela said, a hint of disgust in her voice. It had been years since he'd heard the term, the same disgust bubbling in his gut. "I pity your past, but your skills will make the second exchange I ask far more interesting."

He felt the air shift again, and though he could not see any signs of her derivation magic, he knew she was trying to taste the room again. It was as violating as if he stood naked, having his body inspected by prying, judgmental eyes.

"What is the exchange you propose?" Ophiera said.

Kiela turned her full attention to the paladin, her jaw set with an unreadable expression. "I ask that you lend the Enclave your power over Erum's Flame."

"To what end?"

"Retribution, of course," Kiela said, clearly understanding the depth of meaning. She began to pace with deadly grace. "Beyond the Shole is an oasis— the Verdigris Fount—that edges the ancient border of Odestal and the Ailuro clan territories. Darkness plagues the land, a Stigma that consumes all it touches. No magic the Enclave wields can cleanse it as it spreads. But your flames can end this plague. If you purge the Verdigris Fount, I will divulge everything I know of Pyra and her precious portals."

"You know of the portals?" Ophiera spat.

"One could not know Pyra without knowing of her life's work."

Inside, Jasper screamed for Ophiera not to take the bait. The Odestal asked too much, and like all contracts, this one had not been well defined. Loopholes were the preferred path of those with power, especially warlocks.

"Who says the Aether will work against this plague you speak of? It was not very effective against the girta's poison in the Shole."

Kiela smiled again, though her eyes looked hungry suddenly. "That is due to origin. Centuries of the Enclave's knowledge, pain, and blood were poured into the creation of the girtas. The amount of suffering contained in one of their needles requires far more of Erum's flame to purge than you likely realized. But the Stigma, well...that will not be a problem, as you already know."

Again, Jasper watched the wheels turn behind Ophiera's skeptical gaze. He was glad she was fighting with wit rather than her sword, but it was a battle he wasn't confident she could win against the warlock. While he suspected this Stigma was related to, if not the same as, the ichor, he wasn't sure if Ophiera had reached that conclusion yet.

"What you ask does not seem to be a *fair* exchange for simple information," Ophiera said quietly.

Kiela laughed softly. "And yet a mere whisper of information has brought you here, has it not? You learned that Pyra corresponded with the Odestal and traveled all the way here to find her. Well, I heard a rumor as well...the white fires of Erum destroyed the Stigma that plagued a man in Krysas. So, it seems we have both gone to great lengths over *simple* information."

Ophiera blanched, her eyes falling to her gauntleted hand. "The only reason I was able to cleanse a *person* of the ichor was because he was my ekath! I could not do so again to another, not without claiming their vespers, too."

"And Pyra did far more with the Odestal than mere discussion," Kiela added in what Jasper interpreted as fair exchange. "What I ask of you is not to cleanse a soul but to cleanse the land of the rot that infests it. The Verdigris Fount is key to our city's survival—we cannot lose it to the Stigma. I believe what I ask of you should be easy, especially after leveling a village the size of Iluka."

Even Jasper could not hide his shock this time. He didn't understand how the warlock could know of Iluka's fate or Ophiera's role in its demise. The Enclave had closed its borders and removed all and any trade with Krysas, and yet, somehow, so much information had traveled.

Ophiera's words were visibly stuck in her throat at the mention of her folly. And in her moment of weakness, Jasper found strength.

"How do you know about Iluka?" He asked.

"The Enclave seeks freedom, not isolation. Even if the rest of Erum has forgotten us, we refuse to disregard the world we created. There is a greater purpose to this life beyond pride and tradition..." She turned back to the paladin, her eyes softening. "You have my sympathies regarding the souls of Iluka. But just as I know you sundered the sands, I also know the Vespula Brotherhood was truly responsible for the destruction of your village. And the blight in Verdigris fount is one and the same."

Ophiera shook slightly, a familiar look settling in her eyes. While Jasper had his suspicions about the Brotherhood and their reach, he assumed they had been chased from the city by Enclave rebellions.

"I agree to the exchange. I will destroy the Stigma in exchange for Pyra's knowledge and whereabouts, but I only promise my power—nothing else. My companion remains free to choose his fate."

A foreign warmth settled in Jasper's gut, this time not from Kiela's derivations. While he had dedicated himself to Ophiera, she still considered his freedom. It was the only time someone had considered his choices in this forsaken place.

"I accept those terms," Kiela smiled.

Ophiera turned to Jasper, "What do you wish to do?"

"Wish? I hardly know the meaning," he said solemnly, repeating her words. "But as I said, I will follow my lodestar wherever she leads me."

With pleasure, he watched as his words caused her cheeks to flush.

"Ah, you have an ekath *and* a lover? Progressive." Kiela chuckled.

"We are not lovers," Ophiera said sternly.

The strength with which she denied Kiela's assumption stung Jasper needlessly.

"Regardless, we depart within the hour."

Jasper chuffed. "That's hardly enough time to prepare for travel across the Shole!"

"You won't need to prepare a thing, my little Forged One. I'm nothing if not a gracious host and will provide everything required."

Jasper took a breath to argue, but he felt Ophiera's gentle touch against his arm.

"The sooner we deal with this, the sooner we can return."

The pain lacing her last words struck him in ways he wished to ignore at the moment. But her bonded pain was palpable as ever. And while he didn't trust the warlock, he did trust Ophiera. If this were her wish, then he would fulfill it, regardless of his hesitancies.

Kiela dropped to her knees, meeting the eyes of her fox. In a loving gesture so contrary to her nature, she caressed the black-tipped ears of her familiar. "Iku, fetch Alzerbez and tell them we are ready to ride to the Verdigris Fount."

"These foreigners will think me some measly errand dog," the fox replied, rolling his bright green eyes.

Kiela laughed. "Do not fret; your true nature will become obvious to all as we travel."

Iku held his head up in pride as he slinked away into the night.

At Ophiera's questioning gaze, Kiela spoke as she gathered items from the tent. "Alzerbez is a close confidante—one who is just as desperate to see the Stigma removed from their ancestral lands. They are of the Ailuro clan."

Jasper stilled a moment at the mention of their soon-to-be companion. The druids were rare, even within the Enclave. In truth, he had never knowingly met one until yesterday, when he'd watched the Autarch Syrina berate Ophiera. And even then, she'd maintained her form.

"I hope no one is vegetarian," Kiela mumbled as she packed a large quantity of dried meat and insect rations in a sack.

Jasper's skin crawled at the sight. He knew precisely what the Odestal preferred to eat, and it was not meat or fruit. Hell, she had even called him delicious as she tasted his essence in her derivations.

An icy breeze entered the tent with Iku's return. He shook his fur, a thin layer of frost sublimating from it.

"They're not happy about the hour at which we called upon them."

Kiela frowned. "They need so much sleep these days."

"Needs versus preferences are debatable," Iku said with an air of exasperation.

"I've packed enough provisions for our guests, I think. And we'll fill our water skins as we depart..." She turned to Ophiera, "I'm sure you'd prefer to bring your own bed dressings, yes? Am I forgetting anything else?" she mused, considering her pack.

Her uncertainty may have been endearing had he not known why the Odestal princess was confused by the need for sleep and sustenance.

"How far is our journey?" Ophiera asked.

Iku yipped excitedly. "I can get us to the border of the Verdigris Fount by sundown if we leave before sunrise. Then, we will rest for the night in the jungle and make for Megrim Spa in the morning."

"*You'll* get us there?" Jasper asked. "As a guide or what?"

"Better. Though it goes against my better judgment, my ekath trusts you enough to ride upon my back."

Jasper's jaw dropped behind his cowl. "Ride? You barely come to my knees—has she fed off you so much your brain has addled?"

Growling, the fox turned to Kiela, who instead giggled with a hand over her mouth. "Ah, the Forged One knows our ways, Iku! Don't worry. You'll soon show him what the Enukaja clan of Nijeka is truly capable of."

Suddenly, an enormous creature prowled into the tent. As if myth became reality before his eyes, every rumor Jasper had heard of the druids was proven true by the presence of the beast. Ophiera immediately clasped her claymore, but Jasper put his hand over hers, holding it still against the hilt.

"Don't—" he whispered in her ear. "This is the druid—this is coalescence magic."

The air grew thick in the yurt as the creature before them began to shiver. Their fur matched the sands of the Shole, ocherous gray with darker patterns splotched irregularly. White stripes contrasted the blackish olive spots, all converging into a beautiful, chaotic pattern. And as with all the Ailuro, they held two colored eyes—the left a deep, sapphire blue and the other bright, yellow-green.

The creature stared into the room menacingly.

"Alzerbez, don't be rude. At least greet our companions before we depart."

With a growl that caused Jasper's legs to buckle, the clouded fur rippled violently. He clenched Ophiera's hand over her blade and felt her fingers tighten around the hilt as they watched the fur retract into their skin. Though their front claws protracted, the gleaming talons soon transformed into thick fingers. Muscle and bone twisted, echoing against the canvas as, from their head, sprouted long, silver braids of hair, the same shade as their fur. Neither of their ears was whole; both were shaved from the sides of their head.

Jasper felt sick recognizing the sign of one who had resisted the Registry. As the dual-colored eyes fell on Ophiera, the person standing before them growled, loosening their voice.

"We are Alzerbez," they said in a guttural voice, "Wielder of Coalescence."

~ Forty Three ~

MEMORIA

I dreamt of her again.

I never thought I'd miss a soul more than Berwyn, and yet I feel painfully empty without her. It is to her I owe everything, and she to me...to be so indebted to another soul that cannot be by my side is pure torment. And yet it is a torment we both bear willfully, with an understanding that duty comes above all else. It was something Berwyn could never understand, and perhaps that was what I loved about him, while the opposite is why I loved her.

This place is not what I expected. And in my lowest moments, I find myself wondering how much easier it would be to give in...to give up...to go home.

And yet, knowing what waits at the end of this life prevents me from doing such. For Myronor, I must persevere. For the soul of my son, I must succeed.

* * *

Now that the revolution of the Enclave has settled, the Consortia is back to making ridiculous requests. After my report on the Phratries was received so well, they have now requested a new report on the Cloister of Tanvik. When Glamwell informed me of the request, I laughed until tears poured from my eyes. Alas, the Consortia truly enjoy burying their history so deeply that they must dig for it everywhere else.

I don't understand their sudden interest in a religion that those of Tanvik barely speak of, but I have a feeling I will require Rheta's guidance on this matter. She was indispensable for my report on the Phratries, though sending texts and tomes back and forth across the sea is both cumbersome and painfully slow. If I could only make more progress on my research, then perhaps...well, it doesn't matter. Truthfully, I do not know if there are even any materials to reference regarding the Cloister. Whilst in Iluka, the little I heard of the Cloister seemed to mostly be fisher's tales—great brutes in golden armor, conscripted by the Magistrate to save our souls and faceless white-robed strangers tasked with easing or stalling the passing of souls to the Aether. Yet, in all that time spent in Tanvik, I never once encountered a paladin and heard only rumors of a cleric—the Justicar of the Cloister.

I must be careful with what I reveal in this report. Between my prior knowledge and the bits my little fox has shared with me regarding the Aether and its protectors, I must limit my findings to uncommon knowledge, not myth and legend. Once the Enclave has settled into their new role as rulers of their own fate, I will visit Birozahran. Though the Consortia, as usual, destroyed most of their written history, the clans of the Enclave have kept their history in their own way. The little fox said she would sponsor me anytime I wished to visit...

* * *

To begin my report, I must emphasize that little is known of the origin of the once-thriving order known as the Cloister. What I have compiled here is all I've been able to gather from books and documents amongst the archives of the Magistrate, as well as a few select pieces hidden within the Embassy library here in Krysas.

Once the most revered religion in Tanvik, the beliefs of the Cloister and the Book of the Aether have declined significantly over the years. However, it is not only within the cultural ethos of Tanvik that the Cloister has become a myth. Within the Magistrate itself and other archives across Tanvik, little is written of the elusive order. Few books, accounts, and histories can be found. Even the Magistrate has seemingly "lost" the original doctrines, establishing the agreements between the Cloister and the Magistrate. I cannot begin to guess when the appointment of a Justicar of the Cloister began, along with the tradition of conscripting the Cloister's disciples into service. Therefore, the majority of this report concerns recent history with a dash of mythos. The Cloister, despite its decline, still holds a significant political role in the Magistrate, which will be explored in the following report.

We must first begin with the act of conscription, as this is the most influential role the Cloister has played in the Magistrate and what many citizens of Tanvik recognize as the primary role of the Cloister. From what I can ascertain, the act of conscription was once viewed as a necessary service to the people of Tanvik. And while the tradition of conscripting the Cloister's paladins and clerics to the Magistrate has now dwindled in popularity and practice, it has not died. At the time of this report, only *a single cleric remains in the Magistrate's retention—the appointed Justicar of the Cloister, Aleksander, Hand of Mercy. The Justicar has been the sole member of the Cloister serving Tanvik for some time now, though he was recently joined by Uzziel, Hand of Retribution. As a recent conscript, the new paladin has filled a long-standing vacancy within the Magistrate. For many years, Tanvik went without conscripted paladins, to little consequence, it would seem. However, the sudden conscription of a new paladin cannot be justified by data or facts, and thus, I must embellish history here with my interpretation and opinion.*

The decision to conscript a new paladin lacked any warning or advertising, if you will, that has vexed many politicians and scholars considerably since. Historically, a new paladin conscript was something to celebrate—a small festival was often held, or at the very least, a ceremony of appointment in Feyralis. But most recently, the Magistrate has kept relatively quiet regarding any business surrounding the Cloister. There are rumors that a new paladin may soon be conscripted, replacing the Hand of Retribution with another golden pawn. Personally, I interpret this smoke and mirrors as a sign that the Magistrate may finally be cutting ties with the Cloister. Personally, I believe it is in the best interest of the people of Tanvik.

For decades, the people of Tanvik have protested the appointment of the Justicar of the Cloister. Each member of the Magistrate has historically represented a specific region—Feyralis, the Sloughmire, the Southern Coastlands, the Jungles of Ruin—all with unique terrain, customs, and history. However, the Justicar of the Cloister is called such because they have no land or people to represent. Rumor speaks that they are supposedly representative of the Burnished Highlands, yet the northernmost realm of Tanvik is nothing more than an abandoned wasteland. Therefore, the Justicar of the Cloister solely represents the church's interests with one-fifth of the voting power, and yet none of the people or resources like the other realms.

Now, given their representation of the Burnished Highlands, I found it prudent to at least summarize this distinct realm of Tanvik for context. In the handful of accounts documented, the Burnished Highlands can only be described as a destitute and deadly land. The peaks bordering and scattered throughout the highlands spiral so high that the air completely disappears near the summits. There are descriptions of geysers spewing endless streams of poisonous gas that constantly seep into the deep valleys. And within some of these valleys, molten earth flows in rivers of burning white and red. A close colleague of mine in the Magistrate archives has had a fascination with the area for quite some time, and if these are the only descriptors of the area she can uncover, I must trust there are no more to be found.

Regardless of land, the question of politics remains: Why should the Cloister represent so much of the Magistrate when they contribute nothing to the people or society? That is because, at one time, they contributed far more to Tanvik's society. Firstly, to understand their contributions, we must understand their order and the roles of the disciples within. From the little information available, I gathered there are three Oaths each disciple of the Cloister may be bound to—Mercy, which we call the clerics; Retribution, the paladins; and Sacrifice, the priests. There are rumors of a fourth Oath lost eons ago, but as this is a rumor with sparse evidence, I will focus on the three that are clearly defined.

These Oaths dictate their skills and their purpose, all based on the runic scars blistered into their arms. Now, where this becomes further complicated is in their echelons—only two have been reported in recent years, the Hands and the Keepers. Hands are thought to be executors of the Aether's will and are permitted to leave the Cloister when conscripted by the Magistrate. The Keepers, however, are bound to remain wherever the Cloister may be and uphold the traditions of their order. It is speculated that there were additional Oaths and echelons in the past; however, few records exist of what they may be and what their purposes were. For that reason, I will focus solely on the Oaths and echelons in service to the Magistrate currently.

While there are no records of a priest leaving the Cloister, the clerics were previously one of the most valuable members of Tanvik society.

Hailed for their ability to heal, the Hands of Mercy were one of the few citizens exempt from the taboo of witnessing vespers. Bound to Mercy, they mastered the rites to heal by manipulating the holy flames. And if healing failed, they at least eased the passing of a vesper back to the Aether. As their numbers dwindled, so did their importance in Tanvik society. And while the paladins remained, they have not been held in favor by the people for as far back as records exist.

As the Magistrate's arm of justice, the goal of the paladins is to seek Retribution for souls stolen from the Aether. According to the Book of the Aether, any vesper freed from its vessel by sin, in other words, murder, is freed from the cycle of reincarnation through the Aether. Supposedly, this act of sin leaves a mark on the offender's soul, some indicator of guilt that only the paladins can sense or correct. Those with the Oaths of Retribution seek out and cleanse the tainted soul as recompense for the one stolen. It seems odd to me to solve an unjust death with more death; however, little as to the reasoning or reckonings behind these actions are to be found. Regardless of reason, it is understandable why the people of Tanvik viewed the paladins, in their golden armor and deadly weapons, as a threat rather than a savior. Perhaps it was a political choice to no longer conscript a Hand of Retribution of late, or perhaps it was that there were none available to recruit.

With the lack of popularity, so has followed the lack of recruits for the Cloister. Fewer and fewer families dedicate their offspring to the honor of the Aether, and it seems the majority of recent recruits are abandoned, and unwanted vagrants plucked from the streets of Feyralis. I'm certain other areas of Tanvik also donate orphans to the Cloister's cause. Still, it is in Feyralis where the rare priests, covered in black robes, are seen combing the streets with food and drink to usher unwitting children into their caravans. Again, it is difficult to judge the depth of truth in these stories—are they mere myths to scare children into listening to their parents, or does the Cloister truly recruit their disciples in this way? Who is to say?

Certainly not I, for I am but a mage residing in Krysas and have little opinion as to the ongoings of a dying religion, other than to bid it good riddance.

~ Forty Four ~

ATONEMENT

As Myronor's eyes drooped, he lost focus on the words scrawled across the pages. For hours, he had pored over the tomes in the library, searching for any information related to the Cloister and the Oaths that bound their disciples. But if he thought his library in Feyralis was scant in details regarding the Cloister, his mother's collection was even more so. Despite Pyra dedicating an entire bookcase in her library to the religions and belief systems of Erum, her report to the Cloister was the most information he had found thus far.

While she had gone to great lengths to summarize *The Paladins of the Cloister,* she had provided none of the embellishments he had come to expect from a scholar of her stature: little history, lore, or details—merely vague statements and benign political opinions. Only her journals contained sparse information of interest, and he wasn't sure how much more of those he could stomach to read. In search of portals and Oaths, he had only found disappointment in the life his mother led.

But now wasn't the time to allow Pyra to ruin anything else—his only goal now was to find a way to break Ophiera's Oath to the Cloister. It was the only way to truly save her from the searching eyes of Uzziel and Aleksander, who he hoped were long on their way back to Feyralis by now.

Myronor pressed his palms against his eyes, trying to will away the fatigue in the darkened library. He hadn't slept at all last night nor since the arrival of the Chaplain and Justicar that morning. While he knew the Cloister was hermetic, he hadn't fully appreciated how unprecedented their visit to Krysas was until reading the report. In all of Pyra's writings, there was not a single documented time the Cloister had left Tanvik, let alone visited Krysas.

Something strange sat with him now, given a moment to reflect on the events of the morning. Hadn't Glamwell said something about the aerodock? It seemed impossible, given that no aership existed in Tanvik, let alone one the Cloister might use. To this day, the Consortia remained tight-lipped about their imbuteria, especially the spellcrafts required for creating ship flight. Despite his mother's complaints and efforts, she had been unable to negotiate for any aership knowledge. It was a favorite point of contention with Eliana...

Reaching for a quill, Myronor began jotting down additional questions for Glamwell. He still hadn't heard from the Steward regarding Aleksander and Uzziel's departure. While he tried reminding himself it had taken Jasper days to prepare the *Berserker* for her voyage, he couldn't help but worry about how long it was taking Glamwell to report back. The sooner the Cloister was on their way back to Tanvik, the sooner Myronor could rest.

But as he wrote in his journal, question after question continued to race through his mind until all that was left was the white noise of unknowns. He found the low hum of ceaseless thoughts like a lullaby, ushering his head down onto the desk in hopes of escape. Forehead to the table, he inhaled the smell of parchment and ink, desperately trying to find anything to center his thoughts.

What he wouldn't give to feel Ophiera's mind against his own right now. She'd always had a way of anchoring him, providing some pointed questions or strange thoughts that jarred him out of himself. He closed his eyes, picturing her face clearly in his mind, allowing the imagined sight to ease the ever-growing ache in his chest...

In the blink of an eye, Myronor stood in a dark, silent room. Somewhere from high above, a pinhole of light widened as it descended into a beam. Far across the room, he squinted to see the form of a person illuminated by the light. Though he could not make out any facial features, he could never mistake the shape of her body, the curves of her musculature. With a rattle in his heart, he started forward towards Ophiera.

His footsteps quickened, becoming thunderous as he ran. Bound by the circle of light and yet as still as the darkness, she stood without armor or clothing, framed only by her silken white hair hung loose around her. Though her violet eyes stared ahead, there was an unfamiliar vacancy in them. It was as if she were asleep while standing.

Myronor knew at that moment he was dreaming. But rather than awaken, as he often did when he became *aware* inside a dream, he forced himself to delve deeper into lucidity. More than anything, he wanted to see her, to talk to her, to touch her, even if it was a pure fabrication of his exhausted mind. But when he finally reached the edge of the circle of light, Ophiera remained still as stone, unblinking and unresponsive.

"Ophiera?" He asked aloud.

She didn't blink or flinch. It was as if he wasn't there...or rather, *she* wasn't there. Searching for her through the ekath, Myronor was met with an unfamiliar, vacuous feeling that caused his heart to panic. Empty did not properly describe the lack he felt in his soul. Dream or not, the ennui of her presence broke him. Dream or not, he found himself suddenly desperate to *feel* her again.

Stepping into the circle of light, he wrapped his arms around her broad shoulders. Her skin was warm, and yet she felt stiff, as if...as if...A few stray tears transformed into sobs as he buried his face in her hair. She couldn't be...she was still warm...this was a dream...she couldn't be...

"Don't cry for me."

Drawing back, Myronor looked fervently at her still blank expression, hardly believing his ears. He took her face in his hands, running his thumbs over her lightly freckled cheeks while examining her still-vacant eyes.

"Ophiera?" He whispered.

She blinked.

"Ophiera, my love, please," he begged.

"Is that what I am?" She said, her lips barely moving with the question.

Myronor let go of his breath, smiling as the tears continued to blur his vision.

"Of course—you are my everything, remember?"

Again, she blinked, and he swore he saw more facets in her jewel-bright eyes as if she were slowly coming back to life. The *need* for her to be—to be here, to be herself, to be with him—overwhelmed all others.

Myronor pressed his trembling lips against hers. She took a sharp breath and wound her arms around his shoulders. Embraced against her, connected by soul and lips, he felt a moment of wholeness—a moment, incomparable to any others, of true, undeniable completeness. But suddenly, her corporeal form disappeared in his arms as ash filled his lungs.

He choked away the dust covering his chest, where Ophiera had just been held against him. The cloud of gray soot settled into a pile on the floor where she once stood. The sensation of completeness he felt a moment before swung violently opposite, leaving him desperately hollow.

"No!" he screamed as the void of her flooded his heart.

Blinding, an orb of pure, white light rose from the ashes. Shimmers of gold swirled violently within the pale shade of her vesper, just as he remembered, and if his heart hadn't shattered at the sight, it would have been beautiful. But even through the pain—even knowing this was a dream, he couldn't take his eyes off the glorious manifestation of her soul.

But something wasn't quite as he remembered.

Twisting within the purity of her shade, a coil of bright blue danced. He reached a trembling hand toward the beautiful orb, feeling the draw more powerfully than ever. And as he did so, the streaks of azure swirled even more fervently than before. Yet when his fingertip brushed against the searing hot surface of the pale orb, it disintegrated into white smoke, dusting his hands in a diminishing luminescence.

Myronor dropped to his knees, kicking up the ashes as the light above diminished to nothing. Why did she vanish every time he reached for her? Silent screams reverberated in his chest, begging himself to wake. But the darkness clung to him like wet clothes, suffocating and weighty.

Like a moonless night, he could feel her absence swallow him whole. A vacancy so crushing he couldn't move, couldn't think. Is this what it would feel like if she severed the ekath? If she left this world without dragging him along with her?

No.

This wasn't real.

He had to remember that...she wouldn't...

This wasn't real!

With one last attempt to force himself awake, Myronor threw himself onto the ground. But instead, as could only happen in dreams, he never hit the floor. When he opened his eyes, it was to a vertical wall of still water.

If Myronor hadn't known he was dreaming, he would have blamed Kaikora for the strange trick. But at least now, his subconscious had provided him a means to wash Ophiera's ashes from his hands. He reached his hand towards the surface of the water, and the reflection strengthened as he approached, mirroring like Kaikora's eyes when she cast. The desperation in his reflected gaze, reaching a gray-dusted hand out toward the water, should have been strange enough to wake him. But something more pulled at his features than pure despair, keeping him in dreams...

When did he ever have freckles across his cheekbones? And his eyes...weren't his eyes blue, not violet? The moment he broke the surface tension, the wall collapsed, and a burning pain, quite contrary to the coldness from the water, crashed against him. As the veil of water fell, an explosion of white flames overtook him, and he watched in horror as the water evaporated to steam and his arms caught fire in smoke. Ignited from his fingertips, the flames crawled up his arm, disintegrating his clothes—and *him*—to ash. As the fire spread, so did his pain, all while he watched his body disappear, crumbling beneath him.

"Myronor!"

With a gasp of chilled air, he jolted, knocking the stack of books from his desk.

Dazed, he finally recognized the dark stone library. Despite wishing for nothing more than to be awake, his heart stammered in a frenzied rhythm while the lingering burn of fire trickled down his spine. Breathing heavily, he looked towards the slashed windows, realizing the disappearance of the light of dusk into night. Moments of a dream had equated to an entire day wasted in painful sleep.

"Are you alright?" Kaikora's voice boomed from behind him.

Another stack of books crashed to the floor as he jumped from his chair. Clutching his chest, he took a few deep breaths.

"That is the worst possible way to ask someone if they're okay," he hissed. "And, no, I'm not!"

The shaman still held the basin of water in her hands. Since she had evoked this vigil, she'd carried around the bowl like a beggar on the streets of Feyralis. No wonder his nightmare contained water...and fire...and...

"Is it Ophiera again?" She asked, looking him up and down. "Does she burn?"

"No, though, the draw of the Aether would have been a far better experience than what I just dreamt."

At least if she had called upon the Aether, he could have felt her soul through the agony. Instead, he wasted precious time, sleeping instead of searching—screaming instead of dreaming. He crossed the room and snatched the cold lantern of antracinders. With the slightest bit of mana, he cast a wind onto the dim stones until they glowed bright enough to illuminate the room. After he set the lantern atop the desk with a thud, he began sorting through the books he had toppled.

"Perhaps you should sleep some more," Kaikora offered. "You have not rested properly since Ophiera departed."

"And I doubt I will until she returns, so what difference does it make..."

The shaman, with her scrying bowl, came to sit beside him. And in a rare, foul mood, he wished nothing more than for her just to leave. Kaikora had been a great help these last few days, but shaking off the despair of his dreams required him to drown himself in a book.

"I know the ekath is causing you pain."

"You always *know*, don't you?" He snapped in a bubble of rage. But the words weren't his own.

She raised her eyebrows, staring at him with a look of concern. Her mouth fell open, but rather than argue, she looked down at her hand, still dipped into the bowl. For a few moments, she remained silent, allowing Myronor to refocus on sorting through the mess he'd made of the books.

Where did he even turn to next? He had made little progress on anything since Ophiera left. With only an imbued stone of unknown purpose in his possession and knowledge that the Cloister pursued his ekath, what was he to do about any of this? Like the night Rheta informed him of his mother's death, he wished...he wished he could just walk away from it all. When did the Brotherhood and Aud become his problem? Why hadn't he just stayed in Iluka with Ophiera when they had the chance? For all his talk of fate, he was sincerely despising his own.

"Myronor," Kaikora said with an urgency in her voice. And yet, it wasn't enough to make him look up from his journal. Neither was her sigh—nor the crackle in the air that indicated she used some portion of her mana for something.

"Mistress!"

Myronor's hand froze midair with a tome in hand. The cruel voice laced with such elation, echoing in his library, was an affront he could not comprehend at the moment. In Kaikora's hands, he saw the bubbled vision of Marvena's cell within the bowl she held.

Quietly setting down his tome, Myronor turned his full attention to the scrying bowl in her hands. Though the angle from the bucket of water only showed the ceiling of the darkened cell they left her in, he could hear every single one of Marvena's pathetic whimpers.

"Mistress, I knew you'd come for me; I knew you'd set me free!"

"What did you tell them?" an icy voice rang in the room.

Something sounded off in the Mistress's voice, as if distorted by something physical or perhaps magical, to change the tone. It was unnatural, echoey, and full of hatred.

"I said nothing," Marvena began quietly. "Nothing of consequence, at least. I taunted the mage to try and find the paladin's whereabouts, just as you instructed."

"Then tell me, where is the Aspect?"

For a moment, all he could hear was Marvena's ragged breaths echoing through the rippling water. Myronor held his breath, hoping beyond hope that only he and Kaikora still knew where Ophiera had traveled.

As part of the agreements with the Ashen Order, the Yeoman and her people remained unaware of Ophiera's destination. All they knew was that Jasper had set sail with her as an escort with the intent to find Pyra. As with most of the Order's doings, the fewer people who knew, the better. But as Marvena breathed in the dark, Myronor couldn't help but worry.

"I...I'm not completely sure, Mistress."

"You're not sure? Or you don't know?"

"I'm sorry—she disappeared from our trackers nights ago, and we have yet to find her trail since. It's as if she disappeared into thin air!"

The silence rippled through the scrying basin.

"So then what, pray-tell, compelled you to risk revealing yourself to the mage and his companion?"

Again, the cold silence clung to Myronor's skin, sending a shiver throughout him. Whoever this Mistress was, her voice commanded respect, and her quiet, even more so.

"He...I think he found a keystone."

"What?!" The Mistress's question echoed violently.

"Mistress, I'm sorry—I tried to steal it, to acquire it for you, but that shaman of his, she nearly drowned me in the streets!"

"I wish she had, and rid me of your incompetence!" The Mistress shouted, echoing in the dark chamber. "Am I to understand, then, that in a span of a few days, you have lost the whereabouts of the paladin and allowed the mage to acquire a keystone?"

"I—maybe?" Marvena began, trembling over her words. "There is a chance it wasn't a keystone, and just...just..." Her voice trailed off, overtaken by the Mistress's cold laughter.

"Have you done a single thing right in your life, Marvena?"

"I...yes, yes I have," Marvena said, her voice gaining in strength. "I destroyed Iluka as you requested, and I led the paladin back across the sea as you asked. I know the navarras didn't go as planned, but—"

"But nothing! As long as the Aspect is alive and running amok, nothing we do matters! Kill her, capture him; that has always been the plan since Pyra disappeared! And yet you failed miserably at both, at each opportunity!"

Myronor listened intently, attempting to control his quickening breath. Ophiera had suspected a connection between Pyra and the Brotherhood long before...and now he had proof.

"Please, Mistress, let me repent—"

"Silence!" The hiss rattled the bars of Marvena's cell. "Your failures are unforgivable. Redeem an ounce of your pride and tell me where Myronor is now."

"Back to the Embassy, I think—I assume—he always has that gargantuan shaman with him now instead of the paladin," Marvena sniffed, childish and pathetic.

"And you've had no luck infiltrating the Embassy, correct?"

"Not without effort. As idiotic as the Steward acts, we cannot break his defenses. But Myronor will venture out again, and when he does, I'll bring him to you! Release me from here, and I swear, I will not disappoint you again. Please...please..."

"As I said, your failures are unforgivable," the Mistress said, her voice frosted and harsh.

"Please, no..."

Myronor gazed in horror as the water violently rippled across the basin. Sweat mingled with tears down Kaikora's broad features, and the dark sensation of the world ripped asunder flowed into the room.

"May the Void consume us all," the Mistress hissed before Kaikora dropped the bowl, spilling clear water across the library floor.

~ Forty Five ~

CLADE

Iku's transformation from knee-height fox to a beast the size of a troynt shouldn't have surprised Ophiera, not after watching Alzerbez shift between a wildcat and a person several times over. But now, from the back of a giant fox, she observed the desert landscape change with the rise of dawn. Sheepishly, she wished Iku could have grown just the slightest bit bigger and run just a little bit slower.

Kiela rode first on Iku, her slight frame taking up little room in front of Ophiera. Meanwhile, Jasper rode behind and pressed hard against her back as he tried his best to avoid slipping off the back of Iku. At least, that's the excuse she made for him remaining so close to her.

Trailed by Alzerbez, running as their four-legged form, she realized she had never traveled with so many people, let alone with those so uniquely gifted as her company now. Everyone here was...powerful. She could sense in their presence, in the way they conducted themselves, especially with her. They didn't fear her and, in truth, nearly patronized her.

She still found it bothersome how much the Enclave knew of the Aether. Meanwhile, the Cloister did not ever once mention the Enclave. She supposed she shouldn't have been surprised, given they barely acknowledged mages in Tanvik beyond what she needed to know for training or duty. The wool had been pulled over her eyes for so long, and yet, even when free, she didn't bother to learn more of the world.

"We shouldn't leave the road," Jasper mumbled behind Ophiera.

"*You* shouldn't leave the road, my little Forged One," Kiela hissed, turning to glare at him. "We know how to navigate our land."

"Call me that again, and I swear—"

"What does that term even mean?" Ophiera interjected, hoping to silence Jasper's threat. They had bickered on and off since their departure from Birozahran, and if it must continue, at least she could learn something from it.

"You might have been considered Forged, too, had you not awakened Erum's Flame," Kiela said in her sing-song voice.

"Forged Ones are those not born to wield mana, yet still possess some due to imbuteria or other means," Jasper grunted. "It appears I'm the only one amongst us."

"But I wasn't born with mana," Ophiera said defensively. "The Aether gave me the scars of my Oath."

"I had hoped you no longer sucked at the tit of the Cloister," Kiela said cruelly. "It still surprises me how the wayward children survive this world with such little truth in their lives."

Ophiera did not appreciate being called a child by a woman half her size. While she understood Kiela's point, her own doubts about the Cloister were weight enough without the woman questioning her experiences and intelligence. But strangely, her curiosity overrode the streak of pride Kiela so accurately plucked at...slightly, at least.

"Instead of mocking me, you could explain your knowledge without cruelty. Like an adult."

Kiela took a deep breath, licking her teeth beneath her painted lips. It seemed Ophiera had also plucked at something beneath the cold expression.

"The brands you wear only allow you taste of power—borrowed through imbuement of your very flesh. But you wield your true mana now. The Cloister made you a *paladin*, my sister, but your soul was born to wield Erum's Flame."

Ophiera stared at her gleaming gauntlets, processing Kiela's familiar words. Hearing her doubts so brutally confirmed wasn't as hard a blow as it used to be. Still, it was hard knowing yet again that people, even across the sea, knew more about her scars than she did.

Her view of the Cloister had already been shattered over and over throughout this journey. So then, why did she still struggle to let go of the shards that remained? Like the over-ripened fruit that Jasper tossed to her back in Krysas, the harder she gripped the splinters of her Oath, the more she bled.

Myronor, Kaikora, Jasper, and now Kiela all echoed the notion that she was more than her scars. But if that were true, why did the brands weigh on her life so heavily? Up until recently, all she had was her Oath. But as her life took on more, it seemed her Oath had less and less hold on it.

Everyone else saw the Cloister for what they were, while Ophiera had remained voluntarily blinded. She did not know which agony to prioritize—the fall of her Oath or the drag of the ekath. Both tore at her now as they traveled across the desert, and she wondered how she could possibly help the Enclave with anything when she was so easily destroyed by truth and distance.

"Oath or not, don't let doubt cloud your judgment," Jasper breathed in her ear. "You are the berserker—a fierce inferno, not a dwindling ember. That is who you are, with or without scars."

Ophiera should have guessed he would have sensed her turmoil, sitting so close to her. But what she hadn't expected was his attempt to comfort her rather than taunt her.

"You should not declare what makes someone who they are—it is not for you to decide," Kiela hissed, hearing the rogue despite how quietly he whispered. "Mana is just as key to *who* a person is as their very soul. Before the Purge, my people mastered all the manas Erum offered, and when the Consortia took our magic, it destroyed us more thoroughly than death alone ever could."

The vitriol in her hiss caused Ophiera's skin to crawl as Alzerbez snarled to their side. Even Iku tensed beneath them as the collective hatred warmed the very air. And suddenly, Ophiera felt exceptionally tired.

"Control yourself!" Jasper growled. "We can't aid you if we're drained."

"T'was an accident," Kiela said, her voice returning to the coy sweetness. "My point is, in the Enclave, mana is who we are. Have you not thought about who you would be if the Cloister never found you?"

Ophiera chewed her lip, reminded far too painfully of the questions Myronor often asked her—pointless, uncomfortable questions about what *could* have been rather than what was.

"As everyone continually reminds me, I am what I am, with seemingly little say in the matter. Thus, I find it pointless to wonder *what if.*"

Kiela smiled as she lovingly ran her thin fingers through Iku's sumptuous red fur. He made a satisfactory noise that reverberated through his whole body—a sensation of such contentment that Ophiera felt herself grow envious. The ekath tightened, uncomfortable, and desperate for relief.

"Yet you've changed your very soul *by accident*. And you could do so much more if you allowed yourself a little imagination. If you limit yourself to what could have been, you will never forge the path of what should be."

Silence fell, interrupted only by the soft sounds of paws in the sand. Ophiera didn't understand why Kiela pushed her so hard on the subject of, well, herself. She sensed she was being manipulated, but not maliciously. Neither Iku nor Alzerbez added to the conversation, and for some time, they traveled in a pinched quiet.

"See how they toy with you?" Jasper said under his breath. "This is why I say you cannot trust the Enclave."

Ophiera nearly elbowed him in the ribs, but the collective hisses from the three surrounding them made it unnecessary. She had a feeling he would be scolded enough without her intervention.

"The Enclave never makes empty promises," Kiela spat. "That type of dishonesty only comes from your kind, *anathema*."

"My kind? You don't even know where I'm from."

"I don't need to—the smell on you says it all."

"Didn't you call me delicious before, princess?"

"And like food, your existence is inconsequential to me, you filthy—"

"Will you both shut up?!"

To everyone's surprise, it was Iku's voice that rang clearly across the desert, silencing everyone.

"We're mere hours into this journey, and I'm ready to throw you all from my back—yes, you especially, Kiela. You're too old for this nonsense, and so am I. Let us enjoy the silence of the desert for a while, please!"

As Iku commanded, the party continued their trek across the desert in silence. With the sun perpetually obscured by gray clouds, Ophiera found it difficult to track the time of their travel.

At some point, they left the silken sands of the Shole and ventured into a cragged landscape of cracked desert. Here, the sundered ground was peppered with more dark obsidian stones, protruding violently in all directions. In the distance, the cold of the desert distorted the horizon, causing mirages of levitating peaks of monstrous dark rocks.

Again, despite Jasper's constant warnings, she couldn't help but find the Shole beautiful. After so many years of traveling across Tanvik, she never knew places like this could exist. There was so much of Erum she had never seen and even more beyond. Other worlds, like Nijeka, where Iku and Mallow ventured from, and even the dark realm where Aud resided, piqued her curiosity far beyond the dancing sands.

Perhaps Kiela was right—allowing herself to consider *what if*, whether past, present, or future, filled her with a satisfaction she so seldom allowed herself. And for the first time since climbing onto the fox's back, she felt her shoulders relax as she mused over the possibilities of what she would see next.

A heavy weight fell against Ophiera's back. From the corner of her eyes, she noticed Jasper's head resting on her pauldron, eyes closed and mouth slightly agape. Whether due to boredom or just exhaustion, he somehow had lowered his guard enough to fall asleep.

The warmth of his weight pressed against her carried with it both comfort and guilt. Last night, beside him, had alleviated the tension of the ekath in a way Ophiera didn't quite understand. And yet, he'd claimed her his lodestar, a ridiculous way to dedicate himself to her for reasons she also still couldn't understand. Had she not brought him only turmoil? And had he not brought her frustration? Why, then, were they so drawn to each other? Especially when her heart was filled with longing for another.

As Iku weaved through a patch of stones, Jasper began to slip against her smooth armor. Reaching behind her, Ophiera took his arms and wound them around her waist, holding him in place. She couldn't help but smile, thinking how the grumpy bastard chastised her last night for daring to sleep, yet here he was, passed out on the back of a fox.

"You're sure you're not lovers?" Kiela asked, breaking the silence.

"We are not," Ophiera said pointedly.

"But you care for him?"

"Yes—I can care for another without being their lover."

The warlock laughed. "Are you and your ekath lovers then?"

At the pulse of the tether, she felt her face flush. 'Lover' was not a word she had ever expected to apply to herself. Yet, recalling their ventures alone in the Embassy before this journey made her flesh crawl with a need her soul knew could not be met.

"Yes," Ophiera said. "We are."

"I can't imagine the pain of this separation," Kiela breathed, genuinely sympathetic. "I've rarely parted so far and so long from Iku. We are not lovers, obviously, but we've been bonded for over two hundred years."

"H-how long?" Ophiera said, unable to consider the politeness of her voice.

Iku chuckled beneath, vibrating her armor in his amusement.

"That is why the Ailuro prefer to undergo the rites of coalescence," Alzerbez growled, speaking for the first time since they departed. "The whole can never be separated, even in death—for those of us who can survive the rites, at least."

Ophiera chewed on this knowledge for a moment, struggling to comprehend how souls could fuse. Then again, she didn't think it possible to tether souls either.

"I imagine it was quite terrifying to undergo the birzhan with no knowledge of it," Kiela said quietly again. "I would be curious to hear how you managed to survive such an *accident*, as you called it."

"And I would be happy to tell you," Ophiera said, gripping Jasper's arms a little bit tighter, "after you've told me of Pyra."

Kiela laughed. "Ah, you're a quick learner. I can see why the Forged One worships you."

The word 'worship' made Ophiera's heart sink. As he leaned against her, sleeping in his exhaustion with her, she resisted the meaning of it all. She did not think what he felt for her was anything more than confusion, but the argument to Kiela died in her throat.

None spoke until they arrived at the edge of the dark stone peaks. The bluffs did not float as arctic mirages suggested and appeared far smaller than expected. Like the tricks of the sea, the desert had its illusions that Ophiera found both fascinating and frustrating.

Iku slowed as he carried them along the winding paths, cramped between the peaks of glossy stone. In the shine, Ophiera caught the surreal reflection—three darkly mirrored individuals upon the back of a great fox stalked by the clouded leopard. Strange how Alzerbez's ears were intact in this form, yet not in their other. The idea behind the fusion of souls was something she wished to know more about, but unlike her ekath, she knew when not to pry.

What truly caught her eye in the reflection was Jasper's slumberous face. His dark curls had fallen over his eyes, and his full lips hung slack from his strong jaw. With his thick, dark eyelashes, his features were both youthful and vigorous. Before, she thought of him as beautiful as Myronor, but as she studied him without a tormented expression, she realized he erred more on the side of handsome. Kindness dominated her ekath's features, but strength favored Jasper, and she enjoyed looking at him more than she should.

It was hard to believe such innocence was hidden beneath Jasper's tormented mask, and it pained her to consider she had contributed to his suffering. But perhaps if he could achieve peace in sleep, he could experience it awake as well. Maybe once this task was done, she would be able to witness his calm while awake.

When the path ahead finally opened and they moved away from the cramped path, she breathed a sigh of relief. As she peered beyond the crowded rocks, the ground began to change from stone to lush vegetation. Kiela had described the Verdigris Fount as an oasis, but from this vantage, no plant stood taller than a shrub. She didn't understand what she was seeing until the group vacated the shelter of the stones in full.

Like a verdant gash into the land, the deep scar of a forest was inset into the ground. Amongst the thick green leaves and dark coniferous needles hung vines bearing poisonous-looking pink and blue flowers. The palette of colors scattered amongst the dark green jungle reminded her of the crystals inset into the lift tunnels of Krysas.

Again, Ophiera never knew a place like this could exist. The words "beautiful" fell from her lips before she realized she had spoken.

"The Verdigris Fount always has been," Alzerbez purred in appreciation. "While the Odestal mastered the Shole, the Ailuro conquered the Eternal Taiga. And together, our clans have shared this little oasis between the two—long before the Consortia formed."

With a snort, Jasper awoke violently. His arms tightened around her waist, and she felt the moment of fear tremor through his body. "Where the hell—oh...oh wow..." he trailed off, gazing over the Verdigris.

"We'll descend into the jungle and make camp for the night," Kiela said. "The Stigma has likely spread, even to the edge of the jungle, so we must tread carefully."

Iku followed a path only he seemingly knew, leading them down into the depths of the lush forest. The canopy quickly enveloped them in darkness, and though Ophiera was accustomed to seeing in the dark, for once, she felt outmatched by others in the party. Jasper held a mastery of the shadows, while Iku and Alzerbez relied on their natural ability to see in the night. And she doubted *anything* escaped Kiela's luminous crimson gaze.

The depths of the basin, however, were not exempt from the cold of the Shole. Ophiera's breath fogged before her in the chill of nightfall, her energy falling with the light. The cold sapped her constitution quickly as she blinked away the frost of exhaustion. It didn't help that Jasper kept his arms around her after waking, providing her with a contrast of warmth, like a campfire at night. And yet, the ache in her chest grew ever more, preventing her from dozing off as they rode.

Alzerbez stopped before a gnarled, overgrown tree with a trunk wider than the *Berserker*. In all her years in Tanvik, Ophiera had never witnessed a tree this enormous, even in the Jungles of Ruin. In the dark, the magenta vines covering the bark nearly glowed dimly like the Moon Tide, winding upwards through thick branches that held needles rather than leaves.

"We rest here," growled Alzerbez, maintaining their leopard form.

Iku flicked his tail agitatedly, "Alz, you know I'm not very fond of heights."

"We remember, but given the Stigma, it's best to remain far off the ground."

Kiela dismounted first, allowing Ophiera to follow. When her greaves clunked against the ground, she felt the surge of the Aether, angrier than ever. Like her first steps in Krysas, the difference in *feel* of the Aether was astounding. And yet, in her exhaustion, it did little to stir her scars. It was the ache in her chest that caused her to stumble, worse now that she stood, throbbing in reminder.

She didn't understand how she could feel so tired after only riding all day. But as she stretched her stiff limbs, she watched Alzerbez gracefully lope up the tree.

With a sigh, Kiela removed the leather-wrapped parcel Iku carried on his side and returned their weapons. Ophiera reached for her claymore, enjoying the security of the hilt in hand again, while Jasper twirled his knives. He hadn't been particularly fond of storing their weapons for travel, but he kept his comments to himself upon their return.

With fluid grace, Kiela swept up her intimidating weapon. The scythe reminded Ophiera of the shaman's trident, a weapon that held a purpose beyond violence. Ornate and jagged, the crescent blade was carved from crimson stone that resembled the stingers of the girtas. The handle was suspiciously stained with dark splatters, apparently rubbed into the grain rather than wiped from it.

And yet the Aether never whispered calls for Retribution in Kiela's presence. No one in their party was anathema, as far as she could sense. And yet, how could they have rebelled against the Consortia without murder? Perhaps the Aether didn't consider it a sin to kill those who attempted to enslave you. Was that not retribution at its core? The circles her thoughts ran were nearly as exhausting as the journey.

"I must repeat, I *really* dislike heights," Iku groaned. The surrounding air vibrated as he assumed his more diminutive form, shaking his fur in a blur of red.

The first branch of the tree was twice Ophiera's height from the ground, yet the fox jumped and landed in graceful silence. Up he went, loping between boughs until he reached the glowing eyes of the druid, only pinpricks against the night.

"Do you require assistance?" Kiela asked Ophiera.

Gazing upwards again, Ophiera could not fathom how she would reach the bough *without* assistance. But Jasper stepped between her and Kiela, wrapping his hand around her golden vambrace.

"We'll be fine," he said sternly.

With only a glare to announce her departure, Kiela jumped straight up into the tree, loping between branches with ease in a blur of red. The crimson haze of her magic surrounded her, highlighting her skin beneath the revealing attire before she disappeared into the cluster of limbs the other two had reached.

Ophiera turned to Jasper. "You better have brought the hoist from your ship, or else I'll be sleeping on the roots here. I could never jump that high, even without my armor."

Jasper smiled at her, the expression melting away some of her annoyance. In a blur of movement, he yanked her by the arm, flipping her sword, armor, and all over his shoulder before she could blink. Just as she inhaled to protest this manhandling, he pushed off hard from the ground, forcing the air from her. Her stomach swayed as the forest floor rushed away from her.

A moment later, her feet touched upon a rounded branch within the clustered area. She swayed from the rush, groping to maintain her balance on the thick branches.

"A little warning would have been nice," she seethed at him, holding the trunk for balance.

"I'm not very nice," he shrugged, dropping their tattered bag at her feet.

"Take this opportunity to rest and recover," Alzerbez said from above. They stretched out upon a large branch, yawning with a flare of all their teeth. "Kiela and Iku will keep watch for the Stigma."

"Oh, now I can sleep soundly," Jasper muttered under his breath.

On another branch, Kiela lay lounging with Iku across her lap, running her fingers behind his ears as she glared silently at Jasper.

No matter how quiet he thought himself, it never seemed quiet enough.

Ophiera sighed, growing tired of the continuing tiff. Truthfully, she was tired of everything. She lowered herself, armor and all, down onto a bow and leaned her back against the trunk. It certainly wasn't the most comfortable of sleeping positions, but it was the best she could hope for in a tree while wearing full plate mail. Jasper crouched beside her, studying her for a moment.

"Are you ill?" He asked, removing his glove and touching his knuckles to her forehead.

She leaned away, fighting the urge to lean into his touch. "Just exhausted."

"How?" He asked, dragging her face back to his to examine. "We rode on Iku all day, and yet you look as if you ran alongside him."

"It is her ekath," Kiela said. "We draw further from her anchor, so let her rest; she will need it for tomorrow."

"I didn't ask—"

"But she's right," Ophiera interrupted. "My chest has ached all day with the draw, and it has only grown worse in the last hour. I'm struggling to...to..."

Her words came out as a groan as her chest heaved with pain. The sudden wave felt like the arrow that had pierced her heart, quick and sharp.

"Ophiera? What's happening?!" Jasper growled.

She clutched her chest as it reached a pinnacle, unable to breathe or speak through it. This pain was...different. Neither a call to her soul nor a phantom pain of physical trauma, but an ache of...

"Heartbreak," Kiela said, her voice quiet. "He suffers from heart, not from body or soul, but the drag is just the same. Close your eyes, sister, and let his pain draw you to rest—both your souls need it."

~ Forty Six ~

MEMORIA

Following the success of my first experiment, I decided to take some well-deserved vacation time away from the Consortia. Of course, as an Ambassador, I could not travel unguarded and thus requested Glamwell to accompany me. The fools thought I'd set sail to return to Tanvik—even Glamwell thought as such. But when I usurped the aership and turned our sails northeast towards the Shole, he nearly lost his mind. That was until he saw the skeletal middens from above—the spoils of the Purge. As I suspected, I was not the only one who sought truth in the desert.

My time with the Enclave has confirmed all of my worst fears. Most consequentially, the origin of the Consortia and the lies they have perpetrated. They have poisoned the world with the notion there is but a single power—one mana—one magic—superior to all the rest. Mages—the term the Consortia coined to call themselves—what I have called myself—are those souls born with the mana of the Void, but there are countless other manas—all suppressed by the Consortia. Their lies, perpetuated by their destruction of all other options, have established imperialism over mana and buried what was once common knowledge—the source of the Void and its connection to the Aether.

The Enclave knew. Long before the Purge, when their people spanned dozens of clans, each privy to unique manas and mystics, they knew. United in their diversity, the glory of their civilization has all but been erased by those who wish to dominate. The Purge, justified by the removal of wrongful manas, was, in truth, purely genocide. Only three clans remain, and they now rule the recently freed city of Birozahran. The Civ, the Ailuro, and the Odestal clans—derogatorily referred to as necromancers—the druids and the warlocks by the Consortia and by me, before I knew better...

I wondered why these three were spared, but after spending time in Birozahran, it is clear they were not. The Purge was intended to be absolute, but the three remaining clans survived by refusing to be exterminated. Bonding their souls to anything but the Aether, the birzhan rites they implemented spared their deaths. I knew my little fox was unique, but by the Aether, I had no idea the rarity of such a soul until coming to study with her in Birozahran. I knew our souls were kindred in our sufferings, but to walk amongst a city of souls bearing the burdens...has been overwhelming, to say the least.

They call me a Wielder of Riftwalking but refuse to acknowledge me as a wayward child. I don't mind not being referred to as a child, but many still think of me as an anathema. If only they knew what I set in motion for them, of what my little fox sacrificed for their freedom. But alas, the only path is forward, and forward I must go, though I do not know how I could possibly return to the Consortia after what I've learned here.

Zadok has shared much with me, all in fair exchange, that only confirmed my suspicions about the Consortia. They are thieves who have built an empire on the corpses of the Enclave, castrating those they couldn't kill by forcing them under the Registry. In Feyralis, we placed the Consortia on a pedestal as the apex of our world—the most advanced city-state in Erum, the most potent magic, the best imbuteria...But I know now they are nothing more than barbarians—worse than my own lineage of souls. And the more I learn of Tanvik's origins, the more I know my research is essential to the fate of Erum.

In Tanvik, the Phratries have always known they were descendants of the Enclave—the mother clans, as they often call them. Of course, their origins were all but wiped from existence during the Purge. But long before the Consortia declared war on the clans, some had migrated to Tanvik, establishing many of the cultures we recognize today. The mages of Feyralis and the shamans of the Southern Coastlands are the most well-known of the wayward children, but unsurprisingly, there are many, many more, including those of the Cloister. I left that little tidbit out of my report to the Consortia, but oh, how it intrigued me when Zadock began telling tales of ancient clans that wielded Erum's flame. When I shared what I knew of the Cloister's disciples, the priests, clerics, and paladins who controlled the holy flames, he scoffed and revealed the greatest intrigue of all.

The Phratries' and the Cloister's mana have weakened over time—pathetic shells relative to their ancestors. The Cloister especially has fallen to disgrace in the eyes of the Enclave. Their control over the Aether has become so diluted that they now rely solely on imbuement, forced upon null recruits, that allows them to absorb and manipulate the holy flames, as they call them. The Oaths scarred upon their arms are nothing but imbuteria, apparent to any who knows it well, which I admit is few in Tanvik. The practice is illegal, yes—but even more of an affront is the purpose of the runes.

Upon cross-referencing with Rheta's information on the Cloister, I've come to understand the true meaning of their echelons. Interpreted initially as rank, they are a reflection of the quality of imbuement. The Keepers refer to those who are imbued but unable to wield their mana consistently—the priests and clerics, those who are bound to serve the Cloister. They must remain near the font to be capable of anything useful.

Meanwhile, the Hands refer to those successfully imbued with flames, which few of their order have been deemed for the past few decades. Rheta claims there is another—the Aspects, as she calls them—an echelon so rarely mentioned in tongue or tome that I wouldn't have been surprised if Rheta was mistaken in this rare case. But when Zadock revealed the truth behind the Aspects, the truth of Erum and the destruction they herald...

The beginning of the end looms closer than I dared imagine.

~ Forty Seven ~

ILLUMINATION

Lantern rattling, Myronor dashed to the entrance room as quickly as his trembling legs could carry him. There, he found Kaikora seated cross-legged before the odd, metallic hearth. Her broad shoulders rose and fell slowly as she meditated. And for a moment, he hesitated, wondering if it was worth disturbing her.

But he needed her interpretations of Pyra's writings too desperately. He needed someone to confirm he wasn't going mad.

"Read this," he said breathlessly, thrusting the journal into her upturned palms.

She took a deep breath without opening her eyes.

"Later."

"Kaikora, please..." He begged, voice breaking.

Eyes still closed, she wrapped her large hand around the worn journal.

"And what do you hope to gain by my reading this?"

Myronor swallowed. "The truth?"

"And you think that will help you?"

"I thought *you* would help me."

Her stormy eyes flashed as she looked down at his mother's journal. The book seemed so small in her hands as she ran a thumb along the stacked pages. She flipped the tome open to the bookmarked entry without his guidance.

Impatiently, he paced the room while she read. The frown never left her face as she flipped from page to page, slower than he would have liked. But then again, she hadn't stopped frowning since overhearing Marvena's fate.

Neither of them knew exactly what had happened after the Mistress's threatening words. Kaikora received word that when the Yeoman's people arrived, the cell was left open and empty. Dead or escaped, Marvena was far from their grasp now and even further from Myronor's mind. The only fate he was concerned about now was Ophiera's, and the journal Kaikora was slowly closing, held the clues.

And yet, she didn't say a word.

"Well?" Myronor asked.

"I agree with Pyra's judgment of the Consortia," she said.

He'd never claimed to understand her mood, but her manner tonight was beyond anything he'd come to expect. Kaikora had always been enigmatic but never cruel.

"Did you see the parts about imbuement?"

"Yes," Kaikora said quietly.

"And the Cloister?"

"Yes."

"Damnit, Kaikora!" He shouted, throwing the antracinder lantern against the nearest stone wall. For a moment, he regretted his outburst, but as she continued staring at him stoically, he found his anger only flared hotter. "You said we need to be honest with each other! So, for once in your life, be forthright and tell me if what my mother wrote is true!"

The shaman closed her eyes again, facing the hearth without seeing it. She took a few deep breaths as if she were the one who needed to calm themselves.

"Her words are true."

Myronor sank into a nearby armchair, his legs suddenly weak. And yet she continued.

"The origins of the Cloister, the Phratries, and the dilution of power—is all the truth. Tis why the sight is a rare gift now and why my tattoos hold far greater value beyond the aesthetic."

She flexed her thick arms, the ripple of muscle causing the swirls of green-black ink to move as if alive. Myronor's eyes wandered through the fluidic designs spanning her torso and arms. And where before he saw nothing but art, now he saw the twisted symbols. Like Ophiera's scars and the writings within the dark stone, the signs of imbuteria were undeniable.

"So Ophiera's Oath holds the same power as your tattoos?" He asked.

"Yes...and no," Kaikora said, opening her eyes. She stared into faltering antracinders still scattered on the floor, unblinking until her eyes began to water. Tears ran down her sharp cheeks before she spoke again.

"My tattoos only enhance the mana I already possess—a conscious choice by the Phratries elders. But the Cloister's Oaths...as Pyra said, they are given without consideration and take something in exchange."

"What do they take?" Myronor asked.

"The kindled's will."

He watched the tears of truth stream down her grimace, trying to draw a breath. But he knew too well that taking someone's will was not akin to binding their soul.

"So the runes *do* bind Ophiera to her Oath?" He asked.

"Yes...and no."

He put his face in his hands, quelling the scream poised behind his pressed lips. "Kaikora, please—I'm begging you, just answer me."

The shaman slowly rose from her perch before the hearth and stood beside him. She placed a gruff, placating hand on his shoulder as if the gesture supplied some comfort. But now her touch felt more like a brace than an embrace, as if holding him down to brand him with the truth.

"Ophiera is bound by much, including her fear of extinguishment—which is not a punishment dealt by the Aether itself, but rather a rune blistered upon her arm." Kaikora paused, allowing him to let go of his shaky, held breath. "The Cloister brands all their kindled with the extinguishment rune as a failsafe to punish those who stray from their Oath. Oaths that are themselves dictated and enforced by the Cloister, not the Aether. So...while the runes do bind her to her Oath, it is in threat of pain and torture by the Cloister, not any meaningful consequence to her soul by the Aether."

Myronor clutched his chest as pain beyond the ekath constricted his breath.

Her Oath *was* a lie...

It wasn't the Aether that held her to its will, but the Cloister—the same that now sought her over the sea. She had escaped their will before, though, hadn't she? Away in Iluka, she had retired from her Oath without even realizing it. She had tasted freedom until he had come along and dragged the Aspect of Retribution from her peace. But had the Cloister truly dictated it all?

"What does it mean that she is an Aspect?" he asked through clenched teeth. "You said before her brands were rare, and Pyra confirmed the same."

"Those called Aspects are those who possess the mana of the Aether. They are impossibly rare and difficult to identify, at least until they are kindled. Only then does the Aether interfere with their brands, often becoming incomplete or distorted. There are theories upon theories within the Phratries as to *how* the Aspects come to be, given the loss of their lineage, and how the Aether contributes to their existence, their powers, and armor...All I can tell you is that the flames have always been her destiny, regardless of the Cloister's attempt to contain her."

Myronor remembered his and Ophiera's first night on the road together when she told him of her kindling. All the pain and suffering she had endured...for what? So the Cloister could brand her with their mark, control her power, and force her to submit to their whim? But again, for what? If the Cloister knew what an Aspect was, why did they treat her so terribly? Why did Uzziel despise her so deeply?

Despite the madness of these questions, there was a more pressing query he needed to understand. Ophiera once confronted Kaikora about her Oath shortly after they escaped the Brotherhood encampment. The shaman then hinted at knowing more of her power than she let on, and yet she had never mentioned any of this to Ophiera.

"Kaikora," he hissed, struggling to draw breath. "How could you keep this all from her?!"

She squeezed his shoulder gently, but he shook her hand away. He didn't need her comfort; he needed her to explain! To tell him why, after serving Iluka alongside Ophiera for years, she had never set herself free from the yoke of her Oath.

"I didn't require the sight to know that my words could never convince her," Kaikora said shakily. "And if I pushed the truth, it would have only driven her further away from her fated path."

Myronor glared as she paused, daring her to stop the explanation there. With a sigh, she continued.

"Further from me and that which was destined. If she knew the truth before the Magistrate summoned her, she wouldn't have gone. She would have never left Iluka, never found you, never saved you, never awakened to the power she was born to unleash. While the sight never revealed to me the full extent of her path, it did grant me glimpses of more suffered paths if I forced the truth upon her."

As Kaikora's words sank in, the weight of her honesty crushed him. All these years, she knew Ophiera toiled for nothing—the guilt and the pain her Oath caused her were all meaningless. And yet Kaikora watched.

"How could you ever claim to care for her while letting her believe she was nothing but those damned scars?" Myronor growled, feeling the unfamiliar anger drag across his heart again.

Kaikora held stock still as the tears continued to run down her face. "I mourn for her suffering each day of my life, Myronor. But I do not regret my choices."

His earlier rage continued to clench tightly around his chest, wondering why he was the only one left with regrets. Ophiera had been lied to her entire life by the Cloister, by Kaikora, and even himself. He was no better than the rest, a regret that ate at his very soul as he sat there, reeling beneath the shaman's judging gaze.

It was he who had pulled Ophiera away from her peace, he who forced her power to awaken, and now, his mother's meddling drove her out into the desert. Kaikora may have chosen to keep her in the dark, but it was he that dragged her out into the sun, only to burn.

A burn that he now shared, radiating from his heart down his arm.

"Myronor? What's wrong?"

He couldn't answer as the sensation overtook him. Collapsing to the ground, he clutched his chest as the fire blazed through him. His breath hitched as visions of a dark jungle flashed behind his tear-filled eyes.

"Ophiera!" He bellowed, writhing against the cold stone.

Kaikora's lips moved, but he heard no words as the ekath dragged him far away into a frigid jungle.

~ Forty Eight ~

SAVAGE

Ophiera's heavy eyelids snapped open to the sounds of screams. In the pitch black of the forest canopy, she sensed the others were already awake—sending both relief and worry that she was the last to wake. She blinked to adjust her eyes to the darkness until she could distinguish the outlines of the others in the tree.

Kiela stood far out on a branch, barely bending the bough, scythe held relaxed at her side. Crouched further back, on a thicker limb nearby, Jasper wore his cowl low, eyes staring in horror at something below. She couldn't see Iku and Alzerbez, but she supposed that was their intention.

The shrieks pierced the cool night air again, sending a collective shiver over the group. By the sound alone, Ophiera felt her entire body tense as if transported back to the night in the Sloughmire. The taint of Aud was alive and well here, except this time, there was no Myronor to hold her invisible through the night.

Ophiera rose to her feet, leaning heavily on the trunk for balance. Her armor usually made little sound, but amidst the tense air, her movements sounded thunderous. As the shrieks from below continued, Jasper glanced back at her and placed a shaking finger over his mask to hush her.

Guiding her gaze below, she could just make out five decrepit figures twitching and circling the tree. Their state of decay distorted their forms—some with bloated abdomens and crooked limbs, stumbling across the ground on twisted legs. Three of the figures teetered on two feet while the others crawled on four—all of which made her stomach churn in disgust.

"The Stigma began in the nearby village of Megrim Spa," Kiela said solemnly, without attempting to whisper, "but we all failed to contain it."

Jasper shook his head before crawling back from the bough, moving to stand beside Ophiera. He trembled with every movement, mirroring the leaves in the gentle breeze.

"We were there when the Stigma began," Alzerbez growled, still unseen somewhere in the tree, "and we will be there when you end it, child."

Alzerbez's voice carried such pain hidden within the leopard's growl, layering tremendous pressure on her to succeed. Ophiera swallowed down the lump forming in her throat. The burden of their words and faith weighed on her at this moment, greater than her Oath ever had. But unlike her Oath, ridding the world of the ichor was a burden she felt honored to carry.

Beside the tree trunk, Ophiera gripped her claymore tightly, preparing for the task set before her. She glanced at the blue ribbon and dim crystal still dangling from her sword. Mallow had yet to reappear since the night the girtas attacked, and in this, she found relief. The familiar shouldn't bear witness to what she was about to face, let alone relay the task to Myronor. But as she stepped towards the tree bough, calculating her descent down, Kiela held out a staying hand.

"Save your strength, sister; the jungle will take care of these stragglers."

At first, Ophiera wondered if this was one of the Enclave's nuanced phrases whose meaning had been lost in translation. But as she listened against the night, she heard another sound beneath the afflicted shrieks and bodily drags below.

A faint rustle of the foliage.

"Stay silent and still," Alzerbez whispered, barely audible.

Unsure if Ophiera sensed the fear in the familiar's voice, she looked to Jasper in confirmation. Despite the fox's instructions, his entire body trembled in the dark. Like everything in the Shole, whatever slivered through the jungle now drew terror from beneath his cracking facade. He inhaled sharply, eyes fixated on the forest floor. Following his gaze, Ophiera glimpsed what had caused every soul in the trees to hold their breath.

Vines, barely noticeable, rippled through the underbrush like gentle waves. Raying outward from a distant origin, the front of the undulating forest floor converged on the tree. Ophiera felt every beat of her heart beneath her breastplate as she watched a thick tendril silently crawl up the afflicted's ankles. The other creatures either didn't notice or didn't care as the vines overtook their bodies, winding around each decrepit limb and twisting over their blackened mouths and noses. Only then did the shrieks begin, quickly muffled by the binds. From somewhere in the distant dark, a vibration began, sending a wave of violence that shook the entire forest. As the vines squeezed in unison, blackness splattered over the night as the sounds of squashed flesh and snapped bones reverberated off the trees...

Ophiera swallowed the burn of sick rising from her gut. Spots of ichor, mixed within the blood and entrails, sprayed the forest in a hiss of acrid smoke. Wherever the ichor touched, life burned away to nothing, leaving scars of burning underbrush and dissolving vines.

Disgusted as she was, Ophiera deemed the loss of greenery a small sacrifice for the destruction of those abominations. The forest floor continued to undulate as the vines retreated elsewhere, yet no one spoke or moved. She wasn't sure if it was caution or mourning that kept Kiela and the others still as stone. Jasper, on the other hand, trembled like the leaves in the wind, wide, empty eyes staring into the silent night.

She wasn't certain what drained his nerves so thoroughly—the remnant gore or the sudden silence of the jungle. Quiet enough to hear the wind blowing through the leaves at the top of the canopy. And quiet enough for her to realize that it was not the *wind* that she now heard. From the corner of her eye, she saw them—slowly creeping upon the only movement in the tree—Jasper's shaking form.

"Vines!" Ophiera yelled as she swung her claymore across a set of tendrils.

At her cry, Jasper melded into the shadows, escaping the trailing stems that had managed to avoid her blade. Out on the bough, Kiela remained stoic as before, her only reaction the strange red haze surrounding her body. The cloud of angry miasma expanded outward, shriveling the vines that reached for her. Somewhere above, Ophiera heard the scratches of claws against wood, reassuring her that at least the others were distanced enough from the encroaching climbers. But she had no such skills or luck.

Thick, waxy tendrils wrapped around Ophiera's legs and dropped her to her knees. Before she could swing her sword, they were yanking her down from the thick bough she stood upon. She hissed as the vines continued overtaking her torso and arms, forcing her to grope wildly for her fumbling sword. In her bare palm, she managed to snatch the crystal and ribbon adorning the hilt of her claymore before it fell from her grasp. The clang of her claymore against wood grew further and further away as vine after vine continued to weave around her.

As they had done to the afflicted below, she could feel the vines squeezing the life out of her. And though she felt her breaths draw shallow with the pressure of their ever-coiling grip, her armor prevented the worst. Her only fear at the moment was what would happen when the creepers reached her unprotected head. No matter how many times the ekath had proven her wrong, she was fairly certain she couldn't survive her head being squashed like an over-ripened fruit.

The scent of leather and sea salt flooded her shallow breaths as the vines across her chest began to release their hold. "Kiela!" He barked, slashing at the never-ending growths. "Help!"

In a flash of red, the tendrils shriveled to brittle straws, breaking and crumbling. But Ophiera's relieving breath was short-lived as yet more vines cinched across her ankles and dragged her down from the tree. As she fell, the vines surged upwards, catching her midair and tightening around her like cold, waxy chains. If only the Aether had bestowed upon her a helmet along with her armor...

With her bequeathed gifts in mind, she ignited her arm, burning the vines in a hiss of white fire before they choked her. And once again, free of the tethers, she fell. Perhaps it wasn't the wisest decision to burn the vines that held her aloft, but falling free was still better than being crushed to death.

Her mind changed rapidly as her backside met the forest floor below. The impact forced the air to vacate her lungs again. Surprisingly, the fall was actually worse with armor. The solid metal provided little give and only added weight to her sore limbs as they knocked against the ground.

She hadn't even a moment to process the aches and pains of the fall before the vines overtook her again. This time, they flowed overtop her, attempting to crush her further into the ground. She felt the roots of the tree grind against her back while the snapping of wood echoed in her ears.

In a flash of white flames, the weight of the vines disappeared in a cloud of ash. Coughing on the remnants, Ophiera tried to pull herself up from the divot in the ground formed by her armored body. Thankfully, she succeeded in protecting her clenched, unscarred fist from the ignition, still grasping the ribbon and crystal.

Against the dark, the crystal flashed wildly, and in the strobing light, she saw the entire forest floor undulating towards her. Before she could even think of Mallow, the tendrils converged on her again, wrapping her up in heavy, frigid throngs. Beginning to grow desperate, she searched for the Aether, wondering how much of this jungle she could burn before angering the Enclave. But just as she tried to call forth a blaze of white, the vines yanked her from the ground.

Prioritizing threats as they came, she covered her head with her arms. As the vines formed another tight cocoon around her, she tried to summon the mana within, but as fast as she burned, more vines appeared, never letting her touch the ground. With her mana rapidly draining and her constitution consistently fading, she struggled to fight against the persistent drag of the vines. The tendrils overwhelmed her, thrashing her violently before dragging her deeper into the forest.

As her stomach lurched and her head swam, Ophiera couldn't tell how long or how far she'd been carried. All she could surmise was the vines *knew* not to allow her to touch the ground as they carried her through the jungle. Her stomach churned, the journey far from gentle. And she couldn't help but wonder what had happened to the others. Had the vines squeezed the life out of them as they had the Stigmatized? Or were they, too, being dragged through the jungle now?

Suddenly, the tendrils stopped dragging her and instead turned her up, disorientating her in the air. She couldn't tell up from down for a moment, and only when her eyes stopped spinning behind closed lids did she have a moment to consider. Pressure built behind her ears as the blood rushed to her head. Why were the vines holding her upside down now? Even more surprisingly, why were they beginning to loosen their hold?

Ophiera opened her eyes to find the world spinning in every direction. A gurgling sound drew her eyes downward, taking a moment to focus. Below her head, a gargantuan flower rose from a murky pool of water. Radiating in all directions, the same thick vines that wrapped around her now had weaved a platform around the lily-like petals so wide they nearly reached the shores of the overgrown pond. Centered in the glossy, orange flower, a hole opened, quivering like a muscle rather than a plant. Inside, barbs of bright green rippled in welcome.

As the gurgling sound continued, a single stamen protruded forth from the ominous opening. Ophiera couldn't fight as another vine wrapped itself around her jaw, squeezing painfully as it held her head in place. A cloud of spores exploded from the stamen, burning her eyes and nostrils. Try as she might not to breathe, she choked, forcing an involuntary inhale.

She felt her body fall limp only a moment before her mind went dark.

The numbness was welcome after everything she had endured. But a sharp pain in her chest reminded her of the darkness meant.

Are you in peril again, love?

The relief she felt as Myronor's mind connected with hers made all her suffering worth the trouble. His voice was like a soothing breeze, drawing her from the numbness in a gentle embrace.

Jasper was right...This place really is a death trap.

Myronor's smirk caused her heart to race, even in this state. *Is he with you this time, at least?*

He was...But I don't know if he or any of the others avoided this fate.

Ophiera's mind raced ahead of words, hoping beyond hope they were able to escape in time. The idea of Jasper's vesper coming to rest in the place he never wished to be broke her heart in ways she didn't understand.

I wish I had never left, she admitted.

I wish I had left with you.

Ophiera held on to Myronor's sheepish expression as they exchanged regrets. In the darkness of her mind, his pale, golden hair shone nearly as bright as his eyes.

It's best you're not here, Ophiera said, remembering why she was able to see and feel him so clearly, *then we'd both be dead.*

You're not dead yet.

Though his words said otherwise, her thoughts felt precariously thin—as if a thread was holding her entire being. She supposed that was accurate—a thin blue tether held her soul in place now, one that shook with the effort of keeping her.

Perhaps she had finally pushed the limits of the ekath.

Stop with that nonsense.

Perhaps this truly was the death she could not escape from.

Take what you need from me, and death will never find you.

She didn't understand.

Take what she needed?

She needed air...

She needed an antidote...

She needed to be free of these vines.

And yet the tether shook violently to keep her aware of these needs.

Take more of my strength, Ophiera. Please, you have to fight!

The beseeching voice forced her to focus on the thinning tether. A sudden influx of warmth poured into her heart. And like a parched traveler drinking from a stream, the first drop on her tongue only made her desperate for more. The energy she felt innervating her could not come fast enough. And yet, the more she drew, the more Myronor's face faded from her mind.

I can't keep hurting you like this, Myronor.

You're not doing anything—I'm offering.

I can't...

I need you to stay alive, love. For me.

She felt herself slipping as if pulled away by the tide. Myronor offered her a hand that, if she took, could drag them both out to sea.

She couldn't risk him.

She could never.

Ophiera!

"Ophiera!"

As Myronor disappeared from her mind's eye, a bleary vision of upside-down trees drew into focus. Through cracked eyelids, she saw a pale light dancing between the trunks. Her body, still paralyzed by the toxin released a moment ago, slowly began to descend toward the gaping hole of the flower. And even if she had the strength to fight the vines, her mind was flitting in and out of consciousness so quickly that she couldn't focus on anything besides the sensation of Myronor in her soul. Though she could no longer hear Myronor's voice against her mind, she could *feel* him clinging to her consciousness. And she feared they would not survive another face-off with death. What was the point of taking so much from him if she was only to be eaten whole by the noxious flower?

Again, a light pulsated in the dark between the narrow gaps in the trees. She focused on it, curiosity breaking through her ennui. And as the light grew closer, she could make out a gray leopard, followed closely by Iku, carrying Kiela, illuminated in red.

"Ready yourselves!" She commanded, her burning eyes locked onto Ophiera. "Jasper, on my mark!"

Before she could feel the relief of hearing Jasper's name, Ophiera watched the warlock launch herself from Iku's back. Through the air, Kiela twirled gracefully with her scythe balanced in hand. The arch of her descent left only one possibility for her plan.

After a thick *shing* sounded above her, Ophiera plummeted suddenly towards the undulating mouth. Just as the sickly sweet scent of nectar overwhelmed her, something slammed hard into her side. The smell of lilies was quickly replaced by leather and sea salt, and despite being mere inches from being devoured, she was overtaken by relief.

Jasper had survived. He was safe and, at this moment, saving her.

Together, they landed hard on the shore of the pond. Though her mind was awakening quickly now, her body still had no movement or feeling. With surprisingly little effort, Jasper propped her up against a nearby tree, facing the monstrous flower that nearly consumed her.

A glimmer of the scythe caught Ophiera's eye as it fell into the chasm of the mouth. And as if someone had punched her in the gut, she realized Kiela had dropped within.

She tried to scream, to fight, to do anything to stop the plant from folding its petals up over its mouth and trapping Kiela inside. But her dread turned quickly to darkness as her consciousness waned yet again.

Stay awake!

"Stay awake," Jasper hissed, slapping her cheek.

She barely felt his strike through the numbness, but she did feel Myronor lingering in the dark. Though she couldn't *see* him, she held on to him as Jasper held on to her. The rogue took her by the back of the neck, tilting her head upwards as he uncorked a small bottle. He poured the contents into her mouth as she watched the plant monster begin to shake violently.

"K-K-Kiela," Ophiera begged, barely able to utter her name.

"She can take care of herself," he growled, unconcerned. "You, on the other hand, are more like a doormat for death."

He removed a blade and began untangling the weave of dead vines still wrapped tightly around her. Unlike those falling to her sides, the vines emanating from the closed flower writhed uncontrollably. She wondered, sickeningly, if this was how it digested its food.

But just when her horror reached its peak, the flower began to distend. Bulging outward, the closed petals shriveled at the ends, and a wisp of red haze escaped from the top. At that moment, Ophiera realized just how poorly she had mistaken who the *actual* predator was in this jungle.

The water around the bloated drosera shook just as violently as its body. A loud *pop* resounded through the jungle, and in a glow of crimson, the bulbous body vaporized to nothing. All that remained where the gigantic flower stood was an orb of dark red flames silhouetting a slight woman at its center. Wherever the miasma touched, life shriveled away, leaving nothing behind but the cratered hole flooding with water. With her head and arms thrown out, Kiela arched her spine unnaturally amidst the wrathful, bloody blaze.

The red tendrils retracted into Kiela's body. Her eyes remained aflame, glowing in the darkness. She leaped gracefully, somersaulting towards the bank, scythe in hand, eyes locked on Ophiera.

"Are you well?" she asked, her sing-song voice plagued with worry.

Ophiera's mouth hung agape, and not just from the paralysis. Though the warlock had just been inside the belly of a beast, she appeared utterly pristine; no trace of dirt, blood, or water marred her dark, transparent dress.

"F-fine," Ophiera breathed. "Thought...you were...a meal."

Kiela giggled girlishly. "On the contrary—the drosera was quite delicious."

"What a thing to say after being swallowed whole," Iku yipped, appearing beside Kiela. Alzerbez wasn't far behind, though it was startling to see them transformed back into their human self.

All three examined Ophiera closely.

"Drink," Jasper interrupted, again holding the bottle up to her mouth.

Like a helpless child, she lay embarrassingly useless before them all. But she swallowed her pride, along with the potion, and noticed some feeling return to her fingertips.

Alzerbez crouched and took her closed fist in their rough hands. They tugged the blue ribbon from her grasp, with Mallow's crystal attached, studying it before their dual-colored eyes. To her surprise, a smile crossed their lips.

"You have a good friend in Nijeka, child. Had she not helped us track you, we may not have found you in time."

"Another surprise," Iku yipped from beside Kiela. "Rare for a familiar to help anyone beyond their chosen. You are quite unique."

"And an idiot," Jasper growled, glaring at her. "There were ways to warn us of the vines without drawing them onto yourself!"

Ophiera bristled. She knew his tendencies for cruelty when frightened, but her tolerance waned. Or perhaps it was simply Myronor's response, still lingering in the ekath. She could almost hear him whispering, *You're not nearly as stupid as he is.*

"We should move," Alzerbez said, rising from their crouch. "The commotion likely awoke more of the stigmatized, and there are still several hours before dawn."

They phased mid-jump, landing as the gray leopard in a massive tree near the pond. Loping upwards, they let out a chittering sound that beckoned Iku to follow.

Kiela sighed, kneeling beside them instead of chasing after her familiar.

"Your aura is exceptionally weak," she said, examining Ophiera. "Allow me to share the burden of the drag, for your ekath's sake."

As Kiela stretched her hand towards Ophiera, wisps of the red haze emanated from her nimble fingertips. But Jasper grasped the warlock by the wrist, yanking her away.

"She doesn't need your foul magic," he spat.

Kiela glared at his hand, still as a coiled snake. With a pang of pity, Ophiera realized that his habit of grabbing the wrong women without permission was about to reach a pinnacle of consequence.

"Foul is your etiquette, little Forged One," Kiela hissed, yanking her arm from his grasp. "I am ascendant to the Odestal, and in these lands, *my lands*, your slights against me justify your death! You will not dishonor me again with your *filthy* touch, or I will show you how foul my magic truly is."

"Go ahead, princess—I've already survived the worst your people have to offer, but I'll be damned if I let you violate *her*!"

Ophiera could do nothing to stop the conflict from escalating before her eyes. Though she was at the center of it, a whisper through the ekath encouraged her silence.

"You have no idea what she needs," Kiela hissed. "But I promise, very last on that list is *you*."

"I'd rather be last on her list of needs than top of the list of those who use her!"

Jasper took Ophiera by the arm and hoisted her over his shoulder. With a forceful push, he leaped up into the tree, leaving Kiela's gaze burning behind. After reaching a thick bough, Jasper leaned her back against the trunk of the tree. They were too high for her to see the corpse of the drosera below, a choice she knew was purposeful. She didn't understand how he could be so inconsiderate and considerate at the same time.

Annoyed as she was with him, the returning pain in her chest was far more distracting. With trembling arms, she was able to sit herself up a little straighter.

"Don't move yet," he said, crouching in front of her with a water skin in hand. "The drosera pollen isn't quite the same as the girtas toxin, but they share some alchemical origin. Water sometimes helps the antidote work faster with the *natural* form."

Glaring at the water skin he offered, Ophiera used what little energy she had left to turn away from him. She couldn't really explain why she refused him other than the gnaw of annoyance permeating her gut. The way he spoke to her as if she were a child, the way he was so cruel to Kiela, only to turn around and try to care for her, was a conflict she couldn't contend with at this moment. Not when her chest already ached so painfully.

"Don't be an idiot," Jasper muttered.

With a cold sniff, she closed her eyes, not wishing to see Jasper, or anyone else for that matter. The only presence she needed right now was the pain of the ekath and the lingering feel of Myronor's thoughts within hers.

Roughly, he took her face in his hand and drew her mouth to the open waterskin. She didn't have the strength to fight him or the water gushing into her mouth, and instinct begged her to swallow. He only removed it from her lips after half the bag was drained. With his thumb, he dragged the ripple of water away from her lips.

"Kiela was right to call you a child," he grumbled. "Every time I look away from you, you're throwing yourself into the arms of death!"

"I do not throw myself anywhere!" She hissed, gaining strength. "*You* are the one continually dragging me around!"

"How else am I to protect you when you so willingly seek the quickest path to the Aether?"

"I don't need your protection!"

"Could have fooled me! Twice now, I've witnessed your face absent of life, only see it blink back into existence through that spirit rope madness."

"That madness is what prevents my death, not you!"

"Do you not think he feels it, too?!" Jasper spat, all warmth leaving his amber eyes. "Or do you just not care?"

"What—how dare you!"

"Then why make such reckless choices with him tied to your suffering?"

"Choices?" she hissed, rage pushing her past the hurt of his accusations. "I didn't choose any of *this*."

"Maybe not," Jasper said, his voice faltering as his eyes fell to her arm. "But you choose to fight as someone who has nothing to live for. Life or death—how the battle may end—makes no difference in how you approach it. *Those* are choices."

"I choose what is necessary."

"No, no, no," He laughed mirthlessly, resembling a sob. "You do what first comes to mind. You call me apathetic, yet I have always cared deeply about one thing, and that is my own survival. I know how to keep myself alive, but you, you act with such utter indifference to your very life. I don't know how you survived before he bound your soul to yours! And I don't know how he stands it all when I can barely tolerate *sensing* it!"

Despite the antidote, Ophiera's heart fell numb against his words. All the rage, all her annoyance, extinguished and reignited towards herself. Her own life or death was never a priority while upholding her Oath. The priorities of most of her life had been skewed by the Cloister, viewing her existence as expendable...a tool to be used until it wore down or broke. With only luck and her Oath deciding the timeline, she even wished for fate to intervene early, if only to free her from service.

"I never thought my life would mean anything to anyone else," she whispered.

"It does, and not only to him." All the ire had left his voice as he brushed the hair from her face. "I may not be your ekath, but I *feel* the draw of your soul each time it dwindles. It's as if all air has been sucked from the room...as if someone is drowning me under a sheet of ice. Thanks to these blasted scars, I *feel* what you feel and must assume he does, too."

"He does," she said, biting her lip. "He feels it all...when I burn, when I'm injured, when I'm pained."

"It is his boon to bear for binding you. Though I must give him some credit...the weight of your suffering is a hefty burden to bear."

Jasper skated a calloused thumb across her bottom lip; the desperation in his voice and touch shivered across her skin. The ekath thrummed along with her pulse, and she hated how much Jasper's touch reminded her of Myronor—of an affection she didn't deserve but craved as if owed to her.

Despite everything that had happened tonight, she wanted nothing more than to feel Jasper's lips on hers, against all of her, without armor or inhibition. Her heart spun in loops, confusing itself between Jasper's touch and the lingering feel of Myronor in her soul.

He leaned close again, and for a conflictingly selfish moment, she thought he would kiss her. She wasn't sure she had the strength of body or heart to resist him...but to her relief and frustration, he pressed his forehead against hers.

"Can the mage also feel how your heart races?" he asked huskily.

"Don't be cruel," she said, twitching her face away from him.

"If my affection is cruel, then what is yours? What is love if not *prevention* of suffering, and yet you continually, *knowingly* cause it."

With a waft of leather and sea salt, he stalked away. At the end of the bough, he crouched, gazing over the edge towards the dark forest below. His shoulder shook as he retook the watch, leaving her with nothing but guilt and exhaustion.

~ Forty Nine ~

BLINK

A vision of blurry gray eyes and bronze dreadlocks slowly replaced that of a dark, tumultuous jungle.

"Myronor?"

Kaikora held a lantern aloft, examining him closely as he shut his eyes against the lantern. Instead, he groped for the tether, trying to drag himself back to Ophiera. The despair left by Jasper's words lingered within his own heart, the loudest echo of pain despite everything else she had endured. He needed to return to her; he needed to explain to her just how wrong the rogue was in his understanding of *love*.

"Sir, are you back with us now?"

Despite his efforts, Myronor's eyes snapped open. Behind Kaikora, the shadow of a pink figure moved closer.

"Glamwell?" Myronor groaned.

"I had to fetch him," Kaikora said, dangling the Consortia medallion from one thick finger. "He could hear your screams through the doorway and wouldn't stop ringing that Aether-forsaken gong."

Dragging himself upright, Myronor reclaimed the medallion with a shaking hand. This wasn't the first time Ophiera had dragged him into the darkness of her turmoils, and yet, he felt weaker than he had before. By the dwindling glow of the antracinders, he must have been unconscious for hours already.

"Sir, can you tell us what happened?" Glamwell asked, kneeling beside Kaikora.

Myronor eyed Kaikora wearily, silently hoping she possessed some excuse that didn't rely on revealing the truth. But for once, even Kaikora appeared uncertain about how to proceed.

"Let me be more specific," Glamwell said with a nervous chuckle. "Can you tell us what happened to Ophiera and the others? Is everyone safe?"

Before Myronor could feel the peculiarity of his question, Kaikora jumped to her feet. She wrapped her mighty hand around Glamwell's throat and held him with toes dangling off the stone floor.

"Ooh, ow, careful of my jewelry," he sputtered, groping at her wrists but otherwise relatively calm.

"I should have known you were a spy," Kaikora growled.

"Espionage is rampant in all forms of government, so yes, yes—you should have known."

"To whom do you feed information? The Consortia? The Brotherhood?"

"Neither," Glamwell replied calmly. "And I will be happy to explain everything in exchange for his answer to my question."

Worry etched his features, not in the face of Kaikora's might but in the face of the possibility of Myronor's answer. And though his body remained sluggish, his mind ran ahead, regaining speed.

Glamwell never knew the details he was asking now. The thoughts that had buzzed around his head for days suddenly began to fall into place.

"The people that I saw were unharmed," Myronor said. "Except for Ophiera, of course."

Glamwell smiled with more relief than should have been allowed, given that Kaikora still held him by the throat. She shook her hand and glared at Myronor.

It took Myronor a few minutes to convince Kaikora that this discussion was best undertaken peacefully. Once she'd released Glamwell, the three gathered around the dwindling antracinders, and Myronor divulged everything he had observed in his vision of the jungle.

The vestiges of the ichor, the giant plant creature, and the petite woman riding upon a fox in a haze of red. When he began to explain how Mallow had helped track Ophiera through the jungle, however, the image of a leopard shifting into human form tripped up his words.

It took him a moment to untangle his memories from Ophiera's and to distinguish the recognition he felt from his mind and not hers. Without the eyepatch, he'd only barely noticed...but how had the earless shopkeep transformed into a leopard? And how could they possibly be in the Shole *now*? Jasper needed nearly a week of travel to reach the Shole, and though an aership could manage the trip in a day or two, none were welcome in the desert any longer. There was no denying the person who had examined the crystal held in Ophiera's hand was Alzerbez, as he recalled they'd called them, but changing into a leopard? Was this...

"Sir," Glamwell sighed loudly. "Usually, I wouldn't mind the long pontification—dear Pyra used to trail off mid-sentence constantly. But time is of the essence, so I will make some assumptions about your thoughts and help you along. Alzerbez, of whom I assume you are hung up on, is a druid. They are a Wielder of Coalescence, as are all Ailuro, and thus, they are able to travel through crystals much like your sweet Mallow. Of course, the process requires some adjustments, given their conjoined souls, but once established, they may travel freely between attuned crystals. Alzerbez has established theirs between shops in Krysas and Birozahran for years. So, now that we've cleared that up, can you please continue with what happened after they freed Ophiera from the drosera?"

Myronor eyed him wearily, mulling over the idea of a fused soul and not wishing to speak any further. The way Jasper had simultaneously scolded and confessed to Ophiera had left its mark on his own heart. The strange mixture of guilt and desire churned uncontrollably in his heart amongst remnants of Ophiera's allure and his repulsion of the rogue.

"They discussed resting before..." Myronor began, wiping the sweat from his brow. "Before they arrived at...Megrim something?"

Glamwell clapped his hands together. "I can't believe it...they're actually going to do it."

"Do what?" Kaikora growled, glaring at him with narrowed eyes.

Collecting himself, Glamwell smiled widely at them both. He seemed different from usual—his facade of silliness lifted, revealing watery eyes filled with hope.

"First, I must apologize for hiding myself and my intentions from you all. The plan was always to observe you first, and be honest later."

"And exactly what were you observing?" Kaikora asked, her voice a growl.

"Everything—intentions, behaviors, tendencies. Pyra's son or not, Myronor is part of the Consortia, and any member of the Consortia is a threat to us."

"And who is *us*?" Kaikora barked.

Glamwell's eyes widened as if surprised by her confusion. "The Enclave, of course."

"But you're not..." Myronor trailed off, searching for signs. His eyes lingered on Glamwell's ears, perfectly rounded, with no trace of a pointed end or scars. He ran a bangled hand over his hairless head, lingering over his exposed ear.

"The ends were clipped when I was a babe—they heal better the younger you are. Many of us were hidden from or by the Consortia. It was thanks to Pyra that I discovered myself and my brethren."

"*Who* are you, then?" Kaikora demanded.

Myronor took her literally a moment before remembering the Enclave's ways.

"Like my kin, I am a Wielder of Hollow Vessels, though far less adept given my late start."

Myronor recognized the term from his mother's journals, though he struggled to envision Glamwell as one of the Civ. When Myronor thought of the clan that extracted the power of their vesper as a source of mana, a bubbly man in pink robes did not come to mind. Then again, he'd never *met* a necromancer before. Almost like the paladins of the Cloister, the art of necromancy was used more to scare children into behaving properly than believed to be real. But he had *witnessed* the reality. Instead, Ophiera had—his mind lingered on the skeletal monstrosities that had overtaken Ophiera, haunting his silence.

"While I am Civ, many consider me less, given my upbringing and dual position here within the Consortia. The life of a spy is a lonely one. Pyra used to tell me that she, too, belonged nowhere and everywhere all at once—a curse that became a purpose. And I would guess that's much how Ophiera feels at the moment, too."

"And what do you care about her feelings?" Myronor asked, a sudden fury causing his words to hiss.

"Erum's Flame is our salvation," Glamwell said, dropping his gaze.

Myronor's stomach churned as more shattered pieces of the puzzle fell together in his mind.

Glamwell was a spy...a spy that told him of Pyra's dealings with the Odestal...a spy that had left a trail of bread crumbs that he and Ophiera followed so unquestioningly he found it laughable now.

"You baited Ophiera to the Shole," Kaikora growled, fist clenching, "Was Pyra ever in Birozahran?"

"I have never lied," Glamwell said with a dark expression. "And you, Kaikora, understand how dire our situation is. For years, you have felt the darkness infesting our lands—*your* lands—tormenting the Aether as it spreads. Neither your sight nor the Wellspring can provide you counsel any longer, not on paths the Stigma has touched. Past, present, and future are shrouded, splattered with ink from beyond our world, obscuring our story. We must decide how to end it."

"What do you know of the ichor?" Myronor asked, unable to stop his curiosity.

"I know you harbored Aud's taint when you arrived in Krysas...I was fully prepared to watch Pyra's only son succumb to the darkness...to witness the downfall of Krysas as you became Aud's thrall. But instead, *she* saved you, and everything I thought I knew lost meaning."

"Explain," Kaikora barked, unsympathetic to his diminishing demeanor.

"Do you know how many souls I watched succumb to that blight?" Glamwell whispered. "Despite everything we tried, no magic or medicine could purify the corruption from those it touched. We witnessed an entire village become putrid shells of themselves—we had given up hope until Erum's Flame arrived in Krysas."

"So you lied...to use her," Myronor said in a shaking voice.

"Used, perhaps, but not without fair exchange. And I must re-iterate, I didn't lie," Glamwell added curtly. "You must understand that the situation you've walked into has centuries of discourse beneath it. Pyra understood...she was one of the few who did. And she knew Erum's Flame was our only hope to defeating the Stigma and ending Aud's assault on our world."

Yet again, another something, another someone, sought to claim Ophiera for their own. The Brotherhood hunted her, the Order recruited her, the Cloister pursued her, Jasper coveted her, and now even his mother, along with the Enclave, had used her.

She was *his* ekath, *his* everything, and yet, they endured this torture of separation for a supposed greater good. A greater good that he was slowly suspecting was another one of Pyra's schemes. His mother had somehow ruined much in his life without being a part of it. And now...

"Is my mother alive?"

Glamwell stared solemnly into his eyes, neither nodding nor shaking his head. "I believe so."

Kaikora took a deep breath, crossing her thick arms. "Then where is she?"

"That I do not know. We—Kiela, Iku, Alzerbez, and I—aided Pyra in many ways. Before she disappeared...we were each given tasks and secrets to keep from one another. So, while I do not know where Pyra is, it is likely one of them does."

With each bit of information revealed, Myronor felt his composure slip. Hearing confirmation that Pyra was alive jostled his heart more than he cared to admit. This entire time, he thought *he'd* been at fault for dragging Ophiera out of retirement. Because of him, she had been summoned; because of him, her soul was now bound to his. But now he learned he wasn't the fisher dragging the line; both he and Ophiera were caught in Pyra's net, trailing behind in her wake.

Myronor licked his lips, tasting the salt of his tears trailing down his face. And in that moment, he could only laugh.

"Sir, I'm not sure what's funny, but—"

"What's funny is that I was arrogant enough to think my mother named me her successor because, on some level, she believed in me. Despite my reluctance, I wanted nothing more than for her to think me capable of completing her research...of being an Ambassador. But it seems as if my only purpose was to recruit a paladin...to deliver her to the Enclave's doorstep. That's why it's so hilarious, isn't it? I'm completely unimportant in her schemes..."

"Sir, you misunderstand—"

"I understand perfectly well!" Myronor shouted, no longer certain if he laughed or sobbed. "Everything Rheta told me, everything the Order knew, everything Pyra wrote! She had us all hooked, dragging us along only to reel us in when the time was right...and I, her only son, was nothing more than a baitfish!"

Myronor couldn't speak as the hysterics overtook him. For the first time in his life, he was laughing without joy, crying without sadness. He felt everything and nothing all at once as his perception of purpose crumbled around him. The hows and whys that he so desperately sought in the world suddenly meant nothing.

Warmth enveloped him as a vision of pink took over his tears. Glamwell embraced him, holding him against his chest and letting his tears soak into his robes.

"To Pyra, to Ophiera, to the Enclave, you are more than you know...*your* gift is as rare as Erum's Flame, and even if you were not her ekath, love is the most powerful mana. As one, you and Ophiera are more powerful than any soul that has ever crossed Erum. Which is why, sir, time is now our greatest enemy."

The kindness of his words was quickly lost as Myronor focused on the last sentence.

"Enemy?"

As their gazes met, he knew the answer before the cursed words fell from the Steward's lips.

"The Cloister travels to Birozahran as we speak."

"What?!" Kaikora snapped. "*You* were supposed to send them back to Tanvik!"

"I tried," Glamwell proceeded, "But they made clear their intentions to search the desert the moment Myronor dismissed them. I delayed them in Krysas as long as I could, legally, at least. Only moments before you fell to your fit, sir, did I receive word they were departing the Aerodock to travel through the Shole."

Myronor clutched his chest as if his own heart caved in at the thought of the Cloister. He thought the flower monster had been the latest threat to Ophiera's life, but if the Cloister captured her, he'd lose her forever. The thought alone drove him to madness, and the pain of the ekath only added to the chaos.

"We must leave for Birozahran now," Myronor said. "If we intercept them there—"

"We cannot leave," Kaikora interjected. "The Order has tasked us to find the portal—"

"I don't care about the portals!"

"You must!" Kaikora barked, her eyes widening as if in pain. "This Stigma is nothing compared to what lies beyond the veil! Aud waits, poised to rush the door *your* mother created, and once they possess the key, this world will be plunged into chaos!"

Myronor paused a moment, letting the bitterness of the shaman's words truly sink in. For once, she didn't sound neutrally benign—she was frustrated with their situation and, more importantly, with him. He wondered if this was the first time someone else's machinations had so gloriously outwitted her. Or perhaps she honestly thought that he'd choose Erum over Ophiera.

"The only thing I care for is Ophiera. And *you*, of all people, should agree it is her life that matters most! Not only is she your friend, Kaikora, but you have said yourself we stand no chance against Aud without her!"

"Stop arguing!" Glamwell shouted, moving between them. "There is a solution that will satisfy all parties. If you will, please come with me to the library now."

The Steward patted his pink robes as he stood, waiting for them to follow. Weak as he felt, Myronor pulled himself to stand and follow Glamwell's swift steps, with Kaikora nearly stomping on his heels. The weighted stone felt even heavier in his pocket now.

Through the library door, Glamwell did not lead them to any stack of books or scrolls as Myronor had expected. Instead, he stood before one of the slitted library windows facing the sea and turned to them both.

"As I hope you've understood by now, the portals Pyra developed required a gateway and a keystone on each end of the connection," Glamwell said quietly. "She entrusted us with portions of her work...each of us with a piece of the puzzle. Alzerbez possessed a keystone, while I..."

Glamwell reached within his scant, pink robes and drew forth a string of glowing silver beads. Though Myronor had never seen anything like these before, he was reminded painfully of vespers, only the size of pearls and bound in a line by a leather tassel.

Between his thumb and pointer finger, Glamwell pinched one of the beads, pulverizing it into shimmering powder in his palm. Myronor watched, transfixed, as Glamwell dipped two fingers into the iridescent powder and reached for the empty stone space between the windows. He began sketching with the substance, drawing a series of unique runes Myronor had never seen before in the shimmering pigment from his palm. And under his breath, he sang a chant in a language Myronor *did* recognize.

He hadn't heard Ophiera sing in ages in the mournful tongue Glamwell now matched. His mother's writings had provided the truth, but it wasn't until his moment, as that language spread across a morose tune, that the link became apparent between the Enclave and the Cloister.

When Glamwell's song ended in a trail of hums, the drawn runes ignited in a vibrant flash. After reaching their peak of brightness, the symbols absorbed into the stone, disappearing and spreading like water splashed on sandstone. In their place, a line of blue light traced along the slitted window, much like a doorframe. Though Krysas was carved from dark stone, only now did he see a difference in the stone of this window. Rather than the rough, granite-like texture of the city itself, this particular window had been framed in a smoother, glassier stone, much like the stone he held in his pocket.

"Why do I have a feeling this keystone *doesn't* take us to Feyralis?" Myronor asked, holding up the dark stone.

Glamwell nodded, forcing a hiss from Kaikora. She was unable to hide her displeasure as a grimace fell over her face. She growled, "If not Feyralis, then where does it lead?"

"Another piece of the puzzle," Myronor said wistfully, repeating the words. There was no sense in being depressed about being set up and used by his very own mother. As Ophiera would say, the only path was forward. "I suppose *I* am, too, correct?"

Glamwell nodded again.

Heavy against Myronor's palm, the stone felt suddenly weighed with purpose, more than it had before. Despite Kaikora's bewildered expression, *he* knew exactly where this keystone would take them. All that ran through his mind now was that he should have followed Ophiera into the desert from the beginning. Their suffering had proven over and over again to be completely and utterly pointless. But he refused to make the same mistake twice.

"Kaikora, I'm going to Birozahran to find Ophiera," Myronor said. "You do not have to follow, though I wish you would see beyond the Order."

Kaikora glared at the Steward before turning her sour expression on Myronor.

"It is as Glamwell said; I cannot *see* Ophiera, nor you, nor myself. I cannot decipher the risks or consequences of any choice...but without the sight, I am beginning to care less for fate and more for my friends who are in clear need. I wish to stop the Cloister from claiming Ophiera."

With a curt nod, Myronor accepted the shaman's word and turned his attention to the path forward.

"Where is the other gateway located? I mean, we're not going to appear in someone's home or the middle of the street, right?" Myronor asked.

"I'm not sure," Glamwell said, shaking his head in denial. "Pyra kept many secrets. We must tread carefully."

Risk or not, it seemed this was the singular path before them. Myronor stepped forward to the gateway, feeling the slight hum of imbuteria resonate between the arch and keystone. He wasn't sure what to do next—a lifetime of hesitancy regarding his power stalled him a moment, reconciling how even to channel or summon his innate talent. In the past, he had only acted on instinct, teleporting when he or Ophiera fell in dire straits. In fact...*she* was truly the only reason he had ever spanned. And with her face held in his mind's eye, a surge of power welled within him.

Myronor held out the black stone, concentrating on the runes within. Black turned blue as the inscription synergized with the light surrounding the archway window. As swirls of azure reverberated around him, he felt the familiar compression of the air and, with it, a crushing dread.

But this time, he refused to return to the dark place. He would simply use it, just as Aud intended to use him.

With a steady breath, he poured his mana into the stone, all the while resisting the pull toward elsewhere. The air around him rippled, but no darkness surrounded him. Within the archway, the dark ocean view transformed into a distorted reflection of the library itself. At first, he thought the portal itself was reflective, like the surface of a pool. But as he studied the gateway, he realized it was the glossy stone walls of a cave that mirrored the view of the library.

"Excellent work, sir." Glamwell smiled, stepping forward to take him by the elbow. He had not realized he swayed, nor how costly activating the portal had been. "Rest a moment—I'll go through first to ensure the area is clear."

It was strange watching Glamwell approach the only darkened window amongst a wall of predawn incandescence. As he walked through the archway, his bright pink robes fluttered slightly against the dark walls of the cave.

Kaikora readied her trident and, with one final glance back at Myronor, followed the Steward through the gateway.

Alone in the library, Myronor hesitated.

Suddenly, he felt the weight of his mother's neglectful accomplishments laid before him, staring into the foreign land beyond. She had truly created portals with her magic. *His* magic. Was it for this purpose she had left him and Berwyn behind? When one could create something so powerful, how could it not take precedence over everything else?

He tried to suppress his darkening thoughts as he stepped through the gateway. A weight pressed against his chest, much like the sensation of walking beneath a waterfall. Frigid and heavy, deafening and suffocating, yet the discomfort disappeared the moment he arrived on the other side, stepping into the cool air of a dry cave.

Glancing behind him, Myronor could see the inside of the library framed within an alcove, the shelves of books, and various balconies juxtaposed against smooth, glossy stone. A doorway directly into the Consortia Embassy seemed a terrible security flaw.

Where before he had channeled his power through the stone, he now withdrew it. The portal disappeared, returning to a dark, glassy stone wall hiding the signs of imbuteria carved deep within. Pocketing the stone, Myronor turned to the others.

"Where are we?"

"Beneath the city," Glamwell said in a cautious voice. "Clever, clever Pyra...of course, no one would look here...Follow me quickly."

From an inner pocket of his robes, Glamwell dragged forth the string of beads once more and proceeded to wrap them around his hand methodically. The orbs pulsated with the rhythm of his circling hand, a maneuver of clear routine and purpose. Pale, silver light emanated from them, lighting the cave enough for Myronor to see the dendrites of tunnels branching off in every direction. Mesmerized by the pulsating beads, he followed behind the pink robes, moving swiftly toward a passage to the right.

"Are we sure the Odestal will welcome guests at this hour?"

"The Odestal overlords do not sleep," Glamwell smiled. "But I warn you, only the Odestal heirs, myself, and Alzerbez knew of Pyra's research. The other Autarchs knew of her and the power she wielded and welcomed her as a wayward child. But if they knew of the depth of Pyra's dealings...let's just say it is best to keep silent in all matters of the Consortia and Pyra."

Kaikora and Myronor remained close, examining the indistinguishable tubular paths. No direction seemed to make sense along the winding trek, but Glamwell strode on confidently until a spot of light shone ahead.

"Perfect," Glamwell muttered. "The passage above will take us directly into the Odestal Tabernacle—the clan's territory within the city. We must search for the Autarch's yurt first."

"Search? You do not know where he resides?" Kaikora asked with a hint of accusation in her voice.

"The Odestal are nomadic people, and after the Purge, well, we all found ways to keep our traditions alive. The yurt moves throughout the Tabernacle, but it will be easy to spot for me."

"Why are we bothering with the Autarch?" Myronor asked. "We know Ophiera is in the jungle somewhere; should we not leave to search for her there?"

"And then what?" Kaikora snapped. Her frustrated mood spilled over again as she turned on Myronor. "To best aid her, our purpose is to intercept the Cloister, and the easiest way to do that is to request the Enclave's aid. Their aership will arrive any hour now, and Ophiera is far better off away from the city. From the sounds of it, the Odestal clan is likely the only clan willing to hear us out, given their connection to Pyra. Are you not an Ambassador? Shouldn't these political games be your ideas, not mine?"

Myronor felt the burn of shame, knowing Kaikora was right, of course. The ekath had pulled him towards the irrational choice, though he could never call searching for Ophiera the wrong choice.

"Fine. Lead us to the Autarch."

Glamwell nodded. "Follow me. Do exactly as I say. And whatever you do, do not mention the Consortia."

The path rose behind a line of yurts, sparsely populated and growing denser the deeper from the wall they fell. A few individuals here and there meandered about with large satchels or carts, navigating the chaotic paths between yurts. A few tall, black hoodoos penetrated the endless sea of tents, and from every direction, Myronor heard the trickling of water. Though he knew the city was often referred to as the heart of the Shole, he hadn't expected there to be flowing water in the center of a desert.

Glamwell led them between the thick rows of tents, and while his stride remained confident, Myronor could not understand how he navigated the place. There were no paths, no signs, no landmarks, only flags of a splattered, slitted eye that hung from some of the tents. But soon, they halted before a cluster of large yurts with many emblems hung about, and Myronor knew there was a method to his madness. Glamwell peered around the corner of the tent they had approached. Myronor and Kaikora joined him, eyeing a guard clothed in the same dark tabard standing outside the largest tent. Glamwell turned to them, mouthing the words 'stay' before marching forward.

After the two men clasped hands and smiled, they spoke in low tones that Myronor could not hear.

"They know each other," Kaikora said under her breath. "The guard is glad to see the Consortia remains ignorant of him...but he's wondering why he returned to Birozahran so suddenly..."

"Has the sight returned?" Myronor asked.

"Not quite, though I can read the words as they cross their lips," she smiled. "He beckons us now."

Glamwell waved frantically, holding the tent flap ajar. Kaikora led, as Myronor followed quickly and quietly. Once past the flap of the tent, Myronor walked directly into Kaikora's broad back. His vision danced as if he had struck a stone wall, but as she moved aside, he saw why she had halted dead in her tracks.

A man in black robes, his blood-red eyes gleaming, stared them down. At his feet, a beautiful silvered crimson fox lay, her sharp yellow gaze inciting the same disquiet as the man.

Myronor's mind tickled with recognition.

As he had with the Chaplain, Myronor *recognized* this man, though he had never met him. Not only from Ophiera's memories but from the color of his eyes—Kiela possessed the same crimson gaze. While he assumed they were related, the man's ageless appearance of translucent skin and dark hair made it difficult to guess the relation.

Glamwell followed last into the tent, whispering to Myronor and Kaikora as he passed. "Let me speak to him first."

"There's no need, Glamwell," the Odestal said, stepping towards Myronor. "As Autarch of the Odestal, I, Zadok no Enukaja, welcome all wayward children amongst our clan—even the son of Pyra, Wielder of Riftwalking."

~ Fifty ~

AFFLICTION

While Jasper normally found the perpetual shade of the jungle a comfort, today, he only wished for more light. Last night's catastrophe had left him jumpy, suspecting every dark vine of undergrowth was out to get him. Exhausted, he remained alert by agitation alone.

If only the Stigma had not disgusted him so…if only he had not let fear whittle his guard down. Without Ophiera's moment of warning, he would have met a violent death. Even as he watched the vines drag her away into the jungle, he had allowed his terror to maintain control. And as much as it pained him to admit, if it were not for the Odestal princess ordering Alzerbez to search for Mallow's signs and Iku to give chase, Ophiera might have been swallowed whole by the drosera. With quick, calculated decisions, Kiela had remained calm and in control. And for this, Jasper despised her even more.

At first, he believed the warlock was heartless, exemplifying the apathy he so desperately sought before. But as he watched her leap into action to save Ophiera, he sensed her emotions as clear as the red haze emanating from her. She had felt nearly as terrified of losing Ophiera as he was, and yet, she shut the emotion off like a floodgate when the time came to act. It was a mastery of oneself he had never witnessed before and one he envied greatly.

Far ahead, Kiela led their party through the jungle. The warlock took the lead this time, using her derivations to clear a path forward through the dense forest. Iku, of course, followed closely behind with Alzerbez, in their leopard form, alongside him. Meanwhile, Ophiera trudged along, lone and silent, far behind the three and a reasonable distance ahead of him.

Since departing for Megrim Spa, she hadn't spoken a word to him, nor he to her. From behind, he watched her white braid swing like a pendulum, consistent and mesmerizing against the dark green surroundings. That was until he saw the smear of azure that adorned the hilt of her claymore. The blue ribbon tainted the craftsmanship of her weapon, much like the mage himself tainted her.

Quickly, his thoughts grew bitter, knowing that were it not for the mage, Ophiera wouldn't be alive. Then again, none of this would have happened were it not for the mage. There would be no need to venture into the Shole and no need to face the girtas or the Verdigris beasts. No need to discover the fate of Pyra Ebontide.

A new fury quickened his strides as Jasper caught up to Ophiera. She pretended not to notice him, only fueling his foul mood.

"What will you do if they refuse to tell us of Pyra?"

A shiver of tension crossed her shoulders before she sighed, "I don't know."

He scoffed. "Should I remind you that they have no reason to provide you information *after* you've cleaned up their mess? But they have every reason to hold it over your head."

"Kiela gave us her word," Ophiera said quietly. "And she's given me no reason to distrust her."

"She has also given you no reason to trust her."

"She defeated the drosera last night to save me. That seems reason enough."

"She *devoured* that drosera, and her reasoning was self-motivated. She needs you alive and well to do her bidding, to use you as everyone else has."

"And you're somehow exempt from this?" She spat, still refusing to turn and face him as she walked ahead.

He recalled their duel on the cliffside, feeling a moment of shame for his behavior. Though truthfully, his actions that day still set him apart from everyone else.

"Maybe I have used you, but never your power—I have never asked you to burn."

She recoiled at his words and remained silent for some time. He needed her to understand who these people were; she needed to learn of the danger she faced. No matter the experience she might have with the Stigma, she had never dealt with a warlock, let alone any of the Enclave. Kiela had already laid claim on her, calling her sister or whatever other nonsense she'd spouted. He feared what might bind her back in Birozahran after she completed this task.

"If we get nothing from this other than ridding Erum of a drop of that pestilence, it will be time well spent," Ophiera finally said in a harsh tone. "This Stigma is the same vileness from the Sloughmire, the same ichor that nearly took Myronor from me, and that is reason enough for me to burn."

"Not for me," Jasper grumbled. "If only I had let the ichor claim him on my ship—"

In a blur of gold, Jasper fell hard against the forest floor. Stars flashed across his vision as he held his aching jaw, hoping it wasn't broken. Ophiera flexed her golden gauntlet, glaring down at him with drawn features. It was the first time she'd faced him today, and the first time he realized just how exhausted she looked.

"*You* never had to come," she said in a trembling voice. "And mark my words, if you wish death upon my charge again, I will ensure you beg for your own!"

Jasper wiped the trickle of tangy blood from his lip. Examining the crimson smear on his glove, the demons began their screams of indignation.

"Doesn't threatening me violate your precious Oath?"

Cold metal rang in his ear as she drew her sword swiftly against his neck. Every muscle in Ophiera's drained face strained in a deranged expression, a mixture of agony and anger.

"Do not dare speak as if you know what binds me!" she screamed. "Of what I must do!"

Before his very eyes, her rage unraveled, and once again, he found himself adrift on a boat in a storm. Nothing more than a cowardly pirate upon the beach of Iluka, facing death at the hands of the berserker woman. Genuine fear trickled down his spine, no longer craving the danger she exuded but trembling before it.

She would kill him if he pushed her. And yet, the demons within called for it.

A pair of crimson eyes peered over her golden pauldrons as Kiela placed a gentle, slender hand upon the blade of the sword. Ophiera didn't flinch as the warlock pushed the blade away from his throat and into the dirt nearby. Her dark, full lips barely moved as she spoke.

"My sister, I cannot imagine the pain you suffer. Come with me."

Ophiera hesitated, her fury fading into anguish before relinquishing her sword to her back. With one last furious glare, she followed Kiela's lead, leaving him laid out in the dirt. Stunned, he watched as Kiela placed an arm around Ophiera's armored waist, enveloping them both in a thin haze of red energy.

Jasper's stomach lurched. He drew himself shakily to his feet, but before he could draw his blades to put an end to the derivations, Alzerbez had stepped before him on two legs. Even in their human form, they exuded a wild air, with no ears and differently colored eyes. He didn't wish to fight the druid and moved to walk around them.

"Leave them be. She needs help you cannot provide, Forged One."

"Help? With what?"

"As if you don't know; you prod at her with the accuracy of an arrow aimed straight at her heart."

"I do nothing of the sort," Jasper spat. But still, they wouldn't allow him to pass.

"You really are that oblivious..." they sighed. "Can't you see her soul is tormented—the ekath is tearing her apart. She draws from him to survive, and now must knowingly cause him agony as she prepares to set the Stigma ablaze. Could you march on, knowing that you would subject your soul bond to the torture of the flames?"

"She doesn't have to burn if you tell her of Pyra's fate," Jasper spat. "Don't pretend to be noble when you and the warlock need her in prime condition to clean up your people's mess."

Jasper caught a glimpse of Ophiera and Kiela over Alzerbez's shoulder. The two women now spoke in low voices, too low for even Jasper to hear. Through the red haze, he thought Ophiera's shoulders looked more relaxed, the lines of her face no longer contorted in anguish. Still, if Kiela truly wanted to help Ophiera, she would simply reveal Pyra's location without this exchange of favors.

"There are things more important than suffering," Alzerbez continued. "We are all ekatma here; we at least understand her strife in a way you cannot. Why do you think the soul-bonded are so rare?"

"Maybe people aren't meant for that type of commitment," Jasper murmured.

"Fool," growled the druid. "Most *die* during the rituals, even amongst the Enclave who have practiced the birzhan rites for centuries. That is why only the heirs of the Odestal bind with their familiars, why the Ailuro are so few in number, and why the Civ die so young. Even those who survive the rite often go mad as ekatma! And while you may have suffered much in your life, you cannot imagine the agony of two souls bound but forced apart."

"My suffering has only been caused by filthy innaturals like you."

They sighed, shaking their wild locks in disappointment. "It is truly pathetic how certain you are our people will hurt her, yet you have harmed her most since your arrival to the Shole."

Alzerbez's skin turned suddenly, and with a growl, they shifted while catching up with the others ahead. Jasper stood still alone, immobilized by conflict. Had he really caused her pain?

From the night he'd held the knife to her throat, he had been abhorrent. He'd left her to suffer alone on his ship, abandoned her to travel the Shole alone, and now, only served as a burden amongst the three Enclave.

As Jasper stared at the four ahead, he felt out of place again. His was the only unbound soul amongst them. But he had chosen to serve Ophiera, to follow her, to dedicate himself to her, and yet, he had driven her to the brink with his childish behavior.

"Come! We must discuss strategy," Alzerbez roared, twitching his tail at Jasper to catch up with the group.

The burn of shame only worsened as he approached. Ophiera seemed better, though still wary of his gaze. Meanwhile, Kiela seemed to burn a hole through his head with her crimson glare.

"Megrim Spa is near," Alzerbez said, pacing as he spoke. "The Stigma cannot send its thralls out in the daylight, but we must still watch our steps for the taint within the ground."

"I should go alone," Ophiera said quietly. "If I lose control, and anyone is near me—"

With two slender hands, Kiela grasped the sides of Ophiera's face. Jasper thought for a moment that she intended to kiss her, but she smiled as she studied the paladin's defeated expression.

"You wield Erum's Flame, sister," Kiela said in her sweetest voice. "You control the very fabric of existence! Do not let the Cloister lay claim to your gift, for it is *you* who is the gift. Allow nothing but vengeance to guide your hand, and our souls will be safe within your grasp."

Ophiera nodded against the warlock's hands, the slightest smile crossing her lips. It seemed Alzerbez was right. It was he, and only he, that had caused Ophiera harm. Looking away, Jasper's eyes fell on the stone nearby.

Covered in vines, only now did he recognize the obelisk of black, carved with familiar sgraffito. Reaching a gloved hand, he pushed aside the tightly wrapped greenery and studied the pictographs carved into the stone.

"Was Megrim Spa one of the aqueduct control locations?" Jasper asked.

"Ah, so you're not *so* dumb," Kiela turned to him with a satisfied smile. "The village was one of the five control stations usurped during the rebellions. Another reason we must resolve the Stigma here and now."

"What do you mean?" Ophiera asked, glancing between Jasper and Kiela.

"There is too much history to explain properly," Iku interjected, his tail low between his legs. "But in short, the aqueduct here feeds into Birozahran. When the village fell to the Stigma, we closed the aqueduct to prevent it from reaching the city. But as this darkness spreads—if this taint flowed into the city, the Enclave would fall to subjugation, yet again."

"And if the Enclave falls to the ichor, all of Erum will shortly follow," Alzerbez added grimly.

Jasper felt the sudden tension ripple across the group. He felt the desperation and grief radiating from Kiela, Iku, and Alzerbez in unison, overwhelming him. They truly believed that if the Enclave became thralls of the Stigma, the world would surely follow. They truly believed Ophiera was their only hope...

Anger ebbed into empathy as the gravity of their situation suddenly weighed heavily on his chest. This wasn't a matter of a favor, of exchange—this was a matter of survival. Threat of death drove the Enclave's decision to withhold Pyra's location in exchange for salvation, and he, more than anyone, understood the drive to survive.

Only recently did the Enclave attain their freedom from the Consortia, but they now faced the threat of the Stigma. Jasper had always viewed derivation magics as vile, but perhaps...perhaps their magics were more testament to their perseverance than perversion.

Everything had been taken from the Enclave, and yet, they persisted. Everything was lost, and yet they survived. His only fear now was the cost that came with that survival and how it would weigh on Ophiera in the task to come.

* * *

The ruins of Megrim Spa loomed before them, reclaimed by dark moss and tendrils of overgrown vines. As the party marched through the ruins in solemn silence, Jasper observed carefully. It was a habit to inspect every minute detail of his surroundings, even if the surroundings happened to resemble a living nightmare.

A blackened sap oozed from the trees bordering the clearing of the village, their branches thin and barren of leaves. In some places, the ground itself appeared darker than the forest, stained with a substance resembling dried blood. But he knew it to be the Stigma by the small bubbling mounds of blackened ichor sundering the ground.

Alzerbez did their best to avoid the ichor as they led a trail through the abandoned village. The ichor and infrastructure grew more frequent as they progressed. The abodes, whether made of stone or wood, only consisted of archways, often of various sizes and odd shapes. Jasper guessed they likely accommodated the various forms of the druids. The sorrow leeching from the others prevented his imaginings of how the village might have appeared before, inhabited and untainted.

Jasper could see the weight of the destruction on Ophiera's pauldrons. Her footsteps were heavier than usual; her fists balled as her eyes darted over abandoned homes and decaying forests. The desecration only grew worse the further they traveled. And the scale of the task finally hit him. How long would she need to burn to rid this place of so much vileness? So far, it seemed too much.

Through the worst of the desecration, they finally reached the village proper. As with most Enclave settlements, a font signified the center. But this one appeared quite different from others he'd known.

The dark, shallow basin was not filled with bubbling groundwater as expected. Instead, a nightmare of viscous tar gurgled within, the thick sounds sickening Jasper nearly as much as the stench. Dragging his cowl over his nose and mouth, he wished the cloth covered his eyes as well.

He didn't need to see the draped limbs pouring from the basin like the ichor itself. He didn't need to see bones and flesh of both hand and paw alike. Just as Col had described in the Sloughmire, the dead monstrosities roaming the night must have returned to the fount by day.

Alzerbez hissed, their eyes darting wildly around the scene as streams of tears dampened their fur. Iku stood beside them, his head hung low in mourning. And Jasper wished again for the gift of Kiela's apathy.

"They didn't deserve this fate," the fox sniffed.

"That is why we come to avenge them," Kiela spat, all sweetness in her voice gone.

And for a moment, Jasper felt her rage flicker as her control faltered. Like the crash of a wave, her heart unleashed nearly toppled him in its brevity.

He and Ophiera were intruders on their grief, and yet, the paladin stepped forward, just as solemn as the rest.

"I will do my best to honor your kin," she said, bowing her head to Alzerbez.

"We know...and we will all bear witness to your justice."

The emotion emanating from the druid didn't quite match the literal meaning of their words. To Jasper, "bear witness" meant something nearly nefarious—to spy and report back. But the druid's stance and voice all spoke to a deeper meaning, as if something honorable, shared between kin.

Kiela and Iku bowed to Ophiera before retreating several paces and entering one of the ruined hovels. With their tail swishing agitatedly, Alzerbez hesitated before bowing and trailing behind them, leaving Jasper and Ophiera alone.

"Go stand with them," she said quietly. "It will be safer there."

But he found he could not move.

"Won't this be painful?" He asked naively.

"Excruciating," she breathed. "For me and Myronor...and I suppose you as well, if you can sense it. For that, I truly am sorry."

"Don't apologize to me. I've only added to your burden since we set sail."

"That's not entirely true," she said with a sad smile. Tears welled in her eyes, stalling the words he sensed at the tip of her tongue.

Jasper stepped closer, wiping the escaped tear on her freckled cheek.

"Is there nothing I can do to ease this task?"

Ophiera met his gaze, her eyes suddenly ablaze. She removed her sword from her back, holding the hilt to him. The blue ribbon and shining crystal were adorned on it again.

"I would entrust this to no one else, Jasper."

He grasped the sword, hand beside hers, but she didn't let go. She stared at him with such pain that he could not help but reach for her. When the palm of his hand cupped her jaw, she leaned into it, closing her eyes. As he did last night, he pressed his forehead against hers, feeling her shaking breath through his cowl and everything else in between. Through her determination and apprehension, he felt how his touch brought her a moment of comfort. He felt her heart ease as they breathed together in unison.

Why had he been so cruel before when *this* truly satisfied him? To comfort, to protect, to serve her and only her—his berserker, his lodestar.

"What would you ask of me if things go awry?"

Ophiera smiled sadly before kissing his palm and turning away. Leaving his hand outstretched in the air, she stepped toward the pool of death, looking back at him over his pauldron.

"Run," she said before igniting her arm in bright, holy fire.

Jasper gazed upon her in equal horror and awe as the flames traveled across her body, slowly engulfing her in flames. The golden armor gleamed before darkening against the brightness, like slag floating in molten iron. With slow, deliberate steps, she entered the nightmarish pool, her flames rippling through her hair and undoing her braid. The dark water churned from her blaze, sloshing outward around her waist as if repulsed by her presence. And to his utter disgust, the protruding limbs of the dead began to twitch and twist towards the threat to their repose.

Hesitantly, Jasper took his place by the others, leaning against the doorframe of the hut. Even from this distance, he was unable to withstand the sensation of searing skin so near and dropped, resting on his laurels. The warm brush of soft fur against his shoulder alerted him to Iku's presence, and with the fox beside him, the sensations nulled to a tolerable level—another trick of the familiar, welcomed in this moment.

Jasper refocused on Ophiera. The writhing vileness hissed and smoked as it burned against her armor. Reflecting the pale flames, the black liquid retreated from her blaze as if an invisible barrier existed between her and the ichor. Swirling and churning, the ichor rose high in the air—its only path of escape upwards. And in a wave of repellence, the darkness crashed over her, engulfing her in shadow.

Jasper's screams matched Ophiera's as she erupted into a pillar of flame. Iku's presence couldn't block out the agony shattering his soul. As he watched the fissures of white flames spread across the ground through watering eyes, he bit down hard on his lip and forced himself to silence. If she could endure the pain of the flames, then he, as her sworn, must do the same. Her suffering was his both his punishment and penance for the years spent running from her—for failing her. The least he could do was bear witness to her power, transforming his shame into pride as he swallowed her agony whole.

From her pyre, a vile plume of smoke rose, followed by the tendrils of white flame and smoke spidering across the ground. And for a moment, he feared she had lost control. For a moment, he envisioned an entire village caving in beneath them. But as the ground burned, he noticed the flames travel in distinct patterns—following predestined paths—a precision burn.

"She's magnificent," Kiela breathed from behind him.

"Glorious," Alzerbez said.

Iku yipped softly, "Cautious, too."

With his snout, the fox indicated the circle of emblazoned runes around the abandoned hut they stood within. No fissure of flame penetrated the protective circle inscribed in a language Jasper painfully recognized. Turning away from the symbols, he forced his still-watering eyes to bear witness to the white flames and screams that never dwindled.

~ Fifty One ~

RESTITUTE

In the yurt, Myronor was acutely aware of falling to the cold sandy ground. He was also vaguely conscious of Kaikora, Glamwell, and Zadok hovering above him with concerned expressions. Like the times Ophiera had burned before, he remained with himself, unable to think or speak over the agony of the phantom flames. As his skin seared and his screams grew, Myronor wondered when, if ever, the pain would end.

"Their bond is powerful," Zadok said quietly, kneeling beside him.

The Odestal Autarch had barely welcomed them before the fit had taken Myronor. What an impression he must be leaving, screaming and writhing before the red-eyed clan leader.

Zadok held out his hand above Myronor's chest, and through watering eyes, he followed the red tendrils of smoke that traveled from his slender fingertips. The wisps of derivation embedded themselves into his torso, dulling the pain enough for his screams to subside. Whatever the Autarch cast upon him, it relieved his agony to a smolder of pain.

Zadok grunted as he closed his eyes.

"What's wrong?" Glamwell pressed.

"The pain is exquisite. I'm impressed he has withstood her unabated before."

Another wave of fire shook them both, forcing more whimpers to escape Myronor's lips.

"S-s-he's never—" Myronor began, swallowing another wave of pain, "b-burned like t-this."

"I see," Zadock said, running a placating hand across his sweat-covered forehead. "Child, her soul cries for yours—not in the way of life or death, but for something deeper of heart. If you want to ease this pain, stop resisting it. Don't try to bear this for her, but rather, meet her there."

The Autarch's words made little sense at first. But Myronor grew more desperate for relief every moment, even with the help of the red magic. Closing his eyes, he grasped in the darkness of her suffering for the tether. And the moment he found it, his world erupted in white flames, deafening him with their roar.

To his surprise, the pain subsided, and through the brightness, he searched for the amethyst eyes he desperately wished to see. Amongst the flames, a gleam of gold caught his eye. Ophiera's damascus armor shone like a beacon, drawing him as a moth to a lantern. Her hands were outstretched, fingertips dancing in the lick of the flames with a set jaw and closed eyes wet with streaming tears.

Ophiera?

She gasped, her eyes widening and reflecting the fires surrounding her. He found he could do nothing but stare, drinking in the sight of her amethyst eyes softening with something deeper than shock. Tears trickled down her freckled cheeks as she smiled—a vision of perfection that he could not have possibly imagined.

With a few swift steps, Myronor reached for her through the flames. He no longer burned with pain but with a need for her and her alone. Trembling as he took her face in his hands, he felt the heat of her skin and the moisture on her cheeks. She was tangible, real, and the feel of her alone relieved the never-ending gnawing in his chest. He didn't understand how this could not be a dream...But her eyes held more than tears, more facets of realness that proved his love was truly in his arms again.

And her lips...

A kiss had never relieved so much suffering before. She moved her mouth with his in a fervor that surpassed the fires they withstood. She even tasted as he remembered, and he swore his lips would never leave hers again.

I don't understand, she said, her voice grazing in his mind. *How is this happening?*

Does it matter? I only care that you're here.

She smiled beneath him and, if possible, ramped his heartbeat even more.

Your lack of questioning only makes me more suspicious this isn't real.

I don't have a need for answers anymore, he said, weaving his hands through her hair.

He felt her lips pull away from his, confused by his thoughts. But he dragged her back to him, kissing her more fiercely than ever before. In all his years on Erum, he'd never needed something as desperately as he needed her right now. And she deserved to understand why.

You are my answer, Ophiera—the destination of all paths, the resolution to all uncertainties, the final chapter of every book. You are my soul, my love, my life—You are my everything, and with you, I need nothing more of this world.

Though she said nothing beneath his embrace, he felt his words reverberate through her beneath his embrace. The flames drew closer and closer, yet never burned, as her lips danced with his in growing intensity. With a flare of fire, his clothes disintegrated to ash, and piece by piece, her armor fell from her body, all vanishing into the white flames until there was nothing left between them.

Ophiera ran her scarred hand up his chest, cupping his jaw before pushing him down into the flames. As could only occur in the depths of their consciousness, he fell back against the white fire, feeling nothing but the warmth of her embrace. Her lips never left his as she straddled him, both of them equally bare and equally desperate. His hands found her hips, remembering and memorizing the curves of her body against his over and over again.

The moment she took him, every nerve in his body lit up like flames. As one, just as they were meant to be, Myronor felt his very soul forge with hers as she began her rhythmic dance against him. And in the fires, he lost himself wholly to her.

For what felt like a glorious eternity, more than lust and love were exchanged between them as they melded. Images of the desert city and jungle vines flashed through his mind as she lost herself atop him. And though in the memories he *felt* the stings of the girtas for himself, the squeeze of the drosera, and the caresses of Jasper, they were nothing compared to the pure bliss of their reunion now.

For one disappointing moment, he wondered how much of his memories were being transferred to her. But if she had witnessed his endeavors with Marvena, the Cloister, and his travel to Birozahran, she didn't act on them. She only continued to love him in ways he so desperately needed. Though the white fires surrounding them reminded him of *why* they were together at this moment, he knew it couldn't last. Eventually, she would stop burning. Eventually, she would be gone from his soul again.

Don't, she said, her thoughts as frantic as her kisses. The flames licked over his flesh, wrapping him in a possessive heat that should have felt wrong, but with Ophiera, it only felt right. *If I have to burn for eternity to keep you with me, I will, Myronor. You're my charge, my ekath—mine.*

And though her words only ignited more flames from deep within his heart, something shifted darkly within the tether. He tried to ignore the dreadful pull, like a tide drawing from the shore, that threatened to take him from Ophiera, still burning in white flames. But as the fires began to sear his skin, and her skin turned to ash, a devastating darkness overtook him, leaving him alone with nothing but a surge of immeasurable agony.

***

"Syrina, calm down—"

"I will never be calm with two *anathemas* in our midst!"

"They're not *anathemas!*"

Myronor cracked his eyes open, recognizing Glamwell's voice. With his cheek pressed against the sand, he struggled to focus in the dim yurt. Only a pair of thick ankles and the end of a trident came into focus, though there was plenty of movement beyond.

"The pale-haired one bears the filthy signet! His clothes look and *smell* of Consortia, just as *you* do!"

"The Consortia may claim him in service, but he is of Tanvik! A wayward child—both he and his companion. Now, please, Syrina, be reasonable."

As the room came into focus, Myronor recognized Zadok standing beside Glamwell near the mouth of the tent. Between them and Kaikora glared a tawny lion that nearly disappeared against the canvas, so similar in color. As it roared, Myronor's gut lurched painfully, and his ears ached.

He'd read of the lion familiars in books—drawn as shaggy-maned, monstrous versions of his little Mallow. But in person, there were far fewer similarities than differences compared to his cat.

"Reasonable is me not tearing out their throats," the lion growled, surprising Myronor again. He had no idea familiars could speak aloud, let alone threaten other souls. From the few bits known of the Nijeka realm, he had come to understand they were relatively peaceful. At least, his Mallow had always been.

"Under the laws of restitution," the lion continued to growl, "I claim the pale-haired *anathema* for the Ailuro. The other child, well...whether you are born or Forged, it doesn't matter—out of my way or suffer the same!"

"I will not allow you near him," Kaikora said, digging her trident further into the sand.

The ekath's drag kept Myronor pinned to the ground, unable to intervene. He watched, helpless, as Kaikora's trident twisted in the sand before rising out of sight. As sand sprinkled across his cheek, he felt the air crackle. And with a roar, Syrina pounced.

The sound of teeth grating against metal curled his spine, but he could only see the dancing sand scatter upon the floor. Suddenly, the sound of rushing water and growls stopped his heart, but before he had suffered a single splash, pink robes flooded his vision. With his arms beneath his own, Glamwell dragged Myronor from the conflict, clenching the glowing beads in his closed fist. As he settled him against the yurt wall beside Zadok, the Steward returned to stand guard between the ensuing battle and the Autarch.

Myronor couldn't look away from the violence. The lion now had the shaman pinned, bearing down on the trident that only just held her at bay. From the stone font, Kaikora drew water like a lasso, wrapping around the throat of the lion and drawing her backward. Syrina gnashed her jaw, trying to bite *through* the metal handle. And by the protesting cries of creaking metal, it appeared she might soon succeed.

Snap.

The shaman's trident broke in two, though she held on tightly to the pointed end. Snapping jaws had only been held back by the water leash, and only just—Myronor watched in horror as the razor-sharp fangs inched closer and closer to Kaikora's neck, the water dwindling and dripping into the sand.

But as the water pooled on the ground beneath the lion's belly, he realized it fell with purpose. The shaman nearly relaxed as her eyes mirrored over with the slightest twitch in her lips. Again, the air crackled, and the pooled water exploded upwards with the force of a geyser. A painful roar shook the entire yurt as the water punched the soft center of Syrina's abdomen. As she toppled to the ground, her roar died to a hiss, which soon became gasps.

While the lion struggled to pull herself upright, Kaikora rolled to her side, flourishing her broken trident at the font. The sea glass whined with power as spears of water rose behind her, each aimed toward the struggling lion. She placed the edge of her weapon against Syrina's throat, teeth gnashed.

"Yield!"

But the lion refused to budge.

Eyes wide, Myronor noticed her two different colored irises held identical whispers of fear. As Kaikora inched the spears closer, the lion closed her eyes tightly in refusal.

At a loss for words, Myronor couldn't believe the Ailuro Autarch would accept death over defeat. What was the point of fighting all these years to free her people if she were to just die at the hands of a stranger now? With his thoughts whirling, he watched the scene with bated breath, waiting for one of them to call the other's bluff, but neither budged.

"Tis not their way," came a voice from the yurt entrance. A man with no hair and only white eyes stepped into the tent. "The Ailuro fight to the death when challenged."

Kaikora huffed a breath. "Those were not the traditions I learned in the Phratries. Had I known, I would not have challenged her."

"Much has changed since the Purge, my child."

With a deliberate splash, Kaikora released the water spears, spidering around her. Only Myronor and Glamwell twitched with surprise. Slowly, she removed the trident from the lion's neck, holding the half weapon lax at her side.

"Well, Syrina," said the bald man. "You're lucky the child is merciful."

"It was not mercy that stayed my hand," Kaikora replied, her gray eyes resuming their usual glare.

The lion dragged herself back upright, shaking out her mane, tail held high. "*You* were lucky, child, not I."

"I was underestimated," Kaikora smiled.

Syrina snorted as her fur began to shiver. The air itself seemed to vibrate as she stood on her hind legs, claws retracting. With a final diminishing roar, a dangerous-looking woman had morphed before them. Her dual-colored eyes narrowed as she rolled her shoulders, stretching her back.

Myronor finally had enough strength to allow his jaw to drop. Syrina was not a familiar, but one of the druids his mother had written about. Why hadn't she expressed more awe and surprise in her writings about such fantastical magic? The ability to switch forms...

"I, Autarch Thryne of the Civ, Wielder of Hollow Vessels, offer myself as a mediator of this dispute," said the bald man, stepping into the room. "Though this involves my son and two closest brethren, I will do my best to remain unbiased."

Myronor glanced back and forth between Glamwell and Thryne, weighing the truth of his words beneath his shock. The resemblance was inarguable—the shape of their crowns and the slight curve at the edge of their eyes, even their amused expressions, juxtaposed with a regal stance, mirrored their relation. But he wished Glamwell had given him some indication he was the son of an Autarch earlier. Perhaps Pyra had instructed him to keep that secret as well.

Syrina's leather armor creaked as she stepped toward Myronor, pointing an accusatory finger at the pendant dangling from his neck. "There is nothing to mediate—this one is clearly *anathema*! I cannot allow this fifth in our home!"

Thryne turned to Zadok, his nonexistent eyebrows raised in question.

"He was not born of the Consortia," Zadock answered calmly, joining Thryne and Syrina in the center of the yurt. "He is a Wielder of Riftwalking, like his mother, whom I sponsored before with approval from you and Syrina's predecessor. I see no qualm with offering sponsorship to a child whose kin was once so welcome amongst us."

Thryne turned to Glamwell with a strange expression in the whites of his eyes. "Is this true, my son?"

"Yes," Glamwell spoke. "He is the child of Pyra Ebontide, through and through."

Silence fell in the yurt, but Myronor noticed Zadock's knuckles turn white at the mention of his mother's name. He must have surely known her well to elicit such a response.

Myronor opened his mouth to ask what he knew of Pyra, but with a curt nod from Kaikora, he promptly shut it. The tension in the room would not be cut with his questions...

"And the other," Thryne began, staring at Kaikora with admiration, "is truly a Wielder of Tides, made more by the marks of a

Forged One decorating her body. How else could she have bested you, Syrina?"

The woman growled, very nearly as she had in her lion form. "Wayward children or not, they are both too known by the Consortia, much like your son! I retain my stance on *that* mistake and refuse to allow it again! None associated with Pyra Ebontide are good for our people!"

Thryne's eyes hardened clearly despite their pure white appearance. And while Myronor absorbed their conversation with the aid of Ophiera's blurry memories for context, he was struggling to keep up. The history between these individuals was deep and painful, yet by their reactions, Pyra had seemingly been involved in all of it. He was coming to realize there was much she'd kept secret, even from her journals.

"Syrina, the Odestal are well within their rights to sponsor these children. With two of three in favor, you have been outvoted. Again."

The finality in Thryne's words stilled the room. Despite Syrina's clenched fists, she held her tongue in defeat. And while the interchange may have seemed like a win for Myronor and Kaikora, he worried they had only increased Syrina's hatred of them. Both animals and people behaved erratically when backed into a corner.

A low call of a horn in the distance shook the very walls of the tent. While Myronor and Kaikora jumped at the suddenness, the three Autarchs exchanged meaningful glances. Before any could speak, Syrina shifted back into a lion and fled from the tent with a roar.

As Zadok followed her, so did Thryne, but as Glamwell trailed his father, the Autarch turned his gaze to his son.

"Stay with the children," he said. "We will handle this."

As the two Autarchs left the tent, Kaikora came to kneel by Myronor's side. Still slumped against the tent, he rolled his eyes as she ran her rough hands along his chin, reaching his pulse point with a grimace.

"I'm fine, Kaikora," he said, trying to dissuade her from examining him. "You were the one in a fight."

"You barely had time to recover from the last draw of the tether," she said, forming a cup with her hand and summoning water into the space within. "Though I must admit, without Zadok's interventions, you would have fought a much harder battle than I."

With her full lips, she breathed across the surface, imbuing more than ripples into the now-glowing waters. She placed her hand against his lips and tilted. He sipped the liquid from her hands, the relief flowing through him. Like enchanted food, Though it did nothing to relieve the dull, aching pain in his chest, at least he regained the strength to support himself.

"I saw her, Kaikora—we...I don't know what happened, but it wasn't a dream—it was real, and we...exchanged, or I don't know what to call it, but I'm beginning to remember things she has endured these last days as if they were my own sufferings."

The shaman summoned another pool of restorative water in her hands and indicated that he should drink it.

"Was the exchange mutual?" She asked, a worried pinch forming between her brows.

"I believe so," Myronor said slowly, knowing what Kaikora truly asked. His memories...well, they were quite damning. The keystone, Marvena, the Cloister, and the shaman's confession to *knowing* the fallacies of Ophiera's Oath.

"She must know Aleksander and Uzziel pursue her now," Myronor said quietly, turning to Glamwell. "We must find her as soon as possible!"

Glamwell knelt beside them, his expression quite crestfallen compared to his normal pep. "I know you are desperate, but you must understand the horn you just heard—that is a warning from the aerodock. No Consortian aerships are permitted in the Shole; thus, I can only take the alarm to mean the Cloister has arrived here. If we flee now, we may be intercepted, or worse, followed to her. Until the Autarchs decide if they will sponsor their presence in Birozahran or not, we must stay put."

"But we came all this way—"

"And unfortunately, walked into the middle of a feud that has reached a boiling point," Glamwell said solemnly. "You have faith in your ekath, yes? Then, trust she will make the right choice with the knowledge you exchanged with her. We are still a step ahead from where we started, and that...that is something."

~ Fifty Two ~

EXONERATE

His boots were moving long before Ophiera fell beneath the water, and yet he couldn't move fast enough. Fear fueled Jasper's sprint toward the basin, counting every moment without her in sight. When he finally reached the font, he plowed straight into the tepid, clear water, slowing him abruptly. Wildly, he groped in the shallow waters until his fingers grazed hot metal. And with a great heave, he dragged Ophiera's limp body to the edge, watching with horror as bright red blood flowed down her lips.

"Ophiera?" he panted, not realizing he was out of breath. The back of her breastplate was hot against his chest, and with a trembling hand at her throat, he felt for a pulse.

The strong *thrum* beneath his fingers brought more stillness to his hands than any amount of ember whiskey ever could. But the blood still flowing from her gently parted lips concerned him.

"Your screams were felt for miles, sister," Kiela's voice cooed from behind him. The others had joined, taking vigil at the edge of the basin. But none were seemingly concerned over Ophiera's state.

Kiela's crimson gaze fell on Jasper, sending an involuntary shiver through him. "Allow me to repay her sacrifice and stop the bleeding, at least."

Nodding before he could think, Jasper watched the warlock dance her slender fingers before Ophiera's slack face. Thin tendrils of red haze trickled forth, the red magic flowing through her parted lips and wrapping around her throat. Any reservations Jasper held towards derivation magic disappeared as she stirred in his arms.

"Ja-Jasper?" She rasped, looking up at him with those eyes he would never forget. The sound of his name, even on her bloodied lips, filled him with a warmth so rarely felt.

"I'm right here," he said, wiping the strands of sopping hair from her face.

And to his detriment, she smiled before her eyes slid closed again.

"You have earned all the rest, I promise," Kiela said, enervating Ophiera with a pulse of red magic again, "but first tell us the fate of the Stigma."

Without opening her eyes, Ophiera mumbled, "All...gone..."

"All of it?" Alzerbez growled.

She nodded clumsily, eyes still closed. "Spread...far...sorry...long...time..."

With a shiver of the air, Alzerbez returned to their human form, a bit of magic that still caught Jasper off guard every time. The druid grasped Ophiera's hands and knelt before her in the font, so low their silvered hair dipped into the water. They pressed her gauntleted hand to their forehead and began to sob in earnest.

Iku and Kiela stood on either side of them as all three mourned and celebrated at once. Behind him, he could hear Iku's whimpers, and even Kiela could not contain her sniffle. Their combined emotions caught Jasper's breath in his chest, and before he could muster a resistance, tears began to fall from his own eyes. The relief and sorrow clung to them all, even Ophiera, whose silent tears flowed down her freckled cheeks.

"Thank you, dear child," Alzerbez said, finally speaking as they pressed their forehead to her gauntlet. "The Enclave is indebted to you, forever and always."

In his arms, Ophiera tried to speak, but a trickle of blood was all that escaped. Jasper caught her head as it lolled backward against his shoulder, wiping the red from her lips.

"She needs rest right now, not praise," he growled, unable to contain himself.

Kiela's laugh tinkled as she cast the tendrils again, surrounding Ophiera in a haze of red as she fell utterly limp in his arms.

"Rest she shall get. Iku, may she recover on you as we travel?"

"Certainly," Iku yipped, fur shaking as he grew in size. "Anything for her."

As Jasper held Ophiera in his arms, he sensed the three Enclave held her with equal strength in their hearts. Their feelings of adoration, nearly worship, were all too familiar. While he knew the Stigma was dangerous, even from Col's accounts in the Sloughmire, he had never fully appreciated its direness until now. The relief in the air demonstrated just how desperate the Enclave was to be free of it and how much they owed Ophiera for destroying it.

Jasper lifted her from the basin, holding her close as the water rushed from her golden plate mail. Though he was reluctant to place her on Iku's back, he did so, knowing it was for the best. Even with his strength, he certainly couldn't carry her back through the jungle in his arms. After he settled her gently upon Iku's back, draped forward on her stomach, Kiela began siphoning life from a nearby growth of grass, causing it to brown and shrivel.

"We leave for Birozahran immediately," Kiela said. "Alzerbez, I beg you to travel ahead and call off the girtas. Iku and I will be shortly behind with these two. When you arrive in Birozahran, inform the Autarchs of her feat—I'm sure even Syrina will wish to honor her."

"As you wish," they said, shivering once more into the leopard. The dual-toned eyes fell on Jasper as they growled. "Keep her safe."

Before Jasper could acknowledge or scoff at this plan, the druid had torn off into the jungle. While he agreed that calling off the girtas was a priority, there was still a matter of fair exchange. The entire reason Ophiera suffered now as she did was to find Pyra's location, and that should be addressed before any sort of celebration took place.

"I will honor our word when she wakes," Kiela purred in his ear before leading Iku away from the basin. "And I'm sure even a Forge One will be invited to the festivities in Birozahran."

Without much of a choice, Jasper followed along on the other side of Iku.

They traveled out the exact route they'd entered upon, through the ruins of Megrim Spa. Despite Ophiera's hours of burning, the land and ruins remained relatively the same. Open fissures from where the ichor burned from deep beneath the ground were left smoking, but unlike Iluka, the ruins of the village stood. He wondered if this was a purposeful act or a lucky coincidence, though he realized how little he needed to ponder. Ophiera wasn't one to repeat her regrets.

Everyone kept their silence as they left the clearing and ventured back into the depths of the jungle. While Jasper considered himself relatively quick on his feet, he relied heavily on the scars carved into him to keep pace with Kiela and Iku. The two traveled with a vigor that seemed natural to them yet required his full effort. It truly dawned on him now how much the Odestal princess had held back in their journey here.

For some time, his thoughts were replaced by reminders to breathe as the warlock set a brutal pace. With a haze of red, she siphoned the life from the plants nearest the path as they moved, transferring the energy back to Ophiera and Iku in regular intervals. As much as Jasper's skin crawled at the sight of the derivation magic, he appreciated Kiela's focus on restoring Ophiera.

The day passed in a blur of dark jungle and chilled breaths. Jasper distracted himself from the exhaustion by focusing on Ophiera, watching the mesmerizing reflections in her armor cast by the evening sun barely penetrating the dark canopy. Even without the dancing shadows, it would have been difficult for him to avert his gaze from her.

Throughout his life, Jasper had found himself more often disappointed with people, especially after he spent any amount of time with them. Col had been the only exception to this rule, at least until Ophiera had reappeared in his life. The more time he spent with her, the more he admired her and the more certain he became that she was his lodestar. But she wasn't only his.

He felt a moment of pity for Myronor on the other end of the spirit rope. She had burned for hours, screaming as her only outlet. It was hard enough to be nearby while she cleansed Megrim Spa, let alone to be tethered to her. Perhaps the mage had more spine than he had given him credit for. Perhaps he had been wrong to deem him unworthy of her. At least Myronor helped her survive herself. Hell, even the warlock could use her disgusting magic to help revive her...but he...he was worthless to anyone but himself—especially Ophiera.

"Do you still hate the Enclave?" Kiela asked, her dark-painted lips pursed in the darkening forest.

It was a strange question to ask out of the blue, and he wondered if she had *tasted* his mood growing foul. For once, it had little to do with her.

"I don't hate you," he said, his voice raspy with disuse, "but I don't fully trust you or your people either."

"So predictable," Kiela laughed. "But understandable. The Forged Ones have every right to their hate."

The warlock left her comment dangling in the air, waiting for him to take the bait. But if she had expected some sort of response, he wasn't about to give it to her. Yes, he despised Birozahran. And the Enclave. And magic. Everything Kiela was and everything that brought him torment. But for the first time in his life, thinking about any of the three no longer caused acid to boil in his gut. He wasn't sure why his fearful demons were suddenly subdued, but he had a feeling the unconscious, armor-clad berserker of a woman had something to do with it.

"Do you think Ophiera trusts us?" Kiela asked, following his gaze.

"Yes," Jasper said with a clenched jaw, "But she trusts far too easily."

"For someone who has suffered so much, her heart remains surprisingly fragile."

Jasper stared at Ophiera, her eyelashes twitching against her cheek. She looked nothing like the woman from his dreams now, and yet, this version felt far more threatening to his heart. *He* was the fragile one, after all—the weak one—the one who would surely break if he had to endure what Ophiera had just endured.

"Truthfully, I don't believe any part of her is capable of breaking."

A snort slipped past Kiela's painted smile. And yet, he didn't find anything he had just said to be of any particular humor. Which meant she was yet again going to goad him.

"But did you not swear to protect her?" She said in a cloying voice. "From what are you protecting her, then, if she is so unbreakable?"

"One can suffer without breaking. And those who won't break suffer constantly. The least I can do is help minimize that for her."

Again, Kiela snorted, causing a flash of annoyance to heat him beneath his collar.

"And what would you do if *you* were causing her suffering?"

Jasper slowed his pace, holding himself back. Her question reflected Alzerbez's earlier accusations, ones he did not take lightly.

"Do I act as someone who would willfully cause her pain?" Jasper asked defensively. He wished his voice had sounded more outraged and less desperate.

"Not purposefully," Kiela said with a closed-lipped smile. "I can taste your worship for her. But admiration, dedication, infatuation, attraction...none of these feelings are *love*, little Forged One. Don't tear at her heart simply because *you* cannot understand the difference."

Now, it was Jasper's turn to snort. The word *love* only crossed his vocabulary when referring to drink or coin. And given the trials and tribulations of the Enclave, he doubted Kiela's definition of the word was any less warped.

"I don't need a lecture on love from a warlock," he spat, only concerned with using that word long after it left his lips.

"Am I not the most qualified to lecture you?" She responded, ignoring the slight. "I know both the pain of her soul and the loneliness of your heart. My ekath is not a bond of romantic love, but it is a bond so strong that no love can compare or withstand. I am doomed to be lonely and yet never alone for as long as I survive."

Yet again, Jasper wished he could not sense the truth of her emotions. The ability to *feel* what others felt was more curse than gift, especially now. He had viewed the soul bond of the Odestal as an abomination of magic and preferred it that way. Hate and despise were easy paths for his heart. But understanding the consequences of sharing a soul bond with a familiar was something he had never considered or wanted to feel. And yet what she described broke his heart, as if smashing a mirror.

"How are my feelings any of your business, anyway?" Jasper growled.

"You make them so by allowing them to leach into your aura," she replied, back to her taunting tone. "But truthfully, I fear for her ability to be swayed and misled. She has a problem with her *perceived* obligations to others...to you, to her ekath, and to that damnable Cloister."

Jasper toiled with her wording for a few moments, trying to wrap his brain around what she meant. But between his physical exhaustion and pure frustration with her audacity, he decided not to concern himself with her opinions, only her promises.

"The only obligation that needs to be met at this moment is sharing Pyra's location. And once we have that, we're sailing back to Krysas, back to her ekath, because no matter who or what she feels obligated toward, nothing will ever be more important to her than *him*."

Kiela smiled before departing his side, retaking the lead and siphoning the overgrowth of the jungle to clear their path ahead.

* * *

Night had fallen over the glittering sands of the Shole by the time they emerged from the crater jungle. Jasper found it to be an oddly disquieting sight without the threat of the girtas bursting from the ground. But for the first time in his life, he was eager to reach Birozahran as soon as possible.

Despite Kiela's frequent innervations throughout their hours of travel, Ophiera remained unconscious upon Iku's back. He wasn't sure why she had yet to wake, but her apparent discomfort was beginning to worry him. Her eyebrows remained tightly knit together, her lip trembling as if trying to speak. It was hard to believe that only this morning, they'd first stepped into Megrim Spa, and only hours before, she'd finally stopped burning.

"You need a rest, Forged One," Kiela said, nodding her head towards a cairn stone protruding from the sands.

Pride, not parch, held his tongue in silence, but the warlock must have tasted his fatigue already. She smiled as she steered Iku toward the blackened glass stone without waiting for his response. By the time they'd reached the cave entrance, Jasper was reluctantly relieved she had suggested it. He hadn't realized how thirsty he was until he heard the tinkling of the aqueduct font within.

Kiela studied Ophiera with a curious expression as Iku and Jasper drank their fill. He'd come to realize the warlock was quite the opposite of the paladin, not only in appearance but in expression and manner. While he could read Ophiera better than anyone, Kiela remained perpetually veiled. But thus far, she'd proven herself nothing but true to her word, even if he couldn't sense her motivations or emotions alongside.

"No!" Ophiera screamed as she bolted awake on Iku's back.

With quickened, panting breaths, she threw herself to the ground, and the crash of armor on stone reverberated throughout the cave. Scuffling backward until she hit the wall of the cave, her panicked, incoherent words echoed through the tunnels.

"Ophiera, I'm right here," he said, kneeling beside her, "everything is alright."

He knew all too well how it felt to wake up in a strange place without any recollection of how he got there. But the sheer terror welling behind her eyes felt more damning than simple confusion.

"Uzziel!" She screamed. "In Birozahran!"

"Who?" Kiela asked Ophiera as she eyed him with a knowing look.

"Chaplain...Cloister..." Her eyes darted through the cave, from face to face, unseeing any of it.

"C'mon, it was just a dream," Jasper said quietly, hoping to calm her even a bit. The dread pouring from her was beginning to drown him, too.

"Not a dream," she said, her words growing more frantic. "My-ronor...when I..." She paused, placing a shaking hand over her chest. "We exchanged everything as I burned. I'm still struggling to recall *everything*, but I know he is already in Birozahran. I know he came for me...to stop the Cloister from finding me."

The words fell from her mouth as the same terror overtook her again. She continued muttering to herself incoherently, trembling beneath her plate mail. Jasper could only watch as she curled in on herself and began rocking. The diminishment of herself at the mere thought of the Cloister reminded Jasper of his response to the Shole.

"You're certain, sister?"

Ophiera nodded, her hand clenched over her heart. "I can feel his soul is closer now."

"Alzerbez has likely arrived in Birozahran by now," Iku yipped with hackles raised. "We can make for the city and rendezvous with—"

"No!" Ophiera shouted. "I can't go...Uzziel...he will..."

Jasper felt his hands begin to shake against the terror in her voice. But more powerful than her fear was his resolve to refuse to let her break. Whatever Kiela wanted to call his feelings for Ophiera, they compelled him never to lose her again, even to her-self.

Slowly, he leaned into her line of sight, hoping to catch her darting eyes. But like before, she didn't see him. Throwing caution to the wind, he grasped her by the jaw, pulling her to face him. The shock of his grip returned some of the fire to her gaze.

"Ophiera, listen to me," he growled, "No matter who or what comes for you, I will never let them touch you."

Her eyes widened as if only just now realizing he was here. And yet he could only find relief that she at least saw him now.

"You can't stop them," she whispered between trembling lips. "My Oath—"

"Means nothing to me!" He spat, watching the defiance return to her expression. "I've sailed this world to and from more times than you've spoken the word *Oath*. And I promise you, nothing is more sinful than forcing someone to do something against their will. Don't let the scars they forced upon you control who *you* choose to be."

He felt slightly abashed, repeating the words Col had once spoken to him. But wasn't that precisely why he was so drawn to Ophiera? They were the same in so many suffered ways.

"I'm nothing without my scars," she murmured.

"Those are not your words," he replied, more gently this time. "You were Iris, a poor excuse for a consort who stowed away on my ship and dispatched two navarras with your bare hands. You were the Warden of Iluka before the Brotherhood and Aud destroyed our home. You *are* the Wielder of Erum's Flame here in the Shole and Myronor's soul bond from now until eternity. And to me...You are and will always be my lodestar. Can't you see, Ophiera? You are *everything* without those damned scars, and it's time you proved it to those who imposed them on you."

There it was; the fire had finally reignited behind her eyes, dim behind the terror but burning steadily. She took a deep breath, stoking the flames until her gaze seared into his own. He let go of her jaw and stood, holding out his hand. With her golden gauntlet, she took his offer and came to stand beside him.

"I'm sorry," she said, her voice low but steady. Her grip remained firm as she closed her eyes. "I lost myself far too easily."

"You did," he exhaled, lacing his leather-gloved fingers through hers. Despite the cold armor, he felt suddenly warm. "But I'll always be here to drag you back."

"I know," she murmured, "Thank you, Jasper. "

The affection in her voice satisfied a part of him he thought lost. So much of his existence was spent on keeping himself shielded from others that he forgot how it felt to help shield another. If she, the berserker, could rely on him for anything, perhaps his soul wasn't so damaged, after all.

Ophiera let go of his hand and turned to others, fully herself and fully determined. "Kiela, how will the Enclave handle the Cloister in Birozahran?"

The warlock was unblinking and expressionless. "They will be tested, as you were. But I doubt they will be sponsored."

"Why not?"

"Because they are no longer wayward children," she shrugged. "The Autarchs will know they are Forged Ones by the scars they bear and not true descendants of the mother clans. They should be banished, if not killed."

Jasper watched as Ophiera's gaze fell to the ground, chewing her lip. But something about the warlock's *blankness* stirred his distrust.

"How certain are you they won't be sponsored?"

And there was his answer. The warlock's demeanor shrank ever so slightly, even though she said nothing.

"My ekath's silence is because she doesn't wish to reveal the weaknesses of the Autarchs," Iku said, stepping in. "Personal politics lead to her uncertainty. I, however, prefer to remain unbiased and one step ahead. There is a chance the Cloister will be sponsored. But regardless of whether they are sponsored or not, Ophiera must get as far away from the Cloister as possible."

"Which means we cannot return to Birozahran," Jasper said.

Iku nodded.

"While my scars agree, I know that Myronor and Kaikora are awaiting our arrival there," Ophiera said. "We cannot leave them behind."

"I'm not suggesting we do," Iku continued, circling Kiela's skirt. "My ekath and I will travel to Birozahran and retrieve all of our companions. You and Jasper will make a run for the port. Assuming your ship can accommodate the extra cargo, we will rendezvous with you at the ship and swiftly escape to Krysas before the Cloister has even begun their search of the Shole."

Jasper smiled to himself. He was finally understanding why the Odestal took on their familiars as soulbonds. Up until now, he had given Kiela all the credit for her swift plan to save Ophiera from the drosera. But seeing how quickly Iku turned a plan out, he realized more and more the power of their unity.

"I welcome all sorts on my ship as long as we're sailing away from the Shole," Jasper said to Iku and Kiela. "I can lead Ophiera through the desert while you travel to Birozahran. If you continue to keep the girtas off our backs, we can make it back without stopping."

Kiela nodded. "Iku and I will do what we can to convince the Autarchs to deal with the blasphemers ourselves. Then, I will deliver your ekath to you, sister. This I swear."

With a flick of her wrist, Kiela summoned a bag from Iku's back in a flash of red. She thrust it into Jasper's chest, revealing the provisions she had packed long ago. "You are both weary and weak. Eat or enervate, whatever you wish, to regain your strength. And as you do, I will fulfill my fair exchange."

With a red-hazed hand, she reached for Ophiera. As the small red tendrils melded through Ophiera's breastplate, the furrow between her brow softened. Kiela stepped forward, pressing her hand against the chest armor, the crimson glow brightening as she channeled.

"Sister, what I will show you cannot be unseen. Are you sure you are prepared to learn everything of Pyra Ebontide?"

Ophiera nodded without hesitation before her eyes rolled back, her eyelashes jerking as if in a fit.

"What are you doing to her?" Jasper asked, surprised by the lack of anger in his voice.

"Flooding her with memories," Kiela said quietly. "It is an unpleasant process, and she won't be able to understand them all, at least not anytime soon. But it is the only way to ensure she learns of Pyra's fate. I'm willing to share with you as well if you care to learn."

Jasper hesitated, unsure if he wanted to know. Remaining unaware of Pyra's doings was the safest option and the preferred option. But as he watched tears pour from Ophiera's eyes as the red magic pulsated through her, his decision was made.

"Show me," he said. "Show me everything."

~ Fifty Three ~

ABSCOND

Myronor wasn't chained to a post, but he might as well have been. The last time he spent this amount of time in a tent was under Marvena's torturous watch. And yet now he felt more desperate to escape than he had in the Brotherhood encampment.

All day, Myronor had been treated like a piece of furniture by the endless stream of Enclave guards clad in tabards of black and red. They frequented the yurt, whispering news to Glamwell while ignoring him and Kaikora. And even then, the Steward only relayed the bare minimum of the news.

Outside the yurt, Myronor caught bits and pieces from gossiping people passing by. The tone of their voices held more meaning than the words themselves, only adding to Myronor's desire to leave. People spoke of a golden-clad child—of *Forged anathema*—of an unknown aership at the city's unused aerodock. And sprinkled in amongst the gossip were the hushed fears of a clan war between the Ailuro and Odestal.

From what Myronor gathered from Glamwell, the negotiations with the Cloister were going poorly, and the tests were not to blame. Now that he recalled *all* of Ophiera's memories, he understood the severity of their tests—and they were supposed to be quick and decisive. If the Autarchs had subjected the Cloister to the same tests, the results would have been known, meaning the delay in their decision was due to something else. All Myronor could guess was that there must have been a disagreement between the Autarchs. But Glamwell spent his downtime in privacy, turning the glowing beads in his hands as he hunched behind a tapestry.

A chilly breeze dragged Myronor from his bitter thoughts. He thought another guard must have arrived to deliver some more news he wasn't meant to hear. But he'd only caught a glimpse of the sunset outside before he noticed the gray leopard stalking within.

Kaikora stood, broken trident raised protectively before him. She would likely never view a druid in the same light after her encounter with Syrina, but Myronor recognized the dual-colored eyes set in ashen fur and relaxed.

"Alzerbez," Myronor said, finding amusement in the mild surprise that rippled through their whiskers. He'd only seen them in their human form before, and yet he recalled the beauty of their patterned fur as if he had seen it countless times before.

"Greetings, son of Pyra."

"Is Ophiera with you?"

"No, but we left her in good company," they said, turning their slitted pupils to Kaikora. "We hear you're the child that bested Syrina...It's a shame you didn't kill her."

Glamwell made a "tsk-tsk" sound from behind them both, drawing attention to his presence. The leopard laughed, or at least that was how Myronor interpreted the pulsating growls.

"Brother, we did not know *this* was your part in the puzzle. We're glad to see you've upheld Pyra's wishes."

"We all do in the end, don't we?" Glamwell said with a smile. "But why are you here without the others?"

"Kiela sent us ahead to bring word of the Stigma's cleanse, but we became ensnared in the Autarch's debates upon arrival. It seems the Cloister is overshadowing our victory in Megrim Spa."

"A victory that was impossible without Ophiera," Myronor said tersely. "Tell me where the hell she is!"

The leopard's eyes narrowed as they stalked towards him. While not nearly as threatening as the lion, Myronor had to admit Alzerbez looked far more dangerous as a leopard than a shop-keeper. A low growl trickled from their throat, almost hidden in the sounds of the desert winds. Clenching his fists, Myronor held his ground as Alzerbez circled him wordlessly.

"She is your ekath, is she not? You should be able to answer that yourself, child. Do you know nothing of—"

Again, the tent flap suddenly opened to reveal another four-legged creature.

"Iku?!" Glamwell yelled, rushing to the crimson fox.

"Thank the crystals, you're all here!" the fox said, yipping excitedly as the pink-robed man threw his arms around his neck. "I thought tracking down Alz was going to be more difficult."

Myronor recognized the fox, but now he appeared minuscule, even smaller compared to Alzerbez, who was stalking toward him.

"What happened?" they demanded.

"We rode as fast as we could," Iku said to them all. "But we were forewarned of the Cloister's presence. Kiela is with her father now, trying to stop the inevitable again. Alz, what the hell is Syrina thinking?!"

The fox seemed to skip key pieces of information that would have helped Myronor understand what was going on. But

Glamwell's expression suggested that Iku spoke only terrible news.

"Can someone just tell me what's happened to Ophiera!?" Myronor interrupted, uncaring of anything else.

The fox stared at him pitifully. Slowly, his keen gaze moved from Kaikora to Alzerbez and back to Glamwell.

"Ophiera awoke just outside the city...thanks to you, she knew of the Cloister's presence. We decided that Ophiera and Jasper would cross the Shole, back to *Berserker,* while Kiela and I rode here to sway the Autarchs against the Cloister. But we arrived too late. It seems Syrina has agreed to sponsor the Cloister, even though the tests did not go well. Zadok and Thryne tried to reason with her, but negotiations turned violent. And now...well, this is the start of a clash we all knew was coming but have no business being a part of...any of us."

Alzerbez growled. "After all the progress we've made, she decides to go for the throat of the Odestal."

"We always knew she suffered after the rite," Glamwell shrugged. "But this goes against everything we've built."

"Regardless of reasons or consequences, we must leave the city now," Iku said. "She's ordering Ailuro guards to lockdown the Odestal tabernacle, including the tunnels. Then she plans to allow the Cloister to search for Ophiera—she doesn't know—she thinks she is still housed within the Odestal Tabernacle—they are coming soon."

"What does Kiela advise?" Glamwell asked.

"To flee," the fox hissed. "We must leave at once and rendezvous with Ophiera and Jasper on the *Berserker.*"

Myronor rose to his feet, dusting the sand from his clothes. He felt surprisingly calm, given the direness of the situation. But he felt Ophiera in his soul, more than he had in far too long, which eased so much of his tension. The promise of their reunion kept his heart steady and his mind focused.

"I'm ready," Myronor said, and to his relief, Kaikora joined his side. "Please, Iku, lead the way."

The three Enclave took a moment to squat in the sand, discussing paths and strategies as Kaikora and Myronor listened anxiously. They all needed to remain hidden, except for Glamwell and Alzerbez. Before they snuck from the yurt, Iku cloaked himself in shadows, just as Jasper had before. Keeping his curiosity at bay over the powers of the foxes, he cast his invisibility charm over Kaikora and himself.

The Tabernacle was quiet yet abuzz with the onset of night. Nearly every one of the yurts illuminated the darkness, occupied with shades of movement, and yet they never crossed another soul as they wove between them. Countless footprints in the sand masked their own, and by the time they reached the edge of the Odestal Tabernacle, it became clear why.

Before the gate to the Odestal territory sat an entrance to one of the caves and a dark bear pacing before it. He had a feeling the tunnels below were swarming with Ailuro guards, and sure enough, a pale panther emerged from the depths.

"Tunnels are clear, and patrols are set," growled the panther.

"Good," the bear said, "orders are to remain here to ensure no one else—*sniff*—wait—*sniff*—it can't be..."

"It is," Alzerbez interjected loudly, not even attempting to hide their presence. "But as always, we won't be here for long."

The bear reared up on its hind legs. "Alzerbez, any other day, I would be thrilled to see you. But haven't you heard? The Tabernacle is on lockdown, along with the rest of Birozahran, on Syrina's orders. She will kill you if she finds you here."

"That's precisely why we're leaving, Feyr," Alzerbez said in a friendlier-than-usual tone. "Syrina's war is with the Odestal, not the Civ. We need to escort Glamwell out of the city, as per the Autarch's request."

The bear groaned, sinking back down onto all fours. Myronor tried to calm his breathing under the shaking jowls of the formidable beast. "Sands only know we don't need another dead heir. But Alzerbez, if she catches you, of all people, with him—"

"She hasn't yet, and she never will."

A tense moment passed between the gray leopard and the dark bear, their dual-colored eyes unblinking as they exchanged more than just a silent stare. Myronor didn't understand how a shopkeeper could hold such sway over the druids under Syrina's command, and yet the bear bowed their head before stepping aside.

"There are no guards assigned to the Eastern sewer. Be swift and safe."

Alzerbez nodded without speaking before taking a heavy step forward. Myronor did his best to stay as close to Glamwell as possible, trying to step in each of his footprints while Kaikora followed behind. He only had a moment to worry if they remained hidden before the stalking panther's hiss stopped him in his tracks.

"Feyr, I smell a fox," she hissed, eyes darting over Alzerbez and Glamwell.

Myronor tightened his grip on Kaikora's wrist, preparing for the possibility of a fight. But Glamwell only rolled his eyes as the heavy paws approached.

"What do you expect?" he said, his voice no longer jovial but deadly serious. "The scent of their kin lingers everywhere in the Tabernacle."

"This is more, something—"

"It is more!" Glamwell shouted, his voice echoing off the stone walls. "You smell the guilt of turning on our brethren over something as pathetic as Forged power!"

The three guards recoiled in unison, as if Glamwell's words had physically lashed them. And while Myronor had witnessed Glamwell's serious side a few times now, he couldn't believe the power of his command. Even his hair stood on end, responding to the waves of mana emanating from the Steward. And without waiting for another altercation to break, Alzerbez stalked away, and Myronor didn't hesitate to follow.

The politics of the Enclave clans were beyond anything he had prepared to contend with, even after consulting Pyra's writings. He knew their history was brutal and their liberation even more so. But it was strange to him how much respect Alzerbez seemingly held amongst their people. And Glamwell...a seemingly idiotic Steward turned spy turned powerful Civ heir, was too much to process.

Yet, at the moment, Myronor realized he didn't care much about processing or understanding any of it. What did any of it matter in the face of the Cloister threats? Ophiera, and only Ophiera, dominated his thoughts, her whereabouts the only question he needed answered. The politics of the Enclave meant little to him when he could feel the ekath drawing him back to her.

Once clear of the Ailuro guards, Alzerbez and Glamwell picked up their pace. Winding through the hoodoos and sandy paths of the main city, they entered what Myronor recognized to be the main square of the city. Though his memories were no longer his alone, he relished in the recalled sensation of wonder and awe from when Ophiera first saw Birozahran. There was a sense of belonging she felt here that she had seldom experienced before, and one that Myronor wished he had felt when entering the ancient city. But now, as he fled through the abandoned streets in the cold of the night, he felt quite the opposite of Ophiera's recollections.

Where she saw a city of hope, he now only saw betrayal. The life the Enclave had built, free from the Consortia's chains, was being threatened by one of their own. He would never understand what drove Syrina's choices, but there was no forgiveness for her betrayal of Ophiera. She had sold Ophiera out to the Cloister in some petty power grab, and now, they fled the city, all in some wild hope of escape from whatever disaster was about to ensue.

It didn't have to be like this...

It didn't have to be so cruel.

Kaikora's arm shook suddenly in his grip, alerting him to Alzerbez and Glamwell disappearing beneath the ground. For a split second, Myronor thought they had spanned away until he glimpsed the entrance to a dark cave.

Following the path, they descended into a downward-sloping tunnel of blackened glass. Glamwell had removed the glowing beads from the pocket of his robes, illuminating the shining cave. Iku, visible now, eyed them all with glowing eyes before turning down one of the branching tunnels.

Myronor lifted the invisibility charm over himself and Kaikora and followed without question.

"Where are we going?" Kaikora asked, inspecting the walls of the cave with her fingertips.

"Through one of the abandoned sewers," Iku said quietly. "It's our only path out of the city."

Glamwell chuckled. "Probably the only secret of Birozahran we managed to keep from Pyra."

The sound of his mother's name echoed in the cave, reminding him of who truly led their steps. It might be Iku leading them, single file, through the dark, narrowing tunnel, but it was all because of Pyra. Pyra had interfered with them all, pulling the strings of every decision he and the others had made long before they even knew each other. Had she known of Ophiera before she had saved his life? Had Pyra known this was where her choices would lead her only son?

Shaking his head, Myronor focused on the darkness. Glamwell's glowing beads were the only light, but the blackened stone walls seemed to absorb everything. The closeness, the staleness of the air...

Myronor tried not to think of the dark place where Aud resided. He tried not to think of a cold, dark cave with chains and fires.

In fact, it was best just not to think. Running his hand along the smooth, cold stone, he tried to center himself in the present. But as he ran his fingers over the walls, he realized they were soaking wet.

Iku came to a halt, and both Alzerbez and Glamwell moved to the walls of the tunnel, allowing Myronor to see forward. Before them, the tunnel sank into a rippling pool of crystal-clear water.

"It's flooded?" Myronor whispered.

"Aqueducts and sewers carry water," Iku replied, his voice inflecting with sarcasm.

"What the hell do we do now?" Myronor asked, remembering what could be found in the sewers of Feyralis and feeling nauseous.

Glamwell shrugged. "We've all undergone the birzhan in one form or another, so it's never been a problem to hold our breath long-term."

"I'm certain his concern has little to do with holding his breath," Kaikora interjected, her nostrils wide as she inhaled the stagnant air. "And I personally refuse to swim in shite, no matter the circumstances."

Hunched beneath the low ceiling, the shaman pointed her broken trident forward as her eyes turned reflective. Myronor smiled, his lips cracking from the lack of emotion of late. But he was equally pleased not to have to swim in *shite,* as he was by the fact Kaikora had actually sworn.

"Oh, wonderful!" the fox yipped. "Wish you had been here when we retook the city! My fur smelled for weeks."

"Lead the way, sister," Alzerbez growled, slinking against the wall to allow her to pass.

With heavy steps, Kaikora forced the water back as a familiar energy crackled around her. Like pushing a boulder through the tunnel, she used the sea glass trident to carve their path through the humid aqueduct. As they progressed, walls narrowed in, quickly snuffing out any of Myronor's momentary joy from before. His heart raced as he imagined what would happen if Kaikora suddenly stopped channeling. Their lives felt a little too dependent on a singular thread, but he had to remember everyone but Kaikora was ekatma here.

Any other time, any other place, Myronor would have pressed them with every question he ever had regarding the process of the soul bonds. He didn't understand a thing about the necromancers or how the druids could fuse their own souls. And while the most familiar bond to him was between Kiela and Iku, he couldn't imagine being bound to Mallow in such a way. And while the thoughts spun, the desire for answers again fell away.

The air grew suddenly cold as the ground began to incline. And as Myronor climbed out into the dim light of the vast desert, he inhaled the frigid, dry air. Outside the city walls, he couldn't believe the vast emptiness of the Shole. Both the sands and skies sparkled, illuminated by the dual moons hanging high above. The sight was breathtaking, as was the temperature.

Despite the Consortia's garbs of tight leather and cape, they provided little shelter against the frosted winds of the Shole. With a trembling hand, Myronor cast to transmute his cape, extending and thickening it against the bitter cold. But to his dismay, the blue light flickered in weakness. He didn't think he'd used enough mana to warrant such trouble yet.

Beside him, Kaikora stretched, and he realized sheepishly that she wore even less than himself. But as she twisted her broad shoulders back and forth, he didn't notice a single goosebump on her bare skin. The elements of Erum seemed to perturb her little.

"Where is Kiela now?" Alzerbez asked, sniffing the air.

The fox closed his eyes, his tail no longer swishing back and forth. "She's still at the old aerodock...the Cloister's aership is there...but they haven't...wait...she's...Kiela, what the hell are you...oh...oh no..." Iku's eyes snapped open as his fur shivered. "We need to go! Now!"

The air warmed briefly as Iku's body expanded, growing to a formidable size. He glared at Kaikora and Myronor, tail swishing irritatedly now. "Quickly! On me!"

Kaikora and Myronor leaped onto his back without hesitation as Glamwell climbed onto Alzerbez. With the echoes of sand grinding beneath their paws, Iku and Alzerbez bolted alongside the city walls. The wind whipped with their speed, stinging Myronor's eyes until they watered. He didn't understand what or why they were running—until a deafening rumble reverberated across the sands.

Ears ringing, Myronor craned his neck upwards to see chunks of stone and dust falling toward them. Before he could blink, Iku took a harsh turn away from the wall and out into the desert. The fox carefully dodged each projectile falling from above, and though Myronor trusted his skills, he couldn't help but flinch at every thud in the sand.

"What's happening?" Myronor called.

"She'll explain when she lands," Iku called back, veering hard to the left to avoid a large piece of sandstone.

Myronor didn't understand, but ahead, he saw Glamwell staring back at the wall with a grin. Following his unblinking gaze, he turned back again to view the wall. A half-circle bite had been blown away, filled with a circle of glowing, red light, and scattering debris. Screams echoed across the sands, and the orb of light suddenly ejected from the city as if launched by some ancient war machine. But Myronor sensed the mana shaking through the air and ground, stronger and more violent than any invention he'd ever encountered.

"Make room!" Iku growled back.

And before Myronor could ask for what, Kaikora slid a thick arm around his waist, pulling him hard against her. He was too confused to feel self-conscious over her bare chest pressed between his shoulders. Beneath him, he felt Iku slow and shift as the pursuing red sphere caught up with them. As Myronor gazed upward, he felt warm air trickle down like misty rain as the orb hovered above. Inside, a slight woman bearing an enormous scythe smiled with darkly painted lips.

"Kiela?" Myronor breathed, recognizing her instantly from Ophiera's memories.

Iku adjusted his trajectory again ever so slightly before the woman landed gracefully in front of Myronor. A strong scent of cinders and smoke overtook the air as her magic retracted, but to his surprise, her blackened dress remained perfectly intact, apart from a bit of dust.

"That was close, Iku," Kiela shouted, gazing back at the city wall.

Myronor couldn't help but look back, examining the decimated city wall, appearing like a chipped tooth along the horizon.

"You could have told me this was your plan!" Iku barked.

"Why?" She simpered. "So you could argue it was too dangerous?"

"It *was* too dangerous! You might have destroyed the aerodock, but you failed to blow up their aership—"

"*Failed* is harsh, Iku. I did enough damage to slow them down, at least!" Kiela hissed. "And if Syrina hadn't interfered at the end, it would have been a very successful plan."

Myronor placed a hand over his heart, massaging the uncomfortable twang of the ekath as he listened to their bickering. It reminded him far too painfully of Ophiera, holding back any words he might have had for the Enclave.

Alzerbez slowed their pace, joining beside Iku as they rode away into the desert. "Kiela, you know that this act will solidify the war between the Ailuro and the Odestal."

"Don't you dare blame me for Syrina's delusions, Alzerbez!" She snapped, her voice commanding as the air shivered around them. "Our clans have been on the path to war since she assumed the mantle of Autarch! *She* began this madness by allowing the filth of the Cloister into our home! And you are just as much to blame for the state of our clans as I am."

Alzerbez shook their head, both acknowledging and ignoring her words—a moment of quiet hung in the air before Glamwell chuckled loudly.

"I, for one, am overjoyed to see you again, Kiela, especially in your natural element."

Her teeth shone brightly between her darkly painted lips as she grinned at Glamwell. "I'm glad to see you, too, Glamwell, though I much prefer you out of your element."

Myronor cleared his throat loudly. As interesting as their exchanges were, there were more pressing matters at hand.

"See, Kiela, you're being rude!" Iku yipped. "Introduce yourself, at least."

Kiela reared her crimson glare on Myronor and Kaikora, and for a moment, she assessed them up and down. Her expression was one of someone examining an interesting pile of rocks. But when her eyes found Myronor's again, her harsh features softened, and a sad smile crossed her lips.

"They know exactly who I am, and I them. All that matters now is that we reach the port as fast as your legs will carry, Iku. Our sister waits."

~ Fifty Four ~

CAREEN

*R*un.

It was the only word that kept Ophiera moving—the mantra she repeated to drown out the whispers of Uzziel's voice crawling in her mind.

Run.

The Cloister had come for her. Within the blurred memories from Myronor, she saw him—heard him—feared him. She didn't wish to think of what would happen if he found her...

"Ophiera?"

Her lungs burned now just like they had in the Sacramentum. It was as if she could not draw enough air, no matter how hard she gasped.

"Ophiera!"

She couldn't go back.

Not to the Sacramentum...not to Uzziel.

The brutal punishments, the endless torments—she had been unable to stop them before. He had always controlled her—completely and absolutely.

"Damnit, Ophiera!"

She crashed hard against something.

Blinking the sweat from her eyes, she recognized Jasper as he stepped in front of her. He held his own against her, barely yielding an inch against the force of her impact. Drawing heavy breaths, he rested his hands on her pauldrons.

"Slow down a minute."

"Can't."

"You need to drink something."

"Can't—stop."

She tried to push through him, but he held her still despite her efforts

"You're dehydrated!"

He pushed a waterskin before her face. Thirst clawed at her throat, but her gut screamed in protest. Her vision tunneled, focused on the road ahead. Turning her nose away, she moved to push past him again.

"Don't be an idiot," he spat, grasping her by the jaw.

The leather glove felt cool against her heated cheek, but his forceful grip ached her tense jaw. Unable to fight, she conceded by parting her lips. Cool water flooded her tongue, relieving the ache in her throat as he watched her drink.

Why was she letting him do this?

Touch her...

Replenish her...

Stop her.

If she couldn't stop him, she would never stop Uzziel.

Run.

Her heart stammered again, panic crushing her breath. She swallowed the last of the water before spitting the spout from her lips. His grip tightened as she tried to continue their flight towards the *Berserker*.

"Let go of me!" She growled, yanking away from him to no avail.

"Never!"

The tone of his voice drew her to his amber eyes, smoldering in the gray light of the Shole. This time, they held no apathy, no question or fearful desperation, only a determination she had rarely seen grace his beautiful face.

"Ophiera, I swore to keep the Shole from taking you," he said in a low tone, "and I won't let the Cloister touch you either."

His firm and final words siphoned away some of her panic. Rough as he was, Jasper understood her fear. He alone understood the burden of their scars, even if she had not fully realized the threat of the Cloister until now.

"You can't stop him, Jasper."

He leaned close, pressing his forehead against her own. Their perspiration mingled along with their quickened breath, still winded from the trek. She found far too much comfort in this gesture.

"It is not *him* I'm worried about. You've been traveling at an absurd pace, non-stop, for nearly a day. We both know we will dry up in this desert long before we reach the sea if we continue like this." He drew a slow, deep breath, and Ophiera found her matching his respiration without trying. "I know the fear of your heart…the beast you allow to dictate your actions while the injured parts of you retreat to safety. I know you must do what you must to protect yourself, Ophiera, but then let me take care of the rest. Let me replenish you…let me guide you…let me protect you."

Ophiera continued drawing the same heavy breaths as Jasper, trying not to doubt his words. Her hesitancy had nothing to do with trust but everything to do with their situation. In truth, she trusted Jasper with far more than her life, but all promises fell empty when measured against the Oaths of the Cloister—against the reality of what they faced.

Kiela had shown her far too much in their exchange, and now her heart was breaking as the truths devoured the lies, carving a void in her soul that only fear seemed to fill. Every target had shifted and changed, and now she was left to wonder why she bothered to fight anymore.

"I know," Jasper said, pulling away from her. He brushed the soaked stray hairs from her face, still holding her steady in the desert. "There's too much in the world we don't understand. Pyra, the Order, the Enclave, Aud, the Brotherhood...it's too much, far too fast. But all we need to do right now is reach the ship."

Ophiera blinked, confused for a moment. She stared at the sands, recalling all the problems chasing her now. There were far greater concerns beyond the ship, far greater foes, and far greater pains. But Jasper, as if reading her mind, shook her shoulders until she looked back at him.

"Once on the *Berserker,* we can worry about the future. We can decide what to do next; we can face whatever we choose to face. Or...or we could simply run away from it all."

She froze, staring at his set jaw and warm eyes.

"R-run?"

He nodded, smiling as he licked his lips. "The *Berserker* can outrun any problem, Ophiera. Out at sea, the only problems we face are the currents and weather. We could go anywhere...and leave this mess that Pyra created behind us."

Her heart stammered at the plea in his voice, at an option she had never considered. Despite *run* being her only goal since leaving the others behind, it had never crossed her mind that she could keep going. Could she really just run away with Jasper?

Ophiera cared for him in ways she knew she shouldn't and yet couldn't help. Though he fought her at every opportunity and knew precisely what to say to get under her skin, he also offered to release her from every obligation, satiating a desire she had suppressed for the majority of her life. Iluka had provided her with a taste of freedom, and he, like Iluka, represented a choice she so rarely experienced. And yet, at the prospect of freedom, she hesitated.

"You know I can't," she murmured.

"Because of Myronor?"

She nodded, and a waft of his leather overcoat brought her comfort despite his words. It was unfair how deeply her heart drew to them both, and yet, it was her soul that prevented her from giving in to Jasper's plea. The pain of leaving Myronor behind was a mistake she would never make again.

"You'd still choose him after what Kiela revealed in her memories?"

"He is my ekath," she whispered, trying to repress the revelations of Pyra.

There was too much she didn't understand, too much left to process before she could pass judgment. But if what Kiela had shown her was true...

"Kiela said it wasn't too late to sever the bond. You could be free of all tethers, Ophiera. Free of the Cloister, free of the mage. Free to run with me."

His rough thumb skimmed over her lips, and her body responded, betraying the drag on her soul. She had spent her entire life running from the truth. And now, the truth was she wished nothing more than to lose herself in Jasper's grasp and the promises he made.

"Let go," she said, her voice lacking conviction.

"Is that what you wish?"

"I barely know the meaning," she murmured, repeating the words from the night in the cave.

His amber eyes burned with passion, destroying the final remnant of his apathetic mask. She had thought him beautiful before, but as he held her in the desert sunrise, she felt as if she had never seen him properly.

He both tore her down and propped her up, caused her pain, and siphoned it away. He understood her conflict and shared her violence. Together, they worked seamlessly and matched in power, and yet, despite their strengths, they shared far too many flaws. As he held her now in the Shole, she remembered their nights spent embraced as they traveled and guiltily wished for just a few more.

Myronor would always be her ekath, but in some twisted way, she loved Jasper nearly the same. And yet, for vastly different reasons. She never knew her heart could have room for anything more than Retribution, but both Myronor and Jasper had carved a place there.

Suddenly, Jasper's hand tensed against her jaw as his eyes darted to the sand. She listened to the wind now ruffling his dark curls. And the sound rolling over the dunes filled her limbs with leaden sand.

"Aership," he hissed.

Jasper reached for her arm, cloaking them invisible both before dragging her back to a full sprint. Armor clanking and leather whipping, they ran towards the crest of the distant dune overshadowing the port. The sounds of snapping sails grew on their heels. And while she knew Jasper's cloaking kept them hidden, her scars itched with the encroaching presence.

The Cloister had come.

Her legs burned, even worse now than her chest. Hand in hand, she and Jasper crossed the peak of the dune, looking down at the port. The *Berserker* sat docked, pristine in the decrepit port. Freedom was so close she could taste it, but despite her panic, she knew they couldn't leave without the others.

"Wait," she hissed to Jasper, still tugging at her arm.

He heeded her words as she closed her eyes and felt for the tether. Like a vivid memory, she saw the Shole from the back of a familiar fox. The landscape flitted in and out of focus, flashing between the port that stood before her and the skeletal middens they had passed some time ago. In the sky above, she suddenly saw it: a pale ship adorned in bastardized adamantrium pulling away from the sprinting fox. Thrice the size of the *Berserker*, the Cloister's aership traveled thrice as quickly, too, overtaking them as it sailed toward the horizon. She watched with panic in her heart as a slight woman sitting in front of her tossed orbs of red haze in the flying ship's path. Dark smoke billowed at each impact, but the ship only seemed to slow a bit. She looked down at her own hands, now flickering in familiar blue as she attempted to cast. But in the pit of her gut, she felt her mana drawing from a quickly emptying well.

Opening her eyes, Ophiera surfaced from the link, standing firmly back in port. The others were not far behind, even though the Cloister would surely reach the *Berserker* first. But as Myronor's soul drew closer, his warmth replaced the fear in her heart with burning resolve.

"The others are near," Ophiera said to Jasper. "Kiela managed to slow them but Uzziel is still coming. If you go prepare the ship to sail, we may all still escape with our lives."

"And you?" he asked from the wind, still cloaking them both from sight.

"I'll distract the Cloister until the others arrive. Then, we flee on the *Berserker,* assuming your talk of her speed wasn't just a pirate's version of a fisher's tale."

"Ophiera—"

"Don't," she interrupted. "I would only ask this of someone I trust, Jasper. I trust you not only with my life but also with the lives of every soul I've ever cared for who rides this way. You have always given me the strength to choose, the strength to fight. So, please, fight beside me this time, not against me."

She felt his grip tremble against her gauntlet, though she couldn't see his face. The slight pops of explosion grew louder on the winds, as did the low hum of the aership.

They were running out of time.

"The *Berserker* will easily outrun that floating junk heap the Cloister calls an aership," he growled. He pulled her into an embrace, the smell of sea salt and leather nearly as comforting as his chuckle. "Show them who you truly are."

Jasper descended to the abandoned port first, leaving Ophiera alone on the road at the top of the dune. She felt for the Aether beneath her feet, finding solace in its burn even if she could not call upon it. Since the cleansing of Megrim Spa, the call of its fury had been subdued, sated even. And a part of her wondered if it was the Stigma that had called her to the desert all along.

Her calm faltered with the breeze as the foreign sounds of the aership grew louder. The grip of panic wrapped around her heart again, but this time, she was able to resist its crushing grasp. It was no longer just her freedom the Cloister threatened now.

Pyra knew. Like Kaikora, it disturbed her how much she had known. And while Ophiera reserved judgment for her actions, there was no denying the conviction behind Pyra Ebontide's doings. She had discovered the truth of too many things in Erum, including the Cloister.

And it was for that truth she descended to the abandoned port. Jasper may think she was reckless, but she wasn't without a plan. Uzziel would be easier to face on the white stone road, close to her escape route Jasper now readied. And with the ruined pillars of the abandoned port, there would be no room for the aership to land. From the port, she could see the sand dunes clearly and distract the Chaplain while the others arrived.

Slowly, her fear transformed to rage. Everything the Cloister had done was a slight against her. But what she *chose* was most important to her now. And with Myronor in her soul and Jasper at her back, she stood steadily on the road as the aership rose over the horizon.

Tendrils of smoke trickled from the side of the hull as the vessel sailed through the air off-kilter. The monstrous ship shifted its burned and torn sails as it slowed its approach and began circling. Her braid whipped across her stony face, caught in the torrid of its approach.

As it hovered above her, she caught a glint of golden armor through the blasted hole in the hull. And even from the shadows, she recognized the man glaring down at her. Framed by shards of blackened wood, Uzziel's hateful eyes pierced her soul the same as always. But though her spine straightened with a twinge of fear, more than anything, she found strength in his disdain.

With a whistle of air against metal, Uzziel dropped from the ship, landing heavily on the white stone road. Dust rose around him, framing the hammer shouldered against his pauldron. She recognized the double-headed pommel of the weapon he'd chosen after emerging from the Sacramentum as a Hand of Retribution. As he glared at her with hate-filled eyes, she deflected the visions of dark rooms and cracking bones by gripping her claymore tightly and readying it before her.

"Stand down, Aspect of Retribution," he said, smiling at her with a wolfish bearing of his teeth.

She hadn't heard his commanding voice since her conscription, though the memories of his arrogant tone had echoed in her dreams ever since she'd left the Cloister. Yet, rather than buckle beneath it as she had so many times in the past, the sound of his demands only straightened her spine.

She brandished her claymore in silent defiance.

"I said, stand down!" He shouted, his smile falling to a grimace. "Your Chaplain commands it!"

"I only answer to the Aether," she spat, tightening her grip on her sword.

He took a heavy step towards her, assessing her up and down. For a moment, he glared at her without recognition, wary of her. And all she could think to herself was *good*.

"The Aether and the Cloister are one and the same, Ophiera. Now stand down."

Ophiera smiled mirthlessly, tipping her claymore downward, pointing toward him. "Is a puddle of mud the same as the sea? I think not."

Uzziel's expression froze. Whatever he had expected from her, it was not disobedience. His anger was palpable, even from this distance, and again, Ophiera found it far more empowering than threatening.

"Heed your Oath and do as your Chaplain commands!" He shouted, voice echoing off the ruins of the port.

For a moment, she swore the hammer still shouldered on his pauldron flashed, but as Ophiera drew a slow, deep breath, she decided it was a trick of the light.

"Why would I listen to someone who breaks their own Oath?" She asked coldly. "The Brotherhood ravages the Aether, Aud steals souls across Erum, and yet you, Hand of Retribution, waste your time chasing *me*."

With a clunk of armor, Uzziel took a heavy step forward.

"To be clear, I am no longer chasing—I have caught. And now, you will answer for abandoning your Oath by returning with me to the Cloister—willingly or by force."

Recognizing the threat in his words, Ophiera scanned the horizon for signs of her companions. Violence was inevitable, and while stalling wasn't typically her tactic of choice, she had to admit it was working better than expected. The longer she dragged this out, the better their chances of escape.

"I never abandoned my Oath," Ophiera said, brandishing her claymore held within her scarred hand. "I've not broken any law of the Magistrate nor committed any sin against the Aether. There is no reason for me to return and even less for you to be chasing a retired paladin."

Uzziel examined his arm, clad in the poor excuse of golden armor. Beneath the preposterous gauntlet, she knew their scars read nearly identical, at least in Oath. But she had come to realize her scars were far more like Jasper's than Uzziel's—carved into her only to do the bidding of someone else—scars she refused to allow to control her anymore.

"I thought you'd understand by now," Uzziel growled, a sneer spreading across his darkening face. "Retribution may have been our gift, but our Oaths have always been to the Cloister itself. And you have already broken that Oath by not obeying your Chaplain's commands."

His admission struck Ophiera like a physical blow. It had taken her so long to realize the truth of her Oath, and yet she still clung to some childish hope that Uzziel remained in the dark. At least, if he were truly ignorant, she could forgive his warped choices that led them to this moment.

"How long?" She rasped, her voice breaking with rage. "How long have you served the Cloister, knowing our Oaths the Aether were all lies?"

He laughed. Like the countless times outside her cell in the Cloister, he relished in her despair.

"Served? Ophiera, I *am* the Cloister! While you wasted your life rebelling against their will, I rose to claim it as my own! I suspected long before we were ever kindled that the Aether had no will of its own. Like wind beneath the sails, the holy flames only power the demands of the Cloister. And as such, you too, Ophiera, belong to the Cloister. Meaning *you* belong to me."

The possessiveness in his voice sent a horrific chill down her spine. Everything she ever feared was coming to light, all spouted from the mouth of the soul she despised the most. And yet, though her legs trembled ever so slightly against the stone road, her grip tightened on her sword. She realized, with a bloom of resolve in her heart, that the parts of her that were breaking under his glare were parts she was glad to be rid of. The Cloister, the obedience, the cruelty—she would never allow him to control her again.

"You know nothing of the Aether," she said, feeling the roar of flames beneath her feet. "And not a soul on Erum has claim over me. Not even you, Uzziel."

Her tongue had barely grazed her teeth with his name before he lunged.

Another flash of light reflected off his hammer as he swung down, blunt and merciless. Sand and grit bit into her palm as she rolled, tucking her claymore to her side. The crash of steel and stone indicated she had dodged the blow by a humiliating margin.

But she judged him too quickly.

Before she could return upright, Uzziel bore down on her again, hammer bright against the gray sky. With her heart hammering, Ophiera rolled again, claymore still clasped tightly, as he continued his endless pursuit.

The dance continued and her boots skidded across the sandy stone while Uzziel's hammer swooshed beside her armor. Her breath hissed between her gritted teeth every time she dodged, realizing how quickly he was closing the distance between them. She had hoped to exhaust him before engaging, but it seemed after every swing, he rebounded even faster without so much as breaking a sweat.

As her lungs burned with the dry, cold air, she did her best to remain on the road. If she couldn't access the Aether through the mysterious stone, neither could he. But there was only so much space on the road.

Ophiera hesitated a moment, avoiding the sands, only to allow his hammer to graze her pauldron. The mistake threw her off balance enough that she knew the next blow would meet its mark. It seemed the time had come that needed to fight back.

Dropping to her knee to brace herself, she swung her claymore upwards, meeting his hammer in a deafening clang. The sand ground between her armor and road, the force of the blow reverberating through her very bones. Panting harshly, she managed to keep him at bay.

"You never did practice your breathing," he growled, pressing down upon her.

The familiar words served as ignition to the Aether beneath her. And while she could not call upon the white flames through the road, the mirrored fury empowered her just the same.

"You never minded your business," she hissed before sweeping her legs outwards and catching the backs of both his knees.

As he fell backward against the stone, she rolled quickly away. On her feet, she prepared for another swing, but it seemed her dodging dance had drained him of *some* of his stamina. Clumsily scrambling to his hands and knees, she refused to let him stand up yet.

With a cry of anger, Ophiera drove her greave into his gut. The sight of him curled in pain triggered a flame in her heart of the likes of which she had never felt before.

She kicked again. And again.

Her vision tunneled in a fury, dampening the clang of denting mental resounding through the Shole. She wanted him to feel every ounce of pain he had ever inflicted on her. She wanted him to suffer—to beg her to stop. Blood spurt from his curled lips, only enticing her to continue. Her legs shook with the force behind her next kick, but a tug in her chest caused her to falter.

Myronor was near. She couldn't hear him, but she felt the warmth spread through her body like the tingle of a stim potion. Every nerve in her body pulsated with relief, alleviating the tense hatred coiled in her muscles. She made the mistake of looking toward the desert, hoping to see her ekath and the others. But all she saw was a shimmer of gold before a sickening crunch of the hammer slamming against her abdomen.

Swept off her feet as if she weighed nothing, Ophiera slammed backwards against one of the remaining stone pillars. Stars swam before her eyes as she gripped her claymore with the agony of each attempted breath. Try as she might to draw air, none would come, and her vision swam with crumbling stone and dust.

Get up, Ophiera!

The moment Myronor's voice brushed her mind, she found her breath. Blinking the dust from her eyes, she gazed beyond the Uzziel barreling towards her to the sand dunes beyond. The silhouette of a fox bearing three riders next to a leopard with another forced a smile from her bloodied lip.

Myronor, you must lead everyone to the ship!

I'm not leaving you to face him alone!

I'll be fine! Jasper is readying to sail—make a run for it and I will follow shortly!

As if in slow motion, Ophiera watched as Uzziel charged towards her. She had let her rage get the best of her, but not again. She wasn't here to seek retribution against, Uzziel—she was here to protect Myronor and the others who rode with him.

Spitting blood as she rose from the rubble, Ophiera met Uzziel's strike with her claymore. The clash reverberated through her, shaking more dust from her armor. For a moment, Uzziel let the shock of her resistance flash across his cruel gaze before he began to chant.

The familiar words of the language she had tried so hard to forget caused the Aether to roar in protest. And though the road remained intact, blocking the holy flames from reaching Uzziel's call, it didn't stop the runes carved into the handle of his hammer from igniting in blinding white light.

"Pathetic," she growled, finding the strength to speak with the hypocrisy of the imbued weapon before her. And yet, even with flashing runes, he could not push her any further.

"I would rather wield the weapon the Cloister created than be one," he groaned, strength faltering beneath her blade.

The slight against her only drove her to burst forward, breaking the bind with Uzziel from her. With her elbow locked in place, she pivoted all her strength into the swing of her riposte, driving her pommel against his chest plate. Like his blow to hers, the attack launched Uzziel into a violent crash against another stone pillar.

As the white stone crumbled around the Chaplain, she sought the cries of fear radiating from the tether.

We're nearly to you and the ship! Run now, Ophiera!

Ophiera understood all too well his urgency. But she could only leave the battle safely once everyone was aboard the *Berserker*. Funny how there wasn't a doubt in her mind Jasper had readied the ship—her only worry was that they wouldn't be able to outrun the Cloister's aership, hovering and smoking from above.

"I told you, Ophiera," Uzziel growled, rising from the rubble with a deep gash across his cheek. "You belong to the Cloister."

With another rapid chant falling from his lips, the hammer shook in his hands. But this time, rather than charge Ophiera, he slammed his weapon onto the ground.

A resounding crack pierced the air as the stone slab road below them crumbled to rock and sand. Before she could raise her sword, her greaves were buried in the debris, and the Aether surged within her. But something within the flames felt terribly wrong.

Uzziel chanted, and the runes beneath her gauntlet began to burn. The sudden agony overtook her, searing away the strength of her grip. With a softened *thud*, her claymore fell into the shaking sands.

The rhythmic growl of Uzziel's chant pulsated with his approaching steps. And as the Aether screamed beneath her skin,

Ophiera found she could do nothing but yield to the pain. She couldn't move. She couldn't speak. Building and bubbling beneath her scars, resisting the cataclysm building within required all her strength.

"Your disobedience will not go unpunished," Uzziel said before leveling his hammer with her arm.

The runes of his weapon pulsated in tandem with the agony of her searing scars. A rope ladder unfurled from the hovering aership, but the pain prevented Ophiera from registering it in full. Her vision flashed, her soul screamed; she barely heard Uzziel's guttural chants over the pounding in her ears.

White flames ignited from the ground beneath her. Ophiera's scarred flesh became numb for just a moment before a lash of holy flames wrapped itself around her runic arm. Every carved symbol in her flesh ignited with scorching heat, a pain that outstripped any memory. Her very soul was on fire, filled with nothing but pure, terrifying agony.

She watched through tear-filled eyes as Uzziel's gauntleted hand reached for her, plucking away a single fiery chain and affixing it to his hammer. Pinned to the ground, she felt pain pulsate with the carved runes of his hammer.

"Your first task, Aspect of Retribution, is to destroy this port and everyone in it."

Uzziel's words reverberated through the fiery chains now embedded in her arm. She felt the Aether respond, searing through her against her will and only to his. Her lips parted, a scream ripping free as she suppressed the surge of endless flames pouring into her.

~ Fifty Five ~

RENUNCIATION

"And you just left her out there? Alone?!" Col hissed as she followed Jasper from his cabin.

"I had little choice!" Jasper snapped. "But if you and Felix can finish readying the last sails—"

"Go! Go to her now!"

Thanking the sea for Col, Jasper fled the *Berserker* as fast as his feet would carry him. It was hard enough witnessing Ophiera shatter in the desert at the mere thought of facing the Cloister. There was no way in hell he would leave her to face him alone now that his promise to her had been fulfilled.

On deck, Jasper cloaked himself against the sounds of clashing metal and the hum of the aership echoing throughout the port. Above, a faint trickle of smoke still escaped the imbued hull of the blasphemous golden ship. And as he dropped his gaze to the port, he noticed two blurs of metal dancing on the road. Quickly and silently, he moved over the decrepit docks, trying not to cause any further damage to the rotten wood. As long as Ophiera held her own and the Chaplain did not notice him, perhaps they could end this now rather than flee. Ultimately, the choice was hers.

Movement on the dune lured Jasper's gaze away from the battle, relieving as it was frustrating. Shadowed by the hoary sky, Iku, bearing three familiar riders and a leopard with another, began their descent into the port. Alzerbez and their rider led the charge, and for one foolish moment, Jasper breathed a sigh of relief. But he heard Myronor's yells roll across the dunes before a loud crack pierced the air.

A cloud of dust rose from the white stone road, obscuring Ophiera and Uzziel. All Jasper could make out was a white glow of light igniting within the haze.

Jasper didn't understand...was she calling upon the Aether?

As the dust settled, he saw Uzziel march towards her, but she remained unmoving, dropping her sword in surrender.

She couldn't.

She *wouldn't.*

The moment she sunk to the ground, flashes of white flames drew her arm in chains. He remained unaware of his own moving feet carrying him forward. Uncloaked, he sprinted toward her terror-filled gaze, unable to know truly what was happening, only knowing he needed to reach her. But like in his nightmares, no matter how hard he pushed, he simply wasn't quick enough to reach her before Uzziel climbed up the ladder. Fiery chains held Ophiera to the ground, a singular link connecting her to the bastard's weapon upon the aership now.

"Tell me how to free you!" Jasper yelled, kneeling by her side the moment he reached her.

"You can't," she groaned through clenched teeth.

Her entire body shook violently, rattling the white chains as tears streamed down her face.

"There must be a way!" he growled, reaching for the chains in desperation.

But she tore her arm away from him, a wave of pain spreading from her to him like the flames. A fissure opened beneath her, crackling outward towards the port. While he managed to dodge the veins of fire, he couldn't escape the hopelessness in her cries of agony.

"Take the others and flee!"

"No!"

"Jasper, I can't hold the Aether back much longer!"

"I won't leave you, Ophiera. I swore—"

"You must!" She cried, her trembling free hand reaching for his face. All her fierceness had disappeared behind her eyes; all of her purpose burned away. "Jasper, please...As long as Myronor survives, so shall I. But...argh!" Another fissure opened beneath her, causing the ground to rumble beneath them. The blood vessels in her eyes began to burst, tainting her amethyst eyes with crimson. "Jasper, please! I will never live with myself...if I hurt you. S-s-save them first...then, save me."

With a trembling hand, he wiped away the bloody tears marring her freckled cheeks. Her words were damning enough if he couldn't sense the desperation pouring from her. In his heart, he knew it would utterly destroy her if he stayed...if he allowed her to hurt him or any one of the others that road this way. There was no escape for the berserker woman who haunted his heart all these years. Despite his promises to never abandon her again, he was being asked to do just that. But this time, he left her side not because of his cowardice but because she asked it of him.

"I'll come for you," he whispered, voice breaking as he pressed his forehead to hers. "Like the lodestar, I'll find you!"

Despite the pain etching her features, her lips trembled into a smile. "I know."

Ophiera pressed her lips against his, desperate and terrified, as she sealed his promise with a kiss. She moved her mouth against his with a fervor that would forever hold him to her will. With one last hiss between her teeth, she pushed him away from her and screamed, "Run!"

Scrambling to his feet in the shaking sand, Jasper snatched up her golden claymore, abandoned by her side, and fled. His heart broke with every step away from her. Tears blurred his vision as much as memories of the past, threatening from the edge of his psyche to obscure the present. He was on the edge of losing not only Ophiera but reality itself. The demons within threatened to take him away from this horror, and yet, the sight of Alzerbez and Iku sprinting down the sand dune kept him focused on the present.

"Everyone to the *Berserker*, now!" Jasper screamed, pointing the golden claymore toward the docks.

Alzerbez curved on a dime, carrying the man in pink robes straddling his back straight to the dock. And while Iku hesitated a moment, he sprinted towards the pier all the same, only slowing a moment as the mage threw himself from his back. Stumbling in the sand, Myronor ran towards Jasper. Though he knew it was the screams from behind him that drew propelled the mage's frantic steps.

"Get to the ship!" Jasper spat, catching the mage by his cloak with his free hand. He started dragging him away with him, fulfilling his promise as the ground shook with her screams behind him.

"We can't leave her!" Myronor cried.

As if any amount of tears and screams would help her now.

"Escape is our only hope to save her," Jasper growled, continuing to drag him across the sands toward the *Berserker*.

"Ophiera!" He screamed, clawing at Jasper's arm. And like a tidal wave, the emotions pouring from the mage drowned out his senses. His knees shook with the threat of collapse as his heart tore in every direction. In all his life, he'd never felt a pain quite as damning as this. It was hard enough listening to the mage's words without feeling every ounce of his despair. But for *her*, Jasper needed to remain strong—something the mage could never do.

"If you die, so does she! You are her only hope of surviving this!"

"You swore, damnit!" Myronor roared over his shoulder, his pain now turning to anger. "Don't do this without me!"

A blue glow caught Jasper's eye. Regardless of how he felt about the mage, there was no denying how desperately Myronor loved Ophiera. But that love would be the death of her now.

Without a trace of remorse, Jasper stuck the claymore in the sand. Holding the mage steady, he pinched the soft spot between Myronor's neck and shoulder, hard and with purpose. The pressure point sent his crazed eyes rolling as he fell limp in Jasper's arms. Relieved of his pain, Jasper found clarity in his purpose and hoisted the unconscious mage over his shoulder, along with the claymore. And as he ran to the ship, he dared one final glance at Ophiera.

Her body trembled in sync with the sands. Head thrown back, she screamed to the sky as the flames crawled up her arm toward her agonized gaze. Her bloodied eyes met his for the last time before flames engulfed her in full. But as always, her message was clear.

Run.

The others had reached the *Berserker* long before Jasper carried Myronor across the docks. White fissures of flames ruptured from the pyre that was Ophiera, burning the parts of the docks still anchored in the sands. While the surf served as some protection against the Aether, Jasper knew their only guarantee of safety would be far out at sea.

Col stood on deck with Felix, her shock turning to despair as she read the plan etched on his face. Her dark eyes were filled with tears, and she was unable to speak the words she must. Again, Jasper would bear the burden of doing what needed to be done.

"Hoist the sails!" he bellowed.

Felix looked at him in disbelief. "But, captain, Miss Ophi—"

"Is about to blow this port to hell! We must flee to stand a chance of surviving her!"

Felix's eyes widened with horror as if he saw a monster standing before him. And for a moment, Jasper wondered if that was exactly what he had become. But all his guilt of abandoning Ophiera to suffer alone dissolved when he remembered her lips pressed against his. The promise he made to her, to save them all in order to save her, thundered through his veins. He wasn't running away this time for just his life—he was fighting for all of their lives.

"Now, hoist the damned sails!" Jasper barked for the last time, driving the tip of the golden claymore into the deck of the ship.

Felix stared a moment at the stuck sword but heeded his command with haste. With his first mate taking the helm, Jasper settled the unconscious mage against the mast on deck. He gazed around, looking for the others.

Kaikora stomped across the deck, joining Col at the helm with her broken trident and mirrored eyes. He didn't understand what or why she was casting until the ship lurched suddenly away from the dock. The sound of crackling air and frothing water still couldn't drown out the screams.

Every scar on Jasper's body itched with the need to look away from the shore. But he needed to see what all of this was for. The pillar of white flames reached toward the sky as the sands shook violently around her. As the dust rose higher in the air, the sputtering flames twisted the air, forming a vortex of swirling clouds around her. The hovering aership swayed against the drafts, still attached by the singular flaming chain.

Closing his eyes, Jasper tried to remember all the times he had witnessed her cheat death. She would survive this...she had to. And if she didn't, well...he promised he'd always find her, and if that meant in the Aether itself, so be it.

"Don't look away."

Jasper's eyes snapped open—he hadn't sensed Kiela join him. At his side, she, too, stared unblinking at the shore, regal and stiff, with a hand resting on Iku's bowed head.

"I don't know if I can watch this," he whispered, heeding her word but regretting it by the moment. Ophiera's screams pulsated through the fires as if...they were her.

"She suffers this torment for us," Kiela said coldly. "Fair exchange demands we bear witness to her pain so that when the time comes to avenge her, to give the Cloister their fair exchange, *nothing* will stay our hands."

The vehemence in her voice sent a chill down Jasper's neck, but it was a welcome relief amidst the chaos of their escape. Kiela seemed to be the only one to understand the necessity of their abandonment—an admirable distinction from the mage stirring behind him. While Ophiera burned, the man she loved could only whimper.

Whimpers that quickly transformed into screams.

Jasper turned away from shore to find Myronor still crumpled in a heap beneath the mast. Though his eyes remained closed, his face contorted in pain as his cries resonated with those from shore. Bending low, Jasper tried to apply the pressure points again, hoping to at least silence the echoes of her agony, but they did nothing to quiet him. Throwing himself against the deck, Myronor began writhing with his back arched and hands clawed. And despite Jasper's desire to simply throw the worthless wretch overboard, Ophiera's words echoed in his mind.

With a slink of black robes, Kiela joined him beside the mage and placed a slender hand over his heart. Hazed, red tendrils sprouted from her hand, piercing Myronor's chest as his screams died and his limbs held still.

"What are you doing to him?" Jasper asked.

"Sharing the burden," she said in a quavering voice.

Her slight shoulders shuddered as the scintillating light from shore reached its apex. Iku whimpered alongside the two, but Jasper didn't need to be connected to anyone's soul to know Ophiera's breaking point was near; he could sense her pain carried on the wind.

Suddenly, the screams fell to silence, and in the collective quiet, all eyes fell to shore. Jasper watched time freeze as if every speck of dust, water, air, and soul braced for what was to come. The single white pillar of flame flickered violently and mutely before a blinding flash blazed everything in white light. As his eyes stung with pain, a thunderous roar rumbled over his ship.

The rolling force that followed knocked all the air from Jasper's lungs before throwing him off his feet. Her detonation rocked not only him but his ship, swaying sickeningly as his back slammed against the deck. He allowed himself a moment of awe, admiring his lodestar's strength for holding back that amount of power for as long as she had. But he had witnessed enough during the rebellions to know what followed.

Struggling to draw breath, Jasper stumbled back to his feet. He didn't have the chance to check on the others before facing what came their way from the shore. Taller than the navarra, a wave of impossible height rolled towards the ship. Never before had he contended with a surge *from* shore, let alone a tidal wave of frothing gray water bearing the debris of the abandoned port. As fast as the *Berserker* could sail, she wasn't built to break a wave like this.

"Everyone below deck!" he yelled, unable to mask the doubt in his voice.

Iku whimpered nearby, drawing his attention away from the wave and, instead, to Kiela and Myronor. Both lay collapsed on the deck, unconscious but breathing shallowly. The force of Ophiera's cataclysm through the ekath must have been too much for them to bear. His only comfort came from the ragged breaths Myronor drew, knowing that at least it meant Ophiera still lived. But panic took over as the boat began to list, tilting with the shifting waters and sending their limp bodies sliding down the deck.

Holding the mast, Jasper snatched Myronor by the neck of his cloak while Iku used his teeth to drag Kiela by the hem of her dress. But the greater threat still drew closer—the wave bearing down on them shadowed the deck as sea spray misted the air.

It would be fitting, Jasper mused, that Ophiera would destroy the ship christened in her honor. Fate had a strange way of reminding him that his path had never been his own. He could never escape *her*. And truthfully, he never wished to.

"Hold on!" Kaikora roared, her voice carrying above the chaos of the sea. She slid down the deck between them, eyes glazed in mirrors and jaw set. Broken trident raised high, she stopped herself with her bare feet against the railing near the port side. The crackling of her mana pierced the air as she drew herself up to full height, stabbing the sea glass forward. For the first time in his life, he rejoiced in having a mana user aboard his ship. But to his dismay, the wave never slowed.

As the wall of sea and debris blocked his view of all else, Jasper took a deep breath, resolved to his fate. He had done as Ophiera asked, but like all the times he tried to do what seemed right, this would end in miserable failure. Dragging Myronor against his chest, he hoped the ekath could at least convey his sorrows to her before he returned to the Aether.

Though sea spray drenched his leather overcoat, the crash of the wave never came. Lost in his emotions, it took him a moment to realize what Kaikora was doing—or fighting, rather. In her outstretched arm, the longest point of her trident met the frothing surface of the wave. And as if carving a slice down the middle, the wave split asunder, deflecting to both sides of the ship. The shaman's body shook violently against the force, her bronze dreadlocks whipping behind her as the air continued to crackle and pop. But Jasper knew she would not yield as the two monstrous waves veered around the *Berserker*, rolling out to sea with the promise of havoc elsewhere.

The ship righted, matching the flat water of the sea before them. Kaikora dropped to her knees, breathing heavily and dripping in seawater. Jasper set Myronor down against the leveled deck and rushed to the shaman's side.

"I see why Col is so damn fond of you," he said, offering her a hand. To his surprise, she took it and stood beside him.

"I refuse to fail the Warden any more than I already have," she growled, glaring out to the now visible shore.

Every conscious soul on board drew their gaze toward the port, or rather, where the port used to stand. Though the pillar of flames had extinguished, all else remained obscured in smoke and sand—all except a fiery, white chain rising from the cloud of ashes like a torchbearer of defeat.

The hovering aership emerged, its hull scorched but triumphant in its survival. It stopped, hovering a moment as the white-hot chain ratcheted upwards into the blasted side of the ship. Jasper held his breath, knowing who must hang at the end. But nothing could prepare his heart for the sight of Ophiera's bare, battered body, swaying lifeless in the smoke. Armorless, her white hair fell in curtains over her sand-covered skin, and stark red blood trickled from her eyes and lips. Foot by agonizing foot, Jasper watched his lodestar dragged into the damaged hull, wishing he had never left her to face this alone.

He wished himself unconscious as the mage lying at his feet.

He wished she'd taken his soul for her own in Iluka.

And though he wished and wished, he hardly knew the meaning anymore.

~ Fifty Six ~

LODESTAR

With favorable winds and Kaikora's continual coaxing of the sea, the *Berserker* sailed for only two days before Krysas loomed on the horizon. But Jasper viewed the city through the porthole of his cabin, where he had remained since departing the Shole.

While Col and Felix worked diligently to maintain their speed, only his first mate had dared disturb him in his wallow. But despite her efforts, even Col only brought him despair, as the pale fire cloud continued to reflect in her dark, swollen eyes.

Jasper had fought off the low morale permeating each corner of his ship as long as he could, but within an hour of sailing from the destroyed port, he'd locked himself in his cabin. Every slumped shoulder, every weary eye, sigh, or sniffle from those aboard his ship struck at him like a hot iron. At least now, alone with ember whisky and silence, he could maintain his sanity against the emotions saturating the ship.

Though he sat at his cartography table, map at the ready, it was difficult to look forward when so much had been left behind. The tracing paper and charcoal remained strewn about, the untouched remnants of Ophiera's final departure from his ship. Even the empty flagon had gone untouched, toppled over on the floor, just as she had been that day. The memory of her drunk and passed out against him lingered in his mind like the scent of ember whiskey in his cabin, both causing him more pain than pleasure.

For years, he'd suffered the waking nightmares of the past, obscuring the present. But it seemed only the horrific memories overtook his consciousness—never the good ones. If only he could lose himself in the memories of holding her or fighting her, but each time he tried, the visions were overtaken by an agonized kiss of white flames. Dust now settled over every trace of her, leaving him ever more uncertain of his decision to leave her behind.

Jasper had broken every promise he had made to Ophiera. And no amount of whiskey numbed him enough to forget the plea in her eyes, the desperate feel of her lips, and the blood that ran from both as the Cloister dragged her onto their ship. He had failed her in all ways but one—but he didn't wish to think about the unconscious mage in his cabin below either.

Knock, knock.

The sound only reminded him to take another swig from his flask. As his throat seared, Col entered his cabin with skeptical, exhausted eyes.

"Are you back to check on me or *him*?" He sneered, knowing none of this was her fault and yet despising her sorrow just the same.

"Neither," Col said quietly. "Kiela asked to speak with you."

The unexpected request sobered him slightly. He hadn't spoken to any of the Enclave now aboard his ship, the warlock least of all. Col had said Kiela remained holed up in the water-stained cabin with Iku, unwilling to see or speak to anyone as she recovered from the cataclysm.

"How long 'til landfall?" He asked gruffly.

Col stared blankly across the room, fixated on the golden claymore leaning in the corner. The moisture was beginning to well beneath her heavy lids, but she shook herself to stillness before muttering, "Less than an hour."

Jasper took a deep breath, sitting up from his slump. "Send her in."

Col raised her eyebrows at him, giving him one last chance to reconsider. Whether it was his tone with her or his choice to meet with Kiela, he didn't know nor care to know. As he drew his flask to his lips for another drink, his first mate left the room.

He assumed Col, like him, was worried the warlock would sense his weakness and prey on his misery. But he quashed his ugly thoughts with visions of white fire. Ophiera trusted him and Kiela. And if a paladin, trained to judge, to decide life or death by her own hand, could keep an open mind to the Enclave, then so must he. Throughout their journey into the Shole, Kiela had only been an asset, a help, even at great cost to herself. And yet, as he heard the quiet steps outside his door, he recognized that one could respect a person without enjoying their company.

The door opened, and Iku entered with his luxurious tail deflated, the tip brushing against the floor. His agitation was palpable but not alarming enough to hold Jasper's attention away from Kiela as she followed him inside. Despite her former ageless appearance, she looked as if she had aged ten years since setting sail. The dark circles beneath her dulled gaze were only highlighted by her cracked, painted lips. She took Ophiera's seat across from him, examining the contents of the table without touching anything. Neither said a word for a few moments.

"Myronor is still unconscious," she said quietly.

It wasn't a question but a statement. She must have sensed his life force in the cabin below, where he lay under Col and Jasper's constant watch. But he wasn't sure what use the observation was in the moment and remained quiet.

"It is problematic," she added.

"I find the silence quite peaceful."

"We need him awake in order to find her."

"Do we?"

"Yes."

Jasper sighed. "And you're telling me this because...?"

"Because I know what you're planning," she said stiffly.

Staring at the worn piece of charcoal, Jasper did his best to maintain his composure. "I'm not planning any—"

"I taste how your sorrow has now soured to desperation," Kiela snapped, lively once again. "Combined with your penchant for the bottle and an inability to control your newly discovered emotions...well, it's a breeding ground for rash decisions. You plan to sail to Tanvik and begin your search for Ophiera. And the only reason you sail to Krysas first is to dump the unwanted cargo off your ship before you depart."

Despite his best effort, Jasper's body tensed, and he felt a rare flush creep up his neck. He had not spoken of his wishes, not even to Col.

"Taste, huh?" He growled. "Did you *derive* from me again without my permission?"

Her darkly stained lips curled into a smile without teeth. "While you've drunk enough to numb your heart, trust me when I say if I derive from you, I'd ensure you felt every moment of it. I only sense what you put forth, and I don't hear you refuting any of it."

Jasper said nothing for a moment. It was true that wherever the Cloister had taken Ophiera, he would follow. Certainly, Uzziel was not returning her to Krysas, which left Tanvik as the only option.

But the Cloister had remained hidden for centuries, unknown to scholars and merchants alike. And he was determined to start his search for it as soon as he offloaded the *Berserker*'s excessive crew.

"What do you plan on doing about it?" He asked, hoping to find any way out of her interference. But as she pressed her lips together, he knew he would regret contending with the will of a warlock again.

Jasper barely noticed the red-hazed tendrils extending from her delicate, raised fingers. Before he could stand, they embedded themselves deep within his chest. The moment they penetrated him, everything fell from his control; his limbs became weightless, his heart lighter, and his mind...his mind felt clearer than it had in days. Blissful nothingness overtook him as her predatory eyes glowed with the spell.

"I promise you no harm," she said, her voice reverberating strangely. "But the information I divulged to you and Ophiera—Pyra's whereabouts, her intentions, her research—cannot be known to any others. Not until we have reclaimed Erum's Flame, because, without her, all is lost. Therefore, Jasper, I bind you to silence in all matters surrounding Pyra."

His heart palpitated, violently and dangerously, but just as quickly as it beat, it stopped. A shiver ran through his body before he became enveloped in indifference. Finally, he felt the mindless apathy he had sought all these years, the pure blissful ennui. But the heavy weight of existence returned to his limbs as the tendrils receded, and his heart began to beat again.

Kiela's eyes bore into him, watching for his response.

"What the hell was that?" he spat.

"Your people call it a curse."

"That's been my whole damned existence, princess, so you'll have to be more specific."

She rolled her eyes. "Your words will go missing if you speak of Pyra or any of her doings."

Defiantly, Jasper opened his mouth with Pyra's name on the tip of his tongue but found his breath caught. Despite being able to recall all that Kiela had confessed as they fled the desert, he could not utter a single word regarding the mage's mother. Even at the mere *thought* of her, he felt his throat constrict.

"Do you hate me again now?" She asked, head cocked as she evaluated her handiwork.

In the past, her *curse* would have enraged him. But two days of drunken mourning for Ophiera had drained him of hate. What he found more upsetting was his desire to feel the weightless side effects of Kiela's magic again. There was a numbness with subjugation that he hadn't felt in years, yet continually sought at the bottom of a bottle.

"What I find most upsetting is that you threatened my life in the jungle for touching you, yet you perform derivation magic on me now without my consent. I don't care for hypocrites."

As Iku sidled beside her, Kiela watched him serenely before her lips formed a dark line, pressed in thought.

"I am, indeed, a hypocrite. But more importantly, I am ruthless. And I always honor fair exchange, so for your forced silence, I swear on my ekath that I will do whatever it takes to find Ophiera."

While Jasper believed her words, curiosity overtook his trust. "Why is she so important to you?"

"That is a complicated question," Kiela said with a smile. "Personally, I'm quite fond of her soul...her aura is a shade so seldom seen in this world. But more importantly, more *practically*, it is because Erum's Flame is key to our survival. We have arrived at the precipice, and we, as souls of Erum, must decide the fate of our existence. Pyra knew but remains out of our reach for now. The shaman might have understood, but no longer sees our future. And the only Wielder of Erum's Flame lies in chains held by imposters while her equal lies unconscious below us. The direness of our situation has peaked. And there is no time left for fairness or justice—no place for piety or democracy. We must act, even at the expense of others."

Jasper glared at his map, unable to meet her gaze. Her words affected him in a way that so many others had failed to. While they all preached the end of days, the direness of the ichor and Brotherhood, Kiela spoke without an ounce of self-righteous swill. She wasn't trying to convince him of anything, but instead simply stating her plan while providing the unspoken option to get out of her way. Both Ophiera and Kiela lived by their convictions—no wonder the sisters of flames had grown so close so quickly.

"For the record, I disagreed with the whole curse strategy," Iku interjected, his green eyes sympathetic. "I thought simply asking you to keep your mouth shut would have been sufficient."

"That would have been the most straightforward option, I daresay," Jasper grumbled.

"Perhaps it would have worked had you been someone capable of controlling your pettiness," Kiela said, rolling her tired eyes again. "You would have thrown the knowledge of Pyra in Myronor's face, given a chance. And her secrets must stay as such until Ophiera is free."

Again, she read him with a dangerous accuracy. Jasper may have saved the mage for Ophiera's sake, but it had been only for her; he still despised the idiot, more so now than ever. Nothing would have satisfied him more than reminding Myronor that he and his insane mother were at fault for all that had happened. But at the thought of the woman, he felt his throat constrict slightly.

"Cursed it is, then."

"I promise it is nothing personal," she said, shrugging.

How many times had he ended deals with the same 'it's not personal' speech? Rather than grow angry, he found himself admiring the warlock's ruthlessness, as she called it. Kiela always seemed a step ahead of everyone, and right now, that was a powerful asset to his cause.

"My only purpose is to find Ophiera. Do whatever you wish to me, princess, as long as it does not get in my way."

"We will get her back," Kiela replied with a fierceness that uplifted his mood.

The rage in her statement felt more promising than anything else. Cursed or not, he did not need to reveal the sins of the past to find Ophiera. And given Kiela's ruthlessness, as she called it, he knew she would be an asset rather than a burden.

"I've always been willing to work with a devil," he said, pulling his flask from his coat and raising it to Kiela.

She watched him drink with voracious eyes. "Devil, huh? I like that better than *warlock*."

Jasper's heart stuttered a moment as her tongue maneuvered around the word. After he calmed himself with a drink, he offered it to her in a truce. With slight hands, she sniffed the contents.

"Does this drivel really make you feel better?"

"Not like it used to."

Her eyes never left him as she took a drink, smacking her dark lips. She handed it back to him, and in one swig, he drained the remainder of the contents.

"Libations tend to dilute the ache of the soul," she said, placing a hand over her chest, "but tis a fleeting relief with more consequence than benefit."

"Are you telling me to stop drinking?"

"I only seek to inform— I personally don't care how you poison yourself as long as it doesn't interfere with freeing Ophiera."

Exactly what he had hoped to hear.

The confidence with which she spoke and acted was unmatched by anyone else on this ship, even more than Ophiera. His lodestar held her fair share of doubts, worries, and shame—all placed there by the damned Cloister.

Sudden screams came from below.

"Myronor," Kiela breathed.

She rushed from the table in a whirl of black with Jasper at her heels. As he followed her and Iku into the room, he faltered against a wall of agony. On his bed, Myronor's back arched unnaturally as his limbs jerked, grasping the linens with clawed hands. His pain suffused over everything, and Jasper felt himself fighting against it like a current as he approached.

The scarlet wisps of Kiela's magic converged on the thrashing mage, silencing his screams and reducing the flow. Gathering himself, Jasper joined her by the bedside.

"They're forcing her to burn," she said through gritted teeth. "Talk to him!"

"Why?"

"Through him, she may..." she hissed, taking a pausing breath. "T-tell us...where..."

Jasper approached the bed and leaned over the restless man. With a gentle slap, he tried to focus Myronor's attention, but the blue eyes rolled endlessly in dark, sunken sockets.

"Where is Ophiera?"

Myronor's lips moved, but no words came out.

"Where!?" Jasper demanded, grabbing his lolling head by the chin. His skin was sallow and slick with a cold sweat as he mumbled.

"D-dark...Jasper..."

Even without Kiela's hitch in her breath, Jasper knew the words spoken were not Myronor's.

"Ophiera?" He asked, his voice breaking against his will.

"Please...find...me..."

The blue eyes rolled one last time, and Myronor's body went limp.

Kiela ended her spell, swaying slightly on the spot. Without thinking, Jasper reached for her elbow to stabilize her sway. The crimson glare she shot him nearly made his knees buckle, but when he did not let her go, she smirked. Her arm felt shaky and feeble in his grasp, a great contrast to her typical, intimidating demeanor.

"*That* is why we need him," she said, gently removing her arm from his hand. She graciously leaned her body against the hull. It would have seemed an unassuming stance to anyone else, but Jasper read the exhaustion in her shaking legs. She looked delicate, almost frail now. Her thin frame leaned hunched against the rough wood, glistening with sweat.

"Are you alright?"

Kiela nodded, but as Jasper raised his eyebrows, she smirked sheepishly. "The pain takes much to suppress. More than I expected."

Iku squeezed his way between them, nuzzling his ekath in comfort. He watched her fingers weave into the crimson fur, closing her eyes in satisfaction. No red haze came forth, but he knew she re-innervated through the ekath. The expressions of contentment upon both faces felt too intimate for his eyes.

Instead, he turned his attention toward the still and silent mage. Again, his shallow breaths were a good sign that Ophiera survived, but he remained unconscious.

"Why won't he wake?"

"I'm unsure," Kiela said.

"How about a guess, then?"

She sighed. "It's possible that Ophiera drains him as she burns against her will. Or perhaps I take more than just his pain when I interfere. Regardless, his aura is threadbare...it will be some time before he wakes again."

As Jasper watched the mage, he sensed the weakness, too. And a bubble of unwanted pity towards the worthless man burst in his heart. How was Myronor to help them find Ophiera when he suffered as much? They had only gleaned information that, frankly, he'd rather not know—she burned in a dark chamber and called to him for help.

"Rest until we land," Jasper said to Kiela as he walked to the cabin door. "You look exhausted."

"Don't start worrying about me now."

"I don't want you feeding on my crew."

Iku growled. "Kiela would never taint her palate."

"Well, there is one person on this ship I would consider tasting again," she simpered, soothing Iku with a caressing hand while gazing at Jasper.

He left the room impetuously.

Hearing Ophiera call his name catalyzed his frantic need to find her. In his cartography room, he pulled countless maps from the cubby holes of his desk, carrying the rolled parchments in armfuls back to the table. After the scrolls tumbled from his grasp, he returned for more. He repeated this until nearly every piece of cracked leather and aged parchment lay in a mound upon the table, with a few stragglers on the floor.

Without acknowledging his reflection, he adjusted the light reflector above his table, filling the room with the burning colors of sunset. Silently, he cursed himself for spending the past two days wallowing in inebriated misery when he could have been doing something productive, something useful.

He began unfurling the first of many maps when a knock on his door announced Col. He raised his eyes to meet hers as she entered, and he found the look of amused pity she reserved only for him.

"I wondered when you'd start looking," she said with a sad smile. She leaned over his arm, staring at the first map he had begun to scour. "I didn't know we even had maps of the Burnished Highlands?"

"I have maps of everywhere," he growled, throwing the first fruitless scroll across the room. Reaching for another, he felt Col's agitation seep from behind him.

"Is that really the best place to look?"

"Col, what is it you truly ask?"

She sighed. "If the rumors are true, that the Cloister resides in that wasteland, do you really expect to find it marked on a map?"

Jasper rolled up the second useless map and tossed it beside the other. Two down, several dozen more to go.

"You know better than anyone, Col, that sometimes what is missing from a map is more important than what's been marked."

Her silence allowed him a moment of victory before delving back into his search.

The rumors Col spoke of were precisely that; while everyone in Tanvik associated the Cloister with the Burnished Highlands, that was chiefly due to the Magistrate's division of power, rather than any factual evidence. The only people who claimed to have *found* the Cloister were drunk vagrants spinning tales in exchange for food or clout, and even then, no one believed them.

Obviously, the Cloister had a physical location, though Jasper firmly believed no one actually *wanted* to find the Cloister. The people of Tanvik were satisfied to turn a blind eye to the Magistrate's conscription of the paladins, happy to ignore the rumors of the Cloister's training. Even Jasper had remained blissfully ignorant until that night upon the beach of Iluka when Ophiera had demonstrated firsthand the power the Cloister truly wielded. Perhaps it wasn't very smart to search for a place most were content to pretend didn't exist.

Jasper himself had only viewed the wastes of the Burnished Highlands from a distance, but it had been enough to convince him never to set foot in the realm. Scholars preached that Tanvik itself was born of earthly flames, from liquid rock that exploded out of the sea in fire and brimstone. Remnants of that chaotic history could be found in the Burnished Highlands—tales of geysers, corrosive waters, and toxic plumes. Some grounds were so hot they melted the soles of boots, while other mountainous areas towered so tall they held snow year-round. The Burnished Highlands were a place forgotten by the living, a realm of death that surpassed even the Shole. But at least maps of the Shole existed.

Col strode to the table while pulling a headband upon herself, pushing her plum, wild hair from her eyes. She rummaged through a pile of scrolls before her, splitting a few away from the mound. She began to scan the maps and toss the discards into the pile he had already started.

"Col...I—"

"Captain, there's no need to explain—or apologize—or thank me." Her dark eyes lifted from the map with significance. "I want to find her, too."

For perhaps the first time since knowing his first mate, Col misinterpreted his intention. Certainly, he appreciated her more than words could ever convey, but he had not intended to thank her. He wished only to warn her.

Ironically, it was Col who had first pushed him to find a purpose other than his own survival. And he had found one in Ophiera. The paladin had set him free from a prison he had created by himself and forced him to live for something. But the Cloister had taken his purpose—held her hostage and inadvertently replaced his newfound meaning with another.

No matter the cost, no matter the consequence, he would find Ophiera. Those who stood in his path would find no peace, only a reckoning long overdue. Vengeance was not only his purpose but his promise—to his lodestar, to himself, and to every soul on Erum that suffered at the hands of that power-hungry Chaplain. Glaring at the golden claymore, still dusted in gray sand and dried blood, he forged his oath. He would free Ophiera from the Cloister for good by carving the vile order from Erum forever. Beneath his leather overcoat, he felt his own scars burn in accord—they would never see him coming.

ACKNOWLEDGEMENTS

I never thought I'd be able to write and publish a fantasy book, let alone two, and neither would have been possible without the epic support of my family and friends. My spouse and our cats are just as much a part of this book as the first, providing endless inspiration and love. I can get a bit obsessive and a little bit messy, but for some reason, you still love me unconditionally. My sisters deserve a medal of honor for fielding endless text messages in the middle of the night asking for opinions on character names, fonts, and covers. To be fair, you both drive me as crazy as I drive you. Nicole, my eagle-eye editor, work spouse, soul sister, the list goes on, I'm forever blown away by your tenacity and infinite capacity for care and compassion. My exceptionally talented friend Kelly helped me in so many ways, I can't list them all, but you get all the credit for this gorgeous cover, my beautiful tattoos, and for always having my back--our brains connect in the best ways. Oddly enough, I must also give a shout-out to my pottery instructors for their endless enthusiasm, not only about ceramics but any creative endeavor any of their students pursued. And yes, I took pottery classes while writing this story and working full time... So I really must also give thanks to some awesome coworkers who didn't cringe when I told them what I do on the side, and in fact, supported me wholly! Needless to say, I truly couldn't have stayed sane without all my loved ones' tolerance and support. Who knows what will come next, but like Ophiera, I know I won't face it alone.

Thanks for reading!

If you enjoyed The Aether
Unravels, please rate, review, and
connect with me online!

You can find more information
on the characters, terminology,
world-building, and everything
in between on my website.

www.cgwynn.com

@c.g.wynn
TikTok, IG, Threads

9 7989 87 8 66 83 2